'The undiscovered country,
From whose bourn
No traveller returns.'
SHAKESPEARE: HAMLET: ACT 3, SCENE 1

# No
# TRAVELLER
# RETURNS

ANNE-LOUISE MATHIE

Matador
9 Priory Business Park,
Wistow Road, Kibworth Beauchamp,
Leicestershire. LE8 0RX
Tel: 0116 279 2299
Email: books@troubador.co.uk
Web: www.troubador.co.uk/matador
Twitter: @matadorbooks

ISBN 978 1800462 045

British Library Cataloguing in Publication Data.
A catalogue record for this book is available from the British Library.

Printed and bound in the UK by TJ Books LTD, Padstow, Cornwall
Typeset in 12pt Adobe Jenson Pro by Troubador Publishing Ltd, Leicester, UK

Matador is an imprint of Troubador Publishing Ltd

*To my loving husband, Mark,
who has shared so many adventures with me.*

# Prologue

On the coast of the Mediterranean, the sea is never far out from land, so there is always a sense of a clear boundary. Where the sea stops, the land begins. I find this assurance of a neat border strange and troubling.

In contrast, during my childhood years on the west coast of France, I was familiar with the Atlantic Ocean which merged seamlessly with the land – one moment isolated, swirling grey depths of water, and the next, waves which were on intimate terms with the sand dunes and the gorse scrub.

For a woman born in Les Landes, the Mediterranean Sea and coast were alien to my spirit. The high cliffs of the calanques were hard and brittle and jutted out in proud challenge to the waves below, which, in their turn, held themselves aloof from the land, as if they knew their own place. The coast was an undisputed border.

Most of all, it was a border which kept me away from him.

A human body is a type of border. It announces, 'These are my limitations. I occupy this space; you can't get past me.' I suppose that this explains humanity's fascination with ghosts. In the murky world of the after-life normal borders don't appear to exist.

The border between two human beings is only truly breached in the most intimate act of sex. Only too recently, I had appreciated this borderless unity of flesh in my daily life. Now, the unrelenting nature of the Mediterranean land and sea borders seemed even more cruel.

Twenty hours earlier, I had watched the physical borders of the man I had loved so profoundly, dissolve not in intimacy but in death, as he fell into the surrounding earth. I knew that the maggots would rapidly have taken my place in crossing the border, as they always do in a very hot country. 'To the dust you shall return' says the funeral liturgy. To my mind, dust was a warm, clean and tangible substance, compared to the cold and messy process of decomposition which was even now taking place.

It seemed particularly cruel that the only man to delight me, amuse me and inspire me should have ended up as a dead body. I was no longer young enough to be deceived by the illusion of immortality, but I was still outraged by the idea that a whole person could suddenly be tossed aside as unnecessary, and within a few seconds be reduced to a decomposing piece of rubbish.

How I hated the border of the sea which separated us and cut me off from his decomposing body. How I hated the man-made border between countries which exacerbated our differences. How I hated the physical border which announced with complete finality, 'On this side you are part of death; on the other side you are part of life.'

I didn't turn to the side of the living with any sense of relief. As I sat on the harsh stone, my lower body pricked all over by tiny thistles and thorns, which grew in the crevices of the rock, I was inert and cut off from all feeling. In a more dramatic gesture, I might have been ready to throw myself off the calanques, but I didn't have the energy or the willpower to do that. I leant back into the crevice, knowing that there was no comfort, but in some masochistic way enjoying the feeling of the jagged rock and thorns piercing my body.

If I wanted anything, I wanted to stay there for ever, defy the borders of countries, sea and human beings, and will myself to decompose, so that my body might be indistinguishable from the earth around me, as his would be – not with some hope of joining him in an after-life – but merely to cease from the impossibly painful process of living.

After six hours immobile, I forced myself to stand and confront the unimaginable process of meeting other people who had avoided his fate because they were protected by a border.

He could have been too, but he chose not to be. Without me there to help him, he had made a bad choice. But choices are the lot of the individual human being and not one of us can make correct choices for another.

# BOOK ONE

# Chapter One

What I remember from those early years is the sense of always having done something wrong.

I can't altogether blame my mother for it. It was a feeling which I absorbed rather than anything she said. For her, everything was wrong. Top of the list was all the work she had to do. The work of a farmer's wife in the 1930s was back breaking – endless drudgery – and, if there was no joy to relieve it, no sense of fun and especially no love present, then it was hard to imagine a prospect which was grimmer.

The warm red colour of the herringbone patterned wood on the outside walls of the houses gave the illusion of romance; but inside, there was a hard-beaten earth floor, no electricity and a tap and a WC outside in the yard.

Since those days, I have seen country people farm the small holdings at the back of their houses and been conscious of their pleasure in watching vegetables grow and become part of their daily meals. However, I cannot remember that pleasure in nature from my childhood. My father was not skilled in agriculture. He had inherited the house and the plot from his parents. My parents only had me to feed, but the expression on their faces revealed that life gave them little joy.

In my adult life I have found that I have a store of natural optimism built into my personality, but I never discovered this trait of character until I left home. My first abiding memory was that everything was doomed. And I could not make it right. Making everything right was too much of a burden for any six-year old; and for this particular six-year old, it was certainly not possible because I inherited a complete lack of practical skills from my father. I also remember the flatness of the countryside, the endless ditches and the stagnant water in the outlets of the lake. In my imagination, they all joined to cause disaster for us as a family. That sense of disaster entered the house and presided over the three of us. It was present in the smoke grained table where we ate, in the stone slabs where my mother prepared the vegetables and the occasional meat which my father hunted. Disaster lurked in the chairs which were broken and twisted and which no one had managed to repair, and in the stuffing, which was half escaping from the horse-hair long seat, where my mother sat to mend by oil light.

It was soon clear to me that my mother did not consider my father to be much good at anything. She once told me that she had been fooled into thinking that he had something to offer her when they got married. She saw clearly that he inherited the land and the house from his parents. What she did not perceive was his own lack of country skills. If there was a blight to be caught, then my father's vegetables had it. If there was a bad frost, then it attacked the produce of our field. At the beginning of their lives together, my father had made excuses for his misfortunes. Then he had whined and felt sorry for himself and he had finished by being sullen and resentful.

At first my mother had been willing to help put things right, because she was a naturally practical country woman. But early on she made the fatal mistake of making fun of her husband's incompetence and then she had become frustrated by his unwillingness to help in any way.

I was not a help to my mother's drab existence. I was one more mouth to feed. But, worst of all I inherited my father's inadequacies and so, even as a five or six-year old, I got in the way. If only I had been able to make her laugh as I carried in the potatoes or washed the carrots, I might have charmed her into enjoying my company. My biggest mistake was that I was a dreamer. Somewhere in my imagination I reached out to another world, which I hardly knew existed, but which was more than the drudgery of everyday life.

From the beginning my mother was irritated with me. When I was supposed to separate the sticks from the vegetables., I used them to draw shapes in the earth. When I was supposed to help water rows of beans, I would watch how the rivulets of water formed patterns on the ground.

My mother resented that I was always escaping in my mind from the task in hand. When she bullied my father, he withdrew so she could not hurt him. She was far more successful in bullying me. I soon learnt that I was just an irritation.

I only remembered one time when my father was able to relax. That was in the coldest part of winter when there was a fire. With the forests around us, there was always a plentiful supply of wood, and by the fire, my father would tell the ancient, mythical stories which came from Les Landes – an area which existed even before the land was dredged and planted with forests. I often wondered whether this ability to tell stories had attracted my mother to marry my father in the first place. Had this been their form of courtship – sitting down together on an old wooden form while he told stories? Perhaps it was that magical world which made her forget or even ignore his inadequate husbandry. I only knew that those were the first stories which held me, which made my life bearable, which gave me a picture of life away from this drab existence, where no one spoke or sang during the day, where duties were performed but life was not lived. This was my life, until, at the age of six, I went to school.

# Chapter Two

Most people remember their first day of school as being momentous, and it is usually anticipated, sometimes with fear, usually with excitement. My schooling just happened one morning without warning. I had woken up as usual, helped my father sweep out the yard, and fed the chickens and goats. I washed my hands in the yard tap and went inside for my small breakfast of porridge, softened by hot goat's milk. After these chores I was always hungry, and the food tasted delicious.

My father stood next to the table where I was eating and said 'You're coming with me now, Marie. You're ready for school.'

My mother was busy around the table in the kitchen and she sounded scornful, 'Much good will it do her, here in this place.'

'Annie, you know that they all have to go to school now. It's the law.'

My mother scoffed again. 'Reading and writing never helped anyone. All she needs is a husband who can work, especially as she's the image of her father and won't work for herself.'

I hung back afraid. I had no idea what they meant by reading and writing and school. That was grown up language which I ignored. But I knew already that I did not work hard enough for my mother. What followed was usually a clip round the ear. Again, my father was being shown to be inadequate. I saw the well-known hardened look of pride and sense of inadequacy. But the conversation did not end in the same way as it usually did – in silence and resentment.

'Marie, wash your hands again and bring your cap.'

'And leave me to wash up of course.'

'As you say, you are better at it than me.'

I'd hardly ever heard my father answer his wife back and I was astonished. I had no idea what was happening, but I obeyed and got myself ready to go out.

I walked with my father through the bracken and low undergrowth as I had done thousands of times when he went out to trap rabbits, or, if he was feeling adventurous, hunt the wild boar which were numerous in our area. My father was so soft hearted that he did not often go hunting, but such occasions were times of companionship, smelling my father's smell and experiencing freedom in the land which surrounded our house. My mother resented me going on these expeditions because she knew instinctively that I preferred my father's companionship to hers. I think my father could have been a teacher, if he had received an education. Even around practical tasks he knew how to teach. He let you draw alongside his activity and copy the parts you understood. He never made you do something you had not learnt to copy first. If you got it wrong, he just took over from you. It was not the skills which I learnt from him which drew my affection. It was the half smile, the sense that we were doing something together and that he enjoyed my friendship. Teaching is often shared discovery and out in the countryside there was no one to tell us off.

However, on that first day I knew the excursion was different because I had to take my cap, normally reserved for special community occasions. I had no idea where we were going, but I was happy to leave the house and the morning chores to go with my father.

It took us about an hour to get to the small school room, built in the clearing of the forest. By way of introduction to the experience of school my father made two statements.

'Marie, it is good to learn to read and write. Then you will not have to stay on the farm all your life.'

Looking back, that seems to me to have been the most extraordinary statement of enlightenment. Generally, the country people of our area could not envisage any other life apart from their own. There would always be questions of family continuity and who would look after parents in their old age. Choice was not something which was offered in our small community. The possibility of a different future was placed in my mind that day, and, even though my mind could not hold onto the stone which had skimmed the surface of the shady pond, it had penetrated deep into my subconscious.

Then, my father made another surprising statement – 'It is good for a child to meet other children.'

To anyone in society today that is a commonplace, but in our backward, rustic life, children were little adults who were only there to work. I had no understanding of the implications of what my father had said, and I felt unsure.

'There now.' My father brought me out to the opening of a village where there was only an old moat house, much the same in structure on the outside as our own house.

'It's up to you now. In you go,' said my father, without further explanation. 'Don't come home in the middle of the day. It's too far and it's not worth it.' With that, he turned back the way he had come.

I stood there watching as one or two girls and boys made their way through the door. Clearly that was what I was expected to do as well so, cautiously, I followed them.

A young woman, the teacher as I later found out, was standing by the wood burner, writing down names in a book as the children entered the school room. She saw me and asked me my name.

'Marie Leclerc.'

'Come in Marie, and welcome to school.' She gave me a smile, which confused me. I had seen a few half smiles from my father when he was feeling affectionate. However, I had never been the recipient of a full smile, like this one. It transformed my day; it transformed my life. It made me feel that I could cope with anything. It is a sensation which I have never forgotten. Subconsciously I have always been searching for the quality of that smile in every face I have looked at.

The first morning of learning was an extraordinary one – the first invitation to sit at a desk; the first awareness that my name distinguished me from others; the first realisation that I could respond to instructions without being reprimanded. The jibes of some of the boys at the back meant nothing because the goddess at the front, who had favoured me with a smile, was the only one who mattered. She seemed determined to see the best in me.

All age groups were together in the same room and there were only three other newcomers. While she was listening to the older children read, the teacher gave us new pupils an instruction.

'I am going to give you a slate and chalk and, while I am busy, I want you to draw a line, in whatever shape you wish, and then later to tell me what that line means to you.'

The whole idea of representation was a new one but, somehow, I understood what she was talking about. I thought about the straight lines I had drawn with a stick in the yard at home. I thought about the line of the heron diving for his fish, but the line which I thought was the most interesting of all was the one the wood pigeon makes, when he has stayed in the top of the trees but then gradually circles in a spiral above the yard, stops on the wall and then circles again to pick up the grain meant for the hen. That was the combination of lines I drew.

Afterwards I explained my choice to the teacher. I was worried because I saw that the other children had drawn one straight line each and I thought I would be in trouble for being different. The teacher gave me another of her smiles,

'That is a wonderful line to have drawn, Marie, and you have explained it perfectly.'

I would have done anything to keep that smile focused on me. I did not realise that there were others who were less appreciative of my efforts and that in school life, they could be as significant as the teacher. For the rest of the morning I was ignorant of this dimension of life. I thought I had never experienced happiness like this.

# Chapter Three

In the mid-morning we were let out into the yard to play. This area must have had the same dimensions as our own farmyard, but, as a school yard, it had been left empty. Everyone seemed to know what to do and I followed them.

'What a wonderful line you drew,' whispered the boy behind me.

The other children started to laugh. By the time we were outside someone turned around to say, 'And how perfectly you explained it, Marie.'

I could not have analysed the tone of voice, but even I knew that they were not the same words of admiration as my teacher had expressed. In my house I craved words of admiration. Everything which my mother told me was about my clumsiness and lack of understanding. That was why the words of the teacher had been so extraordinary. I had been basking in her approval for the last half hour. It had continued through the first exercises of copying the alphabet onto the slate. I had tried extra hard so that I would earn the teacher's approval.

Leaving the classroom for the yard was like waking up in a bath where the hot water has cooled without you realising, and where you had stayed too long by mistake. I reverted immediately to knowing that I was no good. Even the three children who were new like me did not want to play with me. They sensed that I had been rejected by the school and they were happy to belong to the majority. I squatted down in the corner of the yard by the wall watching. Most children ignored me. One girl knocked me off my balance as she deliberately came too close.

'Sorry,' she mocked. 'I didn't know you were watching the pigeons.' Everyone laughed. I picked myself up off the ground humiliated.

Everyone started to walk back into school. Before the break, I had been eager to do well; now I was unsure. Did I prefer the admiration of the teacher or the approval of the other pupils? It did not occur to me then that I could enjoy the pleasure of the work for its own sake. My teacher, sensing that there was a change in me, said little but congratulated other children on their progress. A little bit of misery trickled down the windowpane of my soul. After an hour of further work, we were dismissed. I trailed reluctantly behind the other children but, to my surprise they all left the yard. Was it already the end of the school day?

The teacher came out as the last one left. 'I thought your father said you couldn't go home at lunch time, Marie, because you live too far away to get back for afternoon school?'

Oh! So, I was to stay here? Doing more work without the other children! That would have pleased me.

'Shall I go back to the book again?'

Mlle Tessier laughed. 'Of course not. It's your free time. Where is your lunch?'

'I don't know.'

'Your mother hasn't sent lunch with you?'

I couldn't imagine my mother sending anything with me. That would have signified approval of my doings.

I hung back uncertainly. Everyone else had gone apart from one older boy. I hardly dared look at him, wishing that he would go too. I did not want to anticipate a whole stretch of time when I might be tormented by him.

'Alain stays over at lunch time. He will show you.'

I realised later that Alain was not thrilled about having his isolation disturbed. For the three previous years of school he had enjoyed the peace, away from his noisy family and the constant need for chores. He sat down with his back against the wall, where the midday rays of sun reached.

'You can share my picnic if you like.'

I stared at him – the third shock of my day. Someone was offering to give me something unasked. At home I had to be grateful for every piece of food because it was undeserved.

Alain grinned. 'But make sure you ask your mother for something tomorrow.' He stared at me for a moment, when I did not respond.

'Or bring something yourself, if you can.'

That moment encapsulated two amazing revelations. One was that it was possible to be generous. The other was an unspoken understanding that things at home might not be so easy – that my mother might not be like others who would respond to requests; but I could do something about it. Even in a home of negatives, I was not powerless. Looking back, I often think that I learnt the most important lessons of my life on that first day of school. I learnt that, through my teacher, encouragement changes all the ways we tackle challenges. That, from the taunts of other children, other people are not necessarily going to approve or enjoy it if you do well. That generosity for no other reason than the joy of sharing with another human being, is one of the most beautiful things on earth. That understanding that other people's circumstances may not be as easy as your own is the way to forge relationships. Those perceptions became the bedrock of my life and I owe those values to Mlle Tessier and Alain. In my mind over the years I have always come back to those two people, the formative influences of my life. For some reason, despite the bad beginnings which fate had given me, superimposed on that badness was the deep understanding those two human beings gave me. In fact, I could say that I was open to the beauty of what they taught me, because their light showed up in contrast to the darkness of the bad early experiences. If I had come from an averagely pleasant family, that morning might not have appeared so extraordinary. I might not have appreciated with such clarity what I had been given.

With a face which showed no emotion, I squatted next to Alain with the midday sunshine still covering us. I had not anticipated that he would talk as well as share his lunch with me.

# Chapter Four

I had no idea then that Alain was giving up something much more important than food, when he shared his lunch time with me. He was giving up his solitude. As a boy growing up in a loving but very busy family, lunch time was the only time when he could reflect in solitude. Suddenly, breaking into the silence, was a little girl whom he did not know, and who had showed already that she had no idea how to mix with others.

He handed me pieces of cheese, rough country bread and raw vegetable pieces. In our home we did not make cheese, so this was a new experience. We munched in silence.

'You know,' said Alain eventually, 'you shouldn't take any notice of what those boys say to you. It doesn't matter…and anyway, they will soon stop when they are used to you. You go on learning in the way you want to. If the teacher likes your work, then that's fine, but the main thing is whether you like what you're doing.'

How did he know what I didn't even know myself? That I was more scared of what others thought, than of what I truly wanted. But Alain, as I found out, had an extraordinary understanding of people. He himself did not care what anyone thought about him. Early on in my school career he was trying to relieve me of a burden. He didn't even know me, but, instinctively, he understood my fears.

'Don't slow down because of them. Don't do anything to please them. They're not worth it and they won't be pleased with you either.'

I munched on a radish. 'But won't they spend all their time trying to stop me?'

'No. They're giving you a challenge. How far will this girl go in sticking to what she really wants? They want to pull you into the herd.'

'The herd?'

'Yes, you know the goats stick together if they're let loose in the countryside, outside the yard.'

As a country child, I could see immediately what he meant. It was, I suppose, my first appreciation of metaphor.

'When they find that they can't keep you back, they will let you go and ignore you.'

And so, during that lunch time, I learnt more important lessons. Don't be afraid to ask questions. Don't be afraid to learn differently if it works. Don't be afraid to persevere on a path which reveals your own talent. Follow to the end what you want to do. I had only been in that building for four hours and I had been taught the most valuable lessons of my life. It has taken me the rest of my life to truly appreciate them. And all because I was privileged to have the most wonderful friend by my side, in addition to a gifted teacher in the classroom.

I didn't say much more to Alain that day. If he had feared he might have a chatterbox with him for the rest of his school career, he need not have been afraid. I was brought up in a dour, silent atmosphere, oppressed by duty. There was not enough space for extra talk and certainly not for laughter.

'You can go anywhere you want within the confines of this village,' he advised me, as we drank our water from the outside tap. 'But don't go too far into the forest because you won't be able to hear the school bell at the end of the lunch break.'

'And,' he added with a smile, 'When you learn to read, you can bring a book with you.'

I did not then understand that Alain's family read books as a normal part of their lives. Yes, many of them were religious books, but as people they were open to the idea of learning from books. In my family, reading was something you needed for checking bills or reading a government announcement. It had nothing to do with acquiring knowledge or pleasure. In order to survive on my parents' small holding, you had to work from dawn to dusk, and by that time you were so exhausted, that if you managed to sit by the fire for an extra hour without falling asleep, you were lucky, and, even then, there were jobs such as repairing and sewing which could only be done in the evening.

In those early weeks of autumn, I sat with my back against the school wall, enjoying the sun, or I wandered down the track where there were two or three houses or into the nearest entrance to the forest. I did not wander far. It was not the different physical environment which attracted me to school. It was the atmosphere of learning and freedom which I now know was not easy for any teacher to create, especially in a conservative rural area. Mlle Tessier managed to do just that.

I returned home at the end of the day, longing to share what I had experienced and forgetting in those few short hours what home was really like. As I returned that day to the farmhouse, which was empty, and then into the back yard, where my mother was swilling the pigs and my father was working at tying back some overlapping branches, no one looked up at me. It was as if they were in a concentration camp with guards watching over them in case they communicated with the enemy. Neither of my parents looked up, greeted me or asked me how my first day of school had been. By contrast, I was still living in the glow of the sun from a faraway country.

'I learnt to draw letters and my teacher is really nice.'

'Well, don't get used to someone being nice when you come back here. There's work to be done. Get that pinafore off and start to help with these animals.'

I turned away hurt. Surely someone must be interested in the world-shattering things I had learned! And what about all the people? The bullies? The shy little girls of my own age? Alain?

Something told me not to say anything about Alain. If my parents forbade me from speaking to him, my lunch times would no longer be exciting. I kept him in my own country. In fact, I kept all my experiences of school in my own country from now on.

My father paused in his sawing of branches. 'And the other children? Did you play with them?'

'Humph.' My mother's back held itself in a rigid arc in front of me, as she bent over the pigs. 'Glad someone's able to play when so much work needs doing.' I looked past the back to my father's enquiring face.

'I met the other children, Papa…', but I paused. He was listening to me, so I took advantage of having an audience. 'I need some food to take at lunch time. Everyone else lives near enough to go back for dinner.'

15

# Chapter Five

Without my having to ask again, from then on there was always some food left out for me each evening. I suppose that must show something about love. Neither of my parents wanted to acknowledge my need, or to be glad about giving. But it was provided – usually the leftovers from supper or in the summer some extra salad from the vegetable patch. Can love be there, when it is not articulated? Yes. Some people do not know how to express their love in words. They fear that, if they speak out, they will look foolish, or someone will take advantage of them. Since those days, I have found out that the omission of words does not mean that love does not exist. When I remember my home, I only remember the hardness, the lack of forgiveness, the inability to laugh. But when I think of that small offering of lunch left out, I realise that someone must have thought to give it. My mother always appeared to resent my schooling, as if it was a deliberate trick to deprive her of a helper, but, perhaps underneath that hard exterior, she was proud of the fact that I received an education. If only she could have expressed that pride in some form of affection!

Something strange happened on the next day when I brought my own food. I found myself wanting to sit away from Alain, guarding my food for myself. He was unperturbed by my move, always enjoying his own company to the full but I had not taken more than two mouthfuls of the delicious sausage which was left from our meal of the previous night, when it stuck in my throat. There was no joy in keeping it all to myself.

Alain looked up as I crouched down next to him in the yard.

'Decided to join me after all?'

I nodded and passed him my napkin full of food.

He laughed. 'Don't worry. I can't eat it anyway.'

'What do you mean? Are you sick?'

'No. It's the rules. In my family we can't eat sausage.'

'Why not?'

My curiosity about his answer was almost greater than my relief that I did not have to share any of my food. I had succeeded in making a gesture of generosity and at the same time keeping all the food to myself. Oh, the joy of selfishness and self-righteousness combined!

'It's our religion. I'm Jewish.' The word meant nothing to me.

'Does that mean you don't have to go to church?'

Alain laughed. 'Don't worry. We have to do plenty of other awful stuff instead.'

'What sort of stuff?'

'Praying three times a day … reading the Torah…obeying all the rules.'

'What sort of rules?'

'How long have you got? Millions of them. It's worst of all for the women. They have to prepare all these rules about preparing food.'

I thought about my mother's joyless preparation of food in our house.

'Yes, the older girls help her a lot. I'm the oldest son, so I'm supposed to read the Torah and pray, especially as my father isn't Jewish.'

'So, you don't have to go out to some special place like church?'

'Normally we would have to go on a Saturday, but we live too far away to walk so we don't go… at least only on special festivals or if we go to stay with the family in Bordeaux.'

'That's like us with the church and with school of course.' I paused. 'Perhaps living in an out of the way place is a good thing.'

Alain laughed. 'I think it is. It saves you having to obey even more rules than you already have to.'

I thought of the priest and the children who went regularly to church and of how I had envied them, because they were going to a special place. But then I saw how awful it would be – being forced to go every Sunday and missing out on being in the forest by yourself.

'You're right anyway,' continued Alain. 'Here, I can go for a walk when I want to, sit and be quiet, except when you're talking to me, and read by myself.' He shut his eyes for a moment as if recalling his large family. 'I like

17

my family of course, but there's never any time to be quiet and no time to read by myself.'

End of conversation. When Alain took his book from his pocket, that signalled the end of talk.

I always had more questions to ask him. If my teacher was the depository of new skills and new facts, Alain was the source of my knowledge about the world and exciting ideas. I suppose he gave me what my parents could not. But he himself needed to learn about the world outside his small farm, and he learnt it through books. It was a great hunger within him, and my presence was superfluous to his learning.

He gave me so much that I in no way resented his desire to be private at times. As time continued in the school, I too would bring books to read at lunch time and in the winter months, we were allowed to eat and read, sitting next to the central wood burner, while Mlle Tessier disappeared to her own small house nearby.

Alain most of all provided me with a sense of security and was a bulwark against the other children. They did not attack him, merely left him alone and I profited from his protection. He told me that early on in his attendance at school, they had occasionally called him 'Jew boy'. His family tradition was to ignore insults, but Alain did not follow traditional ways. One lunch time he had faced them down and fought each one, with the teacher finally intervening and reporting to their families. They never attacked him again; neither were they his friends, but he did not care. So long as he had the right to wander the forests and read, he was happy. And that's what he taught me to do – at first just a little at lunch times in his company, but then, when I was older, we would meet up at other times and explore and read together.

# Chapter Six

The winter days grew shorter and the two-hour lunch break seemed a long time in the middle of the day. At home we sometimes broke the ice on the pail of water which we would bring in from the yard for our morning wash. Winters in the South-West of France are often bleak, but not many of them offer freezing temperatures.

By the time late November came I had been through the school primer, arduously copied my alphabet onto my slate several times in succession and had caught the magic of reading.

I use the word 'magic' advisedly. It seemed to me not only a sort of magic that those tiny black marks could be deciphered and transferred to my slate, but it was also a sort of 'magic', because of the way in which they transformed my world. Even at the age of six, I could honestly say that I had worked every day since the age of three, helping my parents and copying what they did, not out of some play ritual, as so many children do, but because the small holding, symbolising our whole existence, was so labour intensive that we needed a three year old, if at all possible, to participate. I suppose that if I had been part of a large family as Alain was, there would have been other people to share the chores. A large family might have meant more mouths to feed, but it also meant more people to help. As I grew older, when I saw and knew more families in the villages, I saw eight-year olds who were so efficient and skilled that they could do most jobs, except for the heaviest and physically most demanding chores, as ably as an adult.

In my parents' experience, this was not the case, and later in life I wondered whether this was part of the reason that disappointment, frustration and anger hung as heavy clouds in the atmosphere of our small home. Most couples in the country could expect one healthy son to take on the responsibility of the small holding. Even if daughters moved away after marriage, as single girls, they contributed both to the outside chores and the comfort of the indoor environment, sewing quilts, cutting and sewing blouses and skirts. My mother received none of that help, so that she was worn down by the extra work she had to do.

Not only were there no other children to help, but the two adults were unequal workers. My father had inherited the small holding from his parents, but he had inherited no real sense of how to excel at farming or manual work. If my mother thought she had a 'catch' in her husband who owned a traditional wooden and brick house of Les Landes as well as the surrounding acres, she soon found out that the reality was different. Land is of no use, unless you know how to make it productive. She did and he did not; so, she was the one who ended up doing all the work. As I became older, I often blamed my mother for her lack of humour, her lack of demonstrative affection and her lack of encouragement, but the truth was that she was disappointed by the reality of life with my father. That might have been true of many local marriages in those far off days in Les Landes; but for most people there were compensations and the most obvious one was a large, loving, and ultimately useful family.

Instead, my mother had the misfortune to have me. I suppose that I must have inherited my father's lack of practical skills. At least he had been brought up to exercise them, even if imperfectly. By contrast I was a child with almost no practical skills and with no willingness to learn. Therefore, I was a source of irritation to my mother. Before I went to school, I would trail after her, sometimes being asked to do jobs and at other times trying to help. The results were disastrous for both of us.

The first time I fed the pigs, I dropped half their swill on the way from the barn to the yard. The pigs had less than they were expecting. The trail between the barn and the yard was a complete mess. I had no idea how to collect it up again and my own fingers were filthy. My mother cried out in vexation, as she had to do the job again by herself, do more clearing up and clean up a child, who came indoors afterwards and placed filthy hands on all the furniture.

'I may as well have done it myself in the first place. Now I have twice the work to do.' And she shooed me away in disgrace up to the loft where I was left without dinner so that I would learn about my sins. But I did not learn. I just felt more and more hopeless and learnt that everything I did for my mother was unacceptable. I was unacceptable as her child. I felt sorry that my mother had to put up with me. I was the one at fault.

When I say that learning to form letters and read was a sort of magic, I mean that it was a magic which transformed me in my own eyes from an incompetent, unlovely child to one who not only understood something completely for the first time in her life, but I also saw that I was able to succeed. The result was that I had the extraordinary experience of being praised by another human being.

Thinking back as an adult, I now realise that my teacher was probably quite young and plain with round glasses and a kind face. However, during my school days, whenever I thought about her, she was in my imagination as an angel in one of the stained-glass windows of the church. It is also true that when I returned home to be reminded again of my incompetence and laziness, I only endured the misery by remembering the two most wonderful people in my life, Mlle Tessier and Alain, and I was always longing to go back to them.

Once I was able to copy the letters of the alphabet, I soon learnt to put them together, and then I started to read. There were no books apart from the Bible in our house, and to find that there were books which told stories or gave information about my world was an extraordinary experience and filled me with wonder.

When I learnt to read, it was the greatest gift anyone gave me, because, ever since, I have cherished reading books more than anything else, not only because books are the key to information and learning but for themselves. They have transported me from misery to any imaginary world of adventure and delight more often than I can remember. They have enabled me to escape misery. They have saved me from boredom. They have given me personal hope because they have informed me of other cultures and peoples, different to my own. Through books I have met people who have spoken to me about my problems. I have learnt to understand the point of view of others, to empathise with those who are completely different to me in character and training. I owe more joy and delight to books than to anything else in my life.

And all that started in the classroom with Mlle Tessier.

But despite my rapid progress under Mlle Tessier's instruction, it was Alain who really led me into the knowledge and understanding which books had to offer.

As usual the other children, especially the older ones in the school, were scornful of my progress.

'So which page is our darling Marie on in her primer?' they taunted from the back of the class. The children of my own age were silent. They could not make the same progress as I did, and they were silent and uncomprehending. They did not taunt me as the older children did but they did not understand how wonderful it was to decipher the letters and words. They were slow because it was a burden to them. Reading for them was like trying to thread a needle for me. They did what they had to do, and, when they failed, they had to persevere. The only difference was that my mother had been a dismissive and bitter teacher when I failed to make progress in domestic matters; in contrast, Mlle Tessier knew how to encourage all her pupils in their scholastic struggles.

'Yves, you are making progress in forming your 'ds'. Well done.' And six-year old Yves would be inspired to keep going with his dull work.

For the first time I experienced a sense of superiority and scorn. I looked across at Yves and thought, 'He is still copying letters while I am putting words together.' My success led me to be mean. How can success, rather than failure, lead you to be mean? I have never understood why, but in my experience of life, I have proved that it does.

Mlle Tessier looked up at me as she walked along the rows, perhaps relieved that she could reprimand her best pupil.

'Marie, concentrate on your work please,' she said sternly. 'You should not be listening to my advice to Yves. You have plenty to do yourself and when I come to you, I expect to see that you have completed that section.'

I was stung with humiliation. My angel had found fault with me. How unfair when I was so much better than anyone else! But Mlle Tessier taught me a great lesson by her reprimand. Don't judge anyone else's progress by your own. You are only answerable to yourself and your own standards. I know that even now when I see the terrible mistakes that others have made in post-war France. How can I judge the actions of others? I am only answerable to myself. If Mlle Tessier encouraged me to make progress with my studies, it was Alain who demonstrated to me how to devour the content of books. During those winter months he would bring books to our lunch time break and nothing would disturb his concentration or interest in them. When we could not go outside, he would sit next to the wood burner in the school room and steadily work through one book after another. He could hardly wait to finish eating and wash his hands. His hunger for books was greater than his hunger for food. He not only read every book Mlle Tessier could find for him, he brought books from his own home and from a library in faraway Bordeaux. He was not aware of my presence during those lunch hours. He was in a different world.

# Chapter Seven

I was six when I went to school and Alain was ten when I first met him. We were to have eight years of reading, learning, talking and exploring together before the German invasion changed our lives. He became my greatest companion. Alain had such a sense of being 'different' from the other school children, and such a sense of indifference about what anyone might think about him, that not only was he left alone by the other children, but I also profited from his reputation. At school I was known to be unnaturally clever, interested in books and learning in a way which was not normal in our community of villages, but any deeper bullying which I might have suffered, was absorbed by Alain's personality. I was protected by a larger person. Behind his back they classified his difference as his Jewishness, his bookishness, but, although a loner, he was known to be amiable and fair in his dealings with the other children. And, while Mlle Tessier must have adored her one outstanding older pupil, she was wise enough not to show favouritism. In some ways, Alain did not need a teacher in the same way as I did. Alain would have found books and learning if you had left him by himself in the middle of the forest. His homelife and his religion nourished him and his self-belief in such a way as led to his complete self-confidence. In contrast, with my joyless and critical parents, I needed Mlle Tessier. I needed her encouragement and her patience. I needed the fact that she could cherish the gifts which I possessed, and she did not assume that my lack of practical gifts meant that I was useless.

The children of my own age grew up in the local villages knowing that they were skilled in husbandry, animal rearing, home making, and sewing. No doubt other pupils came from unhappy homes or were the offspring of indifferent marriages. But their skills were honed at home, were useful in day to day life, and were needed in their households. They were satisfied that they were appreciated and needed as part of their large families. School was an unfortunate intrusion on their lives which the government forced them to endure. Many of the families in our community resented mandatory schooling and the government which put it into practice, more than they later resented the German invasion. Cut off on the western edges of the country with little interest in politics, theirs had been a traditional way of life for centuries. They did not really care whether it was a Vichy government or not. The one thing which made them resent the Germans was the number of sons who had been lost in the previous war, but even that was because it had caused hardship through loss of workers on the land, rather than the battles themselves. We were nowhere geographically near the battlefields of the Somme. We were not those who had heard the bombardments or those who nervously waited near the Maginot line for the next invasion of their country. As French men they would be loyal to their country, but in practical reality, they were more loyal to Les Landes and the wider area of la Gironde. These areas were huge tracts of land sandwiched between the centre of France and the Basque country just south of us. The Landais cared, neither for what they saw as the primitive Basque traditions, or the meddling politics of France. They only cared about their small holdings and their forests.

Those who were not small-time farmers were forest workers. If reading and learning dominated my life between the ages of six and fourteen years, then so did the character of the forest, which opened extraordinary worlds up to me. I not only walked through the forest to school, and enjoyed the escape into solitude, but at the age of eight I was given an unexpected gift – a bicycle.

The bicycle was the obvious means of transport for any poor peasant in Les Landes. The forest workers used them to get to and from work, especially to the paper factory which was not far from the coast. Generally, women did not use them because most of their lives revolved around the house, their small holdings and their families. Some families had a generic bicycle for whoever might need it, especially when they sold local produce at the village or town markets. My father used his bicycle for this purpose but sometimes to get away from the house and have a smoke by himself. Occasionally I had sat on the back wheel for a ride.

But my life changed when one day Alain said at school, 'You know, Marie, my sister Alice has a bicycle she hardly ever uses. Would you like it? It would get you to school much more quickly than walking and you could use it in the summer when we go into the forest.'

'But I don't know how to ride.'

'You'll learn in half an hour. It's easy. Anyone can learn.'

'What will my parents say? Where will I keep it?'

Worries and doubts crowded in, before it occurred to me that I could be grateful for the offer and say, 'thank you'.

'Surely your parents wouldn't object if they knew it was a cast off that no one else used.'

I was doubtful of their response. They were proud and introverted. They would be suspicious of contact with any other farm and I couldn't imagine what my mother would think if she knew that the bicycle came from a Jewish family. Instinctively I knew enough about village politics to know that Alain's family was different to ours, and something told me that I should not mention anything about a bike coming from Alain's family. At the same time, I was thrilled. I was used to the idea that Alain was generous with his time, friendship, ideas, books and lunch. The gift of a bike was not an extraordinary idea in that sense. But as something to possess which meant that I could go off into the forest as far as I liked, it presented me with an extraordinary opening. I did not even consider the fact that it might cut the time from my journey to school. School was of such value that I would have walked for hours to get to it. The fact that it took me longer to get home than anyone else satisfied me. It meant that I had less time to do chores at home and less time to be shouted at. The ten minutes at the beginning of the day before I set off for school was the worst time of all.

Alain, as usual, understood my fears and hesitations.

'Tell you what,' he said. 'If you don't want to take it home, there's an old wreck of a hut just outside the clearing here. You could leave it there for lunch times in the summer and when you find the right time to tell your parents or find somewhere to leave it near home, then take it.'

And that was how, surreptitiously, I acquired a bicycle at the age of eight. It was my first possession outside my parents' sphere of influence, and I loved it from the moment I first fell off it into a muddy patch and immediately got on again. It became the symbol of my new, independent life.

# Chapter Eight

When Alain was fifteen years old, he passed the exam for the lycée, the selective school in Bordeaux. No one in our school had ever sat for the exam and passed it before, so it should have been a cause for enormous celebration. For Mlle Tessier and for me it was. Our teacher was very careful not to show favouritism, but it was still clear that Alain was the most intelligent and self-motivated pupil that she had ever taught. No teacher could have failed to have pleasure in teaching him. The modern term, 'learning enabler' was the correct one for her role. Some village school mistresses could have made his experience a sour one, because he would have showed up their own lesser intelligence and lack of learning. Mlle Tessier's great quality in teaching was that she was humble and that she did not ignore either the local child who was struggling or learning enthusiasts like Alain and me. The rest of the village was guarded about acknowledging Alain's achievements. His fellow pupils did not understand him, or indeed barely spoke to him, but they admired him and were not jealous, because they in no way aspired to his achievements. The adults in the community were indifferent to his success. He was not a catholic and his future academic career would not affect their lives amongst the small holdings and forest plantations. Bordeaux was like a far-off country and if he chose to emigrate, then it was no business of theirs. What his own family thought about it I had no idea. Knowing as I do now, how much the Jews prize book learning, I can only imagine that his mother, at least, was very proud of his achievements.

'What did your parents say, when you told them?' I asked him one lunch time as we biked out to a forest clearing to have our lunch time picnic. For once we were not reading at school.

28

'Oh, it's not very important to them,' he replied calmly.

I was confused. 'But I thought there were all these books at your house.'

'Yes, there are but mainly books about Jewish learning. They come from my mother's family because they're Jewish. My father's different. He's a local farmer like everyone else in these parts and he's not interested in books.'

'Do you read the religious books too?'

'Yes, of course. You know me, Marie. I'll read anything in print just to see what it's all about.'

'And is it any good?'

Alain thought for a long moment as we parked our bicycles up against a tree trunk. 'It's amazing and there's lots of wisdom there, but there's an awful lot about how you have to obey the rules better. And I've had quite enough of rules in my life.'

'Me too,' I agreed with my mouth full of rye bread and home-made paté.

He laughed. 'Marie, you don't the meaning of the word 'rule'. You can only know it properly if you've been brought up as a Jew.'

I was annoyed by this attitude of superiority in suffering. 'How do you know? You've never been a Catholic.'

Alain glanced at me lazily. 'When it comes to laws about how to eat and how to keep the sabbath the Jews are way in front of anyone else.'

It was unusual for Alain to show off about anything and, even in this minor matter, he was not interested in the competitive angle of the conversation.

'Go on then. Tell me about the law keeping of the Catholics.'

I had been too willing to show off. Coming from a very nominal Catholic background, I did not actually know very much about my own religion and was embarrassed and evasive.

'You can only eat fish on Fridays.'

'And do you?'

'No,' I had to admit. My father enjoyed catching fish, but my parents did not care about the rules of religion. 'We're not very strict about it but some Catholics are.'

'In that case you don't love and live rules like the Jews do. And you're talking about a rule for one day?' Alain laughed. 'That's nothing compared to the rules my mother is supposed to keep in the kitchen all the time – the one about not having meat and dairy at the same time, for example. Not that she does. A family way out in the country like we are can't possibly do that, at least only occasionally when Great Uncle Reuben turns up.'

'Who's he?'

'He's my famous Rabbi uncle in Bordeaux. Fortunately, he's too busy looking after his synagogue most of the time to worry about us. And he didn't really approve of my mother marrying my father. Also, when the rules go crazy like on Shabbat, he can't travel this far anyway because he's got to be near his synagogue. My mother is always scared that he might show up some Friday and see that we don't keep the rules.'

'Is Shabbat like our Sundays?'

'Yes, but worse. You can't do anything you want to.'

'Some Catholics are like that too with Sundays. Cecile at school told me that she's not allowed to do anything on Sunday, apart from going to church and Sunday School. She gets bored but at least they have nice food on Sundays.'

The great sadness of Alain's life was that his father died the following summer, just before he left the village. At least he had known that Alain had passed the exam and fortunately his Uncle Reuben and Aunt Jeanne understood the situation and offered to give him a free place in their home, so that his mother did not have to provide for him. She was now overburdened with looking after their small holding herself and bringing up the younger children, but she insisted that Alain made the most of his opportunity.

When Alain went away at the age of sixteen, my life at school became a lonely one, but Alain had bequeathed me far more than his presence. I had inherited his love of books to such an extent, that I never felt lonely. I stilled missed his companionship. There is something amazingly companionable and pleasant about reading silently in the company of someone else who enjoys it. Especially in winter I missed his presence round the wood burner and his ability to answer any question I posed. Instead, I had to rely on my own thoughts, what I could discover in books and my own conversations with Mlle Tessier who became much more inclined to stay in the lunch hour and chat once Alain had gone, though she was always careful to do it under the guise of staying to tidy the school desks rather than being guilty of showing favouritism towards a pupil.

My bicycle too gave me a reason never to be lonely. From the start I had loved the feeling of independence, the freedom it gave me to leave family and school without anyone interfering with my plans. After a time too, I enjoyed the feeling of adventure, the fun of discovering new places which were unknown to anyone but me.

My relationship with my parents was already growing more distant. My contribution to the daily chores had always been badly received. It was clear that I was never going to be a helpful, practical child. My mother complained about my ineptitude and lack of availability, just as she complained about my father's attitude. Why had she been left – the only woman in Les Landes to do all the farming, all the mending and the cooking, she asked herself; but secretly she was proud of what she was doing. It was backbreakingly hard work and she must have often been exhausted but it was her work and she achieved something in doing it perfectly. The fact that she had to struggle alone rather than share it gave her great satisfaction. As the years went on, my father was wise enough to become one of her admirers because she needed to maintain that position. If he allowed her to boast about the work she did, he was left in an uneasy peace, and so he played his part by admiring her and doing some of the basic jobs on the farm but also going off by himself to hunt in the woods. She would receive his contributions to her kitchen disdainfully and then silently dismiss him. It was an armistice of sorts between the aspirations of her youthful days, when she thought she was doing well by marrying a landowner and her disappointment in the reality of what he was like and the lack of children to help her. It made for a silent home but one in which both sides kept behind clear boundaries and one in which I was more and more ignored.

If I cleaned out and fed the chickens, looked after the pigs after school and helped with some preparation of food, I was left alone. For a bookish child, who enjoyed roaming the countryside, this was a perfect solution. It was more difficult in the winter when there were less daylight hours,

31

but I always managed to explain that my book reading was my school homework and I was left alone.

For the first year I concealed my bicycle in the abandoned hut near school, but, later, I discovered a similar shack not far from my own home and made use of that as well. That meant I could leave home early as if I needed to walk a long distance and then cycle off to some remote place in the forest before school began. After school I would ride most of the way home and, with an apple saved from lunch, sit against the bark of a tree with my book.

I would ride down the long winding tributaries of the lake, overshadowed by the branches of the trees and stop wherever I wanted to, look, listen and discover. I knew the tap of the woodpeckers, the distant flash of colour of the kingfishers, and spotted the nests of the wood pigeons after the whirring of their wings showed that they had anticipated my presence. Sometimes the tributaries would open out unexpectedly onto sunny and sandy banks. The heron would be there silently waiting to take its own fish. If I suddenly surprised one, he would be off, his luminous, heavy wings flapping over me, but if I had perched on the opposite bank reading, he would accept my presence and stay. While I studied, he worked for his food – a companionable agreement between friends. Then there were the straight unmade roads leading to little hamlets secluded from each other by the forest. I would pass by the front of the houses, wondering whether their small holdings were like ours. Occasionally I would recognize a face from school, but generally anyone I saw seemed in their own little world cut off from mine.

I would pedal round the huge lake at Aureilhan, stopping in the summer to paddle and swim in the cool waters. I had been taught to swim by Alain, who also demonstrated how to be unashamed of stripping off to underclothes and plunging in. Then we would lie drying by the sun and enjoying a quiet rest after our exertions.

It was while cycling round the lake at Aureihan that one day I was surprised by the sight of a large house in the distance. It seemed suddenly to appear from nowhere, and I was fascinated. How come I never seen it before? And who lived there?

I didn't dare to ask my parents, because then they might have worried about how far I was travelling on my bicycle, so I decided to ask Giles and Patrice at school because they lived on the other side of the lake at Mimizan.

'Oh, that's where the English aristocrats come!' they explained, as if such a venue was the most obvious place you would expect to find in Les Landes.

'What do you mean the English aristocrats?' I asked amazed.

'Very rich English people come there every summer to hunt around the lake.'

'So how come I haven't seen it before?' I wondered.

'Because you go around with your eyes shut?' suggested Patrice, glad to find that he had some information which was news to the stuck-up little know all from the further parts of the countryside.

Giles, his brother, was a little kinder. 'You wouldn't have seen it before because the trees were not cut back from the lake. They've only just done that and built the steps down to the lake. They go across on boats to the other side.'

'But why have the English come here?'

'Because of all the hunting round here.'

'Hunting? You mean like my father does?'

Patrice laughed. 'Yes, but I expect they're a bit better at it than your father. And of course, they have servants to do it for them.'

'Why do they have servants?'

'Because they're lazy and rich and think that ordinary people are there to do their work for them.'

That was the first time that I heard about the division between the rich and the poor and saw the emergence of a beautiful manor house, built in the style of a famous house in South Africa, called the Woolsack. To be honest, the idea of having ordinary people to help you with your work sounded an excellent idea to me and a good reason to be rich, but I knew better than to admit that to Patrice and Giles. Their dad was the leader of the communists in our village and I knew from gossip in the school yard that they hated the rich. I said little and continued to marvel at the fairy tale creation which appeared on one side of our lake in Aureilhan.

It was my first realisation that foreigners could come and live in Les Landes.

# Chapter Nine

The invasion by the Germans and take over by the Vichy government happened so gradually as far as our country area was concerned, that I was almost unaware of it. I was fourteen years old in 1940 when we started to hear rumours about it, but politics were never discussed at home. In fact, nothing was discussed at home so any sort of awareness of a wider political life did not exist. With Alain's advice I had progressed from story books to the classics and gradually to concepts and argument, but those ideas were mainly mediated through stories, especially through history, rather than pure philosophy.

Mlle Tessier was a wonderful teacher of French history. At school we had worked through the French Revolution to Napoleon and then we had made our way through the Great War. Everyone in the village was intensely patriotic and hated 'the Boches'. I only knew that they had killed older children's fathers whose names were on the war memorials in the villages. But why they had fought and what the consequences were, I had no real idea.

Older pupils came to school with stories about how the French 'Vichy' government had done a deal with the Germans. Alain's contemporaries had left school long ago, and I was by now part of the oldest batch of thirteen and fourteen-year olds at school. The boys were always huddling together and talking about how they were going to fight the Boches. I felt like saying, 'And ending up on the war memorial like your dads,' but I kept quiet. Several years of schooling and being part of the school playground had taught me that it was not worth arguing with the received wisdom of the day.

I knew too that I was due to leave school sometime soon and the thought sent panic waves through me. I loved being taught by Mlle

Tessier and I had access to so many books which she herself had found for me since Alain had left. The thought of going back to the farm and working with my parents brought a feeling of dread into my life. Surely, I reasoned, if Alain had gone to another school in Bordeaux, then so could I. However, I could not imagine my parents giving permission for such a move. I didn't even know whether girls were allowed to go to such places. But the possibility of further learning and being able to leave home was so exciting that I would hug myself with the sheer joyful anticipation of such a move. Sometimes I would ride through the forest on marked and unmarked paths at tremendous speed, inside my head just willing another future to happen, rather than the mundane one which was more likely. Occasionally I would throw myself down on the ground with my knees up above me, and I would clench them against my body in sheer determination.

In the school holidays Alain would return home to find me and we would set off on the forest tracks again. He knew better than to announce himself at my house. He would wait for me near the empty huts near to my school. Even though my parents now knew that I had a bike, I kept it in hidden places.

One summer, when rumours about the coming invasion and war were rife, Alain was waiting near the hut at the end of the school day. I was particularly glad to see him, because I had a better chance of learning about what was going on from him than from anyone else. Besides, he was not impatient with my questions and did not treat me as though I was stupid.

'What's happening to our country, Alain?'

For once he did not jump back quickly with an answer. He wheeled his bike alongside mine, looking serious.

'I'm not honestly sure at the moment Marie, but it's not looking good.'

'Why? Isn't it good to make peace with the Germans? Then not so many people will die as last time. After all you might have to join the army when you're eighteen.'

'Yes, that would be awful,' he admitted. I could not imagine the laconic Alain caring enough to fight. And he would hate the marching and the shouting and the violence. Then he added, surprisingly,

'But the alternative might be worse.'

'What do you mean? How can anything be worse than war and people killing each other?'

Alain looked very serious, which was unusual even when he was explaining a piece of complex philosophy. 'Because at least in war you have a chance to stand up and fight for what you believe in. But if the Germans invade, we will just cower and let them take over. And it will be the end of people like me and my family.'

'What do you mean?'

'Don't forget, Marie, that I'm from a Jewish family.'

'What difference does that make? You're French and anyway, it's only your mother who is Jewish. Being Jewish is a religion like being Catholic.'

'I'm afraid that it's a lot more than that as far as the Germans are concerned.'

'What do you mean?'

'Have you heard of a man called Adolf Hitler?'

I had heard the name when some of the boys at school were talking amongst themselves. My parents didn't even own a radio. They were isolated in their own little world of work and the small holding. Daily survival was their only aim.

'Hitler has persuaded the Germans that all their troubles are because of the Jews in Germany.'

'I thought that all their troubles were because they invaded us in the Great War, and we defeated them.'

'People might say that, but, for whatever reason, Hitler has told the Germans that the Jews have brought them down.'

'Even if they had,' I commented reasonably, 'That's nothing to do with you. You haven't brought him down.'

'But don't you see? I am part of it. That's one of the things I've seen in Bordeaux. I might laugh at the whole religious thing. I might laugh at the rules, but I am inextricably caught up with it. It's part of who I am.'

'But I've always liked the part of you, which questions everything and sees the stupidity of all those rules.'

I was astounded. Here was my hero, my role model, the one to whom I owed my birth as a real person. He had helped me to reject my identity as part of an ineffective and dysfunctional family, buried in the forests of Les Landes. And now this hero was saying that he wanted these rules after all. If he wanted to adopt the rules of his family, then maybe I would be forced to retreat into the suffocating rules of mine. I had been born and raised as a tortoise encrusted in a hard shell, and, since going to school and meeting Alain, I had crept out of my hiding place to look at the real world and be part of the forest in Les Landes, which had been almost submerged by the sea. I had found that the land was continually reverting to the way it was before the forests were cultivated one hundred years before. If you tried riding through the sand which had accumulated on the path, you nearly always got stuck or fell off. In the end you made better progress if you pushed the bike.

'Thanks Marie.' Alain was laughing in his old familiar way. 'I need your reassurance that if I like breaking the rules it's OK. Actually,' he said, reverting to his former seriousness, 'You're right. I haven't forgotten that the rules annoy me, and I don't believe in most of them, but Jewish people have the right to have their rules like anyone else if they want them. But it's true that living in Bordeaux has given me a different take on them.'

We remounted our bikes and cycled to a familiar spot, a small lake, where teenagers sometimes fished, and which was not far from a hamlet. We flung our bikes down and lay down under a tree, finding our bread and cheese and salad and the greengages which grew locally. I had been to the store in the barn and rescued a few which had evaded my mother's persistent effort to turn them into jam for the winter months.

'What have you been up to in Bordeaux?' I asked full of curiosity. 'I thought you were going to a better school there and you would tell me more about the books you've been reading.' I didn't say that I had been hoping that he might have saved one of two from his store for me during the school holidays.

'Well I have read more books. Don't worry. But I've also had a different sort of education as well. And it's all down to Great Uncle Reuben.'

# Chapter Ten

'I thought that was the part of Bordeaux you weren't looking forward to?'

Two years before, Alain had been looking forward to his lyceé education. With his personality, he didn't see it as a privilege, but more as his right. If I had been in the same situation, I would have been worried about whether I was going to pass the exam and then whether I would be up to the standard of the others at a big school in the town. In contrast, Alain had an extraordinary quality of not caring what others thought. He knew that he merited further education. Whether others at a school in Bordeaux thought he was as good as them or not was a matter of complete indifference to him. He wanted to learn more so that he would have more opportunities in life. It was all about his decision, not about an opportunity given by others or by a government.

Alain lay on his back, sucking grass and staring out over the tiny lake, which was like the forgotten smaller brother of the huge lakes, including Lake Aureihan, which stretched right across the region of Les Landes. There was a sense of intimacy in this lake which encouraged the sharing of confidences. We were in our own tiny world of a small hamlet and accompanying water supply, far from either the big towns or our own small holdings.

'You're right of course,' said Alain. 'I just lived for the experience of the lycée at Bordeaux. I was even annoyed with my mother for making me board with Great Uncle Reuben. I did not want my own freedom to be curtailed by annoying family ties or by ridiculous religious laws. Why should my new world have been restricted by petty traditions?'

It seemed a reasonable question, even though I thought he was lucky to be restricted only by traditions. Alain might complain about the laws of his religion, but I knew that his family, even after the death of his father, experienced laughter and discussion and sharing. Mine did not even have the excitement of debate and argument. Apart from the occasional electric sparks which flew from the three of us when we disagreed, no one talked enough or even cared enough to have a quarrel – a word which seemed to suggest you should listen to your opponent and disagree with his ideas. My parents did not know what an idea was. When I was in their company, my ideas were frozen deep within my body, so that they could not be expressed.

Alain continued his explanation. 'However, I had to be fair to my mother. The education in a lycée is free but you need to live somewhere, and your parents must pay for a boarding place. My family have enough food and a place to live but we're not rich especially since my father died. There isn't enough money to pay for extra lodgings.'

Such practical problems had never occurred to me before. I seemed to have jumped from the surprise that I could be allowed to learn freely when I first went to school to the assumption that a school would give me anything I needed, in order to learn. Alain's explanations about his boarding needs that summer taught me for the first time that things weren't quite so simple.

'The only solution was for me to live with Great Uncle Reuben and Great Aunt Jeanne. To be honest it wasn't a great idea from my point of view. No young people to keep me company, no one pleased about me doing secular learning. A watchful eye being kept on my behaviour and not being allowed to do anything on Shabbat, apart from go to the synagogue and be miserable. But it was the only solution and I took it with bad grace.

But I was wrong. In the event I was wrong about a lot of things.'

I sat up and changed my position, lying on my stomach and giving Alain my full attention. I watched him carefully as he talked. In all my years of talking with him, I had never heard him admit that he was wrong about any of his ideas, which was strange, since he was such an unassuming person.

'First of all, I was amazed at how much I missed my family. I had always been annoyed when my little sisters made so much noise that

I couldn't hear myself think and I couldn't get away from them in our farmhouse.

But I missed them – their laughter, their silly games. I even missed my brother telling me how stupid I was to cherish book learning so much. Instead, when I returned from the lycée, I had all the time and silence in the world, and I missed the family atmosphere and the interruptions. I almost started to look down on my own appreciation of learning. It suddenly started to look rather pompous and shallow.'

I had no idea what he was talking about. How I would have loved to be released from chores to do what I loved – reading. I wondered at my friend's new perspective.

'To be fair to my great aunt,' continued Alain, 'She took care of all the chores and no doubt followed all the religious laws without bothering me. She even made a fuss of me, asking me if I wanted more food and worrying that she didn't look after me like my mother. Great Uncle Reuben, of course, would disappear each day before dark and go off to say 'mincha'.'

'What's that?'

'Jews are supposed to pray three times a day in groups of ten men, and that group is called a minyan.'

'Three times a day? It sounds worse than church!' I knew that my school friend, Alice's, grandmother went to church each evening to say compline but three times a day sounded excessive to my ears.

Alain laughed. 'Yes, well, to be fair to him, he never tried to persuade me to go with him. And he always asked about my day at school. I wasn't used to such close questioning and, to begin with, I found it very intrusive. I thought he might be trying to find fault with the school, and I felt I wasn't allowed the bit of me which was private and which he wouldn't understand. But, after a time, I realised his questions were genuine. He was really interested in my studies, because he wanted to understand me better. No one in my family had ever asked me about school before. He also asked me some searching questions about what I was reading. The man, who I had assumed to be an old, deluded, religious Jew had a few ideas in his head worth thinking about!'

'What about the school itself? What was that like?'

'Oh!' Alain was dismissive as if that was hardly the point of our conversation. 'The usual mixture… mostly those who had to be there because their parents wanted them to be…but a few serious learners of course.'

'Don't worry,' he laughed, as he saw my surprise, 'Not so many offspring of ignorant farmers as at our 'école primaire'. You'll be alright when you arrive on the scene.'

I turned away, blushing and awkward. As usual, Alain was uncomfortably aware of what I really wanted. I was embarrassed that he guessed the extent of my ambition, and that he also understood why I was so keen to question him about his experience.

'I don't think I'll have much of a chance,' I muttered and then shouted and giggled as he tickled me with grass stems. 'Anyway,' I said trying to hide my self-interest and sensing that my next question might be more important to Alain than our discussion about the lycée, 'Tell me about your great uncle and aunt.'

A couple of boys who were fishing had set up near us.

'Let's go over the other side where's there's more shade,' Alain suggested.

I was surprised. Usually Alain did not care who heard what he had to say, and we had been comfortably installed with our picnics and with our bikes parked near.

'I don't want anyone listening, Marie,' he said after we had gone through the upheaval of moving further away. 'People don't understand.'

'Understand what?'

'What it's like to be a Jew now. They don't understand.'

I crouched down by the lake, watching the ripples caused by the frogs jumping in. Something was happening which I did not understand. For the first time in my experience, Alain was concerned about what someone else thought. For the first time in my life it might matter that my best friend was a Jew and that he could not trust some people in the village. It was becoming a world where the old values were not so certain.

# Chapter Eleven

'During the week I was totally preoccupied by the demands of school.'

'Was it hard?'

'Yes.'

I was surprised. I would never have thought that Alain would find book work hard.

'It was rewarding but it was hard. Not everyone cares about the work and some people struggle with the standards expected. But there are some really clever people at the lycée …and the teachers demanded high standards.'

'But you got on alright?'

'Yes, I could cope with it, but it was a struggle.'

My face showed my surprise.

'OK, Marie, just because I like reading it doesn't make me a genius, though of course I've returned all the way to St. Paul for you to flatter me. I'm lazy too.'

'Yes, of course I am,' he added quickly seeing my face. 'Just like you, I've never wanted to help with chores at home.'

I was puzzled at his assessment. 'But that's because I'm no good at them so it's pointless.'

'But also, probably like me, you're lazy. You like using your mind but not your body. Anyway, that's not the point. It was natural for me to like the reading, but I had to start working at things like presentations and essays. There are formal ways of doing things at a lycée and if I didn't bother with them because I thought it was a waste of time, my prof soon told me.'

'Are they nice?'

'Some of them are alright, but there's no one really like Mlle Tessier, which reminds me, I must call on her soon this holiday.'

'Great. I'll come with you.'

'Yes, that would be good.' He paused and went back to his earlier conversation. 'It was my experience of Shabat which changed my view of my religion. We've always had a kind of Shabat at home, but I soon saw that it had been very lax.'

'But I thought you didn't like the rules.'

'It's strange. I didn't before and I still object to them in my mind. But I saw something else in Bordeaux. I saw the joy they took in the rules and how it made them feel special.'

'How can you take joy in rules?'

'I don't know but Reuben and Jeanne do.'

'They took the whole week anticipating Shabbat, and all they seemed to have then was more prohibitions. But it made them feel special.

Here in the countryside, especially as my dad wasn't part of it, we never mixed with other Jews except when there were visitors from different places or family get togethers. In Bordeaux it was different. There was a whole group of them at the synagogue. Yes, I guess it's a bit like church, so you'd think that meant more people being miserable but for some reason it actually meant more people having fun.'

'Fun?' I asked indignantly. In no way did I associate my occasional experience of church with fun.

'Yes, there was this amazing veneration for the Torah, not just for what it says, but for the book itself.'

'But it's an old book, with loads of rules which aren't relevant to now,' I protested.

'I agree in theory and I would have said the same thing myself, before being in Bordeaux. But I've changed.'

I was jealous. Part of who Alain was, was his being perfect. I didn't want him to change and grow away from me.

'Well don't change too much. I liked it the way you were before.'

He knit his eyebrows together and looked at the other side of the lake where we could still see the boys fishing. 'You can't stop change, Marie. It's not just me who is changing. It's the world too. It's changing fast.'

Later, Mlle Tessier nodded in agreement when Alain repeated this sentiment. We had been received with great enthusiasm and affection by our village teacher, just in time to share our 'goûter' with her. She even found some slabs of chocolate to go with the bread. I hardly knew what chocolate was. It seemed to me not only delicious but highly sophisticated. I was being admitted to a very special group of people even though I knew I was only there because of my association with Alain.

'It's true the world is changing, my dears, and not always for the better.' I looked from one to the other astonished. Mlle Tessier was the most kindly, positive person I had ever met. How could she, who was always so optimistic, be saying such things?

'Oh,' I said airily. 'It's just because of the last war. Old people are just scared it's going to start again.'

'That's not surprising,' said Alain, looking at me solemnly, 'when you consider all that they lost last time.'

I felt rebuked. I thought that my comment had been clever and offhand, but Alain judged that I was being insensitive and uncaring. I was ashamed and did not want to join in with any more of the conversation. Instead I listened to my teacher.

'If that were only true, Marie. If we could only dismiss this as the fear of old people who want to live in the past. Unfortunately, this is quite a new threat.'

'It's going to affect everyone, especially my family.' Alain and she appeared to have agreed on this view of a coming war in advance.

I was puzzled. Why would the Germans target Alain's family?

'I've told you before, Marie. It's because we're Jewish.'

'Well, just don't say,' I said, my naivety showing once again. 'If you don't say anything, they'll never know.'

Alain reached over and rumpled my hair, half in exasperation, and half in tolerant affection.

'I don't think it's quite that easy. In the end they always know.'

'Can't you get out before they come?' asked Mlle Tessier seriously.

'Get out?' I repeated incredulously. 'You don't mean leave us?'

'I certainly would if I could, but I can't,' replied Alain to our teacher, ignoring my interruption. 'Reuben and Jeanne will probably try to go and

44

some of the richer ones in the community. But I'm not leaving my family here. There's no way they can leave. My mother would lose her livelihood. And besides, you just can't walk out of a country with twins who are three years old.'

'And no German army would want twins who are three years old,' I added. Surely this was an added advantage, I thought.

My teacher and my friend looked quietly and knowingly at each other. I realised that I was not part of their adult conversation. For all the notice they took of me, I might have been the same age as Isabelle and Amélie, the twins.

'And yet you have something so precious with Reuben and Jeanne, Alain.'

Another reason to be amazed. How did Mlle Tessier know so much about Alain's family and way of life? I stopped asking questions and listened.

Alain nodded enthusiastically. 'They're just amazing. Incredibly devoted to each other and to G-d and the community.'

'What have they taught you?'

Alain considered carefully before they answered. 'Jeanne taught me about love and always putting others before yourself. Never before have I seen soup stirred with such love.'

I couldn't stop myself interrupting. 'What do you mean?'

'She doesn't just make the soup as well as she can. She puts part of herself in it, and it's the part which always seeks the best for other people and sees the best in them.'

'Especially Reuben?' queried Mlle Tessier.

Alain laughed. 'Especially Reuben. She puts up with his absent mindedness, leaving her while he goes off to study or to visit someone, and she always waits for him, without any bad feeling and cares for him with even more love when he returns.'

'That sounds like love,' commented our teacher.

Alain considered the tribute. 'Yes, it is love, but it's not of the sentimental sort. It's a total giving of herself.'

'And your great uncle?'

'Reuben bumbles about all over the place, making more noise and being clumsier than anyone I have ever met. But when you see him with the Torah, you see a different man. He's transfigured. He chants, he sways and his whole face is alight.'

'And,' said Alain, turning to me and anticipating my response, 'In case you think it's about an old book with no relevance, of course technically you're right. I have no idea whether I should follow its teaching. But it's what the book does to him which is so extraordinary. It makes him something more than himself. Don't ask me how, but I've seen it Saturday after Saturday. And the other men were bathed in its light too, when they put their prayer shawls on and said their prayers. The music isn't even beautiful, but it possesses them. It turns them into something greater than themselves.'

'I think that's the opposite of Nazism,' commented Mlle Tessier, showing an extraordinary understanding of the subject for a rural primary school teacher. 'Nazism takes hold of you so that you become less than yourself.'

'How do you know?'

'I've seen it on the newsreels in Bordeaux. Those men are drawn into the war machine of the Nazis so that they lose their individuality and become part of the monster of hate.'

'And the Torah transforms them so that they become part of a great love,' concluded Alain.

I hardly dared breathe. I was hearing things which I could not understand but which I knew were important. I knew that I would never forget them. I repeated them over to myself under the pine trees and along the beaches. They delineated my world, more than the restrictions of a world dominated by the Nazi invasion, which spread over Les Landes inexorably over the following year.

# Chapter Twelve

Such analysis was only a small part of my world that summer, but I had time to absorb it and take it in so that it germinated in the furthermost reaches of my brain. Too much idealistic talk would have overwhelmed me, and I would have rejected and forgotten it.

During the three months when we were free from school, there was a great monster drawing near to us, but at the time we were only aware of its shadow, and even that shadow seemed a long way away, when we looked over to the other side of the inlet which draws down from the Atlantic ocean to the city of Bordeaux.

I might have remained ignorant of the shadow if I had not heard about it from Alain and Mlle Tessier, and when I occasionally listened to the gossip at the centre of the village. One evening, when I had come in from the forest to my own house, I heard it mentioned by my parents. I found this quite startling and frightening. My parents never talked about anything serious at mealtimes. On many occasions my father would avoid the meal table and pick up some leftovers later. The obstinate silence between them was something I was used to; it was accepted as the norm, and was, I suppose, reassuring. They no longer cared for each other, had nothing to say to each other so we all three knew that that was the way life was. Their increasing silence over the years was easier to accept than the recriminations and bad feelings of earlier times. When I was younger, I was always aware that a quarrel or a silence might break out and that perhaps I could prevent it. Nowadays there was just a solid silence.

When, one evening, I arrived home at the last minute to eat and both my parents were there, I had no anticipation of any conversation at all and certainly not a significant one.

'You going out all over the place, will have to stop,' said my mother abruptly, as she ladled out the cassoulet.

'Why?' I asked, suddenly worried. Was I being asked to do more chores at home? Perhaps she just wanted to curtail my freedom? Had she heard about Alain being back and wanted to stop our friendship? It was a curious thing that my mother must have heard about Alain from the villagers and been aware of our friendship, but she had never referred to it.

'Because of the Germans coming.'

'Well they're not here yet.'

'Don't frighten the child, Annie,' said my father. It was unusual for him to challenge anything my mother said.

'It's all very well your saying that, but she's got to know about it, otherwise she'll have us all in trouble.'

'Why would I get anyone into trouble and why would the Germans be interested in me anyway?'

'It might not be you they're interested in, but it might be that Jewish friend of yours.'

I put down my spoonful of cassoulet slowly. I was shocked. It seemed that my mother not only knew about Alain but knew that he was Jewish.

'He's a friend, whether he's Jewish or Catholic or anything,' I retorted heavily. 'No one's going to stop me being friends with whoever I want.'

'In that case we'll all die in our beds and you'll be the first.'

'Enough, enough,' said my father, anxious to be a peace maker, 'No more talk about dying.'

'Maybe you don't want to see it coming, like you put your head in the sand about everything, including the way this farm works. But at least with my hard work, we have enough to live on, but if she gets us into trouble, we'll have nothing.'

'I won't get you into trouble. I'd never bring Alain near here.'

'You'd better not,' said my mother standing up. 'I don't want any dirty Jew near my farm.'

I stood up, outraged by my mother's insults and criticisms.

'Don't worry. I wouldn't bring him anywhere near this family. He's much too good for you.'

For the first time in my life I had the courage to say what I thought and to storm out of the house. I was very, very angry. How dare she insult and criticise my best friend, the one who had brought me friendship and learning and humour and all the good things of my life! Without him my life was nothing.

'Come back here, you lazy little good for nothing.'

For the first time in my life, my mother's words had no authority over me, and no power to hurt me. With that insult to Alain, I had passed out of her sphere of influence.

Furious and alienated by my mother's attitude, I fled into the forest. That evening in mid-summer, as the daylight was at its longest, I picked up my bike at the deserted barn half a kilometre away and I rode it furiously through the forests and down to the sea. It was a good hour's ride, but I used all the energy I had to push down the pedals at top speed, even as I turned up the slight incline where the trees thinned out, before riding down to the beach among some deserted houses and finally to the sea itself.

I left my bike under a small bridge where carts and bikes and the occasional car or lorry passed over a tiny tributary, and I walked on foot up the sandy causeway to where the spur of land looked out across the sea. In the silence as the shadows lengthened over the waves and the sound of the waves seemed to increase as the twilight darkened, alone on the sand I wept. I wept for my parents' lack of love. I wept for the inheritance of the farm which was wasted on me. I wept for the injustice of belonging to a family who failed to appreciate the genius of my friend. And I wept for a country which was giving permission for my world to change against my will. I wept until there were no tears left and I sat on the sand looking out to sea, unable to understand anything at all.

After a time, I was soothed by the soft air and the crashing of the waves and I regained the energy to walk back to my hidden bike and ride home. I crept up to my mattress under the eaves of the house and slept, unable to work out anything else in my head.

My mother had crossed a line. From then on, I stayed in the house as little as possible. I did my chores on the farm in the early morning, but I never stayed any longer than was necessary. Sometimes I took no food for the day with me. I did not want to eat what I had been given by people who had no understanding of my friendship and what was important to me.

As soon as I could, I sought out Alain mid-morning and we rode through the forest into tiny hidden clearings, along the coast, finding hidden ponds behind the sand dunes and disturbing the haunts of birds who had nested for years along the banks of the stagnant outlets of the lakes.

We had cycled these paths so often over the years that we had no need to tell each other where we were going. Instinctively, we would take it in turns to lead the other where we wanted to go. We would take books, munching on cheeses or dark hard remains of country bread or some fruit. Occasionally we would forage on nuts and berries which we found in the undergrowth.

'Marie, why do you bring so little from home to eat these days?' said Alain when we were sharing his lunch.

'I don't know. I don't want to eat their food.'

'Why not?'

'Because they're not worth it.' I hesitated. I did not want to repeat my parents' comments to Alain. I scorned them. I did not want to repeat those derogatory words in case they had some negative power over him. I also wanted to protect him. I couldn't bear for him to be hurt by their stupidity. It was perhaps the first time in my life that I did not speak honestly and openly to him.

'Well you must get enough to eat, otherwise you'll fade away.'

'That's why I'm stealing yours.'

He laughed. 'I don't care if you are, but you are eating at home too, aren't you?'

'I suppose so.'

'Marie, you're looking incredibly thin. You must eat.'

It was my turn to laugh. It was the first time I could remember ever being described as either fat or thin. It had never occurred to me before that I could be delineated or criticised by such a description.

I picked up my bike.

'Hang on a minute. I was just going to read.'

'Not yet,' I said, pushing my bike over the steep wooden bridge, which was rickety and had been probably put up there by poachers.

'Follow me and see what I've found.'

I pedalled ahead, glad to be the initiator, glad to show him the place, which I had discovered by chance earlier on in the summer when I was still at school. It was the most perfect place of isolation. The first thing that you saw was some water pipes linked to an old water mill, now disused. The pipes were encased in mud and grass but if you followed them along, the casing widened, filled up with old leaves, swept in by the wind of previous seasons and you could crawl through. Just as you thought you couldn't crawl through any more the pipes came to an end. They must have been connected at some point to a bigger system, but just as the pipes came to an end, the ground abruptly fell away and, if you weren't careful, you found yourself rolling downhill into an enlarged hole with a rowan tree growing at the bottom.

'What do you think?' I was enjoying the look of disbelief on my friend's face.

'It's extraordinary. How on earth did you find it?'

It was pouring with rain one day on the way back from school. I sheltered in the pipes and found I could get my bike in there too. Then I just kept on going.'

'Wow …peace at last. Such a find definitely merits you having some of my food!'

We sat back against the rowan tree. An apple, a book, a place undiscovered by the world. What greater happiness was there?

# Chapter Thirteen

For a long time after the Vichy government had taken control and the Germans were in occupation of the country which was not part of 'the free zone', we saw or heard nothing. Les Landes is cut off in so many ways from the rest of France. It's not that there are big ranges of mountains in the way like the Pyrénées or the Alpes Maritimes. Instead it is cut off by a nothingness that is not only spatial but also psychological. It is spatial because there are hundreds of small, insignificant roads which need to be negotiated as you go further west. It is spatial because there are vast hectares of forest which discourage anyone from entering because it is so easy to get lost there. But the psychological barriers are far greater. Any invading nation occupying enemy territory cannot afford to use men and resources in such an outlying and insignificant place. It is insignificant because of the people there. For centuries the people of the land have been the poorest of subsistence farmers. Since the cultivation of the forests in the late nineteenth century, conditions of living have improved. Although most houses and plots of land are owned, they are not owned by rich landowners. Either they are basic wooden buildings passed down from generation to generation like my father's or they are tenanted small holdings. They are not important economically or politically. In fact, I would now say that the people there are the most politically inept or innocent I know. In the days before the war, one or two families in a village would have a radio, but people like my parents, who lived isolated from others, or those in tiny hamlets had almost no contact with the outside world.

By contrast Bordeaux was the buffer town sheltering us from the larger world. Anyone wanting to influence the region politically, would station themselves in Bordeaux and that is what the Germans did. Bordeaux had some significance because of the inlet to the Atlantic Ocean which could shelter even big boats. Down the river you could glimpse any activities of a fledgling navy, though generally the Germans concentrated on Brest further north as a naval centre and incapacitated enemy ships there.

As word in our area spread about the invasion and the capitulation of the French government, people were either angry or resigned. The older generation remembered the terrible loss of their men in the Great War. Children, like me, had no memory of it but shrines and memorials had been built in the centre of all the villages with the names of the fallen proudly inscribed on them. It was recent enough for many families to have lost their male breadwinner, and the loss of a male worker in a subsistence farming community was a serious one. As a result, some people were bitter and angry but more because of their economic situation rather than anything else. There were great love relationships which were torn asunder by the war, but generally the Landais are a practical, taciturn group of people who do not talk openly about romantic love. The French may be famous for their amorous prowess, but most of that uninhibited showiness has come out of a Gallic nature, enhanced by Hollywood, not out of our land. Many people were resigned rather than angry. They accepted the inevitable. The Germans invaded, and the government compromised or did too little too late. The people of Les Landes had never felt the presence of war in all the terrifying force of trench warfare, as the French had in the north of the country. In the early years of the Second World War, they felt it as a reality to be endured rather than actively suffered. It did not affect their everyday working lives. Some people even thought that the Vichy had done the right thing in accommodating the Germans. That way the carnage was less, and the task of heroics could be left to those who had more to give in a major war. As far as they were concerned, England and Russia could get on with the messy job of fighting and leave France out of it. Naturally, we could all feel sorry for Belgium, Holland, Czechoslovakia and Poland, but these were merely names on the map of the world. Their suffering meant nothing to us especially as so many of them had had their borders enlarged or shrunk according to the whims of neighbouring empires down the centuries. Better to sit it out and get on with selling our food at the market.

The markets were of course not only the place for commerce but the preeminent place for gossip. That was where my mother had heard some idea of what was going on and reported it to my father and myself.

'They say the Boches are settling in for good now.'

'Let's hope England fights them if we can't.'

'Great. Let them get on with it if they are so strong.'

I was amazed by my mother's indifference to the fate of our country.

'You mean you don't want France to fight for herself?'

My mother shrugged her shoulders and pushed aside a stray wisp of greying hair which had had the temerity to leave its place in her ordered bun at the nape of her neck.

'If they've got the men to do it in these rich places, then let them do it. Let the people from places like the Woolsack send people over – they're rich enough and they've spent enough time stealing our animals. All I care about is whether we have enough to eat. For some reason I care that you have enough to eat too. Though why I can't imagine as you seem so ungrateful and do so little to help.'

My mother's behind as she moved away to cut the bread managed to demonstrate her self-righteousness. The accusation of ingratitude or ineptness no longer stung. It was the constant background to my life at home, but I no longer felt the guilt. In fact, my lack of practical gifts exonerated me. I was better off not helping. I had no experience of how a happy family could help each other, even when some members were not domestically gifted.

What did surprise me was her comment about caring. She had never suggested before that she might work, day and night, on our small holding because she cared for my father and myself. That word caught me by surprise and held me transfixed for a moment. My mother continued moving backwards and forwards from the table. I hardly dared to look at her – her lined face and her sharp lips drawn up in permanent disappointment with her lot in life. But the phrase 'I care' made its way into the hunk of bread I was using to mop up the stew and I ingested it.

I was also surprised by her knowledge of what went on at the large house known as 'Le Woolsack.' Lake Aureihan was quite a long way from our small holding. What did my mother know of the English aristocrats who came there each summer?

Later in the night in the attic bed I brought her knowledge and claim of caring out for analysis. Could it be that my mother cared? Naturally she cared about eating herself; I had always assumed that there was no way out of her way of life and its economic circumstances. In truth, I reasoned, there probably wasn't. In the 1930 – 40s we were not thinking about a modern way of life where a woman could leave personally distressing or distasteful circumstances and start again somewhere else. Such a move would have been inconceivable in our rural society. In my attic bed I fell asleep still thinking about those two words, 'I care.' In the end I concluded in my self-centred and inexperienced fourteen-year old head that part of her 'caring' for us meant having enough for herself, because she couldn't have one without the other.

Since those days of childhood when our family seemed destined to remain for ever in Les Landes, I have learnt that the phrase 'I care' hides more than it reveals. A person may be profuse in their affirmations of caring and show very little in their actions. In contrast to other temperaments, a person may be difficult and say very little, but somewhere there is a spark of real caring which reveals itself in action. My regret in later life was that I knew my mother so little when I lived with her, that I failed to understand her.

By the next morning I had turned my back on my parents' house. I still needed it for sleep and food, but I disassociated myself completely from its attitudes.

I was fourteen years old and full of idealism and a sense of adventure. If my parents were cowards, I was determined not to be. Maybe that was how I could make an entrance into a world they scorned.

Throughout that first summer of the occupation, I still read and talked with Alain and Mlle Tessier and I continued to bike everywhere. At the same time, I hoped that the larger world out there would approach me, and I would find my destiny. It was a waiting to grow up, a waiting to discover who I was.

For the first time Mlle Tessier became easier for me to understand than Alain. I felt the tension and waiting in Alain too, but it was different.

55

For the first time we became male and female, not in any way biologically or sexually but in our pursuit of rôle models. For the first time I saw that he was different to me and not just because he was better or cleverer or older.

All three of us waited but the waiting meant something different for each of us.

In the long summer holiday Mlle Tessier would often visit her parents, who were now elderly, in Bordeaux. It had never occurred to me until now that she, who had been brought up in the comparative sophistication of the city, had chosen to become a village schoolteacher in rural Les Landes.

I called in on her when she returned from one of her visits.

'But why?' I asked full of incomprehension and the transferred frustration I would have felt if I had been her and made her choice of career. At the same time, I felt shy about challenging my beloved teacher so directly. 'Why bury yourself here when you could have been meeting people in the city?' I asked anxiously.

She laughed. 'It's easy to think that where you are, is not the best place. Marie, you think that, because you are in the country and life is not exciting enough for you, all that would change if you moved to the city. But excitement isn't the only draw. It's where you feel at peace in yourself.'

At fourteen I had very little idea of what she meant. I only knew that I wanted her, with all her talents, to aim higher.

'But how can you bear it – the ignorance and slowness?'

'People may be stuck in their traditions here, but people can be just as narrow minded in the city too.'

I doubted it very much. 'With all that learning and ideas around them?'

She looked across at me affectionately. 'You can have learning right next to you and not be interested in it.'

'How?'

'Think about children brought up in houses where there are great libraries. They don't necessarily want to read those books. Think of rich people who own those books. Often, they just want to possess them for effect. They're not interested in investigating and learning all the time.'

I was so starved of learning that I couldn't imagine anyone not being excited about having books in their house.

'But,' said my teacher in a dreamy way I knew was genuine, 'I love the rhythm of the country. I love the trees, the chance to wander in the forest, the lovely satisfying food which some of the families here have given me.' I hadn't realised that school families gave to Mlle Tessier. I thought that Alain and I were the only ones who appreciated her.

She saw my surprise. 'You see, Marie, different pupils receive different things from their teachers. And who's to say that the son of a country farmer doesn't get as much from learning as the child of the city? And besides I have the occasional pupil like Alain or you who make teaching an exciting opportunity.'

I stared at her. It had never occurred to me that I should be exciting to teach.

'Why have you never married, Mlle Tessier?'

She became suddenly quiet. 'My fiancé died in the Great War. I have never met anyone else whom I wanted to marry.' Something in her voice stopped me from asking any more questions. Marriage never seemed the most attractive proposition to me, even though I knew that a lot of girls my age wanted it. Life was for living not for tying yourself down to a life of drudgery and silent mutual antipathy.

I felt so sorry for my teacher spending her life in our backward villages rather than in the exciting life of 'elsewhere'.

She read my face. 'Don't worry, Marie, I have quite enough to occupy me and satisfy me here. Anyway,' her voice lightened and hardened at the same time, 'if you're looking for action, I fear more of it is going to arrive on our doorstep than we might ever want.'

'Do you mean the Germans?' I couldn't see how they were going to be interested in our villages.

'It's not the Germans in themselves. It's what they represent and how others will react to them.'

'React to them? How do you mean? Kill them?'

'Yes.'

'Good.' I approved of direct action, rather than talking and prevaricating, which was mostly how I would have summed up the desire for action in our villages.

'You mean someone is going to fight back?'

'Yes. I know you think that will be good, Marie, but it's also dangerous.'

'Dangerous? Well, of course it's dangerous. What good would it be if it wasn't?'

'But, Marie, you think danger is always exciting. But it's also shocking and brings great sorrow.'

'You mean when people get killed?' Then, remembering her fiancé, I added, 'I'm sorry, Mlle Tessier, you must have suffered terribly.'

She smiled. 'It's alright. It's some years ago now. I've had time to get over it and rebuild my life. But what I now know is that there are worse things than being killed.'

Worse than having your dreams, your life being cut off? I couldn't imagine anything worse.

'Like what?'

'Seeing your loved ones suffer. Like thinking your friends might be traitors. Like being constantly afraid of evil.'

Evil? What was that? I knew nothing about evil, only the stultifying slow dirge of humourless endurance and lack of joy. At least evil sounded something positive against which you could fight.

But Mlle Tessier reflected deeply. 'It's not something to be romanticized, Marie. It is something terrible and it brings great suffering.'

I had no idea what she was talking about. These concepts were far beyond my almost fifteen years of experience.

Was it chance or some sort of fate, that our conversation turned to Alain?

'Will Alain carry on at the lycée at Bordeaux?' I asked.

'I have no idea. I'm sure he will want to because in his third year there he can take the entrance exam for the 'Grandes Ecoles'. He should stay from the point of view of his education. But whether it's too dangerous for him now, I don't know.'

'Too dangerous for Alain?' I was shocked. Why would the German invasion affect Alain in particular? I knew that his education was vital for him, not only as the means to a future profession, but vital for his mind and energy. I missed Alain but his identification with the world of Bordeaux stimulated my own dreams. If he could do something amazing, maybe there was hope for me too.

My teacher saw that I had not grasped the truth of what was happening. 'Marie, you must understand. This is more than a war like the Great War.'

'More? What with all those people on the memorials killed? I thought that France was going to avoid all of that.'

She sighed. 'Losing all those people in the Great War was terrible, there's no denying that. And I should know. I thought my life had ended when Francis was killed. And all the families round here lost fathers and sons and providers. But we were all proud of them and what they did. But this, what the Germans are doing now, even fighting against it, isn't going to make anyone proud.'

'But Alain's only eighteen. Why should it affect Alain? And, anyway, the Vichy government isn't at war with the Germans.'

'No, but they're protecting something more than our safety.'

'What?'

'The evil which has been unleashed by Germany.'

Here we were again with words and ideas I could not grasp.

'What evil?'

'The evil of killing Jews…not just Jews, anyone they don't like or are different to them'

'You mean killing Alain's family. Why? Why are they so important?'

'An interesting question, Marie. Why are they so important?'

I waited for her answer and it was a long time coming.

'I think they're important because they are a direct challenge to the myth of Nazism.'

Despite struggling to understand, I wanted to learn from my teacher.

'What is the myth of Nazism?'

'It's like a story they've told themselves that will make it alright for them to be more important than anyone else.'

'What is the story?'

'That they are special, chosen, more intelligent and beautiful than anyone else.'

'But they were defeated in the Great War.'

'Exactly. That's why they're so angry and why they have to convince themselves of the truth of the myth.'

'But I thought that no one believed in myths any longer.'

'Of course, everyone believes in myths…it just depends on which one, people choose to believe in.'

'But science has disproved myths.'

'Has it? Maybe, that's a myth by itself. Rationality is in charge.'

'But surely it is and should be?'

'No and when times are bad it's even less in charge. People act according to instinct.'

'What's that got to do with the Jews?'

'Because the Nazi myth says that the Jews are in the way.'

'Well from what Alain tells me the Jews in Bordeaux aren't going to be in anyone's way. They're too busy obeying rules and keeping Shabbat to bother anyone else.'

'On the contrary, I think you might find that the Germans think they're very much in the way.'


We waited and waited. I returned to school under Mlle Tessier's guidance and Alain went back to Bordeaux. The Germans seemed to spend their time organising themselves in the big city and ignored us.

One lunch time a few weeks after the summer holiday, when I went to collect my bicycle from the disused barn, Alain was waiting for me.

'Whatever are you doing here? I thought you were at the lycée.'

'I am…I was; I'll be going back in a few days after the weekend, but I've come to ask you for help.'

'Me?' I was surprised and pleased. How amazing that the brilliant and successful hero of my childhood wanted some help from me.

'I haven't much time now, but have you come to ride out for lunch?' he asked, knowing my daily routine.

'Yes, I felt like a lunchtime ride today. Before long, it will be getting too cold to ride just for pleasure. I'm taking advantage of the autumn weather.'

'I thought you would. That's why I came. Go out as usual, Marie, in case anyone notices anything strange. Then meet me later when school finishes at the end of the water pipes and don't say anything to anyone about seeing me.'

'Of course not. They'll not be thinking about you anyway. Everyone will assume you'll be back at the lycée in Bordeaux at this stage of the term.'

'Alright, but don't assume what anyone thinks these days. Just be on your guard if anyone asks any questions.'

'd'Accord.' I wheeled my bicycle through the old rusty door. 'Don't worry. I won't say a word. See you later.'

I pedalled at top speed through the forest. The pace of my pedalling often reflected what was going on in my mind and my emotions. My mind was whirring, and my feet and the energy of my whole body took on that restless movement. I turned right and left in quick succession through the forest. It was still warm enough to be outside without a cardigan or shawl but the faint autumn wind stirring in the branches had begun to be cooler. I had ridden almost instinctively to the small lake near the hamlet where Alain and I had so often talked and read together.

My mind was full of questions, but I was excited too. I had brought my book from school, but, instead of reading, I wanted to sift through my ideas and the possibilities which occurred to me. If Alain was in danger, why was he returning to Bordeaux? And why would the Germans, who seemed to me to be completely engrossed in their own internal organisation, be interested in a eighteen-year old boy? And why and how was he involved? Oh, the excitement of being chosen, of being confided in! Perhaps I wouldn't have to wait to be the age of a lycéenne for life to start opening up for me! I still loved reading and having conversations with Mlle Tessier, but school life had begun to drag a little since the rentrée. The restlessness of adolescence was beginning to stir within me. I wanted to grow up, and perhaps, whatever was going to be told to me after school, would be the first step of that process.

I did not know that this last afternoon of the village school was the last afternoon of my childhood, of my innocence.

# Chapter Fourteen

I was in a state of restless excitement by the time I left my bicycle near the water pipes and tumbled down the slope towards the rowan tree.

'You have to tell me about the 'pèlerins', Marie.'

'Sorry?' It seemed like an incomprehensible language which Alain was using.

'The 'pèlerins'. The pilgrims along the road to St. Jacques.'

I stared at him and then replied impatiently, 'Of course, I know who the pèlerins are. But what has that to do with you and Bordeaux? You are the last person I would be expected to be interested in such religious myths.'

The pilgrims would sometimes walk on the route from Bordeaux down to the mountains in the south. There had been less of them in recent years. No one had the time or the belief to seek out the blessing of St. James at some shrine in Compostella in Spain. There were devout Catholics in France of course, but most people did not have the leisure to spend trekking across country just for the sake of religious devotion. The few who came were thought to be monks and nuns from further north. They were respected for their religious beliefs but everyone in our community thought that they were a little strange. Most Catholics were superstitious and enjoyed placing a few gifts in the wayside shrines. I remembered that some religious people in our community left gifts of food which the pèlerins, wearing their distinctive cockle covered capes and hats, sometimes picked up. Hard working, small time farmers of the Gironde might not be able to do anything as fancy as a pilgrimage, but maybe they were earning a bit of God's approval by helping those who made the journey. Apart from the atheists and communists who were virulently anti-clerical most people in our rural community had a superstitious admiration for genuinely religious people.

But why would my Jewish friend be suddenly so interested in Catholic pilgrims?

The question returned to me and preoccupied me. I was impatient with learning and geometry, because I was invaded by a profound sense of inquietude.

That afternoon my journey through the pines and then out into the more open countryside had led to the question, 'What is happening?' and, underneath it all, 'Why are such changes happening?' and the even deeper thought, 'What is happening to our culture and civilisation?'

'They're coming for the Jewish community in Bordeaux.'

I didn't have any trouble identifying the 'they'. 'How do you know? Have they said so?'

'We don't need them to say so. It's happening all over Europe and it won't be any different in Bordeaux.' The certainty in his voice precluded any doubt.

'If you stay quiet, perhaps they will ignore you. After all they've got a whole new country to organise, quite apart from a war in other parts of Europe. Have they really got time to worry about a few ------?' I didn't know how to finish the sentence without being disparaging.

'You mean with a few old yids who don't really matter.'

I was silent, puzzled by the bitterness I heard in Alain's voice which had never been there before. Was this delightful, urbane young man becoming a stranger to me?

'No, don't worry, Marie, I'm not shocked by you…'

'But I didn't mean it like that,' I protested, hotly, horrified at how he might be interpreting my questions. 'You know that's not how I see your family and friends in Bordeaux. But I can't see how an invading power could care so much.'

'Yes, interesting isn't it? They think we are rubbish, sub-human, so you'd think they would ignore us. And yet they want to spend all their energy and the resources you rightly say they don't have, in getting rid of us.'

'If they want to get rid of you, why don't you all just move to a different place?' I asked reasonably with a child's total lack of understanding of how you might move whole households of people geographically.

'So, where do they go to? Family in a different town? Out here in the forest with your family? And you think they would leave us alone after that?

'If they find you annoying to have around or they don't want you in an important city like Bordeaux, yes.'

'Marie, I think they find us more than annoying to have around.'

'So, what are they going to do about it?'

'Kill us.'

I almost laughed. Surely that was why the Vichy government had not opposed Germany – so that the terrible carnage of the Great War would not be repeated? It was annoying having the Germans in France of course but the families in our villages who had suffered cruelly in the generations before were relieved that the carnage was not going to be repeated.

'I think,' said Alain slowly and gazing at the top of the rowan tree which lay aslant along the bottom of this miniature valley, 'that you can go on compromising and giving in to evil but one day you have to face it.'

'Evil?' I picked up on the word with enthusiasm. Ideas were something I was far more familiar with in conversation with my friend than mad people movements. 'You've said yourself that it doesn't exist. Patrice says that his dad says it's a word which has been invented by the Catholic church to keep us back from making advances.'

How well we had absorbed that lesson. Like Patrice, I also thought that evil was an old-fashioned myth, which was irrelevant to our modern world.

Alain ignored my point. 'It's like the ancient dragon… it's been asleep for a long time. But I think it's beginning to awaken.' Alain turned over suddenly. For once metaphysical argument was of no interest to him.

'Marie, we haven't got long. Otherwise someone will notice that you're not back home.'

I was puzzled and thought he was being neurotic. When had anyone ever noticed that I wasn't back home? Our fellow countrymen did not care, and my parents were used to my long absences. And when did Alain ever care about what anyone else thought? That was partly why I loved him so much.

'We don't have much time to plan and think. Tell me more about the pèlerins and do they still turn up round here? Come on quickly. I'll tell you why later.'

I explained a little about the route which the pèlerins usually took. They walked towards the coast and then cut alongside the coast until they reached Bayonne to the south and then, apparently, climbed the first foothills of the Pyrenées to St. Jean Pied du Port before disappearing over the Spanish border. I concentrated hard on the memory of those figures and what people had told me in order to help Alain.

'They usually travel in twos or threes.'

'Only that number? Never in a big group together?'

'No, they seem quite lonely, as if they like being in a small group and occasionally they're just one at a time.'

'And do people mind them?'

'No, I don't think so. Most people don't think about it very much. Everyone round here is busy cultivating their land. It seems to them that being a pilgrim is a strange occupation. Local people…put up with them. Maybe they even admire them, but no, they don't want to be like them. They are just different.'

'Do they dress in a certain way?'

'Yes, they have large floppy hats and rather old cloaks and they always have shells on their clothes and staves to help them walk, I guess, especially when it comes to the mountains.'

'And where do they get those clothes from?'

'I've no idea… maybe the convents or monasteries further up into the north of France.'

I had only a very vague idea of what constituted a monastery or a convent. I had little formal teaching about Catholicism either from the church or school, but I remembered history lessons from Mlle Tessier when she talked about how monks and nuns had contributed to the French way of life. We saw very little of such religious people round our way. The forests of Les Landes had been planted in the mid nineteenth century. Before that they had only been very sparsely populated by poor subsistence farmers. There had never been much interest in religion and no money for building monasteries and convents. To me the monastic orders were a strange idea for people who lived elsewhere, who believed in God in an extreme way and who dressed strangely.

'Where would you find things like that out from?'

I thought carefully. 'Church? I know Cecile at school. Her parents are always going to church. They might know.'

'Marie, could you find out for me?'

'I expect I could if I asked her. But why all this interest in religious characters? I thought you had enough in your own religion.'

I was puzzled. Alain had never been interested in the Catholic religion before. And what had this to do with the Vichy government and the German occupation?

Alain leant back against the rowan sapling which grew not far from a tiny underground spring. There was just enough room for him to stretch out full length.

'I don't really want to tell you, but I think I'll have to.'

I was hurt. In our younger years we had shared confidences without fear. Talking to each other had been like talking to our own selves, only better because we had responses which were different and interesting. Alain saw my expression.

'Marie, it's not because I don't want to share with you, or even that I don't trust you. It's because I don't want you to get hurt.'

'How could I be hurt by finding out about the pèlerins?'

'Because some of my people may need to escape from Bordeaux.'

'Why?'

'Because bad times are coming for Jewish people in France.'

'What sort of bad times?'

'Being badly treated, possibly even killed or shipped over to Germany to labour camps.'

I stared at him, utterly convinced of the craziness of what he was saying.

'Why would anyone want to do that?'

'Because they are Fascists, Marie, and Fascists hate Jewish people.'

'Well they're stupid then, aren't they?' I said with my fifteen-year old conviction about the nature of stupidity.

'I think they're stupid too,' agreed Alain patiently, 'but that doesn't alter the fact that they're the ones in power.'

'Besides, France wouldn't allow them to do that.'

'I'd like to believe that too, but the Vichy government are under the authority of Germany, not the other way around.'

'OK, I've got it. The Vichy government are cowards – lots of people say that – but the real French people won't allow them to do that sort of thing.'

'Are you sure?'

Now I was angry with Alain. How dare he think that ordinary French people would be so hateful as to turn on one group of people who were their fellow citizens?

'Marie, I'd like to think that what you say is true. But when people are threatened themselves, they do terrible things. I don't trust human nature. And the Jews have been persecuted here before.'

'When?'

'Heard in history of the Dreyfus case?'

'Vaguely.' I remembered some passing history lesson which seemed unimportant at the time.

'What we learn from that is that a minority people are used as a scape goat when things go wrong.'

'But why the Jews?'

He laughed mirthlessly. 'Why indeed? If I could answer that question satisfactorily, I could do something about it.'

He sat up in a purposeful manner and continued.

'All these questions need to be answered and I hope we'll have lots of time to talk about them in the future but for now I have to be practical. Marie, you're my friend and I trust you completely.' I glowed with pride. 'But you're my dear friend and I don't want anyone to hurt you for helping me.'

'Oh, don't worry about that. I'm not important enough.'

'You may only be fifteen but if you have knowledge which they want, I wouldn't put it past them to cause you a lot of trouble.'

I rocked forward to sitting on my heels, prior to getting up, determined and strong in my youthful convictions.

'It's alright. I'll just ride off into the forest where they can't find me. I know it better than they do.'

Alain laughed, instantly more relaxed. 'When I see you pedal through the forest, I believe you. No German could catch you.'

'Exactly,' I said, contemptuous of German skills clearly so inferior to my own.

'No German motorcycle could get through where I go.'

'I'm sure they couldn't. You're unassailable, I forgot.'

'So why do you want to know about the pèlerins?'

'Because that might be a way of getting some people out to Spain.'

'You mean pretending to be pèlerins?'

I jumped up, excited and purposeful. 'Great idea. I'll find out all about them. Don't worry, I'll be a perfect spy. No one will ever know why I'm asking about them. I'm starting to feel very interested in Catholic religion. So far I've been denied all knowledge of it.'

# Chapter Fifteen

I found myself with a new purpose in life. During my school years I had discovered an amazing and wonderful preoccupation. It was called learning. I now realise that, though this an ostensible reason for the existence of most schools, it is often the activity which is least present there. My experience was different. In school I was permitted to learn, encouraged to discover for myself and praised when I was successful. During the first six years of my life I had been starved of praise, and I had become very hungry. I was lucky because academic success came naturally to me, whereas to most of my contemporaries at school, learning was an irksome chore. I also had the good fortune to acquire the friendship of a truly amazing person who was four years older than me but who became my best friend. For the nine years of my schooling so far this was enough for me, along with communing daily with the forest, lakes and beaches all around me when I walked and when I went on my solitary cycle journeys. If the war had not come, I would have continued with this pattern of living for at least a year, before I found out whether I too could have sat the exam for the lycée at Bordeaux.

But now something different took hold of my personality. Yes, I wanted to help my friend; yes, I wanted to be considered useful by an older hero. But there was something else too. I could take on a further exciting role. I had always loved stories. I suppose that when we are young that it is our identification with stories which forms who we are. We try a best fit approach. It is as if we have a cardboard cut-out and we try to see whether we are tall enough or shaped right for each role. As we grow to maturity, we reject those shapes which we cannot fit into. I kept trying to fit into several different cut out shapes for much longer than many of my contemporaries. They were far more content than I with the nearest cardboard cut-out – the housewife figure, the mother of children, the market stall holder, the farmer.

Alain's call for help offered me another positive and romantic possibility – saviour of the oppressed. It galvanised me into action. Even as I was cycling away from my encounter with Alain, I had plans circling in my head.

To begin with, I had a problem to solve. How could I find out the needed information about the pèlerins without arousing suspicion?

Most people in our community were averagely religious. My family put in the occasional church attendance for Christmas, Easter or the Ascension but lately my mother had declared herself too preoccupied with the farm even for that. There were a few people in the community who were even greater non-believers than us. There was the odd communist or atheist in the villages, but they were generally not vocal in their beliefs or lack of them. Some of them sat on our local councils. Those of us who were born and brought up in Les Landes were an apathetic lot when it came to ideals and philosophy. We might have boasted about our doubts and criticisms in the Hôtel du Centre, but they were just words. We were content to leave the real action to the radicals in Paris or Bordeaux.

Therefore, the problem was – how was I, who had never shown any interest in religion, going to ask questions about the pious life of a pilgrim without provoking more questions and suspicion as to my motives? How could I do it quietly?

I spent much time pondering this question as I cycled to and from school. Feeding the chickens first thing in the morning or eating my picnic near the lake, I went on mulling it over in my head until I found the answer.

I always sat in a double desk in the school room with Cecile. Unlike some pupils who shared desks, we were not great friends. We were both the odd ones out in our class. I was on my own because I was consumed by a love for learning and had no time for anyone else who did not – that is, the other pupils in my school. In truth, I do not now know whether any of them were intelligent or not, but I had dismissed them as inferior or at least different, years ago, when I first met Alain. No one else came anywhere near him in my estimation and he so dominated my mind during the first eight years of my schooling that I had no room in my heart or imagination for anyone else. I did not care what anyone else thought of me, because I did not consider their opinion to be of any value. I now know that mine was an arrogant, superior and totally unjustified attitude, but at the time, I never doubted its accuracy. I was also the odd one out for another reason. My parents did not mix with other adults from the village. I wasn't sure of the reason why, but it didn't worry me that we were a family apart. If I did not consider any of the local children worth mixing with, then their parents were probably going to be equally inferior in my eyes. My mother was completely preoccupied with keeping the farm going and complaining about her husband and daughter. My father was too much of a loner, a solitary hunter and a dreamer. Why would he want to talk to anyone else? My mother did sell her goods at the weekly market and I sometimes went to help her, but she insisted we kept separate from others and we were generally too busy for socialising.

I suppose the main reason that we did not mix with other families was that we were not practising Catholics. Looking back, it amazes me that my mother, who was full of self-righteousness about hard work and cleanliness, was not religious. She took me to Christmas Eve Mass (la veillée) and the feast of the Assumption and sometimes to the vigil of Easter Eve but she resisted all attempts of the curé, Père Christophe, to visit her or to show any interest in us. My father did not even care about the most basic religious festivals. He once told me that his faith in the church or even in God had run out in the trenches, though he had only been old enough to experience the last six months of the Great War. I could not imagine my dreamy father to have had anything to do with guns or fighting. He belonged to the magic of the forests and the silent lakes of La Gironde.

Not every family in the village was religious but those who were did the job properly – weekly Church attendance, Sunday School, buying one of the weekly Catholic publications and of course supporting the social events such as the dances in the village hall. These latter were the only part of religion with which I would have liked to be associated. The young people seemed to have fun dancing and they were allowed to stay up later on those Saturday evenings. Once or twice I had come back from a lonely bike ride and seen the village hall door open with lights and decorations behind and the local music band playing. It was a world which was denied to me.

There were also a few ardent critics of religion in the village – the communists and the atheists. However, there were not any serious atheists. Those who called themselves by that name were bitter about the church for personal reasons, and, as my mother once tartly observed, because they were interested in protecting their wallet from the priest. In other words, they did not want to pay the tithe, either in money or in food. The communists had adopted their own religion – alternative meetings, with readings from Marx instead of the Bible, and this took up as much of their time as church attendance for the Catholics. Some of the keener ones went off to Bordeaux or Dax or even Toulouse for rallies and to support strikes but most hard-working farmers and forest workers in our area did not have time for such irrelevancies.

Cecile was not as much a loner as I was. She was a podgy, white faced girl who had a vacant expression; but she was kind – even sharing some of her sweets at break time with me. The reason the other girls did not like her was because she was extra religious. Her parents were the curé's favourites – probably because they were better off than many and so gave more on the offering plate. I could hear my mother's cynical comments in my head.

If anyone knew about the pèlerins, I thought, it would be Cecile. But how to ask her? I was known as an oddity at school. Other pupils put up with me, but I did not share confidences with other girls. If I suddenly shared too much or asked too much, it would look strange. Alain wanted information but he said that I must not arouse suspicion. I was of course thrilled to be given this special task by my hero, but how to fulfil it, needed all my ingenuity. What would appear normal in my school?

I ruminated on the problem as I rode my bike through the forests. Should I ask Mlle Tessier directly? I did sometimes chat with her at lunch times and of course I loved and trusted her but instinctively I knew what Alain was telling me. Don't trust anyone. She was intelligent and would see immediately beyond the questioning. How could my information gathering appear normal?

Two days later it came to me. Rather, it was fortuitously given to me by my schooling. We had to write a sort of mini project, on a subject of our choice, which had to involve some research. Everyone groaned. Most of the pupils did not know how to involve themselves in any sort of learning apart from rote learning and copying. They did not want to research anything. Even Maurice, the most intelligent of my contemporaries, thought it was a waste of time.

'I could be learning more important things for my exams,' he said annoyed with this interruption to our normal way of learning. He was planning to take the lycée exam in a year's time in Bordeaux.

I decided then that this was my opening.

'But it might help you learn more.'

'Trust you to like what Tessier says, little stuck-up cloud girl.'

I had retained my nickname from the question I had asked on the first day of school, but it was used without rancour. Generally, my intelligence was regarded as odd, rather than something to be jealous of.

'Besides, most people don't have the books they need at home.'

'That's why Mlle Tessier is offering us some of hers.'

'Well I'm going to the library at Bordeaux.'

Someone turned on Maurice who came from a richer family than most. 'It's all very well for you. Most of us don't go there.'

'I have to go when Papa goes to the next meeting.' This was from Giles whose father was a committed Marxist.

I thought hard. This was an ideal opportunity. Asking questions of another pupil would not be suspect because it was part of what we had to do, and everyone knew that I adored Mlle Tessier and was likely to excel at the task. However, Catholic traditions were not known to be my area of interest. I had to introduce this idea carefully.

'I expect that Marie's going to choose a topic we've never heard of.'

I was known for my reading of books on philosophy and history and geography, my favourite subjects.

I said, 'This time you might be surprised.'

'How's that?'

'I can't get to Bordeaux. I've read Mlle Tessier's books anyway and she stressed it should be about personal research. I thought first I'd do it about butterflies in the forest.'

This idea attracted scorn from my school mates. 'How can you do research about butterflies? They're just there.'

'Exactly. They can be drawn or painted, and you can find out about what they do. But, you know, I'm not much good at art, so I've decided against it.'

'OK. So, what are you going to do?' Everyone looked at me curiously. I was normally the one who had ideas, though I didn't normally share them very generously.

'I've decided. I'm going to ask Cecile about the Catholic Church.'

'Cecile! You're going to base your project on her!'

'And why the Catholic Church? I've never known you be interested in it!'

'Exactly! I don't know anything about it. Time to change my ignorant ways!'

Giles was horrified. 'You don't mean you want to be part of those hypocrites?'

Another girl, Alice, was mortified. 'How dare you say we're hypocrites? What about you communists?'

'What about us?'

'You say you care about the workers, but you only care about the Bolsheviks.'

'Well of course we do. We learn from them for all of us.'

'You're never learning for me. Papa says you'll destroy France.'

'A fat lot your Papa knows about anything important.'

The conversation descended into a private argument, but this gave me two pieces of luck. One was that everyone would remember the fight between Alice and Giles, not how it started, and it gave me another idea. My research project would explore two contrasting beliefs – Bolshevism and Catholicism. That was how, quite innocently without arousing suspicion, I would garner information about the pèlerins.

# Chapter Sixteen

If the validity of learning can be gauged by how much we remember later, then that educational project must have been one of the most effective of all times. I became fascinated as much by the subject of Bolshevism as by the subject of the monastic way of life.

In the interwar years Bolshevism was spreading like a religion throughout France. In our area people were too poor and consumed by the needs of work to take much interest in it. In the large towns of France, it was rampant, led by the intellectuals, but taken up by the factory workers who were disillusioned with Catholicism and had no aim in their lives. It was not popular amongst the field workers of Les Landes, because their poverty was not of the same sort as those in our industrial towns. Life was hard for them; having enough to eat depended on the vagaries of the weather and the luck of good crop response. There were two other factors which absorbed people – their own farming skills and being outside for most of the day. The small-time farmers of Les Landes could make a living if they were skilful enough and many of them were. Their small holdings gave them enough to eat and some more to sell at the market if they were successful enough. Open air work made them healthy and tired them out. Many had inherited their small holdings down the generations. They had heard that the Bolsheviks wanted to do away with private property. The average farmer in our locality wanted above all else to hold onto his land. My parents were typical in that they were very suspicious of the Communists.

'Thieving so and sos, who don't know any better,' commented my mother, dismissing the whole philosophy of Lenin and the Russian revolution in one sniff. My father usually said nothing. Exchange of ideas was not something which happened comfortably in our household.

However, on one of our joint trips into the forest, my father made a surprising comment. 'Don't mock Giles' father. You don't know what he's suffered.'

My father rarely said anything about the Great War. He had only been conscripted in the last year and he had served without distinction. For me it was what old people like my father had done and had no relevance to my life now.

However, everyone knew that Giles' father had come back without an arm, a potentially very serious handicap for a farmer, particularly as it was his right arm.

'Those men saw terrible things, Marie.' I was far too absorbed in my own preoccupations to ask what terrible things he meant.

'They were ordered to do terrible things by the officers. They will never take orders like that again and I don't blame them. That's why they're Communists.'

'I thought the Bolsheviks had to take orders from Lenin.'

My father laughed. 'You're more correct than you know, Marie. We all end up taking orders; the only question is from whom?'

'So, who do you take orders from, Papa?'

We stopped in the middle of the path, the sound of the woodpeckers tapping very clearly audible from the side of the path.

'Your mother of course. She runs the farm. No,' he added in case I wanted to intervene, 'She does a good job and I can come out here almost whenever I want. I am free here.'

'Don't you want to achieve anything, Papa?'

'It's too late for me now, Marie. But it's not too late for you. You can achieve for me.'

That was the moment when I became determined that I would indeed achieve something for my dreamy father, who, by taking on a farm to which he was wholly unsuited, gave up the will to achieve anything and resigned himself to taking his wife's orders.

'Find out more about Bolshevism for your project, Marie,' he advised me later when he heard about it, 'but don't be taken in. Men become Bolsheviks because they are bitter with their lot, not because they believe in it.'

'Some of them must.'

'Sure. The idealists, the intellectuals but they'll do well out of it, just as they do well out of being aristocrats and factory owners.'

Against the background of my father's cynicism I started to learn more about Bolshevism from Giles.

Giles could hardly believe that I wanted to learn something from him. He was a heavy-set large boy with carroty coloured hair which he was always trying to tame and hide. He told me that he was not interested in communism himself. He had been forced to attend too many marches and rallies by his father and he just wanted to be allowed to fish in the lakes of La Gironde without needing to think further. It seemed that attending the weekly gatherings of the cell was as boring as attending church.

'In fact, worse,' said Giles, as he helped me with my project one lunch time when it was pouring with rain. He had stayed at school and brought his own lunch, even though he lived near enough to go home.

I was amazed and touched by his unselfishness. I had never considered that someone, who I had dismissed as ignorant, might want to help me.

'At least at church there's some music and pretty girls to look at.

My older brother – he's interested in what Papa does. He goes to all the rallies and even goes and teaches at the factories, but me?' Giles shrugged his shoulders philosophically, 'I'm just happy being around the farm and helping. I can't wait till I can leave school and start work full time. I'll save up so I can find my own place and have children myself.'

That must have been what my father had been destined to do, I thought – only it had not worked out as he had imagined.

'What do you mean – teach at the factory?' This was a workmanlike Bolshevism about which I knew nothing. Alain had taught me about Marx, but how it worked out in the day to day life of the French worker I had little idea.

'They find little groups of dissatisfied workers at the factory.'

'How do you find them, if you don't work there?'

'Yeh, well the people who work there know them. They find them, sometimes at the marches and protests, and strike action, and then invite them to the study group.'

77

It was again beginning to sound like the extra keen groups at the church who met at the priest's house during the week.

'And do many of them come?'

'Enough.'

'Enough for what?'

'Enough to stir up trouble in the factory, to be the forward movement of the revolution.'

'Giles, do you think the revolution will come?'

'Who knows? I don't really care, except it has come in other countries hasn't it? Look at Lenin and Stalin.'

'Will it come here?' I somehow could not imagine the conservative traditional culture of Les Landes changing.

'To be honest, Marie, I hope it doesn't. I want to till my own land. I don't want to hand it over to 'the people'. I can't see how any cooperative could do a better job than individuals who care for the land.'

'So why does your father want it?'

'Because of the war.'

'But lots of people fought in the war and not all of them want Marxism.'

'Some of them do …people like my dad, who saw what happened at the Somme and Ypres…how the ordinary soldiers were led to death, when they had no interest in it at all.'

'What about the civil war in Russia?'

'Well at least they were fighting for their own beliefs, not for the beliefs of the generals. Yeh, OK,' conceded Giles the farmer, 'I've heard a lot about it…I'm not touched by it… I want to stay out of the way…but I understand their arguments.'

'War's already started in France,' he added, 'and this time most of us don't want to fight the Germans. Better to live at peace with them and work together.'

'Work together? What for? Nazism?'

'Yeh, well I guess the Nazis will disappear sometime and at least millions of us will not have died in the process.'

I thought about Alain and his fight for his people.

'I hope you're right, Giles.'

'Me too… I just don't want to get into politics. It's not worth it. I hear too much about it at home.'

If I had learnt passionate thinking from Alain – ideals which were pivotal for his life, talking to Giles over the weeks taught me prudence, the desire to guard the land, the belief that nothing worthwhile had changed down the centuries. My father may not have worked the land as he should, but he still had the right to own it, and the freedom to go out hunting and fishing. With the Bolsheviks we would never have such freedom or such ownership. It turned out that with the Nazis, although we still had ownership, we didn't have freedom, especially the freedom to pursue our own ideals.

The point about my project was to find out about Catholicism and the pèlerins, but oddly it was my conversation with Giles which had a greater effect on me. It raised questions which went on bothering me throughout my adolescence and adulthood.

If we were better off with communism, why did it not speak to my heart?

If it was a fairer system, why not embrace it for everyone?

The French bureaucrats, even in Les Landes, where no one really cared about politics, were more afraid of Communism, than they were of the Nazis. What was so terrifying about it? Was it just a case of those who were mediocre, being scared of what high ideals might bring? Or the rich being scared of losing their money? Perhaps it could never work anyway. The masters would always be in power. Stories filtered back to us about what was happening in the civil war in Spain. Somehow it was inevitable. The bosses would always win out…why bother arguing? Better to get on and enjoy the fruit of the land, such as it was.

But I did not deal in land. I only dealt in ideas. They drew me, they invaded my brain and my imagination. I thought about them as I pedalled amongst the pine trees, as I lay down besides the lakes and as I lay in my little kingdom, cut off from the world around me, cocooned by grassy slopes and a rowan tree.

Although I had shown Alain this place and we had met there together, it was pre-eminently my little kingdom, where I sifted through ideas and dreamt. My dreams would change through the weeks. One moment

I would be a successful lycéene in Bordeaux and even go to university there. The next moment I would emigrate to Russia and become a co-propriétaire...another moment I would marry a French landowner but not like my father. This one would be rich enough to give me the lifestyle I needed...mainly access to a library of books with days spent on the beautiful beaches of Les Landes. Perhaps I could meet the English owner of the Woolsack House and marry him, and he would give me all I wanted. It is impossible to be brought up in Les Landes, without your mind being affected by the rhythm of the sea crashing onto the shelving of the sand dunes and hearing the piping of the sand martins. You might be the most idealistic communist or the greatest academic in the world, but you would always return in your spirit to those sounds. The English aristocrats seemed to like it too. That was why they returned to Lake Aureilhan each summer, even though, since the advent of the Germans, they had returned home.

And then there was the question of variety and freedom. Why shouldn't Cecile's family practice the religion of their choice? Going to church sounded to me a poor way of spending Sunday, when you might be pedalling freely through the forests, or leaving your bike at the edge of the sand dunes and settling down with a book and a casse croûte, but there were undoubtedly other compensations – harvest suppers, mid-summer dances for the young people and a sense of belonging with God on your side. As occasional attenders my family had the worst of both worlds. We were not free to enjoy our lack of religion, but we were also criticised by the local curé, who always had something to say in his Christmas sermon about those who only came on special occasions and thought they were fooling God.

I could see what he meant. If God had any brains at all, he would not be fooled by our family – by the stiff, special occasion clothes which my mother forced me into in order to appear religious – by the bickering and long silences which went on at home. What were we doing there? I once asked my mother. All she could reply was, 'You're as bad as your father. You have no respect. We must be there for the major festivals. What would people think of us if we were not there?' Such an answer left me with more questions than answers, but I knew better than to pursue them.

The lecture afterwards would end with the familiar refrain – Why do you want us to be so badly seen by our neighbours? Why did my mother have to work so hard with her lazy husband and daughter who did nothing? The unspoken answer to the last question did as good a job as any Roman Catholic dogma in encasing us in guilt.

As I could not expect my parents to understand my objections, I repeated them to Alain, who always understood the point of questions. To my surprise, he was completely tolerant of my mother's sense of self-righteousness.

'Well my dear, she's just keeping up with what everyone else does. Can you blame her?'

'But she's a hypocrite, pretending to be good when she isn't.'

'Most people are hypocrites in some measure.'

'Well they shouldn't be.' In my fifteen-year old zeal, I was annoyed with him for his lack of condemnation of the obvious deficiencies of my parents.

'How can you live with someone if you're not honest with them?'

He was thoughtful in his response. 'Perhaps it's harder to live with someone if you're too honest.'

'In that case I'm only going to live by myself.'

Alain rolled over and tickled my chin with rough grass blades. 'I think that will be a blessing for everyone.'

I asked Cecile, did everyone believe what they were taught in the Catholic Church? I knew she had been taught her catechism at her first communion. I had seen all the girls in my school being herded together in their white dresses and veils. Seeing them look so special, I was envious of their beauty and their certainty in what they were supposed to do.

Cecile hesitated. I would have expected her not only to be a good little prig and say the right thing, but also, as someone who showed no sign of ever thinking for herself, to have believed unerringly in what the curé taught her.

'To be honest, I don't know, Marie.'

I had brought pen and paper to write things down for my project in the empty school room during lunch time; but I feared to write down such an answer. I hardly dared to breathe. If I showed the wrong reaction,

Cecile would revert to all that I expected from her – lack of thinking, self-righteousness and certainty of her fate in life. To realise that she might not know something filled me with excitement. Could she be a free thinker too?

Cecile could not live with the enormity of what she had first intimated. 'Yes, of course I believe it. It's our faith. It's what the Pope tells us.'

'How do you know that what the Pope says is right?'

Sadly, I had lost her. Her uncertainty had disappeared under the glare of infidel interrogation. She glanced at me surprised. 'What the Pope says is always right. He's in the line of Jesus, who was the Son of God.'

'How do you know he is?'

'Because the curé tells us, Besides,' said Cecile scornfully, her response an always fail-safe method of withdrawing from rational argument. 'Everyone knows that, Marie. How can you be so ignorant?'

I was used to that line of argument. Because I didn't know something or didn't understand something, it meant that it was my fault. I had an inbuilt fault line in my internal workings.

Usually at this point in the argument, I would stamp off in a bad humour or argue my opponent into the ground. But this time I tried not to forget that there was another more important purpose behind my questioning.

'So, Cecile, what would you say are the most important parts of the catechism?'

This was meant to set her at ease. She could talk about the facts of the catechism learnt by members of the Roman Catholic faith rather than the validity of her own personal belief system.

'I suppose about Jesus dying and rising from the dead … and about Mary being always a virgin and being the perfect mother of God and about the priest giving us absolution after confession.' She then went through different points of the catechism and I diligently wrote them down. Then I tried to subtly change the subject of conversation.

'Tell me about becoming a nun or a monk. Is that the best thing to do if you are a Catholic?'

'Not necessarily,' said Cecile carefully. 'You have to be specially called to that and of course you have to be really holy.'

'How do you know whether you are holy enough?'

'I suppose the curé will tell you.'

'Would he ever tell you that?'

'Me?' Cecile laughed, now quite sure of herself. 'Of course not, Marie, what an idea! I'm nowhere good enough. I just want to grow up to marry a farmer and have children like my mum. I'd like to be good at appliqué work like her too.'

Somehow the Cecile who was unsure about her own holiness was a much more attractive character than the Cecile who never doubted what the curé told her. The question now for me was whether I had put her at ease enough for me to find the real information I needed.

'And what about the pèlerins we see around here? Are they also holy? Are they ever ordinary people, I mean ordinary church-goers, or do they have to be the frères or soeurs?'

# Chapter Seventeen

Alain and I had arranged to meet two weekends later, when he would be at home from the lycée in Bordeaux. It had to be a weekend, he said, otherwise people would think it was strange.

It was unusual that Alain, who had never cared what anyone thought about him, now commented all the time about what other people might notice. He tried to explain himself to me.

'Marie, for myself I don't care what anyone thinks, and I probably won't ever.'

'Well that's a relief. I was beginning to worry that you had changed. I never want to care what people think.'

'Yes, I agree. Marie, have I really taught you to be such an upstart?'

'Apparently, so don't start regretting it now,' I said secretly proud that he saw me as such a close disciple.

Alain had not wanted to meet me near the house or near the school where I normally left my bicycle. Instead, we went straight to the water pipes near the water mill with the steep drop down into the tiny valley. I had been there so often by myself in the last few weeks that it now seemed too small to share with Alain's increasingly big and gangling frame. But it was the only place where we could be sure of secrecy.

'Marie, things are getting serious. You must understand that if you want to stay safe, you must blend in with everyone else.'

'But I don't want to be safe.'

Alain threw up his hands in desperation.

'Don't you understand, Marie? I'm not talking about being safe and unadventurous and not exploring new ideas. I'm talking about not dying.'

I was silent. This sort of talk sounded unfamiliar. Why would a few Nazis in Bordeaux make any difference to us in Les Landes?

'The curé says that it's better to have a few Nazis around keeping order than a whole lot of Bolsheviks in control.'

'That's because he doesn't understand what the Nazis will do.'

'And you, an 18-year old lycéen, do?'

'It's not a game. I know I don't understand everything. I'd like to think that Pétain will keep the worst of the Nazis at bay, but I'm not very hopeful.'

'Why not?'

'My uncle has received messages from his brother in Poland. They're rounding the Jews up.'

'Well the French won't let them do that here.'

'Hope you're right, Marie. But Uncle Reuben thinks that everything is going to get worse.'

'Maybe he's just scaring everyone?'

'Maybe, but Uncle Reuben's not stupid. He knows a thing or two.

Look, Marie, when everyone is getting along fine, it's OK to stick out and be different. You have that freedom. But when the enemy is here, you need to melt into the background.'

'I never thought to hear you say that.'

'It's not that I want you to think the same way as everyone else. In fact, you shouldn't. You must have your own standards, not give in like everyone else will. But for your own safety in public you must not stand out as being different, even if you are deep down.'

'You mean like a spy story?'

'Exactly like a spy story.'

That was better. I was comfortable in the realm of spy stories. You could read those and know that the good would triumph despite some dangerous moments on the way.

'But are you so sure,' I questioned, 'that the Nazis will triumph, and that people will give in to them?' I told him about my project and about talking with Giles and Cecile. 'From what Giles says, his dad really goes to a lot of trouble to be different. It doesn't sound as if he would be afraid of the Nazis.'

'Yes, Giles' dad is very brave.'

'How do you know?'

'I've heard him speak at the factory. He makes people stand up for what they believe.'

I was amazed. 'I thought you were studying hard at the lycée?'

'I am but I still have free time. I like to hear what people think, not just in books. There are some amazing Marxists. Maybe we will need their courage.'

'There you are you see. You're not alone. And I've even been surprised by Cecile. She's not as dim as I thought she was.'

Alain laughed. 'Oh Marie, glad you've decided you're not the only one with a brain.'

I was indignant at his unspoken criticism of my arrogance.

'I don't think I'm the only one with a brain, but let's face it, brain power is not the strong point of most of the children at our school.'

'Perhaps, but in the coming years, loyalty might be more important than brain power. By the way, what did you find out about the pèlerins?'

The pèlerins, Cecile had told me, were keeping up a tradition which had started in the Dark Ages, when it was rumoured that the bones of St. Jacques, the brother of Jesus, had been brought to Compostella in Northern Spain. From then on and especially in the Middle Ages, the Catholic faithful had made pilgrimages from all over France, to show their adoration of this saint, and to hope that their sins would be forgiven, as a result of their pious devotion. One of their routes passed near to Aureilhan and St. Paul-en-Born and continued, following small roads and paths parallel to the coast until they passed near to Bayonne, before cutting inland towards the villages just before the mountain pass.

'Do they travel in groups?'

'Yes, quite often, especially when they are part of the religious sects and they stop at the road shrines and local churches for devotion.'

'Where do they get the shells from?'

'Don't know. Maybe the beaches where shells normally come from.'

'Possibly. Thanks, Marie. You've been incredibly helpful and I'm most impressed by the way you used the project as a pretext for questioning.'

I glowed with the honour of being praised by my hero.

'In the next few weeks, can you get me some of those shells, the biggest you can find?'

'There are only a few on our beaches. They're not full of shells.'

'All the more reason for you to go where you know you can find them. And do it unobtrusively. You shouldn't have too much trouble. Everyone knows you cycle everywhere. Take your school bag with you and no one will know what you are doing.'

'How long do I have to do it?'

'About two weeks.'

'Fine. I can do it. But why, Alain, what are you going to do with them?'

He hesitated. 'Best for you not to know.'

'You mean you don't trust me?'

'I wouldn't trust myself if the Nazis tried to get information out of me.'

'You mean torture?' I asked amazed. 'Why on earth would the Nazis be concerned about a few pilgrims and their shells?'

'There's no real sign of torture, at the moment, to be honest with you, but there might be in the future. It's already happened in Poland when the 'goy' has tried to help the Jews.'

It was the first time in our relationship that Alain had used a word like 'goy' to describe me. I knew that he wasn't trying to show me disdain; but for the first time I felt that I was 'other' to him.

'Poland's a long way away and they resisted the Nazis and now the Germans are on the way to Russia. In France we've welcomed the Nazis. It's got to be different here.'

'Has it? I wouldn't be too sure of that. Polish Jews thought that ordinary Poles would defend them. They didn't.'

I was dismissive of such gloom. 'Well, it shows what cowards the Poles are. I'm always going to be your friend.'

And I meant it. Alain was more important than anyone else to me, even my family. I rolled over in the grass towards him. He held me close for a minute, and then started to pick stalks of dried grass off me. The action was more like that of an older brother than a best friend.

# Chapter Eighteen

There were not vast quantities of shells on the beaches of Les Landes, but I knew exactly where to find the best ones. On the other side of the small coastal town of Mimizan, on far side of the inlet, the forest was particularly dense. And between the forest and the sand dunes, there was an area, almost trapped in between, which was neither beach nor forest. It was grass mixed with some sand, which had blown off the main sand dunes, and there were small ponds and inland lakes, which surprisingly consisted of fresh water, like the large lakes dotted inland round Les Landes. It was a small ribbon of land which not many people visited, because it did not have the charm either of the beaches or the forest.

Most people who lived in the area went to fish in the big lakes or hunted small game in the bushes, or low-lying forests. If they came to the coast, they either came to visit family living in the town who welcomed visitors in the heart of summer from those who lived inland, or they came with their children for a picnic by the sea on a day's holiday.

The area I was searching and which I knew well appealed to neither group of people. I came here regularly for two reasons – for solitude, especially when the mists and fine rain were driven off the sea and hung in low clouds over the small stretches of water – and secondly, to see the birds, which enjoyed landing on these lonely waters. Of all the place I enjoyed going to on my own, this one was the best because I never had to hide from anyone else who appeared unexpectedly. For the fisherman or hunter or swimmer or family picnicker, it held no particular attraction. Unless you had explored the area, you would not imagine that the pine forests stopped before the sand dunes. Only, if you stood on top of the sand dunes, were you aware that there was an empty space and even then, most visitors were not curious about it.

I knew, from long experience, that this was the place to find shells. They were blown from the seashore up onto the high dunes and then down again to this empty space. Most of them were either tiny or broken up by the buffeting of the wind, but a few of them were large enough for my purpose. It took me a few visits to collect enough to give to Alain.

We had arranged to meet again down the hole beyond the water pipes. I carried them there triumphantly, after I had placed them in my school bag which also acted as a bag for merchandise on market days. I wrapped them carefully in a scarf, which I had borrowed from my mother to protect my head as the autumnal rains started.

'These all right for you?' I queried nonchalantly. It was like producing the best homework ever for my teacher.

'Wonderful, Marie. That's just what we need. And no one saw what you were doing?'

I looked at him askance. 'Does anyone ever see what I am doing?'

He grinned. 'Stupid me. The disappearing ghost, I forgot.'

'Especially, my mother says, when chores need doing.'

'I guess your mother doesn't appreciate you reading a book instead.'

'No, she thinks it's a waste of time. But this isn't a waste of time, is it?'

'It certainly isn't. Marie, could you sew them onto some woollen hats or broad brimmed hats if I found them?'

'Not if you want neat sewing.'

He laughed. 'Don't worry. I wouldn't have asked if I wanted that.'

'What do you mean?' I asked suspiciously, ready to take offence even though I knew I had no talent in that direction.

'Don't be stupid, Marie. You know you're a book worm and a thinker, not a sewer. If I bring the hats here and put them under this tree, could you start sewing three or four onto each hat, the way the pèlerins would wear them.?'

'Sounds like the worst job you ever gave me.' I was reluctant to show my ineptitude even to please my best friend.

'I think I'm better at finding information for you.'

'You probably are, but I don't want anyone in Bordeaux to do it. A neighbour might see and start to guess.'

'What's so terrible about guessing about pilgrims?'

'Because they're for Jews, silly, and normally they wouldn't be interested in Christian pilgrimages. We mustn't give our neighbours any idea of what is about to happen. And, yes, there might be neater workers around here, but I don't trust anyone apart from you to keep their mouths shut or not to ask questions.'

I glowed with pride. I was the only one worthy of his trust.

'OK I'll try and get a thread and needle from my mother.'

'I suppose she won't be suspicious of you, but be careful, because normally you don't do any sewing. If she finds you with a needle and thread, you need to have a story to hand.'

Shells! Information! Needles! I was dismissive about his worries. I was an arch-spy entrusted with a secret mission. It made life much more interesting and it was all a game to me. There was no real risk attached.

In the event, stealing a needle from my mother's sewing box was much harder than I expected. She counted her needles carefully and she had different sizes for different tasks. I stole one away, used it to thread some cotton, which I had stolen from Mlle Tessier's desk at school, and over a couple of lunch times and after school sessions, found a way of binding the shells to the hats Alain left me. My mother was still complaining about the loss of a needle when I decided that I would have to admit that in some way that I was the culprit. The needed excuse came my way when my father pinned out the skin of the truffles in the forest. My father and I would collect them at this time of year, and he would have his own bigger pins to use.

One night I went into the forest and collected truffles on my own and then pinned them out in the back room of the farm. It wasn't long before my mother found out what I had done. She was very angry with me for wasting her shiny needle for such a purpose and I was sent to bed with no food. But at least the needle had been restored to its rightful place, and there was no possible connection with shells and hats.

One day a week later, Alain was there at our rendezvous again.

'Marie, it's going to happen in the next few days. The group of pèlerins are coming through and you have to take them some food.'

'How am I going to get that?'

'I can bring some here from my mother's farm, but they need quite a lot to see them through the next week. Can you find some at the market or some things left over from your small holding?'

And that was how I became a scavenger and a thief. If I helped my mother at the market, I would steal some milk or loaves of bread. I siphoned off some rabbit stew from the stew pot which was often left on the oven top at home for days. I found lots of windfall apples from a nearby orchard. I transported all of these to our little valley.

Alain was impressed. 'I'm going to tell you when they're about to come through. You must take them this food and then lead them the back way through the forests to the coast. You know the ways where no one will see them. It's mainly this part which is most difficult. They mustn't be seen in the villages or towns. Otherwise people will be suspicious, and we won't be able to use the route any longer.'

'You mean there will be others coming afterwards?'

'Of course. There will be a hundred or more over the next few weeks. If a local person stops to speak to them, they will soon get suspicious.'

'Why should they be suspicious of someone who looks like a pilgrim?'

'It won't take long for them to realise they aren't part of the faithful. Most of them look too Jewish. We'll only be able to use the disguise for so long.'

'Why can't they just go in cars and get to the Spanish border?'

'Because the Nazis are blocking all traffic out of the city, especially going South. Also, there's no petrol available.

We've had to find them forged passports. We'll be able to get them over the lower slopes of the Pyrenées on foot but only for a limited time. Will you help?'

'You know I'll do it. I'd like to anyway.'

'You're just about the only French Gentile I know capable of saying that at the moment.'

# Chapter Nineteen

Two weeks later I saw the sign that the pèlerins would be passing through. We had agreed on one horizontal slash on the bark of the rowan tree on the evening they were coming. That way, if our hiding place was ever discovered, no one would be able to interpret the sign. I had to keep a tally of how many there were, so I didn't inadvertently miss any arrivals.

Up to that point the whole thing seemed like a harmless school game. It started with a school project, then proceeded to finding shells, borrowing a needle for an inept piece of sewing, but the knife marks on the bark of the tree told me that I was involved with intrigue. I was still excited by the plan rather than scared. At my age and in my corner of France I was so cut off from national events, that I had no idea of the significance of helping to rescue those, who might be considered as enemies of our nation. I had no understanding of French fears and enthusiasms.

Who were the Jewish people? Why were they disliked? Why would anyone think that they were a threat to France? At my house no such subject was ever discussed. We didn't even get newspapers. My only link with the Jewish people was Alain and in my eyes he was perfect. We rarely saw his family in the village because they didn't come to church, they lived even further in the countryside than we did, and they didn't sell very much produce at the market. My family did not mix with other people, so, as far as I was concerned, they were very private people just like us. If they kept a few strange food laws, so what? My own parents had their own peculiar fetishes and Alain's family did not attend a synagogue and only kept the Sabbath in the same rudimentary way as we kept Sundays. By marrying a non-Jew, Alain's mother had cut herself off from the more orthodox community in Bordeaux.

Watching out for and helping the pèlerins started as an adventure on behalf of Alain but, when I saw the first blade mark on the tree, I realised that it was rather more than that. I returned to our house for tea, wondering how I could pass on some food to the travellers. During the meal, I saw my chance as I noticed that my mother had stored some lentil stew in the larder. I found some empty gourds in the outhouse where the pigs were kept, washed them out and ladled in some of the stew. With the chunks of cheese which I had been carefully saving near the chicken run and some more windfall apples, I reckoned it would keep them going for a couple of days. After tea, I went out cycling again, carefully hiding my treasure in a linen bag used on market days.

'You're not going out again, Marie.'

I half turned, hoping my mother would not see me with the bag and ask what I was doing.

'Just going for a quick run before dark. I've fed the chickens.'

'Fine. Don't be too late. Otherwise you'll never get up for school in the morning.'

I felt almost guilty that my mother, normally so acerbic in her comments, was being particularly nice, when her daughter was up to no good.

'No, I won't be late. I just want to enjoy the last of the autumn before the dark sets in for winter.'

'Just like your father. He can't bear not to be outdoors, instead of helping indoors.'

'We're natural outdoors people. I'll see you later, Maman.'

I said this through a half open door, as I made my way to where my bicycle was kept in an outhouse. Then off I went, riding swiftly through the trees, as the dusk fell on the woods. It was a strange light, not one I was accustomed to, but I used its cover to get away as quickly as possible.

I pulled my bicycle down into one of the ditches which lined the roads in that part of France. They were frequently filled with water, but not at this time of year, when there had been very little rain throughout the summer.

It seemed to me that my task was a strange one. I had never hidden food before or expected to meet strangers like this. It felt as though that evening did not belong to my life and for once I would have preferred to be helping my mother with the chores or finding my way to the attic to read.

The four strangely dressed figures appeared a long way off down the straight road, each with a pole to guide them. Their pace was kept back by an older woman, Alain's great aunt I assumed, and they were keeping step with her and so came quite slowly. I emerged from my ditch before I needed to so as not to startle them.

As Alain had instructed me, I nodded to them courteously and asked them no questions.

'Sirs and ladies, you are welcome to our lands in the name of the route de Compostella. I greet you in the name of St. Jacques.'

'Greetings. Are you a fellow pilgrim?'

'One day I may be but for now I bring you refreshment along the way.'

'We thank you. We are in need of rest and food.'

I guided them through the trees till we were out of sight of the road and then I drew out my gourd with the lentil stew, just a small serving for each of them, but enough to give them some essential nourishment.

The older lady was particularly glad to be seated against the bark of a silver birch and to be eating. They finished off the provisions with an apple and shared a water bottle. I opened the travellers' bags and placed more apples and cheese inside them. This would keep them going for a few days.

'Thank you.' The oldest man in the group spoke softly and politely to me. 'Our great nephew has spoken of all you have done for us. We cannot thank you enough but now we must continue.'

I was fascinated. This was Great Uncle Reuben! I had imagined a huge man with a flowing beard, but this man was small and slight and clean shaven.

I gestured to the woman who must have been Great Aunt Jeanne. 'Do you not think she needs to rest more?'

'Maybe but we don't have a choice. We must continue through cover of darkness. People are less likely to see us that way or to be suspicious. This,' said Reuben pointing to his clothes and hat,' is a reasonable disguise for a quick glance, but I don't think it will satisfy those with suspicious minds.'

I tried to set his mind at rest. 'I don't think anyone round here is suspicious. Everyone is too tired from working on their land to care. Most people are indoors now for the night. You have nothing to be afraid of.'

'Maybe but we already have the experience of neighbours in Bordeaux, who used to be our friends, but who now draw away from us. I wouldn't willingly trust anyone. Besides we have several days' hard walking ahead and we must make a good start.'

'Yes, you're right. It will take you at least a week to get to St. Jean, but people are used to the pèlerins there, further south. You will have no problems.'

'I trust you are right, my dear, but how long the paths over the mountains will remain open no one knows.'

It seemed to me quite unreasonable that they would not be open, but I decided not to argue my point. They must go as soon as possible.

I led them back to the roadside and sent them off with clear instructions for the night. They were to continue to the courant of l'Especier. I would find them tomorrow after school on my bike when I would have more provisions, which had already been hidden in our small valley. From there I would send them on their way south. Others would pick them up and provide for them at Hossegor and then Bayonne. I had no idea who these guides were, but Alain had assured me that different people were involved.

I left them on the road and sped back home. The whole episode had jolted me. I was excited but also afraid. For the first time in my life I had things to hide from my parents which were more than ideas or discussions or books. I was helping those who were unwanted in France and I had no idea what my parents would think about my actions. After school the next day I had to get down to l'Especier with more food and then get back home before bedtime and without rousing suspicion. I needed a better story than just being out late. It was not unusual for my parents to tell me off for being out too late, but it was unusual for me to be out after ten o'clock in the dark evenings.

It was the fisherman from Contis who gave me the story I needed.

# Chapter Twenty

During the long summers in Les Landes, there are fishermen out every night on the beaches. They merge into the white sand and the surf and the sky as the night descends low onto the horizon. There is an essential quality of silence and stillness about any fisherman. I have been aware of it as I sat beside my father on the banks of the small rivers locally. But on the coast the quality of the silence is absorbed and made prominent by the sound of the waves on the edge of the Atlantic Ocean. When the sands are not edged by people or by towns, but by miles of pine forest, cut off by the dunes and the high wind which has banked up the sand as a defence against the invasion of the beaches by any other creature, the quality of silence, alongside the sense of the insignificance of all humanity, is extraordinary.

I had cycled through the forest very frequently. I had run through the area of small lakes and bird breeding grounds behind the dunes and in front of the forest on a regular basis, stopping to watch the birds and the voles and the water creatures. But when I came across Armand, with his line extended from the beach to the sea water, I knew that I was in a different country.

I didn't even speak to him or look out to sea to find out what he was catching. I just knew that he was part of the bigger environment in a way which I could never be. I was like a tiny toy-like observer of a bigger world of which he was an essential part. I wanted to sit there and watch with him. I found it fascinating and soothing all at once. Words were unnecessary. He was part of something which I could only observe.

I think now that in those early days of the invasion I was frightened of being asked to be part of a world where there were threats and murders and of doing something about it by bringing food to those escaping. To merge into a bigger world, where I was not capable of doing anything, except being still and an appreciative observer, and being drawn into the wonder of it all was very reassuring.

I had wandered down to the beach in that early autumn, because somehow it was far too ordinary a thing to cycle straight home after being involved in hidden plots and helping foreign undesirables. If I really wanted to get home quickly without facing uncomfortable questions from my parents, I should have returned as quickly as possible. But somehow, I could not cope with the change from the dramatic to the ordinary without anything in between.

I was drawn by the gap in the dunes which happens at l'Especier beach and provides an easy access to the sea, which has an aura of calm continuity, whatever crazy things human beings are doing to each other. It was there that I encountered Armand. I say 'encounter' because 'meeting' was far too ordinary a word to explain, how I was drawn by the power of the sea and that physical environment which he inhabited.

For some time, I just stood there, looking out to sea, just as he was doing as a fisherman. Then silently he beckoned to me as he drew in his catch and then handed me bait to help him, as he fixed his hook. There was no sense of danger, of concern about being with an older man in a lonely place. I was happy to be with the 'otherness' of the sea and the horizon. I was also happy to be in the company of another human being.

Later, when I arrived back home and questions were asked, I was able to explain with total innocence how I had helped fix the bait for a fisherman.

'Wasting your time with fish just like your father,' observed my mother, confirmed in her view that the bad traits of her husband were passed on to her daughter.

I resented her criticism of my father. 'Papa catches fish for us too,' I replied.

'Yes, that's true sometimes, but it's nothing to the time he wastes out there.'

'You might be glad of a few fish if war comes.'

It was the first time that the possibility of war had been mentioned in our family. Surprisingly, having never consciously absorbed the subject myself, I now mentioned it as casually and certainly as if I believed every word that Alain had told me.

'Don't tell your father.'

'Why not?' I was curious. It suddenly occurred to me that my parents might have had private conversations about which I knew nothing.

'Like many of our men folk, he saw more than enough last time. We want peace. I hope Pétain brings it for us.'

'Peace at any price?'

'Yes, the price of not killing the next generation of young men.'

I didn't dare mention the people who might be crushed as a result. I was about to mention Alain's people, the Jews, but I stopped myself. I knew that to mention a subject which had not been discussed in our house, and which might relate in some way to fleeing pilgrims in the area, would be only to pique my mother's curiosity as to the source of my knowledge. I decided to go to bed, knowing that I had a new secret to guard – the secret of my understanding of what was happening to the Jewish people and my opposition to the Vichy regime.

I knew instinctively that in order to stifle any suspicions which my parents might have, I had to go more frequently to the coast and establish an interest in sea fishing. I started that routine immediately after my first visit even though for months there were no new pèlerins to help. I genuinely loved the experience of being by the water's edge and being involved in the fishing. I went enough times to bring back a few fish to contribute to the cook pot, so that my outings became a new routine, rather than anything extraordinary.

It was several months before I was given notice that another group of Jews needed escorting. More members of the Bordeaux synagogue decided to leave. To begin with they had thought that the French would protect them, and the Germans had begun the occupation without too much aggression, but as the occupation tightened its hold and more news filtered through about camps in Germany, more Jews decided to follow the example of Alain's Great Uncle Reuben.

In the succeeding months I became an established courier and skilled in how I gave directions and found food for the pèlerins. After the delivery of food on the coastal road, I stayed in the area for the experience of deep-sea fishing with Armand.

I had not seen Alain for some time, but one day after school, I found a note next to my bicycle, 'See you at our special place but destroy this note first.'

I found my way to the water pipes and hid my bike inside the grassy tunnel encasing them, then crawled through the last part of the pipes and dropped down into the hole below. Alain and I hugged as comrades and equals for the first time.

'They keep on telling me how good you are, Marie, and I haven't heard a word of suspicion from anyone local.'

'Except that you aren't around to hear any of it if it exists…But no, as far as I know, no one suspects.'

I told him about my meetings with Armand beside the sea.

'Be careful you don't tell him anything by mistake. Don't even tell him about the path you take to get there.'

I laughed. 'Don't worry. I won't. Armand and I don't talk to each other about anything or anyone. He is the epitome of the silent fisherman.'

'Good. Sounds safe but still, be careful. Don't always approach him from the same direction. Don't let there be a pattern in what you do. Taking fish home on other nights sounds like a good idea. Have your parents noticed anything about your activities?'

'They don't notice anything about me anyway,' I retorted scornfully.

'You might be surprised,' he said. 'When it comes to noticing, the whole French population is becoming more suspicious, and your parents won't be any different.'

'Suspicious of what?'

'As the Germans clamp down and Vichy is in their pay, loyalties and enemies will be established. People here just don't want trouble of any sort. They want to be allowed to get on with their small-time farming. They don't want their consciences to be troubled.'

'Why should they be?'

'Because you can't let a whole section of your population be persecuted and sent to die without doing something about it.'

'Will your family be persecuted, Alain, do you think?'

'To be honest, I don't know. On the face of it, they're the most relaxed non-observant Jews imaginable, who just blend into the hamlets near St. Paul and Eulalie like anyone else. But who knows how others might see them, once the Germans start signalling out the Jews for trouble?'

'And what will you do if that happens?'

He looked grim. 'I don't know, Marie. You can't just remove a woman with six children from their house and over the border to Spain that easily. They haven't got enough money for a start.'

'Money! Why do they need money?' I asked naively, as one who had no idea what it meant to earn my living. 'All they're doing is walking and I'll find them free food.'

'I know you will and everyone in the community is already grateful for what you are doing. But plenty of people don't provide free anything. And getting three-year old twins to walk across a mountain range without attracting attention is almost impossible. And once they're in Spain they've still got to find a way of surviving.'

'What about the communists? They hate the Germans. Perhaps they will help.'

'I don't know. Yes, they hate fascism but whether they love the Jews enough to save them, I don't know.'

'Alain,' I said suddenly. 'Why don't you go to Spain? Maybe you should go now yourself.'

'Maybe, but I'm not leaving my mother with the twins and other children to look after herself. If I can't save them, I can't save myself.'

# Chapter Twenty-One

When I first heard about unrest and problems, it was not from Alain but from Giles.

Giles was due to leave school very soon, but his future was unclear because of the occupation.

'My father says it's not the time to study now,' he complained to us at break time in the winter, as we all huddled round the wood burner in Mlle Tessier's school room.'

'Why not?' I had become much more sympathetic to Giles recently. He would never have Alain's magnetism, but he genuinely wanted an education so he could leave the village behind. He wanted to go to agricultural college so that he could farm more productively in Les Landes in the future.

'Because there's more and more trouble brewing with the Germans and my father doesn't want me in Bordeaux.'

'Then, why does he spend so much time there?' asked Cecile, sounding unusually provocative.

'Because he cares about the unions and what will happen.'

She looked at him dismissively. 'If he didn't stir things up, then everyone would be at peace.'

Giles turned on her with contempt in his eyes. 'You mean just accept the Germans and everything they are doing, like your precious Catholic leagues?'

Cecile sensed the attack. 'My parents want law and order. The cardinal says we should respect those in authority.'

'They're only in authority because they invaded our country.'

I was amazed at the level and intensity of this discussion. Our school room was not known for the quality of its debates. Normally there was whispering and giggles from the girls over the latest village romances or expected births and exchanges about rival village sport contests from the boys.

Why was everyone suddenly so concerned about the Germans who were far away? I realised that the animosity between Cecile and Giles came from their parents' activities and the views they were hearing at home. Unlike the example of my own home, families were sharing a variety of attitudes and loyalties with their children.

'Papa says that the only way to get any action against the Germans is to keep going with union meetings and strikes in the factory.' Giles was proud of his father and sure of the rightness of his views.

'How do strikes in the factories help?' I couldn't imagine the Germans being deterred by a few strikes in the factories.

'Because they show that the workers reject the Nazis, and the Germans need them to produce goods.'

'Surely you mean that they reject the bosses. They're bringing chaos to France – that's what Communists always do.' Cecile was as well instructed by her parents as Giles was by his.

He turned on her. 'So, you'd rather just accept what the Germans are doing?'

'I'm sure it won't last very long. Then we'll be free to take up our lives again and not so many people will have been hurt.'

'Oh yes?' Giles was cynical about this happy outcome. 'Nice idea, Cecile. Unfortunately, people have been 'hurt' already, like a few thousand people who have been killed during the invasion.'

'And what about the English and the Free French in London?' This was from Gervais, a boy in our class who loved to use his fists.

'What are the Free French?' I asked innocently.

Gervais was dismissive of my ignorance. 'And I thought you were supposed to be the clever one. Don't your parents listen to the broadcasts?'

'What broadcasts?'

'Honestly, Marie, I wonder about you sometimes. What's the point of having your head in a book, if you don't know what's going on around you?'

I thought about my mother's attitude to the wireless. When did she have time to listen to music and entertainment? She had far too much work to do on the farm.

'Alright. I accept what you're saying. Now you tell me, who are the Free French?'

'The people who got over to England to join the Allies, when Germany invaded. The most important one is Charles de Gaulle.'

'Maman says he's dangerous.' This was from Audrée, one of Cecile's friends.

'Of course, he's dangerous, stupid. If there's an invasion or a war, there's no point doing anything unless it's dangerous.'

'Well, I don't want anyone dangerous round here. I just want our village to be left in peace.' Some of the girls sympathised with Audrée's fears. They huddled closer together over the stove as if they preferred to be left to their own girlish interests and this other talk could be handed over to the boys.

'You're living in France,' announced Giles loftily. 'No one's going to be left in peace.'

'Not if people like your dad stir up trouble.'

Giles turned away from warming his hands to face Cecile.

'My dad fought for this country in the last war. He's not the one who brought the Germans back. They're here and they're going to cause trouble.'

'Not if we keep the law and don't do anything bad.' Cecile repeated her well learnt lesson.

Giles now had a mission to tell us what we should believe. 'Don't you realise? They're going to take the men! Yes, of course they are.' This was added in the face of widespread incredulity from his audience round the fire. 'They've already started taking men in their twenties for forced labour to Germany.'

'That's only in the big towns.'

'Yes, that's the start. They will be going after us all in time.'

Could this involve all the families round here, not just the Jewish ones? I was curious. 'What would you do, Giles, if you were taken off to Germany?'

'Run away.'

'Where to?'

'England or Spain.'

103

'Anyway, it's not likely to be us they take. We're too young.' This contribution was from Artur, Giles's friend. 'It's more likely to be our fathers.'

'I don't want my dad to be taken away.' Little Régine, aged nine, was on the verge of tears.

'No one's taking your dad away, Régine,' said a reassuring voice from the back of our group. Without our knowledge, Mlle Tessier had re-entered the school room.

'You mustn't be frightened. To begin with we are a rural community and the Germans need men on the farms, to help produce enough food.'

'In other parts of France, they've already started taking people.'

'I thought it was just the Jews.' This was from Cecile.

I turned on her. 'What do you mean, "just the Jews" and who told you about them?'

I had spoken too quickly, drawn in by the heated discussion and anxious to know more about what was going on around me.

'I heard about the Jews in Poland. They were talking about it in the Hôtel du Centre last week, when I went to buy matches for my mother.' Poland sounded a safe distance away, I thought.

'Poland resisted Hitler. That's why the Jews are in trouble there. Our government will protect the Jews here.' Cecile was completely confident in the actions of her own country.

'Of course, you're right,' I agreed docilely. 'Don't be known for your interest in the Jews,' I heard Alain's warning in my head. Remain innocent and no one will think about you when questions are asked.

Giles was less compromising. 'Who will protect the Jews? The Vichy government? You've got to be joking! They can't protect anyone except themselves.'

'That's a terrible thing to say,' said Cecile shocked. 'Marshal Pétain will look after us. He protected us in the last war.'

'My dad says he's not going to lead us out of trouble now.'

'Children, we need to get back to class.' Mlle Tessier intervened before the rival groups in our class turned on each other.

I was glad. I had often complained in the past about the lack of intelligent conversation in our school. Now, I wasn't sure I wanted so many different conflicting opinions.

'I didn't realise that people felt so strongly,' I ventured to Mlle Tessier, as I helped her pack up the books at the end of the day.

'I'm afraid, Marie, that that's not the end of heated discussion in our villages.'

'I've never heard them be so definite in their views about anything before.'

'That's because it's already affecting people in their homes. This is much more than an intellectual discussion, Marie, fascinating as that might be.'

I hesitated. Mlle Tessier had always been so keen to show me that good discussions involved understanding multiple different points of view.

'What do you think is going to happen, Mlle Tessier? Are we all going to be pulled apart?'

She stopped. The soft light above her on the wall highlighted her face and the flames from the wood burner lit up her arms full of books.

'I think trouble is coming. I thought that it would escape us, tucked away here in Les Landes, but now I'm not sure. The Germans are watching everything which goes on. They are not pleased by people's disdain for them.

Be very careful, Marie. They are not to be trifled with.'

# Chapter Twenty-Two

Giles proved to be a helpful informant about what was going on amongst local people. Since he had given me so much local information which I could use in my project about religion and politics in Les Landes, our conversations had continued. Ironically Cecile, whose help I had needed to find out the details of Catholic pilgrims, and whose desk I had shared in the school room, had no long-term effect on my understanding of local belief systems. She was a reliable informer but demonstrated little engagement with the subject matter she gave. She was a conformist who found enough meaning for her life in the traditions she had inherited from her parents. For as long as those traditions gave her joy and satisfaction, she had no reason to question them. I might have ignored her by summing her up as 'dull', but the truth was I could have benefitted from her certainty, her confidence and her satisfaction with the family she had been born into. It was the exact opposite of my own inheritance.

After Alain had left school, I had never turned to other classmates as friends. Alain had such an extraordinary effect on my life, that it was impossible for anyone else to fill his place. If, subsequently, my days at school were lonely, they were, in my estimation, adequately filled by my own imagination, internal dialogue and voracious reading habits, with the occasional invigorating injection of visits from Alain in Bordeaux during the holidays.

After my questions about the Communist Party which were meant to deflect any curiosity which others might have felt about my interest in the Catholic pilgrims, I began to have the odd, genuinely interesting conversation with Giles. It was not sudden, just a gradual loosening up of relationship and communication. I had been moved by his ownership of a different world vision to that of his father. True, his was the conventional desire for a future more in keeping with the traditional ambitions of generations of 'landais'– inheriting the farm, making local produce profitable, looking for a marriage with a local girl, enjoying local festivities and dances, often hosted by the local 'mairie' or the Catholic church. If Giles found fulfilment in these, it was at least because he had thought through the options and made a conscious choice. He also wanted to farm more profitably and that was his reason for his interest in higher education.

In doing that, he had also rejected his father's loyalties. Over the next few months, as Giles lingered before going home at lunch time or arrived early at school, having completed his early morning chores in good time, our occasional conversational exchanges lengthened. He had none of the originality of thought shown by Alain, but he was an acute observer of motive in others, and, being less of an idealist, saw more clearly the reality of his father's passions.

One morning he arrived at school looking tired and he did not display his usual attentiveness in completing his morning's work. Unusually he stayed at school during the lunch break joining with me round the fire. I shared my lunch with him.

'Thanks, Marie. You're right. I'm so tired I can't even be bothered to go home.' Giles' farm was only a ten-minute bike ride from the school room and usually his mother, an excellent housewife, had prepared a tasty meal, made from leftovers from the night before. There was good food as well as conviviality at the Delamares' table.

'You must be tired if you can't be bothered to eat your mother's main dish. What were you up to last night then?' I was curious because early morning rising in our community usually necessitated early nights.

'There was a special union meeting at the match factory in Bordeaux last night and my father wanted me to accompany him.'

'Why?' I knew that Giles wasn't interested in politics, so there must have been some special reason for him being there.

'He's often at the union meetings, hearing about conditions, seeing if he can support strikes, campaigning for better wages, speaking about lay-offs and redundancies.'

'That sounds good to me,' I said. 'I wonder then why people talk about the communists bringing trouble.'

'Yes, well they do bring trouble, but it depends whether you're the one who's suffering.'

'It sounds like your Dad is sympathetic to those who are suffering.'

'Of course, he is, there's no doubt about that…that's not the problem.'

'What is the problem then?' I was young enough to want to paper over the complexities of right and wrong, but Giles was more worldly wise than me.

'He thinks the communists will change all that.'

'But you don't.'

'I think they want to change it, but they'll change other things at the same time, which isn't quite so good.'

'Such as?'

'Individuals being able to farm for themselves.'

'Ah,' I said knowingly. We were back at the root of Giles' desire – land to farm and self-sufficiency. 'Surely communism needs farmers.'

'Yes, but only those who will work with quotas and certain amounts of land and the state owning all the land.'

'Yes, well I can see that wouldn't suit most people here.' I shifted comfortably down my hard chair to get my body nearer to the warmth. All this talk about farming quotas seemed a long way removed from anything I might be interested in. Giles was a decent school friend, but in my head, I was far more interested in Plato and Herodotus and the history of Aragon and the old kingdoms of France than the question of who owned the land.

'So, if you don't care about it, why did you go?' I had heard Giles talk about his father's visits to the factories before. I thought that the clandestine nature of the visits sounded romantic, but Giles was anything but romantic. When he could, he stayed at home on the farm with his mother, while his older brother, Patrice, learnt about his father's political interests.

'My father said I should go and hear what was happening.'

'You mean he wants you to be a communist.'

'No. I think he's given up on that one. Besides he is reasonable, despite being a communist. He wouldn't force his family to do anything. Patrice is genuinely interested, but I'd rather stay on the farm.'

'Sounds boring to me.'

'Maybe, but I love it. I know I can make something of it, and I don't want the communists destroying what I love.'

'So, what was special about last night?'

Giles suddenly put his feet down away from the comfort of the burner and turned to me, his face earnest.

'Marie, you won't tell anyone will you?'

'No, of course I won't.' My heart was beating fast. Someone else was about to confide in me as well as Alain. Could what Giles have to say have any effect on Alain's family?

'Because I have to tell someone, otherwise I'll go crazy.'

'What happened, Giles?' I didn't even bother to affirm my trustworthiness. My whole body looked the same as before, but inside every nerve was taut, as I waited for the story to be divulged.

'I'd been to those sorts of rallies before…the big ones and the small groups. Loads of speeches about the conditions of the factories and the bad pay for the workers and about how following Lenin and Stalin would change all that. But this was different.'

'How?'

'When the shop steward – I mean the unofficial one. They call them that though the union isn't allowed to exist…it's their own hierarchy of power. When he started to speak, it wasn't a swagger or even a loud voice. It was almost whispered but it was serious. I could feel it …I was almost shivering, and I'm not usually affected by what they say.'

'What was different this time?'

'They talked about the Germans, about how at the beginning they just checked that everything was running smoothly but didn't get involved in the day to day running because they trusted the 'patron'. But things have been changing recently. There's more and more of them watching the shop floor, asking the 'patron' who the trade unionists are, who are the secret communists.'

I was unimpressed. 'I expect they're just wary. After all, they are fascists, aren't they? They're not going to like the communists.' That simple binary of opposites was already firmly established in my head. So long as they left us alone in the villages and towns of La Gironde, no one, including me, really cared.

'It's a bit more than that. I think they're going to cause us real trouble.'

'What, here in Les Landes? My dad says they will leave us alone. They might be policing the rest of France, but we're out on a limb – unimportant.'

'But we're still in the Occupied Zone and Bordeaux is still a major city.'

'Oh well, Bordeaux!' I was dismissive of Giles' fears. Even the Jewish escapes from Bordeaux seemed removed from my everyday life. My work of supplying food and making sure they were on the right route was more like an exciting game.

'Marie, I'm serious. It's going to affect all of us.'

'How?'

'My dad says they're going to get workers for their arms factories in Germany.'

'What? From Bordeaux?'

'And here.'

'But then they won't have people to run the factories and farms here.'

'They'll get older people and women to do that. The young men they consider dangerous will be taken to Germany.'

'Giles, does that mean you might have to go?'

'No, I don't think so. Not yet. But it could affect Patrice and my dad.'

'Alright … but not especially the communists?'

'Yes. I think especially the communists. They're the dangerous ones because they're against fascism.'

'But I thought Russia was the German ally.'

'True but they're still scared of Stalin.'

'From what I've heard, I'm not surprised.'

Giles ignored my gibe, which was not based on any real knowledge of the situation, just hearsay.

'It was scary, Marie.'

I was silent. It sounded terrifying. The menace of the war and the German occupation had just moved one step nearer to my everyday life.

# Chapter Twenty-Three

Giles' fears proved to be correct. In 1942 there was a cull of men of military age who were sent to work in the munitions' factories in Germany. His father, along with various military-aged men from Bordeaux, were sent away. Patrice and Giles remained, as did most of the farmers in our area. But there was an aura of foreboding. Les Landes had been touched. Vichy was no longer the trusted government who could save us. Marshal Pétain was still venerated as a hero of the Great War, but there was no confidence that Germany would merely leave us to our own devices.

I turned sixteen and my parents wanted me to leave school. Mlle Tessier was keen for me to sit for the lycée in Bordeaux, but my parents were adamant.

'If you go to Bordeaux while the Boches are there, there is no knowing what will happen.' For once my parents were in complete agreement with each other. Bordeaux spelt risk and risk meant that their only daughter could be in trouble.

'But why should I be in trouble?' I argued. 'The Germans are not interested in me. I'm only a sixteen-year old girl.' My parents were going to use the invasion as an excuse to stop me having what I had always wanted – an education and a way of escaping from the stranglehold, the narrowness of home!

But my parents were unmoveable and without their permission I could do nothing.

I talked about it with Mlle Tessier who sympathised with my disappointment but who was far more reasonable than I was.

'Wait, Marie. All is not lost,' she counselled. 'I can understand your parents' point of view. For now, Bordeaux is a dangerous place.'

'That's their excuse. The truth is they want to keep me at St. Paul so that I can work on the farm and never have a life.'

'Maybe, but there's an opportune time for everything. They can't take away from you your reading and your lively mind. The war will end one day and then your time will come.'

'Oh yes? By then I will probably have been married off and be a good little housewife just like Cecile and all the others.' I was frustrated and bitter that my teacher was not on my side.

She laughed. 'Marie, I can't imagine you as a good little anything. Remember, it's up to you what you become. If you choose to settle down in this area, then that's your choice. But there will be opportunities in the future when all of this is over.'

'Oh really? You mean when I'm too old to have an education.'

'Marie, you're never too old to have an education. Education is what happens when a mind expands. That can happen at any age.'

I left the room in anger and despair. No one understood. I was sixteen and I could not imagine anything happening in my life beyond the grand old age of twenty. Life ended at such an advanced age and I would be dead without achieving anything. The only person who could be trusted to understand was Alain, and I saw him only rarely. Even the flow of pilgrims escaping over the Spanish border had diminished. What Alain himself was doing, I had no real idea. He seemed to be staying on at his lycée, as a sort of 'moniteur' or assistant. Apparently, it allowed him to earn and to study at the same time for entrance to the 'grandes écoles' – the top universities in France. That Alain would end up going to the best that France had to offer, I had no doubt. In the summer of 1942, he came back briefly to our area to check on his family and to find out what was happening.

I was still biking through the area and reading more of Mlle Tessier's books, though now I doubted that I would ever use them to pass an exam.

To my amazement, when we finally met up again down the valley across the pipes, he sympathised with my parents and Mlle Tessier.

'Marie, I know you don't see it, but they have a point. Bordeaux is a very dangerous place to be.'

I drew away from his hug and sat with my back against the bark of the rowan tree.

'Well you seem to be managing alright in all this danger.'

'Only because I've been at the lycée for the last two years so I'm not new. The Germans notice new movement.'

'Are you trying to tell me that there won't be a new intake at the lycée next year?'

'No, there will be, but the vast majority come from Bordeaux itself. It's a natural progression from the 'écoles secondaires' of the town. No one will be interested in them. But you're different. You're from the country and you'd have to find a 'logement'. That's difficult and costly and all education is uncertain right now.'

'Thanks,' I said bitterly. 'I thought that at least you would understand.'

'Marie, you know I back you all the way. I think you're fantastic. You're clever and you've got loads of initiative. No one will ever be able to keep you back.'

'Well, everyone seems to be trying.'

'You must have a better view of yourself than that. Let's see what happens in the next couple of years. Either Germany is going to take over the whole of Europe or they're going to be defeated by the Allies.'

I had only vaguely heard about the Allies. 'Is that England? But I thought Pétain was saying that they are our enemies.'

'You obviously haven't been listening to the radio.'

'We don't do radio in our house. You've forgotten. We only 'do' – keep working and if you're lucky disaster won't strike.'

Alain laughed. 'I'd forgotten. Sorry. But surely your dad had to give up his hunting gun like everyone else?'

'Yes, that's true, though my father finds other ways of hunting so it's not the end for him.'

'OK but the Free French aren't finished.'

'Who are they?'

'De Gaulle. He's in England rallying free Frenchmen everywhere and going abroad to the colonies to find them.'

'But are they strong enough to fight the Boches?'

'Not for now, but we should wait. And don't forget the Americans.'

'What about them?' The American were so distant to my mind that they might as well have been aliens from another planet.

'They came in at the end of the Great War and they may do it again.'

'But everyone loves the maréchal.'

'They do for now because he represents stability; but there are already rumblings against him.'

'What sort of rumblings?' I was amazed. No such controversies ever reached the world of our little farms.

'Marie, Vichy and the Germans are doing terrible things to the Jews and the Communists. There are train loads of people being taken away in the middle of the night, when they think no one can see them.'

'Where to?'

'No one knows but there are rumours in the Jewish community. They start by being herded into the camps like Gurs in the Pyrenées, not far from here and in Drancy, which is a northern suburb of Paris. But they are sent on and there seems to be camps called concentration camps set up.'

'You mean like where Giles' father has been sent to work?'

'No. Those are labour camps. Not that those are nice either. If you are too weak or unhealthy you could die there, but this is more than that. They're sent to die in those camps.'

I was silent. Suddenly my own future didn't seem so important. I turned to look at Alain. He was staring at the little piece of sky you could glimpse from our valley.

'If they send the Jews there, does that mean they could send you there too?'

'I think I'm too young for now, but yes, they could.'

'So why don't you escape like Great Uncle Reuben?'

I sat up. In my mind I was already organising his disguise and his food and, of course, I would be involved in the rescue plan.

'I think I'm needed here, Marie. No one's taking any notice of me, but the moment they do, I'm off to the forest with the maquis.'

'Who are the maquis?'

'Those who are resisting the Boches.'

'But can they? I mean are they strong enough to do that?'

'No. But they're gaining strength all over France.'

'But if you're a Jew, you're more at risk of capture. Why don't you just go over the Spanish border?'

'Because of my family. No, I don't mean the ones in Bordeaux. They've already gone. I mean my mother and the little ones.'

'But the Germans won't be interested in them. They're too unimportant.'

'Not if they're only interested in having workers, I agree; but if they want to exterminate the Jews, they will want them.'

I was picking up the fallen rowan leaves with my fingers and methodically taking them apart with my fingers.

'Alain?'

'Yes?'

'Why do they hate your people so much?'

'G-d knows.'

'That's not an answer.'

'No, but you can find lots of other answers and none of them give you an adequate answer. Jealousy because they are so successful in business? Anger, because they resent their defeat in the Great War? Because the Jews don't have the same religion as the majority? I honestly don't know, Marie. But they do.'

'Well, I don't hate you.'

In response, Alain laughed. He tickled me and pulled my hair and I cuddled up to him.

'I don't know why, my little one. I'm always asking you to do things for me. I may need you, Marie, or my family may.'

'Well, I'm here for you.' It was the most natural statement in the world. The rest of the world might fall apart but he would always be my special friend.

'So,' Alain said, suddenly changing the subject. 'If you're not going to be allowed to pursue a great academic career, what are you going to do?'

'I'm going to work as a waitress at the Hôtel du Centre. At least my mother isn't deluded enough to think that I would be any good on the farm.'

'In that case, she's not so stupid after all! The Hôtel du Centre sounds like the perfect solution to me.'

# Chapter Twenty-Four

With my mother's approval, my new life began. In the past I had imagined two scenarios. The one extreme was the world of my fears, chained to the farm by my mother's orders and constantly berated by her for my incompetence, stifled so that I never read a book again, occasionally escaping to go hunting or fishing with my father. The other extreme was the life of the brilliant student, amazing my teachers and fellow pupils with my intelligence, and passing my 'baccalauriat' at the highest grade and disappearing in a blaze of glory to some exalted position in France or, better still, to adventure in the wider world. Although the second one seemed to be the most unlikely, the first one, to be fair, was not what my parents were likely to choose for me. Who would want a fellow worker on a farm who was more of a hindrance than anything else? Perhaps my mother might have hoped that I would marry a hard-working farmer, but, then, it was more likely that I would go to live on his farm than he come to mine. Although my mother was disillusioned by the outcome of her own marriage, she was not spiteful enough to want the same fate for her daughter. My position as waitress and barmaid solved the problem of which fate to choose. While it meant that I could no longer study and have a 'brilliant academic career', it also meant that I did not have to work at home. From my parents' point of view, I was safe in the local community and I was earning a wage which helped the family.

The biggest surprise, as far as I was concerned, was that I found a social outlet which I had never experienced before and which I enjoyed. Having kept myself isolated at school from all but Alain, I had no idea that I might enjoy the gossip and the passing conversations of bar life. I was amazed by how many interesting people there were in the little town of Mimizan, how much the 'proprietaire' knew about them, and how well informed was the senior bar maid, Thérèse, who worked there. If Thérèse had been at school with me, I would have despised her for her lack of academic ability, but as the senior in my place of work, I respected her and learnt much about my neighbours in the town, as the result of her chatter. She kept an eye on me, told me who to avoid, who was mean with their tips, and who was dangerous when they drank too much.

I also discovered that I had unexpected talents. I knew how to be charming to the clientele, how to show interest in their lives, how to give someone an encouraging word, even when they were wasting hour after hour at the bar with endless apéritifs, because they clearly had nothing else to do with their lives. I found that I looked forward to going to work and was glad to be out of the farm for so many hours. Apart from my day off, I even spent less time roaming the forests, lakes and beaches of Les Landes. Most mornings, if I had worked late the night before, I was too tired to do very much before going back to work.

To begin with I had to concentrate on getting the prices and the change correct, and I needed to know the tastes of the regular customers. By the time I had learnt that, I had more spare time for gossip and for discovering the interests and points of view of the regular customers.

Patrice and his friends were regulars. Now that he had lost his father to the labour camps, he was the one who was the leader of the local communists.

'If you want real change round here, you'll be backing me for the 'mairie' in the future,' he would boast.

I couldn't help thinking that no one in our communes wanted change, and that his claim would never have much appeal to locals.

'This isn't Bordeaux, you know, Patrice. Better to go to the unions there, like your dad did.'

'Better to be rid of the Boches first,' said another knowingly.

Such a statement was the first of many which ran along predictable lines.

The older generation of drinkers didn't have much time for such fighting talk.

'Life wasn't so much better before the Germans were here. Every government has promised us better wages and conditions ever since the Great War, but nothing has changed.'

'Yes, they're all 'salauds' – the aristocrats and the government workers. We may live in a republic, but we were still like the peasants to the English aristocrats at Lake Aureihan. They were the ones who had all the money and ordinary, decent folk like us were just left behind.' M. Dupont, a local baker, stubbed out his cigarette in his beer glass, a habit which always enraged me, as I had to clean out the glasses.

'Yes, it doesn't really matter who's in charge – Germans or the French – they're all as bad as each other.' Paul Monier thought he was agreeing with the others while enjoying his own pessimism, but this was a step too far for Patrice and his friends.

'You think you can confuse an honest Frenchman with the dirty Boches.' André, Patrice's friend, stood up to confront Paul.

'Oh, sit down, André.' Yves, the pharmacist intervened. 'He doesn't know what he's saying. None of us want the Boches, but none of the last lot in France belonging to the third republic were much good either.'

'If only we had Blum back in power. He was a real socialist.'

'No, my friend, it was the Jews, like Blum, who caused all the trouble.'

'That's the line Pétain and Laval and all the Vichy people take. They just let the Germans walk all over us.'

'Better than die in their war like the last time.'

Silence descended on the core group of old men in the bar. No one wanted the deaths and the injuries and the absences of the last war. Great war memorials in the centres of the villages were not enough to replace the real fathers and husbands who were lost.

However, the younger generation were not so sure. They still clamoured for glory, for the chance to prove themselves.

'The unions will show them.' Patrice was sure of his loyalties.

'Show them what, my young friend?' came a voice from the back of the room.

'That you can't keep the workers down. That the reds will overcome the Fascists.'

'Under the reds in the factories, we've had strife and higher prices.' Monsieur Morel, caretaker at the local church, spoke up. 'At least the Fascists keep everyone in order.'

'Sure! They keep everyone in order – their order. So that all the money goes to Germany and our men go there too.'

'Yes, look at what happened to my dad.' Patrice was the only one in our village, whose family had really suffered in the war so far. 'My mum never hears from him. Anything could be happening. He's working for slave wages to keep the German war machine going.'

'Better that than keeping Stalin's war machine going.' M. Morel's tone of voice did not invite sympathy. Patrice was the only one in the group who had suffered for his beliefs. All the men, even those who had no interest in his communist beliefs, wanted to support Patrice against M. Morel.

This was where Thérèse stepped in. She knew exactly how to diffuse these arguments and the bad feelings which threatened to tear our village apart.

'How about another round, Messieurs?'

'What do you think then, Thérèse?'

Thérèse swung her hips and looked round at her admirers.

'I say bad luck to Patrice's dad for getting taken by the Boches. But don't let the unions take away more of our men.' She continued, looking round them all flirtatiously in the bar, 'There aren't enough of you as it is. Don't let the reds get people sent to Germany.'

'Quite right, Thérèse. We want to stay with you.' Someone pinched her bottom and she stopped for a moment to sit on someone's knee. This was my cue to collect more dirty glasses and move over to the bar to pour another round.

I realised that I had come to the bar not just fill the glasses but to learn more about local politics. It was to have its uses but then, so was the art of compromise and peace as practised by Thérèse.

# Chapter Twenty-Five

In the bar I heard endless talk of how the Germans were evil, or not so bad, or even that they promoted order, according to the politics of the individual. It was a make-believe world where we could all push the chequers around on the board. If you sent so many workers to Germany, there would be fewer armies coming from Russia. If you had more soldiers from the Free French in Britain, you would have more real French patriots who emerged in France. It was fascinating. Everyone enjoyed discussing the different possibilities because none of them really touched us.

Everything remained the same and different views enlivened the conversation until someone noticed that the Woolsack House, which since the Occupation had been empty, had more recently been taken over by German soldiers.

'Why would any Germans want to be in such an out of the way place?' Most people in the area could not see any advantages in being such an impractical venue.

'I always had my doubts about that place,' ventured M. Morel. 'Owned by foreigners who are capable of anything,' he added darkly, as if the Woolsack had been used by the Gestapo for years, rather than being the playhouse of rich English aristocrats.

'But the English are on our side, M. Morel,' Thérèse pointed out.

'Oh, are they? Well, I've always had my doubts about them, bringing their servants from London and Paris.' For a true Landais, it didn't much matter whether it was from England or Paris – they were both suspect as foreign parts.

It wasn't long after this conversation that the German Feldcommandant and two of his junior soldiers decided to visit the Bar du Centre.

We had no warning of their coming and no idea why they were there. Why could they not stay in Bordeaux and contain their nastiness there without travelling down the long straight forest fringed roads of Les Landes? Or why could they not stay drinking at the Woolsack where foreigners had always conducted themselves shadily with parties and drinking extravaganza?

My shift that day started in the early evening, when they had already arrived.

Thérèse pulled me into the back kitchen before I served that night.

'Listen, Marie, they're here – the Boches.'

My eyes widened. It was like being told that the witch in Hansel and Gretel had arrived in the village. Surely, they couldn't exist in real life!

'They're here and, Marie, it doesn't matter what you think. Just treat them like normal customers.'

'How will everyone else react?'

'Leave them to me,' said Thérèse. 'You just concentrate on filling orders, like you usually do.'

'What will Patrice say?'

'Nothing, if I have anything to do with it,' said Thérèse. 'We don't want them here of course, but the best way of getting rid of them, is to make them think that their journey here is pointless. The more tolerance we show, the less reason there will be for them to come back.'

'Do you think the local men will allow us to be tolerant?'

'They'll do what I say.'

I believed her. Thérèse was magnificent. I had my first glimpse of what could be done when a clever woman was in charge.

'They won't take any notice of you,' she added kindly. 'You're too young. Don't be especially nice to them but don't refuse to serve them or be rude to them.'

I stared at her. How were we to manage the enemy in Mimizan? Or were they really the enemy? Not according to M. Morel from the Catholic church. According to him, it was Patrice and the union men from Bordeaux who were the real enemy. But I liked Patrice. I linked him in my mind with his brother at school. Giles was my friend and not interested in communism or politics, but Patrice had a right to his views.

I felt extremely nervous as I entered the bar that evening. It was a very quiet atmosphere. People's normal conversation was silenced. I began to collect the dirty glasses, hardly daring to glance at our German visitors.

'So, who are you then?'

Immediately it felt strange to be approached like that, so directly. No one had ever had any need to ask that question, even though I had never frequented the bar before I worked there. Everyone in the commune knew who everyone else was. I felt a shiver of alienation. I paused as my finger pads touched the tops of the beer glasses.

'I'm Marie.'

'Ah Marie, and how long have you been working here?'

'Two months.'

'And is it a good job?'

'Yes, certainly. I'm treated well here.'

'Good. Then you will know how to treat us well then in the future, won't you?'

I wasn't sure about the logic of that idea, but Thérèse had told me to keep them happy.

'Yes, Sir.'

Feldcommandant Jurgen Gross moved indifferently from me to his beer on the table.

His assistant tried to treat me with the contempt I deserved but the younger one, a blond-haired boy who was no more than eighteen years old, smiled at me.

I tried to ignore him, but the smile reached to me as a person. It felt like a genuine communication between two young people, and in my short life I had experienced very few such relationships. He was the enemy, but he was a young person. I tried to half smile with the side of my mouth, without giving anything away.

Unusually there was silence in the bar. We couldn't talk about Patrice's father or the unions in Bordeaux or the Catholic Church. These subjects were now too dangerous. Whatever anyone felt, they did not want to air their views in front of the Germans.

'Your beer is very good, mademoiselle.' The Feldcommandant turned his attention to Thérèse, whom he felt instinctively was the one with the real authority.

'I'm glad you like our French beer, Monsieur.'

She was polite but her pointed reference to the origin of the beer made her position clear. At the Hôtel du Centre we did not serve German beer.

'We will always enjoy the products of France and especially what is grown in your wonderful Bordeaux 'vignobles'.

'However,' continued the Feldcommandant, 'don't confuse them with English rubbish.'

'There's no English 'vignobles' that I know of, monsieur,' said Thérèse lightly as she swept around the bar.

'No. So make sure you don't listen to English news.'

'Why would we do that, Monsieur?'

'Because I have been told that there are those in this area who listen to English lies.'

We all knew what he meant. Anyone who had a radio listened to the regular BBC broadcast from the Free French.

'I'm sure, sir,' said Thérèse with great charm and gaiety, 'that we are all loyal French people here, sir, with no links to Englishmen.'

'I hope so, Mademoiselle, And no links to the Spanish communists either.'

The Feldcommandant's eyes searched the customers of the Hôtel du Centre. They were mild, cultured and rational. Nevertheless, there was a threat underneath his words.

I was going about my job of taking and receiving orders but, in my head, I felt the threat.

Did he know about what I had done with the 'pèlerins'? Did he know about my links with Alain and my adventures down the coast? It seemed a long time since I had done those trips but somehow his presence warned me not repeat them.

Thérèse answered for Patrice when she said, 'We understand that the communists have been defeated by General Franco. That is the end of the matter as far as we are concerned.'

'Good, mademoiselle,' said the Feldcommandant, rising from his chair, 'so we have nothing to disagree about. No doubt, I will be patronizing this charming establishment again with its French wines and its delightful French citizens.' He bowed towards Thérèse, the acknowledged leader of the bar and left with his two young assistants.

There was at least a fifteen – minute silence when they left, as we all recognized the seriousness of the situation. We had been noticed. If they had come this far from Bordeaux, it had been for a purpose. All of us had been warned – no interest in the Spanish, no listening to the English radio and no links with the communists.

Without saying anything, all of us chose to ignore these threats in our own way.

# Chapter Twenty-Six

The first visit to the bar by the Germans both frightened us and made us more purposeful. Even Monsieur Morel was affected.

'I will always support the Catholic Church,' he boasted one evening, 'and the Catholic Church can stand up to the Germans.'

'Oh really?' queried Patrice, 'And that's why the Pope is not criticizing the Nazis?'

'He doesn't support the bad parts of Nazism, only the good parts,' protested the caretaker.

'And is he speaking out against the bad parts?'

'Ah well,' he hesitated.

'Of course, he's not. He's just told the faithful that this year will be dedicated to the immaculate heart of Mary, as if that's what we need, when they are murdering Communists and Jews.'

'There are some Catholic priests who are speaking up against injustice.'

Surprisingly this came from Léon, who did not normally support religion in our village. Our own Père Francis had spoken against the persecution of the Jews in last Sunday's homily. Such a stand carried dangers and would give him a reputation.

Patrice was determined in his support of the Unions. 'If we keep on saying the same thing in the factories across the country, then Nazism will be defeated.'

'How can we have any effect whatever, if no one on the outside helps us?' This was from André.

'That's why we need to listen to the Free French on the wireless.'

'But he just warned us not to.'

'So how does he know what we do at home?'

'And how can he stop us? Is he going to send a whole army to find out who is listening to the wireless? I don't think so.'

I made no contribution to this general discussion. If anyone knew that I had helped the pilgrims, I would be in serious trouble.

It was to Alain that I voiced my fears next time we met down the valley through the water pipes.

'Alain, do you think you'll send more pèlerins?'

'I think we've passed that stage now, Marie.'

'What do you mean? Surely there are still Jews who need to escape?'

'Of course, but it's not so easy to do that openly.'

I had thought that I had been involved in a masterful intrigue, but Alain seemed to see it now as a simplistic operation.

'It was great to be able to send some more people like that,' he explained. 'but I doubt we'll be able to do it again now.'

'Why not?'

'Because the situation is more serious now. The Germans are on the lookout. If they've been to Mimizan, and are stationed at the Woolsack, it means that they are aware that there are stirrings.'

'But, even if there are, there's nothing they can do about it. So far there's only been three soldiers and Les Landes is a huge area.'

'Yes, but they're getting more knowing. Before, they were content just to occupy and to oversee what everyone was doing. Now they're actively looking for Jews.'

I was worried by his words. 'That means they're looking for you, Alain. You have to be careful.'

'Don't worry. I'm more than capable of being careful. I can disappear here any time I want.'

'Maybe we should leave some food supplies here.'

'Maybe we should.' He paused before continuing. 'But I'm not the problem.'

'Then who is?'

'The people in the towns who have nowhere to disappear to. And not just the young men, who are free agents. It's the families who are at risk.'

'You mean the children? Surely, no one wants to kill them! What point would there be in that?'

'The point, my dear friend, is that you get rid of Jews completely.'

'But why would you want to? I just don't understand. OK, they want to get rid of their religion.'

'It's not just the religion. It's the people who make money they don't like.'

'But the children don't make money.'

'They will in the future. They want a Europe without Jews.'

'They're mad.'

'Maybe but that's what's happening.'

I was perplexed by this mad reasoning, but I was more worried about my friend. 'Alain, why don't you go now before it's too late? You could set off on the road for Spain tonight.' I jumped up in distress. 'Go now, this minute. I'll bring you food for the journey.'

Alain laughed. 'Thanks, Marie. I know I can rely on you. No, don't be offended by my laughing. I'm serious. I know I can rely on you and I appreciate it more than you can imagine.'

We held each other close without saying anything. He desperately wanted the assurance of my friendship. I desperately wanted to save him. We wanted to protect each other from the terrible world beyond our little bolt hole. We wanted to assure ourselves that we would be alright, despite the madness of the people around us. Our friendship was based on laughter and jokes and reading and discussion and playing tricks and riding our bikes through the forest and having long conversations lying on the banks of the lakes but we were being invaded by a world which wanted nothing of this innocent enjoyment.

'Marie, you have to understand that I can't leave my family especially my mother with the twins. They're too young to escape and my mother is too unknowing about the real dangers. This is the only world that she knows.'

'But if she knew that that world is dying?'

'She does know somewhere deep down, I think, but she can't cope with it. She won't leave their farm.'

'Damn the farm,' I cried with the exasperation of youth. 'Surely their lives are worth more than the farm.'

'It's just that in her imagination she can't move past the farm. It's the only life she and my father knew. And taking three-year old twins anywhere without them making a noise and holding everyone up is almost impossible.'

'All the more reason for you to go. At least you can survive for them.'

'I can't survive knowing that they're going to be captured.'

I felt my anger rising within me. Why waste a life as beautiful as Alain's because of three-year old twins? They weren't going to escape anyway so why not give Alain a chance instead?

'Marie, I might need you to help me.'

'Of course, I'm going to help you.'

'I might need you to bring us food, or even hide some of them.'

'You know you can rely on me.'

'But it's dangerous and I don't want you to be hurt.'

'If you get hurt, I get hurt too. If you get safe, I feel safe too.'

'Marie, start building up food stores here, a bit at a time. I know it's difficult with rations, but, do your best.'

'There's always more food on the farm than we need and, even at the bar, there's extra food. No one will know.'

'I'm hoping the Germans will ignore families, way out in the countryside like mine is, but I'll always be on the lookout. No one's really safe in this country anymore.'

'You and I can be safe down here.'

'Yes, but I can't stay safe if my family are in danger.'

'I'll keep you safe.'

Alain pulled me to him laughing. 'My darling Marie, I trust you completely.'

That was the happiest day of my life.

# Chapter Twenty-Seven

The 'pèlerins' came again several times and I kept my word, finding them food, but these days I needed to meet up with them after midnight so that I didn't lose time from my job.

The German soldiers didn't come near our village again and I felt that everything had returned to normal.

Then, one late night, while Thérèse and I were doing the last washing up of the day and clearing away in the bar, there was a knock on the kitchen window. Outside was Patrice, looking worn out and scared. Thérèse drew him inside quickly, making sure first that no one was watching in the back yard.

Patrice sat down at the kitchen table with his head in his hands. 'It was terrible,' he sighed. 'I don't know what will happen. I agree with those who say we should not stir up the enemy, but it's going to cause problems to us as well, even out here. The Germans are capable of doing anything and now they've seen me out here…' He was shaking, almost, I thought, crying.

Thérèse poured him a shot of brandy.

'Get that down you, Patrice. And when you're feeling calmer, tell us what's been happening. Marie, make sure all the lights are off, and the blinds are down in the front. No one must know that Patrice is here. At the first sign of anyone around, we need to get him through the outside toilet in the yard.'

Thérèse seemed to know exactly what to do. She calmed Patrice and made me feel that all could be well.

Patrice at last felt able to talk. 'There have been people in the union talking about getting back at the Germans. I go to the union meetings, keeping up my father's traditions.'

'That's a good thing to do, Patrice. Your father was a good man.'

'Maybe, but he's in a labour camp now. And I don't know whether he would have agreed with what the union people did.'

'What have they done?'

'They've sabotaged the Paris/Bordeaux line and one of the Paris Feldcommandants was killed. Now they're talking about revenge.'

'On the communists?'

'Yes, but not only them.'

'Who then?'

'Ordinary people. They could come here and pull ordinary people out of the village and shoot them.'

'Surely, they'd take people from Bordeaux, not that that's alright either. But why come all the way here?'

'Because they want to hurt everyone, and everyone knows that this is the way to Spain.'

I tried not to show too eager an interest. No one had interfered with my activities so far.

'That's crazy,' said Thérèse. 'Even if people choose to go to Spain this way, it's nothing to do with us.'

'That's not how the Boches think,' said Patrice knowingly.

I kept up a calm exterior but inside I was terrified. Those German soldiers might come here and kill? I was so preoccupied with this awful possibility that I didn't really care if they came and killed everyone else. I just didn't want them to come and kill me. I felt sick at the thought. Maybe they knew already and were coming to get me? Or what happened if all the people in the village knew and gave me up or, if there were revenge attacks, they came after me later and killed me then?

There was a noise outside. It turned out to be a drunk going home after everyone else had left a nearby bar. But we were ready to put Patrice in the yard. We went silent and waited until the drunk had passed.

This was how life was going to be from now on. I knew it. The rumours, the person passing too close and me being constantly fearful, anticipating the terror of being put up against a wall and shot, or, even worse, hung. If I was taken to be hung, I would be screaming all the way there, no matter how undignified it was.

Thérèse got Patrice to stay in the outside toilet for the next three days, bringing him blankets and food when he needed them. No one else in the village knew where he was, and he wouldn't go home and risk putting his family in danger, until the reprisals had taken place.

And they did take place, far away in Bordeaux, a few days later. It was, as Patrice had predicted, mainly the communists in the unions who suffered but also their families, innocent people who had had nothing to do with the original attack. I'm ashamed to say that I felt such relief and joy when I heard the news, that I felt light-headed for several days. Let the problems happen miles away in Bordeaux, in another country, where I could not be touched!

The night of Patrice's visit, my life changed. For the first time I realised that I would not automatically be protected. My parents were far from perfect; but I had still felt completely protected by them. Up until that night the world was such that, no matter what mistakes I made, my parents would look after me and make it come out alright in the end. That night I lost that illusion and I found myself to be a snivelling, frightened creature, who had no principles and no courage.

In the mornings before going to work I would often retreat to the small bolt hole below the water pipes. There I felt safe from parents who had no desire to allow me to follow my ambitions, or the village society who didn't have much time for me or my family or the Germans who wanted to destroy Alain and his people. The joy of biking round the forests and lakes had disappeared. I continued to borrow books from Mlle Tessier, who was generous in her desire to sustain my love of learning, and I immersed myself in romances, philosophy and history books. Sometimes I would take food from the farm and stay in the valley till the time was right to go to work. I would store food which would last in a secret hoard near the tree trunk, in case Alain needed supplies.

One morning I found Alain there, already helping himself to my supplies.

'I didn't see your bike.'

'No, I came on foot. You must be careful to hide your bike well.'

'I always put it in the pipes.'

'Yes, but not always far enough in. You must cover it with tree branches.'

'What? Each time?' That seemed to me an unnecessary chore which would delay me each time I came. 'Surely the Germans won't be in this corner of the forest looking for my bike,' I said almost jovially, as if the idea was a ridiculous joke.

'They may not be here today, but who knows what will happen tomorrow? You must take extra care now, Marie. It's when you're careless that things go wrong.'

'Careless?' I repeated surprised as I munched my way through a wizened apple. 'Why should I worry about being careless? The Germans aren't looking for me and my hideout.'

'No, but one day they will look for me and they'll use you to trail me.'

'They don't know anything about me, so, how can they?'

'You said yourself that they were at the bar a few weeks ago.'

'They must just have been looking round the whole area.'

'Yes, but they're on the attack.'

'What do you mean?'

'Occupying France hasn't been as easy as they expected. Their pride is hurt. Instead of having an easy time, they're starting to be on the lookout for rebellion and they will crush it – just to show who is boss.'

'Like the revenge for the communist sabotage you mean?'

'You heard about that then?' Suddenly I realised that Alain would not have known about Patrice's visit to the Hôtel du Centre in the middle of the night. It was the first time I realised that in the secret world of intrigue, people had to keep information from each other.

'Word got back to the village,' I explained carefully. 'There are communists at the 'mairie'.'

'It won't stop there, you know.'

'What do you mean?'

'These people… these Nazis.'

'Are all the soldiers Nazis?'

'Yes, they are because they are all ultimately following what the Nazis want.'

'Maybe they're just afraid of doing anything else.'

'May be but there's a time to be counted. A time to decide whether you want to be human or not.'

O God, that's it! Do I want to be human? Or do I want to play at enjoying life and being successful?

I looked at Alain, with his straight nose, the slight remains of acne on his face from when he was younger and his brown eyes, and I knew that he was the best human being I had ever met. But did I want to be like him, whatever the cost?

'Alain, I'm frightened. For you and for your family but also for me.'

If the truth be told, I thought, especially for me.

'So am I, Marie. But if we let this go, then there won't be any more humanity left.'

'But if I'm not there, I won't care if humanity is there or not.'

'You have to care. We all have to care. Otherwise we might as well completely give up on the human race.'

I knew that I just wanted to stay down this bolt hole, so that I didn't have to think about humanity.

'Maybe I'll just stay here.'

'I'd like to join you, but I can't leave my family.'

'I'm not sure that I care so much about my family that I'm prepared to kill myself.'

'That's because they're not at risk, but mine are.'

'I promise you, Alain. I'll help you, if I'm brave enough, but I'm not sure I will be in the end.'

'You've been brave already.'

'But I didn't realise what it was all about. Before now, it was a bit of an adventure.'

'If you were in the same position as those people, would you want someone to help you?'

'Of course.'

'Then just think about how you'll feel when it's all over, if you don't offer to help now.'

'At least I'll be alive.'

'Yes. But think about the guilt.'

'I don't care about guilt.'

'You will because guilt corrodes all the life you have and makes it a misery.'

I had nothing more to say. We hugged each other fiercely, kissing each other passionately, not out of lust, but out of desperation and the desire to cling to life in each other.

Guilt corrodes. How often have I learnt that truth ever since I was taught my first lesson about it down by the water pipes?

# Chapter Twenty-Eight

Inevitably, they returned to the bar – the Feldcommandant and the two young soldiers – debonair and charming, as before. They appeared as people who were walking on stage for a performance; the blond hair of the young lieutenant was beautifully brushed; the eyes of the commandant were wise and shrewd; their uniforms were immaculate. However, their reception by the village audience had changed. The village was no longer an innocent and attractive rural idyll. People were hungrier and tougher but there was a feeling that now we knew what occupation was all about. We knew how the young communists in the factory and their families had paid with their lives for what the resistance had done, and we had no more illusions about the courtesy of German soldiers.

As usual, Thérèse held us all together in a masterly way. She managed to serve drinks so that no one could accuse her of being impolite, but at the same time no one could think that she wanted to serve the enemy. We all took our cues from her. We could not go too far in our rudeness because we had to live alongside these people, and we did not want any intrusions into our village life. But any show of being too charming would have earned the anger of Thérèse and no one thought it worth their while to make her angry. She was the authority we lived with day by day, not that of the Germans.

When the Feldcommandant had finished his drink, he got to his feet slowly and carefully with an announcement made to us all. 'It has come to my attention that there are people round here who are listening to the poisonous mis-information of the British broadcasting system.

Do not trust them. They will bring you to an ignominious defeat. De Gaulle has no real power. The British do not even like him. They are letting him play the pirate leader, but his way will lead to disaster for France.

But also, and this is to warn you with the highest of motives, Messieurs and Mesdames, if my soldiers find that you are listening to these broadcasts, you will suffer.'

'Like the communists suffered?'

There was a sharp intake of breath, an almost communal reaction from the café clientele. We knew that Jules should not have said it. I was surprised. Jules was an old and seasoned drinker at the bar. No one thought he had anything inside him apart from red wine from the Bordeaux vignobles.

The Commandant ignored the gibe and answered the question.

'Yes, like the communists suffered. They were badly led.'

'No one 'leads' the farmers round here. Each individual does what he wants,' chimed in one of the regulars.

'In that case you may find that others suffer for the foolishness of individuals.'

'So, you will shoot someone else if a wireless is found in one man's house?'

'No. We will shoot the man himself.'

'For listening to a broadcast?' The representative from the 'mairie' sounded incredulous.

'You people need to know who is in charge. Even if you don't listen to us, listen to what the French government is saying.'

'What the Vichy government is saying.' By using those words, Jules made it very clear that he did not regard the Vichy as the real French.

The German turned around to face him full on. 'And who are you, Monsieur?'

'Jules …le Frang'

Until now I had regarded Jules only as the hopeless alcoholic of the village, but the way he said his name without any fear and looked the Feldcommandant in the eye, made me hesitate ever to stereotype him again so dismissively. He was not afraid to say what he thought, and he did it with dignity.

'Well, Monsieur Le Frang, that is the only government you have, so I suggest you take some notice of it.' Then, moving towards the door, he turned back to speak to Thérèse. 'I will be back, mademoiselle, and I expect this village to behave with respect.'

The threat was fulfilled the following day when three armed cars full of soldiers arrived in front of the ancient church. With the help of loudspeakers, the commandant announced that each family was to bring its wireless to the town square. They were to stay there for two hours while the soldiers searched the houses. If any radio was found, the head of the family would be shot.

Families came and presented their radios to the enemy, sullenly and unwillingly, but no one wanted to sacrifice their lives for a radio. In the search, not a single extra radio was found. In this way the Germans exerted their will over the population of Les Landes and we hated them for it.

Confident that they had taught us a lesson in submission, they returned to Bordeaux, their cars laden with the radios which had been sacrificed.

In doing so, they not only deprived us of vital information from abroad, but also music and radio shows from Paris. With radios we could imagine that we still lived the ordinary French life of before the war when people enjoyed their entertainment. Now they had no means of escape from the effects of the invasion and it hardened their desire to the see the end of the Germans.

In the bar, word soon got around that a couple of radios had been salvaged.

Thomas, one of Patrice's friends, walked into the bar a few nights later, looking full of confidence. He was 19 years old and had been hiding with Patrice in the forests which bordered the beaches, returning to Patrice's farm every week or so to collect food and more clothes. Both these young men knew that if they were caught, they would be sent to one of the labour camps or, even worse, to join the Germans who were fighting against the Russians on the Eastern Front.

Thomas swaggered into the front of the bar, looking at the other customers, who immediately seemed old and diminished in comparison.

'A good job someone had the guts to hide one.'

He wanted to be questioned further but no one gave him that pleasure, partly from shame that, in contrast, they had given in so docilely to the German demand.

Thérèse came and put her hand on his shoulder in a kindly gesture. 'Thomas, get out of here. The Germans can come back at any time.'

'Don't worry. We have a look out. You can't exactly disguise the Boches when they visit.'

'If they find you, that'll be the end of your freedom,' someone warned.

Thomas turned defiantly round. 'We're not all so scared that we even bring our radios to their feet.'

'It's not about being scared, young man,' said Giles, an older man who had married late and had a young family. 'It's about protecting our families.'

'Yes,' added Thérèse, as she came by with an order. 'Don't get yourself killed for the sake of a radio.'

'Or someone else killed.'

'I wouldn't be so stupid. What I've got, no one will ever find.'

'If you have one, don't boast about it. You don't know who has ears.'

Thomas seemed ready to reveal more, but then thought better of it.

I was slipping home at nearly midnight, when a hand reached out and grabbed me. It was Thomas. I felt shaken and anxious to get back home.

'Don't do that to me. I don't want anything to do with you.'

'But you have already.'

'What do you mean?'

'Come on. Not here. I'll walk you back home.'

'I've got my bike.'

'Well, ride it through the village. I'll see you at the end of the lake in ten minutes. We need to talk.'

And with that he was off into the shadows.

I wasn't sure that I wanted to talk with Thomas. The Communists were far too dangerous for my liking, but I was curious about why he thought he had a connection with me.

The village was quiet. I cycled past the shuttered houses and up the road, left through the woods and up to the point of the lake near a small bridge where the ducklings and otters swam.

Thomas joined me from nowhere as we walked over the bridge, up the other side of the lake, where, before the war, there had been boats for rent for local couples on a Saturday afternoon.

'Marie, you needn't be afraid.'

'I'm not afraid. Why should I be?'

'I know all about what you've been doing.'

I laughed confidently. 'What? Working at the Hôtel du Centre?'

'Sure. And all your work on the coast.'

'I've never worked there.'

'No, but you've helped people there.'

I was silent. If Thomas knew, then anyone else might and the Germans might too.

'Don't worry. It's only Patrice and me who know.'

'What do you know?'

'How you've helped the pèlerins.'

'I don't know what you're talking about.'

He laughed. 'Sure...but, Marie, we've got to trust each other.'

'Why?'

'Because the more we trust each other, the quicker we'll get rid of the Boches.'

'I don't want to get rid of them. I mean, I don't care about them. They're not affecting my life.'

'They already have. No don't answer that...and they will again.'

'What makes you think that?'

'Because things are getting trickier for them in France and, as it gets worse, they'll come looking for more trouble.'

'If they come looking for more trouble, I don't want to give them any.'

'Marie, we don't have any choice.'

'You might not, but I do.'

'I thought you had more fight in you. Patrice told me his brother said you were always arguing in school.'

Arguing in school seemed centuries away. Down by the shadows in the lake I was quickly turning into a conformist who wanted safety at all costs.

'That wasn't real life.'

'But Armand, the fisherman, said you were helping now.'

I was stunned. The silent deep-sea fisherman. What did he know?

'We're looking for helpers for a network of resistance. Armand wants to help, and he said you would want to as well, because of what you've done already.'

'That's finished now. I don't want to do any more.'

'You've got to help France be free.'

'I'm not helping France be free. I'm looking after my own skin.' In the daylight I might have been ashamed of my cowardice. But in the night shadows, I only wanted to continue with my own little life. Continuing to work at the Hôtel du Centre and going home at night suddenly seemed very attractive.

'You'll regret it when we're the heroes.'

'I won't regret it, when you're the dead heroes and I'm still alive.'

'I thought better of you.'

'Well, you were wrong, weren't you?'

I pushed my bike through the soft mounds of sand which collected by the lake shore. I stopped and looked at where I imagined Thomas' face to be. There was a tiny slither of moon casting light on his earnest face.

'Thomas, I wish you and Patrice the best of luck. But don't bring your communists round here. No one wants you and I don't blame them.'

'That's not what Alain told me.'

I had left Thomas behind as I pushed the front wheel through the sand. The pronouncement of Alain's name made me stop suddenly.

'What did Alain tell you?'

'Just that you were very brave and always found a way round problems.'

'Alain had no right to tell you that.' It was the first time in my life that I had criticised Alain. I felt like a traitor, but I wanted life to be simple, to save myself from further complications.

'Thomas, I'm not interested in being part of your network. I don't want to know about it. Knowledge brings trouble. Now, go.'

'If you ever want to help, just bring food to one of the bird hides by the smallest lake behind the sand dunes. We'll know how to get it to the right people.'

I left him, but it was my own words which were my undoing, not his powers of persuasion. 'Knowledge brings trouble' sounded more like my mother's words than my own. And hadn't I always wanted the knowledge which brings trouble? What other sort of knowledge was worth anything worthwhile?

# Chapter Twenty-Nine

I took the food. How could I not? It was some time since I had seen the pèlerins on their way, but it was still relatively easy to find some extra food on our farm. Once a week on my day off, I cycled towards the coast. I knew where the ancient Maison de la Forestière was, and the hides were only twenty minutes further into the forest, behind the sand dunes.

Curiosity also made me wait to see Armand, the silent fisherman. He had said nothing to me before except how to attach a fly to a line, so how did he know so much about me?

I found him one night, still patiently reeling in his catch. We stood amicably next to each other in front of the huge ocean. Quarrels between nations, never mind between individuals, seemed of very little importance in this setting. It seemed hard to start a conversation with him.

'How did you know about me?'

'I don't know anything about you.'

'But you told Thomas about me and he told me.'

A long silence.

'It's better not to use names.'

'But how did you know?'

'I fish and stay still, but, when I hunt, I move about. A hunter is used to seeing things which are hidden.'

'That means I could get into trouble.'

'Not from me you won't.'

'How can I be sure of that?'

'You can't. You have to trust.'

Trust – that terrible word! How could I trust any of them?

'Little girl.' For some reason I didn't mind being called 'ma petite'. It seemed appropriate when faced with the ocean and alongside a man who had used his skills for survival for so many years unaided. 'Little girl,' he continued, 'It's better not to talk and not to use names. Keep your mouth shut, especially in that bar.' So, he knew about my job as well, I thought! 'But, if we're going to preserve our freedom, we have to take action against them. And we have to do something with others who want the same as us.'

'Even the communists?'

'Even the communists.'

'But I thought they wanted chaos.'

'I don't think they want chaos, but, even if communism brings chaos, that's better than what we have at the moment.'

'Which is?'

'Oppression, people dying not only for what they believe; but for who they are.'

'And it's worthwhile fighting against it?'

'Yes, because all over France there will be some people who fight against it.'

'And will we win?'

'Eventually. But, whatever the result, it's the right thing to fight for.'

His words went far out to sea and then came back, carried on the incoming waves. The idea of right. Not the idea of obligation as preached by my mother, but the idea of right, instead of wrong.

'Armand, do you believe in right and wrong?'

'Yes, my little one, I do.'

'Why?'

'Because, despite the dictates of politics and religion, both of which I reject, there's a right way to treat people and a wrong way.'

'How do you know you are right?'

Armand hesitated. The furthermost light on the horizon was mirrored on the spume of a wave far out to sea.

'Because I feel it deep within me and, I feel I have to do this.'

'Maybe I should do it too.'

'Yes, but, little one, only do it if you feel you should, deep within you.'

'And what if I'm afraid?'

'Being afraid needn't stop you doing what is right.'

'You mean I can be afraid and do what is right at the same time?'

'Yes.'

'How should I start?'

'You already have with the food. Did you bring it for the boys today?'

'I haven't given it to them yet. I came to see you first. I wanted to know whether what Thomas said was true.'

'And you've found that out.'

'Yes, I'll be going now, and I'll take them the food and then get back home.'

'Don't be too curious, little one. Only know what you need to know. Then you'll be doing what is right and there are limits to what you can tell anyone.'

And that was how I became a 'runner' for the Resistance group in Les Landes. When I delivered the food to 'the hide', after I had left Armand, I acquired new confidence. It wasn't a personal favour. I was doing what was 'right'.

Somehow, I wasn't surprised when I heard Patrice's whispered instructions later that night.

'Marie, in the next few days, there will be a packet for you, left in the toilet in the yard at the 'Centre'. Pick it up at the end of your shift. And bring it here, as soon as you can.'

'What happens if I can't?'

'It's important that it leaves the bar as soon as possible. Is there anywhere you can hide it if you can't get here immediately? No... don't tell us. Just think. Away from people's homes.'

I thought about the miniature valley where Alain and I used to meet.

'Yes, there's somewhere. Yes, it's hidden. The Boches won't find it.'

'Remember they might watch you.'

'It's right the way through the forest, far away from the road. I'll know if they're watching me.'

'If you think they are, get rid of it. Do you smoke?'

'No.' Women of my mother's generation did not smoke, and I was not allowed to. It was a man's recreation.

'Start doing it a bit. Then you'll always have a match on you. If necessary, hide in the forest and burn the documents.'

'Documents?'

'Yes, the passports you'll be bringing us.'

'What if they ask me what I've been doing?'

'Tell them anything.' Patrice thought for a moment. 'Giles told me you were always reading. Keep a couple of books in the hide-away. Tell them that you're keeping up your education until the war is over. Anyone who knows you will agree. Mlle Tessier will back you up.'

'Why would she do that?'

'Because she cares about this too.'

'You mean Mlle Tessier is part of this?'

'Let's just say she is sympathetic. You don't need to know any more.'

My instinct, brought out on parade before me by Armand, was correct. If it was confirmed by Mlle Tessier's involvement, then it must be correct. She who had wanted me to be educated and be ambitious, she wanted to help the Resistance too. I felt satisfied as I went home that night.

'Marie, you must keep up your strength,' said my mother next morning, as I yawned my way through the farm chores before work. 'You are out far too late at night and then you can't get up in the morning. Why?'

For once I gave my mother a truthful answer. 'Because I want to keep in touch with the forests and sea which I have always known. I don't just want to work at the Hôtel du Centre.'

# Chapter Thirty

The move from supplier of food for escapees to courier of false passports, money and identification documents seemed at first to be a big one. I was now intentionally a member of 'the resistance', not just a helper of my best friend, Alain. With this knowledge came more responsibility, but instead of more fear, it brought me more focused determination. Armand's words had converted me to the necessity of doing 'right', even if it involved only the vaguest instinct about what being on the side of 'good' meant.

To begin with, it felt like a real risk to check the outside toilet in the yard behind the bar. The first time I found documents, my reaction was one of intrigue and curiosity. I was sure I had not seen a stranger passing by. Who had done it and what journey had these documents gone through to arrive at this inauspicious place?

However, after a few months, it became second nature to check. Every ten days or so the documents would be waiting for me at 11 O'clock when I left work and I would hide them in the piggery at home until the next day or occasionally cycle through the lanes and forests and deposit them in the bolt-hole immediately. Because it involved what I had always done – riding the forest trails near the lakes and beaches of Les Landes, it seemed the most natural thing in the world, and I comforted myself with the thought that no one would be surprised if they met me doing this. I reckoned that if I ever saw a German tank or motorbike coming towards me, I would easily see them in advance, because the lanes were so straight, and I would have time to dive into the nearest part of the forest. I was so much part of the forest habitat that camouflage came naturally to me.

I felt truly happy. While I regretted the loss of my education, I was being socially educated at the Hôtel du Centre, and for the first time, I found other people attractive and interesting. I had lots of time to observe and to listen to the clientele, without having to give my opinion, and that was restful. Collecting glasses, taking orders and washing up was easy and did not make impossible demands on my rudimentary practical skills. Thérèse was far less demanding than my mother had been, and she was also a wonderful protector. If anyone tried to flirt or be difficult with me, Thérèse was there to ward off trouble. To be fair to the village community I grew up in, no male took serious advantage and went no further than a playful pinch on the bottom and a wink. My youth also protected me, the fact that I was unused to more sophisticated society and I found that my reputation at school had gone before me. I was a know-all, a reader, the school-teacher's favourite and therefore held in awe by many of the local men.

The combination of all these roles meant that when the Germans next called at the bar, no man or woman there would have ever suspected me of subversive activity and would have been outraged by any German suspicion about my involvement in resistance work.

I was a local young girl from a non-practising Catholic and a non-communist family, who had a reputation for being reclusive and miserable but otherwise harmless, young, innocent and reasonably pretty without being outstandingly beautiful, who unfortunately was known to be clever, which would never be an advantage in the marriage stakes or in acquiring a farm in the economy of Les Landes. Who could be more harmless and ineffective?

The German Feldcommandant ordered the drinks for his men, which were served punctiliously and without unnecessary charm by Thérèse. This time he was accompanied by three young men, one of whom had an unfortunate level of acne on his face. I felt sorry for him. He looked as though he should be at home with his mother in Germany, not catching rebels in an enemy country.

'So, mademoiselle,' he addressed Thérèse courteously as she placed the schnapps on the table in front of him. 'Do you have anything unusual to report in your community?'

'There is never anything unusual here,' she replied equably. 'This is a farming community. We are not known for our originality of thought.'

'Indeed, indeed,' replied the commandant, placing his hat and leather gloves on the side of the table as he picked up his glass. 'So, in that case, you would notice if anything unusual happened?'

'Indeed, Herr Commandant. We would all know about it because it would enliven our lives so much.'

'In that case, you may be interested to know that there is a supply line to the Resistance rumoured to be going through this village.'

Thérèse laughed, a natural, easy laugh, which showed how unperturbed she was by such an idea, because it was not possible.

'You flatter us, Herr Commandant. No resistance movement would stop here. We are far too conservative and dull to be of any use to them.'

'Maybe, but you have communists here.'

'Only Monsieur Delmare, who was interested in the Trade Union movement in Bordeaux, but he went long ago to work for you people. There is no one left with the same political interests as he had.'

'Except that M. Delmare had several sons and at least one of them, a certain Patrice, was also a member of the party.'

'Patrice moved out of the village when his father was deported. No doubt he didn't want the same destination as his father.'

'Maybe you are right, or maybe he is still in the area working for the resistance.'

'We know nothing about any resistance here.'

How glad I was that Thérèse was in charge, that she knew how to answer these difficult questions! My heart was thudding with fear as if I had been caught out by my mother when I hadn't done the chores properly. Should I excuse myself and be checking the outside toilet now or should I avoid it all evening? I decided the least conspicuous action was to stay exactly where I was, and blend into the bar, just as in my travels I blended into the forest.

'We will see about that, Mlle Thérèse,' said the commandant suddenly becoming determined and efficient. 'You will all stay here in this room, no one to move, and my men will check the whole premises.'

I held my breath. Even if they found documents tonight, they would not necessarily trace them to me, but, if they did, that place would never be safe again.

Conversation all but ceased. We stared into our drinks and tried not to think about what they might find. Even the most apathetic drinker in Mimizan that night, or the man who was the most pro-Vichy supporter, wished that nothing bad would happen, nothing that would put our village in the spotlight.

Fifteen minutes later the soldiers returned; they had been through all the rooms upstairs, the kitchen where the glasses were washed, and they had found nothing.

Everyone was relieved, even those who had no knowledge or enthusiasm for the Resistance. We were to be left in peace again. We were who we said we were.

I quickly checked again before I left. Nothing was there. Either by chance or because the network had been warned, it was not the night for a drop.

# Chapter Thirty-One

That was the night I realised there were traitors amongst us, and that the network was being watched, even if I personally was not suspected of being involved.

1943 – things were tightening up all over France. The Germans moved from the Occupied Zone to the Free Zone. There was no place now in the country which did not feel the pressure of the occupiers. And the roundup of the Jews and anyone associated with them, started in earnest To begin with it was the 'foreign Jews', people who had lived in Alsace in the eastern regions of France, those who had come from Poland or those who were supporters of Bolshevism. Not that any of these should have been condemned to arrest or death, but somehow French people rationalised it. It was, I found later, what people always do, when nasty things are happening in their country. Don't get involved and it won't touch you. Don't ask too many questions, because then you will be able to persuade yourself that it is all justified, because it is only people who are 'undesirable' who will be arrested.

It was when ordinary Jewish neighbours and children were taken away that people began to wake up and stirred themselves to action – even in a place as sleepy as Les Landes.

One day when I was spending some precious time relaxing in my hide-out beyond the water pipes, Alain appeared. I hadn't seen him for some time, and he looked pale and dishevelled, with a growth of rough beard. I realised that he had become a man, and a man who was unwanted by our society.

'Alain, I must get you some food.'

'Marie, I want more than food.'

'What do you mean?'

He grinned, looking for a moment like the care-free youth I had known at school centuries ago.

'I want some peace and quiet and a good book.'

'Welcome to my kingdom, monsieur. You can have both freely here.'

'I know. It's wonderful. He looked round at the tiny valley which was hidden from the outside world by the undergrowth and water pipes.

'Let me enjoy every moment.' He slumped down in the grass and picked up one of the books I had left there.

'Rousseau? I can't believe we actually spent time reading this, Marie. And the discussions – do you remember them, with our feet next to the wood burning stove in the school room?'

'Of course, I remember, though I would have thought that you had plenty of discussions about philosophy at the lycée since then.'

'Maybe, but none of them were as good as ours.'

I was secretly pleased. 'Why was that?'

'Because you didn't argue with me, Marie. You had plenty to say but you weren't scoring points off me. It felt like you were a discoverer too.'

'I was.'

'Yes, you were, and it was great.'

He pulled me down to him and I felt the wonderful familiarity of his arms.

'Marie, I miss that life so much.'

'Me too.'

'Sure, but you get boredom and village gossip, and I get constant danger and evading the Germans.'

'Do you never feel safe?'

'No, never, not now, and none of our people do. We're always waiting for the knock on the door or the confiscation of identity papers.'

'Where will it all end, Alain?'

'I've no idea. I suppose in my gloomiest moments, when we're all dead, but at the moment, I can't even foresee that ending. I'm just surviving from day to day and trying to get a few other people to survive.'

I was silent. I had no idea such a life existed. In comparison, mine seemed very ordinary and uneventful.

'Surely, someone must rescue you?'

'Sure, but when? For now, these mad men are ruling the world.'

'Surely the British will arrive sometime or the Americans.'

'Yes, I just hope we won't be all dead by the time they come.'

I didn't comment but I knew instinctively that when he said 'we', he meant his own people, not the French and not me. There was a clear demarcation line between us.

'How are you surviving now?'

'By moving to different houses and villages all the time. Never stopping one place more than a couple of days.'

'Well you must stay here. At least it's safe here.'

'Yes, it is…it's paradise. But do I have the right to be safe when others are in fear of their lives?'

'You're not making them more unsafe by being here.'

'True.' He turned around where he was sitting and looked at me searchingly.

'Don't get me wrong, Marie. It's wonderful to be here. It feels wonderful. I just want to lie down and sleep.'

'Well, why don't you?'

'I will for a few hours but first I have to give you some instructions.'

'What sort of instructions? You mean you have some documents for me to take to Patrice?'

'No, not this time, though that's been a wonderful job, Marie. They've given quite a few new identities, not just to Jews, but to socialists who want to get to Spain.'

'I didn't know you were helping the Communists.'

He grinned impishly. 'When we were arguing with Giles at school about his dad and unions, who'd have thought we would end up on the same side? In truth, we often are on the same side, because lots of Jews, especially the East European ones, are communists.'

'In that case, they're likely to get it twice over?'

'Yes …but you can only die once.'

Silence. We were talking about death as though it were part of a game that some people took part in. I shivered. I wasn't sure I wanted to be part of that game, but I could choose. The Jews couldn't.

'What do you want me to do?'

'You know there's a camp at Gurs?'

I'd heard of it. It was a holding camp for refugees, people who had come to live in France, escaping from Russia or Germany or anywhere else where normal life wasn't possible. I had only the sketchiest idea of how people lived there or how long they stayed.

'There are lots of Jewish children there,' Alain continued. 'But soon the Nazis will start to clear them out.'

I was shocked. 'Surely not children! Surely they will be sent somewhere else?'

'Don't fool yourself. There are plenty of Jewish adults who are fooling themselves. They think their children will never be taken away. They could be wrong, even though they don't want to think about it. But, like you, they think no one could be evil enough to kill children.'

'Kill them?'

'Kill them. We have plenty of evidence that adults are being killed in camps like Auschwitz. The children will be needed to make up the numbers.'

'What numbers?'

'The number of Jews the Germans are demanding from the Vichy government.'

'And they will just be sent? I can't believe that any French government would do that.'

'I don't want to believe that either. But before my belief is put to the test, we have to get those children out.'

'From Gurs?'

'Yes… they have to get to safety in Spain or Portugal or possibly North Africa.'

'What about the Free Zone?'

'Possibly, but it doesn't really exist any longer, and all the evidence is that once the allies close in, it won't make any difference at all. Then any escape to the South and North Africa will disappear.'

'So, you want me to provide papers for these children for the route of St. Jacques?'

'I want you to do more than that.'

'What?'

'I want you to be a courier.'

'Me? You're joking, Alain. I can't do that. I have no means of travel. How would I get time off my job to do it without creating suspicion? And Gurs – how would I get there? I've never ever left Les Landes in my life.'

'No, that's true, but you're young and resourceful. I agree you've no experience of travel and we'd have to find a valid reason for you to be off work. But, if I could arrange that, would you do it, Marie?'

I wanted to please him. I wanted to fight against evil. I found I wanted to use my ingenuity. I was pleased and flattered that Alain thought I even had any. Within me, I wanted to travel too, to see other landscapes. It was ultimately the adventure which attracted me.

'I don't know. I suppose so, but how are you going to make everything work?'

'I'm not sure, but we've got the possibility of a partnership with Père Julien.'

'The Catholic priest in Léon?'

'Yep.'

'I thought the Catholic church were all cowards and friends of Vichy.' I'd picked that much up from Patrice who was no lover of religion.

'Some of them are, but a few good men, especially the ordinary priests, want to do something to help. Between you, Marie, you could take children out of Gurs.'

'I've never looked after a child in my life.'

'You're not being asked to play with them. This is a life or death situation. You won't find them a nuisance.'

I was ashamed of myself. These children were fleeing in fear of their lives, and I was worrying about how good I was at entertaining them. And how would I get on with a curé? I'd hardly even met one; we were not the most popular sort of parishioners. It raised all sorts of doubts in my mind, but my curiosity had been roused. I knew deep within me that I would never be able to stay working in the bar, while imagining what would have happened if I had said 'yes'.

'I don't know how it's going to work out in practice.'

'Neither do I fully, at the moment. I was waiting to see what your answer would be, before I made a solid plan. What will you do, Marie? Will you help me save these children?'

Put like that, I wanted to help him, my dearest friend and hero. It also gave me a thrill of adventure which my dull life in the village could not give – what an exotic and self-centred mix of motives!

'Get me a good plan and I'll do it.'

My reward was for the first time the experience of a passionate, adult kiss. It was the start of my adventure.

# Chapter Thirty-Two

I didn't hear any more from Alain for about two weeks.

Then one night as I cycled home after work, a figure stepped from the shadows. He was young and athletic, and I assumed he was a friend of Patrice and Thomas.

Père Julien immediately challenged my stereotype of a Catholic priest. I had a hazy memory from childhood Christmas celebrations of our own priest, who was old and had a stern, disapproving countenance. This one was young and cheerful, and there was no way I could have recognized him as a priest in ordinary life.

'Marie, I've heard all about your work.'

I was cautious. Was he trying to get information from me? I didn't respond.

'Don't worry,' he laughed. 'I'm not going to ask about it. I know better than to do that. But we need to meet somewhere in private.'

'At the nearest point of the lake, underneath the wooden bridge in ten minutes.'

I flung out my proposed rendez-vous and went off into the night. I knew enough not to stay around a contact anywhere where I might be seen.

'I forgot you were so experienced in this sort of life,' he said to me later as we huddled underneath the little bridge. 'You seem so young'

'I've grown up fast in the last year.'

His voice sounded serious, though I couldn't see the expression on his face in the dark.

'Many of us are doing things which a year ago we could have hardly imagined.'

'Has Alain sent you?'

'Who's Alain?'

That was when I understood the extent of the resistance, and the necessity of secrecy. 'Need to know' was the only safe way to operate, even though in our small village, we seemed miles away from the real threat.

'I have my contacts and my orders, and I'll just tell you what you need to do.'

'Right. Tell me.' I was practical and focused. Whatever was necessary, I would do.

'You need to get yourself some time off from the bar in a week's time.'

'All right. How long for?'

'I think it will take us about a week.'

An idea had been forming in my mind. My mother had an aunt living near the central Pyrénées area. Maybe I should arrange a visit. The only problem was that I needed to persuade my parents of my interest in a great aunt who I had never seen. If they guessed about my involvement in the Resistance, they would be furious, but, more seriously, they might be vulnerable if German soldiers started asking too many questions.

'I'll sort it somehow. I've got an idea.'

'Good girl. Let's say a week on Monday, cycle down to Léon and the church in the centre. Do you know it?'

'No, but I can cycle there easily. I do it all the time. I'll find the church.'

'Right. Come to the first confessional box by 11am. I've got the papers. We'll go from there.'

'I can't cycle to the camp. It's too far.'

'No, you can't, but I have a car.' He said it with some pride. Indeed, it was unusual for anyone at that time to be driving a car, even if they owned one, because petrol was in such short supply.

'My car is an important part of my pastoral work in the area.'

I'd no idea what 'pastoral work' was, so if he was trying to impress me, my reaction must have been a disappointment.

'Don't worry, my friend. I'll be taking you on some very strange visits this time. Do you think you could turn into a good novice nun?'

'You mean someone who's training to become a nun?'

'Yes.'

'The trouble is I know nothing about religion.'

'Ah well, your education could be about to begin.'

He laughed softly. 'I'll tell you what, Marie. The most important commandment is 'Love your neighbour as yourself.' As you know all about that already, I think you have enough knowledge to be a sister.'

'I just hope the Germans don't ask me about theology.'

'I doubt they will. They're not terribly knowledgeable themselves. I have no doubt you will make a perfect nun.'

'And then what?'

'And then you'll find out.' And he was off among the shadows of the trees before I had time to answer. I stayed there watching the water voles feed their young on the bank of the lake underneath the bridge, completely oblivious to the crazy activities people were involved in around them.

I had a week to prepare my excuses and to ask permission from my parents. Since my work in the bar had begun, our relationship had changed. Their authority had disappeared. My mother still worked hard on the farm and grumbled about my father and me, but her position of 'ruler' had changed. I brought her some of the money I had earned and occasionally I would still help her sell things on the market, but I was no longer a child and I had left her jurisdiction. I had always loved my father, but he treated me as much more of an equal and, with his hunting activities increasing, in order to give us more food, he was often away for a longer period of time. For the first time, I noticed the grey around my mother's hair line and the frown lines on her forehead which were also worry lines.

'Maman, Thérèse at the bar says I can have a week off soon.'

'It's alright for some. I haven't had a week off once since coming to this farm.'

Rather than being annoyed at her martyr's attitude, I tried to use it to my advantage.

'I'd been wondering about Tante Hélène at St. Palais.'

'Why ever would you wonder about her?'

'You used to talk about her when I was little. And I've often wondered what she was like. I thought of using my holiday to pay her a visit.'

'What an extraordinary idea – suddenly going to see an old woman you've never met before.'

'I know but we have so few relatives, and I thought it would be interesting to see her. And take a closer look at the Pyrenées too.'

'How would you get there?'

'By bike down to Léon and there's a bus from there.'

Follow what's likely to be the truth was one of the rules of information giving in the Resistance. You're less likely to make a mistake that way and your interrogators are more likely to believe you.

'You could have spent a week helping me here.'

'I know that, Maman,' I said artfully, 'But you know how I always get under your feet and annoy you. This way I will have been somewhere different. I will have met up with an old relative and you will have had a more peaceful time on the farm without me.'

That was the difficult part over. Persuading Thérèse that I needed a week off to visit an elderly relative was easy.

'We'll miss you, Marie, so hurry back. Don't stay and become her slave. We need you here.'

I was touched. I enjoyed my job at the bar, but I had no idea that my service was appreciated. Perhaps my village wasn't so bad after all.

# Chapter Thirty-Three

What to take with me on my journey was something which preoccupied me for several nights. I'd need at least a change of clothes, but I didn't have much more than that and the question was where to put them.

Fortunately, my mother's practical advice was invaluable. For the first time in my life, I sought her help and we sorted out the problem in a way which mothers and daughters had done over the centuries, but which I had never experienced before.

From her bottom drawer near her bed she produced a linen bag which I had never seen.

'I sewed this myself before I went away with your father.'

'You went away with my father?'

I was astounded. They seemed to me to have been quarrelling all their lives and to have avoiding each other in the farm as much as possible.

'Yes,' she said proudly and quite shyly. 'We were among the first couples in the village to have a 'lune de noces.''

'Where did you go?'

'Up to Arcachon.'

'Fancy you being so fashionable.'

'Fancy indeed.' My mother quickly reverted to her customary way of speaking. 'I should have known better that it was the only good time we would ever have.' The bitterness in her voice was clear.

'Did you have a good time?' I wanted to get her back to the memory of something pleasant.

'Yes, we did. We went to the fair and danced and walked on the promenade like a proper couple, even if we weren't so well dressed as everyone else.'

'You should do that again, Maman.'

'What? With this war going on?'

'Alright,' I conceded. 'Maybe when it's over.'

'At the moment it doesn't feel as if it will ever be over.'

For the first time it occurred to me that my parents might be suffering, that this war might be impacting their lives as well as mine.

'I guess it will have to be over some time. But Maman, do you really mean I can borrow your beautiful linen bag to go and see Tante Hélène ?'

'Better for it to be used for something than just sitting in that drawer.'

It was true that my plans for education and getting away from the area had been delayed by the war, but in some ways the war had given me a different adventure – a job, a camaraderie with other people in the village and the opportunity to be involved in rescuing people in trouble. For my mother, it had brought only increased poverty in an already hard life, less opportunities to go to the marketplace, and no relief from the boredom and drudgery of everyday life on the farm. For the first time it occurred to me that I was rather lucky.

I hadn't many clothes and I thought that if I was going to be a novice helping in church work, I should take a couple of head scarves to cover my hair. I had had no opportunity in the village to buy smart clothes. My skirts and blouses were what my mother had made me while I was still at school and I still wore these even when I was working at the bar. I filled my bag with extra food which did not make my mother suspicious as she thought that with limited food supplies all over the country, it might it difficult to find enough food at Tante Hélène's.

Early next morning I set off through the woods and bracken and my heart was singing. I had forgotten the dangers I might encounter. All I could think of was seeing a town I had never visited before, enjoying being with the curé in a role I had never known, going to the Pyrenées and being trusted enough to be useful to a whole new group of people. I stopped for my early picnic breakfast at the Cap d'Homily and saw the waves from the vantage point of the cliffs in a way I had never seen before nearer to home. I was on a completely new adventure and potential opposition and the Germans meant nothing to me

The church at Léon was right at the centre of the little town, on a crossroads surrounded by a local commerce and one or two cafés – a much more bustling centre than our own little village. On market days, before the war a market had stretched from the church at the top of the hill right down to the far side of the town which consisted of several small hills.

I leaned my bicycle against the wall of the church and went inside. The morning mass was just finishing, and I crept into one of the confessional boxes, wondering whether Father Julien would have even noticed that I had arrived. I carried my linen bag slung over my shoulder. I was a young member of a family who was on her way to enquire about the welfare of a great aunt in time of war and occupation.

I had to wait some time before Father Julien appeared in the priest's half of the confessional box. It was a good place to have a whispered conversation, and I knew enough to intone the opening words, 'Bless me, father, for I have sinned.'

The words struck me as ironic. Whatever else I had done in my life, what I was doing now did not strike me as sin.

'Right Marie, this is the plan. Wait till I have gone into the vestry and unrobed and put away the silverware from Mass.

Do you have a scarf round your head? Good. I also have a sash and badge from the local house of the sisters. Don't worry. They're used to lending me things for some of my journeys. It wouldn't fool the Germans for very long if they investigated but it's enough to pacify a few bored soldiers at the roadblocks. There tend to be more of them as we get towards the mountains a bit further south.

Meet me in my car at the other side of the church. The locals are used to seeing me go off visiting in the area. With your clothes and a head scarf, they won't think anything more about it.'

Outside the church, suitably headscarfed, I followed instructions and found myself sitting in a battered 'deux chevaux'.

'How come you got a car like this and petrol?' I asked. Most priests went everywhere by bicycle.

'Old Père Jacques, who was the priest before me, was very much loved in this town and he had bad arthritis. The parish saved up before the war so he could get around in this. When he died, I took over and I was lucky enough to inherit this.

And the good Lord must have known about my needs, because I've had plenty of use for it, since the Resistance got going.

Now tell me about yourself, Marie and where does your great aunt live?'

I explained that she lived at St. Palais not far from Pau. Julien thought it best if we tried to find her first, let me stay for a couple of days if possible, and then I should find an excuse to meet up with him again, before getting to the camp at Gurs.

His first job while I was with my great aunt would be to take several children to stay with families in the foothills of the Pyrenées. Three of the eleven-year old boys were at particular risk. They looked older than they were and, if the Germans descended on the camp, they would be taken off for deportation. Father Julien would have to find a safe haven for them.

'Does that mean a work camp?' I enquired

'That's what they say, but we have good reason to believe that it doesn't mean that at all. It means a death camp.'

I was puzzled. 'But surely it would be better for the Germans to use them as workers in the war effort?'

'That's a logical statement, Marie, but these people are not logical. They have a bitter, twisted philosophy and they want the Jews dead.'

'But why?'

Père Julien sighed. 'Who knows what's really going on? The Jews are accused of bringing Germany down and even taking jobs in France, according to Vichy. But I think it's about jealousy.'

'Jealousy? Of what?'

'Jews are amazingly clever and successful. They work hard and they do well. If your country isn't doing well, then you either use their expertise, or you say that they are depriving you of prosperity.'

Could jealousy really deprive you of all common sense and lead you to kill people? I wondered.

We each spent our time in the car with our own thoughts about the situation. The forests on either side of the little coast road which we were following were thick with pine trees like they were in my own area, but the country was opening out. After we had passed the clearings in the forest and small holdings, like those of my parents, larger fields could be seen, and the land became even flatter. This continued until we saw signs for Bayonne.

'I'd like to show you Bayonne. It's a beautiful city, but I don't think we have time to stop today. We need to get up into the hills.'

Soon we left the pine forests and coast behind us and the countryside changed to gentle hills and pasture where sheep were grazing. In the late summer sunshine, it seemed like the most peaceful country imaginable. No one could have imagined that France was at war.

But it wasn't long before we came to a roadblock.

We had our identity papers in order. Father Julien explained that I was a member of his church, thinking of entering a convent and that I was on my way to see a great aunt who was ill. The soldiers looked bored and waved us on.

'It's not a bad life for them,' said Julien. 'At least at the moment. Better luck to be sent to occupy France than to be sent to the Eastern Front. But how long it will be good for them, I wouldn't like to say.'

'It feels as though they'll be here for ever,' I remarked. I wasn't even sad or angry about it. The reality of occupation was now part of my life.

'Ah, but they won't be. And when the allies come, there will be some real fighting.'

'Will that affect us?' I asked anxiously. I didn't want real fighting in my village.

Julien laughed. 'Marie, you're doing some real fighting now.'

'It doesn't feel like it.'

'No, but it is …it's all working towards getting rid of the Germans.'

If fighting meant hiding in the woods, bike rides and stealing some food, it was all part of the adventure. I shut my mind against thinking what else it might mean, even if not to me, then to Alain or Patrice or Thomas.

The gentle hills under the warm sun of the late summer were beautiful. I noticed the red-roofed farmhouses and the signs in Basque. The buildings were very different to the rustic houses of Les Landes. We crossed a river and meandered up along the foothills with the occasional peak looking down on us. As the day wore on, we came to some more small towns and then to the outskirts of St. Palais.

'Do you know where you're going?'

'Not really, but it's called l'Hirondelle, and it's just west of the church.'

'Do you think you could find it if I drop you by the church? I want to get to the camp before the curfew sets in and I don't want to be noticed round here too much.'

"I'll find it,' I said, more confidently than I felt, as I saw the church in the distance. 'Leave me there.'

# Chapter Thirty-Four

I spoke to an old man tidying his chrysanthemums near the church and he showed little surprise at my request for directions and pointed up the hill to a large white building with an untidy perimeter of vegetable garden. My mother would have been proud of me, I thought, in even noticing that the area needed work. I was pleased because it was an obvious way to offer help. Even better, we would not have to spend hours trying to pursue a conversation which neither of us really wanted.

I knocked at the door and was greeted by a lot of barking. A little later the door was partially opened by an elderly and rather scruffy looking lady. I tried my best to look casual, friendly and enthusiastic, though what she would make of a visit by a great niece about whom she knew nothing, I could not imagine.

'Tante Hélène ?' I tried tentatively.

'I am Hélène, yes…Who are you?'

I started my rehearsed answer.

'Speak up girl. I'm a little deaf. What are you saying?'

'I'm Marie, the daughter of Annie in Aureilhan.'

'Yes? Annie… my sister's daughter? The one who wanted a farm and got one with a man thrown in?'

As a description of my parents' marriage, it sounded a little direct, but reasonably correct.

'Yes, that's right. I'm Annie's daughter, Marie. I came to see how you were getting on in the Occupation.'

If I wasn't very convinced by my own credentials, neither was she.

'Well, in that case, it's taken you long enough. As you can see no one takes much notice of us either way. There's a few Boches nearer to the town centre, but they don't take much notice of me out here.'

She looked me up and down. 'You'd better come in.' She led me in to the sparsely furnished front room.

'Sit down girl. I was about to have my apéritif before eating. What do you want?'

I was taken aback by being treated automatically like another adult. 'I'm not really used to drinking.'

'Nonsense. You're French. I'm not one of these skinflint, no pleasure people, like your mother and I've no use for you, if you are. What are you having – anis, porto, vin blanc?'

I went for the porto because it was generally sweeter than the rest and easier on my untutored palate.

My choice seemed to please the old woman.

'Yes, I like a nice porto too. We're not so far from Spain and Portugal that we can't appreciate their drinks.'

I looked round the sitting room, which adjoined some glass doors. The side-board was huge – reflecting the fashion of the Great War, and very clumsy, as though it had been inherited rather than chosen. The easy chairs were scratched and some of the stuffing was emerging from the cracked covers. The dog had made its home in one of them.

'Sit down, Marthe,' said Hélène, talking to the dog as though she was some over-energetic child, rather than a dog.

'You don't mind the dog, do you? What did you say your name was?'

'Marie. No, I don't mind the dog at all.'

Being brought up on a small holding, I was used to animals but not animals as pets. I wasn't in the slightest afraid, only bemused by a dog being given so much house room.

'Good, because Marthe's my friend. She's got more sense than most humans.'

It had never occurred to me that you could feel like that about an animal. For me animals were the noisy, smelly, dirty creatures who needed looking after. But when I looked more closely at Marthe, I could see what Hélène meant. She was intelligent and sympathetic and was unlikely to let you down.

In Hélène's ménage I learnt very quickly about the delights of an apéritif before a meal, about the companionship of a dog, about how having a home didn't have to mean perfect tidiness or cleanliness.

'How long are you thinking of staying then? I assume you are.'

I hadn't expected such a direct question so soon. 'Would three nights be too much?' I asked diplomatically, feeling somewhat embarrassed about my imposition on an aunt I had never been interested in.

'Say what you want, girl. If you want to stay three nights, say it.'

I had to admit defeat. 'Yes, I would.'

'Well then, three nights it is, though I'm a bit curious about why you should suddenly want to come, when no one in your family has bothered about me before.'

Obviously nice noises about wanting to help the family were not going to impress this particular lady. I thought a near approximation of the truth might be a good idea.

'To be honest, Tante Hélène, I had heard you mentioned in the family and I never have any opportunity to go anywhere and I thought it might be a fantastic opportunity to go exploring.'

'Mmm.' My new-found aunt eyed me up and down. 'Well that at least sounds a bit more honest. And what I remember of your mother, I would think she can't imagine anyone wanting to leave her precious farm.'

I felt as though I should defend my mother a little. 'To be fair, she does have to work hard to keep it going.'

'You mean she wants to work hard to make everyone admire her. No, no...' she held her hand up against a possible reply. 'Don't answer. I don't expect you to be disloyal to your mother.

But now you're here, you can make yourself useful and keep an old woman company. I'll show you where everything is and then over dinner you can tell me all about yourself, not your family. You look like a young woman who has plenty to say for herself. Come along. Set the table while I boil up the soup. Fortunately, there's plenty of it because I always make enough to last several days.'

This was the beginning of my three day stay with my new-found great aunt. It had originally been a convenient excuse for my clandestine activities, but it soon became an experience for its own sake.

I had never lived with anyone who enjoyed life quite as much as Tante Hélène. She was old, deaf, and hobbled because her hip hurt her, but she had an ability to enjoy life which was infectious. She said exactly what she thought; she acted exactly as she wanted to, and she did not care what anyone else thought about her. How she came from the same family as my mother was a mystery to me.

'It was all to do with the circumstances of life,' she said, but I thought it had more to do with personality. My mother's mother who had long since died, had married a man who never owned anything and who wasted what money they had on drink. When I understood that, my mother's desire to marry someone who owned his own small holding and might choose to work night and day to make it more prosperous, made much more sense. In contrast, Tante Hélène had married a local accountant, who liked the good things of life and who had been extremely sociable. He had died before they had had any children much to her disappointment, but, as she had been left a widow with a small but adequate pension, and a large vegetable garden and house, she had become satisfied with her own company.

'And of course,' she added, 'I love looking at the mountains.' As I found out the following morning after my arrival, you could see the peaks of the Pyrenées in the distance from her windows and garden. When she had been younger, she had walked them with her husband. Now, with an awkward hip and arthritis, she could only admire them from a distance but, as she said, they still made a difference to the enjoyment of her garden and her walk round the side of the house and down the hill to the local bakery each day.

I had used Tante Hélène as an excuse for being in the area, but I found that I enjoyed my stay with her more than I expected. I found out a lot more about my mother's family. Although helping her meant practical work in the house and garden, I found that it was very different from helping my mother. Hélène accepted a reasonable standard of work rather than a perfect one. Sometimes she enjoyed talking but at other times she was silent, but it was a companionable, non-intense silence. In contrast to living with my parents, it did not involve a complicated emotional relationship. Hélène (she quickly wanted me to drop the title 'tante') said what she thought, treated me as an adult, and had a waspish sense of humour which I appreciated. She was not well read but she was intelligent, and she showed an interest in the books I had read at school. When she sat down at the dinner table, it was for a time of relaxation. We listened to the radio together, even programmes from the Free French in London.

'Don't you know that could be in trouble for that?' I enquired innocently. Until then, we had not discussed the war or the occupation.

In reply she snorted and reached for a cigarette. 'Do I care at my age? I have no time for the Germans but so far, they have left me in peace. I don't think they are interested in an old woman like me.'

'They've been bothered about old people in our area.' I told her about the forced collection of radios and about people being shot in reprisals in Bordeaux.

She let rings of smoke escape through her fingers.

'If they're bothered about things like that, they must think they're losing. Only someone who fears loss of power could give such ridiculous punishments for such trivial things.'

'They might be trivial,' I said with feeling, 'but if your family gets shot, you might be forced to take them seriously.'

She poured herself more wine. 'So that might be the advantage of having no family. They can't hurt someone you love.'

It was only when I thought about it later that night, that I realised the logical conclusion of what she had said. If they can't hurt someone you love, that must mean you had no one to love. For the first time it occurred to me that it was not a desirable situation.

During those three days we established our own little routine. Hélène did not 'do' early mornings, not, as she explained to me, because she was sleeping late, but because she didn't want to be sociable before 11 in the morning. After our coffee together in the kitchen, she would take me outside, and show me what she needed doing in the garden and we would work together for two or three hours. Then after what seemed more like a snack than a lunch, there was some straightening up of the house and the washing to do. In the early evening there was a long, leisurely apéritif, followed by a dinner, mainly consisting of vegetables from her garden but supplemented by lentils and occasional pieces of meat. The radio was turned on in the evening.

'I've enjoyed having you, Marie,' she said on our last night. 'I wasn't expecting you and I'm not entirely sure why you're here, but you're alright.'

I raised my eyebrows. What she had said seemed like a compliment. 'Thank you.'

'Yes, you're better than your mother and your grandfather, come to think of it. Miserable old sod.' A pause while she let her judgement of my family take effect. 'What are you going to do now? How are you getting home? What was that about a priest you said?'

'Father Julien. Yes, I'll be going back with him tomorrow. He's been visiting some of the flock, especially people in the camp.'

It was a risk to link Julien with the camp, but it seemed reasonable to think that he might be helping with the refugees there.

'Oh! You mean the camp at Gurs?'

'Yes' I was surprised that she knew about it, but I later learnt that it was well known in the region of Pau.

'I've heard that there all sorts there – foreigners, communists from Spain, Jews…the lot.'

'Julien was asked to go and help give communion for a few days.'

Hélène looked at me quizzically. 'So how come you went with him? I've never known any member of our family to be religious.'

'We're not, but someone from school knows him well and told me that he would be going.' Cecile had come in useful again. She was religious and therefore must know about the movements of local priests. I hadn't seen Cecile for months, but it seemed like a harmless piece of lying.

'So, you're going back with him tomorrow?'

'Yes, I'm meeting him at the bottom of the hill by the church at midday.'

'If he comes another time and you can get a lift again, then you can come here. I don't mind you.'

It wasn't exactly an effusive appreciation, but I felt more genuine affection from her gruff, 'I don't mind you,' than any more elaborate protestations of emotion.

'And I don't mind you either, Hélène. Thank you for having me. I would be glad to come back.'

'Humph.' She turned from the table to busy herself with the washing up.

# Chapter Thirty-Five

When I met Julien the following day outside the church, I felt as though I had grown up a little, relaxed a little, and was more confident. He too seemed to be in a good humour.

'I've got a job for you to do, Marie.'

'Great. What makes you think that I can do it?' I wasn't sure that I could meet the expectations of this optimistic priest.

'Right. I'll tell you as we go along.'

We got into the car and drove along towards Gurs. I was so immersed in his plan that I had almost forgotten about Tante Hélène.

'I've given the papers and passports to my contact in the camp. He's sorting out which adults and which children should go.'

'How do they select them?'

'With difficulty. It's awful, because you feel as though you're making a decision about who is going to survive and who is not, but it's got to be done. No room for sentimentality or everyone will be damned.'

'It doesn't sound very fair.'

'It isn't but the alternative is to do nothing and let them all die. We can only save some of them. That's the reality.'

'How will he choose them?'

'He'll choose those who have the character to survive and those who haven't got parents who hang onto them.'

'Surely the parents want them to survive?'

'In theory yes, if they thought about it logically, but a lot of the adults are in denial. They know that the Germans and Vichy are after them; they know about the rumours of the death camps, but they still don't want to know.'

'I don't blame them. Who would want to know about things like that?'

We were driving along beautiful lanes with the autumn sun fingering the just-browning leaves of the silver birches, edging them with a glorious burnished orange. Death camps seemed like a figment of the imagination.

'Me neither, but they are shutting their minds to reality. They might think that Jews are unpopular, or the Germans don't like them but somehow they are deluding themselves into thinking that the children might be a passport to safety.'

'And they definitely couldn't be?' The normally smiling priest looked very grave.

'They're definitely not. I suppose no one can really imagine that there is such evil in the world which could willingly kill children merely because of their ethnicity, but…' The sentence was left ominously unfinished.

'Father Julien?' I looked up at the far peaks of the Pyrenées which at each turn of the road were coming nearer.

'Yes?'

'Do you believe in evil?…'

It now amazes me that such a deeply philosophical question could be relevant as we took a ride, in a 'deux chevaux' in a beautiful rural region of France. This was a conversation between a young, unworldly teenager who had never considered or experienced religion for herself and a Catholic priest who had been trained to believe in God and the devil. It was, to Julien's credit, that he never showed shock that I did not understand religion, nor did he treat me as though my opinion was not worthwhile.

'Yes, I do, Marie.'

'So, what is it then?'

'I don't believe in a devil with horns and a pitchfork…but yes, when you see what the Nazis are doing, you know that you're up against evil.'

'You don't think that any Germans can be good?'

'Not all Germans are Nazis. And probably most of them back in Germany don't know what is happening.'

'And anyway, some of them go to church. Alain told me.'

'Who is Alain?'

'A friend from school.'

'You can go to church and still be evil, Marie.'

'Wow! That doesn't make a whole load of sense.'

He laughed. 'No. It doesn't...hey!'. His face had an impish grin, as he continued,

'All this deep theology is worse than being at the seminary, training for the priesthood. Let's get to more practical matters.'

'All right. What's going to happen? What are we going to do?'

He changed gear to tackle a very steep hill and the deux chevaux forced its juddering way up a narrow, bending road, and I hardly dared to believe that it was going to get there. Suddenly we were above a valley and driving at right angles to a perpendicular drop below.

'We're going to challenge the power of death, Marie.' It was my turn to grin at such preposterous language.

'If you say so, Julien. You're the religious expert here.'

'I do say so.'

'Fine. Convince me. Give me the details.' I was ready to be a convert.

'The papers I've already taken to Gurs – they're in the hands of the section leaders there. Teenagers will head out with them over the next fortnight.'

'Do they know what they're heading out to?'

'To a certain extent. All the groups have got packs of food to keep them going. But they'll have to rely on their own ingenuity.'

'Especially if they're teenagers who's going to lead them?' I'm a teenager, I thought. Would I be able to make it over those huge peaks which now rose into view as we turned down from the road which hugged the side of the gorge, before rising upwards to an even dizzier height. How long could you climb, just relying on your own feet?

'Some of them are led by group leaders who are seasoned resisters, but many of them are only 18 or 19 years old.'

'Do they know the route?'

'Some of them do, the ones who were brought up round here who know the mountains. Some of them have been recruited from far afield, places like Lyon or Marseille in the Free Zone.'

'So how come they've come this far west?'

'This far west is as good a way as any for getting out of the country. We used to use the eastern route past Nice to get down into Italy.'

'I thought Italy was Fascist too?'

'Yes, in theory, but they've always been a different sort of Fascist.'

Julien paused as he negotiated another hair pin bend. The cattle on the side of the road were feeding high up on the meadows. The hay had already been gathered in. These were the last weeks before the early winter rains started, and the cattle would be taken into shelter further down the mountain.

'The Mediterranean Fascists are different. Don't get me wrong,' he added, as he saw my raised eyebrow before concentrating on the road again. 'Any sort of fascist is bad news. But I guess it's the Mediterranean factor. Perhaps they drink more wine than the Germans.'

'Like the French do?'

'Yes, but French wine doesn't seem to have opened the heart of Vichy. Anyway, whatever, the Germans have taken over the part of France which was occupied by the Italians. There are lots of Jews hidden there. Some of them have moved over here to do something useful.'

'How can Jews rescue the Jews?'

'You mean without getting arrested themselves?'

'Yes. Surely the Germans will suspect any Jewish leader.'

'That's true but things are so desperate now, it's a matter of getting them out by any means at all.'

I thought of Alain, continually moving between Bordeaux and Aureilhan, guiding others to freedom but never escaping himself.

'Why don't all Jews just escape?' I was typically annoyed by the frustration of it all, especially when it meant that my friend was in danger.

'Easier said than done. You've got to have money and papers and friends. Also, now the children are being attacked, the adults are reluctant to leave them.'

'But there must be adults who don't have children themselves?'

'There are of course, but it's a strange thing, Marie. The Jews won't willingly abandon their own people.'

'Isn't that good?'

'Yes, it is, but I don't think we're quite so loyal to our own people.'

'Maybe not…but here you are, on your way to rescue them'

He laughed unselfconsciously. 'You're right, Marie. Maybe I've been doing us down. And you're part of the rescue operation too. In which case, you can congratulate yourself.'

After the lower slopes of the Pyrénées the land had become flatter again, and soon we were coming down into the camp which was Gurs.

I had never seen a refugee camp before. At first sight it was beautiful, but, on closer inspection, the buildings were prefabricated and flimsy. It was the magnificent backdrop of the mountains, which gave the illusion of beauty.

Our little car entered through the barriers and armed guards came out to check our papers.

'How on earth are we going to get past them on the way out if we are taking children with us,' I asked Julien as he wound up the window again.

'Don't worry about it,' reassured my optimistic, and, I now realised, experienced priest escort.

'They're actually a lot better than they appear to be. They've got to keep up the illusion of being fierce armed guards or they'll only be in trouble themselves or get replaced by tougher ones. They make it relatively easy for us to get past them.'

'Do they know you already?'

'They're bound to. They're not stupid and they'll have their suspicions, but they'll turn a blind eye to what I'm doing.'

We got out of the car near a large wooden building which turned out to be the camp refectory.

'Aren't the guards trusted by the Germans?'

'Well of course they are Vichy guards, but there's Vichy and there's Vichy. There's actually quite a lot of good Vichy-ites, as well as bad ones.'

'So how do you know the difference?'

Julien flung his cassock into the back of the car, as if he was getting rid of his real identity. 'You don't. You just have to trust your luck.'

'I thought you believed in God?'

'Well OK then. Trust God then.' He rumpled my head scarf. 'I was just making it easier for you as my little atheist…'

'I thought I'd been converted into your little novice?'

'Yes, I forgot. Just testing your beliefs, ma soeur. Come on.'

I followed him into the refectory where he was greeted by some of the older moniteurs and monitrices.

'Salut, Père Julien.'

'Salut, mon ami!'

'Everything OK ?'

'Sure … Eveything's OK for me.'

We made our way to a small room on the far side of the refectory. It was set out as a rudimentary chapel with chairs and kneelers and a rough altar table and cross. Children and teenagers and adults started to make their way into it, and the room was soon packed. To my surprise Julien brought his rosary out of his pocket and turned to the altar where the sacrament had been prepared.

It was the first eucharist that I had ever attended, and I assumed it would be a sham but to my surprise there was a sense of real sincerity and integrity on the part of the participants. The service was repeated three times because there were so many people who wanted to take part. To begin with I was impatient for it to be over, so we could get into the real reason for us being there, but Père Julien didn't seem at all anxious or hurried.

'There's all sorts of reasons for my spending time doing the Saint Cène when I arrive,' he explained later. 'First of all, it establishes my credentials as a genuine priest. There will be inmates here who will give Jews away to the authorities if it means they can gain their own freedom. No one knows who they are, but our best defence, is to be who we say we are.

Secondly, many of these people feel desperate inside, however happy they may appear on the outside. The Saint Cène gives them something to relate to outside of themselves, the feeling that God may be in control, despite all the chaos going on here. And lastly, and most important of all as far as I'm concerned, it's for me. It makes me know deep inside myself that this is all part of my service to God. It gives me strength.'

This third point was completely beyond me. I assumed that this was part of the craziness of being a priest in the Catholic church, a sort of extra gene that the rest of us didn't have.

The real business of rescuing children from the Nazis was what interested me and the mechanics of that were about to be explained to me after our supper in the refectory. What was theology compared to real people?

# Chapter Thirty-Six

The whole camp came together for a rudimentary meal in the refectory. Despite the uncertainties of people being threatened with deportation, the mood was resigned and gentle. Most people felt safe, explained Julien, because they had been there for some time, the food was adequate, and they were near to beautiful countryside. War was a long way away and no one can go on worrying indefinitely.

The newer, younger members of the camp were more on edge. They were generally young men, who were communists and who had fled the civil war in Spain and who had been placed in the camp to keep them away from communist agitation in France. Some of them were experienced fighters who were skilled in action and who were now bored and frustrated. Some of them were angry with the Vichy government and some of them were questioning the exact future for the stalemate of Occupation. Others were hopeful that America would bring about the desired result – the end of Nazism.

Julien and I met with a small group of local leaders, including a small number of trusted teenagers. I was introduced as Lucie from Toulouse, who had been visiting the sisters in Julien's town of Léon. Julien looked round at the band of leaders.

'Right. So, the papers I delivered last time? Any news from the groups who have used them so far?'

One of the section commandants of the camp, André, replied. 'No, Father. They were sent out as you instructed. So far we haven't heard anything.'

'That may well be good news. If anyone had been detained by a roadblock, the chances are that they would have been brought back here.'

'Not necessarily, Father. They could have been transferred to another camp. Or the Nazis could just be biding their time till they saw if any others left from here. Or they could have put pressure on them to give more information about what was going on here.'

'You mean that the authorities will be here soon?'

'Either that, or they are just waiting for the next group of people to leave before they act.'

Julien was silent for a few moments. You could see him working through the likelihood of these possibilities. What risks should he take or allow those in his care to take?

'I think the only answer to these unanswerable possibilities is to act fast but in secret. In any case, if the Nazis arrest them now, it won't be any different to what they were planning all along.'

'You mean the final solution?'

The question came from a nervous looking young man smoking in the corner of the room, who sounded more knowing and better educated than the rest. It was, I remember, the first time I had heard the phrase 'the final solution' – a phrase which, after the war, became so familiar and which was, even in that camp, pregnant with doom and a euphemism for tragedy to come.

Julien turned towards the speaker. 'That's the phrase the Germans give it – one which is pure evil. Don' t let's go into its meaning, Maurice. We need to act now. If we can't do anything, we can't; but at least we need to try.'

We were all affected by his words and his resolve. At that point I could have no more withdrawn my support from his plans, than I could have ceased to be French. Some of us felt worried; some of us felt inadequate and afraid; and some of us felt desperate. But we all wanted to follow Father Julien in whatever he decided.

The tension passed and jokiness suddenly became the norm, as if we were just a normal group of young people who were completely relaxed with one another. Julien alone became business like and serious.

'Maurice, here are the papers for your group of youngsters, and here is the map which tells you which villages to go through. Learn the map and the names of the safe houses in the next two hours and go before midnight. Did you get them all prepared with essential belongings like I told you to last Thursday?'

'Yes, they're all, ready to go. I've got them prepared over the last few days.'

'You can wake them up tonight?'

'Yes.'

'Go and get some extra food for them all from Alice in the kitchens and, Maurice, may God go with you.'

The priest and Maurice, who I now saw was little more than a teenager himself, gave each other a bear hug in the doorway, and then the younger man was gone.

'Sylvie and Jacques.' Julien signalled out a young couple sitting in the centre of the group. 'You've probably got the most difficult group – not old enough to be totally independent and not young enough to be just up for an adventure. Here are the papers for all of them and here is the money. We can afford to give you a more direct route, because you're going to act as their parents, and be taking them for an educational trip into the mountains.'

'You don't think they're a bit young for the parental role?' someone asked.

'Oh well, country bumpkins start families very young. The Germans don't know much about your way of life. Your best bet is to be full of life and enthusiasm and show the children the flowers and animals around them.' Sylvie and Jacques didn't have anything to say. They left to return to the dormitory where the children would be sleeping.

'Now,' Julien said, turning to me. 'Lucie, it's your turn. I'll give you the papers tomorrow morning. You'll have to keep them yourself because your group of children are between 8 and 11 years old so there can be no pretence that you're their mother. This is where you become a seriously religious girl taking your group from the colonie de vacances up into the mountains.'

'I hope I'm not expected to give them religious instruction.'

'Actually, I've packed a little book for you of verses from the Scriptures to read every day. It will give you the feeling of being more authentic. You'll meet the children tomorrow morning and the bakery van from the village will take you on the first part of the journey.'

'And then?'

'And then you're on your own. You'll have a map and a route with barns to stay at, but, if you sense trouble, go off the road. Look out for the roadblocks and any lorries of soldiers passing by. If you're not sure, keep off the roads and use the pasture, especially lower down.'

'I assume we're going to the Spanish border?'

'Yes, but the best route with such a young group of children is to head up west to the Basque country and then over the lower hills. The Germans aren't so vigilant there.'

'What happens if we can't get food?'

'I'm giving you ration books for each child. The Basques are known to be sympathetic. They're an independent group of people who don't like invaders of any sort. You'll need to be ingenious and make your own decisions.'

'Father Julien, I've never done anything like this before,' I protested, with hundreds of unanswered questions going on in my head.

'You're right, child. But then none of us had, before this started. I wouldn't say my training in the seminary had prepared me for this.'

'What happens if we can't get through or I fail in some way?'

'I don't think you will. It might take you longer than you expect. There may be adventures on the way, but the alternative is death, and there can't be anything worse than that for these children. As far as the parents are concerned, you're their last chance.'

No one left in the refectory seemed the slightest bit sympathetic to my objections. I had one night to get my resolve together and put aside my fears.

# Chapter Thirty-Seven

I had a feeling that I was going to bed as one person and waking up as another and that change was not just about a change of name. I went to bed in a cramped cubicle at the end of a dormitory full of girls. Marie – a country girl who had always slept in an attic by herself on a farm, one had taken lone risks in a countryside which she knew well and loved and into which she could disappear at any moment. I woke early in the morning before anyone else, contemplating my new persona. I was Lucie – a Catholic novice, who regularly helped a priest, who was a member of the Resistance movement, ready to look after eight little girls aged between 8 and 11 years, who were leaving their parents and fleeing for their lives. What would happen if they didn't want to come with me? I had no siblings and rarely mixed with people from the village and knew nothing about looking after children. What would happen if they all hated me? It was strange but that question bothered me far more than how I was going to travel inconspicuously with eight children up the foothills of the Pyrenées toward the French/Spanish border. I might have a new name, but I had not acquired the necessary skills of child management overnight.

Fortunately, I did not have to persuade them to come. It had already been decided for them.

By 7 in the morning, with the outline of the mountain peaks in the distance silhouetted by the rising sun, I was softening my 'bout de pain' in the hot milk which had been provided for breakfast in the canteen.

By 7:30 my charges were inside the refectory, each with one bag of belongings and looking sullen and completely out of touch with the reality of what was happening to them.

I observed them as they came in separately, wide-eyed and uninterested in me. I already had my own linen bag with a change of clothes and all the necessary papers for my charges. Father Julien came in immediately after the girls arrived.

'Now girls, here is my fellow church worker, Sister Lucie. She is going to look after you while your parents can't be there. She knows what is best for you, so try to be as helpful as possible for her.'

One of the girls was more outspoken than the others. 'I don't see why we can't make the journey over the mountains with our parents.'

'Because, Annette, we haven't got the right papers for them yet, and we need to get you to safety as soon as possible.'

'That means my parents might not be safe. I want them to be safe too.'

Father Julien was experienced at countering these objections. 'Of course, you do. We're working very hard on getting those papers, but grownups can leave the camp at a moment's notice. It's harder for children to do that, so, as we've got papers for you, we're taking our chances while we can. Your parents will be able to join you in Spain later.'

I looked down into my empty milk cup, trying to get some of the departed warmth into my hands. I knew it was a lie. It was probably too late to get the parents out. These children would never see their parents again. How was I going to effectively lie to them for a whole week? I had no idea, nor did I know how I was going to talk to them as convincingly as Father Julien did.

Suddenly I stood up. Action was needed.

'I'm Lucie, girls and I'm very pleased to have you with me. We're going on an adventure together, so I hope you're going to help me as much as possible. Starting with the way we're leaving the camp – has anyone here been in a bakery van before?' Fortunately, there was no answer.

'Neither have I but I love the smell of bread first thing in the morning and we're going to have that pleasure right now. Come on. Pick up your things. Whose bag is that?'

I pointed to a school satchel over the other side of the table.

'It's mine,' whispered a shy little girl, who seemed embarrassed about being signalled out.

Suddenly inspiration came. I was about to tell her she shouldn't forget things, when I remembered how much I had hated being told off as a child. 'Well, we don't want to leave that one behind, do we? It looks almost new. Did your mum buy it for your first day at school?'

She nodded shyly.

'I think it's going to be just the right thing for our little outing. It's got to have lots of pockets for the things you need. So much better than my old linen bag.'

She smiled uncertainly and I swept her up and her bag and went outside. The others all crowded round.

'I'm going to get to know you all. Here's the papers we need. And, ah yes, here's the baker's van. I'm going to call your names as you get in and, remember, if we have to stop because someone wants to check the van, you have to be completely quiet.'

Rose, Alice, Florence, Annette, Anne, Laurence, Marthe, Annick. They all trooped past me into the back of the van and I leaped in after them. I smiled encouragingly. 'I can't think of a nicer way of travelling than being surrounded by smells of the 'baguettes' we've just eaten.'

'Sister Lucie, where are we going?'

'We're going as far as St. Palais, where the bakery is, stopping there while the driver fills up with his next supplies, and then to the village of Bastide. And then, we'll see.'

No one wanted to talk which was just as well, because I had nothing to say. I went over the girls' names, over and over in my head and checked them against their identity cards, so that I could not be caught out by an official who might not believe that I was their teacher.

St. Palais could be a difficult place Julien had warned me. There were lots of soldiers stationed there and they were on the lookout for runaways. Sure enough, on the outskirts of the town, the van was stopped. Inside we hardly dared to breathe but then we were off again over the cobbled streets of the town, until we were driven to the back door of the bakery and the van doors were flung open.

'Hey, little ones, before we stack the bread rolls, here's some for you to eat so you don't get too hungry.'

The rough and ready bakery owner passed round brown paper bags filled with croissants and home-made jam and patisseries filled with vanilla cream.

'And you too, sister, have something to fill your stomach, instead of your soul.' He enjoyed his laugh at my expense. I felt a bit guilty about my spiritual inadequacies, but I was happy to eat the croissant.

'How ever did you manage to get jam?' I was amazed as I put my teeth into the delightful gooeyness. We hadn't had access to sugar at home for months.

The baker leaned forward and touched his nose. 'Don't ask too many questions sister, but let's just say that this year in Pau, there's been a record number of plums. And the government can't eat them all!'

The van was filling up again and, when they had finished their food, I got the girls settled down for the next part of the journey, travelling north west. Filled with croissants and plum jam, I felt so much more hopeful about our future and decided to sit in front with the driver. Now away from Gurs, I felt relieved and hopeful that the girls were not going to be sent back.

We were just past the church on our way out to the next village, when we turned a corner, and there they were – three German soldiers on a roadblock.

'Tell them about the girls, Bernard,' I said to the driver who looked startled.

'Tell them right at the beginning. They're bound to find them and better to look as though it is all planned.

'If you say so, Sister,' replied Bernard dutifully.

'Papers please,' ordered the German soldier courteously.

I handed over the papers of the girls as well as my own.

'Who are these?'

'They're girls from my church. We're staying at a colonie de vacances near Pau and I'm taking them on a special three-day retreat into the mountains. It's for educational as well as religious purposes.'

'What are you doing in a baker's van then?'

'Well, sir, you wouldn't believe how difficult transport is in war time. Buses don't run like they used to, and petrol is so expensive. Bernard here said he was coming to the village and I and my girls took advantage.'

'So where are you staying, mademoiselle, for your educational retreat?'

I had to find somewhere which sounded convincing.

'For the first few nights we're staying with my great aunt.'

'Oh really?' The German soldier was polite but sceptical.

'Yes, she just lives at the top of the hill. The girls are going to get some experience in helping her to harvest some of her vegetables and fruit and we'll be going up on foot into the mountains for reading and poetry and identifying flowers.'

'Where does your great aunt live, mademoiselle?'

I pointed up the hill past the church.

'In that case she won't mind the girls being delivered by truck.'

'Of course not.'

'Well, get them in then.'

My first job was to make sure that the girls did not panic. I tried my best smiling voice, and reassuring tones as I opened the van.

'Girls, you won't believe what luck we're having today. Not only did we get a lift with the patisserie van, but these soldiers are giving us a lift, up to my great aunt's house. You know the one where we're going to help with the garden?'

They stared at me uncomprehendingly but understood enough not to contradict me.

What was my great aunt going to say?

She heard the lorry arrive even though she was in the back garden. She came out to see what all the noise was about. If she was surprised to see me, she showed nothing.

'Yes, officer, what seems to be the problem? I see you have my great niece with you?'

'This woman is your great niece, is she?'

'Well of course she is. Haven't I just told you?'

Tante Hélène must have been down in the garden for a 'pause cigarette' in the middle of the afternoon.

I quickly intervened. 'I arranged it all when I visited a few days ago. I don't often get from the church to see Tante Hélène and I thought it would be the perfect opportunity to bring my girls round and teach them the ways of gardening.'

'So, you don't mind eight girls staying with you, madam?'

The officer was amused but beginning to be bored. Aunt Hélène showed no surprise at all.

'I would be disappointed if they hadn't come,' she said loftily as if she entertained eight children every week. 'As my niece says, they are here to learn about the gardening and to help me with the autumn tasks.'

'Now, officer, if you'll excuse us, we have to set up camp for the night. Come along girls,' and she firmly ushered them into the house and closed the door on the German soldier.

# Chapter Thirty-Eight

'Girls,' said Hélène, taking charge as if was her natural place, 'Leave your bags and coats down here and we'll go straight into the garden.'

All eight of them followed her out meekly, with due deference to this old woman who held their futures in her hands.

'I've got secateurs and hoes here…plenty of everything. I'm not going to learn your names just yet. I'm an old woman and I'll have to write them down to remember them.'

I had no idea whether any of them had worked in a garden before in their young lives. But, with Hélène giving them brief instructions, they were soon at work.

'And you, what's your name?' She put a hand over her forehead, as if she was rather forgetful.

'Lucie. Sister Lucie,' I supplied for her.

'Yes, Lucie, while the girls work here, you go upstairs and see what you can find for the sleeping arrangements. There are plenty of sheets in the landing cupboard. They come from my mother's time, but they're perfectly serviceable. Just look and see what you can do with the beds and mattresses separated. Later you can take the cushions upstairs and make some extra places to sleep. Find whatever you can. But don't touch my room. I'm an old woman and I'm not going to have eight little girls disturbing me late at night when I can't sleep.'

While the girls worked and after Hélène had given me her instructions, I found all sorts of sheets and eiderdowns and bolsters upstairs. The girls would have to sleep three of them on the bed springs, three on the mattresses and two on extra cushions but there were two extra bedrooms upstairs and plenty of room.

Then I went downstairs and found as much food as I could. There was some of Hélène's soup to which I thought could be added more water and whatever could be picked in the garden today and some rough, dry loaves. It was fortunate that the girls had started their journey earlier with croissants and jam from Bernard's bakery.

The girls appeared to be enjoying their work in the garden, and, after their initial nervousness, loved the dog, and were amused that its name was the same as one of the girls. I could see them all gardening from the bedroom window and any suspicious soldier would only have seen exactly what I had told them.

We got them to bed by eight o'clock. As they went upstairs, Hélène had a word of advice. 'Well Sister Lucie, I think it's a good idea for you to go and have a little goodnight prayer with them.'

'But they're Jewish,' I objected.

'Don't say any more. Any child would feel the comfort of a prayer and I thought you were supposed to be a sister?'

I looked a little embarrassed. 'I don't know any prayers myself.'

'You mean your mother has brought you up as a godless heathen? I'm not surprised. But surely you must know the Lord's prayer?'

'I suppose so.'

'I think you'd better get them to learn it if they're going to sound like good Catholics. But for now, go and ask God to bless them. It doesn't matter which god – any will do,' added my aunt airily. 'And then come back down. I think you have a little explaining to do.'

It wasn't so difficult to ask God to bless them and it was true that they all felt reassured by my bedtime prayer and kiss. One of them, Annick, started crying.

'I want my mummy.'

I found that I instinctively knew what to say. 'I know you do, Annick, but mummy sent you away to be safe. She doesn't want you to be unhappy.'

At this point, the child next to her turned over and gave her lots of hugs and I left to go downstairs.

'Right,' said my aunt companionably, 'let's have the apéritif we missed earlier on, and you'd better tell me what you are doing here with these children.'

'Aunt Hélène, you were amazing. You looked as though it was completely natural for you to be receiving all these children.'

Hélène sat down next to me with her absinthe, smiling to herself.

'I thought I did rather well myself. Nothing is calculated to make me feel angrier than seeing one of those meddlesome soldiers interfering with our way of life.'

'You don't mind them being Jewish?'

'Good gracious, girl, why should I? One of my best friends at school was Jewish. We all lived together perfectly happily till the Germans arrived. And anyway,' added Tante Hélène , taking a companiable drag on her cigarette, 'These girls are little children. What sort of government or country would want to do them harm?'

'But they do.'

'Exactly. If they do, they aren't worth taking any notice of at all.

But, down to business,' she continued. 'What exactly are you planning to do with them? And,' she added tartly, 'I might have known that it wasn't just an innocent, 'be nice to a great-aunt-visit' in the first place when you arrived last week.'

I looked embarrassed. 'It's true that I needed to come down here to the camp, but I did think that it was a great opportunity to visit my mother's family.'

'Umph.' Hélène looked at me quizzically, as if to assess my honesty.

'Anyway, the question is what am I going to do with you all now you are here. I assume you didn't mean to be here this time round?'

'No. It was only the roadblock which took me by surprise.'

'Where are you planning on going from here?'

I told her about going north west, and then crossing the mountains not far from the coast.

'Good idea. I'm trying to think how we are going to get you there. I know some farmers round here who would help.'

'They wouldn't be worried about getting into trouble?'

'The Germans aren't terribly interested in us country folk. Besides you've already proved that you're a Catholic sister getting yourself to a colonie. I think you need to stick to that story.'

Here was my great aunt, who I had only met five days ago, planning an escape route for eight Jewish children!

'I can see I'm going to enjoy this,' she said as if in answer to my thoughts.

'Now let's work out how we're going to organise food for the next three days, while I get some transport arranged.'

How about a night cap before we settle down for the night?'

# Chapter Thirty-Nine

Tante Hélène organised us as if she was used to organising classes of children.

'Ah,' she sighed, when I asked her about this. 'That is because I used to organise the village scouts a long time ago.'

'What does that mean?'

'Goodness, Sister Lucie,' she mocked me playfully. 'Where have you been all your life? Did you never have a scout group in your village?'

'I've never heard of them. Maybe they were part of the church.'

'In your role as 'religieuse' you certainly should know about them. They're a uniformed group who help us do good things and learn how to camp and look after themselves in the open.'

'That sounds useful. Maybe I could have done with some of that.'

'There's plenty of things you could have done with on that farm of yours.'

'Such as what?'

'A bit of fun and love, I should say.'

I was taken aback. Was my home really lacking in such necessities? And where did fun come into it all? It suddenly occurred to me that that was why I liked my job in the Hôtel du Centre so much. It was fun.

I was also amazed at the girls' attitude to Hélène. They treated her with respect and did exactly what she told them. In fact, they took more notice of her than of me.

'It's no good, Marie,' she said to me in private one evening after they had all gone to bed. 'You've got to get alongside them a bit more. Listen to them when they're feeling upset and help them to make up when they quarrel.'

I felt annoyed at all these expectations. Surely, I was doing more than could be expecting by leading them to freedom?

'But I've never done this sort of thing before,' I retorted. 'I was an only child. I don't know how they're feeling. I just want them to get on with what they've got to do without complaining.'

'You took this job on,' my aunt warned me sternly. 'Don't get me wrong. It's a very worthwhile job. But you've got to enter into the spirit of it all. They've got to want to be with you.'

'What happens if they don't?'

'You've got to get them across those mountains and it's not just a case of organising the route. They've got to want to be with you. They're very young children who've had to leave their parents. It's very hard for them. You need to be understanding.'

'And you think I'm not?'

'I think you expect too much of them.'

'That's all very well.' For the first time I felt angry with my great aunt. 'But I've never done this in my life before. I don't know what I'm doing. And I'm not used to looking after little children. I didn't ask to do the job. They've got to take what they get.'

I saw her relenting a bit in her attitude to me. 'I know it's tough, Marie, and I admire you for doing it. All I'm saying is –listen to them, have a laugh with them, think about them being homesick.'

'I'll try but I'm not sure I can do it, Tante Hélène.' I was close to tears myself. I was only a sixteen-year old with no experience of life.

'You've got this far. Come on, girl, you've got plenty of grit. Tomorrow I'm going to see my friend, Olivier, the farmer over the hill. I've got a little proposal for him and, if he'll listen to me, I've got every reason to think it's going to work. We're going to get those girls out and away.'

Next morning, having given me a list of jobs for the girls to do round the house, Hélène was away, and I was left in charge. I tried hard to listen to the girls as well as organise them. I silently invited them to draw near to me as we dusted Hélène's bedrooms and chopped up her potatoes for the night's soup. Hélène had suggested some questions which would allow the girls to open up about their feelings. Even though this wasn't a natural process for me, I needed to try hard, if I was to gain the girls'

193

loyalty and trust. Without that, she said, I would not get the girls working together with me. Escape was far more likely if we were a unified group who trusted each other. I wasn't sure about the emotional investment, but I wanted to complete my assignment.

Florence seemed to be dusting more assiduously than anyone else. The others all flicked their dusters, much as I would have done, if I had been asked to dust at the same age.

'So, you're good at this, Florence. Did your mother show you how?'

Wrong question! Florence immediately burst into tears. I had to take her aside and hold her. I didn't know how long to do it for, but I knew technically that that was the correct way to show concern.

'Are you worried about your mother, Florence?' In my mind I had rehearsed exactly the right answer for this question. To my surprise Florence's muffled voice could just be heard. 'No, I'm worried that I'm not doing it right. She would be so angry with me for letting her down.'

My heart surged forward in empathy. Here was someone else whose mother had huge expectations of her domestic gifts! I had been letting my mother down like this for the last sixteen years.

'Well, Florence.' I drew away from the little girl with the pale face and dark plaits which were especially curly at the end. 'You know what? I think you're doing brilliantly. I've never seen such dusting. I can't do it half as well as you. Tante Hélène's going to be so impressed by the time she comes back. You can tell your mother from me when you see her that you are better at it than any of us here.'

Her little head was raised in query. I recognised the look. She didn't believe she could be genuinely praised. Jewish children weren't so different to me! I don't know how I came up with that answer. It wasn't because of any gift or experience with the young. It was because I understood how she felt. I was still reliving my childhood.

'Will you really tell her that?'

'You bet I will.'

And then I realised that from her point of view I wasn't just praising her. It was because I was affirming that she would see her mother again. Simultaneously with that understanding came the knowledge that I was being a great liar. It was very unlikely that she would see her mother again and I knew it. I also knew that it was acceptable to lie to her because it gave her hope and she needed hope in order to escape.

I went downstairs to check how the potato peelers and choppers were getting on. Annette, Laurence, Alice and Annick were all crowded round the chopping board and pan, throwing potatoes and carrots into the boiling water.

'Great, girls, we're going to have some amazing soup tonight, I can see. Now you can see the point of digging up those carrots yesterday.'

'You know what, it's a lot more fun than I expected,' said Alice.

'Yes, especially when you tell me silly stories about the boy in your class who brings you cauliflowers.'

They exploded with laughter and then stopped, hands to their mouths, aghast.

'O sister Lucie, we're sorry. We didn't mean anything by that. It was just something silly which happened in Alice's class in the camp.' I suddenly realised that as a religieuse, I was expected to disapprove of such goings on.

'Bringing you a cauliflower? Well, that's a new way of a boy showing he likes you.'

I decided to play the relaxed Catholic sister. Most of the old ones I had heard about from Cecile at school appeared to be disapproving and distant, but why shouldn't the young ones be a bit more relaxed? They all stared at me. Then Annette, the spokeswoman for the group said quietly.

'You're a bit different than we expected from a religieuse, Sister Lucie.'

I decided that I had gone far enough with the sympathy. 'Now don't expect me to be too broad minded, girls. How's that soup coming along? It's not going to have enough in it at this rate.'

The work of the day moved on, but the tension was broken. Hélène was right. Everyone felt much closer to me and I enjoyed their companionship over our bread and cheese lunch. I started to teach them some traditional French songs, which some of them, from stricter Jewish backgrounds, had never sung before.

'It's good for us to sing together,' I explained. 'It's the sort of thing that girls from a French colonie de vacances do. We've got to act the part.'

And suddenly we were transformed from a group of individuals with a leader whom they had never met, to a group who were working together for a common purpose which was dangerous but important.

Towards evening Tante Hélène came home and we were ready to listen to her plans together.

# Chapter Forty

There was almost a festive atmosphere when Hélène returned. She had only been away from the house for one day, but already the girls had missed her. She fussed around them as they served the evening meal, asking them about their day, laughing at some of the stodgy dumplings they had made and having a little grumble about the state of the kitchen, which had been left with a few splashes from the soup-making.

'I really don't know girls. Where have you been brought up? Did your mothers, not teach you to clean up as you were going on?'

Annette with the pigtails looked solemn. 'We're sorry, Tante Hélène. We'll be extra careful when we wash up from now on.'

I reached over and pulled her plaits. 'Don't worry, Annette. We'll do it together. It will get sorted.'

'I'm going to sit down with a cigarette while you're doing that. I've had a busy day and need a rest,' explained my aunt.

'Has it been busy today because of us?' Annette still looked worried.

'Yes, my dear, it has been and I'm an old woman. But,' she smiled up at the child reassuringly, 'I haven't had so much fun for ages. My bones are aching and creaking, but inside I'm laughing.'

I organised the girls into teams for clearing, washing and wiping and putting away and, after they had gone up to bed, I made what passed for coffee in war time and sat down with my great aunt.

She had advice for me. 'Give them a bit of time and then go up and say goodnight. And yes, you do need to give them a kiss as well as a prayer.'

'Would a nun do that?'

'Not all of them are cold and distant. And anyway, this is in your role as children's leader, never mind being a nun.'

'Alright, if I must.'

'Humph…Actually you've made progress in that area.'

'How do you know?'

'I could see how they were with you over the meal. A few more laughs, a bit more relaxed …you're getting there.'

'Alright. Thank you for your confidence in me,' I said tartly.' I'll go and do the favourite auntie bit, while the coffee brews. Then I can see you're dying to tell me what you've been up to today.' It was obvious to me, that while I was only doing my duty, Hélène was enjoying every minute of her unexpected drama.

'Yes, I admit that I haven't had so much fun in years. When you come down, Marie, I want you to tell me how you got into this.'

And so, when I returned after the goodnight ritual, I explained to Hélène how I had started helping the pilgrims, progressed to working with the communist, Patrice, over papers and money, and had finally taken this journey with Father Julien.

'And you're still only 16?'

'Yes.'

'You must have a lot of ability, Marie. Not many people have done all that by the age of 16.'

'It must be the war. I haven't had any choice.'

'Of course, you've had choice! We all have. It's true that the war had given you the opportunity of joining the Resistance. But you've taken that opportunity up.'

'I wanted to go to the lycée and study like my friend, Alain.'

'When the war's over, you'll have to continue your education.'

'It might be too late by then.'

'Nonsense! It's never too late if you really want to do something. Besides, your job at the bar sounds good fun, even if it's not developing your brain.'

'Tante Hélène, do you think I'll ever make anything of my life?' I was desperate for her affirmation.

'There's no question of it. You've got the brains. All you need is the determination. Mind you,' she said, pausing to put a cigarette on one side and sip some more coffee. 'Life does throw some strange bi-paths at you, which you were not expecting, but, if you've got talent, you'll make the most of them.'

'Is that what happened to you?'

'Yes, my husband was my route out of the claustrophobic world of poor man's farming in les Landes.'

'That's what I definitely don't want,' I said vehemently. 'The thought of living on a farm all my life is terrible.'

'You won't need to if you don't want to. No one knows what's going to happen after the war, but there's bound to be more opportunities for girls.'

'Why do you think that?'

'We're the last country in the civilised world where women haven't got the vote. When the Allies get rid of the Germans for us, women will get freedom too.'

In that sitting room on the outskirts of St. Palais, it was the first time that I heard about the liberation of women, and it all started in my mind because of a conversation with an old woman and our involvement with the work of escape and resistance.

'Tell me,' said Tante Hélène, settling back on the high-backed chair, with her last cigarette for the day. (She told me that she limited herself to five a day during war time.) 'What about this boy it all started with? Alain. Where is he?'

'Still in Bordeaux, I think. But he comes to St. Paul when he can.'

'He must be very brave.'

'To work for the Resistance?'

'Yes, but more to have stayed in France for so long, rather than leaving himself.'

'Yes, he is brave and clever and funny.'

'What an amazing combination!' rejoined my aunt drolly, as if she had never heard of a man with such qualities before. 'I can see he's your hero. No, no,' she held up her hand, as I started to protest. 'He sounds as though he's a good boy and worthy of your admiration. I meant more that it's obviously dangerous for him to stay, so why has he?'

'For his family. He told me that there is no way his mother would leave with a horde of little children. They just hope that they're so hidden in Les Landes that no one will be interested in them. He keeps an eye on them as well as working in Bordeaux.'

'Let's hope he's right. When you're attacked, you help each other. And these girls need help. We must get them out to safety, Marie.

Yes, I know,' she added, reading my thought, 'I'm saying 'we' and it's you who's doing all the hard work, but I like to think that I'm doing my part too.'

'You are helping. You're amazing. I can't believe that a week ago I didn't even know you and now we're smuggling Jewish children out of France together.'

'Life has some funny bi-paths, which just present themselves unexpectedly and you find yourself taking them.'

'That sounds almost religious, Hélène. I didn't expect that from you.'

'Well I'm not religious, at least in the traditional sense. I've only done the basics of going to church apart from the 'scouts' I mean. But, as you get older, you can't help having the feeling that there's something there guiding you. Anyway,' she added in a highly practical tone of voice in case our philosophising went too deep, 'this is getting far too serious for me and I'm out of my depth. I need to get to bed because I'm tired out.'

She did indeed look haggard with the lines on her face revealed in the harsh electric light. 'I'm sorry. We've exhausted you.'

'Don't be silly girl. Stop apologising. Normally I can't sleep because I haven't done enough. Tonight, I'm going to sleep well because I've done some work for a change.' She sat up suddenly straight, without the benefit of the hard back of the chair. 'While the children are asleep, I must tell you what is going to happen the day after tomorrow because we need tomorrow to get prepared.'

'Right, Hélène, you tell me.'

'I've been to see my friend, Olivier, over the hill. He's a farmer and he was friends with my husband over a long period of time. He's a good man and I know I can trust him. Although at some point you'll have to walk with the girls, they're very young and you can't expect them to walk from here to Spain. But the problem is, quite apart from roadblocks, no one has the petrol to drive them or the room to hide eight girls.'

'So, what's going to happen?'

'Olivier, and a lot of the farmers round here now, use horses and carts, like they used to in the olden days. He regularly takes up hay to sell at the towns further west, so it will be perfectly natural for him to be on the roads.'

'But not with eight girls and me,' I objected.

'Indeed, but we've already established that you are part of a colonie de vacances, so it's alright to be joining them. This is the plan. The next two mornings you have to go down to the village boulangerie and look around. See what the roadblocks are doing and ask around, carefully of course. Don't tell anyone what we're planning but get the feel for the German security around the town. You can't expect to avoid roadblocks for ever, but it'll help you get on your way if you can make a good run to begin with.'

I looked at her bemused by such simple planning. 'You mean we're just going off on a horse and waggon with your friend, Olivier, and no one will notice?'

'No, no, of course everyone will notice,' said my aunt impatiently. 'You can't stop that, but you can monitor what they will notice.'

'How?'

'If you have four girls riding on the outside, but the other four hidden under the hay, everyone will know that they're on a trip with a farmer, but it will look as though only half have gone and the rest are still with me. It looks as though you are out on one of your educational jaunts, pointing out to them the beauties of the countryside but the rest are still waiting back at home with me. It's to get out of people's minds that a group of eight girls are escaping somewhere.'

'But what happens if the Germans search under the hay?'

'I don't think they will. If you present them with four and yourself, they'll take that at face value and check those papers rather than looking for anyone else.'

'I see what you mean,' I said rather doubtfully, 'but where will we be going?'

'To La Bastide-Clairence in Basque country. Olivier often goes up there where he gets a good price for his hay.'

'And after that?'

'You'll stay at his friend's barn for a night before continuing with the rest of the journey.'

'OK. Food?'

'We've got tomorrow to get enough food together for you all for the next few days.' She looked at me with some impatience. 'Come on, Marie. We need all our wits about us. Let's get to bed and we can start organising it all tomorrow morning.'

And with that my great aunt heaved her old bones out of the upright chair towards the stairs.

'Good night, Hélène, and thank you,' I called after her, somewhat ashamed of my lack of trust in her scheme.

I heard a snort as she disappeared into the darkness.

# Chapter Forty-One

I wasn't used to snooping around a town I didn't know. In fact, I wasn't used to snooping anywhere. In Les Landes my activities had involved riding at high speed through the forest, not looking out for German soldiers.

That morning, on Tante Hélène's instructions, I went down to the boulangerie with a sack over my shoulder in order to carry the large number of loaves we needed for the next few days. Before that, I went up and down the little roads in and near the little suburb of St. Palais, trying to see if there were any roadblocks. My look-out walks were repeated after lunch and in the evening, the only difference being that I was accompanied by two of the girls each time, so that any spies in the village became used to seeing them. After all, the Germans already knew where we were all staying, and we wanted local gossip to confirm our presence. We went down out of the village and walked along the river side as if we were enjoying the exercise. I deliberately stopped along the banks, pointing out various natural features of the landscape, so it looked as though I was giving my 'colons' nature study lessons.

All day we prepared packs of food, some of which would be placed in the girls' bags and some which would go in separate sacks underneath the hay. Four girls were to ride on top with the farmer and myself, and four were to hide under the hay. The girls were to have exercise books at the ready so that they could learn more about the countryside near the mountains which were more like foothills at this point, but which rose up beyond the village to the higher peaks of the Pyrenées.

In Olivier's farmyard away from any road, I arranged the children and as many food bags as I could manage. Olivier was an elderly, but healthy-looking farmer with very little expression on his face or words to share. I had never been to such a busy farmyard before. It was a much bigger agricultural operation than anything I had seen in Les Landes – tractors parked on the side of the yard and some old ploughs too. In the horse boxes some old ploughing horses waited patiently, and two of the younger ones were being placed in the pony and trap when we arrived. The hay was on the side ready to be lifted on.

'Right girls, you will have enough air to breathe. Hay when it is first collected is prickly, but you'll get used to it. Have you got scarves which you can wind round your hair and faces to protect them?'

Scarves had been part of the escape equipment, so they were quickly produced. The girls were excited at being placed in the waggon under the hay, but Olivier had words of warning.

'Girls, you will get fed up under there and when we go over bumps and holes in the road, it won't be comfortable. Just decide now that you're not going to call out or make a noise and then you won't suddenly have to be quiet if we see people ahead on the road. If you think you're going to make a noise, stuff the end of your scarf into your mouth. You can move your legs a little when we're riding to stop them getting cramp, but not when we come to a stop, especially when there are people about. Remember, if you don't behave properly, everyone is going to suffer, not just you.'

When we had got up that morning for breakfast, it had felt like an adventure. But after the farmer's stern words, everyone looked a little cowed and frightened.

I tried to cheer my charges up.

'Girls just remember that it will only be for today. By tonight you'll be safe in a barn together again. But today we're on the move and there are dangers, especially if the Germans stop us.'

'What will happen if they find us, Sister Lucie? Will we be shot?' Marthe's big brown eyes looked up at me in terror.

'No, Marthe, you won't be shot. We might even be able to get away with an explanation and be allowed to continue. But they might turn us back, or take us to another centre, or send us back to Gurs.'

'Well, I don't mind being sent back to Gurs,' said Laurence defiantly. 'I want to see my parents.'

Annette turned on her, 'Don't be so stupid, Laurence. Your parents sent you here to keep you safe. If you're sent back, it means you won't be. And none of us will be. We have to do what the farmer says.'

I tried to intervene as the girls glowered at each other. 'Laurence, I'm afraid Annette is right. This is the way for you to keep safe and this is what your parents want.' I looked up at the group. 'Don't worry girls. All will be well, but you are the oldest and you must set an example to the others. Now, all of you, promise me that you will do as you're told.'

'Yes, Sister Lucie,' they all murmured dutifully, as Olivier and his wife, Julienne, handed them up to the wagon. Julienne had a sense of humour, which made up for her husband's dour looks.

'You girls, I always wanted to travel on hay ricks when I was your age. They're soft and you can have some quite good tickles.' Suddenly she started tickling the faces of each of the girls, so that within minutes they were rolling around on the hay laughing. Her action dissolved all the tension in the group immediately.

'Now, that was just a taster. Think what fun you'll have when you get to the other end.'

If we're altogether and alive, I thought to myself, suddenly afraid. During the last few days I had felt protected by Tante Hélène against the reality of what was taking place. Now, with the first rays of sun coming over the mountains, but the air still chilly, I realised that I was ill-prepared for what lay ahead.

We turned down towards the end of the farmyard and the lane which led to Hélène's end of the village. The cart stopped outside her house, the door opened, and the four youngest girls came forward, ready for the journey and carrying a bag each which contained extra food supplies.

'Good-bye, my dear little cherubs,' said my aunt. 'I have loved having every single one of you. Enjoy your journey with Sister Lucie and be good for her.'

They kissed her goodbye and I realised that Hélène's words were to all of them, including those hidden under the hay.

'Come and see me another time,' she whispered in my ear. 'And tell me when they are safe.'

I saluted her quickly, anxious to help the girls onto the waggon and to waste as little time as possible.

'For the moment I will go in the front with Olivier, but later two of you can swop with me and sit at the front.'

Off we went, the horses descending slowly down the steep hill towards the church, then picking up speed as we went over the bridge alongside the little river and up the winding valley road.

# Chapter Forty-Two

In the half-light we were silent. Two of the little girls on top of the hay settled down to make up for the sleep which they had missed through their early morning start. Even if it had been the right time for talk between Olivier and me, it was clear that the farmer was not at ease with chat. I had nothing to do but observe the hay in the fields being bound together, the buzzards above us who were hovering over the higher land to our left and the river which followed the road up to the higher hills. Occasionally a farmer would appear outside a farmhouse and wave to Olivier. There was nothing particularly conspicuous about our hay waggon.

Ten miles along the road, down the next valley, outside a small 'mairie', we came across a German road bloc. I warned the girls,

'There's nothing worrying about it. I've got your papers, and, if he questions you, just remember that I'm the Catholic monitrice in charge of your stay at the 'colonie'.

'Papers,' the guard demanded of Olivier, curtly but not hostilely. It must be a good job I thought, for a German soldier. Nothing much to disturb a peaceful day out in the country.

'So where are you going and why?' he asked almost laconically.

'To Bastide, like I always do at this time of year, to get the hay dried and cut and ready for winter. They've got the correct, more modern machines there, and the farmers' cooperative at La Bastide are my friends.'

'And you, mademoiselle, what are you doing with these children?'

'I'm looking after them at the colonie near Bayonne. They've been staying with me at my great aunt's house near Pau. I've got them away from the town, so they can have some exposure to country life. Bayonne doesn't have the same country air as here.'

He examined the papers and walked round the cart. Then he stamped the papers and instructed us to proceed. When we were well past the next village, I called out, 'Well done, girls. You behaved beautifully and he didn't seem at all suspicious.'

That was our only interruption all through the day. We stopped in the early afternoon so that we could drink some water from the stream and have a casse croûte. All the girls needed to go to the toilet in the field and the hidden ones came out, covered in bits of straw but otherwise cheerful. I made them sit still four at a time while the others worked off some energy so that anyone from the road could only see four girls. Then they climbed back into their original places and we set off again.

By the end of the afternoon the look of the farmhouses had changed, and it was clear that we were in Basque country. A misty rain started to descend, and the younger children were becoming wet.

Olivier gave them a measured look. 'Don't complain. You'll only end up a little wet, but I need to worry about my stock of hay. It's far more serious if that gets a soaking.'

But the rain stopped and soon we were turning up the steep hill, which led around a corner to the sharp ascent of the main street of La Bastide-Clairence. Before the war it had been a prosperous little town, with cafes at the service of those who came up for the day from Biarritz. Nowadays no one had the money or the leisure to spend their time sitting in street cafes and so the street looked somewhat neglected. We made a sharp right hand turn up between some farm buildings which lined the road and into a farm courtyard.

'Carlos! Genevieve!' Olivier called out. In a moment two people came around the corner of the farmhouse. Carlos was a farmer of Spanish origin, who was rather more affectionate and demonstrative than Olivier. He tried unsuccessfully to grab him round his neck.

'Good to see you, my old friend.'

'We'll get the hay indoors in a minute, but first let me get these young ladies down and into the house.' My girls giggled and were delighted that such a good-looking farmer was so attentive in helping them down.

'Come into the kitchen,' his wife brushed him aside. By contrast, she was slightly plainer looking, and less effusive than her husband. 'I've got some tea and goûter for you all. Then we'll talk about where you are staying the night.'

'Olivier, don't let the others out here,' I warned. 'Take the horses into the barn and uncouple them. Then send the older girls into the farmhouse kitchen.' The four older girls were all looking a little bedraggled and found it hard to find their feet again.

'Sister Lucie, I've had pins and needles for the last hour. I can hardly feel my feet,' complained Marthe. She limped to the side of the barn.

'Yes, that's why she's been kicking me under the straw to make sure she's still got feet. I can assure you she has,' said Laurence, looking annoyed at her friend.

'And I thought I was going to explode with coughing a few miles back,' continued Marthe. 'The straw really got to me.'

'I couldn't believe that we didn't get stopped again, could you, Sister Lucie?'

Annick's eyes were shining with excitement and the realisation that the escape was actually taking place. I put my arm round them before we left the barn.

'I'm so proud of you girls. You've done really well. And here we are, 60 kms further up the mountains towards our goal. Come on, let's join the others and see what Geneviève has got for us.'

I thought that 'goûter' was an understatement. Heaven only knows where she got all the ingredients. I could only think that she had been gradually storing up rations until she thought she might have an excuse for a bit of a tea party. If she wanted an appreciative audience, she could not have done better than my group of eight little girls.

'I can't believe that this is genuine cream. I haven't seen any since we lived in Paris and Maman made cream caramel choux.'

'And the jam! This is nothing like the watered-down stuff you find in the shops!'

'Madame, thank you so much. This is like a banquet!'

Geneviève laughed. 'Don't mention it, my dears. I thought you might need something special after all that riding in the hay.'

'And I'm afraid,' she added more practically, 'that it's more hay tonight. You'll all be sleeping in the top barn. Carlos will show you where afterwards. I hate not to have you in my house, but we can't risk it with the farmhouse being so near the road. You'll be comfortable there for the night and then you'll come down here for breakfast tomorrow.'

'If breakfast is anything like tonight's tea, you'll have them here two hours early tomorrow morning,' I assured her.

She laughed, a good-natured laugh which accepted the compliment I was giving her. 'Not too early. We don't want to draw any attention to you. The less noise you make to and from the barn, the better. Now, girls, you can use the outside WC here before Carlos takes you up to the barn.'

Sleeping in the barn was another adventure as far as the girls were concerned. We were silent on our way up there, but, once installed, even though we had only torch light, the hay was plentiful and warm.

'Are we changing into night things, Sister Lucie?' Martine as usual was concerned to behave correctly. Living in a refugee camp in Gurs had not changed her upbringing or her character.

I considered carefully what would be best for my group of young girls. It wasn't necessary to change, but I reckoned that there would be nights ahead when 'changing for bed' would be out of the question. Better to preserve some sense of normality for as long as possible.

'I think that would be a good idea,' I answered. 'Then our clothes will feel fresher tomorrow morning. Find your nighties in your bags but try not to tip everything out of the bags so that things get lost in the hay. Nothing must give away our presence to the authorities.'

'Does that mean they'll come after us later,' asked Mireille, understandably anxious about her safety.

'No, but more likely that the people living here will be in big trouble for sheltering us.'

Silence. They were too young to understand what looking after young Jewish girls might mean for Carlos and Geneviève and I didn't want to enlighten them.

Fifteen minutes later I had eight little girls, dressed in nightdresses, burrowing their way into straw beds. We might have been on a family camping holiday.

'Where will we go tomorrow, Sister Lucie?'

'Ah, you'll have to wait till after breakfast to find out. I can't wait for Geneviève's breakfast, can you?'

## Chapter Forty-Three

Once more it was an early call from our surprisingly comfortable beds in the straw. I had slept the night alongside the girls and that changed the way they saw me. I was now one with them and there was no one else for them to rely on. They would have been shocked to know that I had no more idea about the next stage of our journey than they had. That had been part of Father Julien's advice to me.

'In the Resistance you must only do things on a need to know basis, Marie. Then you can't be caught out or betray people.'

'But surely I can't think ahead if I have no knowledge of the plan,' I objected.

'That's an advantage. You'll see,' he had promised when we had been in the car together on the coastal road from Léon. 'For a project like this which is so big, you have to work with other people. But other people are the danger. What you don't know, you can't give away. And circumstances on the ground change, and it's only someone in the immediate area who understands these things. If the Germans suddenly change their normal patrol, it's only the local person who sees that. So, trust me, it's the best way.'

It was true that I felt relief that I didn't have too much knowledge, a sort of lifting of responsibility. It also gave me a strange sense of adventure. Where might we be by the end of the day?

I had predicted correctly that Geneviève would be big on breakfast. She clearly did her own baking and had added pieces of cheese from her dairy farm to give sustenance and soothing bowls of warm milky drinks.

Olivier appeared at the door of the kitchen as we were finishing.

'While my cousin here deals with the business of hay, I'm going to take you girls walking to the next village.'

'How far is that?' interrupted Agnès, looking rather worried.

'About 10 kilometres.'

'10 kilometres!' she exclaimed. I've never walked that far in my life.' Many of these girls, I discovered, were town-bred, despite their enforced stay at Gurs camp. Walking in the countryside either for work or pleasure was not part of their regime.

'Well, it's either walking or you get left behind and discovered by the Germans,' said Olivier gruffly. 'The bus from Bayonne calls at Hasparren before it goes to Cambo-les-Bains. We're starting off there now before it gets light and everyone is out looking at you. Later on, you'll have several stops when Sister Lucie here will give you some interesting lessons. Children from colonies de vacances get fresh air and exercise.'

'We always had a car to take us on days out,' complained Annick.

'Well, my lady, maybe you had a chauffeur too. But you're not going to get one here. It's walking, or nothing.'

'Come on girls,' I said gaily, ignoring Annick's superior airs and Olivier's disdain, 'let's get these bowls washed up and we'll be off. You were cooped up so long yesterday on that hay cart. It'll do us all good to have some exercise.'

'And no talking as we leave here and go through the town. Later in the day, when we get the bus, you can make as much noise as you like, provided you talk about life in a colonie.'

Apart from Agnès and Annick, no one else had any comment to make. We formed an orderly queue at the washing up sink.

In the outside pre-dawn darkness, objections vanished, and fear and apprehension took their place. Carrying our bags, we walked out of the farmyard, silently down the big hill of the main street which was completely deserted. As we came to the outskirts of the little town, we met a few workers getting ready for the day, but they seemed completely unconcerned by the sight of eight girls and their monitrice walking by. Perhaps in time of war you do not want to register what is unusual because knowledge can bring you trouble.

I tried to compensate for the peculiarity of the situation by wishing 'Bonne Journée' to each worker we met and smiling, as if we were doing what was completely normal. Most of them muttered, 'Bonjour,

Mademoiselle,' under their breath and turned their collars up against the cold dawn.

Outside the village we followed the road, which Olivier had pointed out to me the day before, and which led down towards the river. We walked silently, focused on the task of getting as far as possible on our journey without being interrupted by casual conversation. Yesterday's trip on the hay waggon had been exciting. Today's long walk was tiring and for the first time the girls seemed to understand something of the seriousness of the journey they had undertaken.

We stopped down at the river for our casse croûte and water which we had brought with us. Down, away from the road, we broke our silence and the girls gradually rediscovered their voices.

'I can't believe I've walked all this way already,' said Agnès, sounding very sorry for herself.

'Just because you've been taken everywhere by car in your life, you think you're too good for a morning's walk,' retorted Laurence.

'I didn't notice you any further ahead than me.'

'Girls, please stop arguing. We've all made it here. You've walked very well, especially the younger ones. I suggest that before we have our bread and cheese, we take our shoes and socks off and have a good paddle.'

The younger ones had their socks off before I had even finished the sentence and soon, they were scampering around flicking water at each other and dangling their feet above the sides of the river which was running quite fast. The seriousness of our journey and any indignation about having to walk so far were soon forgotten in the playfulness of the moment.

'Girls don't get yourselves soaked,' I warned, every bit the responsible monitrice. 'We've only got a short time to dry out and you don't want to go to sleep tonight in wet clothes.'

My voice was unaccustomed to such domestic warnings. I knew that this was the sort of thing that teachers were supposed to say but it didn't feel like me. It was only the focus of getting the task done and the people to be rescued, which made me say it. I was not a natural monitrice. It was partly because the girls showed such instinctive trust in my decisions that I felt that I should speak with authority over trifling matters.

After lunch we took the road alongside the river until it turned in one direction over a bridge and up north to Dax and Les Landes and then started to wind its way up the hill to another village.

'My feet hurt, Sister Lucie.'

'It's not far now. just up this hill and then we'll get the bus. Come on, Florence. Give me your bag. Does anyone know a song we can sing?'

Some of the older ones had been members of 'les Eclaireurs d'Israel' which was the Jewish equivalent of the Scout movement and they started singing. I stopped suddenly. 'No Jewish songs. That would be asking for trouble.'

'But those are the ones we know.'

'I'm sure that's true but not here. Some of you must know some traditional French songs,' and I started them off with 'sur le pont d'Avignon' and this then jogged their memories about songs they had learnt at school.

Olivier had given me money for the bus fares and to my relief we were at the Hasparren bus stop in time to catch the bus which would take us to Cambo-les-Bains, another twenty kilometres further towards the border.

'You're rather young to have so many children, mademoiselle, aren't you?' The driver winked at me in a mildly flirtatious manner.

'Of course, monsieur, especially as I'm a soeur religieuse.'

'Oh, sorry, sister, I didn't notice the headscarf. What are you doing here?'

'We're from one of the colonies.'

'Isn't it a bit late in the year?

'We've got a special extension from the diocese this year. We're doing work on autumn flora. Then we're going back to school in Pau. It's all part of a partnership between a colonie and a Catholic school,' I lied fluently.

'Ah well, it may be war-time, but youngsters still have a better time at school than I did.'

'Yes, but in war time our youngsters need a break from bad news.'

'Yes, that's true. We all do. Let's hope the Free French get through to North Africa and bring us help.'

'Indeed, monsieur, as long as France finds peace.'

I hoped that that was an acceptable, general wish. I had no idea at the time what he meant by the Free French getting through to north Africa.

215

We had been cut off from the news for weeks, but I thought it sounded patriotic and Christian.

'Be careful,' Patrice had taught me back in St. Paul, 'how you react when people express sentiments about liberty. Sometimes people are just testing you to see where you stand and, if questioned, will report you to the Germans to earn their favour.' I had learnt to be cautious about expressing my support for the Free French in France.

No one stopped the bus or came to check our papers while we were travelling. Two of the younger girls looked as though they were dropping off to sleep in the warmth of the bus, after their long walk.

'Cambo-les-Bains,' shouted the driver, and I hurriedly got everyone to wake up and find their things. 'No one is to leave any of their belongings on the bus. Come on, girls, this is our destination.'

Cambo-les-Bains was an old town, where earlier in the century, wealthy French people had come to test the waters and to live in luxury, even though the town was Basque in origin. Money is not fussy about ethnicity. Cambo is on the edge of the Pyrénées with access to healing waters, and it was ready to persuade any wealthy hypochondriac to part with their money.

I had my instructions, given by Olivier, before he left us by the river. Down the hill overlooking the river's source was a luxury hotel. For some reason Father Julien had a contact in the housekeeping department. We could spend the night there, even have a bed for the night and be looked after. No wealthy spa visitor could have been as grateful for this hotel as we were, when we crept up the back path to the entrance for the domestics. We were lodged for the night in the former servants' quarters which were now deserted. Indeed, there were only one or two elderly aristocrats who hardly seemed to realise that a war was happening. Their own personal safety and satisfaction were far more important to them than any pan-European war. Money has always managed to escape that which is most uncomfortable.

# Chapter Forty-Four

I must have become careless, as we had been free from interference by the Germans since that first encounter outside St. Palais. In the basement kitchens at the back of the huge hotel, where we were fed by the housekeeper, there seemed hardly anyone to meet. The younger staff had all left to volunteer for the war effort and there were only one or two older servants left. They were all delighted to see the children and made a fuss of them.

In the company of one of these employees, I went upstairs to look around and I glimpsed a few elderly clients in the hotel dining room. They had all changed for dinner into clothes which looked as though they had been fashionable twenty years ago. I had wanted to see for myself what sort of people were there, in case there was any sort of emergency in the middle of the night and then I intended to return to my charges. I was totally unprepared to be accosted by a German officer in the long corridor leading past the dining room and into the reception area. When I saw him, I was tempted to run, but I knew that this would only arouse his suspicions.

'Mademoiselle,' he started charmingly, clicking his heels and removing his cap in time honoured courtesy. 'I didn't know that such a delightful guest was staying at this hotel.'

'I…I'm not really staying… I mean I'm just staying for a couple of nights with my godparents who are the housekeepers here,' I stumbled through my explanation. I was really perturbed as to whether I should own up to the presence of the girls or not. Up until now I had always taken the advice of Father Julien – 'Pretend as little as possible. Show the girls but give a good reason for them being there.' However, the thought of this man sitting down with me and questioning me about the background of each of my girls did not seem like a good idea. I decided to chance a lie which did not involve them.

'I'm just here for a couple of nights – a little holiday really. I come from Les Landes and my godparents said I could come and see them. I'm a novice from Léon.'

'I didn't know that novices had holidays.'

'Not exactly a holiday, more a break before I go on my retreat next week. The mother superior gave me permission.'

'And the owner of the hotel knows what hospitality your godparents are offering?'

'I'm sure they do. They value my godparents' work very highly at this difficult time.'

'No doubt. But they value their food rations too, especially for guests who pay a lot to stay here.'

'Of course, sir, but I eat very little.'

'I can see that, mademoiselle, or 'sister' as I should call you, but I'd like to check that your papers are in order.'

'Oh, they are sir. Shall I bring them up to you now?'

'No. I'll come down and see them.'

Panic overtook me. I needed to get the girls away from the kitchen area.

'Of course, sir, but the servants are just finishing serving up and they're very busy in the kitchen at the moment. Please allow me to help with the washing up there which my godmother has asked me to do, and then I can receive you.'

He smiled pleasantly. 'I forgot that a religieuse might use her holiday to help her godmother.'

'I should hope so sir, especially when they're so hard working and they've been kind enough to let me stay. Would half an hour be alright?'

I was about to suggest that he could have a drink in the kitchen with us but decided that such an offer would seem too friendly. A religieuse would be polite to anyone but she would still be French in her loyalties.

'Half an hour would be excellent, only I was going to suggest that you have a coffee with me now in the dining room.'

218

I was suitably impressed by the prospect of real coffee if not by being entertained by a German officer. The residents must be paying highly for such a luxury.

'If you'll excuse me sir, I should go and help my godmother now, because she is expecting me, and it is a very busy time for them with so few servants to help.'

'I will be there in thirty minutes, Mademoiselle.'

I tried not to run straight down the corridor but to walk in a dignified way. Soon I was back down in the kitchen where the girls were relaxing over some food.

'Quickly, girls.' I was reluctant to worry them when they looked so at ease, but I knew that I must not make any mistake now. 'A German officer is coming to check my papers in thirty minutes. You must all disappear. Can they go upstairs to the bedrooms?' I asked the housekeeper who was stirring a white sauce to be part of the tarte au citron for tomorrow.

'Yes, yes. I must let the sauce thicken. Then I'll take them. Make sure they don't leave anything behind them.'

I grabbed a pair of damp socks which Agnès had taken off, hoping to dry them in the warm kitchen. 'I can dry some things later for you, but you must pick up all your things now. Sorry you haven't finished eating.' This was to one of the girls who was toying with the leftovers of some stew.

'Come on. He mustn't see you or suspect your presence. I must have time to clear up your plates too. Now, when we go out of the kitchen up the stairs, not a single word from anyone.'

Instinctively they knew this was serious and not a word was said. One of the little girls slipped on one of the stairs and came out with a loud 'ah' but the others all looked at her crossly and she put her hand over her mouth, as I helped her up and we followed Mme Chinan up four flights of stairs to the attic where they were to sleep.

I turned to give them instructions. 'No one comes up here, but all the same, no noise, at least while that German might be snooping. The guests are too old and deaf to be able to hear anything.'

I kissed each girl to give them reassurance and told them to get ready for bed. I put the three oldest girls in charge of the young ones and told them I would be up in about an hour. 'You can't go to the toilet yet, because they might hear you even four floors below. If anyone is really bursting, there are chamber pots under the bed, but try not to use them. You can whisper to each other if you need to but no more than that.'

I shut the corridor door behind me and sped downstairs. I must clear the plates and be doing the washing up when the officer arrived. I had left the girls' papers in the bedroom with them and had kept mine with me. I just had time to sweep the table clean, tell M. and Mme Chinan that they were now my godparents and make up a quick story of how they knew me in Les Landes, and the officer appeared while I was starting the washing up.

He stood at the entrance surveying the scene. 'Ah, so good evening, Mme Chinan. I see that your god daughter is an exemplary religieuse.'

'Yes, sir, she's always been a helpful girl even before she went into the church and we're glad to have her here for a couple of days.'

He inspected my papers which were of course in order.

'How much have you seen of Cambo, Sister Lucie?'

'Not very much, sir. I only arrived this afternoon.'

'Oh, was that by bus?'

I almost said 'yes' and then realised that, if he checked with the bus driver, he would soon be told about the girls. Happily, Mme Chinon intervened.

'No, no. My husband picked her up from Bayonne. He had gone to do some business there for one of our guests.'

The answer seemed to satisfy him. 'Perhaps I could show you around the town in the morning, Mademoiselle?'

I didn't want to refuse. 'That would be fine, Monsieur. Perhaps before I come back to help prepare dinner for the residents?'

'What a perfect god daughter you have, Mme Chinan.'

She chuckled. 'It must be the advantage of having a god daughter who feels called to be a religieuse.'

He got up from the table bowing.

'Indeed, Madame, though it does seem to be a shame to be hiding such a paragon of virtue in a nunnery.' The he turned to me. 'Nine O'clock outside the front of the hotel too early for you?'

I had hoped to have us leaving Cambo by 9 O'clock so that we would have a full day to walk. 'That would be lovely.' I smiled in what I hoped was a mixture of modest delight and care for my reputation as a novice.

The girls were far more interested in my flirtation with a German officer than with their walking schedule.

'That gives us a whole morning to lie in bed – bliss!'

'And your German officer can't be investigating us as, at the same time, walking out with you.'

'I am not walking out with him, Laurence. Apart from the fact that I am a religieuse, he is an enemy soldier and a German and romance is not part of what is happening.'

'It's a shame,' said eleven-year old Laurence, who obviously thought she knew how romance worked, 'that German officers are so good looking. Maybe if they just married a lot of French girls, all our problems would be over.'

'How can you say that, Laurence, when they're killing our people?' Agnès looked at her in disgust. 'You're so superficial.'

In answer, Laurence flicked her light brown hair away from her shoulders. 'Maybe I am superficial, Agnès, but at least I have some fun.'

Ignoring the quarrel, they all clamoured, 'Tell us what he said to you, Sister Lucie, when you come back.'

# Chapter Forty-Five

I was amused by the thought of the girls assessing my small talk with Commander Schreiben and of my own inexperience in flirting with men. Most of the night before my date I spent in fear – fear that he knew what I was doing, that he would try to catch me out and that I would somehow betray my hosts, and that I would jeopardise the whole escape plan. I had begun to feel fiercely protective of my little girls.

He had arranged to meet me at the top of the hill in the direction of the main town. I was relieved to find that he was not staying at the hotel and that our little tour of the town did not start there.

He gave me a tour of the spa waters themselves, explaining about the special nature of the water coming down from the Pyrenées, and comparing it to several spas he knew in Germany. He gave me the whole talk in a punctilious and organised way and very soon I became bored by so much detail. A few pieces of gossip about aristocratic life in the spas might have livened up his narrative, but Commander Schreiben did not specialise in imagination or frivolity. I was so worried about his possible suspicions that I paid a great deal of attention to what he was saying. He appeared to be gratified by my interest.

'So, mademoiselle, shall we have some coffee in the town?'

Suddenly I was worried that I might be seen by the townspeople as a collaborator and quickly declined.

'Your talk has been most instructive, Commander, but I fear that my godparents will be organising lunch and I need to help them. Besides, I am not sure it would appropriate for a religieuse to be having coffee with a man in public.' At long last religion was coming to my rescue!

'It is only natural for you to be concerned about your reputation, but I would always behave correctly with you, mademoiselle. I am indeed a church goer in my own town in Germany, and I respect the religious beliefs of others.'

'I'm pleased to hear it, Commander,' I replied piously. 'How about you taking me to see the church instead? I've never visited the church here before.'

My suggestion led to another boring recital about the history of the little church and the history of the Basque Catholic traditions. It turned out that Commander Schreiben knew far more about the history of the Basques than I did.

By lunch time I was able to make my excuses and go back to the hotel, leaving the commander in the centre of town.

'What was he like, Sister Lucie?'

'Did he bring you flowers?'

'Did you go for a meal with him?'

'Did he propose marriage to you?'

The questions became more and more improbable – part of the romantic notions of a group of innocent girls. We laughed together, but my reputation had definitely soared in their estimation. I was now no longer just a pious, single religious novice, but a young woman who had attracted the attention of a desirable man.

I felt strangely angry with the German army. These young girls had idealistic reveries about their soldiers whose real purpose was to find them and kill them. How incongruous the disparity between the two different ideals! It made me feel very protective towards my group of girls. They loved me because they now saw me as they wanted to be when they were older. The war, the probable disappearance of their parents, their dangerous escape into Spain – all of that painful reality meant nothing to them in comparison with their daydreams, which were no different to those of any other young French girl at the time.

My tour of the town, necessary in order to allay the German soldier's suspicions, led to a delay in our plans. I felt that we now had insufficient daylight time for walking to the village of Bidarray, which was scheduled as our next stop. I also thought that we might be more visible if I tried to lead the girls out of Cambo at this hour of day. We would have to stay another night in the hotel. We could not risk going down to the kitchen again, so food had to be brought up to them. I volunteered to help serve in the dining room and I was glad that I made that part of my routine as the Commander appeared again for his evening meal. I agreed to have a coffee with him in the reception area of the hotel later. He was so sorry, he said at the end of the evening, that he could not escort me anywhere the next day, because his military duties were calling him away further south for a couple of days. This time I felt flattered by his attention as well as relieved to hear about his imminent departure. It was the first time in my life that I had been invited to an after-dinner coffee by any man, let alone such a good looking, urbane man. I thought that if I had not been Sister Lucie, I might have responded to his interest with some genuine flirtation.

We left the following day before dawn, covering our retreat from the hotel and the town of Cambo in the dark. I had been given clear instructions about the way ahead by the housekeeper – out through the town, along level ground which would gradually become hillier. As the sun came over the hills, we passed the 'foret des lapins' which I had been told about. The girls were transfixed by the sight of hundreds of rabbits scurrying across the field and hills. We put our bags down over the fences and the girls chased the bunnies into their burrows and up the hills. The girls were mainly town children from Toulouse and a couple from Paris and they were unused to such delights. For forty minutes they were shrieking with excitement as they hurtled themselves about almost as if they were entering the burrows themselves. The rabbits, who had become used to war time indifference on the part of humans, since all the hunting guns had supposedly been confiscated by the Germans, must have wondered what sort of crazy nightmare was erupting into their lives.

Shortly after this interlude, we cut up a small road, past a church and alongside some old houses, which were clearly occupied, but which showed no immediate sign of their inhabitants. The girls instinctively walked in twos in silence past them. They had begun to take their own precautions without being asked. Another small lane cut away from that road and soon we were following a narrow but tumultuous river with the water gushing through boulders and drowning out all other sounds. The side of the road became more enclosed by an overhanging cliff face and gradually narrowed until it was a dirt track. Just when we thought the track might disappear altogether, we turned a sharp bend and the land widened and flattened out. The riverbanks became much more accessible and ancient paving stones led from one side of the river across a small tributary. The sound of the water died down and suddenly everyone relaxed.

'Yes, you can all go down, girls. Let's take a break. But take your shoes and socks off first. I don't want you cold and wet for the next part of the journey.'

'You said that a few days ago too,' pointed out one of my charges, dismissively. 'It turned out alright then. We did get dry.'

'Yes, but we were about to get a bus and we ended up at the hotel at Cambo. But there's no bus here and no hotel tonight, so get those shoes and socks off.'

'You mean we've got to walk again after this, even though we've walked for ever this morning?' complained one of the girls.

'Yes, I'm afraid so, Rose. But don't worry; it's beautiful countryside. The weather's still good and you'll enjoy yourselves.'

Rose and her friends looked at me with troubled eyes. They weren't at all sure that my idea of 'enjoying themselves' was the same as theirs. With that statement I believe that I showed how far I had come as a guide and as a leader since the early days. I was assuming that I knew better than them what they wanted, and I was going to make them believe me. With every new incident, they were being moulded into my little group of followers. My class at school in St. Paul would never have recognised my transformation from loner who scorned all group confidences to youth leader. I had started to fit in! As the girls paddled in the shallow water, even jumping from the stones into the water and daring each other to see how far they could reach, I lazed back on the river side thinking about my schooling and Alain. I was glad that I was involved in rescuing his people, but I wondered where he was and whether he had kept himself safe. It would have been far more satisfactory to be hiking up these mountains with him and to be delivering him safe across the border. Sadly, I couldn't see Alain as part of a group, which was heading towards safety.

'Alright everyone, Madame gave us some casse croûte and apples and you can get water from the river to wash it down.'

They were all tired from their play in the water but contented. I wondered how long they would stay that way. As we took the track which led over the next hill and then into the next valley, some of them started to slow down and needed constant chivvying. In the end I took the older ones aside.

'Girls, you've got to help me. Take two of the younger ones between you. I know you're not used to walking but this is the only way. We've got to get to Bidarray by nightfall.'

'Why are we going there, Sister Lucie?'

'Because it's on a back route to Spain. Because it's very small and on a plateau, so you can look around and see what's happening. And because Father Julien has a friend there and he's going to help us.'

'That's alright then. We like Father Julien, so we'll like his friend.'

That sort of simple logic on the part of Agnès cheered them all up. What they weren't prepared for was the cold, ancient church which sheltered them for the night or for the hardness of the pews where they lay down to sleep. But by the time we got there, three hours later, I was glad of any resting place.

# Chapter Forty-Six

I had been told to approach the central village of Bidarray carefully. The back road from Cambo had followed the river round and, apart from the girls being very tired at the end of a long journey, it was not a difficult walk. The road met an old bridge which led onto the main road to St. Jean Pied de Port, but we did not take it. Instead, we skirted round the bridge, and rounded the corner through some old houses and shops of the village, including an old hostelry which was now deserted. A very steep hill faced us.

'I'm not sure I can climb any more,' whispered one of the little girls quietly to me so that the others couldn't hear. She only said what they were all thinking.

'Last one, I promise you. Our resting place is at the top of that hill so let's get there as soon as possible.'

I picked up one of the smallest children who was struggling with blisters and carried her, puffing and panting myself, for that last twenty-minute climb.

We could not see what lay ahead but when we rounded the bend at the top, we were surprised. On a steep incline on the left-hand side was a graveyard looking out onto the valley below, and which backed onto a church building.

If I had not been so tired, I would have been taken aback by the beauty and tranquillity and hidden nature of the town square. The church was four hundred years old and stood at the head of the square. Old houses were built on one side and on the other was an old village bar, but, unlike the one where I had worked, most of it was in the open air, forming part of the square, with vines trained over the top, acting as a shelter and

227

connecting to the plane trees growing outside. In the hottest part of the day it must have been a wonderful place to have a leisurely 'verre'.

We made our way round the front of the church where there was a small fountain and the girls stopped to have a drink. As we entered the church, the bells rang out for compline, the last service of the day. They frightened us with their sudden clamour, but also reassured us that this ancient service had been said in this place for centuries and it would continue, whether there was a war or not.

We stood at the back of the church while the elderly priest continued his devotions and we watched. Whether he was surprised by our appearance or not, we didn't know because he showed no awareness of our presence. If I had never seen such a service take place, it was even more unlikely that this little group of Jewish girls had, but I felt instinctively that they were strangely reassured by it. In the words repeated over the centuries in this holy place, we were being told that God would look after us as we slept. It didn't really matter what religion we had or didn't have, someone else was in charge. Not one of my group questioned or complained about what was being said. We wanted a god to be in charge of our world.

The girls were a little disappointed that Father Julien's friend was so old – a small rotund man with a completely bald head and dressed in his cassock for the service but when he had finished praying, he made us welcome.

'My housekeeper will be bringing you 'cassoulet' for you to eat as soon as I tell her you are here.'

'But Father,' interrupted Agnès, clearly worried.

'Yes, my child?'

'We can't eat it. It's got pork in it.'

He smiled wearily. 'We call it cassoulet, but I think there's everything in it except pork. We don't ask what's in it. It's edible and Jeannine has done wonders with it. But you'll have to eat it. God understands.'

Agnès looked uncertain and Laurence interrupted scornfully. 'You're always worried about stupid things Agnès. Who cares what some old rabbi has told you? We're hungry and we need to eat.'

'It's not an old Rabbi. It's what's written in the Torah,' Agnès said shyly but sure of herself.

The old priest smiled at her, understanding her religious scruples. 'Don't worry my child. The chief rabbi has given you permission to eat but I assure you it's not pork. We wouldn't give it to you knowing your religion. God understands your problem because He is love.'

The other girls turned away from the discussion. No one wanted a theological dispute when we were cold, tired and hungry. I spoke to Agnès reassuringly.

'Agnès let's trust what Father tells us here. He's a holy man and you must eat.'

The priest went off to tell his housekeeper to prepare the food and we put our bags on the pews.

'We'll never manage to sleep here, Sister Lucie. These pews are too hard.'

'Want a bet, Annick? I'm so tired, I could sleep anywhere tonight.'

I had to agree that the pews looked uninviting but by the time the housekeeper had brought us a big tureen of cassoulet, which she ladled into bowls for us, everyone was sleepy. She explained where the toilet was just outside the church and showed us how to wash ourselves in the outside fountain. She then showed us the vestry where in wooden chests a huge number of old cassocks, cushions and blankets were stored.

'You've had visitors before, Father,' I suggested to him later in the church.

The priest's face was unresponsive. 'We are always prepared, Sister Lucie and in winter up here, even our village worshippers need blankets over their knees.'

As I had predicted, the hardness of the pews did not stop us sleeping and we were surprisingly cosy with the supplies from the vestry underneath and covering us.

Father Jérémie had the first service of the day at 7am. We had to store our bedding away by then and wait in the vestry in case parishioners turned up for the early service. Afterwards I took four girls at a time over to the bar, but we sat inside at the back in case anyone should pass by in the square and be inquisitive.

'The café used to do a great trade with tourists before the war, people walking in the hills as well as pèlerins on their way to St. Jean Pied du Port.'

My interest was awakened. 'The pèlerins came here?'

'Yes, it's just off the main road. It's another twenty kilometres up the road over the border.'

I imagined some of the pèlerins I had seen in Les Landes sitting here in the café.

'It's too nice here for a pilgrimage.'

The bar owner laughed. 'You'd be surprised, sister, by what pèlerins expect these days. They're not medieval monks doing penance you know. More likely having a good time under the guise of religious observance.'

Later I asked Father Jérémie about the route to St Jean.

'Yes, at the beginning of the war we often used that route to get people over the border. But not now. It's too dangerous. The Germans always put roadblocks up there and we'd never get through.'

'So how about us? How are we going"

'You'll see. Over another mountain pass near here into Spain. Don't worry, sister. The mountains here aren't so very high and we're sending guides with you.'

'The girls aren't used to climbing you know.'

'True, but it's the only way they'll be saved and even then, we'll have to keep a look out for soldiers.'

'Do they know about this place and what you do?'

We were walking in the graveyard, while the children played among the graves.

'Yes, I think they do. We've had quite a number of people pass through over the months.'

'Aren't you afraid of being arrested?'

Father Jérémie laughed. 'At my age? What can they do to me?'

'Kill you?'

'That's the only thing they can do, sister.'

'But that's terrible.' I couldn't understand his light-hearted attitude.

'Not really, sister. The Bible says that we shouldn't be scared of those who can kill our body but not our soul.'

'I'm more scared of my body being killed than my soul.'

'That's because you're young, sister, and you don't really think your soul matters.'

It occurred to me that I was not sounding like a good Catholic sister.

Father Jérémie gestured with his hand to our surroundings. 'Living with these graves every day puts everything into perspective.'

# Chapter Forty-Seven

We all sensed that important things were about to happen, and we hoped that we would be ready.

'You'll be amazed, Sister Lucie, by what these children can cope with, if they have to.'

'I hope you're right, Father. They are mainly city children.'

The girls were having a rest after lunch, as they were tired after the very early start in church. Father Jérémie and I sat in the grass between two gravestones, looking out over the surrounding hills and valleys. It was a truly great 'look out.' Any advancing Germans could be seen miles away.

'They may be,' he agreed, 'but they want to survive. They may not talk about it, but they know instinctively that it's their only chance. We've had other groups of children here before and they've done it, but now they know that it's more serious than ever.'

'Why is that?'

'Because the Germans are really going for the 'final solution'.'

'I've heard the term before now, and it sounds horrible but what does it really mean?'

'It means that since their conference in Wannasee, they want to get rid of the Jews, not just foreign Jews, but French Jews.'

'But why?'

'I don't fully understand it myself, Sister. Why this terrible hatred? I think they've started themselves on a course of hatred and envy, and now they've got to see it through to the bitter end – almost to prove to themselves that they are right.'

'But how can they think that this is right, when it's so obviously a terrible evil?'

'Indeed, it not logical. It's mass murder. But the point is, Sister, it's happening here in France. The parents of these children are going to die.'

'It's a wonder they could bear to let their children go.'

'Not all of them have. Some of them have clung to the children, as if they might be saved by them. But the parents of these children, Sister Lucie, they knew better. They were wise. And as they were wise, their children will fulfil their wish.'

'Are you saying that these girls know that they won't see their parents again?'

Father Jérémie shook his head and sighed. 'I don't know. They won't admit it, but I wouldn't be surprised if deep within themselves, they know. They are the ones who are saving their families.'

'What happens when they get to Spain? Who will look after them there?'

'There will be people. The Jews always look after their own people. Some of them will go to Palestine.'

'To Palestine?' I was shocked. 'But that's thousands of miles away. Why there?'

'I know, but the Haganah, the Jewish organisation of defence, are already taking them there. They're getting ready for the big fight.'

'What big fight? Haven't they had enough of fighting already?'

'But It's a different fight there. There they will be proud and independent, not just trying to save their own skin. They'll stand up and fight for themselves, rather than running away.'

'It sounds pretty uncomfortable to me.' It was quite bad enough, as far as I was concerned, to escape across the Pyrenées. I had imagined that after that, they might be able to settle down and lead a normal life – not be exposed to more danger and killing.

'I'm glad that I'm leaving them at the Spanish border. That's quite enough danger for me. I need to get back to my job.'

Father Jérémie put his arm on my shoulder in a fatherly way.

'Of course, you do, my dear. You've done a brilliant job in bringing them here. And you're not bad as a 'religieuse' either.'

I laughed. 'I don't know how you can think that. I have no religious background at all.'

'Well, I wouldn't want to test your knowledge of matins and compline. But still, we shouldn't stereotype. God calls all sorts of people.'

I looked at him, puzzled. Such language was alien to me. 'I have no idea what you mean by a 'call' and I certainly haven't had one.'

It was his turn to laugh. 'No indeed, my dear. I'm not wishing it on you. Still it would be foolish to imagine that a call is only for those who are going to be a 'religieuse'. You have lots of other talents, and God may have a different job for you to do.'

'I don't think God has anything to do with it. It's what I want to do that matters.'

He chuckled. 'I think you'll find that God may well have an interest in what you want to do. Otherwise, you wouldn't be here now, would you?'

'This is getting a bit beyond me, Father. Now, can you tell me how I need to prepare the children for what lies ahead?'

'Certainly,' he replied, as we started to immerse ourselves in practical plans for the days ahead.

We waited until the following night before setting out. Father Jérémie was right in thinking that the children had a sense of imminent danger and the significance of what they were doing. During the day, they would play hide and seek round the gravestones and laugh together in the back of the bar, but they looked round fearfully as they crossed the small road in front of the square and held onto me as they settled into the pews to say goodnight.

'Sister Lucie?' came the small voice of Rose that night. 'We will be alright, won't we?'

'There's no doubt about that, Rose,' I replied, trying to sound full of confidence. 'We've come all this way safely and we're not going back now.'

'Sister Lucie?' came another small voice from the pew next to Rose's. 'Please will you pray for us?'

I didn't know how to reply but I managed something. 'I'll pray for you, when I go to bed and tomorrow, I'll ask Father Jérémie to pray for us all before we leave.'

As we gathered the following evening for final instructions, I remembered to ask Father Jérémie to pray for the group.

'What an excellent idea, Sister Lucie!'

'It was Rose and Alice's idea.'

'In that case,' he smiled kindly at the two little girls, 'a great idea to pass on.'

The girls all felt strangely comforted by his words and I saw the older girls mouthing what must have been Jewish prayers after him.

As he finished, we were joined by two mountain guides, one a sinewy, middle-aged figure, and the other a young man with a rope, who gave us instructions.

'We have to go at night, because it's too dangerous during the day. We won't be talking because talking echoes right across the valleys and alerts people to what we are doing. We must stay together unless I tell you differently. We'll stop at various points for cheese, apples and water but you mustn't lag behind. Within ten hours we'll be at the border and Maurice here will go over and see where the guards are. They're not very concerned in such a remote place, and I don't think they'll be looking for children, but we'll hold back until Maurice is sure.'

'Any questions?'

'What happens if there are guards?' asked Laurence.

'We'll be waiting till they've disappeared before we cross. But you must be silent and no crying.'

Eight pairs of eyes turned to him, terrified. I knew that I was in charge of holding that terror in check.

# Chapter Forty-Eight

As dusk started to fall about 7pm we left the church and the square and the café under the vines, as if it were some romantic model of life to which we would never return. We had looked out to the valleys and the hills from the church graveyard, but we had never once looked behind us, and now, we walked the road, leading from behind the square, past the local school and beyond. We turned off onto a path, came around the cusp of a hill onto a steep forest embankment. Although there was no strict necessity for us to be quiet at this point, we instinctively were. All of us were far too scared to indulge in girlish chatter. As we looked down between the trees, Jean-Paul, the younger guide, put his fingers to his lips.

'There are some soldiers on the road. We will wait here till they've passed.'

Immediately, four covered waggons passed us below on the road and we waited.

'Remember. They may come back again, so the moment I say, 'crouch low', do it immediately.'

We half slid down the steep hill, some of the girls letting out little yelps of fear, as they slid on the newly fallen leaves and crashed into the next tree trunk, but there were no signs of the waggons returning.

The going was easier on the road, and we went up and down well above the river which we had been following two days before. Someone had half built a bridge over the water, but it was good enough to walk on, and then we turned up onto a steep incline, with the cliff veering up vertically on our right side.

'OK. If you need to hide, on my signal, you disappear over this left side, towards the river and keep low. There's plenty of trees and vegetation so you don't need to fear discovery.'

The shadows deepened as we reached the end of the road and started on the steep Pyrenean path. We stopped for a moment to catch our breath, and, as the sunlight dissolved, saw the eagles and buzzards, hovering over the next valley, waiting for their prey. Up we went now, over huge boulders which were difficult for the youngest girls to navigate. Jean-Paul and I had to hand some of them over the gaps between the rocks, but they kept going.

Suddenly, ahead, we saw a big bend in the path, as it veered round away from the side cliffs and up and over the mountain.

Someone pulled at my skirt.

'Sister Lucie, I'm afraid.'

'You don't need to be, Florence. Jean-Paul knows what he's doing.'

'I didn't mean that, Lucie. I mean, I can't go around that bend.'

'Why ever not, Florence? That's where we're all going.'

'Have you seen the drop down?'

In truth, I had not been looking down, only up at the ascent ahead. I now saw that there was a sharp drop of 100 feet in front of the bend.

'You'll soon be round that, Florence.'

'No, I can't.' Her voice betrayed her panic. 'I'm not good at heights. My dad and brothers aren't either. I can't go there, Sister Lucie.'

'Do you think I'm going to leave you behind?'

In the half-light I could see her start to tremble violently.

'I don't know. Maybe you'll have to take the others but not me.'

'That's crazy, Florence. I'm not leaving you or anyone else behind.'

'But I can't do it.'

I called over to the older man, Maurice, who was at the back of the group.

'Maurice, we have a little girl here who's afraid of the drop.'

'That's easy. Come here, little one.' She was trying not to cry, as she looked up at the face of the big, old mountaineer.

'In a moment, you're going to get a piggy ride on my back and you're going to shut your eyes and before you know where you are, we'll be up and away. OK? Trust me.'

237

'I suppose so.'

We started off again, when suddenly there was a sharp whistle and the command came back down the line.

'Up into the caves.'

I saw that where the path went around above the sharp drop, there were some dark entrances.

Maurice led the way with Florence on his back and we all clambered up to the caves, the entrances of which were hardly discernible in the vanishing light.

We all turned our backs against the cold, wet rocky sides of the cave and Jean-Paul alone looked out.

There were one or two shouts and whistles on the road far below and a couple of soldiers appeared at the start of the path, but we were not disturbed in our cave. After half an hour, there was a continuing silence. Some of the girls had their heads on my lap and on my shoulder as we crouched for support against the rock. Three of them were falling asleep.

'Wake up, girls. Time to go again,' said Jean-Paul, standing up.

'But what if they come back or they saw us?' asked Annette uneasily.

'Don't worry. They won't. They had a good scout around, but they saw nothing. The entrance to these caves is well concealed if you don't know the area.'

'Shouldn't we stay the night here?' I asked cautiously. 'We would be less likely to miss our footing in the daylight.'

'Yes, and more likely to be caught in the light.' He looked at his watch. 'It's 11 O'clock and we've got four more hours of climbing to the border. We'll be in Spain before daylight.'

I don't know how we had the strength to do those last four hours. It was a steep climb, and I, even though I was fit through an outdoor life in Les Landes, found the going difficult with such precipitous inclines. Some of the girls jumped from boulder to boulder like little mountain goats, but others were tired and not used to such hard, physical exercise. Maurice and I took turns in giving piggy-back rides to all the youngest children. By the time we reached the top rim and crest, I was exhausted. The night at this high altitude had become bitterly cold and all of us were shivering.

I stopped just behind the crest of the mountain to hide behind the boulders while Maurice went ahead to reconnoitre.

'We're just about there, everyone, and there are no guards that I can see. Come on!'

The border was at the top with a steep, sheep path, running vertically from the highest point and down the spine of the pass. Jean-Paul was the first up with two of the smallest girls and he waited some 100 feet below for the rest of us. I followed with the other two youngest girls and then lastly Maurice with the four oldest, who raised their eyes in the dawn light to the barren hills of the Spanish Pyrenées.

We were over.

# Chapter Forty-Nine

Seeing those children go off up the steep path, and not being able to follow them, was one of the hardest things I had ever done. I had avoided sentimental goodbyes and I knew that, when I saw them up that final slope in the dawn light, before they were caught at the other end by Maurice and taken into the refuge, they had imagined that I would be following them. But I had done my job. Once they had been taken on the last stretch to the Spanish border post, they would be met by members of the Jewish Rescue Service. I had to turn back the way I had come. Although, in the next year, I did four more similar rescue operations of children from Le Vernet and from La Hille, none of them affected me as much as that first group of small girls. This was partly because I discovered so much about myself in the process and partly because I began to understand more about the cruelty of the world, in which I lived. I also began to understand more about the goodness of the ordinary French people, who sacrificed their comfort and, in some cases, their lives, to take in the refugees.

I went back to work in the bar at St. Paul, but, over the following year, I was called out four more times by the curé to do the job of rescue. Meanwhile I was supplying identity papers and food to others through the communist escape line. That now seemed part of my normal life, but each time I waited in intense anticipation for the next call from the Father to be involved in the children's escape route. Serving in the bar was now a pleasant interlude of normality between these dramatic events.

I now realise how lucky I was to have had the support and loyalty of the local population, both those who drank in the bar regularly and those who worked there. Since the war ended, I have realised how divided France became in those last months at the end of the Occupation.

Communities were divided sharply between those who turned a blind eye to the atrocities committed by the Germans and those who in revulsion, turned to help those who were being hunted. In a sense no one had the luxury of being neutral. Everyone had to decide whether to be counted and whether to accept the consequences. We were lucky in Les Landes to be spared some of the terrible reprisals which took place in Bordeaux. The gathering Resistance were made to realise that for every railway line disrupted, ten innocent people were shot. If the Germans had been hated for the carnage of the First World War, they were despised and feared for the evil edicts of the Second. Two actions angered everyone – the last attempts to liquidize the Jews, not just the foreigners but our own people, and the children in particular, and the determination to send every French male worker to the labour camps in Germany. Everyone now knew that the Germans were losing the war, but that desire to commit atrocities seemed to grow with the inevitability of defeat. Not all of them. I have no doubt that the young men who had previously visited our Hôtel du Centre in previous months had no desire to be involved in atrocities. They were ordinary, decent young men but they were forced to agree with what the bosses were doing. Those who demurred were court martialled. Ironically, at the time of my greatest activity, there were less and less visits from the Germans in Les Landes. They had more important things to do than visit an isolated bar in a small rural town. But, if they had, I thought that none of the frequenters of the bar would have turned me in. That was the extraordinary, tight-knit loyalty which small farmers in Les Landes inspired.

I had not heard from Alain for months, had no idea whether he was still in the country, when one night I decided to visit our bolthole, more to remind myself of its presence than anything else. I found a copy of Rousseau with a note inside. I responded by saying that I would be there every Thursday morning for the next few weeks. Two weeks later he was already there when I arrived. He was gaunt and starving and the first thing I did was to promise him that I would fetch him some food.

'Thanks, Marie. I'm not sure how long I'm going to last.'

'Why don't you go with the Communists and become a pèlerin like your great aunt and uncle before you?'

He laughed. 'Those were the easy times! Now it's too late!'

I was shocked by the sense of doom in his voice. 'No, it's not Alain. You can go too. We can get you out of here.'

'Yes, I've heard how good you are at the escape routes. Believe me, I'm grateful.'

'I don't want you to be grateful. I just want you to leave.'

'I'm not leaving without my family.'

'You mean your mother and the younger children? How many are there?'

'There's the twins as well as the older two. Impossible to hide them or go over the mountains with them.'

'I'm sure we could do it, Alain. Other people have. I'll get Patrice to get papers for them.'

'I don't think so. They think they're safe. They haven't the will to go.'

I was frustrated by this obtuseness.

'Well, you'll have to persuade them. Give me a week to get a plan worked out. Patrice will get the papers and Father Julien will sort out the transport.'

'So, you're a fan of the church now, Marie?'

He managed a smile at such an idea.

'I certainly wouldn't say I was religious but what Father Julien has done, as well as Father Jérémie, is fantastic.'

'I'm sure it is but I don't think it will work.'

'Let me go and see them.'

'OK. You can try.'

I tried. I did everything in my power to persuade Alain's mother to leave, but in the end, her will was to stay. She lived in an isolated farmhouse where she rarely heard the news. She was subsisting on food from her farm, her little ones were happy, and she simply did not believe in the danger. I left the bar for two days to arrange transport and the papers. Father Julien was to visit them with the car and drive them by night to the border. Alain had money from the Haganah to pay the 'passeurs', for an especially dangerous trip with such young children.

# Chapter Fifty

That night when Father Julien came to collect them, the Germans arrived at the same time. Someone in the village had tipped them off. Alain had come to make sure of their safe passage. On his way there, hiding in the woods, he saw them approach the farm and led them in a different direction, hoping to act as a decoy while the family escaped, but in the end they shot him, took his family and Father Julien back to Bordeaux. Alain's mother and his brothers and sisters were deported to Le Dranet and Auschwitz the following day and Father Julien was executed in prison in Bordeaux.

I was not implicated but I returned to my job with bitterness in my heart, knowing that someone had betrayed us. I could never look at the clientele of L'Hôtel du Centre without suspicion again.

'You know,' said my mentor, Thérèse, 'before this war is finally finished, you have to leave here.'

'Oh yes?' I was cynical about any advice I might receive. 'And where will I go? I don't have a huge choice of options. Work experience? Escape routes and bar work in an isolated village in the West of France!'

'It could be worse. You could have been working for the milice.'

I didn't answer. The mention of that hated word did not merit a reply.

'Marie, you're young and you're intelligent.'

'Am I?'

'Yes, and you know you are. Come on, Marie, everyone knows that you are intelligent, that you are the most brilliant student that the école has ever had.'

'Who says? And anyway, the most brilliant was Alain,' I retorted bitterly.

'Alain was brilliant, it's true, but everyone knows that no one had a chance against you in argument.'

'Who says?'

'Mlle Tessier. She used to joke about it. She believed in you.'

I was amazed. I hadn't heard from Mlle Tessier for months.

'I have an idea which you might be interested in,' continued Thérèse in a determined fashion.

'Really?'

I was cautious. Thérèse had a reputation for ordering things and people according to her liking.

'Yes. My cousin, Lily, has a bar with her boyfriend in Paris. They're always looking for good workers and especially now with Paris in chaos.'

'And why should she have me?'

'Because you're young and strong and I recommend you. Paris is divided between those who supported the Germans and those who didn't. With the new French government and the liberation, they need people who were firmly on the side of the Resistance.'

I didn't know too much about the official Resistance. I only knew about our local group. I wasn't sure that I wanted to be part of Parisian politics. And was working in a bar what I really wanted?'

'Come on Marie,' she cajoled, overriding my hesitation. 'You're good at talking to the clients. You're much too intelligent to carry on doing bar work for ever, but in Paris there will be opportunities.'

'What sort of opportunities?'

'There are lots of newspapers trying to make a go of it after all the arguments in the war. You could easily be a messenger girl for a newspaper and transfer to writing when they see your talents.'

'And in any case,' she added stoutly, 'What else are you going to do? Stay here at your parents' farm until you get married?'

I shuddered. That future looked bleak. I saw what a dead-end my mother had found, and I wasn't even good at the practical side of farm work like she was.

'You've got plenty of links with the communists. You could join one of their papers.'

'But I'm not a communist.' I remembered how ardently Alain and I had argued over Marx.

'Maybe not but you know enough to give you a head start. Plus, all your links with Patrice and the unions in Bordeaux.'

I laughed a hollow laugh. 'I don't think that hearing all of Patrice's ideas gives me the right to say that I'm a communist.'

Thérèse was getting frustrated and I suddenly saw myself like Madame Defarge in the village, always talking about what her Bernard had done and how hard it was to cope when he came back after the war.

'All right, Thérèse. Thank you. I'll give it a go. How will it work?'

'I'll write to my cousin and you take a letter with you just in case it doesn't arrive in the postal chaos.'

And that was how I left my home village in Les Landes and became a Parisienne.

# BOOK TWO

# Chapter One

'Don't think about leaving until those glasses are gleaming.'

Charles of the 'gleaming' eye – the eye that wants to punish me for resisting his advances and for my disdain for the job, and for my inherent laziness.

I will never give way to his advances, though it is the way to have an easier life here. I won't do it, not because I couldn't put up with his physical proximity, but because it has no purpose. If I give in, I condemn myself to an unwanted baby or a back-street Paris abortion. I've heard some of those being performed in the apartment underneath mine, the screams and moaning. And I've seen the grey faced women, hidden under their scarves, staggering out into the street later in the day. Having a baby is unthinkable here. Not that I've ever wanted a baby anyway, but certainly not in a post-war world where there's not enough to eat and no one cares for anyone else.

Charles is right about my disdain for the job. On the face of it there's no difference between the job here and the one in Hôtel du Centre. But underneath the surface, there's quite a number of differences. There are no people here I've known since childhood. I don't care about the lives of any of the clients here. And, most important of all, there's no Thérèse, acting as a surrogate mother and guiding me in the ways of the world.

She got me the job here through her cousin Lily, but Lily only wanted to do her cousin a favour. She doesn't care about me. In fact, she finds me stand-offish. I'm not even good at laughing at the jokes of the customers and I don't flirt with them.

Parisians, I've decided, don't like me. I'm too intense. I don't appreciate their sophistication. Lily doesn't like me because I'm dissatisfied, restless and lazy. I don't care enough about the job to wipe all the glasses until they're shining. I always get away with the least possible amount of work and that annoys Lily, Charles and the other waitresses. I'm proud too. I'm not the only young girl who's been taken on here since the end of the war, but I know I'm the only one with brains and potential.

Most of all I'm homesick – homesick for the old men who are arguing for and against the curé and the church and the communists, who are interested in the control of the local mairie, and who talk about it every night in the Centre but who still take each other's wives butter beans and tomatoes when they're ripe. I'm homesick for the forests and the bumpy rides on my bike. My bottom has become fleshy and dimpled since coming here. I'm homesick for the quiet of the night and the waves breaking as I hide behind the sand dunes. Most of all I'm homesick for the lack of choice – whether to be around others I know or on my own in the velvety darkness. I'm even homesick for the attic where I slept. But not of course for my mother's criticisms or stern looks of disapproval or for my father's look of resignation and disappointment.

This morning I woke up early determined to get away from the street where I work. In the last weeks I've been too tired to get up in the mornings and do anything apart from tidy my room and rinse a few clothes. Today I wandered through the quartier till I came to the offices of 'Le Rouge', which is an offshoot of Libération.

I saw the small downstairs office of what looked like a communist newspaper and acted on impulse. I pushed at the bell.

'Yes?'

'I've come with a message from Patrice.'

'Patrice who?'

'Patrice from Bordeaux.'

The buzzer allowed me to enter.

'Well?' An untidy man with a dirty collar and tie, pulled half-way down his neck looked up at me. He took his cigarette further down his mouth so that he could draw some smoke and speak at the same time.

'Who are you?'

'A friend of Patrice from Bordeaux.'

'I don't know any Patrice from Bordeaux.'

'Well, you should do. He and his father kept the Trade Union going during the war and fought the Boches.'

'What's that got to do with you?'

'I worked with him and he sends his regards.'

'So?'

'I've come to help you.'

'How?'

'To work on your paper.'

'Oh, you mean you're after a job.'

I looked round the untidy office. 'I can help you keep your office in order, run messages and help you on some assignments.'

'How do I know you're any good?'

'You don't. Try me.'

'I don't have the money.'

'You have something and a room up there.' I pointed to the floor above merely guessing that it belonged to the paper and that this man didn't live there.

'That's where Mme Dubois lives.'

'Well, Mme Dubois could do with some extra help.'

'How do you know that?'

'All ladies could do with some extra help.'

For the first time, the man chuckled.

'Right enough. What can you do?'

My mother's training came in useful at this point. 'Clean, make coffee, order your files, clear your desk. Do some interviews for you. Make myself useful.'

'Do you do shorthand?' I hesitated, wanting to lie but afraid that I would be found out.

'In a way.'

'How?'

'Not what they teach you at secretarial college, but I can get by.'

'Hmmm'

'When can I start?'

'Now.'

'Now it is.'

And that was how one morning I moved out of the domaine of the insufferable Charles and surly Lily, and into the offices of Libération. I remembered the name from some of the Resistance workers in Les Landes. The newspaper's early workers had come from their resistance work in Lyons and the North of France to have a left-wing presence in Paris after the war. There were one of a number of communist papers at the time who were trying to establish their presence in de Gaulle's capital, reminding everyone of the work which the communists had done to challenge the Occupation. I still had to clean, but it was 'clean' to make something work better, and something I believed in. I specialised in smiling to make Hervé's job feel better. I ran errands and watched for any opportunity I could find to be useful. I analysed the contents of the paper to find out what their readers wanted. I was paid even less than at the café, but I was convinced that I was on the route to what I wanted – journalism. I was happy and I rediscovered my particular talent from my days at L'Hôtel du Centre in Mimizan – the ability to make other people around me happy, at least in an environment where I felt at home.

# Chapter Two

I was genuinely happy because I had a purpose, not just survival, and I was working towards something which I wanted to do – writing. Not of course the philosophical stuff, nothing as deep as that, but Libération had an agenda – to glorify what the communists had done during the war and to work towards putting the party in power. Not that there was much hope of the latter, with de Gaulle and the Free French swaggering at every possible remembrance parade. Hervé was furious.

'They and that artistocrat come in from years away from the country during the war and act as if they have done everything for France.'

'Well, they have done something.'

Hervé gave me a look of disgust. 'Whose side are you on?'

This was where my training with Alain came in useful.

'I am on your side. I want to see the communists rewarded. They did a lot of good in Bordeaux, but that doesn't mean to say the Free French did nothing.'

'What did they do?'

'Got the broadcasts going, got into Algeria and invaded from the South and got into an alliance with Churchill.'

'And all for the purpose of keeping us down when they got back here.'

'Maybe… But you can't do anything when you're dead, and they helped to keep us alive.'

'You come here as a tea maker and tidier and you start talking philosophy and strategy.'

'That's because I'm not only a tea maker and tidier.'

'So, what are you?'

'I don't know yet but I'm going to do something.'

'You've already started. My desk hasn't been so tidy for years.'

I laughed. 'My mother would be proud of me. I never helped on the farm, but I guess she showed me how to keep things in order.'

'So, not such a bad maman after all?'

'Perhaps not.' My voice was non-committal.

'And where did you learn to think? At school?'

This conversation took place during the 'pause dejeuner', the non-time after dinner in Paris, where for a short moment there is a hiatus in the day – nothing seems to happen.

I told Hervé about Alain and our talks over the feu du bois.

'What was he – a Jew?'

'Yes. But it wasn't his Jewishness which made an impact.'

'What was it then?'

'His humanity.'

'Mmm…' Hervé made a non-committal noise which always meant he didn't want to comment.

'Too philosophical for me.'

'You mean too emotional.' He would not reply on that level.

'Anyway, Mlle Marie from Les Landes, how about finding the fiches on the Trade Union in the 'quartier est' of Paris?'

I busied myself going to the area of the room where those files might be kept. This part of the room had not yet been tidied. I knew that it was my next job.

Hervé looked at the dossiers which I brought him. 'There's not enough information here to write an article. Why don't you go and make yourself useful and find out more?'

'When?'

'Now.'

'What shall I say?'

'You'll find a way to introduce yourself. You seemed to manage with me. Use your friend, Patrice, who came in handy before. Find out what this lot did during the war and then write an article.'

'You'd trust me to do that?'

Hervé grumbled into his cigarette. 'If you don't go soon, I won't trust you at all.'

254

I knew better than to state objections. I grabbed paper, pens and some of the papers in the file. I'd read them before I got there. For now, I needed to get out of Hervé's way before he changed his mind.

'Can I take your bike?'

'If you have to.'

'It's cheaper for the paper than the metro there and back.'

'Mmmm'

Locks were unknown in Les Landes, but I knew that in Paris anything was saleable even an old, rusty bike so I made sure I knew how this one worked.

I hadn't much idea where I was going but I knew that the offices of Libération were in the north central area, and Paris is not a big city. I grabbed several sous from the box of change before leaving.

'In case I need to buy a coffee. Perks of the job.'

I left on my first assignment as a journalist.

I had the address and the name of the quartier but, apart from that, I had no real idea of where I was going. It was early afternoon, so I followed the direction opposite to the sun, remembering my father's advice about direction. 'Work out the direction you need from the sun and you'll always get there in the end.' Slightly harder to do in a congested city than in the clearings of the forest but never mind. I cycled through one chic district, then into poor and bedraggled areas, far more likely as a home for communists I thought. I asked a couple of times for the quartier est, and then the name of the road and parked my bike inside the door at the bottom of the old stairway. The old woman who acted as concierge and saw me coming in responded to my request with the information I needed, and I climbed up to a room, converted to an office, on the third floor.

Outside the door I adjusted my hair, smoothed my skirt and concentrated on being calm for my first assignment as a journalist. But no amount of arranging myself could suppress the mixture of excitement and apprehension inside my body.

'Oui?' a sharp female voice called out in response to my knock.

'Sorry, Madame, to disturb you, but I wanted to talk to the secretary.'

She looked up from her work, narrowed her eyes, and gave me an impassive stare.

'You're doing it. I am the secretary.'

This response was a bit more direct and earlier than I had expected. Clearly rehearsing my feminine charms had been a waste of time.

'Madame, I'm writing an article on Trade Unions in Paris. We're doing a series on the big cities. I've already done one on Bordeaux,' I lied fluently, hoping to sound more experienced and professional.

'For what?'

'For Le Rouge, part of Libération.'

The lady raised a quizzical eyebrow.

'Nonsense. Le Rouge doesn't have the money for that. And Hervé is too lazy to move his fat butt to get down to Bordeaux.'

I laughed. She clearly knew Hervé. 'True, but I'm not too lazy and I come from Bordeaux. I knew Patrice and his father at the Trade Union. It was easy to speak to them.'

'You think it's going to be easy to speak to me?'

'Only with your cooperation, Madame. The Trade Union in Bordeaux did lots of good things against the Boches.'

'No doubt, but the war in Paris was always different. The communists here have always been full of Jews and none of them could move. Otherwise it was the cattle trucks.'

'Of course, Madame, I understand. But don't tell me they didn't join the Resistance?'

She sighed. 'The Resistance, yes, but which part? The part that hated the Jews too, or the part that took risks for them?'

'Madame, I had Jewish friends in Bordeaux.'

'And how many of them are still alive?'

'A few.'

I began to feel nervous, not with adrenaline as before, but with the anticipation of failure. I had to have a story out of this.

'Please, madame, tell me about the trade union here over the last few years. I can help raise your profile.'

And suddenly, in a fast monologue, which I could scarcely keep up with, she did. Most of it was the propaganda and stories you would expect, which, although I scribbled down some notes, I could have almost made up myself. I needed something more exciting.

'And did any of the unionists actively defy the Boches?'

She hesitated. I felt instinctively that she had something worthwhile to tell me.

'One man here, Philippe, went down to the Vel d'Hiv and took four children out.'

'Children?'

'Yes, they were the least noticed. He took them back to Parisian families under the noses of the Germans.'

'And they're still alive now?'

'I expect so. I've never found out.'

'This man Philippe, he did something extraordinary and he belonged to the Trade Union in this quartier?'

'Yes, but it didn't help either the union's cause or the socialist cause.'

'No, it helped the human cause.'

# Chapter Three

I needed to find this man, Philippe. By this time, the secretary and I were on chatting terms and I, rich with my potential story and sous from the Libération expenses box, felt bold enough to invite her down to the café at the bottom of the street for a coffee. Her secretarial work was certainly boring enough for her to want to be distracted.

'How can I find this man, Philippe?'

'Not that easy. He doesn't work here any longer.'

'Why not?'

'Because some of the people in the union disowned him.'

'For rescuing children?'

'For bringing the whole union into danger. We could have been shut down.'

'But he didn't care about that?'

'Evidently not. He thought rescuing children was more important.'

'Sounds about right to me.'

'It's easy for you to say that. You're young and idealistic and at that point in the war, it wasn't so obvious who was going to win, and we had to live under the reality of German rule.'

'You mean, we should only do good things when it's obvious it's going to pay.'

She looked at me under hooded eye lids for a second and shrugged her shoulders. 'It's the way we all survive, Mademoiselle.'

'And yet this man, Philippe, was not a Jew himself? A communist?'

'Yes, but with Catholic origins.'

From what I knew about groups in Les Landes, that was an unusual combination of beliefs.

'Catholic, then Communist, then a rescuer of the Jews? Sounds unusual.'

'Yes, he was unusual. Wasn't good at towing the party line.'

'And what about the other people in the union here? Do they always tow the party line?'

'There's no point in belonging to a cause unless you're going to follow instructions.'

'Even when that means killing children?'

'Children have been killed before, Mademoiselle.'

'Yes. But that doesn't make it right.'

'You're young. Your wrong and right divisions are very clear to you.'

I knew I was being derailed from my purpose. I must return to Hervé with a story; otherwise he would never use me again.

'All right, Madame. I understand what you are saying. The days of occupation were tough for everyone. Where does this Philippe live?'

She hesitated. She didn't know me, and I knew that acts of revenge from every side were taking place in Paris at this time. I sought to reassure her.

'I admire what he did.'

'That's not true for everyone. There were people here who were glad of the Vel d'Hiv.'

'Enough to see the children die?'

'Enough to want revenge for what they saw as France's troubles.'

'Madame, my best friend was Jewish. He gave his life to save children.'

'If anything happens to Philippe...'

'What?'

'I'll be after you.'

She hesitated for a few seconds, then decided to trust me, or maybe it was just easier to get rid of me quickly. '40, rue des Arenes.'

'Thank you, Madam. My article will prove that the communists did something good. Our readers will be reassured.'

Even if that statement was true, it took some time for Philippe to feel reassured.

'Not everyone in the T.U. agreed with what I did.'

'If we all waited for everyone to agree with us, then we'd never do anything.'

'Perhaps you're right. Though, strangely, it wasn't a planned action – more of an impulse.'

'Even better. But why do you think you did it? Something to do with your Catholic origins?'

'Who told you about that?'

'The Union secretary. But she wasn't critical.'

'She might not be, but others certainly would be.'

'Let's just say, monsieur, it was your humanitarian instincts. Our readers will be glad that the communists can have such instincts. It's one of the more frightening things about communists that they don't appear to have instincts, only rules. What happened to the children?'

'No one is to know. It's still too dangerous.'

'Even now after the war is over?'

'We're still too close to the end of the war, despite de Gaulle's triumphal march. There are still communists here hoping for a coup.'

'But not for murder of individuals?'

'Coups bring murder whether you like it or not. Look at Eastern Europe.'

There was at this time terrible news coming in from countries like Poland and what became known as the Eastern Bloc, crushed once before by the great war machine of Nazism and now at the mercy of the Communists who were bringing murder to the streets again. It was hard for me to believe that France itself could be on the edge of such a revolution.

Philippe attempted to explain his convictions. 'I joined the communists because of all they were doing in the Resistance. I'd always had religious doubts even though I was brought up as a devout church goer and, when I saw how the church still supported Pétain and were afraid to condemn atrocities, I'd had enough. The Communists weren't perfect of course but they were honest and seemed to care about ordinary people.'

'But there wasn't much move by anyone, communists or catholics, to condemn the Nazis at Vel d'Hiv.'

'To be fair – there wasn't much anyone could do on a bigger scale. Anything more aggressive would have meant the end for the Communists and then they couldn't have fought at the end of the war and supported the liberation of France.'

So why did you decide to do something?'

'It's hard to say. I kept on thinking about my own children and, if I'd been a Jewish parent, how I'd have been desperate to save my children, even if I couldn't save myself. I went there that day to make myself confront the torment of what they were going through. That way, I couldn't ever say that I didn't know. I hung round the entrance as they went in to be registered. I picked on two mothers with two children each about eight and eleven years old. Old enough to make no noise and to stay hidden. The queue was very long. They were all being registered for death, but that queue was as ordinary as queuing to buy tickets for a concert. How the hell did the Nazis make them do that so quietly?'

'Connive at their own death you mean? Perhaps they thought they were just going to work? Labour camps in Germany. And if they behaved all would be well?'

'Yes, or the desire to be dignified in what was certain death? Or to fool themselves that it couldn't possibly be happening to them?'

'Do you think there were other people who wanted to rescue them? Did you ever ask?'

'No, I didn't. By then I was afraid of organisations. Afraid and sickened by the money which was being demanded by some to rescue Jewish people. I was confused. I just knew somehow that day that I wanted to do something to say that I wasn't part of it.'

'You did well, Philippe. You followed your instincts.'

He didn't respond to my compliment but continued with his story.

'I surveyed them all as they went in. Saw who looked intelligent with the will to live. I had borrowed a van from my friend, – he worked in an electrician's shop. I changed the plates the night before. I walked up and down the queues, even saw one of my fellow communists, who was now a policeman with his dog on guard. I borrowed his dog and cap and gave him a big tip and I spoke quietly to both mothers. I got the children by the scruff of the neck with the dog in one hand, so I looked as though I was punishing them. Everyone in the queue hated me, but the mothers understood. I took the children and they resisted. Even when they heard they were going to safety, two of the children wanted to stay with their mother. I told them that the parents would not be

261

working in Germany, but they would all die, and their parents wanted them to be rescued.'

'And where did you take them?'

'To one of the underground newspaper headquarters.'

'To the Rouge?'

'Yes. It was less risky for everyone than taking them to a family. The headquarters would get trashed by the Gestapo, but they wouldn't know which individual to arrest. They stayed there three days and nights and I took them food from home and different clothing.

One of the workers at Le Rouge who knew about it offered to have them come to her house.'

'That was brave.'

'There were brave people in Paris on all sides who dared to do what was right.'

'And you?'

'I took them to my house instead because I wasn't directly connected to the newspaper. I then arranged to go to my in-laws in the suburbs with my own two children.'

'What did you do for papers?'

'I got forged papers for nieces and nephews and I took them to one of my union contacts just outside of Paris.'

'How did they feel about that?'

'Oh, my friend Antoine's parents were good communists. I told them that the children were part of a communist group who were in danger from the Nazis.'

'And they didn't suspect?'

'Two of them didn't look like Jews and were easier to hide. The other two stayed with Antoine's parents for the rest of the war.'

'They're still there?'

'Yes, but not for long. They're off to Palestine soon. The Palmach have been around. They're orphans of course. Their only hope is Palestine.'

# Chapter Four

'Hervé,' I announced, 'I'm going to write two articles about this, one about what happened in war time and one about what is happening now.'

My boss sighed. He knew that he couldn't hold me back. I was very excited, not just about the subject matter, but the fact that I might, for the first time in my life, be about to earn my living through being a journalist, rather than through working in a bar.

'Be careful, won't you?' he warned.

'Of whom?'

'Anyone. There are still retaliation murders going on against those who worked with the Germans, those who worked with the Jews, the Catholic Church, the Communists, the list is endless.'

I laughed. 'Well, that's just about everyone in Paris. According to you, all of them may want to murder me.'

Hervé sighed. 'It's not that you're a great threat to anyone but you're an innocent abroad. It's what you know which is dangerous, and how that knowledge could be used by unscrupulous people.'

'I'll watch my back, I promise'. I just wanted to find Antoine's family in the suburbs and see what they had to say. I reassured Hervé, 'It should do your fellow communists some good – raise their profile.'

'Let's hope so. They could do with it. Go carefully, Marie.'

Sometimes I thought that Hervé wasn't as hard as he liked to pretend. To many of the reporters and workers at Libération, I could only be 'comrade.' Some of them didn't approve of my working for Hervé as his assistant – it was demeaning, they suggested.

I got the fare for the train out to Domont from the petty cash drawer. It felt too far to cycle, and I wanted to imagine the journey which Philippe had taken with those four children. There were plenty of families going out for the day and I looked at them with their picnics and 'ballons' and 'boules'. Had Philippe staged the same look with the four children that day? For his own children it had just been a pleasant visit to see their grandparents.

The further we went from the city, the poorer it looked. Families struggling with small allotments and outdoor toilets; old women sitting in front of darkened doorways, dressed in black and looking without hope or interest in life. Domont itself looked like a town which was not proud of itself, and which did not welcome visitors. There were no staff at the station. Had there been Germans at the station to check the family's papers, I wondered. I asked for the name of the house I had been given. Again, I used the name of Patrice from the 'usine' in Bordeaux. Make sure the link is with the Trade Union, not the Communists, or the Jews, Hervé had advised me. That's less suspicious.

He need not have worried. I had the feeling that even if I had announced 'assassination squad' as my link, no one would have reacted at Domont. I walked out of the station, down the road, where a waiter in a run-down café was setting up for lunch, and I followed his directions to a big old house.

'Mme Hugo?' I enquired politely speaking to a middle-aged woman, dressed in a shapeless, dingy frock and with whitening roots under her bottle red hair.

'Yes?'

'I'm a friend of Philippe's from the Union in Paris.'

'You don't sound like a Parisienne.'

'That's because I'm not. I'm a Bordelaise, a comrade of Patrice and …'

'We don't know the unionists from Bordeaux.'

'No, but you'll have heard of them. They derailed a few German trains amongst other things out there in the West.'

'Did they? Good for them. Glad to get rid of the sales Boches.'

'Of course, Madame, weren't we all? I'm interested in the children you looked after in the last few months.' The old woman put a hand through her white roots and then carefully lit a Gaullois.

'Who told you about them?'

'Philippe.'

'He should keep his mouth shut.'

'But, madame, you should be proud of what you did. You helped rescue innocent children.'

'We've learnt to be suspicious of everyone. Since the end of the war, we've learnt that one family in this village were working with the Germans.'

'What happened to them?'

'They've left the village. I don't care what happens to them if it's true, but the older son came back from the front and committed suicide. It was all just rumour, but rumour here can get you into serious trouble.'

'But you helped the children of …,' Mme Hugo interrupted me quickly.

'We helped the children of the communist unions in North East Paris.'

'That's what you were told?'

'That's what Philippe told us, and I don't want to know any more. All our lives we've been part of the trade union here at the match factory. The communists helped us, made sure that they kept their jobs. It seemed only right to help the children of some of our comrades.'

'Why did those children need helping?'

'Because the Germans were about to arrest their parents and then what would have happened to the children? No food, no one to look after them.'

'Did you know they were Jews?'

'We guessed of course but as far as we were concerned, they were children of socialists.'

'How long did you look after them?'

'For about a year. They came for them last week.'

'Who came for them?'

'The socialists from Palestine.'

'Why Palestine?'

'They were Jews, weren't they? That's where they'll be looked after.' 'Yes,' she nodded, 'the best place where there will be justice.'

Had she just persuaded herself that the offer was a good one? She must have just been glad to get rid of her charges. I couldn't imagine her enjoying having young children under her roof. Still, I thought, she had looked after them, even though that could have put their lives at risk, and perhaps her husband was more sympathetic to young people, only I couldn't find out because he was out at work when I called.

I left Domont with a heavy heart. I admired the Hugo family for taking children in, but I couldn't see much joy in what they had done.

'Don't start causing problems,' warned Hervé, when I told him. 'Write your article. Show the communists to be heroes of course, but don't get personal, and don't complicate things.'

I wanted to follow his advice, but somehow writing an article without feeling passionate about the outcome was unsatisfactory. Why should I care about the fate of two children I had never met, I asked myself? But I couldn't fool myself. I did care.

# Chapter Five

I had to admit that I felt nervous. Hervé gave me warnings and I took note. I did not follow up on the other two children who had been rescued by Philippe, but I did write two articles for Libération – one about trade unionists in Bordeaux. I changed the names and chose what to keep secret and I wrote one article about trade unionists in Paris. I took some time to write them. The ideas came tumbling out onto the page in quick succession, but I needed to check the right journalistic 'argot' and make them conform to the standard style of the newspaper. I took my advice from Hervé and he was surprisingly generous with his help. Find your own voice, he counselled, but keep within the accepted style of Libération. The readership has become used to it and like it. A bit of freshness and originality – yes, but not too much. It frightens people. Not so different as advice about mixing with new people socially I thought. Be different enough to be noticed but not too different, or people will distrust you. Another skill I needed to learn was how to type and it took me long time to get it right. Hervé was generous in giving me the odd hour to work at my articles, but he didn't have enough money to release me from the tasks of courier and tea maker and chasing around after his needs in the office. In the end it took me two months to write one article, typed in full and to have the other one handwritten.

'What do you want to be called?'

'What do you mean?'

'Best to have a pen name. It brings less attention. How about La Voyageuse Libérée? It will give you the freedom to go elsewhere, if you want to or I want you to.'

I was outrageously proud of myself when that first article was published. It felt as though I had conquered the world. The only sadness I felt was that there was no one to share it with. Alain, whose good opinion I coveted more than anyone else's, was dead. My parents didn't read newspapers, especially politically motivated ones, and would not have seen it as an achievement. Thérèse was the only one who had believed in me and helped me. I decided to send her a copy. I affixed a note, 'Read the article on Page 4. You have helped me, Thank you, Marie.'

'Coming for a verre de vin, Marie?'

Hervé had asked me before, but I had always felt too shy to join him and his friends. Now I wanted to be with other people who might have read my article. We were going to the bar just down the street from the office – seedy, cheap, filled with the dark, dirty fumes of Gaullois, but the haunt of journalists and office staff from other small papers – and I wanted to belong.

Hervé hardly bothered to introduce me. I realised that this group had been meeting for years and, in order to belong, you needed to earn your membership. There were two women amongst the group of 8 – 10 men there – Madeleine, who was in her middle twenties and a hanger on at 'La Révolution Française,' and Pascale, a mature woman who had earned her place with the men in front line journalism and had been part of the Resistance.

No one acknowledged me but I soon realised that they knew all about me. For at least two hours I sat next to Hervé without commenting. The talk was about the hoped-for revolution, the disappointment with de Gaulle, and the need for their papers to speak out and energise the people. Everywhere in the streets de Gaulle was spoken of with admiration. Mme Dubois, whose house I cleaned and where I lodged, regaled me with stories of his courage and leadership. But at the Bar and Tabac du Carrefour, he was reviled.

At last I spoke up. 'Why do you hate de Gaulle so much? For everyone else here he is a hero.'

I sensed the hostility of the silence after I had spoken and felt Hervé's nervous lighting of the cigarette next to me.

'Because he's a filthy betrayer of the people,' said one young man, his eyes burning with anger.

'But he's freed France,' I objected.

'He appears to have freed France, in order to imprison her again.'

'But there will be elections. The people will vote.'

'The people!' Auguste laughed with derision. 'The people always do what they are primed to do. They are being seduced by his talk. They will do what he tells them until it is too late.'

'In that case, you would rather the Free French had not come to Paris?'

Brahim, a tiny North African with gold rimmed glasses turned to me. 'The Free French, as you call them, came by way of the non-free French.'

I was lost in the puns – 'the non-free French?'

Hervé helped me out with the explanations. 'He means Algérie, Marie. The free French invaded France again from North Africa, where the French have been busy imprisoning people.'

'People?' Brahim turned on us both with disgust. 'You mean a whole nation, chained and serving their masters.'

'I thought the Algerians fought with us during the war,' I suggested naively.

'Only because they were forced to,' chimed in Dédé, but Brahim was having none of that. 'Only because they are brave, and no one wanted to be enslaved by the Germans instead of the French.'

'Then you see only enslavement for your people?'

Brahim looked morose and intense. He was clearly more at ease with prophecies of despair than political challenge. 'For the moment, yes, but our time will come.'

'When will that be, do you think?'

That question seemed to cause merriment for everyone apart from Brahim.

'Please don't, Marie. Don't get him started. Brahim is already plotting revolution in France. He has it all worked out.'

So that chimes in with your own ideas of revolution?'

'Yes, we will work together. When we are free from the aristocrats, we will be free from the colonisers too.'

'I think I will go to bed. I have to be up early in the morning to help Mme Dubois.'

'Why do you work as a slave for the bourgeois?' challenged Brahim of the dark, ponderous eyes.

269

'Quite simply because I need to live.'

'That won't happen when the revolution comes,' Dédé assured me.

'Fine,' I replied, getting up and putting my coins on the table. 'Until the revolution then I need to work. Goodnight.'

I made my way through the shadowy street back up to my room. I didn't feel comforted. I had met too many of the bourgeois who were honest and kind to want to do away with them completely. The socialists of La Révolution Française were very different from the communists of Bordeaux and I knew which I preferred.

# Chapter Six

I might have been a slave to the bourgeoisie and forced to work for the middle-aged French woman above the office and I had never been keen on housework but the next morning working for Mme Dubois felt normal and reassuring. I liked the feel of sweeping out the kitchen and making the coffee at exactly the strength she preferred and seeing her pleasure when everything was done in the right way. Small, petty pleasures. Seeing someone else pleased. Was that what I considered to be the purpose of life? Was I letting myself down? Had I moved far away from the ideals of my teenage years in Les Landes?

It was true that I no longer had time to read Zola and Proust. I was involved in serving the bourgeoisie but not all the time. It allowed me to pay my rent and to work for a small salary at Libération. And I was a published writer. Hervé had no problem in commissioning me to write the follow up article to the one about the trade unionists in Bordeaux. I was also surprised that the 'dogsbody' work in the office showed me much about the work of a journalist. I had never been tidy but keeping Hervé's papers and desk tidy was an entirely different matter. It was part of the job and needed to be done well. Being pleasant to the other journalists and secretaries also had its perks. Everyone felt the office was a nicer place to work when I was around. My attitude was excessively middle-class. I did enjoy hearing the great discussions about revolution and freedom. I learnt a great deal about the history of Algeria. But it also taught me to stay apart from the idealists. They were enjoying themselves being superior to everyone else, but apart from that, I reckon they didn't have much fun.

There was one man who met with the group at the café and who worked for La Révolution Française, Antoine, and he was different to the others. He didn't have so much to say, kept himself on the fringe but he was always there as part of the group. For some reason he didn't seem so engrossed as the others in the ideology.

One night, he too excused himself from the late-night session and walked home with me. I let him into the flat, because I knew that Mme Dubois had long gone to bed and that I would not disturb her.

'What drew you to work at La Rév?' I asked him as I filtered the coffee.

'The same as you, I suppose.'

'Which is?'

'The chance to work with a newspaper of note.'

'That's all? No ideology?'

'Only superficially. I feel for their desire not to go back to the old ways.'

'Why? Were you badly treated when you were younger?'

'Of course. It's impossible to get into the Ecole Supérieur, unless you come from the right background.'

'My friend, Alain in Bordeaux, was going to go there if the war hadn't intervened and he didn't come from the right background.'

'OK but someone must have been backing him.'

I thought about his uncle and aunt. 'I guess his extended family, but they didn't have money.'

'No, but they must have had ambition or the foresight to recognize his talent. What did they do?'

'I'm not sure – tailors, I think.'

'In that case, probably Jews. They always look after their own.'

'We can look after our own too if we want to.'

'Yes, but it takes a whole community to do that. And most people aren't that unselfish.'

'Do you want to work for the revolution?'

'No, not really. A small revolution, maybe, but not with this lot.'

'You don't trust them?'

'Do you?'.

I laughed. 'Maybe not. But my problem is that I think I'm just too bourgeois. I'm happy with all this.' I waved my hand over the kitchen as if symbolised all that was counter revolutionary.

'No Marie. The problem is that you don't hate enough.'

I was startled by his response. 'Why is hate so important?'

'You have to feel hate to give you strength to fight against the powers that be. The real revolutionaries in that group in the café all have the capacity to hate. Brahim, on behalf of his country against the colonialists, Marcel against the Gaullists who have denied the socialists the honour of being the real heroes.'

'Hervé?'

He laughed. 'Not Hervé. He just goes along for the talk. He'll never be a revolutionary.'

'So, you don't think Libération or even Le Rouge would last?'

'In a revolution? No way. Hervé will be too busy enjoying his apéritif and boeuf bourguignon.'

'And you?'

He hesitated. 'It depends what they have to offer me.'

'Ah, so you're in it for ambition.'

'I guess so. What else is there?'

'I don't know. I think there are plenty of socialists who are decent people like the ones I knew in Bordeaux. They're a different breed from the ones we met tonight.'

He surveyed me coolly. 'You know, we could do it together? Be on the make?'

'Together?'

'Come on, Marie. Don't be naïve. You could come and live with me. Leave the bourgeois housework.'

'Live with you? From what I've seen of relationships, I'd end up doing more housework than ever that way.'

He moved towards me for a kiss. It was the second kiss of my life and ranked nowhere near the first. It was a utilitarian kiss. It said, let's see how we can make life work according to our desires. I drew away.

'No Antoine. I'm not moving anywhere.'

He laughed full of self-assurance. 'We could start without moving?'

'No thanks.' Do all French men think they are irresistible? I wondered.

'Why are you so cold?'

'I'm not cold. I'm just not interested in the deal.'

'Why not?'

'Because ------------Why do I have to explain this? Because I want more out of my life than just living with someone.'

'You can have both.'

'No, I don't think so, at least not at the moment. I'm young. I'm free. I've just started writing. Why throw it away?'

He was annoyed with me and I was exasperated with him. Why do men have to think that they are worth so much that you would sacrifice everything for them? I stood up.

'Antoine, I need to go to bed. I'm up early in the morning. Thank you for talking to me,' I finished lamely, holding the door open.

'Good night, Marie…' He managed to make that simple phrase as disdainful as he could, and I could not wait until he was out in the street again and I could curl up in my solitary bed.

# Chapter Seven

My profile as a journalist expanded very slowly. I'd written my second article about the children rescued by Philippe when I received an unexpected caller at the office. It was Ann-Marie, from Le Coq Enchainé, another small communist newspaper trying to make a go of it. She was young, vibrant and smiling.

'So, Hervé tells me that you are the writer about the children taken from the Vel d'Hiv.'

I glanced at Hervé for his approval. After all, he was my boss.

'It's all right. I said she could talk to you.'

'He doesn't own you, does he?'

'No, but he does pay me and allow me to work for my rent upstairs.'

'OK. I have a little proposal. Let's go somewhere to talk.'

This felt very grown up. A little spark of fire and enthusiasm spurted up inside me. Someone wanted to talk to me about work, and work meant more writing. However, my optimism which grew to an extraordinary extent in the three minutes which it took us to settle in the Bar du Carrefour, was quickly squashed. Perhaps Ann-Marie sensed my hopes and was being kind to a newcomer.

'No. I'm not offering you a job, Marie. There's not enough work anyway. We don't know how long a communist newspaper will last under de Gaulle. But we would like another article.'

'About what?'

'Where some of the survivors of the Vel d'Hiv ended up.'

'Why would I write that for you and not for Libération?'

'Because Hervé's too slow in realising his assets. Because he's not adventurous enough. Because we want to look at the socialist angle in

Palestine.'

'Palestine?' I'd hardly heard of the place. 'Why would you be interested in that?'

'Because that's where the young survivors are going. They're being taken there by the socialists. We want to see how it works out there. We thought we'd start with the young survivors. You've already written about some of them. You're on their side.'

'How do you know?'

'It's obvious from the angle you gave in the last two articles. You're sympathetic. And,' she added carefully, fingering the saucer underneath carefully almost in embarrassment. 'You weren't here when it happened.'

'Why's that good?'

'Too many people here stood aside when it happened. The communists have already been accused of doing that.'

'Was there anything they could have done?'

'Probably not., but not many people attempted to do anything. It doesn't endear us to ordinary people.'

'As far as I can see, no one else did much either. They can hardly point the finger at anyone else.'

'True, but the others aren't self-proclaimed idealists. We communists are. If we want people to believe in us, we've got to show that we're worthy of trust. Your articles really helped us with that.'

'What about Hervé? Surely I should be writing for his paper?'

'I've talked to him already. He's not interested in the Palestine angle. I can have you for this one as long as I don't steal you for ever.'

'Probably likes me tidying his desk too much.'

'Probably,' agreed Ann-Marie companionably.

'Where do I start?'

'I've got some names for you. People who hid older children long before Vel d'hiv. And several of these children have been taken by the Palmach already, as well as the ones Philippe saved.'

'Where? What for? And who are these Palmachs?'

'The Palmach are the Jewish freedom fighters. They want to start a state in Palestine. They want all the Jewish children who've been saved from the Nazis.'

'Why?'

'Because they say it's the only place where they'll be safe.'

'And will they be?'

'As far as I can see, it's the last place they'll be safe. There's about to be a civil war.'

'Not another one! Haven't we had enough?'

'It's hard to argue with people who've lost 6 million of their own.'

'6 million!' It was the first time I'd heard of such a figure. I was stupefied.

'Right across Europe. That's why they don't trust Europe anymore.'

'So how do I find out about all this?'

'We want you to go down to the Zone Libéré, to the docks in Marseille and if necessary, further along the coast and find out what's happening.'

'And then?'

'Talk to some of the socialists there. Bring us back two or three reports of what they plan to do. But make it how socialists can help their own people. That's good for our readership. Makes them feel less guilty about the children in Paris and more positive about what socialism can do.'

# Chapter Eight

I was so excited I could hardly sleep. If only Alain could have seen me! And I was going to find out more about his people. Most important of all, I had a train ticket in my pocket and an official journalist's pass, a notebook and 20,000 questions to ask.

The train was crowded out. I was lucky to get a seat at the last moment and found myself sitting opposite a nun. Over a twelve-hour journey with numerous stops and announcements, we were bound to start chatting.

I was curious as to what she was doing there. 'Sister, why are you making this journey at such a difficult time?'

'I'm going to rejoin my mother house, ten miles east of Marseille in the Calanques area.'

'So why have you been away from them?'

'I've been in Paris during the war.'

'Why when it must have been safer in the Zone Libre?'

'God doesn't always call us to safety, Mademoiselle.'

I was astonished by her reply. I knew about my own Father Julien of course but I didn't know that there were other religieuses involved in the Resistance.

'I thought that the Catholic Church supported the Nazis.'

My nun hesitated. It probably wasn't the best time or place to be discussing church politics.

'The Holy Father needs to say what will help the country's stability, but that doesn't mean that our mother church doesn't support the persecuted.'

It all sounded like mumbo jumbo to me. 'So how was the church supporting the persecuted in France?'

'There's much I cannot say, mademoiselle. But you can be sure that things happened.'

End of conversation. We both turned back to our baguettes and hard-boiled eggs. I noticed that the little sister under her gold rimmed spectacles and white wimple wasn't as old as I had originally thought.

I started the conversation again. 'I'm a journalist.' I was proud of my new-found title. 'I have written about the support of the communist party for the Jews and other 'étrangers' in France. What did you do?'

She smiled graciously. 'It is not for me to say, mademoiselle, but I'd say to you, read 'En Captivité' and you may be surprised.'

I knew that En Captivité was the organ of the catholic church. Libération and the Coq Enchainé treated it as no better than a Nazi publicity leaflet and would not have anything to do with it.

'You should never assume things,' she added in what I took to be a slightly superior voice which annoyed me. 'Always find out for yourself.'

'And have you not assumed things, ma soeur, by entering into a convent and believing everything you were told?'

The light blue eyes behind their gold rims did not lose their equanimity, as she replied, 'I would never commit my whole life to something I had only found out about second hand. We all need first-hand experience of our chosen life-style before making a commitment.' And with that she settled into her rosary and her reading of the daily prayers.

My own enthusiasm for my assignment quickly waned. By the time I was deposited on the 'quai' at the station in Marseille, I was perspiring, dirty and thirsty. I had been given the name and address of one of Ann-Marie's contacts who lived in the 'Vieux Port' and she said that they would be happy to give me a bed for the night. During the night with the hot weather and the windows open all night, I was kept awake by the constant talking in the streets, the 'klaxons' of cars forcing their way through the narrow streets and smells of a large city without adequate drainage.

'Estaque – that's where you need to be,' said one of the men in the café where I went for breakfast. 'three roads along here on your left. Find André. He works at the port. He'll take you along.'

I was pleased to be given all this ready information, though less pleased by the way my one change of blouse already looked limp in the heat of a new day and a little dirty.

I'd had some difficulty adapting to the clipped vowels of Paris when I moved there but the nasal twang of Marseille was even worse. I only seemed to be able to decipher one word in three. I couldn't work out whether André was going to the port immediately, later in the day or even during the following week. I hung out near his car as the sun became more oppressive and hoped for the best. André clearly loved his little old van. He kept on returning to check one more thing and enjoyed keeping me waiting. It was part of his pose as an eligible bachelor doing a favour to a lone female and it was a role that he relished.

'Are you actually going today, André?'

'Patience, mon amie. Why are so impatient to get to Estaque? There's nothing worth seeing there.'

'I've come to see the refugee boats.'

He laughed. 'Then we've all the time in the world. They've been down there for over a week at least and they're waiting for permission to sail from the British government. I wouldn't be in a hurry if I were you. Have you got your papers in order?'

I had them in my linen bag. 'As long as you've got those and plenty of time, it's all you need.'

'Bof', he shouted, gesticulating with his hand to show that his important business was now finished, and he had time for someone like me. 'I'm ready now. Let's go!'

# Chapter Nine

As we started towards the main gate outside the port, I could see nothing, just more fences and more gates and lots of dirty warehouses, with a strange variety of old engines jutting out from their doorways.

'This is just the first gate. There's at least another three before you start to see the boats properly.' Despite his annoying self-preening, I was glad that André was there. I didn't know how I would have got an entrance without him. He locked each gate behind us. After the third one, I started to hear the noise and smell the sweat of bodies herded together.

'There's your refugee boat, ma belle!'

I looked past his outstretched arm. It looked far too fragile to be an ocean-going boat, almost a glorified fishing boat and it was packed with children and young people shouting and waving placards.

André saw my hesitation. 'You won't have any difficulty getting in there. You're a journalist. They want all the publicity they can get.'

Yes, I could see his point. But how to get the angle which would please a communist newspaper? Fortunately, I had taken the precaution before I travelled of getting the full names of the two children rescued by Philippe. I needed them as a way of appealing to the readership – a personal insight into a political story.

'Papers? Reason for embarking?' demanded the guards at the dock, who looked about fifteen years of age. 'We don't know the names of those on board. You'll have to go through the office down in the gunwales. But if you're family and want to dissuade them from going, I warn you, there's not much hope.'

I reassured them boldly. 'I'm not family. I don't want to dissuade them. It's up to them what they want to do. I just want to reassure the family who looked after them in Paris during the war that they're safe.'

And I'm a journalist. I can give your mission good publicity if you'll let me.'

These fifteen-year olds might be skinny and dressed in mismatched clothes, but they were not easily impressed by talk. They showed me where to go to the official registration office.

Despite being a native of Les Landes and surrounded by sea and lakes, I was no specialist in larger boats but even I could see that this boat left a lot to be desired. I found it difficult to keep my footing along the corridors below even in the calm waters of the port. The cramped office, measuring no more than three foot by three foot and with a makeshift bunk bed in the corner was managed by a young woman in her twenties, surrounded by dirty, torn lists and papers. The heat this far down in the boat was oppressive. I found myself perspiring and feeling sick and I had only been there a few minutes. If this young woman felt any discomfort, she showed no signs of it.

'Yes?'

'I'm a journalist.'

'Papers? Identity?' I explained the politics of my paper and my interest in the two Parisian children.

'Before I look at the lists, why would you want to see them?'

'So, they can explain to me why they want to come on this,' – I waved my hand dismissively at this failing, ancient tug-boat – 'when they could have stayed in Paris in comfort.'

'I can tell you that already, mademoiselle.'

'No doubt, but I want to hear it from them.'

'In case I am deceiving you?'

'Maybe. But for a journalist first-hand sources are always better.'

'And you think I'm not going to Palestine too?'

'I'm sure you are but you haven't come from Paris or been rescued by a communist from the Vel d'Hiv.'

'No. I was left to die by the communists in Poland.'

There was no adequate answer to that sort of statement. 'Could you look at the lists please?'

'Sure. On condition that if you get your story, you change their names.'

'No problem. But what danger can they be in from a Parisian readership?'

'Mademoiselle, you can have no idea what danger any Jew can be in from the enemy.' This young woman made me feel like the enemy and I was annoyed.

'I think I have some idea. My best friend was Jewish.'

'And was he rescued by the goyim?'

'No, he chose not to be. But some of the communists in Bordeaux did a lot to save his compatriots.'

She stared at me impersonally. 'I'm glad. But we prefer not to rely on a few good-hearted people. Better to go where we are really welcome.'

'Welcome by who? The English?'

'The English will not always be in Palestine. The revolution is coming.'

I laughed. 'My communist friends in Paris say the same thing.'

'And you? What are your political convictions?'

'I'm sympathetic but not convinced.'

'But I thought you said you worked for a communist newspaper.'

'Sure. It's my way into journalism.'

'Ah, an opportunist!'

'If you like, but at least I'm honest about it.'

She turned away from the conversation because it distracted her from her real job.

'Actually, you're in luck. The brother and sister you're looking for, Robert and Mireille, are on this boat. They're probably on the top deck with the suicide squad.'

'Sorry?'

'Yes, didn't you know? If the British haven't let us go in three days' time, we have suicide volunteers. That will wake the world up.'

I was horrified by this callous attitude. 'But that's evil manipulation of young people.'

'Is it? They know their only chance of freedom is Palestine. These kids have no family. They've all died in Belsen. They want to help the cause.'

I left, disgusted with the extremity of this view. I climbed up several decks and found Robert and Mireille, happily not part of the volunteers.

'Robert? Mireille?' The two Parisian youngsters looked less gaunt and haggard than many of the teenagers near them.

'I'm from M and Mme Hugo, where you lived in Paris.'

Their faces lit up. 'Please send them our love but we're not going back,' they assured me after I had explained my mission. Even the hair-cuts of these two young people showed that they had been looked after well until recently.

'I'm sure you could have a nice life and a safer life with M. et Mme Hugo.'

'You're right but our parents didn't have a nice or safe life in Paris. They died in Belsen.'

'But you were rescued.'

'That was just a chance gesture of kindness. Of course, we'll always be grateful to those who rescued us, but that doesn't mean that the streets of Paris will always be safe for us.'

'And the streets of Tel Aviv will?'

'No, we may die in the coming war but at least we'll die amongst our own.'

I looked at these two, twelve and fourteen years old, with a new respect. Would I be capable of saying that so calmly even at my age? I knew that I didn't have that sort of conviction. It was the same sort of calm conviction which had sent Alain into the guns of his killers.

'And you don't think the communists of Paris will do enough for you, even though they looked after you so far?'

'We think the communists of Eretz Yisroel will do a lot more for us. We are going to live in a kibbutz. That's real sharing. I didn't hear of any kibbutz in Paris, Mademoiselle.'

That sounded like a better hook for my communist readers.

'Can you show me someone here who can talk about life on a kibbutz?'

'Someone?' repeated the young people confidently. 'Many people, but let us find you our group leader, Angèle.'

# Chapter Ten

I was unnerved and impressed in equal measure. Angèle was a charming twenty-year old from Nice, who explained to me the concept of a kibbutz – total sharing and total equality.

'You know they have been trying such ideas in Russia for some time,' I suggested, in case she thought she was the only one who believed in equality.

'Yes, of course, but it hasn't worked.' Angèle clearly knew the history of the Bolsheviks. 'It doesn't work because it involves civil war and forcing people to live like that when they don't want to do it. But in Israel, it will be different.'

'Human beings aren't that different the world over.' Oh dear, I was beginning to sound like the world-weary M. Arnaud in the Hôtel du Centre!

'But we are a people fighting for our existence. Everyone else has a nation and a land, but we don't. We want only the best. Also,' she added, 'our socialism is different. No one is forced to live on the kibbutz. You only come if you want to.'

'And socialism for the whole country?'

'Yes of course we want socialism to work for everyone, but they have to see it for themselves and make their own decision.'

Angèle flicked her red hair back from her face. In peace time France she could have been a model, a lycéene waiting for her next date. Never had I seen such a commitment to a cause as in this young girl. She made all the discussions I had had at school seem like fantasy and bourgeois dreams. This determination of hers was rooted in real life.

'The kibbutzim will be clearing the ground. We're going to grow vines eventually, but it will take some hard, manual work first.'

'It sounds exhausting to me. Shouldn't you be having fun at your age?'

She regarded me quite coolly as though I was a flippant socialite who had no idea what real life was about.

'You can only have fun if you've been allowed to live. Most of the kids here have lost both their parents. It'll be a long time before they feel like having fun.'

'Maybe you should encourage them.'

'Marie, have you been here during an evening yet?'

'No, I only arrived here a couple of hours ago.' I explained my mission as a journalist.'

'Well stay here all day and stay this evening on the boat. You'll see the kids having fun.'

I looked at the gaunt faces around me. It didn't seem possible that some of them were in their early teens or even younger. No one else was going to do the chores around them. The temperature under the Marseille sun had risen and below deck it was insufferably hot. They were all taking it in turns to spend time on deck but while they were waiting, they were cleaning and helping to prepare the meals.

'No one here is a passenger,' explained Angèle. 'They're all here because they want to be, and they know that it means responsibility and hard work.'

'And they all know and accept it just like that?'

'Marie, you don't understand. They have no family to belong to, apart from each other. Family means sharing the chores. They feel desperate. They're excited by the idea of working together.'

'Do none of them just want to give up and lead ordinary lives?'

'The ones who have given up don't want to do anything. They've lost all hope. There are about ten kids who have cabins near the medical centre. They've seen, greater evil and suffering than anyone should. They don't want to take part, not just here, anywhere. You want to see how people look with no hope? I'll show you.'

Briskly Angèle guided me below deck, three floors down. A nurse was with two of the girls, trying to persuade them to get dressed. They had both turned their faces to the wall. When their faces turned as they were given medication, I saw their blank eyes. It was a relief to go outside and see children scurrying around with mops and buckets.

286

'If you want to see children have fun, come to the dance tonight.'

The word 'dance' for me had connotations of Catholic socials, where you might get lucky and be partnered by a good-looking boy without spots. I should have known that the Jews would do it differently. Looking at the exhausting heat and the condition of some of the children and the multitude of bureaucratic tasks which were needed to get them out of that port, even if the British gave them permission, I could not imagine how anyone would have the energy or space to dance. I myself, having gathered lots of information for my forthcoming article, just wanted to get back to the 'vieux port', laugh at the flirtatious posing of André and have my meal in peace, before a 'quiet night'.

'You'll be surprised,' promised Angèle, a mischievous glint in her eyes, as she tossed back her red hair.

'Come ready to enjoy yourself.'

The food on board was not of a great quality and I was tempted to go back early to my pension, but Robert and Mireille had taken charge of me during the afternoon and had a zeal to show me what a good choice they had made in rejecting the comforts of bourgeois Paris and joining in the communal life of a shabby tub which looked as though it might not survive its voyage on the Mediterranean.

I did notice how much more mature all the teenagers were compared to the average family member in France. They did not complain about chores. They had to work hard, and fashion was not on the agenda – shorts and t shirts only were the order of the day.

'But Marie, you have to dance the hora with us,' said Mireille excitedly.

'But I've never heard of it and I don't come from the sort of family who went to dances.' I remembered looking longingly at the people from school who were admitted to the dances at the church hall. One night I had stood opposite the door in the twilight, hidden amongst the shadows, clutching the handles of my bike, in case someone might tell me off. I gazed in admiration at what I had imagined to be the sophistication of the girls who entered, wearing their specially chosen or sewn dresses. No one gave me clothes like that. Even when I worked at the Hôtel du Centre, I had to offer to work the shifts on Saturday evening, when the other waitresses wanted to go to a dance.

Robert and Mireille laughed at my ignorance.

'You'll see. It's fun.' How could you have fun, I wondered, when all your family had been murdered?

After the meal, coloured lights were arranged on the deck and everyone was hurrying to finish their chores. No one had a change of clothes but some of the girls had tied a brightly coloured scarf over their tee-shirts. The coloured lights cast a soft glow over the heads of these young people as if to give them all a feeling of romance. And then the music started. This was not the music of sedate waltzes or even country harvest dances. This was the music of accordions, playful, enigmatic even sorrowful, yet hopeful. Starting quite slowly, then rising in crescendo and speed, inviting everyone to dance. There was very little pairing off among the dancers. Most of it was in circles, joining hands, twirling and jumping and these children put all their energy into it. They may not have been wearing colourful costumes, but the lights gave the illusion of multi colours and every face was a different shade of skin – pale northern Europeans, Russians, silver haired to tanned Mediterranean. I was dragged to the floor by Robert and Mireille. In truth the music made you want to dance. I had never felt before such a close bonding with a group of people. There must have been more romantic 'liasons' taking place, amongst older teenagers, but none of that mattered. They were a vibrant, heaving mass of young people, shouting and squealing with excitement, ponytails bobbing and loose hair swaying. It didn't seem to matter whether you knew how to dance or not. No one cared about gaucheness. What did matter whether you were prepared to join in, change partners and jump and swerve in all directions. Before half an hour had gone by, I was exhausted.

'Come on, Marie. It's too early to finish yet.'

'Alright, but I need to recover my breath. I'm not quite as energetic as you.'

I wasn't allowed to sit out for long. A young man came to invite me to join in again. I didn't feel oppressed by the invitation or worried about his motivation. The conventionalities of polite society and relationships between the sexes did not seem to operate here. By the end of the evening I had to admit that I was enjoying myself.

I was even forced to stay the night on the boat, sleeping on the floor of Mireille's cabin, which she shared with two other girls. They did not worry about their privacy being invaded by a strange woman. For me it was a totally new experience-sharing a room and being accepted unconditionally by a group of contemporaries.

I had one more night booked in my pension in Marseille, but instead of enjoying the peace, I missed the crazy atmosphere of the boat.

'So, you are in favour then?' Angèle quizzed me before I left in the morning.

'I've got to say it's impressive,' I admitted truthfully.

'Well, make sure you tell the world what we've been doing because not many of them understand.'

'I'll do my best.'

# Chapter Eleven

I kept my promise. The only addition I had to make was trying to understand the whole event from a communist point of view. I had to write about the brave communist, Philippe, who had rescued children from the clutches of the evil Nazis. It had the merit of being true. I suspected that it was more about his personal integrity and humane instinct – a horror of the genocide, his strong feeling of injustice and his desire to do something for the good of others, however small – rather than his membership of the communist party, but as a journalist I kept that suspicion to myself.

France was reeling from the aftermath of the war and was also coming to terms with the truth that people had not resisted the Germans as they should have done. Remembering the bloodshed of the Great War, it was understandable that this time they might have wanted to be more passive. However, what was emerging in post war days, was the truth that not only had many French men and women not fought back against the invader, but they had allowed a monstrous evil to take place in their midst. As families lined up outside the Vel d'Hiv to be carried away to be slaughtered, the French police had supervised them. People shrugged their shoulders in characteristic Gallic fashion, as if to say, 'What could we do? At least with us in charge, they were less oppressed and more humanely treated than if we had left it to the Gestapo.' True in many ways. But it also gave those families an illusion of safety. If the French police were helping, they thought, then maybe they were going to labour camps rather than death camps.

In those days when I first worked as a young journalist in Paris, a collective sense of guilt was beginning to emerge, which would spread right across the country. They had colluded in mass murder. The Vichy government had allowed the Germans to set numbers of Jews who would die and others

290

who would be deported. People claimed ignorance and were horrified by the stories, which were beginning to emerge as Auschwitz, Belson and Ravensbruck were liberated – far too late for most of the occupants. And it reminded France that twenty years before, starting with the Dreyfus case, anti-semitism had been festering under the surface of society. Most people would not consciously have believed what Hitler was telling them about the purity of the Aryan race but subconsciously it struck a chord. There were too many Jews who were successful in French society and the French were jealous. Tragically too, many Jews had fled west from Central Europe, believing that they might be safe there. France had not been able to keep them safe, and French people knew that they had done very little to protect them.

The Communists were sore too about the success of de Gaulle and the Free French. The people who had marched in to liberate Paris were very far from the left politically. They were headed by the old 'aristocrats.' They had fought for France so that afterwards their country would return to the values of the third republic. The communists were horrified by the influence of the right. They claimed, with some justification, that Paris had forgotten that the foremost people in the Resistance were the Communists and they wanted to carry on fighting for a truly liberated France. People were tired of war and wanted stability and normality and it was easy for them to forget what the Communists had achieved in war time. Libération, Franc-Tireur, l'Humanité and Le Coq Enchainé and other left-wing newspapers served to remind them.

My article about Robert and Mireille helped to remind the readership of how proud they could be of actions of party members such as Philippe. It was the second article I wrote, followed by others, and they endeared me to the communist sympathisers in Paris. I still stood outside their political beliefs. I was not a convinced convert. I had had too many conversations with Alain in front of the school room log fire to easily swallow any line of politics wholesale without any argument, but it was an opportunity for me to step into journalism, an opportunity for me to support my old communist friends from Les Landes, but also an opportunity for me to trace the fortunes or misfortunes of Alain's people. I found myself longing to talk to him, grieving for his death, and being obsessively interested in what had happened to other Jews in the country. I remembered those groups of lovely girls who I had taken over the border to Spain and I grieved for all the others who had gone to their deaths for no other reason than their racial origins, and the madness of the Nazi party.

I travelled down to Bordeaux to find out what my friends were doing in the Trade Union down there. Patrice's father was back from his experience in the forced labour camp in Germany and I wrote an article about what he had experienced there and when he returned home. He was a quieter, more reflective man than before the war. He had seen some brutality in the work camps, not just from the camp guards, but as the result of desperate men competing for privileges and enough food rations. As the war had continued disastrously for the Germans, food supplies for the labour camps using enemy manpower, had not been a priority. The men returned to France, emaciated and had difficulty readapting to ordinary family and community life.

The readers of Le Coq Enchainé liked my articles commissioned by Ann-Marie. There was human interest in them, rather than just political propaganda. It also made them, in those dreary post war days, proud to support the communist cause.

I had written my article on Robert and Mireille, who were now safely in Palestine. We knew from the news that the State of Israel had been declared and that the ensuing war with the Arab indigenous population had been bloody, but, while fearful for their safety, I knew that these two teenagers had chosen to be identified with their people instead of remaining safely in France. The kibbutz was the very model of socialism on a small scale that all communists aspired to and hoped for when the country became more stable. I even hoped to be able to see for myself how the kibbutzim were doing if I ever managed to get to the new state of Israel.

I had never discovered the full story of what had happened to the other children who had been rescued by Philippe. I managed to contact Mme Taube, with whom they had stayed, and she believed that Russia was the perfect destination for the children. I had already seen Robert and Mireille with their Israeli friends, fulfilled and with a goal in life. Did the other children feel the same way about socialism in Russia?

# Chapter Twelve

I decided to ask the group who met regularly at the café du Carrefour. I still met with them occasionally, though, since Antoine had shown interest in me, I felt more awkward in his presence. But I needed to ask their opinion about Russia and how Jewish children would be accepted there.

I arrived late one evening when the political debate was already in full flow.

'Ah, it's our blossoming journalist,' Marcel said, laughingly, but not unkindly.

Ann-Marie retorted quickly, 'Just because she's had a brilliant human angle on the story which the readers like, don't belittle her, Marcel. You're only jealous.'

'Mon Dieu! Me? Jealous?' Marcel looked like an actor about to throw a tantrum. 'As usual, Ann-Marie, you don't understand me. You've never done. Human angles are all very well, but they don't get to the heart of where our country should be going.'

'Maybe not, but the readers like it and, if we don't sell, we won't eat.'

Marcel looked up, waving his cigarette in disgust. 'How can you be so bourgeois? You worry about eating while our country follows a fascist leader.'

It was the first time I had heard the word 'fascist' used like this – merely as a description of someone you don't like – and I was shocked.

Ann-Marie, seeing my reaction, patted my hand encouragingly. 'Marie, sit down and forget these idiots.'

'So,' said Brahim, 'is it being an idiot to forget that your country is in slavery?'

Antoine commented drily, 'You may be in slavery, but, if you are released too quickly, you won't know how to survive on your own.'

The little Algerian turned on him in fury. 'We survived successfully for hundreds of years before you French came to enslave us.'

Marcel sighed, 'The French are now enslaved themselves.'

I really felt like leaving immediately. All these people had their own agenda and they were unlikely to be interested in anyone else's story of victimisation. They were too selfish to govern a country, I thought. And too selfish to pursue an interesting story which was not in line with their own ideology.

'Sit down, sit down, ma chérie,' said Ann-Marie, guessing my reaction to the conversation. 'I know you have all these 'fous' to put up with, but somewhere amongst them all there is the desire to do what is right for all.'

I was not convinced but I sat down anyway.

Antoine was a little more quizzical about my work.

'So then.' He looked amused by my initial reaction of embarrassment at meeting him. I had not wanted to see him again but now I could see clearly that he looked at me with complete detachment. My rejection of his manhood had been dismissed and forgotten. There were other girls who would recognise his desirability. I was no longer a serious consideration for him.

'What sort of story are you after now?'

I had nothing to lose by trying.

'A few weeks ago, I went to see a Mme Taube. She and her husband were the other couple who took the children that Philippe brought them, although M. Taube has since died. They were some distant relation of Philippe's and they took the children in as a favour.'

'Oh, back to the Vel d'Hiv again!' Marcel swept his lock of black hair, which insisted on getting in the way of his coffee and cigarette, away from this forehead. 'I'm getting sick of hearing about it.'

I hated his cynical attitude and I wanted to crush him. 'Maybe you're sick of hearing about it because it makes us all feel guilty. People were murdered there. Perhaps we haven't talked about it enough.'

Silence.

Hervé added quietly, 'Go on about those children, Marie.'

'Mme Taube said that when peace was declared some Russians came and took them off to Russia. I want to know why anyone would take Jewish children off to Russia.'

'Because they believe in communism?' suggested Antoine.

'OK, communism in general. I can see that some people will believe in it whatever. But why take Jewish children in particular?'

Hervé commented, 'It sounds like you're sniffing out a story.' He held his hand out to Ann-Marie. 'And this one has to be on us. It's our turn.'

'Oh, come on, Hervé,' said Ann-Marie said in a kindly way to her newspaper competitor. 'You know that if I hadn't got in there, this poor girl would still have been tidying your desk and doing the washing up unpaid. Talking about slaves, what about women? Communism is all about women comrades being liberated too.'

'I don't care who I write for,' I said airily, as if it was the most normal thing in the world for newspaper editors to be arguing about who should publish the writing of an unknown, country girl from Les Landes. 'But this story fascinates me, and it's gone completely cold. I have no idea where to go next.'

Hervé suddenly and unexpectedly took the initiative. 'Where did you say this M. Taube had worked?'

'The cheese factory at St. Berthe.'

'I know it. They always had a militant union there. Is M. Taube still around?'

'No, at least I only saw the woman and I got the impression that she was a widow.'

Hervé was surprisingly directive. 'Go back there but not to the woman. She doesn't sound involved enough.'

'No, I agree. I don't think she cared enough about the children. She just did her duty to please the union people.'

'Then go the cheese factory instead. Snoop around. Find someone who knows something. You can't just spirit two children out of a country without someone knowing something.'

Ann-Marie intervened. 'Hervé, don't be naïve. It was the end of the occupation. Everything was in chaos. Anything could have happened.'

Hervé turned to her more forcefully than I might have expected. 'Ann-Marie, I'm not naïve. Someone in that village will know something. And our budding journalist here will find out about it. And I want her story on our front page this time.'

'It sounds like you've got an assignment, my dear.'

# Chapter Thirteen

I had managed to go to St. Berthe the first time without too much commotion being caused. I knew that the second time would be more difficult. Just outside the city's limits, it was a non-descript, depressing place. It was on the edge of farming country, but not rural in any attractive way. Rather it was a sad offshoot of the city, which had been forgotten. It didn't possess the buzz of Paris or the charm of the country. Its biggest employer was the cheese factory and, as with M. Taube, most of its workers had been there all their lives. Not that this fact engendered loyalty to the firm. It was more a case of nowhere else to go and no other way of making a subsidence living, if you didn't want to commute to Paris or engage with the farming community.

I didn't want to talk to Mme Taube again because I was sure that she was an individual who got by every day with her few friends and memories and was almost completely lacking in curiosity. Her husband had been a loyal supporter of the union, which is why they had taken the children in. The children themselves held no interest for her and she was too unimaginative to think about their future.

Instead, I decided to go straight to the factory and ask to see the union representatives. From the entrance I was directed to a squalid little office which had a leak in one corner of the roof. Even Hervé's office looked organised and up to date in comparison. If there had been union activity here in the past, it was clearly no longer the central concern of the workers.

The bell went for the break for the early workers and as one or two of them made it to the office, I had a chance to question them.

I was cheerful and pro-active rather than waiting for their suspicions to form. 'Good morning. I'm working for a paper in Paris and we're

297

doing a special article about the role of the unions during the war. I was wondering if you could help me.'

The young man who appeared in the doorway looked uninterested.

'I wasn't here during the war. I escaped to the Free Zone and I've only come back here since.'

'Ah, so you were brought up in St. Berthe?'

'Yes, worse luck. It's the most nothing place you can imagine.'

I smiled sympathetically. The young man was after all about my age and I understood why he might be looking for excitement.

'I can imagine. But in that case why did you come back here?'

'Looking for a job. Able to stay with my parents free. Too many refugees in the zone libre who wanted to stay on, liked the south and the sun.'

'Can't blame them for that.' I laughed sympathetically. 'But we all have to earn a living. Do you think you'll stay on here?' I'd already mastered the art of showing an interest in my potential informers because that made it more likely that they would help me. Exploitation, some would say. Real life and getting the job done, I answered myself.

The young man hesitated. It was clearly a conversation he had had many times in his head.

'Look at this place. It's had no money invested in it. The machinery is old. Will it survive post-war improvements and economy?'

He shook his head. 'I'd be surprised.'

'Well, as you say, for the time being, it's a job. Were you about to make coffee?'

For the first time his smile showed him to have a boyish, fresh face. I personally hoped that he wouldn't be condemned to this factory for the rest of his life.

'Yes, would you like one?'

'Yes, please.'

He busied himself heating up the water on the small stove in the corner of the hut.

'Why did you say you were here?'. He grinned again impishly. 'Not that you're not welcome. You're about half the age of most of the women in St. Berthe.'

'I can imagine. I've met some of them.'

'Boring, moaning cows.'

I laughed. 'I guess they've had their troubles during the last few years.'

'Hasn't everyone?'

'Yes, but we need to move on.'

He busied himself with the sweet black coffee and gestured towards a stool where I could perch. 'Here, let me move these.' A whole load of papers were transferred to another pile on the floor.

I looked round the room. 'This looks like my boss's office before I got to work on it.'

'Feel free to do the same here, mademoiselle.'

'Are you the union rep here?'

'Yes, but only because no one else was prepared to take it on.'

'I'm looking for some information about a family who were looked after here during the war. They were orphans.'

'I don't know. Perhaps someone in the town would know. Why come here?'

'I've already asked in the town and met the woman who looked after them. But she said that someone from the union had come and taken them off to Russia.'

'Russia?' He sounded surprised. 'Poor kids. Why would anyone do that?'

I laughed. 'You work for the union? You're supposed to be supporting the socialist paradise.'

He snorted. 'It may be. All I know is that it's cold and a long way away from here. And who knows what's going on there? If Stalin hadn't supported the Nazis to begin with, the war might have been over more quickly.'

'That doesn't sound like the words of a communist agitator.'

He looked suspiciously at me. 'Is that what you're doing here? Undercover?'

I looked genuinely horrified at the suggestion. 'Not at all. I have nothing at all to do with the government. I work for a communist newspaper and I'm finding out what happened to the children who were protected by the communists in the war.'

'But you're not a communist yourself?'

'Not really but I'm sympathetic. I've had friends in the past who were communists and trade unionists, who were good people. But no, I'm not sure I'm anything. Just trying to get on with my life and make a decent living.'

He nodded companionably. There wasn't much difference between the two of us. He didn't strike me as a 'joiner' of political causes.

'OK but I can't really help you as I've only just come back to St. Berthe. But,' he said as a grinning, jovial face with a large nose, marked by skin problems, put his face round the door.

'Auguste! Just the man we need!'

'Ah, might have known what kept you,' said Auguste good humouredly. 'Coffee with a pretty girl. Bonjour, Mademoiselle.'

'Bonjour, Monsieur.' I smiled as charmingly as I could.

'This is Auguste, and, sorry, I don't know your name.'

'Marie.'

'Marie here is looking for someone in the factory who took some kids from the town at the end of the war to Russia. Sounds unlikely to me but would you know anything about it?'

Auguste's large body seemed to fill up most of the remaining space in the small, chaotic office.

'Ah, that sounds like René.'

'Who is René?'

'René is a true believer, Mademoiselle. He thinks the communists have all the answers.'

'And do they?'

Auguste's rich laugh filled the room. 'Do I think anyone has all the answers? Of course not! "Get on and enjoy life while you can" is my motto.'

'So that's why you come to the TU office in the factory,' I teased him.

'Of course, Marie. It's the only place where you can pour yourself a decent cup of coffee and sit down with a fag before going back to the workhouse.'

'And René?'

'René believes in it all. He's hoping for a revolution. But believe me, when it comes, it'll be people like him – bad tempered and intense – who will be in charge.'

300

'And what do you think about that prospect?'

'Not a lot. I'd rather have de Gaulle.'

I laughed. 'You'd better not let the true believers hear you. So how do I find this René?'

'You mean you're interested in him and not us?'

'Unfortunately, from the point of view of my newspaper, yes.' I already liked Auguste far more than any trade union official I had ever met before.

'Meet me at lunch time outside the factory. I'll introduce you to him and we'll see what he can do. Though I warn you, Marie, you'll need all your charms. He doesn't give anything away easily.'

'I can only try, Auguste. I'll meet you outside the main door at 12.'

# Chapter Fourteen

Auguste gave me permission to stay in the little office until dinner time and to make myself more coffee. I amused myself by looking at some of the piles of paperwork, some of which went back to 1940. I also tried to work out a strategy to conquer René, who, according to Auguste, did not have a generous spirit.

The bell went for the dinner break at the cheese factory and at least a hundred men and women made their way outside. I could see why the factory was such a stable source of employment for the area.

Auguste waved at me from the gate and by him stood a glum, older man who I could see immediately would not be delighted by the idea of a conversation with a strange woman.

'René, this is Marie and, if you've got any sense, you'll enjoy the fact that for once a beautiful young woman wants to have a coffee with you.'

René was a calculator. He looked at me shrewdly. 'If she's buying me a coffee, then she must want something.'

'If only you knew, René!' Nudge, nudge, wink, wink, on the part of Auguste. I couldn't imagine how they put up with each other, but Auguste seemed to be unconcerned about how his suggestions might be received. I tried to put René at ease and asked,

'Do you want to go back home for lunch, Monsieur?'

'Of course,' His wife must be less than thrilled by his appearance each lunch time I thought. It probably broke up the most tranquil part of her day.

'Would it be possible to meet for a coffee afterwards before you go back on shift?'

'What do you want?'

302

'I'm told that you were particularly good to a family in this village. I just wanted to know more about them.'

'Why?'

'Because orphans have ended up all over the place since the war. It's been a crazy time. And we're running articles about different destinations of children who became orphans because of the war.'

'Who is 'we'?'

'Libération and the Coq Enchainé. They're both good communist and trade union newspapers. My editor reckons that several families were helped by workers like yourself. They've never been acknowledged properly and it's good for France to know that the unions have been active in doing good.'

He looked at me suspiciously. Probably no one had accused him of doing good to others for a long time.

'I know you want to get back to your home for lunch, Monsieur, and I don't want to intrude too much on your time. But if you had half an hour before the afternoon shift started, I'd be grateful.'

'Alright. But nothing critical of the union should come out of this.'

'Of course not. We want this to be a positive story too.'

'I go to the Café du Pont over there.' He pointed to a bedraggled looking bar on the other side of the town square, just on the corner of a small street.'

'It's the only café where the bar tender is more miserable than his customers,' suggested Auguste. I ignored the gibe and was all politeness.

'It's very good of you to give me your time, monsieur René. I appreciate it. I'll see you later.'

I wanted him to start his dinner as soon as possible, so that he would have time for me later on. 'A toute à l'heure, Monsieur et bon appétit.'

'Well,' enthused the good-natured Auguste when René had gone, 'If he's not man enough to invite you out to lunch, then I will.'

I laughed. 'It's very kind of you, Auguste, but you've given me enough already. And when I drink a coffee with René later, I think it'll have to be on my own.'

'A pity. Miserable old sod. But I know the owner of Café de la Victoire, a much better place than du Pont. Come on. Let's have lunch there. No, don't deny me. My reputation in this town will soar if I'm seen with you.'

Faced with such a responsibility, I could do nothing but submit. In truth, the meal and the wine were very pleasant, and Auguste was a delightful and amusing companion.

'By the way, Auguste. Don't mention anything to anyone about René. I'm just here to report on union activities.'

'No problem, Mlle Marie. No one could imagine that you could write anything worthwhile about René anyway.'

But an hour later over our coffee in the Bar du Pont, I wasn't so sure.

'So how did you get to know about M and Mme Taube's adopted children?' I started.

'Everyone in the town knew about them. You couldn't exactly hide them. We all pretended not to know about how they had come here but everyone guessed.'

'That they were Jewish?'

'Yes. We didn't want to get involved of course. Repercussions were dangerous during the Occupation. Fortunately, they didn't look particularly Jewish.'

'So how did you know?'

'Why else would stray children be around without their parents?'

'But what about the Russian link?'

'They were Russian originally and lots of the Russian émigrés were Jews.'

'Yes, they had to flee two dictators.'

This sort of comment was not acceptable to René.

'The Russian situation and Hitler cannot be compared.'

'No?'

'Of course not. Yes, people were killed when the Bolsheviks came to power, but that was retribution for the terrible injustices of the Tsarist system.'

'And there have been no injustices since?'

'You are like all bourgeois hangers on, Mademoiselle. You cannot have a revolution without casualties. What is important is that there is ultimately justice for the workers.'

'And will there be?'

'There's no doubt about it. Now the war is over, Russia will give opportunities to everyone.'

'So, is that why you sent these children back to Russia?'

'I did my duty as a communist. These children had come as émigrés with their parents. They spoke Russian and French. They needed to be repatriated.'

'Why?'

'Because M. Taube, a loyal trade unionist for so many years, was dying. His wife could not be expected to look after these children alone.'

'But why back to Russia? Why not an orphanage in France? Why not to Palestine?'

'To Palestine?' René looked shocked. 'You are seriously imagining that socialism will triumph in Palestine, with all those English colonialists? It would be madness. I couldn't have sent them there.'

'No,' concluded René, stirring his sugar into his after-dinner coffee, 'I've heard what Stalin is doing for his people, for all the different nationalities in Russia. He's building a special place where the Jews can be Jews and communists. I sent them there.'

'But who with? How could two children like that possibly go alone?'

'Go alone? No, the union had a representative from one of the big factories just south of Paris. He told me about how the Jews were being helped in Russia. I got everyone in the factory to contribute something to help them.'

'And how did the children feel about this?'

'The children? They didn't know anything. We told them what a great future they would have amongst their own people in the first truly socialist country.'

'And where is that just society happening in Russia?'

'Birobidzhan.'

'Where on earth is that?'

'Somewhere in the East of the country, where it's very healthy and the Jews can keep their own culture.'

'And this man? You believed him?'

'Of course, Mademoiselle. He brought me all the articles about it.'

'And that's where Daniel and Devorah have gone?'

'Yes.'

'Did other French children go too?'

'Only those who came from Russian stock. It was for Russian Jews who wanted to live the socialist dream.'

'And that's why you sent them?'

'Of course. It had to be in their best interest.'

# Chapter Fifteen

'Birobidzhan.'

'Sorry?'

Hervé looked up at me askance as though I had just uttered a swear word, which wasn't part of my normal vocabulary.

'Birobidzhan. It's the name of the town or the autonomous region where those children in St. Berthe were sent to.'

'Why were they taken there?'

'Because the union at the cheese factory believes in communism. And some Russian envoy arrived in France at the end of the war and declared that this place was a paradise for all Jewish workers.'

'And is it?'

'I have no idea. I don't even know where it is.'

'Alright. You'd better find out a bit more.'

Just the news that a roving journalist wants to hear from her editor, I thought.

'I looked it up in the geography department of the university library.'

'And?'

'It looks as though it's on the edge of the world. Deep in Siberia.'

'Siberia? That sounds more like a prison camp?'

'I agree but René from the cheese factory was adamant that they were creating a Jewish workers' paradise there.'

'Some people will believe anything.' Hervé looked at me through his cigarette ash with his usual cynicism. I couldn't help but notice that the desk, during my absence, had descended into its ancient chaos again.

'Let's hope for the sake of the children that it's true.' Pause. 'It would be good to find out and do an article on this workers' paradise.'

'The trouble is,' said Hervé carefully, 'that the discerning reader will not just believe any old idealistic formula.'

'You mean you have discerning readers?' I asked playfully. One of my ongoing arguments with the promoters of the communist media in Paris was why they wanted their clientele to believe in communism so exclusively. In my young life, I had already discovered that reality is a little more nuanced than that.

'At the moment,' rejoined Hervé, adroitly ignoring my gibe, 'your series of articles has been about what unionists and communists achieved during the war. We're playing the Free French at their game of 'who has the most heroes?' and we're establishing that some communists have been great patriots and fought the Nazis – just in case people forget that.

Your line, Marie, concerning the human element has worked wonders. We can trot out all the official figures of how many train lines the Communists blew up, but it's the human story which really captures people's imagination. Your article on the ship going to Palestine and the establishment of the kibbutz there really fired people up.'

'Even if you tweaked it so that it sounded as if the socialist paradise was about to be established in the Middle East, instead of being about civil war?' I asked cynically.

'OK. Let's be realistic. Our readers must follow the final line of 'Wouldn't communism be better for everyone?' Obviously, that's the point of a communist newspaper. But what captured people's' imagination was the story of Robert and Mireille being rescued from the Nazis at the last moment by a brave union man.'

'Alright,' I replied. 'The same rescue took place with Daniel and Devorah, so that's not a new story.' I knew in my brief career as a journalist that repetition was death for a newspaper.

'No, it's not, but what happened to them afterwards is. From what you say, life at St. Berthe with the famille Taube was pretty dispiriting, but it was safe, and that couple took a risk, and a big one when they looked after those children. Anyone could have turned them in, and they would have been dead.

So perhaps the line you need here is how the union at the cheese factory closed ranks and looked after them, and that's why René, the sour faced, unimaginative union man, found a solution at the end of the war.

And to be fair to your sour faced René, he did help the widow of his colleague by relieving her of a financial burden when she could not afford it and he did find a solution which was in keeping with children's Russian origins.'

'You mean, René has to be the hero of this story?' I grinned, thinking of Auguste's reaction to such an unlikely pitch.

'You don't have to make him into an amusing, vivacious problem solver.'

'Which he definitely is not. The word 'unimaginative' springs to mind,' I added, remembering the tedious conversation over coffee at the Café du Pont and its drab surroundings, which accorded well with my interviewee.

'Never mind that.'

Hervé rounded up the conversation in a business-like way. It was at these moments that you could see why he was a newspaper editor, who had to meet deadlines.

'Marie, find out more about this unpronounceable and mysterious place in Russia. You may be cynical about its position as the new Paradise, but, get some facts about it and in your article concentrate on the good will of the cheese factory union in St. Berthe.'

# Chapter Sixteen

Finding out the details of a mysterious place in Siberia did not prove to be easy. The two possible sources were Russian émigrés in Paris and more knowledgeable members of the Communist party who had present-day links with Russia. Both had their limitations. The émigrés had chosen to escape their homeland because they hated the Bolsheviks, so, even if they knew of the place, they were likely to be cynical about its acceptability. Most of the original Jews amongst them had disappeared in the Holocaust so no one could really give the Jewish point of view. Pro-Stalin communists in Russia saw everything there as ideal but had little interest in the Jews and just obediently trotted out the party line that a wonderful place was being developed for them in Siberia. The fact that most of the prison camps known as Gulags were also in Siberia, because of its inhospitable climate, seemed to have escaped their notice.

For a few weeks I pursued several lines of enquiry without success. My article remained unwritten, simply because there were no interesting facts to flesh it out with, apart from the escape of the children.

I had met up with the Russian émigrés in their customary Paris café haunts. They were friendly enough, but they were mainly moaners. Their talk centred around what the Bolsheviks had done to them and how many millions of roubles they had lost. When all I heard was how rich spoilt Russian aristocrats had done so well out of the Tsar's regime and that nothing would ever be the same again, I suddenly became a believer in socialism. I heard nostalgic accounts of balls in St. Petersburg and what had happened to High Prince or Princess so and so. I didn't feel very sorry for them because their accounts of straightened circumstances in Paris sounded very much better than those of the ordinary workers in Paris, never mind the poor suffering peasants in Russia. They had not had to endure the privations of the sieges of Leningrad and Stalingrad.

I was more impressed by those who had fought under the banner of the White Army in the civil war. They had at least had a vision for the future of the Russian people which seemed more balanced than that of Lenin and Stalin. On the defeat of the White Army, they had fled for their lives.

As I continued to hang round the Russian cafes, I started to hear other stories of people escaping the Motherland after the war and they sounded like a more promising source of information.

In the previous six months stories of horror had been coming from the concentration camps. Everyone in Paris felt desperate and guilty. They had connived at Jews being slaughtered in these terrible places. But as time went on, other stories started circulating – about how during the non-aggression pact between Hitler and Stalin, the Nazis had invaded the Baltic States and Jews had been systematically murdered. They were not sent anywhere. There was no pretence about labour camps. Thousands upon thousands in the towns and villages of Lithuania, Belarussia and Ukraine had been marched out into the forests and had been systematically shot. Those who had survived had been buried alive with the others in huge communal graves. For the remaining Jews in Western Europe, the sadness was overwhelming. For myself, remembering my best friend, Alain, and his warmth, wit, intelligence and gentle humanity, it was like hearing about an even more gruesome death than his own, a thousand times over. I was appalled by the horror of the human condition. It made me cynical about any 'isms', communism included. If normal German soldiers could do that under the banner of Nazism, so could anyone else under a different banner.

It was in such circumstances that I had met Andreyvitch who had come from Sebastopol to live with his cousins in Paris. He was the first Russian I met who knew anything about Birobidzhan.

He was a tall, lanky man without much personal grace, but his dark eyes were still brooding on all that he had experienced. He was glad, he said, to come to a place representing normal civilisation.

Normal civilisation is only on the surface, I couldn't help thinking. Not very far down is the human ability to turn a blind eye to atrocities.

'Don't worry, Andreyvitch,' said his cousin, determined to be upbeat. 'It's not going to happen again. The western powers have been warned.'

Andreyvitch did not respond to this wishful thinking. He had seen too much evil to be easily convinced by any glib optimism. I knew instinctively that I needed to speak to Andreyvitch at greater length and I was relieved to meet a Russian émigré in Paris who was not solely concerned about his Russian roubles or his inherited art collection.

Quite apart from my investigation into Birobidzhan, I knew that his story was worth listening to. It was connected to my love for Alain, as well as my desire to nose out a story as a journalist.

'Please could we meet sometime and talk about what you have experienced,' I asked as quietly and sympathetically as I could.

'It depends on what you want to do with it,' he suggested solemnly. 'If you want to trivialise it and use it for some cheap journalistic project, then I don't want to. It would be a shameless sacrifice to squander the terrible suffering of my fellow Crimeans.'

'I don't even necessarily want to use it to write about,' I said honestly. 'I want to hear it because my best friend before the war was Jewish and he gave his life for his family. I have never forgotten his heroism or his intelligence or his wit. I feel sick that brutes killed him for no other reason apart from his racial origins. It was a tragedy. And now, every time I hear about his people, I think more deeply about him and what I have lost.'

Andreyvitch regarded me solemnly and searchingly. 'In that case, Mademoiselle, I apologize for attributing unworthy motives to your interest in my story. You have loved one of my people.'

And in truth, I had. It was the first time I realised that I had loved not only my school friend, but a representative of a great people.

'No one can conceive of what it means to wipe a whole village out,' he began. 'Even now I cannot take it in. It means far more to me than the whole story of the war and what happened between nations.'

We had met at a café outside my local area and beyond the usual haunts of the Russian émigrés. I somehow felt that his story was sacred and couldn't be contaminated with the ordinary.

'I had been brought up in Vitesbsk, but my parents were unusual amongst the Jews who were brought up in the Pale of the Settlement.

Jewish culture and education alone were not good enough for their sons. We were sent away to Odessa, in order to stay with a distant relative who was a secular, not a religious Jew. We would go to schul on special holidays but most of the time we were learning by working as clerks at my second cousin's finance firm.'

'And did you enjoy it?' I could not imagine the intense young man I was meeting now, in a finance firm.

'It was tedious, but it was a way to get ahead, so that later we could study poetry or music or whatever we wanted.'

'Did that mean you were away when the Germans invaded?'

'Yes, the whole change of Stalin's position happened very quickly. One minute the Ukraine was Russian, the next it was German. There was no warning.'

'My second cousin in Odessa was more worldly-wise than we were. He was immediately alarmed about the international situation and kept us boys in the capital, got rid of our side locks and made us officially part of his secular staff.'

'When did you discover what had happened to your family?'

'There were rumours in Odessa, but they were so terrible that no one could believe that they were true. After a time, we two brothers insisted that we go back to the village to find out.'

'And you found?'

'Nothing. It was like the village had never existed. We were so confused that we even wondered whether we had gone back to the wrong place. We were strong and determined young men, but we were rushing around the forest, calling out the names of our parents and sisters. My youngest sister, Katya, was seven years old. I could not believe that any man could do such an evil thing as to get rid of her. A Ukranian peasant had hidden two Jews in her barn – she was very brave. They would have killed her too if they had known. She told us that the Germans had herded them out of the forest and shot them.'

'Why did they go willingly?'

'No one could believe that they were all going to be shot. They were told that they had to do some work felling trees in the forest for the army. It was only when they were digging up the ground that they realised.'

313

'I found the place where it had happened. I found Katya's scarf on the ground near where she had died. I hope she died immediately. Some of them were buried alive. The Ukranian peasant said that the grave was still heaving three days later. That sort of suffering is unimaginable.'

Silence. The only possible mark of respect. This man was carrying a heavy burden in cosmopolitan Paris. I was afraid to move him on to the focus of my investigation.

'Andreyvitch, some Russians are saying that there is still a place for Jews in Soviet Russia. Do you agree?'

He stared gloomily at his cigarette smoke, seeming almost to ignore my question. After a time, he continued,

'I'm not sure I think that there is a place for Jews anywhere in Europe, at the moment. I don't want to belong anywhere. I'm not sure I want to go on living.'

There was no adequate reply to his despair, and I could not even try to persuade a man who had experienced such trauma, to give me what I needed for something as tawdry as a newspaper article.

# Chapter Seventeen

Andreyvitch's despair was potent. I felt awed by it. How could I possibly enter into what this man had suffered? In some ways it was worse than the emerging stories of the Holocaust in the camps. Most of the Jews who were alive in Europe had not actually been there. They knew that their relatives had died and wept for them. But they had no sense that they could have prevented it; no sense that, except for a few random circumstances, they might have been part of it. It didn't matter how many times you told Andreyvitch that he had done nothing wrong by being in Odessa at the time of the invasion or that he could not have prevented the massacre. He wished that he had been there so that, even if he could not have protected his family, he could have died with them. He did not appreciate the gift of life apart from his loved ones and therefore he could not find any useful purpose for it.

I grieved for him, but I could not pretend to be in the same position. Even losing my dearest friend Alain was not the same. Was he the love of my life? I had no idea. I wasn't mature enough to make that sort of analysis, but my memory of Alain was becoming hazy. I had turned in my emotions and mind away from him to the desire to succeed in my present circumstances.

Birobidzhan did exist. Of that I was sure. Jewish refugees, including Daniel and Devorah, were going there, but was it going to be successful? Was it a safe solution for European or Russian Jews? And what was really going on in Stalin's domain thousands of miles away?

I poured out my frustrations to Hervé.

He was amused by my passionate concern. 'Well, madam get to the bottom at all costs journalist, there's only one way to find out.'

'Sorry?' I was brought up short by his attitude. Was he mocking my supposed ambition or pouring scorn on my ability and vanity?

'You'll have to go there, won't you?'

'Go there? So how am I going to get to the far side of Europe?'

'By train.'

'By train.' I repeated his words like some crazy zombie. 'Oh sure, I'll just cycle to the Gare du Lyon, and set off on the 8:20. Should be there by midnight.'

'No, no. I'm quite serious. The Russians have a train. It's called the Trans-Siberian express. You get it in Moscow, and it takes you right across the Urals and into Asia. Vladivostock is on the far side, on the Pacific Ocean.'

I stared at him in disbelief.

'OK, so I jump on a train. And who's going to pay for this?'

'Right, so now we're talking practicalities. Libération and possibly Le Rouge too.'

'The Rouge? Since when did they have sort of money? And if Libération has, why haven't my wages gone up?'

'Now, now, that's selfish, capitalist talk, comrade.'

'It's personal survival talk.'

Hervé sighed mockingly. 'You've become a hard-headed woman, Marie, while you've been working here.'

'As it happens,' Hervé added carefully, 'and I hate to admit this, but while you've been writing your articles about Bordeaux and socialism in Palestine, our readership has expanded. You've done well for us. That's why I'm offering you this chance.'

I was stupefied and thrilled and terrified all at once. Surely you couldn't just get on a train and go to the far side of Siberia and come back again!

'Alright,' I responded cautiously. 'You've decided it's worth it and it can be done. What about the small matter of Stalin?'

'What? Our worthy leader? Come, come, comrade. Don't tell me you wouldn't trust him with your life.'

I snorted. 'I wouldn't trust anyone with my life. And news coming out of Eastern Europe isn't exactly encouraging. As far as I can see he's bulldozing his way through Hungary.'

'You mean, liberating them.'

'Pull the other one.'

'OK, so you don't want the assignment. Too much of a risk for you?'

He knew that would have an effect. How would I ever get anywhere in the world of journalism if I didn't take a risk? And I was still a French citizen. Surely there was a limit as to what a mad dictator could do to a French citizen!

'If you're in anyway serious, I'll do it.'

Then I thought about practicalities.

'But how do you get into Russia in the first place? Presumably it's not just the 4th stop after the Gare du Lyon?'

Hervé laughed. 'Yes, I think it'll be a bit more complicated than that. Maybe you'll have to fly to Moscow to start with.'

'Fly?' Such sophistication was well beyond my imagination.

'Yes, flying, Marie. Mankind has been doing it for the last fifty years.'

'No one told anyone in Les Landes about it,' I replied dryly.

'Well now, might be the time to stop being a little Landaise and grow into being a big brave French journalist.'

How I liked that description! What it meant in terms of sacrifice and discomfort I had no idea. I thought I would emerge from a plane journey with a beautiful new aura, ready to conquer the world.

'I'll do you a deal,' proposed Hervé, with immense confidence despite the shadowy nature of the assignment.

'You keep on chipping away at the idea of Birobidzhan with any Russian émigrés you can find and any true believers in the Russian revolution, who might still be hanging around in Paris.'

'The only true believers I've ever met are in the Café du Carrefour and are friends of yours.'

Despite his cynicism, Hervé was unexpectedly loyal to his friends. 'They do have the merit of having brains, which is more than can be said for most of the bourgeois Parisians who suck up to de Gaulle.'

He continued with surprising energy. 'I'll go to the consulate and find out about the visa. There's bound to be a mania for bureaucratic stamps if we're talking about the Bolsheviks and I can always do a handy bit of bribery all for the sake of the cause.'

# Chapter Eighteen

I did quite a bit of research in Paris through the Russian émigrés whom I met in the cafes and literary clubs. They weren't very helpful. As I had already discovered, most of them were long term escapees from the Bolsheviks and had no words of encouragement about Stalin's attitude to anything or his ability to offer safe transport to foreigners. They were mostly completely wrapped in their own problems. You would have thought from speaking to them that they had been in as great a danger as the Jews. There was not a lot of love lost between the two groups. I felt at first hand some of the anti-semitism of Tsarist Russia. The fate of the Jews was an old problem that none of them seemed to care about

Finding Jews who were prepared to talk about Russia was hard. If they had any thoughts about returning to their homeland, they would not openly criticize Stalin and his regime because they knew that spies were listening. They were nervous about staying anywhere but their best hope for being prosperous was to stay in France or emigrate to America. If any of them had money, they chose the latter option. Most of them were cynical about a possible future in Palestine. It was not a comfortable choice and was generally pursued by the idealists and those who were young enough to make a fresh start.

The process of applying for a visa for a defined period was long and arduous and I was amazed at Hervé's energy and enthusiasm in trying to procure one for me.

While waiting, I made an unexpected decision. It came to me quite suddenly one morning when I woke up. As many instinctively right decisions do, it seemed to come from nowhere. I would return to Les Landes and tell my parents what I was doing and see my friends at the

Hôtel du Centre. I had no way of easily communicating with my parents, as telephones were not part of rural France, so I packed my small suitcase, asked for two weeks leave from Libération and took the train first to Bordeaux and then to Labouyère. There would be a few pony and traps driven by farmers going in the direction of Mimizan.

I was excited and apprehensive about seeing my native countryside again. When I got off the train at Labouyère, I was immediately struck by the leisurely pace of the small town and the silence. I had become accustomed to the background rumble of Parisian streets and the air seemed empty by comparison. I managed to get a ride with the father of a former school friend, Annick, as he was driving over to the coast to move some farming implements.

'Annick is expecting her second,' he informed me conversationally as we drove along.

'Her second what?' I asked puzzled.

He returned my puzzled look with a stare of incomprehension.

'Her second baby of course. Little Joel is almost eighteen months now.'

'Oh, how wonderful!' I exclaimed politely. I couldn't think of anything worse than settling down at Annick's age with two young children. 'Who is her husband? Would I know him?'

He chuckled. 'I should think so, seeing as he spent a few years with you in that school room. Fabrice Leleux?'

'Oh Fabrice. I remember. He wanted to be a farmer.'

Silence. Why would you want to be anything else, was the unspoken reply!

After another thirty minutes or so, 'So you don't have a young man in Paris?'

'No…I don't. I have my job to do which keeps me busy. I'm a journalist.' I might as well have said that I was an alien for all the response it elicited.

'Just come back to see your parents then, not to stay?'

'No, no. I'm not staying. I've got an assignment in Russia,' I stated proudly, hoping for an admiring reaction.

'Russia? Where all those murdering commies are? Why would you want to go there?'

'To find out what some of them are up to.'

Annick's father snorted. 'We know what they're up to. No good. Keep out of their way I say and don't let them come over here.'

It seemed that investigative journalism to uncover the truth was not a priority in Les Landes because the population already knew the truth. A convenient way of living, I thought.

We had rounded a pretty bend in the road, where the inland trees were coming into bud in the early spring, and we passed a windmill constructed of local wood, which had been there for a century. Eventually we came to the long, straight roads of coastal Les Landes with more and more pine trees. The lowering sun was just peeping through them, warming us as we travelled on the cart.

'So, has much changed in Mimizan?' I asked, thinking that I already knew the answer. But I was surprised by his reply.

'Well, I don't need to tell you that the Boches have gone and good riddance.' He spat from the side of the cart onto the road surface. 'But the holiday makers have started coming.'

'Holiday makers?'

'Yes, they were starting to come before the war.'

'Were they?' I had never noticed such a breed of people but then I had confined myself to forest paths and usually had my head in a book.

'Oh yes. The old spa in Mimizan has opened up again.'

'And people are coming?'

'They certainly are,' he said cynically but without bitterness. 'Those with plenty of money. Those who made it on the black market and have still got it.'

'I guess it will bring prosperity to the area.'

'So, they say. It also brings noise and too many people on the roads.'

I didn't tell him that compared with Paris these roads were an oasis of quiet.

'Here you are then. Can you walk from here?'

He had put me out at the crossroads of St. Paul en Borne. It was another three miles to my parents' small holding. A few years ago, I would have thought nothing of walking it. Now I found that exercise did not come naturally to me, but the walk gave me time to get myself ready mentally for meeting my parents again.

I pushed open the back door near the back yard and called out but there was no answer. I dropped my bag in the house which had not changed at all. I might have been returning from school four years ago.

My mother, hearing the noise, came in from the back yard where she had been feeding the pigs.

'Oh, so you've returned, have you?'

I went to give her a big hug but here whole stance told me that it wasn't wanted.

'Come to use us for somewhere to stay rather than helping with the work, I see. Nothing's changed then.'

'Maman, I've just walked in the door,' I remonstrated as reasonably as I could. 'Let me help with feeding the pigs while you put the kettle on.'

'Not with those fine clothes, you don't,' she replied, glancing at my workmanlike blouse and skirt, which in Paris would have been considered plain. 'You're a bit above us now.'

'Maman, of course I'm not above you. I've come to see how you're getting on. If you need to finish feeding the pigs yourself, I'll get the water on for a drink.'

'If you like,' and she turned her back on me in order to go out into the yard. I felt rejected, just as I had felt rejected all those years ago as a child. She might have too much work to do, but she wasn't even interested or even happy that her only child had returned for a visit.

I sat down next to the old log burner and had a drink while she prepared supper. The farm had not changed, her attitude had not changed, but physically she had changed. I had not noticed the amount of grey in her hair before. I had never noticed how small she was and surely in the past her face had not been so lined? Had she aged or had I never noticed signs of age when I was living with her? I felt guilty at my lack of care for this old woman who felt like a stranger to me. I asked all the questions, almost like a professional journalist would, and she asked very little back. I was longing to report with pride about my job. She saw nothing about me in which to have pride.

I was feeling disillusioned again and almost wishing I had not come when my father entered, straight from his usual pursuit of fishing. In contrast to my mother, he put down his rod, and gave me a huge welcoming smile and hug.

'And so, our little Parisienne returns. Let's look at you.' He cast me an appreciative eye. 'You've grown well beyond the old folks in the farm.'

I laughed delightedly. 'But I haven't forgotten them.' I knew it was a lie. I forgot them most days, but it pleased him.

'The café in the big city is treating you well then?'

'No, papa, I'm not in the café anymore. I'm a journalist. I write for a paper.'

'Our little girl writing for a paper! That's wonderful, isn't it, Annie?'

My mother had her back to us, stirring the soup and she did not reply.

# Chapter Nineteen

Just as I had in my teens, now it didn't take me long to get out of the house. After the evening meal I went down to the Hôtel du Centre, revelling in my grown-up status as the one who intended to buy the drinks, rather than serve them.

I was greeted with genuine affection by Thérèse and, after chatting to the regular clientele, who were augmented by a few visitors, I stayed after closing hours to chat to her. I told her about my change of job, and she was impressed.

'I didn't think it would take you very long to go places, Marie, and I was right.'

'You were the one who believed in me and helped me to get to Paris.'

'It was just lucky I had a cousin there, though,' she added with a lift of her clearly defined eyebrow. 'I gather you weren't the greatest in the cleaning glasses department.'

I laughed. 'No, it's not my gift, but it was a stepping-stone to something else,' and I explained about the progress of my new career. I also explained that I was hoping to have an assignment in Russia.

'Wow, that sounds important. I hope it's safe, Marie.'

'I'm sure it will be with the right visas,' I reassured her more confidently that I felt. 'It's only a three-month tourist visa.'

'I just hope they understand the idea of 'tourist'. As far as I've heard, it's a workers' paradise or hell, depending on your point of view.'

'Does Patrice's dad still keep up with the communists?'

'Patrice's dad was a changed man once he came back from the German work camp. I think he wants his own fireside these days, rather than any brand of politics.'

'I'm not surprised after what he had lived through. We were relatively lucky here. There was a massacre in the village called Oradour-sur-Glane in the Pyrenées, even though the Germans were on their way out.'

'I heard about it. We French will never forgive them for that. There must have been a less ferocious commander in charge of the mop up operation round here.'

'Thank God for that.'

We talked together about how Les Landes was changing, as there was already an influx of tourists from the Paris area and the spa was being revived in Mimizan Plage, and new roads were being built.

'You'll be like them soon,' laughed Thérèse. 'Coming back here once a year to take the waters.'

'I'll come back here to look at the sea and the forest, never mind taking the waters.'

'Make sure you do. Don't get too high and mighty for us.'

I looked at the back door of the small kitchen which I had used regularly before cycling back into the forest.

'I could not forget this place Thérèse. It's where my life started and had meaning.'

Thérèse moved the glasses off the side sink. 'Don't get too philosophical with me. Do something useful and get these glasses put on the side, will you? I can see why Lily got fed up with you in her café.'

If I wanted a deeper level of conversation, I had to see Mlle Tessier. I wondered how she would seem after all these years in the schoolhouse. She looked older and more forlorn, but her smile was the same as she welcomed me after dismissing her class.

'Come and have a goûter with me, Marie, at my little house. It's so wonderful to see you.'

'And you.' It was more than polite conversation. I realised that Mlle Tessier was just about the only person in the area with whom I could have a genuine exchange of views.

'A journalist! It's wonderful! I can't believe that the shy little girl who wouldn't mix with anyone is doing such amazing things.'

'I think 'amazing things' might be a bit of an exaggeration,' I admitted laughingly. 'So far it's been a bit of a hand to mouth existence.'

'Yes, but that's inevitable at the beginning. You have to start somewhere, and you've earned your place on your own merits.'

She still had the ability to make me feel good about myself, as she had all those years ago when she was my teacher. We talked about the sadness of losing Alain. Again, she was the only one who understood about our friendship.

'He would be so thrilled with you, if he was here today, Marie.'

'You think so?'

'I know so. You helped save his family and his friends in Bordeaux.'

'But I couldn't save him.'

'He chose not to be saved out of loyalty to his mother.'

'I know, I know.' I spoke out my frustration honestly before her. 'But why did he have to die because of his mother and brother and sisters? They were nothing compared to him.'

There was silence. She knew what I meant. It was very unlikely that younger siblings, brought up in the isolation of the forest could have the intelligence, sensitivity and initiative of Alain. In one family there only going to be one person of his calibre.

'The only thing is, Marie,' said Mlle Tessier gently, 'Who can say who is worth saving? Why is one human being worth more than another?'

'But he was. He was extraordinary.'

'I know but that doesn't mean that he was worth more than another human being.'

'In what sense? To whom? He was worth more in my eyes.'

'Yes, but you're not God.'

'Of course not. But who is this God who can choose the wrong human being to be saved? Do you believe in God, Mlle Tessier?'

Silence. There wasn't going to be an easy answer to this one.

'My belief has been tested many times, but, yes, I think I do.'

'With all these terrible murders of innocent people?'

'That's the choice of evil people. But actually, without a God, there's no purpose at all, no point at all.'

'What about just getting on with the accident of life?'

'That doesn't help when you don't feel like getting on with it and there's no reason to do anything.'

I remembered the stories I'd heard about her own terrible suffering after the Great War.

'Have you found a purpose here?'

She looked round at the little schoolhouse. 'Yes, I have. I love these children, not just the clever ones like you and Alain, but all of them. I see their potential and want to help them.'

'Then they're very lucky children,' I declared, wondering how my life would have been without her influence.

'And the communists?' I asked later, after I had told her about my forthcoming project. 'Do you think they could do something good?'

'You never know, Marie. They could. They might achieve something worthwhile for ordinary people.'

'Even though so many ordinary people have suffered in Russia?'

'Ordinary people suffer everywhere. It's only the rich who can buy their way out of uncomfortable circumstances. I think a government for the poor must have it right somewhere.'

# Chapter Twenty

I thought a lot about her words on my flight from Paris to Moscow in May 1948. Perhaps because of a bourgeois fear of communism and the dread of losing property, Stalin's government had engendered fear in France. The Russian émigrés in Paris had nothing but scorn for the Bolsheviks, but, I thought, they were the ones with the most to lose materially. The factory workers had only a terrible life to lose, so why not embrace the Revolution? After the war, de Gaulle and the right-wing parties in Paris stirred up hatred of Bolshevism for their political advantage. What was really going on? I had heard rumours that the Berlin airlifts were about to begin and the start of what was being called 'the iron curtain'. If life was grim in the East, then maybe socialism gave the ordinary citizen something to live for. I would not be prejudiced, I thought, but wait and see for myself. Hervé had warned me in no uncertain terms, 'Whatever you feel, don't let anything negative come out of your reports. And you will need to be careful when you come back, as much as for the sake of this paper as for your own life. We can't let Libération be badly seen in Russia.' I could have retorted tartly that there wasn't much point in going to see the country if I had already decided what I was going to see anyway. But underneath the controversy, I wanted to find out what had happened to Daniel and Devorah. Had the Jews really been given a safe place in the autonomous region as they had been promised?

Whatever the outcome, I was incredibly excited. I had never been on a plane in my life and the taxi journey to Orly alone was enough for me to feel that I was doing something special. I loved the offer of free food and wine and the sophisticated beauty of the air hostesses. The men around me were either French businessmen or Russians. There were very few women on the flight – a bit like Saturday night at the Hôtel du Centre, I thought, giggling in an immature way. They all needed Thérèse to keep them in order.

'What are you doing here, young lady?' asked the unexpected voice of an American next to me. My English was of the schoolgirl variety, but I knew enough to explain that I was a journalist. The man was pleasingly impressed.

'You're very brave.'

'I'm hoping I don't need to be. The Bolsheviks want positive coverage in Western European newspapers, so I hope they're going to treat me well.'

'I can tell you now – they need more than newspapers. They need money. That's why American firms like mine are trying to help.'

I was surprised to hear that the Bolsheviks welcomed American capitalists.

My neighbour laughed at my naivety. 'It depends what we have to sell them. I work for a tractor firm. They need us to keep their agriculture on track.'

'Actually,' he added. 'My firm is sympathetic to their social values. But that makes the American government not very sympathetic to what we're doing.'

'Why not?'

'Because they're terrified of communism. All the Western leaders like Roosevelt and Churchill and de Gaulle are.'

'In your view should they be?'

'For loss of freedom maybe but not for what they're giving the poor. If I was Russian, I wouldn't have my luxury flight and meals paid for by Air France. It's the rich who have so much to fear from communism.'

'So why does your firm support it?'

He laughed. 'Ah well, we're making money out of Stalin's latest five-year plan. It's all to do with being selfish.'

A depressing thought, but I had no reason to disagree. After all we all knew that the black-market profiteers in the war had prospered because they were selfish.

'Anyway,' added my new companion, 'don't let me put you off. Here's to your enterprise!' He toasted me with Air France's dinner wine.

I was terrified by the juddering of the engine, and the wings going up and down outside the window. When we landed, I was sure we were going to crash and briefly asking the god who I had heard about to rescue me. I was sure I wasn't going to survive very long in an atheist country. When I started panicking, I needed more than the party to hold onto!

Getting through customs with my visa was the first hurdle. The woman at the desk was stony faced and questioning. Charm on her part or mine was not called for. I felt guilty all the time though I had no idea for what reason. Eventually I was assigned to a minder, who took me through customs to a waiting car and I was taken to a hotel near the Kremlin.

'Do not say anything to anyone in the hotel rooms,' Hervé had warned me, 'because they will be listening in.' The person assigned to listen in to my room must have found the job very tedious. Also, the pipes were so antiquated that they were continually emitting strange noises. I wanted to go out and explore but I had already been told that it wasn't allowed. My train was not due to depart until the following evening, so I requested a tourist visit to Lenin Square the following day and was duly assigned a guide. The square, with its surrounding onion-shaped roofs, was impressive and I made the obligatory visit to Lenin's mausoleum. Other visitors were weeping with emotion as they saw the great man. I couldn't help but be reminded of the book I had read about Greek peasants venerating and even kissing the relics of their saints, but I said nothing even when I was treated to a lecture about the wonders of the revolution by my guide. The tour was a welcome break from the drab surroundings of the hotel. I can only describe it as grey, greasy, and sweaty with stodgy food and stony-faced workers. My small experience of Alain's community had been one of joy and vivacity. I wondered how any Jewish community might fit into this world of unsmiling faces.

# Chapter Twenty-One

By the early evening, my bag was packed, and I was ready for the taxi ride to the station. I was excited because this was really my entrance ticket into the world of Siberia and Birobidzhan. Before coming I had bought a Russian/French phrase book, but I realised that I should have practised a bit harder with Andreyvitch before coming. Getting anyone distracted enough to pay attention to my queries was difficult. It was as if they all had to concentrate hard on their own duties and it did not allow them any spare time to give to a stranger. I also realised that the presence of a foreigner was unusual to say the least. If Paris was full of refugees, émigrés and the remains of American and British troops, Russia was full of Russians. It was such a vast country and had been cut off from the west for so long because of the revolution, its internal struggles and the war, that foreigners were not an acknowledged species.

I eventually found my train which was a miracle because at one point I had been afraid I was going to miss it and was panicking about staying in Moscow for ever, instead of reaching my intended destination.

When I got on board, I first encountered the carriage dragon. As time went on, I christened her 'Little Miss Bossy Boots'. I was the one privileged to travel under her guardianship. There was no 'the customer is always right' attitude here. But there were some good things too. Each waggon had its own samovar, like a huge tea pot. Being a French woman, I was more naturally a coffee drinker but at least I could get a hot drink on board. I had already been warned about the need to bring my own provisions, but there were also plenty of stops en route with stall holders outside the train on the platform eager to sell their wares.

I needn't have worried about starving. One of the most delightful surprises for me was the welcome I received from the other members of my twenty-bunk dormitory. If I had had the impression from Moscow that all Russians were hostile to human beings in general, never mind questionable foreigners, that impression was obliterated by the warmth of the welcome I was now given. Most of it was through sign language but I was shown which bunk to take, how to get to the toilet, how to lay out my possessions and keep my valuables safe, by friendly fellow travellers. It was as if we were in a completely different country to the one outside the train. It was a mixed carriage but that didn't make it feel threatening. It was more like a holiday camp atmosphere and I started to relax. People wanted to know where I was going and why and all about Paris, which had acquired a status in their minds as the most exotic foreign destination. According to them, even to meet someone from there was an honour. If only they could see me cleaning Mme Dubois's room or tidying Hervé's desk, I thought, then they wouldn't see me as a representative of the city of Chanel or Dior. However, for now I would enjoy my celebrity status!

I had decided to keep a diary though everyone in France had warned me about its necessary limitations. I was not to record names or anti soviet views. As I have always kept a diary to record my innermost thoughts, I was not used to censorship, but I thought I could use my own code to circumvent the restrictions. Also, my memory was such that I easily recorded the content of important conversations and, if their recall acted as a trigger to my own developing ideas, I could easily keep track of them. I had not yet read Orwell's 1984, but I was convinced rather arrogantly that I could defeat Big Brother in my mind and, if necessary, on paper.

The train set off, passing through the straggling suburbs of Moscow, some of which were like shanty towns and others just grey blocks of rabbit hutches. Then one of my fellow travellers called across to me, 'Look!' and I saw new blocks of flats being constructed with one or two already finished. 'New, new. You see Stalin act for us,' the man said proudly, and I realised that I should ignore the unfortunate existence of the shanty town and rabbit hutches and see only the bright new future for the Soviet Union. I decided to play the game. 'Lovely, lovely,' I repeated conveying great respect in my tone of voice. 'You are very lucky,' I lied, knowing that the most rural citizens of France or the workers in the big unions in Paris or Bordeaux were better housed than this. My enthusiasm pleased everyone. I had proved myself a safe person to travel with and soon everyone's food was being shared and that included mine, although I had only some black bread and cheese, bought at the station at an exorbitant price, to contribute.

What struck me about the companionship of that journey was how, despite the leveller of communism and the imposed homogeneous reactions, individuals still emerged. On the parallel high bunk bed across the way from me was a young man who appeared to be an acrobat. He stood on his head, did amazing tricks by contorting his body into impossible shapes and routinely staged one-man exhibitions throughout the journey. As we finished our meal and everyone went out to help themselves from the samovar, the after-dinner party pieces emerged. One man produced a small ukulele and sang piercingly sad songs which touched everyone's emotions and made some travellers cry but they also had such a cathartic effect that everyone felt more cheerful afterwards. Someone stood up between the bunks and proclaimed what I was told was Pushkin's poetry with great drama and was duly applauded. A woman sang light and lilting folk songs and then one or two operatic arias. I felt ashamed. I had been invited to the dinner party and had no party piece to contribute. The entertainment continued far into the night, but no one minded because it was difficult to sleep against the shunting of the wheels and the whistles of the steam.

The next morning, I was awake and peeping out of the curtains and for hundreds of miles it was flat agricultural land. I noticed how basic the farming equipment was – mainly horses and ploughs – and thought my American acquaintance from the Air France flight was going to make a vast profit if he sold here. We began to stop at small stations, and I got down onto the platforms – often a hastily constructed boardwalk – just to stretch my legs and breathe fresh air. The peasants who trailed alongside us looked half-starved and dejected as they offered a few potatoes or some thick lentil stew for sale.

'If you have the money, please buy from them,' urged my neighbour from an upper bunk who spoke some English. 'If you don't, you are their last hope.'

'What about the other people on the train?' I asked, annoyed by his interference. Was I to take responsibility for all these thin faced people?

'Those of us with extra roubles like myself will do, if we can. Most people on this train have saved for months for this journey, so that they can see their relatives or go home after they have finished service with the Red Army.'

The food on offer all looked unappetising but I had an idea. 'How about if I buy a meal for several of us. Would that work?'

'Probably. The car attendant will finish cooking it.'

Sure enough, Little Miss Bossy Boots got to work and then decided who around me could have a ladle of stew. When she finally served it in small dishes, she was so pleased that I had the impression that she herself had provided it for us all. If it was a rather reluctantly given generosity on my part, I profited greatly from the ensuing popularity I gained in my part of the carriage. Even better, my neighbour, whose name was Gregory, produced a bottle of vodka for everyone to share. I was startled by the kick of the warm alcohol as it poured down my throat.

Watching my reaction, Gregory enquired solicitously, 'Haven't you had vodka before?' I shook my head in reply. 'Don't worry. You get used to it. It's the only thing which keeps people going in Siberia.'

'I've been told I'm going to a workers' paradise,' I ventured, disingenuously.

Gregory guffawed loudly and repeated the words to everyone around, the vodka making him bold. Everyone repeated my words with great gusto and laughed and slapped me on the back.

'Enjoy our workers' paradise, dear little French girl.'

I understood the implication and didn't put anyone in danger by questioning too closely. Oh, well, I can survive anything for three months, I thought.

'At least I won't be there over winter,' I said to Gregory.

'No, but summer's bad enough,' he replied cheerfully. 'Get ready for the mosquitoes and swamps and infected water.'

I turned over sleepily to the wall of the carriage, completely overwhelmed by the effect of the vodka.

# Chapter Twenty-Two

The countryside changed. Vast plains gave way to the mighty Ural mountains which were covered with coniferous forests, waterfalls and streams. At times the train went so slowly I could have touched the trees if I had reached out far enough. The heat manufactured inside the oven of an enormous continent was slowly increasing and I could feel its intensity during the daytime stops at stations. The wooden buildings which were home to these small communities seemed to get more and more dilapidated as our journey progressed.

'How on earth do they survive in wintertime?' I asked Gregory.

'Vodka, samovars, communal fires, where everyone sits round with their feet towards the fire, layers of clothing if you're lucky, and of course, sex,' he finished matter-of-factly.

'I would have thought the climate conditions would put anyone off sex,' I suggested, inadvertently revealing my lack of experience in such matters. Any joyful discarding of clothes I had seen in films seemed unimaginable in such a climate.

'Fortunately, no one gets put off sex for very long. Even in the gulags where relationships are forbidden and people work fourteen hours a day in impossible conditions, sex still happens. I know, little girl.' Gregory was not to be contradicted on this matter. I didn't want to ask the question – how do you know about sex in Siberia or the gulags? However, Gregory had no inhibitions about explaining further. 'I know about both, little girl, from personal experience.' We were talking late at night near the samovar. Little Miss Bossy Boots had retired for the night. I'm not sure that she ever slept but she couldn't understand our broken English. Curiously, the change of language allowed me a certain freedom from inhibitions.

'Tell me, Gregory.'

'All right, as long as you don't quote me in the west. I could be sent back again or worse – if it is worse to be executed rather than enduring a living hell.'

'Why were you sent there?'

'To be re-educated. My neighbour snitched on me in the purges before the war. I was accused of reading capitalist literature and pamphlets written by non-communist agitators.'

I was silent as the train's wheels clacked next to my ears and I gripped my cup, still warm from the leftovers of my tea, and waiting to be filled again.

'You mean you were punished because you were reading?' I asked slowly, articulating the idea to myself, so that I could take in the enormity of the deprivation of freedom this entailed. I thought of the life-sustaining elixir which reading had always been to me, how it had allowed me to break free from the stultifying confines of my family background, of how it gave me a platform for conversations with Alain and Mlle Tessier. What country was this, I asked myself, which did not allow people to read?

'How can you stand it?'

'I have no choice. I was born here and, before you ask, you can't escape unless you have money and connections, which most people don't, and, even when they do have, they get caught and punished before they can get out.'

'Then,' I stated slowly, 'it's like a giant prison.'

He laughed. 'Yes, it's a continent-wide gulag, with the smaller ones tucked into a corner of the bigger gulag. But, don't worry, dear little French girl,' he said with a wry grin, as he shifted his weight more comfortably onto his haunches, 'it's all for our good …ultimately.'

'How?''

'Everyone is experiencing more freedom, more equality of material prosperity and more significance as a worker, contributing to the greater success of our socialist paradise.'

'All I can say is that I hope it does contribute to something good because the means to achieve it seem pretty drastic to me.'

'It's not just for now. Generations to come will benefit.'

'But will they be allowed to read?'

He laughed. 'Don't get too obsessed with reading, little one. Most people before 1917 didn't have the leisure and education to read, so it doesn't much matter that they don't have it now.'

'Someone must have been reading,' I objected, 'at least Marx. Otherwise the revolution wouldn't have happened.'

'A few people read, but most people were told about it at night, in the illegal factory union meetings and most people acted on it at the end of a gun.'

'Which end?'

'A small number at the trigger end and most of them at the barrel end.'

'And you?'

'I was only a child when the revolution happened. We lived in a village and my parents objected to their ancient serf farming methods being taken over. But in the end, it was a case of 'do what you're told, or you'll be dead.' They didn't object for very long.'

'They must have been so angry.' I thought about how my parents would have felt if they hadn't been able to farm their land as they wanted.

'No. They were luckier than most.

The Soviet who led them weren't corrupt like some. They at least had basic food. In those early days, millions either starved to death or got caught up in the civil war between the Whites and the Reds. We were relatively lucky.'

'Even though you got sent to a gulag for reading?'

'Luckiest of all I survived the gulag and, when war broke out, Russia needed all the men she could find, so I got released.'

'As cannon fodder?'

'Sorry?'

'in order for you to die on the battle front.'

'Millions of people died on the battle front – the non-readers, the top of the class Bolsheviks, everyone. I'm the lucky one. I didn't die and I'm a free man talking to you on a train.'

'Thank you.'

We squatted on the floor next to each other in companionable silence. I was half asleep and the floor was very hard, but I tried to absorb the suffering of this one man and indeed of a whole nation. I knew I couldn't. But my conversation with Gregory prepared me for the respect and humility I would soon feel as I came to know the community of Birobidzhan.

The train seemed to pass the same scenery for days on end. I almost stopped looking out of the window except that there was nothing else to do. I had brought books, but I wanted to save them for the challenge of boredom in Birobidzhan and, when I wrote my journal, I did it as a clandestine activity deep under the covers of my top-level bunk.

I practised my Russian phrases. I had a few rudimentary conversations in French or English with my fellow passengers, but I was careful not to pay too much attention to Gregory in case he was accused of being a spy or of giving anti-socialist ideas to me. Deep within me, I didn't think anyone would. They all seemed a decent non-political, ordinary bunch of people, but Gregory had already warned me that when someone is accused of treason, that person automatically starts accusing someone else as a means of self-preservation. That was why, in the purges before the war, the whole country had become a seething network of informers and accusers. No one was worse than anyone else – it was just the inevitable result of the system. No wonder then, I thought, that everyone I had met in Moscow, had been stony faced and unsmiling. Even the ubiquitous vodka was more an escape from everyday awfulness and produced a maudlin sentimentality. The French loved their wine, but it seemed to produce gaiety and laissez-faire as national characteristics, not introspective misery.

As we went further East, the countryside changed again. The tundra became sparser, but the trees were softer. The silver birches were just coming into leaf and sometimes, passing along the edge of these woods, you could have imagined yourself in Western Europe. We passed Irkutz, where I knew the first Russian revolutionaries had been banished. With their aristocratic wives living near them, their punishment was to work for years in the silver mines. They could receive visitors in their prison housing. It almost seemed like luxury compared with anything political prisoners endured today. We passed down one side of Lake Baikal, the most extensive and deepest inland stretch of water in the world. The mist was descending as we passed its shores, shrouding the whole expanse of water in mystery. Then on to the wide rivers and distant hills. I was at last receiving the impression of the uninhabited, vast swathes of land which compassed Russia. Les Landes, which had always seemed uninhabited compared with the French cities, now appeared to be small in comparison. I had just started to assume that no one actually lived in these vast tracts of land, when on the bend of one of the smooth rivers, I saw a fisherman. Where did he come from? How did he get there? And was that how to escape from the all-pervasive machinery of the Bolshevik factory? I hoped so. Looking at their idyllic isolation, there might be a bit of hope for the orphans in Birobidzhan, I thought.

Gregory's story did not make me feel hopeful about their fate. On the other hand, I knew that before the war, Stalin had assigned these people autonomous lands and, since the war, had continued to promote them. I didn't really want to talk to anyone about my interest in the Jews. I thought that people like Gregory had enough to cope with just obeying their own national rules without having to be burdened with anyone else's questions.

Now, when we stopped at small stations and when extra passengers joined the train, they often had Mongoloid or Asiatic features. The food which they shared in the dormitory had strange spicy smells, and somehow their presence relaxed the atmosphere even more than before. Stalin – his picture ever-present in the sleeping car – had stern Westernised features even though he was from Georgia and the high collar uniform of all the socialist leaders seemed out of step with these locals who boarded the train. Some of them wore traditional even Chinese dress. I had the strong impression that I had left European Russia behind and that the Europeans were the ones embracing Bolshevik idealism seriously. Out in Siberia the landscape was too vast to be restricted by political idealism.

'Don't be fooled,' warned Gregory, when I shared my impression of the changing landscape. 'The Soviet committees exist here, despite the Chinese food. You can be proscribed here too. Take it all in, think your own thoughts, but be careful what you say, and, even more important, be careful what you allow other people to say. You might be evicted from the country in disgrace, but you will regain your former life. If they are accused of talking to you too much, there will be no escape.'

# Chapter Twenty-Three

The train seemed to get slower each day, and I became more jaded and exhausted and impatient with each hour. At the beginning of the journey it had seemed like an exciting outing alongside mysterious companions and a sense that we were cut off from the rest of the world. Now, conversation was exhausted, especially with my limited Russian and my companions' limited English and French. We had nothing more to say to each other and we knew that we would never meet again, so it didn't seem worth investing in social intercourse. Even Gregory had become a distant figure. I knew that he was trying to get to Japan through the less restrictive border checks in the East. I wished him well; he deserved some freedom; but what would happen to him I did not know and did not really care. We had stopped pretending to be interested in each other. More than anything, I felt dirty, constantly hot and sweaty and there was no place to wash. There was a toilet for each carriage, but it was past the state of being kept clean. At each station someone would appear with water and for a few roubles, we could wash our faces and hands. As a Westener, I enjoyed this luxury, but no one else bothered. When I returned to the carriage, the overwhelming smell of human sweat, and body odour overcame me again – a fuggy staleness. In some ways it was better to stay on the train so that you absorbed it all the time and were not repeatedly aware of its unpleasantness.

I got out at the stations to get some exercise and to savour the atmosphere of these far-away places. Near to two or three of the train stations, there arose the incongruous sight of Orthodox churches. In Moscow they had been largely destroyed, but in these exotic locations it seemed that the State had almost forgotten that they existed. Their golden globes shone in the early summer sun, and this sight impressed the visitor. It was as if unexpectedly the symbol of the mysterious, of the other, of all that could not be explained materially, had remained uncorrupted. Stalin might have put thousands of citizens into prison and the gulags but by mistake he had forgotten these symbols of unsurpassed beauty, which spoke of a different way of seeing the world. In France I had hardly noticed the village churches because I was so used to them as part of the landscape. Here, they struck me as significant as though they were speaking a warning to mankind. 'I have always been here, and I will not be demolished.' It was strangely reassuring, even though there was hardly a priest left in the land to officiate at services.

On the stations I bought all manner of food – partly because I was hungry and partly because I wanted to help the desperately poor people who were selling it. They were humble and appreciative of my custom and the food was surprisingly appetizing.

I began to collect my belongings together. Many of the original members of the carriage dormitory had left to meet members of their families. Other travellers had taken their place but none of them seemed very interested in me. I was just part of the community they had found on the train, and I was ignored. Gregory became more self-preoccupied as we continued our journey through Siberia. Perhaps he was remembering his long years in exile or perhaps he was preparing himself mentally for the strategies of deception and perseverance and ingenuity which he would need at the border with Asia.

'Vladisvostock always belonged to the Whites in the Civil War,' he mused. 'And Americans arrived there in the 30s to support the cause against Bolshevism. There's an 'anything goes' feel to Vladivostock even now.'

'How do the Americans manage to get everywhere?' I wondered.

'Because there's so many of them and because they're so rich and because they're such individuals. They fled oppressive regimes in the nineteenth century when they came to America in the first place. They're always in the business of opposing oppression.'

'Sounds good to me.'

'And me – if they can oppose the Bolsheviks, good luck to them. But the Bolsheviks get more stubborn the more they are opposed.'

So how were the Bolsheviks going to react to the Jews, I wondered. How were they really going to see them?

# Chapter Twenty-Four

My first impression was one of contradictions. Not everything was as it seemed.

I was met by a brass band and greeted by the Mayor. Apparently, I was an honoured guest and I was flattered. I couldn't understand very much of the Mayor's speech but that didn't matter. I understood the point of it, and the repetition of the words 'Comrade Stalin' at various intervals. I was welcome because Stalin had signed a piece of paper saying that, as a foreign journalist, I could come and report on what was happening at Birobidzhan. I knew how to act – receive the flowers gratefully, smile often and be amazed at the state's generosity in every area of life. It was not a difficult part to play, especially as my case was taken off me and I was escorted to a small boarding house in the centre of town where they were used to receiving foreign visitors. I was shown to my room which was basic but adequate and introduced to the housekeeper or cook. There would be a welcome meal for me and other dignitaries at the town hall at 8 in the evening. I was glad to get out of my travelling clothes and use the cold tap in the wash house. Baths were once a week downstairs in the kitchen by prior arrangement with the housekeeper – not much different to the customs of the average farmhouse in Les Landes before the war. Meanwhile I asked for a bowl of hot water so that I could do some minimal washing and the housekeeper was happy to comply. She showed me how to get the water from the kitchen and which pail and bowl to use. The same water supplied the endless samovar system and it was good to know that I could help myself to tea at any time of the day.

The daylight hours were long, and I decided to take a walk around the town. By 5, children were beginning to go home from school, and I enjoyed watching them with their bags on their backs and slates in their hands. The school premises looked remarkably large, if rather cavernous. If I had been expecting the intimate surroundings of my own schoolhouse, I was mistaken. Many of the children, seeing a stranger in the street, greeted me politely, some with the Russian 'Good day' and some with an English 'hello'. I was realising that all foreigners were assumed to be Americans or at least English speakers. Behind the main square was the impressive façade of a theatre with front pillars. I had not expected such an edifice in a pioneer town. This would certainly give me some material for articles, I thought.

After the school children returned home, no one seemed to be around on the streets. I returned to my lodgings to find a dress which would be special enough for this evening's event and applied to the housekeeper for a hot iron to press out the creases. By ten to eight I was ready to be escorted to the Town Hall.

I had never felt so important in all my life as when I crossed the square in that Siberian town and found myself in a wooden building with a dais at one end, the tables set out as for a wedding and everyone standing to attention and silent as I walked in.

For a little nobody, a small holder's daughter from Les Landes, it felt extraordinary, but it also felt rather threatening. I wasn't sure what they expected from me or whether I would be able to give them what they wanted.

I need not have worried. There was an agenda. The speeches of welcome took place. We all ate a hearty if monotonous meal, and I was expected to reply. There was a translator, but I discovered that he was better at translating English rather than French, but what I had to say was not complicated. I was impressed by the welcome and what I had seen in the town. I was looking forward to seeing how they prospered and how the Jews had established themselves there and of course I was grateful to the government and especially to their leader, Stalin, for allowing me to come.

There were polite nods and applause in response but at the same time I did not get the impression that knowing what was going on in this town was going to be a particularly easy job.

'Mademoiselle?'

I turned around as I was walking home across the square. A young man with the red kerchief of the party and shabby clothes was walking alongside me.

'Don't stop to turn to me but listen as we walk along.'

'Right. Who are you?'

'I work at the theatre and I'm a Jew.'

My interest immediately quickened.

'If you want to know what is going on in this town, meet me tomorrow in my office at 10am.' Pause. 'Come with your notebook ready to write an article about the theatre. That's the easy part. But I'll show you other ways to find out about the real business of this town. While you toe the line for the party, you'll be able to find out about other things too in time, if you do it carefully. What is your particular interest?'

'You... I mean, the Jews.'

'Ah!' He didn't alter his pace, but his face took on a quizzical expression. 'And why are you particularly interested in them?'

'Because some French orphans came here after the war and I want to find out what happened to them.'

'But you write for a communist newspaper.'

'Yes, and it was communists in France who helped them to survive and who sent them here.'

'And that is all you want to know?'

'No monsieur. I want to know the real story of the Jews here.'

Silence.

'Ah, well now, in that case you might need a nose for truth.'

'I think I've got one. I'm a journalist.'

'True, but you might need to be a very persevering one and a very brave one.'

'Why brave?'

'Because strange things are happening here. And sometimes it's more convenient to ignore the truth.'

'Do you ignore the truth?'

'I live here. That's different. Sometimes I need to ignore the truth to survive.'

'Don't you survive if you face up to the truth?' asked my daring and very naïve self.

'Perhaps. It depends how you want to die... but, mademoiselle, we are at risk of drawing too much attention to ourselves here. Come to my office at 10 O'clock tomorrow morning.'

# Chapter Twenty-Five

That night the memory of those words about being prepared to die unnerved me. I, who had worked in the Resistance, who had helped Jewish youngsters escape under the nose of the Nazis, felt unnerved.

I got ready for bed unwillingly. It was the first night for some time that I had not gone to bed accompanied by the rhythm of the wheels and the sound of the steam escaping the funnel and I missed them. Surely, I asked myself, as I snuggled into a lumpy mattress and under a coarse but thick eiderdown, you should be glad not to be smelling the sweat of twenty unwashed fellow travellers? The air was still around me and I was glad of that. But the silence and the pure air allowed other thoughts to enter.

Taking dangerous risks is not too frightening when you are doing it from the safety of your own country, even if that country is overrun by an invader. After the risk taking, you return to the normal. The Pyrenees mountains had been my friends and had helped my protégées to escape. When I was in command of my bike, my speed and the sandy paths and pines had been part of my natural environment. It was difficult for a foreign soldier to be better at manipulating the environment than me. I had had the hole round the pipes to run down into and there I had stored my books and provisions – probably only an illusion of safety, but nevertheless I could relax there.

Here I wasn't sure that I could relax. I suspected that the housekeeper was watching me and had been given instructions to report on my activities. The bed creaked every time I turned over. The toilet was a primitive drop one. I had used one many a time in our back yard but defecating near your family is a natural action. Worrying about what the

346

engineer from Moscow, who was also staying here, might be hearing and thinking was a different matter.

But it was far more than physical privations which disturbed me. It was a sense that I was in a big empty prison, thousands of miles from home with no way of escape. During that night I relived the experience of the empty horizons and the thousands of miles of tundra and forest which I had seen and not consciously absorbed at the time. Now in my mind, I reencountered them again. I was so small compared to them that I almost ceased to exist. I was terrified. I have since found that this experience is called 'homesickness' – that extraordinary desire to be back somewhere which is familiar and safe. I forced myself further and further back down into the bed, as if trying to escape from the landscapes which were threatening to overwhelm me.

At the darkest moment, the only way I could give myself relief was by telling myself that I did not have to stay in this place a moment longer. Who cared that Libération had paid for my fare? Did I care about my reputation as a journalist? Not at all! I only wanted to be safe and away from this appalling situation.

I found some relief from making this decision. In fact, I fooled myself into thinking that in coming to this conclusion, the problem was over. I could return to France tomorrow if I so wished. Thus, illogically, being reassured by this certainty, which was completely uncertain, I managed to sleep at last.

I was woken by the baboushka knocking on my door with words which could only have one meaning. 'Why are you still in bed? Wake up!' Then – 'There is tea and food for you in the kitchen.'

At this urgent summons, without any more time to think, I pulled on my clothes from the night before and went downstairs. It was light and my companions from the hostel had already disappeared for work.

If it was coffee which I drank, I had no idea of its provenance but, as we had got used to acorn coffee during war rationing, I did not feel justified in complaining. It was hot and the coarse rye bread was filling.

The old woman hung over me as if she wanted me to be finished and out of the way. It was light outside and I wondered how near it was to 10am and my appointment at the theatre.

I went upstairs and got my toothbrush and toothpaste and came down to get some water to wash my face. The old woman stared at me and I realised that she had never seen such a thing before. I made a huge pantomime of showing her what I needed to do and eventually she gave me two small bowls of water, one to wash in, and the other to help me reuse my toothbrush. She showed me a yard outside the house where there was some sort of basic drainage and stood near me watching curiously as I got myself ready. She seemed very pleased and nodded vigorously and that reassured me. She was accepting me.

I had no idea what time it was but decided to wander around the town before heading for the theatre which was a solid looking building in the central square. It amazed me that it had been built using stone, when the surrounding houses were made of wood and comparatively flimsy. There was a large clock just striking 9:30 as I waited behind the theatre and wandered into the nearby streets. I saw what I took to be a synagogue a few streets away, made of wood like the other buildings but also decorated on the outside and attractive. Two streets back from the town square, the boardwalk over the mud had broken up and soon my shoes were becoming muddy. I had brought some big boots with me, but they were back in my hostel and I decided not to explore any more without their protection.

I pushed open the big heavy door of the theatre and ran up the stairs. At the top, near what looked like a lighting room, was a study and there I found my companion of the previous day, Nicolai.

'Welcome Marie, welcome!' He pushed some piles of paper across the table and got up for me to sit on the only chair in the room.

'I'm so glad you came today. If you want to find out about Jews, this is the place to come.'

'But I saw a synagogue in the street back there.' I waved vaguely in the direction I had come. 'Surely that's the best place to meet Jews.'

'Sure, you'll meet Jews there, at least those clinging to their religion. But if you want to know what's really happening amongst us, this is the place to come and of course I'm the person to tell you.'

'Fine.' I was a little cautious about his sense of self-importance. Presumably there were others in this town who could also tell me what was happening.

'Well, I'm really happy to talk to you. But I thought you said that you had to be careful about what you said to foreigners.'

I looked round at the darkened room, wondering what microphones might be hidden there.

'Don't worry.' He laughed and his bright beard caught the gleam of the light in the oil lamp, which was needed because the windows were blacked out by blankets. 'We're not sophisticated enough in Birobidzhan to have bugs. No one would waste them here. The authorities have other ways of finding out what is going on.'

'Such as?'

'Spies, informers, people who are so scared that they incriminate others to buy their own freedom.'

'Why would you incriminate others if you're scared?' I asked uncomprehendingly. I had never been initiated into the presence of overwhelming terror before. I knew internal terror, but not the sort which pervades every action you take and the air you breathe. I was so naïve that I had no idea what this way of life really was.

'You become so scared that you will say anything that your jailors want you to say under the illusion that they might let you go as a result.'

'And do they ever?'

He laughed mirthlessly. 'They invade every living space of your body until they have suffocated you and you don't have the strength to leave.'

# Chapter Twety-Six

'Tea?'

'That would be lovely.'

'Great. The authorities don't seem to be able to get rid of the samovar, that great Russian answer to all problems. I'd offer you coffee, but we are forced to rely on any supplies someone can bring in from the outside world. There's a group of us who meet in the café. I'll introduce you to them another time. We always celebrate together with any imported coffee we can find, and of course vodka, which is always around in Russia. But I'm afraid tea will have to do for now.'

'That's fine by me. I'd have brought some coffee with me if I'd known. Perhaps someone from Paris will be able to send me some while I'm here. Though since the war it's not been all that plentiful even there.'

He laughed. 'You'll be the most popular girl in Birobidzhan, if you manage to bring coffee.'

'Worth a try then,' I replied flippantly. I found myself able to relax with this young, red haired, bearded Russian Jew, even if we had had a tense start the night before.

While he was out of the room attending to the samovar, I glanced around me. The bookcases were full. I could only decipher parts of the titles and authors, using my basic knowledge of the Cyrillic alphabet. I picked out the Russian greats – Chekhov and Gorky – but some of them were in a different script altogether.

'What are these then?' I asked Nicolai as he returned with the tea.

'Ah, those are the Yiddish greats.'

'I've never heard of those before.'

'What Yiddish or the greats?'

'I've just about heard of Yiddish. I thought it was a minority language for a certain small group of exiles. And I didn't know there were any 'greats',' I added as his face showed some concern. 'Excuse my ignorance.'

'Ignorance it is young lady.' He handed me an old battered cup of steaming liquid and we each hugged our own cups companionably, getting the maximum comfort from the heat, before starting to drink.

'If you want the history of Yiddish, you've come to the right place. Even if you don't, you'd better know and understand it or living in this place won't make any sort of sense to you.'

'Go on then. I'm ready for a lesson.'

'Well, to be brief, when the Jews were kicked out of Spain and the Western European Christian countries in the Middle Ages, they came mainly to the East and, most of the East is Russia. In order to survive as communities, they kept themselves to themselves.'

'Was that for religious reasons?'

I'd never really understood the Jewish desire to cut themselves off from everyone else and I was searching for understanding.

'Partly, but also partly because they were cast off by the Christian population and they had to help each other because there was no one else to do it for them.'

'So how did this language come about?'

'If you know anything about languages, they evolve through isolation and the necessity of use for a particular community. But they also pick up features of the language which is used where they live.'

'So which features would these be?'

'Most Jews went to the Polish and Germanic areas of Europe, but they also went to the Ukraine which for hundreds of years had been independent of Russia.

Yiddish developed as a language, which was partly Hebrew, partly German and partly Russian.'

'Why didn't they just use Hebrew?' I asked remembering Alain talking about the language of the Old Testament and the Palmach on their way to Palestine talking about the revival of the Hebrew language.

'I don't fully know. Languages can be described and explained but aren't always logical. They used Hebrew as a religious language, but it had never been used as a day to day language for so many years, that it was unlikely that it would be revived again in its old form.'

'But they're intending to do just that in Palestine.' I told Nicolai about my experiences on the boat in Marseille.

'Ah well, the whole Palestine obsession.' Nicolai shrugged his shoulders.

'You don't see eye to eye with them?'

'It's a great dream, but whether it can ever work, I've no idea. And for us here in Russia, it's an impossible dream.'

'Why?' I asked, suddenly imbued with the spirit of 'can do anything' which I had learnt from the Palmach and which, months earlier, I had found so inspiring.

'Marie, don't you understand what it's like here? I assume you found applying for a visa and getting in here quite a hard process?'

I nodded.

'Well, I can assure you that's nothing compared with getting out of here.'

My face must have started to show panic. He put his hand reassuringly on my arm. 'Don't worry. I didn't mean for a foreigner. You'll get out of here alright.'

My laugh in response was nervous with tension. His suggestion had brought back to me the nightmare of the night before. I shivered.

He was surprisingly understanding and solicitous. 'You needn't be ashamed of being frightened, Marie. Frankly you'd be a fool not to be, coming to a country you know virtually nothing about and at the end of a brutal war, not to mention an even worse civil war which took place before that.'

'Did that affect here?'

'No, not really. It's the one thing Birobidzhan has escaped. It's had about everything else but not that one.'

'Why not?'

'It's just too far away from everywhere. And the Jews who did come here were staunch Bolsheviks. Ironically, it's one of the reasons they're so unpopular in some other areas of Russia.'

'Such as?'

'The Ukraine to start with. Which makes for more craziness. Some of the people our great leader has sent us since the war are Ukranians, who are not Jews.'

'And so?'

'So – the Ukrainians have a fairly awful relationship with the Jews. Some of them stood aside and watched while the Germans massacred the Jews in their villages. They didn't do a lot to stop it.'

'They probably couldn't.' I recounted briefly what had happened when the Germans were looking for traitors. Nothing. 'There wasn't a big rebellion against the edict. In the end everyone saves their own skin.'

'Yes, you're right. But to make matters worse, a lot of Ukrainians benefitted from the houses and lands which the Jews left behind when they died.'

I commented reasonably, 'Well, who wouldn't? The Jews weren't coming back, and they might as well help themselves. I don't suppose they were made rich by the German invasion.'

'I wouldn't be too sure of that. The black marketeers and the financiers who helped the Germans did well out of it. Anyway, whose side are you on?'

'I'm not on anyone's side. I'm just trying to think about what happens in war.'

'The truth is,' said Nicolai solemnly, as he pulled more piles of paper onto the floor, and lit his homemade tobacco, leaning lazily full length across the table, 'Shit happens in war. But now we have shit happening after the war too.'

'In what way do you mean?'

'People being taken away and murdered.'

'People? Who exactly?'

'To start with the director of this theatre, Solomon Mikhoels.'

'What happened to him?'

'No one knows. He was taken away and a fatal accident was reported. Which according to our leader's 'speak', means he was murdered.'

It was such a straightforward, unemotional statement, and I sat there pondering the enormity of the implications.

'And you worked under him?'

'Yes.'

'And now what do you do?'

'I'm trying to be the theatre director instead of him, which I might say is an impossible job because Solomon was the most brilliant director, firstly, in Leningrad, and now here.'

'But doesn't that put you in danger?'

'Possibly but I haven't got Solomon's reputation, so my death wouldn't be significant. Also, Solomon wrote and acted in Yiddish.'

'But I thought that was encouraged in Birobidzhan?'

'We thought that too, but unfortunately Solomon just did that too well. And the powers that be were jealous.'

'So why wouldn't they be jealous of you?'

'My Yiddish is passable but not brilliant. Solomon was an actor as well as a director and he was brilliant at declaiming Yiddish. I'm not in his league so I don't draw attention to myself.'

'So, you're not trying to produce plays in Yiddish any longer?'

'I do some, especially amateur productions with the school children, but I make sure I do plenty in Russian as well and I also make sure I play the party line too.'

'So, Yiddish will go out of fashion?'

'Ah well, good question, but, no, I don't think so ultimately.'

'Why not?'

'Because of the other poets and writers who are here.'

'Who are they?'

'Most of them you won't have heard of, except perhaps Bergelson, David Bergelson.'

I shook my head. 'Sorry, no. I'm not up on plays and poetry, especially not in Yiddish.'

'You surprise me. You look like the sort of girl who would have read a lot.'

'Thank you. Some philosophy and French literature, but I haven't really had an advanced education. I've been too busy earning my living by waitressing in cafes.'

'In that case, you'll feel completely at home in the Birobidzhan community café. I'll introduce you to the regulars later this evening.'

354

# Chapter Twenty-Seven

I had to wait two days before being able to go to the café where Nicolai's friends met. In between I had to speak to the Mayor and be officially given a tour of Birobidzhan. It could have been dispiriting – lots of flooding and bad drainage and mud, and half-built, inadequate buildings – but I was lulled into acceptance and even optimism by the mayor's accompanying commentary. When the settlers first came to Birobidzhan, they had been almost overcome by the terrible weather, the permafrost, the impossible task of clearing so much forest, by disease and by the lack of resources and by the wild animals. But good socialist citizens always make the most of everything, and, despite thousands giving up and going back to where they had originated, the hardy few continued, and the settlement had been built on the banks of the two rivers.

'Two rivers?' I questioned. I had only seen the tributary of one.

'Yes,' said the Mayor triumphantly, ready to give me as much information as he could. 'The Biro and the Bidzhan. Near here is only the Biro. But, further down,' he said, waving expansively in another direction, 'is the Bidzhan.'

'And what's down there?'

'Factories ------ to keep our workers in production for the Motherland.'

'What about the original plans for farming?'

'They didn't work out so well,' he admitted. 'Blight and bad weather conditions constantly ruined the crops, and in the end, it was decided that machine production was best for us and for our country.'

'So, where does all this machinery get taken?'

'East Siberia and out to Vladivostock and Korea and Japan and west to Irkutz.'

It sounded like the perfect solution to a successful, modern town, but later I was to find that the story wasn't quite so straightforward. Nicolai told me that if the party had not guaranteed the buying of the equipment, then the town would have starved.

The following day I was given a tour of one of the factories. I couldn't help but notice the inadequate buildings and the cramped conditions of the workers. In the lunch break in the canteen, I was introduced to some of them through the services of my translator. One of them had been working for twelve years in that factory.

'You mean all through the war?'

'Yes,' said the old man dutifully. 'I was too old to serve our country on the front line, so I had to stay and work here instead.'

I could only imagine that working in a factory in Birobidzhan, however hard, was a welcome alternative to dying on the front line in Stalingrad.

'Many of the workers have come here since the war,' added the Mayor. 'They are glad to have useful productive work to do and to be here with their families.'

After three days of factory tours, I was ready to accept Nicolai's invitation to meet in the Yiddish café, just off the main square.

After several days in the town, I was beginning to feel much more confident about what I was doing, though I still had to fight against moments of disorientation and panic back in my lodgings, when I was by myself.

I was excited to be going to a café. I was used to the cafes of Les Landes and Paris and I wanted to compare them. I was also excited about seeing Nicolai again.

The café was a bit like an old house hastily put together, where the front room had been made to look like a café. When I opened the door that Wednesday evening, I was overwhelmed by the tobacco smoke. I was used to the smell of 'Gaullois' in Paris, but this was all pervasive, personally rolled tobacco, which seemed to fill up the whole of the small space, so that I was fighting my way through the fog, in order to see the characters round the table. Nicolai moved his chair back the moment I appeared and came to greet me.

'Marie, how wonderful that you have come. Let me present David Bergelson.' The great writer moved unsteadily to his feet and straightened up painfully. He grasped my hand and kissed it.

'Mlle Marie, how wonderful that you have come. I hear that you are going to tell the world about us.'

I was overawed by such expectations. I hoped that my articles for 'Libération' and 'Le Coq Enchaîné' were going to count as 'telling the world.'

'I'm not sure I'm that important,' I replied shyly. 'But I'll do my best to tell Parisian newspapers about what is going on here.'

Bergelson looked in a kindly way at me, his blue eyes twinkling. He must have been over 70 years old, but it was easy to fall under his spell.

'I'm sure you will my dear. But how lucky we are too to have such a beautiful French lady with us.'

I wasn't used to such compliments and didn't know how to react. Luckily a third man rescued me from my confusion. 'Good evening, Marie. Don't take any notice of Dovid. He's been charming women throughout Russia for the last 50 years. I am Yisroel Ermot from Poland and I am delighted to meet you.'

'And me too, Mr. Ermot.' I repeated the polite phrase in French, almost as a child repeats her lessons about introduction. If I didn't know much compared with the editors and writers of the Communist newspapers in Paris, I knew even less about how to converse on equal terms with these men of the world. I had a strong feeling of lack of experience and unworthiness. Why should I be writing about their lives, when they had been suffering for so long in ways I could not imagine?

'Yisroel is a famous Yiddish poet,' Nicolai informed me helpfully but at the same time making me feel even more inadequate. 'He has come here to contribute to our community and to make our newspapers famous.'

I was intrigued. I did not associate contributions of poetry with newspapers. Nicolai understood my lack of comprehension immediately.

'I know, I know,' he said, guiding me to a spare chair which he brought forward. 'Western newspapers don't go in for poetry, but our Shtern here is famous the world over for its cultural contributions. And Yisroel's poetry finds its way into The Jewish Daily Forverts and Di Tsukunft in

New York. They're the leading Yiddish newspapers in America, by the way,' he informed me.

I was impressed. 'That's wonderful. I didn't know that Russia had such close contact with New York.'

Nicolai laughed. 'It doesn't on most matters. Socialism and capitalism don't mix, but when it comes to Jewish culture or Yiddish culture, there's not a great divide between the two countries.'

'No, no.' David Bergelson took his gnarled hand from his cup of coffee and included the room in his gesture, as if he was embracing the whole world. 'We Jews understand what international culture is more than anyone else in the world. That's why they must not get rid of us.'

'Of course not, Dovid, no one is going to get rid of us,' soothed Yisroel.

'Though it looks as if they might try,' said Nicolai with some asperity.

'They'll never offend the Americans, not after the war when they've been allies.'

I remembered the news about the Berlin air lifts and the talk about the zones.

'But,' said David suddenly, 'we're ignoring our guest and I can assure you, my dear, we don't very often have chic guests from Paris. This calls for real coffee and vodka.'

# Chapter Twenty-Eight

It was unusual for me to be the centre of attention in any situation and ironic that in the café, where the most illustrious, literary figures met, I should be given such attention. Ironic too that in a communist country where there was supposed to be no difference between the two sexes, because such attitudes were 'regressive' and 'bourgeois', I was treated as someone 'different' and accordingly, protected. I was also the only woman in the group and the men were full of little gallantries, pulling out a chair for me, standing up when I walked into the room and pouring me the first coffee and vodka of the evening. I had never experienced this before, and I liked it. It appealed to my vanity, my sense of self-importance and my inherent laziness. Where had I, a country girl from Les Landes, acquired such characteristics?

Conversation at the café did not allow for introspection. There were far more serious political and international topics to discuss. Two weeks after my first introduction to the group of Yiddish writers and artists at Birobidzhan, there was news of a disturbing nature. There was a visitor from the Ukraine, Carlos Miroslav. Bergelson gave him an affectionate bear hug when he entered the café. I saw a man of about forty with pinched features as though he had known too much hunger in his life.

'My little Carlos, how wonderful to see you!'

'Uncle David! I have missed you so much!'

I was bemused. Carlos was a giant of a man over six feet tall and I had not been given the impression that David was still in touch with any relations in the Ukraine. In fact, most of them had been killed during the Nazi invasion. Coffee and vodka in plentiful supply were called for from the kitchen.

'Marie, Carlos' family were my family in Kiev,' explained David after we had been introduced. 'When I decided to become a writer and turned my back on the tailoring business of my father in our village, Carlos' family took me in. This man was a toddler of three years old when I stayed there. But,' he continued, playfully punching Carlos in the stomach, 'he's grown a bit since then, so I can't lift him onto my shoulders anymore.'

I soon learnt that Carlos had come to Birobidzhan to buy machinery for one of his factories near Kiev.

'So, how's business in the Ukraine?' I asked politely, hoping to glean more understanding of the industrial situation in Russia as a whole. Such visits from outsiders were very useful to me as a journalist. I wanted to build up a bigger picture of the country, which, I was sure, would come in useful at some point in my work.

'Well, you know,' replied Carlos, good naturedly, stirring his vodka into his coffee, 'Business is all right here as long as you follow the rules.'

'You mean Russia is all right as long as you follow the rules,' Nicolai added.

'Yes, my friend, you are right,' agreed Yisroel. 'The problem is that we Jews are not very good at following the rules.'

'I thought the Jews had plenty of rules of their own,' I suggested.

This comment brought great guffaws of laughter from the table. 'The little girl from Paris is right.' David put his arm round my shoulder and drew me to him affectionately. I can still smell the mixture of tobacco and vodka on his breath, mixed with the whiff of sweat from under his arms as the summer heat intensified. 'We Jews are good at obeying the rules as long as they're our rules. We don't care about anyone else's.'

'And you,' he added, turning to Carlos with a grin, 'weren't even very good with the family rules, were you? Always in trouble, as far as I remember. Never back from playing in the street in time for Shabbat. Your dear mother was always looking disapproving, as you walked in late while she was stirring the soup.'

There was silence after this remark. I didn't dare ask about the fate of Carlos' mother. There wasn't much good news coming out of the Ukraine after the war.

'But what about you, Carlos?' I dared to ask instead, breaking the silence to enquire about someone who was very much alive. 'How come you survived the war?'

'I grew up a good Russian citizen despite all the ways my parents tried to make me into a good Kodesh scholar. I don't regret it. That's why I'm the only one who's still alive.'

'Where were you when the Germans invaded?'

'I had already volunteered for the Red Army and was away training on the banks of the Don.'

'Where's that?'

'Near Stalingrad in the south-east of the country.'

'Where the great siege took place later in the war?' I asked, recalling my hasty reading about Russian war-time history, before I came.

'Yes, though I'm happy to say that I missed that. After I trained, I was sent to Finland.'

'Finland!' I had hardly heard of it. 'Why?'

'Because I had a talent for skiing which they discovered when I was in the army. I spent most of the war skiing up and down Finland on secret missions, and in helping with the defence of the frontier with Norway. I was good at harassing the Germans.'

'Yes,' added David playfully, as the conversation risked becoming too serious. 'He's been harassing other people all his life. It started with me when he was three years old.'

'And who do you harass now?' I asked intrigued.

'Good question, little girl from Paris. I've reformed! I've become a model citizen for our great leader, Stalin. I just buy and sell machinery for our firm which supplies farms in our area.'

'Nonsense, Carlos,' insisted David. 'Once a troublemaker, always a troublemaker. That's why we need to hear from you about what's really going on.'

The atmosphere suddenly became tense.

'I'll tell you later,' said Carlos carefully. 'After we've eaten our borscht and shut the door.'

Everyone ate their soup, schlurping great thick borscht from the side of the bowl and mopping it up with dry, rye bread. Even though I had

361

eaten at the hostel earlier, I joined in companionably. In the last weeks I had become part of the group, accepted by virtue of my foreign and gender status and the constant attitude of inclusion from Nicolai.

Other customers at the café had gradually slipped out into the white night. They knew that these key literary figures went on discussing their poetry and drama until the early hours. I stayed on with them, sensing that important things were going to be said that night.

Yisroel began, turning to David, as if he was the person who really mattered. He was certainly the leader of the group.

'David, you need to listen to Carlos. There's trouble brewing.'

David sighed and put his arm onto Yisroel's shoulder reassuringly.

'Yisroel, my friend, there's always trouble brewing. That's what I've learnt in my 64 years on earth, but what I've also learnt is not to get too worked up about it. Troubles pass just like they come.'

Whether Yisroel was reassured by this or not I don't know, but Carlos looked his uncle straight in the eye.

'No, Dovid, this time it's different.'

'Carlos, you're just a trouble-maker. Sure, it's different but how can it be worse than the Great Patriotic War and 6 million Jews dead?'

There was silence in that small café as the tobacco smoke curled up to the wooden beams of the roughly hewn structure. It was like a moment of respect for all the suffering which had taken place in these men's lifetime.

Carlos continued, 'Of course, nothing could be worse than that, Dovid. No one's disputing that extreme of suffering for so many people but this one's different.'

David sighed again, as if forced to ask, 'Why is it so different? And if you and I survived the greatest threat of all, why not this one too?'

'Because this one comes from within.'

David laughed dismissively but the younger men in the group listened more attentively.

'You mean from the socialist workers' party? Nonsense! I don't believe it. The Jews who were in leadership helped to save Soviet Russia. And Stalin has provided this place as a refuge for us to come to.'

'Maybe but times are changing.'

'They won't forget what we've done.'

362

Yosroel cut in, 'Dovid, think. We know that Solomon has already gone.'

'That's because he was a loudmouth and made more publicity for us than was healthy. They won't forget what JAC did in the war.'

'JAC?' I intervened from the outside of this conversation but fascinated by what was going on. 'Who's that?'

Nicolai helped me. 'It's not a person. It stands for the Jewish Anti-Fascist Committee. They did a lot in the war and David was a prominent member. He made a lot of important speeches in Moscow supporting Stalin in his fight against the Nazis. He had considerable influence in those days and Stalin was grateful for his support.'

Carlos continued. 'Dovid, you must understand that they've disbanded the Jewish Writers' Association in Minsk, Kiev and Moscow.'

'Just window-dressing, dear boy. They have these little fears. Yiddish writers will always go on writing great literature. It doesn't matter whether they're allowed to join a writers' association or not.' He banged his whole arm onto the table and sat forward straining to get his point across.

'They won't forget my speech in Moscow. I helped turn half the population to fight for them against the Nazi aggressors.'

'But, Dovid, those aggressors are no longer there. Moscow doesn't need us anymore.'

# Chapter Twenty-Nine

I suppose that it was one of the chief memories which I will always have of David Bergelson. After all the laughter and the verbal quips were over, he was a man who wasn't needed any more. Sadly, the Yiddish community didn't really need one of their elders because he represented a time which had disappeared. No one really knew what was needed for the future, but I felt the tension in the community, not only in the café where he was in the centre of attention, but in other parts of the town too. There was an undercurrent of sadness and uncertainty.

When I was with David and Yisroel and Nicolai in the evenings, I felt cocooned by their warmth and their understanding and their inner strength. Outside that close-knit environment, it was different.

The mayor suggested that I should visit yet another factory where agricultural machinery was made, and which was further out of the town. I wasn't quite sure of the advantage of doing this, but as I was generally lacking in occupation, I decided to take up the offer.

A man and woman from the cooperative came to take me there from the mayor's office one morning.

It was the start of a beautiful day at the end of May. The spring chill was still in the air, but the sky was bright blue, and the silver birch trees which we passed were sprouting. They could easily have been part of a copse in inland France a couple of months earlier.

'You must really enjoy being here at this time of year.' I tried to make conversation via the interpreter with the stodgy faced lady from the factory. In her dull uniform and with her sensible straight-cut hair, she didn't look like someone who enjoyed much.

'It's alright until the mosquitoes arrive.'

'Oh, when's that?' I asked nonchalantly, with no idea what the word 'mosquito' meant for someone who lived on the Russian steppes. I imagined a few annoying insects who might have appeared on a summer's evening in France.

'In June. You'll know when they come,' she warned me darkly. I almost had the impression that she would be pleased that a soft Westerner would know what suffering was really like.

Her companion was more enthusiastic about conversing with me, anxious to make a good impression on a western reporter.

'You have come to see our factory. It is an honour.'

'I'm sure the honour's all mine,' I replied virtuously.

'It is an honour for us to work for our great party and our revered leader; and it is an honour for you to see it all.'

Ah well, I thought. I hadn't noticed much honour either claimed or sought at the cheese factory on the outskirts of Paris. Perhaps things are different here.

I was taken two miles out of town to some big draughty warehouses filled with noisy machinery. It all looked very efficient and uninspiring. How could I possibly make this part of an article about life in Russia? I found my answer in the workers' canteen, which I visited at lunch time. The food was basic but hot and good – lentil stew with big servings of boiled potatoes.

'We are very lucky here,' a fresh-faced young woman informed me. 'Food is not always plentiful for the rest of the community but here there is food every day.'

'Yes indeed. This is excellent,' I agreed. 'Has it always been like this?'

'Not during the great patriotic war,' claimed an older woman sitting next to her. 'There was never enough then. These young people don't realise how lucky they are.'

Suddenly I felt uncomfortable. Did I belong to the older or the younger generation? This was a problem which I discovered later was to become part of my life in France. The younger worker grinned happily at me, confident that, as far as age was concerned, I was on her side.

'Yes, even when the machinery doesn't work, we get fed,' added a young man sitting further along the table.

'What do you mean – when the machinery doesn't work?' I asked, intrigued.

'The right parts don't always come,' he informed me.

'So, what do you do then?'

He shrugged his shoulders. 'We just send them out anyway.'

'You mean you send them when they don't work properly?'

'Why not? As long as we do our quota and get fed properly, no one really cares.'

'But isn't that a terrible waste of resources?'

'We're contributing to what the Motherland needs.'

'But surely the Motherland needs tractors which work?'

Again, he shrugged his shoulders. Such questions were obviously too difficult or involved responsibilities not appropriate for the ordinary worker.

I asked Carlos about it later that evening.

'Surely you don't buy tractors which are damaged?'

He laughed. 'Marie, you can't imagine what goes on. We make our orders, and no one knows what will turn up. Fortunately, I'm able to travel and see what is really happening on the ground. I get the real stuff, not the dud ones.'

'So, in Russian terms, you're the canny businessman.'

'Yes, and in Jewish terms, I get to see my friends.'

'According to what you've been saying recently, that might put you in danger.'

He hesitated. A bright, optimistic 'can do' businessman, it was not natural for him to be either self-effacing or too serious about himself.

'You have to understand, Marie, that I can't abandon Bergelson. We have too much history together as a family.'

'You mean when you were brought up in Ukraine.'

'Yes, and I'm aware of what he has done since for the Jewish community.'

'What about his own family?' I was curious about them. I had heard it mentioned that he was married, but there had been no sign of a Mrs. Bergelson, as far as I was aware.

'It's almost impossible for anyone outside the Soviet Union to help.'

'So where is she, or they?'

'When Bergelson came back to Moscow before the beginning of the Second World War, his family left. They went to Japan.'

'Japan? The enemy in World War 2?' I was startled. Even so soon after the war, news was trickling back to Europe about the ferocity of the war with Japan.

'I know it sounds unlikely but there was a short time when Japan was receiving all sorts of people.'

'And they made it?'

'Yes.'

'But what happened during the war itself?' Any stories about Japan I had heard involved prisoner of war camps.

'The border with Vladivostock was an easy one to get out of. Dovid's wife and sons got out and then got a boat to the USA before all the shipping routes were closed down.'

Wow! I thought to myself. What makes some people lucky enough to escape and others to stay and face hell?

'A sense of duty,' suggested Carlos, as if reading my thoughts. 'A question of age as well?'

'Age?' I queried.

'His wife was much younger than him. He'd been running all his life. There comes a point when you feel too old and tired to keep running. And you stop believing that it makes a difference.'

# Chapter Thirty

And what of my other fugitives, the people I had secretly hoped to see all along? What about Daniel and Devorah? I hadn't asked about them in the town, because I didn't want to draw attention to them. I had no idea how many Jewish orphans were arriving in Birobidzhan. I had no idea whether such children would be unpopular because they came from a capitalist country. I was learning more and more about prudence and diplomacy, especially when it involved the long-term welfare of others.

My babushka at the hostel was dismissive of my enquiries. 'Just a few of them – orphans. Some of them are Jewish. We don't really want them here.'

'Why not?'

'They use up too much money and food and don't give anything in return.'

'But if they can't settle in Birobidzhan, where could they possibly go?'

Caring about humanity in general was clearly not her strong point.

'We have difficulty enough with the adults, especially those who have forgotten how to work.'

'I haven't noticed anyone in Russia who doesn't know how to work.'

'Ah well,' – she went away to get more cups for tea for my interpreter and his friend – 'those who have been fighting often want to be treated like capitalist lords.'

'I guess they've had a pretty awful time on the front. They need a bit of relaxation.'

'Relaxation?' She shook her head and finger at me. 'That's the word which is the excuse for laziness amongst all the aristocrats.'

Remembering the Russian aristocrats in Paris, I could see her point of view. Most of them wanted to spend their time bemoaning their present situation and looking nostalgically at the past. However, it seemed to me a bit unfair to class all the former fighters and defenders of the Motherland with people like that.

'If they've been made orphans by the war, I'm glad they're being looked after here,' I stated decisively. 'Where would I find them?'

My babushka knew when she was defeated. 'You'll have to go beyond the square and through some back streets, then across the Biro river and ask there.'

Should I take the Mayor's official translator with me, I wondered. In the end I decided that it would be difficult to show too much interest in particular orphans with him around.

Instead I dropped in at the theatre mid-morning to ask Nicolai.

'Sure,' he responded good humouredly as usual, 'I could come this afternoon. Is there a particular reason you are interested in them?'

I decided to explain about Daniel and Devorah and to tell him what had happened to them in France.

'Well that's certainly unusual. Jewish children being saved by communists.'

'You don't think that communists can behave in a humane way?'

'I don't think human beings behave in a humane way when they are under threat.'

'Well, these two got lucky then.'

'I hope they were as lucky in being sent here.'

'That's what I want to find out about.'

'Sure, Marie. How about this afternoon, when I've finished reading this script and thinking about the lighting for next week's performance?'

I went to meet him at 3pm and I was glad to have a friend to show me how to negotiate the mud, the board walks and the rickety bridge. The Biro was flowing fast and furious beneath it.

'Ever followed the river out of town?' I asked Nicolai.

'I'm not the greatest outdoor type but yes, sometimes last summer when I wanted to be alone and think.'

He grinned as he noticed my reaction. 'I'll promise to take you some time, if you promise not to ask me a hundred questions.'

'Do I really ask you so many questions?'

'You're a journalist and a foreigner, so it's likely that is what you enjoy doing.'

'Alright. I'll keep my mouth closed and allow you to think great thoughts.'

He raised his eyebrows in response as we negotiated more mud over the other side of the bridge and then veered off on a rough half made path up the side of the nearest hill. We entered the forest and continued for about a mile round the side of the hill, until we came to a clearing.

Nicolai stopped. 'Don't ask anyone about those children yet. You don't want to expose them to foreign interest and any repercussions there might be.'

'Yes, I realise that. I'd just like to meet the director or leader and find out what goes on here.'

Everyone seemed to be gathered at the furthest house in the clearing. The rest of the buildings – as we realised later, the dormitories, refectory and kitchen – were deserted.

'Who are you? What do you want?' I guessed the content of the question without Nicolai's translation.

A huge man in an army uniform came out of the building. If Nicolai had a small curly red beard which was neatly trimmed, this man had a huge red beard, dotted with white and unkept, though generally he looked clean.

Nicolai explained who we were. I expressed my interest in all that Stalin was doing for orphans in giving them a new start in Birobidzhan. At the mention of Stalin's name, the man's face broke into a huge smile.

'Come in, come in, comrades. Come and have a drink before you meet our young people. They are at school, at the moment, over there,' he said pointing to the distant building. 'Come in, come in.'

I recognized the acorn drink which we were offered but knew better than to point out what it was replacing.

'You want to know everything which is being done for our young people?'

'Yes, of course, but first I want to know who you are and what you are doing here.' 'It's always best to get the personal story,' I added in English to Nicolai, before he started translating what this huge Russian had to say.

'I am Matvey Khazansky.' Matvey stood up and bowed to each of us in a gesture which seemed most un-comrade-like to me, but I instinctively liked it and him.

'I served the Russian army in Leningrad and then I marched west right through Germany. I marched to Berlin and sat in the Bundestag the day we defeated the Fascist pigs.'

Such a boast should have been threatening and militant but somehow it wasn't. It sounded like a phrase he had learnt, and which had nothing to do with his real opinion of Germans.

'What are you doing here, Matvey?'

'I was sent back to Leningrad. Most soldiers were demobbed but I wanted to do more. I offered my services to the Motherland and the party and they sent me here.'

'And what do you do here?'

'I helped construct these buildings last year in the winter, when our poor children were all freezing to death. And now, I look after them. They're divided into different age groups. They all have a teacher in charge of them. We have cooks in this building and I'm in charge of the whole system.'

'Sounds good to me. Where do the children come from?'

'All over Russia. There are orphans everywhere in our country. Do you know how many Russians lost their lives in the Great Patriotic War, comrade?'

I shook my head.

'40 million', he replied solemnly. 'The sacrifice of 40 million Russians to help the West defeat Fascism. And they're not even grateful.' He shook his great feathered beard sorrowfully.

'I think the West is grateful, Matvey. It's just that we lost millions too.'

'Not like Russia.'

'Maybe not but France was invaded too.'

'You didn't fight over every kilometre like we did here.'

'True and there are a lot more kilometres in Russia than in France.'

Matvey liked that. I didn't have the feeling that he felt any personal animosity towards me as a French woman even though I represented a capitalist country.

'You're right. Russia is a great country and a huge country to defend, but we did it.'

'So, who are all these orphans then? Are any of them Jews?'

Matvey looked seriously at Nicolai for a moment, as if he held the answer.

'Yes, of course, some of them are Jews. Our great leader wants to care for them too.' I saw the picture of Stalin stuck behind the oven on the wooden wall of the kitchen. I guessed that in Matvey we had a true believer.

'But there is a mixture. The most important thing is that they are communists. Even if they don't understand it now, they will grow up to be part of our great socialist workers' party and they all revere our great leader.'

'Did all of them come together?'

'No, of course not. A hundred here and there.'

'And when did you first meet them?'

'The first hundred came and were looked after by other families in the town. Then I arrived and took the whole project over.'

I looked at him with admiration. Getting the wood, the buildings, the water and food together must have been a huge task.

'It was a big job, especially in winter. I thought some of them were going to freeze to death, but they didn't.'

'When did all of this happen?'

'It started eighteen months ago. Now we have 500 orphans here.'

As if on cue, children of all ages were pouring out of the big hall which acted as a classroom on the opposite side of the enormous courtyard.

'Come and meet them.' Matvey was on his feet as he spoke. It wasn't long before it was obvious that he loved these children and that they loved him.

'See these little girls here? They're only eight years old.' A troupe of about a dozen little girls bounded up to him. 'But already they're little Pioneers. They make me proud.'

372

No one could hide the laughter and fun of these children as they made their way to the dining hall. Then, as if a sign had been given, the chatter stopped, and everyone turned towards Stalin's picture and started singing the Communist Internationale. They were all dressed in party uniform, some of it of bad quality, but they were all clean and glad to be there.

'And the teachers?' I asked, as we ate our soup and bread with them.

'The teachers are all trained and look after the children as well as teaching them. And the older children look after the younger ones.

Comrade Marie, you are welcome to go with one of the girls' group and speak with them as they do their chores and prepare for bed.'

'But the language barrier?'

In answer Matvey strode across the hall and signalled to one of the young women. 'This is Natasha. Her mother was English and her father Russian. She will translate for you.'

# Chapter Thirty-One

Natasha was a down to earth, practical young woman. She didn't express her emotions very openly, but she was pleasant, and her English was excellent. My own English was making rapid progress in Russia, as I found that many people assumed that I was American and spoke to me in English. I found that officially the USA was the great enemy of socialism and was despised. Unofficially, American generosity was appreciated. It seemed that this was the case at the orphanage too. I was interested in Natasha's own story.

'So, you must have had the chance to go to England at some point.'

'Not really. My mother never encouraged me to go.'

Being a representative of the 'free world' I found it difficult to imagine why any parent would not want their child to visit their own country or even find their future there.

'My mother came from a farm labourer's family in Norfolk. My grandfather worked hard on the land in all weathers. He died very slowly and painfully without anyone to look after him properly because his wife had died before him. My mother never encouraged me to go back. She said that the workers had a better deal in Russia.'

'But I thought that the life of the Russian peasant was very hard here too.'

Natasha smiled. 'All workers have a hard time in any country but at least here there was hope.'

'Hope?'

'Of a future under the communists. Our leaders wanted to make it better for the workers not just for themselves.'

'How did your parents meet?' I couldn't imagine how a farm worker's daughter from Norfolk could easily meeting a young man from Russia.

'My mother was a governess – oh, not to a rich family, but to a middle-class merchant's family in St. Petersburg, as it was then.'

'So, she must have been educated?'

'She could read and write and was especially good at sewing. I don't think that the merchant wanted much more for his daughters and for my mother it was an incredible opportunity.'

'And how did she meet your father?'

'Just before the Revolution when there were trade unions' meetings on the street corners, he saw her going out to buy provisions for the family. By then things were chaotic and she could easily go out at night to buy bread without drawing attention to herself.'

'Except to your father?' I suggested.

There came a glimmer of restrained laughter on Natasha's face. 'Except, as you say, to my father. He fell in love with her just like that and persuaded her to adopt the cause of the workers.'

'What happened to the merchant and his family?'

'They were reduced to one room and couldn't afford to keep my mother anyway. It was convenient for them when she left with my father.'

'Are they still alive- I mean, your parents?'

'No, my mother died of cancer before the war and my father died in the siege of Leningrad.'

'So, you're an orphan too?'

'If you like. But Marxism teaches us to work together with the community, so I don't miss my parents so much.'

'And the children here, do they have a good deal?'

'It depends what you mean. They have nothing materially compared to children in capitalist countries. But here, they will be given a basic education and training for a job. It's the most anyone could expect, especially in these difficult days after the war. Our comrade leader has made provision for them. Come and see.'

I followed her out of the refectory to where her group of girls aged 8 to 12 years old were playing in the courtyard. It was still light enough for them to be playing outside. Some of them were throwing a makeshift ball made of rags. Some of them were playing with wooden dolls and, like children the world over, were engaged in imaginative play together. I wondered whether they played at 'mummies and daddies.'

'They play at being the leader of their youth group and teacher,' Natasha informed me. 'What they've never had, they don't miss.'

She stopped so that I could ask the girls questions about their lives and welfare. Predictably, they enthused about their group of friends and their favourite teacher and who had the best bed in the dormitory. I was shown where they slept. There were latrines at the far end of the school hall, and I was shown a well just outside the complex. One of the children's many chores was collecting water each day for drinking and washing.

'And for washing clothes?' I enquired. The clothes were old and patched but clean – quite an achievement, I thought, with only one well.

'All our children are trained to keep their clothes clean. We don't have servants here.'

'I should hope not,' I agreed, virtuously, but Natasha did not pick up the undertone of irony. 'Actually, on the farm I grew up in in France, we didn't have servants either.' Natasha did not react to the hint about a Western culture being different to what she might have heard.

'That's one thing I find extraordinary,' I confided to Nicolai the following day. 'They meet hardly anyone from abroad and you' d think they might be interested in hearing first-hand what life was like in the West.'

Nicolai smiled indulgently at my naivety. 'Marie, most people are not curious, just accepting and trying to survive. They haven't got the energy for curiosity.'

I thought of my school friends in Les Landes. That was probably true for them too. Survival was far easier for them in France than here, but they didn't have much curiosity. The church dance, who was having the next baby, that was enough for them. They weren't forbidden to ask questions. They were just innately lacking in curiosity. So, maybe it wasn't so strange that it was like that in Russia too. Nicolai explained further.

'When I say that it's a matter of survival, I'm not just talking about getting reported to the Party. I'm talking about survival for their own psyche.'

'What do you mean?'

'I mean that in order to find life meaningful, we've got to think it's worthwhile. It's the best we can do. In order to accept life here, never mind enjoy it, subconsciously they've got to think it's a good one. It's when you don't think that it's worthwhile that you want to escape. There's no point escaping if there's nowhere to escape to. I don't just mean because Birobidzhan is in the middle of nowhere, which it is, I mean because you can't escape from Russia.'

I was beginning to understand the enormity of what he was talking about. My parents' farm had in some ways been a prison for me and I had hated the thought of settling down there. I had had the opportunity to escape – through education, through my good friend, Thérèse, and through my own personality. In France, escape was a choice. In Russia it wasn't. I began to realise how lucky I had been in the accident of birth. I felt humbled by this realisation.

I spent time with Natasha's group of girls. I only had my Jewish escapees to compare them with, and, compared to them, they were docile and straightforward. Instead of prayers from a nun (even a pretend one) at night, they had the thoughts of Lenin. I supposed that the words of the great man droning on as the candles were snuffed out, must have been of some comfort to them. There had existed someone who had supposedly cared for them. I still couldn't help feeling that there was something lacking.

'It's mystery,' I decided at last as I spoke to Nicolai as the half-light faded and we walked back over the river.

'There's no mystery in the words of Lenin. It's too matter-of-fact.'

'Matter of fact is just what you get here,' agreed Nicolai.

'Not altogether,' I thought to myself.

# Chapter Thirty-Two

No one could call the scenery 'matter of fact'. When you first saw the silver birch woods, it seemed no different to Europe, but, as I ventured by myself outside the main part of the town, I began to see the mountains and the rushing rivers further out and the startling blue sky. And the silence. I was used to being alone in the forests of Les Landes, but this was different. There you could always hear the rustling of the wind from the coast in the bracken or among the pine trees. Here the silence was absolute. I emerged one day high above the town and looked out across what seemed to be thousands of miles of tundra and mountains and, a hundred miles away, I could see the tops of the snow-covered mountains leading towards the Chinese border. Birobidzhan was squashed between two rivers, and the town seemed to grow out of the railway station. I saw now that it was a small dot within this vast country. It was as if through the building of the station human beings wanted to say, 'Hey, we've made it; we're getting somewhere in this vast expanse of land and it shows how important we are.' The town clung to this sense of significance. All the shoddy buildings declared, 'We're part of this achievement. Human beings have created something here.' It was only when you climbed higher, lost sight of the town and looked across to the huge expanse of mountains beyond and occasionally, when it was not too misty, saw the jagged snowy peaks, that you realised that human beings were nothing. They could not conquer Siberia.

'Which is why the people got sent to the Gulags here,' agreed Nicolai. 'The environment killed most people without any help from the Communist party. If you escaped the mines or building the railroad, the cold and the mountains would kill you anyway.'

Living here certainly gave you a different perspective on life from the one you gained if you lived in a warm valley, or a quaint village in the west of Europe. Stalin might have got rid of most of the churches, I thought, but he couldn't get rid of the mystery of the mountains. If you wanted to feel the feebleness of mankind, all you needed to do was to climb up a few feet out of the town. However, most people in Birobhidzan, I felt, were too preoccupied with the demands of everyday life to think more widely, but then, I suppose that this is the predicament of all people everywhere.

I had explained the background story of Daniel and Devorah more fully to Nicolai.

'Just go slowly,' he cautioned. 'Get to know the place. Write some articles about the orphanage and how well they are being looked after by the state, before you make too many enquiries.'

I followed his advice. I sent articles back to Paris, sometimes through hand-written letters entrusted to travellers. Once I asked a minor official to telegraph my work from Moscow, when he was visiting the capital. My articles were full of praise for what the Soviets were doing in this little town in Siberia. I had no sense of whether anything was being achieved by this, but Nicolai told me that I should be thinking in a different way. 'If you were threatening the equilibrium here, you'd soon know about it. No reaction means you're alright.'

The small Jewish community was uneasy. The intellectuals and poets talked about the situation constantly over vodka. I wasn't sure how much this was just part of the drama of their lives which they enjoyed sighing over. Nicolai looked at me with pity when I suggested this.

'Marie, you don't understand what it's like to have been a Jew in Europe over the last twenty years.'

'I think I understand a little.' I had told him the story of Alain and his family.

'Sure, but you don't understand what it's been like in Russia and the East. The Jews in France faced deportation and the Holocaust, which was a terrible fate. But for the Jews in Eastern Europe and especially here in Russia, it's been thirty years of persecution and uncertainty.'

'I thought that lots of Jews were involved in the 1917 Revolution.'

'They were. There were Jews in the Politburo. But they've never really been safe.'

'Why not?'

'If they rise to power, it's because their Jewishness has been suppressed. It's not their identity anymore. Instead their heart has been recreated by the Party.'

'And if they're not that important?'

'As long as they lie low and mingle, they can survive for a long time. But when troubles and competition come, then jealousy seeps through, and the Jews always lose out.'

'Why should that be?'

Nicolai laughed with some bitterness, which surprised me, because I wasn't used to that trait in his character.

'If we knew the answer to that, then we'd have all been able to save ourselves.'

A pause as we sat with curtains drawn in the room at the top of the stairs in the theatre.

'Marie, have you ever read Esther?'

'Esther? No, what's that? A play? A novel? It didn't pass by the école primaire at St. Paul en Borne.'

'It certainly wouldn't be part of any school syllabus here either. It's from the Bible.'

'The Bible?' I didn't expect a modern secular Jew to be reading such old-fashioned literature.

'Don't look so shocked. There's some good stuff in it and it helps you to understand the Jews.'

'Impossible!' I joked. 'Understand you lot? I don't think so! Anyway, what's so important about this Esther?'

'Well, they were living as a minority quite peacefully in Persia. And, as luck would have it, the new queen, Esther, was a Jewess. There was a plot against her husband, the King of Persia, and no one knew about it apart from her uncle, Mordecai.'

'So, she got to be important? a bit like being in the Politburo, I suppose!'

'Yes, but what's interesting is how the important politician of the day, Haman, plotted to get them all killed.'

'Why?'

'It's as I was saying, a mixture of jealousy and anger that Mordecai didn't show him enough respect.'

'What happened?'

'The plot was foiled by a mixture of Esther's clever diplomacy and G-d sorting things out.'

'Ah well – G-d – that would really help, having him on your side!'

'Yes, I agree. Only I haven't heard from him lately and things aren't too good here.'

'You mean about the head of this theatre getting murdered?'

'Yes, and the Yiddish writers' groups getting closed down.'

'It might just be chance. The director of your theatre had an accident, didn't he?'

'Yes, except he wasn't the sort to take winter trips on icy roads.'

'Who knows?' I said airily. 'It's probably only a one off and it doesn't matter really whether there are Yiddish writer cooperatives or not. People can still write in Yiddish if they like.'

'Yes, they can, but, before the war, they were being encouraged by the Party. Now there's only a few of them in Birobidzhan, and there's no real market for their work.'

'To be honest, Nicolai, I can't imagine how any Socialist Workers' Party hierarchy is really going to be that interested in Birobidzhan. It's not exactly politically important.'

'True but none of us are comfortable with what is happening.'

'Are you ever comfortable with what is happening? You'd better take a leaf out of Esther's book and ask G-d.'

Never serious for too long, Nicolai laughed.

'Fine. Why don't you come along with me?'

'Where?'

'To ask G-d! I'm going to the synagogue this Saturday.'

'Will I be allowed in?'

'Of course, though only on the balcony with the other women.'

'Isn't G-d interested in me then?'

'Only if you're supporting a man.'

'I thought it was Esther who saved the people from ruin?'

'That was only because she was a queen. Everyone else has to rely on their husbands.'

# Chapter Thirty-Three

Attending a Jewish synagogue in an atheistic country felt like a strange experience. It was one of the most beautiful buildings in Birobidzhan. The church had been despoiled and abandoned but the synagogue was intact and there was a core group of regular worshippers.

I joined the women on the balcony. Some of them were very devout and followed the prayers line by line in the 'siddurs' or prayer books. Some of them just chatted on, ignoring what was happening on the floor below. I had seen plenty of ladies outside the church in St. Paul or Mimizan, having a gossip session outside the door and we had often received the 'end-tails' of that gossip at school the next morning, but it was the first time I had seen gossip take place as an alternative to a religious service and within the service itself. It was pleasant. No one was having to pretend that gossip wasn't important, part of what happened in religious communities. There was a complete openness, and the religious ladies did not turn around and glare at their more worldly sisters. They just pursued their own devotions. I liked the feeling that you could be yourself.

Below us, the men intoned and sang their prayers, read from the Torah and listened to the sermon. I liked the feeling of being an observer. There wasn't the same sense of mysticism as being in a Catholic church – none of the ornate sculpture and colour around a high altar area – none of the effect of a choir singing in Latin – but there was the feeling of something powerful emanating from the reading of the Torah. It was protected by scrolls and velvet. It was kissed and handled reverently. The way the text was read in Hebrew distanced it from the here and now. Of course, I couldn't have understood it whether it was read in Russian, Yiddish or Hebrew, but I had the feeling that the older men were familiar with the

Hebrew text and the younger men listened with respect. There was a sense that this ancient manuscript, imperfectly understood, had been at the centre of the community for hundreds of years. The 'tefillin' and the prayer shawls were also part of what made it special.

I had been invited with Nicolai to a family meal afterwards. It was the end of the Sabbath.

'Normally in the rest of the world, Jews meet in schul on Saturday mornings,' explained my host, 'but here we meet on Saturday afternoons because so many of the men have to work on Saturday mornings.'

'How important is this for you?' I asked the men of the household through Nicolai's translation.

'This is what makes all the hardship of living in Birobidzhan worthwhile,' one of them replied simply, gesturing to the rough-hewn walls and the basic food.

I was humbled by this family's hospitality amidst so much poverty. What had already struck me in Russia was the endless grind of everyday life. I suppose that I had seen it in my parents' farm in Les Landes but here it was even worse. In France it had been relieved for most people by community events and a night at Hôtel du Centre and, if you were lucky, by a happy marriage. But the privations here in Siberia caused by the weather and the very basic economy made life almost unendurable. This man was telling me that he could put up with all this, if he had the freedom to worship and read the Torah in accordance with the customs of his forefathers. Surely it wasn't too much to ask!

'Where did you come from before?'

'Bellarussia.'

'So how did you escape all the persecution?'

'Luckily for us, we came here three years before the war. We were cut off from all the horror; though I have no doubt that our wider family perished.'

'You mean that the war didn't affect you directly?'

'Yes, it did in terms of privations. But we were lucky. I was too old to be called up and our children were too young. We stuck it out here by ourselves.'

'And now you are being joined by other Jews? That must be a blessing.'

'Yes, it is, though,' and at this the old man's eyes twinkled, 'We are set in our ways and sometimes we don't like the new things the others bring.

But,' he continued, 'our children benefit from the companionship of others.' His wife nodded in agreement as she ladled out more borsch.

'What about the orphans who have come, I mean the Jewish ones, do you know anything about them?' They both looked wary of anything controversial being asked but the lady of the house answered for them both. 'We would like them to come to schul, but often those in charge are so busy indoctrinating them in Marxist ways that they don't have time to discover their real heritage.'

'I thought that was why they were sent here?'

'Yes, in theory, but young people won't appreciate their heritage, unless someone really encourages them, and we don't see much of that.'

'Perhaps we could take that up with Matvey?' I suggested to Nicolai. 'I know he's not religious, but he strikes me as a reasonable man.'

Nicolai shrugged his shoulders. 'You could try. You'd have to put it over as a cultural experience in order to get anywhere.'

I tried it out with Natasha next time I saw her. She was rather doubtful. 'Why would they need anything more than the teaching of the party?' she queried.

'Because many of the orphans here come from this sort of background and it's good for them to learn what their parents did.'

'How will it help the future of our country?' she asked pragmatically.

'Because it's hard to do the future if you don't understand anything about your past.'

'I'll ask Matvey.'

He, as I expected, was far more open to the suggestion.

'Why not? Give them a new experience.'

'Or remind some of the older ones of what they once had?'

'On the other hand, it's not really important for the success of our country.'

'Maybe not, but they were sent here because they are Jews by your great leader. Let them experience it and you can tell them how lucky they are that Stalin let them have this inheritance.'

Matvey beamed. You couldn't begin to doubt the wonder of the supreme leader in his eyes. Anything which helped the children understand and appreciate his magnanimity must be good.

As a result, one group at a time of about twenty children came to the schul to experience the prayers and the reading of the Torah. I was hopeful that it might spark a real debate amongst them about atheism and the value of religion, but I was disappointed. The older Jewish families often shared Shabbat food with them after the service and the children were polite and grateful but nothing deeper seemed to have got through to them.

'Why aren't they thrilled by their heritage?' I asked Nicolai, cross that my intervention seemed to be having so little effect.

'Because they've been taught week after week that something else is more important.'

'And do they all automatically believe it?'

'Marie, when you've lost your parents and family and then the party has rescued you, you will accept anything they tell you, especially if, the consequence of rejecting their intervention is that you will starve.'

'Do you think that everyone is as accepting as it appears?'

'Think about it, Marie. Most people accept Catholicism, Orthodoxy, bourgeois good living, Marxism, whatever they are brought up with. We're conditioned to like what our family likes.'

'I don't want what my family wants.'

'That's because you're a rebel at heart, but you're different from most people.'

'Does that mean that you can be a docile revolutionary?'

'Yes, especially if you're a revolutionary of the second or third or fourth generation.'

'How upsetting.'

'Maybe, but society has to become stable to survive.'

386

# Chapter Thirty-Four

I still hadn't found Devorah and Daniel. Every time I went to the orphanage, I hoped that, as I looked at all the children, these two would stand out in some way, but no one orphan appeared to be different from another. After a few weeks I thought that I had waited long enough without interfering and decided to make an enquiry.

'Natasha, I think that here you have children from other countries not just Russia? Am I right?'

She was not at all suspicious of the question. For her it was perfectly obvious that all children throughout the world would want to come to her wonderful country and see what the great leader had provided for them.

'There's a limit to the number of children we can accept, but, yes, we do have some from other countries.'

'Which countries?'

'We have a few from America.'

'America?'

'Yes of course. Families who appreciate the importance of the revolution. Why ever not?' She looked at me suspiciously. 'Why shouldn't they come from America?'

'No reason at all. It's just such a long way, and I thought that America was not on favourable terms with Russia?'

'That's because they haven't appreciated all that Russia did for them during the war and they have tried to prevent the good things which have been going on in Eastern Europe.'

'Such as?'

'Helping Hungary and the other countries invaded by the Fascists.'

'Yes, of course.' Not the place or time for political discussion, I thought.

'That means you have American children here who speak English?'

'Yes, they were sent over by Jewish charities. Their parents had supported the revolution and the American government was suspicious of them as a result. These children are better off here.'

'Good. Can I speak to them?'

'If I can find them. Often, they don't want to be reminded of their nationality. It makes them different from anyone else.'

'I won't embarrass them, I promise you. And it would be interesting to see how much they remember of their native language. Also, Natasha, do you have any French children?'

'French children? I don't know. Not in my section. But Matvey will know. Why do you want to speak to French children?'

'French is my native language.'

For the first time in the conversation, Natasha smiled. 'I'd forgotten. I'll ask for you.'

The American children – five of them in that section of the village – had been dispersed into different groups – presumably to make sure that they picked up the Russian language more easily and were not subversive. Like most converts, they were keener on the cause of Communism than anyone else around them.

'We are very lucky to be here. Our parents always told us how difficult it was in America. No rights. Trade unions not allowed to be very active. Discrimination.'

'In what ways?'

'Against black people.'

In 1948, such an idea had not occurred to me.

'But you're not black.'

'That doesn't mean that we shouldn't care.'

I was humbled by their concern for other people and amazed by their complete acceptance of the superiority of the USSR compared to the USA.

'What they didn't tell you,' said Nicolai, later on when I was telling him about my conversation, 'is how much the American Jews have helped Birobidzhan.'

'In what way?'

'By giving huge sums of money to help settle the orphans and money for buying machinery from Vladivostock.'

'Why would they want to do that?'

'Because they are totally committed to helping Jews everywhere despite their political persuasion.'

'And,' chimed in David Bergelson in the café, listening to our conversation, 'because they believe in Yiddish.'

'What's Yiddish got to do with it?' I asked naively.

Nicolai groaned. 'Now you've got him going. He won't stop now.'

'But of course, my dear Marie, Yiddish is the language which unites us all.'

'Despite political differences?'

'Exactly! It is our common heritage.'

'But how does a language which belonged to the Shetls of the Pale in Russia belong to Jews in America?'

'Because so many Jews in America came from the Shetls.'

'Why didn't they just adopt English?'

'English!' exclaimed Bergelson dramatically, as if I had pronounced a dirty word, and everyone around us laughed. 'Such a barbaric language! Nothing like the beauty of Yiddish!'

'You must learn not to make such sacrilegious statements here,' warned Yisroel, smiling and shaking his finger at me.

'Sorry!' I mirrored his tone of irony with my mock contrition. 'It just shows what a barbarian I am too, even though I come from France. I haven't had the advantage of an education in Yiddish, I'm afraid.'

'Or the advantage of being a Jew and being hounded by the whole world,' commented Georgios drily.

A pause. We drank more deeply into our coffee cups, and the men drew on their foul-smelling cigarettes.

'So, tell me more about Yiddish in America then?'

Everyone in the café groaned. 'Marie don't get him started. We'll be here all night.'

'The night in summer in Siberia goes on for ever.' Bergelson turned to me, bowing. 'And this beautiful young lady from France wants to know about our wonderful Yiddish newspapers.'

'Yes, I do.'

'There used to be nine or ten, four in New York, two in Chicago and three in Washington. Unfortunately, there are only three left in New York now.'

'Why has New York kept them?'

'Because the Orthodox community is larger and more vibrant in New York than anywhere else.'

'You mean that they publish news about what's going on in New York for the Jewish community there. What's that got to do with here?'

'Because it's much more than a small-time parochial newspaper,' interrupted Yisroel knowingly and quite passionately.

'Yes, indeed, it serves to educate and inspire the Jewish community world-wide. We are all interested in it, because they have accepted literary works from us here.'

'Especially Bergelson's,' added Nicolai, without translating for the others. 'He's our most famous writer, and Yisroel has also made a name for himself. The paper gives literary reviews, and poetry, novels in serial form, everything literary and cultural connected with Yiddish.'

'These publications really have an amazing reputation worldwide,' he added. 'But, sadly, they're becoming less numerous.'

'Why is that?'

'I suppose there are less people who know how to edit them, and then there's generally more assimilation.'

I'd heard the word before but wasn't quite sure what it meant.

'Assimilation is what happened to the German Jews before World War 1. They became more like the secular society around them.'

'Yes,' explained Yisroel. 'And it didn't help them one little bit, when it came to the German killing machine.'

'Becoming like everyone else doesn't do any of us any favours. That's why Birobidzhan is so important,' explained David.

'What about the new state of Israel which they're hoping to establish? Surely that's where all Jews can be truly accepted?' I asked.

I shared with them some of my experiences on the refugee ship in Marseille. 'They were all convinced that it was the only way to save their own people.'

390

Bergelson was horrified. 'They're just dreamers trying to create a new culture and language when what they've already got is staring them in the face. Why create a new language when for hundreds of years we've had our own Yiddish?'

Why indeed? But when I recalled the total focus of the young people on that ship, I didn't remember them as just crazy dreamers.

'Anyway, Marie, enough of this intense debate. I'll show you the newspaper produced in New York and translate parts of it for you.' Nicolai offered.

Later, as we were walking back to the hostel, he asked,

'Did you find your French orphans by the way?'

'Yes, I did, though whether coming here has been such a happy ever after story for them I'm not so sure.'

# Chapter Thirty-Five

Natasha found six French children for me. I was so excited, that I had to control myself physically not to put my arms round them as I asked them their names.

Luckily Natasha thought my emotional response had something to do with being able to speak to them in my own language. Two of them were so young that they had forgotten how to speak French. They managed a 'bonjour' and a 'ça va bien', but they had no more to offer. The other four were older and able to speak French. After several weeks coping with Russian and English, it was a great relief for me to be able to speak my own language. Two of them who were older boys, were already earning their living in the machinery workshops. They were puzzled by my questions and showed a complete lack of interest in my own reasons for being there.

'Why didn't you stay in France and get a job there?' I was intrigued. Surely, they could have earned more, working in Lyons where they came from?

'The partisans were coming up from the south. Some of them were communists but most of them just wanted the old ways back.'

'Maybe they were just trying to liberate their country from the Nazis?' I suggested.

'It's no good liberating it from one enemy and working with another afterwards,' answered one of them, a serious twenty-year old, called Jacques.

'What do you mean?'

'One of the comrades in Lyons told us that, unless the party was in control, France would go back to being just as bad as it was before the war.'

'And was that so bad?'

'Of course. The trade unions were suppressed. The poor had no work in Lyon. There were children who were starving.'

It was my turn to show surprise. I had to admit that I knew nothing about the conditions of the poor in cities in France before the war.

'And you didn't want that?'

'We want a fair society.'

'So, what did you do about it?'

'We went with the communist partisans right through France and across Germany and joined the Red Army in Berlin.'

I stared in amazement. These boys – as I considered them to be – not much older than myself, had already relinquished their homeland, fought in a war, joined another army and learnt to speak another language.

'That's extraordinary. You are very brave.'

'No, mademoiselle, we are inspired by the patriotism of the Russian people.'

'And the great leader who has done so much for them,' chimed in the other young man, Stephane, who was smaller than Jacques, with huge blue eyes proclaiming his innocence, and belying his experience of the world.

'And how did you come to be here in Birobidzhan?' I asked, intrigued.

'We got all the way to Minsk with the Red Army and one day, Uri here, heard some people talking about a great new experiment in justice over in the East of the country.'

'We had no one,' Uri assured me, taking up the story from his comrade.' We were tired of fighting and all the other soldiers had someone to go back to. We had no one. Our parents had belonged to the French resistance in Lyon and had been killed by the Nazis.'

'But didn't your parents have friends in Lyon?'

'Yes, people who belonged to the union and who encouraged us to fight the Nazis.'

'Besides,' added Jacques, continuing the story,' It was all chaos. Many of the comrades in the Resistance had been arrested and killed. Many more of them were joining the partisans and were going up north with them. We just got swept up with them. It was that or starvation on the streets of Lyon.'

393

'But,' (I was still struggling to understand their logic), 'I thought that the Americans were arriving from the South from Nice.'

'The Americans?' Uri spat on the ground. 'Who would trust them? They were just there for themselves and their capitalist bosses. They wouldn't be interested in us.'

'People in Marseille and Paris welcomed the Americans,' I pointed out. 'And since the war they haven't interfered with our politics at all.'

Uri and Jacques and Stephane turned away. They weren't interested in my defence of the Americans.

'And what about you two? Where do you come from?' I now felt free to question the two young people who were left. They looked about fourteen and twelve years of age.

'I am Daniel, Mademoiselle, and this is my sister, Devorah.'

I tried not to look too emotionally overwhelmed at this introduction. These two were my real reason for crossing this vast continent.

'How interesting that you still keep the Jewish form of your name,' I commented. The older French boys had now disappeared, and I felt more freedom in what I could say.

'Why not, Mademoiselle? This is the name our parents gave us.'

'Indeed. You are quite right. I am so pleased to meet you. I have heard of you before when I was in France.'

Immediately there was a flicker of interest in the boy's eyes.

'How, Mademoiselle?'

'Don't call me 'mademoiselle'. It sounds so formal. Call me Marie.'

'All right, Marie.' Daniel was correct in the way he spoke without giving any indication of his feelings. He seemed to speak on behalf of himself and his sister. 'How did you know about us in France?'

'I knew Mme Taube.'

'Ah, the lady who took us in after our parents left us.'

'Yes. You remember your parents?'

'How could we ever forget them?' Devorah joined in, suddenly inspired by the memory of her parents.

Daniel explained, 'Nothing was ever the same without them. And now we know that they died in the most horrible way through the Nazis.'

'I know. But they would be thrilled to know that you are both here and safe.'

'You mean that we are alive?' To my sensitive ears, Daniel seemed to discriminate between being alive and being safe in this place.

'I mean that you are alive and well and going forward in your lives.'

'Maybe. If we are really going forward…'

'What do you mean?'

'Whether this is a place which will ever go forward.'

I was amazed. It was the first time I had ever heard one of the orphans questioning the rightness of their situation and destiny. However, I didn't want the conversation to become subversive too quickly.

'Everyone here seems to think that it is a good place. But how did you get on with Mme Taube outside Paris?'

Daniel shrugged his shoulders. 'We were grateful to her and her husband for taking us in, but, after her husband died, Mme Taube hit the bottle.'

This young man was certainly aware of the realities of life, I thought.

'Is that why you decided to come here?'

'Not exactly. The union man from the cheese factory – he told us that it would be better here and that there was no future for us in France. Mme Taube didn't care about our education or future and we didn't have any money or friends. We decided to chance it and came to Russia.'

'And now?'

Daniel looked at me straight. 'For now, Marie, we are both receiving an education and have enough to eat. Whether we remain here in the long term remains to be seen.'

This was the first time I had heard any of the orphans consider any alternatives for their future.

'So, what will happen, do you think?'

'Who knows, Marie?'

# Chapter Thirty-Six

When we met several days later in the top room of the theatre, Nicolai was intrigued by the unusual nature of Daniel and Devorah's attitude to Russia.

'It's the first time I've heard of orphans under Matvey's guidance not believing every word he tells them about the party and Stalin.'

'Perhaps they're free thinkers?' I suggested.

'Perhaps. But, if they are, they will be in danger.'

'How? How can having a brain in your head and thinking about the future lead you into danger?' I was angry. It was almost as if Nicolai wanted them to fail.

'If you think for yourself, then one day your thinking will be expressed in words to someone,' he explained patiently. 'Once you tell someone, it will be out in the open and word will be passed around. Then someone in authority will hear about it and, at that point, you can be reported.'

'You're assuming, that they will share their ideas with someone else?'

'No, but it's unusual for a fourteen – year old to be able to keep their ideas to themselves. And they told you.'

'Obviously I'm different. I'm French and I'm a journalist. Maybe Daniel thought he could speak freely to an outsider.'

'Maybe he did. And maybe he thought it was a lucky chance. I hope you're right, Marie, but I would fear for those two in the present climate.'

'How is it different from any other time in this country?' I was beginning to think that these Yiddish intellectuals were suffering from paranoia.

'I think it is different. Until the end of the war the Jews were friends of Stalin's government. Now they're under suspicion.'

'But why are they? Have they done anything to cause offence?'

'They're supported by the American Jews and the Americans can't be friends with Russia.'

'Even though they've given this country so much money?'

'Perhaps, it's BECAUSE they've given so much money. Socialists are supposed to be superior to capitalists so they shouldn't need American money.'

'So, it's pride?'

'In a way, but also because since the end of the war and the end of the Nazis, they're the only possible threat to Stalin.'

'But Daniel and Devorah are not Americans. They're French and lots of the French Trade Unionists, including their own parents, were friendly towards Russia.'

'I agree in theory, Marie but two orphans aren't representing their country. It's more that they're thinking for themselves and that's always dangerous in Russia.'

'Well, you think for yourself. And what about all those ideas floating around amongst your friends in the Yiddish coffee house?'

'Exactly. You've understood.'

A pause.

I saw a line of cockroaches creeping along the top of the curtain in the blacked out top room of the theatre. I had seen so many in the hostel that I wasn't alarmed but I was intrigued by their orderly progress.

'In that case, you're all in danger.'

No answer. Silence.

'You should try to leave.'

'And how, my dear Marie, would you propose we go about doing that?'

'Applying for a travel visa?'

He laughed – a hoarse bark of a laugh. 'We'd never be granted one and even making the application would immediately put us in danger. It means we want to leave this socialist paradise and so we are not to be trusted.'

I was frightened, angry and frustrated by the fact that you could want to do something, have the means to do it, and yet not be allowed. I had been in rebellion against my upbringing, but I had had the opportunity to leave it behind. I had the mind of the Western European – if you want something badly enough, you can have it. If you didn't get it, it was your own fault, because you hadn't worked hard enough or pushed hard enough to achieve it.

I stared at Nicolai, appalled. In that small upstairs room, our different cultures disappeared. One human being stared at another across the abyss.

The tension was broken by Nicolai moving round the table towards me, pulling me towards him and kissing me hard on the mouth.

'What was that for?' I stuttered, when he had finished.

'That was my sign of appreciation for you.'

'My looks? My Western ideas?'

'No, for being naïve enough to believe that you can do what you want.'

'That's something to be admired?'

'It's amazing. It's beautiful. It's what I long to have, Marie.'

I laughed. 'Well, you can have it quite freely. You don't even have to have it through me.'

As a response, he held my head in his hands and looked at me searchingly. 'You offer it to me, and I want it, Marie.'

'What? A passport to freedom?'

'No. The pure belief that you can act like that. When you are talking to me and looking at me, I can believe anything.'

I reached up to the curls of his beard and ran my fingers through them.

'Nicolai, I give it to you freely. You've got to admit, it's quite an unusual way of declaring your affection for someone.'

'It's probably the Yiddish way – full of romance and idealism and totally impractical.'

The others agreed when we met them later in the café. We had not declared anything to each other or to the world, but subtly we had grown closer. There was something intimate in the way we looked at each other and were aware of each other's physical presence. The other men in the group were far too well-mannered to comment in an obvious way, but they were aware of it.

'So, is Marie going to be part of the Yiddish language culture?' began Bergelson playfully.

'I'm ready to learn,' I answered dutifully.

'I think Nicolai is ready to teach you, aren't you, my friend?'

'Yes, of course, Dovid. Always ready to do a service for the Yiddish language cause.'

'If you want her to hear Yiddish spoken, you must visit the Davinskys on the Shabbat. They speak beautifully and of course you must read my articles in the Shtern.'

'Of course, Dovid. Who could miss those?' This from Yisroel, who enjoyed a joke at Bergelson's expense. There was inevitably a great deal of banter about the desirability of recognising Bergelson's genius. He was an old man and the younger ones in the café respected him.

I felt inspired by Dovid's suggestion, and I followed it up as Nicolai walked me to the hostel that night. 'You know, Nicolai. That's something we could definitely do in order to help us find out what Daniel and Devorah are really thinking.'

'What's that?'

'Invite them to the Davinskys.'

# Chapter Thirty-Seven

The Davinskys were a lovely, older Orthodox Jewish couple who remained faithful to the synagogue in Birobidzhan and who believed that any Jewish orphan had the right to share or continue their religious tradition if they so wished. The teachers at the orphanage could not see any point to the experience, but they shrugged their shoulders and allowed it to happen. They were sure that their charges would see it as a waste of time in the new world of Soviet work.

It was the obvious thing to invite the brother and sister to the Davinskys, not because they had shown any interest in religion, but because it was a way for Nicolai and myself to interact with them more freely. I learnt that, through the wider Jewish community, several groups of orphans had already been invited to the 'schul experience' and a few of them had shown an interest in returning. If we could only make Daniel and Devorah part of a group, hopefully no suspicions would be aroused.

I went back to Matvey and Natasha to see what could be arranged in the next few weeks. The obvious strategy would be to put the brother and sister in the French speaking group with myself as guide and interpreter. We tried to put the Americans in the same group, but Natasha was immediately suspicious.

'By doing that, you are signalling that those with capitalist pasts are special and different.'

'But perhaps they are?' I suggested, as we sat together on the benches in the large communal dining area, after lunch, when the groups of children were given half an hour to relax or tidy their dormitory areas.

'I don't see them as being different,' she retorted sharply, 'apart from the disadvantage of having a western past.'

'Exactly.' I soothed her, playing the socialist game. 'They are at a disadvantage and therefore they understand each other.'

She looked at me suspiciously. 'There is no room for this sort of personal understanding in our socialist workers' society. This only encourages individualism which is bad for productivity.'

I accepted the sermon with good humour. No amount of argument would ever dent Natasha's complete belief in her country's system. I was sometimes amazed because I knew that Marxism had emerged out of dialectics, which implied some sort of friction of ideas. There was no apparent friction of ideas in this orphanage.

'Right, so if we are going to carry on giving these children access to their cultural heritage, how do you suggest we do it?'

By following Natasha's suggested programme, Daniel and Devorah's invitation was delayed for several weeks, but it had the merit of not drawing attention to them.

'And don't tell them about it first,' warned Nicolai. 'That will show your special interest in them, and it also means you won't observe their spontaneous reaction to the experience.'

As a result, it appeared to be ever such a casual invitation but under the surface, every word and nuance of behaviour were scrutinized by myself. I wasn't entirely sure why I thought their reaction to this experience was so important. After all, they had no religious background, so why should this particular ritual make an impression on them? For me, it was something to do with their response to an experience which was so non-materialist and so different to anything they would have encountered in Russia so far.

They kept firmly with the group which had been invited that Saturday and it consisted mainly of Russian young people with a few Serbs included too. They were all polite and had been trained to show no emotional reaction. It was not surprising if they were bored. Once you had observed the strange swaying of the men and their donning of the prayer shawls or looked at the tefillin hanging down from the waist or noticed the leather box of law bound round the forehead and then wound round the arm, there was not much to look at and, as they could not understand a word of the Hebrew, there was nothing to understand, to agree or disagree with. With the boys and girls being separated, Devorah seemed a lot more isolated. I had not noticed before how much she relied on her brother to speak for her, but, when she was alone in the upstairs gallery, she did not engage with the group of girls. She edged closer to me, as if that would save her from having to react to what she saw.

While the boys were in the middle of all the prayer activity going on below, the girls were cut off from the sense of being engaged directly in religion. The few women who were following the siddur sat on one side of the gallery and were engrossed in what they were doing and ignored by everyone else. This allowed the girls to express their amazement at what was happening and to distance themselves from it.

'What an incredible waste of time!' exclaimed one of the girls, not bothering to hide her disdain. 'They could be studying more about the future and about the Party.'

'Or they could be just relaxing and having fun outdoors,' suggested another a bit more realistically.

Devorah, on the other side to me and nearer to the girls, whispered the gist of what they were saying. I wasn't surprised. Nothing in their background or what they had been taught prepared them for this. I didn't react but allowed them to have their say. Afterwards I reminded them that they had been invited to the Davinskys house and that there they should be respectful.

'Why should we be?' One of the Serbians, a dark eyed beauty, tossed her pig tail with her hand, as if stating her superiority and the right to react as she wanted. 'They are not contributing anything to the future of the party.'

'Actually, they already are.' My tone was firm, though I doubt that anything more than my words could be conveyed in translation. 'This couple work in the wood trade just like anyone else here, so they are contributing to the economy of Birobidzhan.'

'They why are they bothering with these out of date, reactionary ways?' This young lady from Serbia was not easily defeated.

'First of all, remember that they have been given the right by your great leader himself, so, if that's how they choose to spend their leisure, then it's up to them.'

'Waste of time, if you ask me.'

'Also,' contributed one of her friends, 'Why aren't they just bored? How can they bear to spend time doing this every week?'

'Because that's how their ancestors and yours behaved in the shetl.'

'Thank G-d that was all done away with many years ago.'

'That may be,' I replied good-humouredly, not interested in pursuing a conversation about the rights and wrongs of Jewish worship, which really didn't have any relevance for me. 'But I bet you won't say no to Mrs. Davinsky's gefelte fish and borsch!'

And indeed, they loved it. I couldn't imagine how the Davinskys had found enough food for us all. I hated to think that they might be laughed at by this confident group of young people, when they were welcoming them into their home. There was something moving about us all being gathered round the table, eating the same meal which had been celebrated for centuries. If the word 'spiritual' means anything at all, it must mean the sense of unity which seemed to bind us all together and which was initiated by the Davinskys' love. Some of the young people drew back from full participation but all were touched by this extraordinary communal experience. I watched closely for Devorah and Daniel's reactions, but they were impassive. It was impossible to tell what they were thinking.

'Well, we've done our bit for the culturation process!' I reported laughingly to Nicolai in the café that night. 'But I'm not sure it's having any effect. I think convinced atheists are pretty hard to touch.'

'Don't fool yourself,' answered Yisroel unexpectedly serious for a moment. 'They're not convinced atheists. It's just that they've not experienced anything else in their young lives, and it's only our experiences which inform us about what is true.'

'And are you informed by your experiences of religion?'

'Of course. I was brought up with it in Belarussia. Oh, I'm not sure I want to attend every Sabbath, but I like to have the right to it.'

'And, anyway, it did have an effect on our two friends from Paris,' chimed in Nicolai.

'How do you know?'

'Because Daniel told me.'

# Chapter Thirty-Eight

In the café Nicolai only gave me brief generalisations. Daniel and Devorah had enjoyed the experience and had particularly appreciated the Davinskys' kindness and were glad that they had been asked to go.

'Good,' said Bergelson. 'At least someone amongst our young people is going in the right direction.'

'I didn't know that you were such a supporter of religion, Dovid,' commented Nicolai with some asperity. 'I thought that you spent all your youth trying to get away from the Pale.'

'Of course, of course,' replied Bergelson, waving his cigar frantically and impatiently. 'What do you expect from a young man, who wants to make his way in life and is being dragged down by his family. But you know perfectly well, Nicolai, that my passion is Yiddish.'

'But, as I understand it, that's not the same as the Hebrew in schul?' I queried. The distinction between and the significance of the two languages was still a mystery to me.

'No, Marie, of course it's not.' Dovid talked slowly to me as I was a child. 'There is a difference. One is a dead, religious language. The other is a vibrant, cultural resource, but even the religious one allows for a different culture.'

'Tell me something,' I asked them, feeling much more confident of my place in this little group of men than I had when I first arrived. 'Explain to me why your great leader allows schul to happen but has persecuted and shut down all the orthodox churches.'

At this point, Yisroel became the person to give me instruction. 'Because Orthodox Christianity was connected with the Tsar and the old regime. You can't have a new political system and have people remembering how the Tsar and Tsarina relied on the church and whole Orthodox religion. It was like a superstition that the people kept on going back to. But our schuls are different. To start with the Pale was never a threat to Bolshevism. It was full of non-powerful people. No one in Russia then or now is going to convert to Orthodox Judaism.'

'So, it's not a threat to the system?'

'Exactly.'

'But surely, it's illogical, if you're proclaiming atheism. To allow any monotheistic faith is a retrograde step.'

Yisroel sat back, one leg over another and ready to say in this small café, where he felt safe, what he must have thought thousands of times, but never had the freedom to declare it. 'Illogical? My dear Marie, what has logic got to do with it?'

'I know that faith is not logical,' I agreed hastily.

'Ah, well now, that's another discussion. We won't go there at the moment. Otherwise we'll be here all night. No. What I mean is, why do you think the Bolshevik way of doing things is logical?'

I hesitated, fumbling for words. 'I thought that if anything is logical, it must be the system here. It's atheistic; it's for the good of the people; it's about everyone being equal.'

'You're partly right. Yes, it's about imposing Bolshevism, which is supposed to be for our good, but, if something illogical helps, like a bit of someone's culture, then it's allowed.'

'Yes,' agreed Dovid, 'it's like the NEP in the 1920s.'

I always found Russian acronyms hard to keep up with. 'What's that?'

'The new system which Lenin introduced after the civil war, which allowed the peasants to buy and sell and make private profit. See what I mean about illogical? It shouldn't have been allowed under socialism, but they needed the peasants, especially the richer ones, on their side. Otherwise the whole economy was going to fail.'

'Yes, but it was only allowed for a certain time,' added Nicolai, 'while it served Bolshevik purposes. Then, when the time came for suppression, under our great leader, then it came big time.'

'And I fear, Dovid,' continued Nicolai turning to Bergelson with some kindness, 'that the same sort of process is going to happen with us.'

405

'No, no, no,' replied Bergelson airily, pouring more vodka into his coffee. 'We've helped Russia. Think of how my speech in Moscow helped the cause of the war. Think of what all we Jews have done for the state and I'm not just talking about the hard-core members.'

'That, my friend, is because you can't bear to think anything else.' Nicolai spoke into the silence after Bergelson's boast. For three seconds everyone believed what Nicolai was saying. But soon the human desire for deception and a quiet life took over again.

'No, you're wrong, Nicolai. It's not just that they will honour our past. Birobidzhan is a model 'soviet', a place where indigenous people can prosper. It shows how other minorities can flourish in Russia too. Besides, we're too far away for anyone to care.'

By about 2 in the morning in Siberia, the daylight is just departing and the chill in the air reminds you of the reality of the impenetrable cold during the rest of the year. Someone had opened the back door so that the tobacco fumes could dissipate in the air, but there was no fooling anyone what the temperature was outside.

Nicolai pointed to the framed picture on one wall of the café. 'Our great leader is everywhere, my friend, and if he decides we have to go, we will.'

I didn't say a word. Nicolai had spoken the last words in Russian without translation, but I knew what the gesture towards the picture meant. I had once seen in a farmhouse in France an embroidered, framed picture of words which proclaimed that 'God is the unseen guest in this house, hearing every word spoken.' It was meant to remind the inhabitants to be careful about what they said, even in private. Here, you only needed a picture of Stalin to send the same message. A religious friend had once told me that it wasn't just your words which mattered. God judged your thoughts too. In Russia, Stalin had taken over G-d's job.

Nicolai had taken to meeting me over the bridge in the forest beyond the orphanage. He once reminded me not to go too far in because of the threat of bears, but when we were visiting the orphanage together, it was a convenient place to be alone. Despite my lack of sexual experience, I was not afraid of Nicolai. He was a considerate lover and, out here in the forest, I felt at ease. It was so much closer to my upbringing in Les Landes and it was buildings which were more likely to remind me that I was in a foreign culture. Was I in love with Nicolai? I had no idea what those words meant. Not, I thought, if love meant what books told you, that the whole earth moved when you were together. But certainly, a far more pleasurable prospect than an awkward fumble and a sense of being used at the end of the night with a Parisian Marxist.

'Does your mind ever stop thinking even when we are making love?' he once asked me, but I knew he was only teasing.

'Probably not,' I had to admit. 'It doesn't seem to have an off switch.'

Nicolai didn't seem to be upset by this admission. He laughed good naturedly.

'Good job I love you as you are.'

I couldn't, I thought, ask for much more.

'Tell me about Daniel and Devorah, then? What made you think they wanted more than the orphanage when you saw them?' I asked him, on one of our excursions outside the town.

We sat together on the springy, turf floor of the forest. It was as good a bed as any for the purpose of making love and it had the advantage of privacy.

'Not Devorah, of course. She's younger and anyway you saw more of her than I did.'

I explained about Devorah nudging up to me during the religious service.

'That's probably because she finds you to be more reassuring than anyone else when her brother's not there.'

'Yes, I agree. I hate to think what would happen to her, if they were ever separated.'

'I expect she'd survive,' said Nicolai matter-of-factly. 'People do. You don't know what resources you have within yourself, until it happens.'

I wanted to ask whether that was what had happened to him, but I felt instinctively that that was not a conversation for today, so I didn't push any further.

'So, tell me about Daniel then.'

'After the service the men have to go to a room and take off the borrowed tefillin and prayer shawl and leather straps before they leave.

Daniel was the only boy who had taken up the offer of getting involved like that. For many Jewish visitors, it's like the possibility of dressing up and entering into the experience, even if they don't really believe. Most of the orphans can't be bothered to do that, but there are always one or two who give it a go.

When Daniel was in the back with me alone, he said "That's important, Nicolai. What we've just done is important."

"Have you ever done it before?" I asked him.

"A few times, a long time ago, with my grandparents when we lived in Bordeaux."

'Bordeaux!' I exclaimed. 'He went to the synagogue in Bordeaux! That's where Alain and his aunt and uncle went.' I had explained to Nicolai something of my connection and friendship with Alain on another occasion.

'The place doesn't really matter,' suggested Nicolai. 'What does matter is that he felt a connection with his past which most of the orphans don't feel. It seemed important to him.'

'Then I tried another question, a more daring one." Daniel, are you and Devorah happy here in Birobidzhan?"'

'He looked at me with his searching brown eyes. "Happy? I don't know what that means. Fed and clothed? Yes. Is there justice and good management in the orphanage? Yes. Do we miss our parents? Yes. Do we understand what has happened to us? No. Do we want to stay here for ever? I don't think so."

There were quite simply too many negative answers. We both knew that a good socialist orphan, even a Jewish one, would always say 'yes' to everything.

# Chapter Thirty-Nine

Nicolai and I tried to keep an eye out for our brother and sister team over the next few weeks, but I had to avoid Natasha's suspicions. I thought she was quite capable of reporting me to some authority and getting me extradited for having a bad influence on Soviet young people. It would have made a great story for my newspaper but, unfortunately, I was not the only one who would suffer. It was those with whom I had associated who would be labelled as 'counter-revolutionary agitators' and who would be taken off somewhere unpleasant. Nicolai mentioned terrible places where you could be lost for years and no one would know what had happened to you.

My relationship with Nicolai was developing all the time. I had never really given myself to someone in this way before and I found, to my surprise, that it was not just a logical sense of choice. I thought that once you had ditched the middle-class notion of marriage, all would be straightforward. You would decide to embark on a relationship and, when you or your partner had had enough, you would leave it. I had reckoned without the tentacles of emotional attachment. Not only was I starting to enjoy the physical side of the relationship, though it was still rather hit or miss, I found that I was feeling attached to Nicolai. I had no idea where our relationship was going to, or how it was going to be pursued when I was back in France, but I found that I was beginning to feel at ease with his mannerisms and enjoy his sense of humour.

As I was walking through the town one day, Yisroel stopped me. His English was broken but understandable.

'You, be carefully, little French miss!'

'I didn't know you spoke English, Yisroel!' I parried conversationally. He grinned, pleased with the compliment.

'I speak good, yes?' He was like a schoolboy in his eagerness.

'Yes, well done, Yisroel.' I clapped him on the back as if the purpose of our conversation was just to show off his rudimentary language skills.

'Be careful, for Nicolai.'

'For Nicolai or with him?'

The distinction between prepositions and their meanings was evidently lost on Yisroel.

'Some bad people not like it.'

I couldn't imagine that he objected to my friendship with Nicolai on personal grounds, so I decided to ask Nicolai directly.

'What's the problem? Why is Yisroel warning me?'

'Because of things which have happened to his family in the past.' He continued as an explanation. 'You'll find, Marie, that this is a common story in Soviet Russia. Everyone has relations who had bad ends. You try to forget about them but in the end, you start fearing for everyone you meet.'

'And Yisroel is afraid for me or for you?'

'Probably for both of us, but especially for me.'

'What happened to his family?'

'Ask him.'

I had to ask him with Nicolai there as a translator in the Yiddish café. His father and mother had been involved with Bergelson in supporting the Stalinist government at the beginning of the war. They had returned to the Ukraine to support the siege of Stalingrad. There, alongside the rest of the population, they had endured unimaginable horrors as the Nazi blockade lengthened. Yisroel's parents had never been anything but loyal supporters of the Soviet regime. They had only talked about their Jewish heritage at home and had always taught their children to be careful in what they said outside. Yisroel had learnt Yiddish as a young child, and, as a natural dreamer, began to write poetry in Russian and Yiddish when he was a teenager. He and his brother had been exemplary members of the Pioneers and the Komsomol and had done almost as much as the adults during the war for Russian victory.

410

'But after the war, that counted for nothing,' said Yisroel bitterly.

'What happened to your parents?' I asked, dreading the answer which I knew must involve more suffering.

'They were denounced by Ukranian peasants who were jealous of them because they had received some extra money from Yiddish speaking friends in the West.'

'Do you mean in America?'

'Yes, and the only reason that happened was because of me.'

'How do you mean?'

'I printed poetry in Russian newspapers but of course that had to be very politically correct. I reserved my emotional output – 'from the heart', as Nicolai translated it – for the Yiddish publications in New York. I was just proud of the fact that my work was being printed in an international magazine, but our neighbours found out about it, and denounced my parents.'

'It wasn't your fault, Yisroel and I'm sure your parents were proud of you.'

'Yes, but we were all naïve fools. My parents were exiled to a camp in Siberia. They would never have survived the winter there. They were too old and worn down by the years of war. I managed to escape here, where no one can punish you for being a Jew.'

'So, why are you worried about Nicolai?'

'Because he's associating with you, and you are Western.'

'But no one knows about us.'

Yisroel laughed bitterly. 'They will. Someone will report it. They know everything.'

I could see his point of view. The older men in the café might tease us about our romantic relationship. I wasn't convinced that anyone in the Mayor's office or the hostel knew anything about it. As far as the orphanage was concerned, Nicolai was my translator. But who knew? I was beginning to understand the paranoia which saw suspects behind every impassive face.

I was worried about putting Nicolai in danger. I was worried about how attached to each other we were becoming. I was worried about where it was all leading and whether I had only been concerned about my personal attachment to this man when I let it begin. Personal relationships between the sexes were quite bad enough anyway, I thought, without having these endless extra complications.

'So, what are we going to do about it?' I asked Nicolai directly when we were alone in the theatre.

'I don't want to do anything about it,' said Nicolai. 'I like it as it is. That's good enough for me.'

'But what about the consequences for you?' I asked, vaguely dissatisfied with his answer.

'Consequences?' He threw his hands in the air dramatically. 'Who knows what consequences there will be? Yisroel's parents thought they were keeping their son under close guard, so that nothing bad could happen. But they were wrong.'

'Perhaps the wrong was in letting Yisroel write for a Yiddish newspaper.'

'Marie, you can't continually betray your own soul. If you deceive yourself, it has a way of getting out anyway.'

'If we stop seeing each other, it won't keep you in safety?'

'Probably not. But if we stop, then we will have denied our love, and that matters.'

It seemed to me that Nicolai was much more spontaneously affectionate than me. I felt much more calculating and I was ashamed of myself.

'I love you, Nicolai, but I wonder where it will all end.'

'Maybe it won't end at all?'

'What do you mean?'

'Maybe I'll be able to leave Russia with you.'

'You really think that's possible?'

I had always assumed that such a journey was not possible. In fact, in some ways I realised that it secretly pleased me, because then I didn't have to worry about the long-term effects of a relationship. It was a convenient ending for which I had no responsibility.

'I've told you before, Marie. It's a prison here; but sometimes you can see a chink of light.'

'Do you think that Daniel and Devorah can see a chink of light?'

'I wouldn't be surprised. I have a feeling that Daniel knows exactly what he's doing and that one day he will move.'

'Maybe we should help him.'

'Maybe we should help them both, and at the same time, help ourselves.'

# Chapter Forty

We agreed that we needed to find a time to see Daniel alone. One feature of the Soviet system which annoyed me and made me very suspicious, was that they hated the idea that anyone could want to be alone. That, I thought, would make me reject the whole communist system. What had I loved more than anything else when I was growing up? Being alone in the forests and by the sea. Life on the farm and sometimes at school was hard. People could annoy me. I reasoned that if you don't have any time alone, and if you don't have nature to nourish you, then it feels as though there is no hope. If you have ideas thrown at you all the time when you are growing up, which inevitably happens explicitly and implicitly, how are you to know which ones are good for you, if you never have time to process them in your own soul? How can you bear the boredom of incessant chatter of people who have nothing to say, if you can't experience silence? How can you get rid of anger in your heart if you never have time by yourself to speak it out?

Soviet Russia hated people being by themselves. They had to be policed all the time and that made me suspicious. If the system was so good, why did people have to be watched all the time in case they rebelled? If you saw how the orphanage was organised, you realised that those young people were never left to themselves. They slept in dormitories. If they weren't in lessons, they were being politically educated or they were doing sport, or they were involved in debates. None of those things were bad in themselves, but what about the time just to be? I was worried about a system that was always trying to intervene, always trying to change people. If a system works, surely it doesn't have to be forced down people's throats all the time? It should be obvious that it works.

'You're just a natural rebel.' I heard Alain's voice in my head. 'Maybe,' I found myself replying to him, 'but we need a few rebels. It's good to question. We need people to disagree. That's how we eventually make things better.'

'That's all very well,' said Nicolai, when we had an unusual discussion about politics in the theatre one day when we were alone there. 'But the Bolsheviks did disagree. That's the whole point.'

'Yes, they did,' I argued fervently. 'But they weren't very good at letting other people disagree with them, and I'm not talking about the supporters of the old regime. What about the sailors at Kronstadt? They supported the Revolution, and then got mown down by Lenin because they were moderates.'

'That's because Communism can't exist alongside anything else. It's everything or nothing. And the Party says that the everything approach gives a better deal for everyone.'

'Not for the people in the Gulags,' I reminded him. 'Not for the people that Stalin didn't like.'

'But Stalin did it for the good of the country.'

I stared at Nicolai, amazed. 'Whose side are you on?'

He ruffled my hair affectionately.

'Just showing you that not everyone has to agree with you.'

'Alright,' I conceded. 'Don't ask me to say that this crazy country is a workers' paradise, because it's not.'

'And France is?'

'No, it's not. It's miserable for lots of the workers, it's true but at least no one's pretending it's Paradise. And you can get yourself off the lowest rung and onto something better. And what's more there are families.'

'I thought you didn't like your family?'

'I don't but lots of them are good. And even I had my great aunt Hélène, who turned out to be a hero.'

'Well, before we make a decision about west versus east, how are we going to speak to Daniel?'

'Our only hope is to get him alone in a place, where it's natural for him to be alone.'

'We've already established that. There isn't a place, especially not in that orphanage.'

'All right then. Where?'

'The Davinskys'

'Doubtful. If he spends too much time there, it will look suspicious to the others. And the Davinskys might get into trouble.'

'How about during schul? The other youngsters will all be looking at the service. They might not notice if he's not there.'

'What about the link with me?'

'What do you mean?'

'I'm a Westerner, but your dear leader has allowed me to be there. I could write an article about the young people's reaction to Jewish culture. And for that I need a translator.'

'So far you've always had either me or the Mayor's translator.'

'The Mayor's translator is no good for either Hebrew or Yiddish. You will have to be unavailable – a bad case of sickness or something. Then I will be able to call on Daniel as my French/Russian translator.'

'What about Natasha?'

'Again, not good enough for the Hebrew stuff. Nicolai, this is the only way this could work and it's better without you being around. The question is, what are we going to propose to Daniel?'

'I can't imagine. He might have his own ideas. Also, you have to see whether he's interested in going anyway.'

'I think he'll be interested. He's too intelligent not to be.'

'There's the Western mind at work, my darling. There's lots of intelligent people who are totally committed to Bolshevism.'

I considered this point carefully. 'That's because they've never known anything else. If you're here and you're an idealist, they you'd put everything into it.'

'Or if you've never been badly treated here. If you've been part of the proletariat, especially in the cities, you've probably done quite well out of the system. Also, if you came from an aristocratic background but were totally aware of the injustice there and wanted it to be better for everyone.'

'Are there people who are that unselfish?' I asked cynically.

'Amazingly, yes. We had people inside the Pale of Settlement who were so delighted, when they were allowed to leave after the Revolution, that they pledged themselves to equal opportunities for all.'

'I hope they're still convinced.'

Nicolai shrugged his shoulders. 'Some of them will be convinced till their dying day because they want to be. Some of them are already bitter and disillusioned.'

'And that includes you?'

'Some people of my generation felt that they had it easy because they weren't involved in the 1917 revolution. They felt that they had to make up for it, by being extra enthusiastic about Stalin's reforms in the 30s.'

'But not you?'

He grinned ruefully. 'You couldn't really see me as a devoted member of the Kommosol, could you? I'm not keen enough on red scarves and improving speeches.'

'I don't blame you. It would make me sick.'

'My little Marika, you are never going to be part of a uniformed brigade, are you?'

'Certainly not, especially after the Nazis. But,' I said practically, evading his teasing and the light in his eye which always heralded more love making, 'we've still got to decide what to do with Daniel.'

'We can't decide that yet. You need a system of interviewing the orphans who are visiting the schul with Daniel as your translator. Then, one time, you have to interview him.'

'Let's hope Matvey and Natasha buy the idea without any suspicion.'

'Yes, I agree. As good Stalinists, they are always looking for signs of backsliding in others. On the other hand, they are such committed believers themselves, they can't believe that anyone else wouldn't find the Soviet experience in Birobidzhan anything other than wonderful.'

'How do people become like that,' I wondered.

'They don't. They're just born differently to you.'

# Chapter Forty-One

As a result of this conversation, we played on what we thought of as the blind spot of the orphanage leaders, brought about by their illusions and vanity. I had good training for that through my work with the Resistance. When attempting to fool the Germans, Père Julien had advised me to look for their blind spot, but also added, 'but don't forget you've got one yourself.'

I approached Natasha, who I considered to be more suspicious and aware than Matvey, and who also spoke English and therefore could have acted as a translator.

'I have something I need for my job as journalist,' I explained to her. 'I want some of your youngsters who have already been to the schul once, to come again, so that I can interview them about any developing reactions they have to the traditional culture.'

'I think you'll find that they see it as more and more reactionary and bourgeois,' she stated firmly. 'They hardly need to come again to repeat that opinion.'

This was an anticipated reaction, but I found that she was indifferent to the whole process. If I wanted to waste my time as a journalist representing a tradition from an obsolete capitalism, then I was a fool, but it was none of her business.

I set up an experiment using the responses of some of the youngsters. I chose them because of their varying personalities and backgrounds, so that there was a chance of an interesting variety of responses, which I could genuinely include in an article for a French communist newspaper. It was all about how Russian orphans were being looked after by the state and how they were responding to their traditional cultural background, which Stalin was good enough to allow them to access. I asked Daniel to be my translator because he spoke my native language as well as Russian and so I hoped that the nuances of reactions by the young people were likely to be better represented and transmitted to my audience.

'How do you feel about doing this job for me, Daniel?' I asked him.

It had never really occurred to either Nicolai or to me that he might not want to do the job. However, we reckoned without the truth that Daniel was a cautious young man.

'I would first like to ask Matvey's permission.'

'Good idea. If he says 'yes', will you do it?'

He hesitated again. 'Yes, on one condition. That Devorah can come too.'

It was my turn to hesitate. I wondered whether the invitation to translate risked becoming too personal and that this might create suspicion.

'Fine by me, but I don't know how I'm going to justify that to the leaders of the orphanage.'

'Saturday is the only day we see each other properly when we're not in our groups. We look forward to it. I can't let her down.'

In most Western orphanages, that would be an understandable request. But in Stalin's Russia, the only family which counted for anything officially was the family, who were your Bolshevik comrades. Wanting to be near your sister might be a sign of dangerous, bourgeois tendencies.

'Let me think about it, Daniel. If we do that, I'll need to include her in the task.'

'You can give her the job of translating for the girls. I know she's quiet but she's good at languages and remembers French well. You could also say it's appropriate, because of the way boys and girls are divided for Jewish worship.'

'We'll try it.'

Nicolai and I held our breath as the process of permission went through as we had predicted. Matvey was full of good humour and quite incapable of believing that there was any ulterior motive behind the request. Natasha was not sure about the inclusion of Devorah in the process. 'In our new society here, men and women are the same and the sooner our young people understand that the better. Dividing the sexes is peasant mentality.'

In my brief history lessons given me by Nicolai, I had understood the label 'peasant' was an insult. Before I came to Russia, I had thought that in a communist country 'peasant' would be a positive description, but apparently not. The peasants, especially the more successful ones, had got in the way of Stalin's five-year plans in the 20s and 30s, and had had to be re-educated, which meant sending them to labour camps and working them to death.

'They understand perfectly the lesson of equality,' I assured Natasha soothingly, 'which of course I totally agree with. It's more because the men and women have completely different experiences of worship and culture in the Jewish scheme of things. A girl might find it easier to be more in tune with the girls' experiences. I'll try swopping them around sometimes. In fact,' I enthused, as if she was helping me in my research, 'that's a good idea! I can write it into my observations.'

'Hmmm.' She looked a little nonplussed at my apparent praise of her attitudes. 'As long as this doesn't become a regular thing, which would not be good for the group as a whole, and, would not help their political education.'

'Of course not. I understand what you're saying. It's only for a few weeks and then everything will be back to normal.'

The process had been devised by us as a ruse for talking to Daniel by himself, but, surprisingly, it became an interesting exercise, in its own right, and made my articles which were being sent back to France, much more interesting and ultimately successful with the readers of my newspapers.

Nicolai and I decided that it would be best if we did not meet up later in the day of the synagogue visits, so that it would give all the right signs of a work assignment being efficiently and objectively carried out and give me time to write up my findings.

The young people did not mind being asked to go back to schul and the Davinskys. It broke up the monotony of everyday life in the orphanage, and, for those who didn't like sport or Pioneer meetings on Saturday afternoons, it was a relief. I promised the participants that their responses would be anonymous and that they would ultimately be supporting the reputation of Stalin's regime in the West. They were young, but they knew that it was a death wish to criticise the regime. Even if it didn't have consequences in the short term, it would be on their file for the future. I had made it clear to Matvey that those contributing to my research must not be signalled out in any way because they had taken part.

Some of them predictably said that the prayers were old-fashioned and redundant in the new post-war world. One or two of them said that they totally rejected their cultural origins and did not want to be reminded of them.

'Of course not,' I assured them. 'I'm not asking you whether you want to be involved in this sort of thing in the future. What I want to know is how you felt about the building you were in and how you feel about what you are hearing there.'

However, some of their reactions were surprising ones.

'I felt safe.'

'I remembered the prayer shawls from when I was a child. In our village they had to be hidden away in case the police found them, so it was surprising to me that they could be used here openly.'

'I loved the food which Mrs. Davinsky gave us. It felt as though it was being made especially for me.'

'It was so warm inside the house.' This was an understandable reaction I thought, when most of the time you live in a freezing barracks.

'I like the rhythm of the old words when they read from the Torah.'

'Seeing it all wrapped up in velvet made it seem special.'

It was obvious to me that the effect of the culture and the prayers on these young people, who were steeped in communism and were in the process of working towards a romanticized future, was like the sun creeping over the icy rivers of Siberia in the month of May. It didn't change the landscape but, deep down, it was having an effect. You would have to be very insensitive to think that this exposure to culture had no good effect at all.

'But we're not here because we assess other cultures in any way at all,' commented Nicolai the next day. 'We're here because some people, especially our leaders, have decided what the future is going to be and that is for our good, whether we want it like that or not.'

'So, what you're saying is, that we're all children and everything has to be decided for us.'

'Exactly.'

'Well, I always was a rebellious child.'

'There are a few still around,' Nicolai assured me, 'Even though most of them have been worn down.'

# Chapter Forty-Two

Since these groups had been visiting the schul, Daniel had been translating for me and, surprisingly, Devorah turned out to be quite adept at this too. Once she knew that the orphanage was asking her to do this task and that Daniel was in favour of it, she became more open, and relaxed. I even caught one or two shy smiles from her. However, when one day, I asked her what she thought of the schul and Shabbat, she was very reluctant to answer. It seemed as if, for her, language was acceptable when it was merely transposing what someone else thought. But using language to express what she thought was completely different because it was if she didn't allow herself to think. I couldn't imagine what Devorah had been through in her young life – hiding from the Nazis in France; accompanying her parents in the queues to the Vel d'Hiv.; suddenly being snatched from her parents and taken in secrecy to a trade unionist family outside Paris and her identity changed; then the death of her adoptive father and the sense that there was no future for her; later, a journey right across Europe to Siberia and learning to adapt to the orphanage in Birobidzhan and having to watch every word she said, as well as learning a new language. She was 13 years old and had experienced more drama and tragedy in three years than most people in their whole lives. My own life seemed settled and secure in comparison.

Daniel translated all the questions which I asked the young people from the orphanage, and their answers with a completely straight, inexpressive face, as if he was concentrating on the technical demands of the occasion rather than getting involved with the emotional content.

After the third Saturday of doing this task, I decided to find out a little more of what he was thinking. We were sitting in the schul after the service, before we went for the meal at the Davinskys.

'Daniel, I was wondering whether next week we could go through what has been said so far and you could check the accuracy of my impressions. Then for one week we won't have any interviews.'

'If you think that's necessary.'

'I do. I want to be completely fair to those who have taken part so far.'

'How about if you and Devorah come alone next week? Don't worry.' I saw immediately the guarded expression on his face. 'I'll explain it to Natasha and make it alright.'

'Marie, you have to be very careful about this for your sake as well as mine.'

'In what way?'

'Things can be read wrongly here, misinterpreted and then used in evidence against you.'

'Yes, I've realised that. That's why I'm checking it all the time with Natasha, so that she can't be surprised or suspicious.'

'I don't think you should bring Devorah along. Let her stay next Saturday. Then we can't be seen to be plotting things together. I don't want her to be in trouble.'

'Is she likely to be, at the age of 13?'

'She could be sent to a different orphanage in another part of Russia, if she is seen to be under my influence.'

That was a bleak thought, but I wasn't going to argue about why he expected such terrible consequences. For a moment it seemed as if Daniel was the adult and I was the carefree teenager.

'Ok,' I agreed. 'I'll explain it's just you I want because you can check Devorah's ideas too, as you are the most fluent in French.'

He hesitated, his brown eyes looking at me straight from his white complexion, which was pinched and glass like.

'I'll wait to get permission from the leader of the boys' pioneer group.'

A couple of days later I repeated this conversation to Nicolai.

'In that case, he's a clever boy. He's not fooled. He knows exactly what goes on here.'

'It must be awful if he feels they've been led into a trap.'

'Especially as it was probably an innocent trap.'

'What do you mean?'

'I'm sure the Unionist man in Paris who sent them over here thought he was doing his very best for them.'

'Nicolai, they're so young. I have to help them.'

'Just make sure that in trying to help them, you're not causing them more problems.'

But I knew that I couldn't just ignore the fate of these two young people who had been led by a series of disasters to Birobidzhan.

'We have an hour before the service finishes,' I said to Daniel the following week. "Quickly check what I have written down from the last interviews. Put a few squiggles with my pen, where you question the translation or the real meaning. I'll give you ten minutes. Then let's talk.'

He didn't reply, but instead took up the pen. We were in the front room of the schul building where you entered from the lobby. What I remembered of that conversation was being surrounded by siddurs which were no longer in use and the cupboard, painstakingly carved by hand to keep the Torah safe throughout the week.

'Daniel, you have to tell me if you are happy here.'

'Why should I tell a journalist?'

'I'm not asking you as a journalist. I'm asking you as a fellow French citizen.'

'I'm no longer a French citizen.'

'What do you mean?'

'When we came here, we had to give up our passports.'

'Did you know what you were doing?'

'Not really. We were all in such a daze and we'd been told we were going to be looked after by the Russian government. There didn't seem to be any choice.'

I groaned. How could such beautiful young people, who had already suffered so much, be duped so easily?

'Marie, our parents were socialists. They believed in what the socialist state was trying to do. We didn't have any opportunities in France. It seemed better to take them here.'

'And now what do you think?'

His face looked sullen. 'I'm not allowed to think here.'

'But you do think, Daniel. I know you do. I can see it in your eyes.'

'How?'

'I just can. You're far too intelligent to just accept everything you're told.'

'Even if I am, how does that help me? I've thought about it, night after night.'

His voice was intense with emotion. I suddenly saw this fifteen year old in my imagination in a lonely bed in the dormitory, isolated and unwilling to talk to anyone else, with not enough covers on his bed against the intense cold, afraid to talk to his sister, horrified by what he had let happen and unable to do anything about it.

'I could help you.'

'How?'

'I'm not sure yet, but there must be a way.'

He gave a dry, hollow laugh.

'That's because you're still living in a world where you can make things happen.'

'Perhaps. But the alternative is to just sit back and let your whole life be taken over by the leader.'

Even in a supposedly safe environment I didn't dare utter his name.

Daniel was cynical about my ability to help. 'Maybe that's the best way. Accept the inevitable and make the best of it. Work hard, get an education, rise in the ranks of the Komsommol.'

'But the problem is, Daniel, you'll always be betraying yourself because you won't believe in it.'

He didn't even bother to argue. He knew that he didn't believe in it, and I didn't know how he was going to hide that truth from anyone else.

'Do you want me to try?' Desperately I asked permission to save this boy from himself. 'And how about Devorah?'

'She will just accept what happens.'

'I wouldn't be too sure of that, Daniel. I know she's quiet and relies on you, but she's not stupid.'

'No, but she may have lost the will to say "no".'

'No human being should lose that,' I said more passionately than I felt.

'The problem is that if we are shown to be subversive, we could be separated from each other and led to a terrible fate. If we lose each other, then that really is the end. We've already lost our parents.'

We could hear the service finishing in the main hall.

'Daniel, let me talk about it with Nicolai. He'll think of a way. I've deliberately not included him in this survey so that no one could be suspicious. Don't show any reaction to what you are doing and hearing at schul. You are just helping me, and I've got permission from Natasha and Matvey and from your great leader himself.'

# Chapter Forty-Three

Although I had ideas buzzing in my head and was longing to speak to Nicolai, I had to wait several days to speak to him alone and in a safe place. By this time, I was aware that the sweet old babushka in the hostel was keeping a close eye on me and was probably a spy and informant. The staff at the town hall were more obviously servants of the state and only interested in conducting me on official business. I found that more reassuring because at least with them you knew what to expect. They weren't any different from bureaucrats in France, only they had more to lose if things went wrong. It was almost a relaxing business going with them to visit a factory because you knew that they would tell you how wonderful it was, and they would explain the development of Stalin's strategy from the five-year plan through to post-war heightened production levels. I was polite and appreciative. There was no point in being anything else. I felt that looking after me was a nice thing for them to do, a break from tedious office work. It was a reassuring formula. They told me how wonderful everything was. I expressed amazement and offered congratulations. I made sure that in my regular posts to my newspapers in Paris, I included something about the state's amazing achievements. I could see in my mind's eye Hervé sitting at his desk surrounded by Gaullois fumes, feet on this desk, looking dishevelled and being completely cynical about what I had written. I was also sure that the papers were being piled up around him in increasing disarray. My house-wifely instincts, which I didn't even know that I had, could make me want to return as soon as possible. Suddenly in that rudimentary Birobidzhan hostel, a picture came into my mind of the electric light switch I had seen in Hervé's office, shortly after I had started working for him. When he was giving me instructions about reorganising the office, I noticed the light switch covered in accumulated dirt, and, the first thing I did on my first morning of work was to clean it. The office immediately felt better. I was sure that, without my salutary influence, that light switch would be saturated with dirt again.

Nicolai and I arranged meetings in the theatre during the day when no one else was around. His little cubby hole upstairs in the grandiose theatre was the most intimate place we could find. To help me, he had procured lots of old coats and blankets so that the table or the floor was not too uncomfortable when we made love. If it had been a film, I am sure we would have been making passionate love against a tree trunk in the forest, or on the forest floor, but I was too aware of beetles or worse which might suddenly appear, curious as to our activities. Nicolai said that I was too easily distracted, and I expect that he was right.

We were also careful about what we said in the Yiddish café. We discovered that half of the group did not want to believe that anything bad could happen in their beloved Birobidzhan and the other half were too frightened and depressed to be reliable confidantes. When you are afraid for your own life, Nicolai used to say, you will seize on any piece of information which might salvage it in the future. Russia, turning its back on overt materialism, traded in information. We were too rich in information and we didn't want other people to guess at our wealth and so become jealous.

As a result, it wasn't until we were in the forest in late June, that we felt free to have a conversation about the plight of Daniel and Devorah. We were feeling lazy after love making, despite my discomfort with pine nuts and insects on the floor of the forest.

'And you're quite sure he wants to go? You're not just reading this from his expression or thinking that he must want to escape?'

'No, I'm sure.'

'But why just those two when there must be others who want to escape?'

'Because they weren't born here. Because they're French citizens and because they've been given a lousy deal by the Union people in Paris, even though they had no idea what it was really like.'

'I can't see how you're going to spirit two young people away under the noses of the authorities.'

'Are orphans ever sent away to another part of the country?'

'Only when they've done something wrong. They'll only end up somewhere worse than this.'

'And what about you, Nicolai? Are you planning to stay here?'

Up until then it had been an unspoken conversation. What about the future? What about our relationship? Would it ever be safe here for a Yiddish speaker?

'I don't know,' said Nicolai heavily with his back to a pine tree and pulling on his cigarette. 'Solomon died. I have a feeling that Bergelson will be next.'

'But why? Dovid has been a loyal Soviet citizen with an impeccable war record. Why would they not reward that?'

'Because they're always frightened. And fear makes you do strange things.'

'How can they be frightened?' I was frustrated by the total lack of logic in the way the regime worked. 'They have more power than anyone else. Why should they be frightened of a few Yiddish speakers in Birobidzhan?'

'Because those Yiddish speakers are supporting a whole different world view.'

'Yes, but it's not a threat. Most people don't want to convert to Judaism. Only a minority of Yiddish speakers are religious.'

Nicolai looked sad, and, as he often did when talking to me, very patient, as if he was talking to a child with limited understanding and brain power.

'It's since the war; the powers that be are terrified of the Americans.'

'But the Americans were their allies in the war.'

'Yes, and that makes them dangerous. They might take the glory away from the Bolsheviks.'

'Alright, but how does American victory affect the Jews in Russia?'

'Because the American Jews give money to the Russian Jews.'

'Great,' I said practically. 'It's fairly obvious that they need it. I'd be grateful if I was them.'

'Yes, Marie, but you're not them. If you accept money from the Americans, you show that not everything in Soviet Russia is perfect and that's treacherous.'

'They're mad. There are slums in Paris. Would we all mind if the Americans gave money to help them be rebuilt? Of course not. We'd be glad. It's just pride.'

'Yes, of course it's pride but it's more than that. If they accept American money, they might think the way of American politics is better than ours and for a one-party state, that's dangerous.'

'Can you really get into trouble for accepting money from the Americans?'

'You can get into trouble for even speaking to Americans.'

'Wow!'

'Because if you have to be top dog no matter what, then you are always looking for enemies to be afraid of.'

'Anyway, it seems to me that Dovid is obviously famous. You are not, so you are not likely to be in danger.'

'True, but I might take up Bergelson's cause and it's not the same as Stalin's.'

'So, would you try to escape?'

'Yes. Even though failing would be dire. Years in the gulag and an early death.'

I shook my head in disbelief. 'And that is what those French workers condemned Daniel and Devorah to?'

Nicolai shrugged his shoulders. 'You can do the wrong thing for the right reasons.'

'You can also do the right thing for the right reasons. Come on, Nicolai, we've got to find a way for all three of you to escape this hell.'

# Chapter Forty-Four

It was the Davinskys who gave me the first glimmer of an idea. It was constantly going around and round in my head – the hell of the future for these young people in this country, which was not theirs, the injustice of their fate and the even worse consequences should I fail. I was the only person who wasn't taking a risk in all this – apart from being escorted to the frontier and my name being blackened. I wasn't so afraid for Nicolai. He was an adult and he had always lived in Russia, and he understood the alternatives. What I didn't realise then was how many people in the USSR faced these bleak prospects. Most of them had lived through the terror of 1937/8, when thousands of people faced arrest, imprisonment and execution with no logic or justice to the trials and no escape. Then they had faced the terrible sacrifices of the Second World War, what the Russians called The Great Patriotic War. And now another shadow loomed over them. When had people suffered enough, I wondered. Anything we had put up with in France during the Occupation was happiness in comparison to this. Even in the despair of war time, if you kept your head down and obeyed the rules, trouble would pass you by. Here, it didn't matter how assiduous you were about obeying the rules, you could be in serious trouble. Not just a bit less food or social ostracism, but years in a prison camp where you would be forgotten. More people died in the Gulag from hopelessness than they did from physical ill treatment. And it didn't even help if you were a fanatical supporter of Bolshevism. There was no way you could win.

One Saturday afternoon I was looking after two children from the orphanage who had visited schul. At the last moment Daniel had been sick and couldn't come to translate but the visit had gone ahead anyway.

Mrs. Davinsky had done a fair bit of translation herself as she welcomed her guests, and the young people seemed happy with that. In fact, I guessed that they might welcome the peace and quiet and the lack of conversation.

Suddenly over the borsch Mrs. Davinsky turned to me. 'I do worry whether these youngsters will ultimately get a chance to understand our traditional Jewish culture.'

'They seem to be getting something worthwhile here, Mrs. Davinsky, and I can assure you, they enjoy coming.'

'Thank you, and, Marie, thank you for encouraging them to come. And I hear from my husband that there are other plans too.'

'What do you mean?'

'Apparently, some of the teenage boys, especially the Jewish ones, are being sent away from Birobidzhan.'

'How do you mean, 'sent away'?'

'They're being encouraged to take up factory apprenticeships in other towns in Siberia, where there is no Jewish culture.'

'Why is that do you think?'

'I don't know. I think so that they can forget where they came from.'

'But surely, they were brought here in the first place because of Jewish culture,' I objected, puzzled by this plan.

She sighed. 'Yes, that's true, but times change and policy in the Politburo changes.'

It was obvious that I wasn't going to walk out of Birobidzhan at the end of my journalistic assignment with two orphans under my arm. But how about if one of them was forced to go to a place further away? Would there be the possibility of being sent to a place like Vladivostock, which was nearer to the border with Japan?

Vladivostock had an interesting history. It had been a centre of support for the Whites during the Civil War. It was on the furthest border of Russia as it met the Pacific Ocean. Dovid's wife and son had escaped over the border and had eventually got themselves to America at the start of the war. Was this idea of an apprenticeship a way of moving Devorah and Daniel further, in accordance with the Party's wishes, but also to a place where it was easier to get out.

Naturally, within a couple of days I had the whole scheme for escape worked out in my head and it was Nicolai who was needed to put forward all the practical objections.

'To start with, if Daniel applies for an apprenticeship, you can't be guaranteed that he'll be sent to Vladivostock. He might be sent further west towards the Urals.'

'Are different factory apprenticeships connected with different centres?'

'Probably.'

'In that case we find which ones are connected to the places furthest east and he expresses a preference for one of those.'

'OK. What about Devorah?'

I agreed with Nicolai that she was a problem. They felt safe while they were together. And she was 13 years old, probably not quite old enough for an apprenticeship and the Soviets had a reputation for separating family members. It was obvious to me that they were afraid of the family unit.

'There are orphanages further east too,' pointed out Nicolai.

I could see problems with this plan. 'But at least this one here understands Jews, and she can go and visit people like the Davinskys. Also, we know that Matvey is a thoroughly decent human being, and I presume that's not true for all the leaders of orphanages in Russia. And, what's more, could she cope with the change emotionally after all she's been through?

I guess it depends on how much the two of them want to escape,' I concluded. This was an admission by me that I could not just bring about someone else's future.

'And you need to think about whether the alternatives are worse.'

Nicolai had already told me chilling stories about the children of the 'enemies of the people', who had been put into children's labour camps, where the conditions were inhuman.

Although the conditions at Birobidzhan were hard – no western child would readily cope with it, I thought – they were nothing compared to some of the orphanages Nicolai had heard about. It was the emotional climate which was important. Matvey might be deluded as to the benefits of Stalinism, I thought, but he genuinely cared for the children and had the advantage of a strong sense of humour. This was a quality sadly lacking in most of the adherents of Stalinism, as far as I was concerned. But then, Russia hadn't had a lot to laugh about for a long time.

'We've got to do some investigating,' I concluded. 'But how we do investigations without arousing any suspicions, I really don't know.'

'You need, above all, good judgement of personality,' said Nicolai sagely.

# Chapter Forty-Five

Next time Daniel came to translate for me on a Saturday afternoon at schul, I suggested the idea of an apprenticeship further east.

'They send people there so that they will forget about their Jewish origins,' he stated, surprising me with his knowledge. He sometimes knew more about what was going on than you might expect from just looking at him.

'But you are not likely to forget about your Jewish origins.'

'I'm not sure I've ever really known much about them anyway.'

'Maybe, but you seem to fit in here alright.'

'Who knows where I fit in? I just want to be able to make my own choices.'

'But, if you moved to an apprenticeship in the east, you would be nearer the border and have a better chance of leaving if you wanted to.'

'And Devorah?'

'Yes, I'm not sure how that would work; but there must be orphanages in the east as well. Then you would be nearer to her and she could go and live with you, once you were established.'

'Perhaps, but it's a bit risk.'

'True, but then everything's a big risk, and do you really want to stay here for ever?'

He merely replied with a searching look.

In the end I decided to ask Matvey. He had a sort of innocence about him, so that it was impossible for him to imagine anyone wanting to leave Stalin's loving care. I explained that Daniel wanted to take an apprenticeship so that he could work hard for his adopted country.

'Of course, that's wonderful,' agreed the red bearded giant, 'but the little sister? How's that going to work?'

'That's what he's worried about too. Do you know anything about the orphanages out to the east?'

For once Matvey looked a little shamefaced. 'I'd like to say that they are all great places but to be truthful, Marie, some of them are in a terrible state. I'm not sure that Devorah would survive in them. Here I'm in charge and I get special supplies for settling Jews, and I know that the Jewish adults here will do everything they can for the orphans.'

'What if I went over there and saw what one or two of them were like?'

'I think to be honest with you, that they will wonder what you are doing and whether you are planning something bad.'

'What if I went by myself, did some investigation about two or three different orphanages, and then wrote an article comparing them with this one here?'

'If you make this one sound too good, we might lose some of our supplies, and people get jealous.'

'Of course, but what if I praise these orphanages and tell the Western world about what a good job they are doing.'

'And how will that help Devorah?'

'Because behind all the praise, I'll be able to see what they're really like and see if she would be happy in any of them. I could do a similar article on the apprenticeship schemes. Look what the Soviet Union is providing for their young people!'

Matvey could not understand irony if he tried. 'Well they are privileged of course. If you think you will get permission to travel, Marie, I'll back your choice for Devorah.'

# Chapter Forty-Six

I laid my plans out carefully so that it would be clear that I had nothing to hide. I talked about it to the babushka, to the mayor's office and in the Yiddish café. I applied for a three-week visa to travel to towns in the Altai region of Siberia and to the border towns near Vladivostock. I telegrammed Libération about my plans. I was excited with the sort of pent up energy I used to have before taking a group of escapees across the French/Spanish border in the war. Nicolai said cynically that the only good thing was that it made my love making more responsive and exciting. I was consumed by plans of how it was all going to work. I had briefly explained to Daniel what I was thinking and asked him to explore with Matvey which apprenticeship schemes he might apply for, but, warned him that, apart from that, he should show no interest in my journalistic endeavours.

The Mayor's office was predictably enthusiastic about my desire to publish the wonders of Soviet schemes for their young people. They also wanted to send their official translator with me, Vladimir, a thick set stony faced young man, who did his job adequately but without imagination. I would have preferred to discard him, but I thought that I needed to play the system as near as possible to the official line, so that no one would suspect anything strange.

The result of all this 'correct political attitude' on my part was that three weeks later I had train tickets, visas and places to go. Leaving Nicolai felt like leaving home. In a short time, I had come to trust and love him.

'Don't do anything silly and get deported while you're there, Marie,' he warned me.

'Why not?' I asked, curious as to his personal motivation.

'Because I might not see you again.'

'And does that matter?'

'Yes, it does. I want to see you again.'

No; not protestations of love; perhaps only a desire to use me as an escape route for himself; but, nevertheless, a firm, meaningful connection. I didn't know him fully, but I felt that our relationship was a good one.

It seemed strange to be getting on the trans-Siberian express again. How much had changed since I was last on it, I thought. I had been apprehensive and shy. Now I was confident and determined. Two months earlier it had felt like travelling to the edge of the planet and I had been afraid that I might fall off the edge. Now Birobidzhan was familiar and comforting. Then, I had no personal connections with the place. Now, I had the most meaningful and intimate relationship I had ever had with another human being. Before I had been living with the nostalgia of my idealistic relationship with Alain. Now I knew what it was like to relate to a real man. Then, I knew nothing about Yiddish culture. Now I had experienced the theatre and the synagogue and the coffee shop where the Jews met regularly. Before, Daniel and Devorah had been part of an interesting story – an excuse to travel and have an exciting journalistic assignment. Now they were part of my personal passion, inhabitants of my special thought world. I was confident and determined. I had enough to occupy me inside my head and I didn't pick up casual conversations with strangers on the train. In fact, I was of no real interest to anyone because I merged into the background. I didn't have any Western food to share and somehow, I looked and felt more Russian. I even thought that there had been a subtle change in people's attitude over even the last three months. There was less curiosity about outsiders and more fear of indiscreet conversations. Nicolai had already informed me about this.

'It's not just the Jews. Everyone is afraid again.'

'Again?'

'Yes, during the 30s everyone was afraid of Stalin's purges. They picked up innocent people all the time. But the war changed that.'

'Because people were fighting Nazism, do you mean?'

'Yes, it was a case of survival and saving our country and so we hadn't a lot of energy for introspection. But everything is changing again.'

439

'Why?'

'Stalin is afraid of the west and we've had too much contact with the West.'

'So, why's he so afraid?'

'Because he's afraid we'll all want to escape the prison. Because he's afraid we'll find out it's not so wonderful over here after all. And he's afraid that the whole of the revolution will seem like a mistake.'

'And was it?'

'Don't ask me. No, of course it wasn't. We needed a revolution away from the Tsars. And, no,' he added grinning. 'We're deep in the taiga here and I'm not afraid that the trees will report me.'

'It sounds as if Russia is changing back into a place where no one really wants to be.'

'Exactly.'

So, how many people on this train were heading towards escape at the far eastern border, I wondered. The prison gets worse, as you head East, Nicolai had warned me. That part of the railway was only built with the slave labour of the prisoners in the camps and they didn't get any chance to escape. There were more camps the further east you went. Most of the scenery through the carriage windows was endless taiga and mountains and rivers but occasionally we would espy a group of forced labourers. They made me feel very depressed. We were free citizens on the train, and we were passing so near them, but we wanted nothing to do with them. It was far easier to ignore them and carry on with our own little lives.

I had three orphanages to visit. The first one was the furthest away from Vladivostock. When I got off the train, I was greeted politely and correctly by my minder and from then on, the whole of the three days was a whitewash. I was only allowed in each room at a designated time. The food seemed adequate, but I was served at a different time and a different place to the children and two children were allowed to sit with me at each meal and answer my questions. They were robots. I could have answered each question myself without asking them.

'Do you have enough food?'

'Yes, always. We are well fed.'

'Do you receive a good education?'

'We have school every day according to Soviet law.'

'What do you enjoy most at school?'

'Soviet history and learning about the way Stalin helped us to prosper.'

'What do you intend to do when you leave the orphanage?'

'Work to make our country great again after the war.'

'How do you think it will be great again?'

'By turning our back on capitalism and doing what the Party tells us.'

In those three days I tried everything possible to circumvent the guards, to speak to real children but without success. Even when I met some on my own coming back from a Pioneers meeting, which had been held in a back shed, they gave me the same answers as the others. The children did not furtively look over their shoulders, fearful of who might be listening. They didn't even need coaching to give the right answers. They seriously believed in what they were saying. They didn't need to be drilled. They were genuine in their attachment to what was being done for them. They were submissive and they were happy. I wrote a report about what I had seen. Any censors would have been happy with it. There were no subversive messages. The only thing I wondered to myself was how I could possibly discriminate between any of these places, when I needed to choose a home for Devorah. Would she settle in? Would she accept the rules as the other children did? What would living here do to her? On the other hand, what would living in Birobidzhan for the rest of her life do to her as well? She would have no chance of escape, but she might be happy. Who was I to say otherwise?

# Chapter Forty-Seven

I had begun to wonder how I was going to write even two articles about the orphanages in the east which would convey any sense of journalistic integrity in Europe. I had not completely forgotten the standards of my own country and I knew that the anodyne comments and banal description which I could give about my experiences were unlikely to interest anyone in France. My only hope was that in writing in such a dead pan way, no intelligent reader would really believe what I was saying. If my present, adulatory reports passed the censors here, I could always add a more controversial commentary when I went back home. I knew too that I would not be going back home in the same way as I came. Three important people had come into my life and whether I left them behind, or they came with me, my future would always be affected by them. It occurred to me that if I wrote anything which questioned the regime in the future, I could hurt them. I could just imagine some Soviet tribunal assigning someone to five years in a labour camp because they had had dealings with a capitalist anti-Soviet journalist. And I didn't fool myself into thinking that all my future articles on this country would not be avidly scrutinized. They were so frightened of the West that someone in an office somewhere in the Kremlin had the job of reading foreign newspapers to find out what dangerous things were being said abroad. The Soviets had extraordinary networks of knowledge. It was about the only thing that they were rich in, apart from forced labour.

It was the notion of forced labour and my sighting of prisoners building a reservoir near a remote riverbank which first gave me a new idea. I was booked in to visit three orphanages and I was unconvinced by any of them as a possible destination for Devorah. Remembering her lambent brown eyes, and straight eyebrows which bespoke honesty and intelligence and affection, I could not imagine her amongst any of these half-starved and correct children whom I was meeting. They were part of a formula and Devorah did not fit into a formula. Better to stay with Matvey and Natasha, who, although they subscribed to the party rules, managed to be human with it.

I had finished my visits to the orphanages well within my allotted space of three weeks and I had a train ticket which would take me to Vladivostock. I wanted to see this outpost of freedom, but I also wanted to visit a forced labour camp as part of the infamous Gulag. It was something I had heard at the last orphanage at Soborisk which inspired my curiosity.

The director of the orphanage, a tired and unkept looking man, who looked as though he was only just surviving in his job, remarked on three children who were getting ready to leave his institution.

'They're going to the camp near Khabarosvsk to join their mother.'

'You mean they're becoming part of the forced labour at their age?' The idea was so shocking that I forgot to be circumspect in what I said. Amazingly Gregory, who must have been more human that I had given him credit for, half smiled.

'No, no. There are schools and children's houses there too. These particular children are going there, because they thought they were orphans, but their mother has just been discovered.'

'How do you lose your children like that?'

He smiled at my naivety. 'Very easily, Mlle Marie. Many people who were sent to the camps were arrested in the middle of the night. Later, no one knew whether they were alive or dead. The children left behind survived, either through finding other relatives who looked after them, or through being sent to orphanages like this one.'

'And,' he continued, giving me a valuable insight into the life of Soviet Russia in the late thirties, 'the location didn't matter. They were just sent wherever there were spaces. And, of course, some of those arrested were not executed; they were sent to the gulag. Also, there's been so much coming and going with the war, that children never rediscovered their parents.'

'So how did you find out about these three?'

'Because their mother, despite being in a labour camp, has been sending out all over the place, to see if her children are still around.'

'I didn't know that you could 'send out' to anyone in the gulag.'

'People go to extraordinary lengths and, if parents had skills or professions, which the labour camp wanted, they might have been treated a bit differently.'

'But what will happen to these children when they get there? Will they become part of the forced labour gang too?' I couldn't think of a worse fate for these children, even if they were going to be reunited with their mother.

'Mlle Marie, the Party would never subject children to such a thing, even if their parents have been the enemies of the State.'

I refused to comment, glad that this non-descript man had such faith in his own government after all this time of serving it faithfully.

'Comrade Gregory, could I accompany them?'

He looked surprised and worried at the same time. 'I'm not sure. I don't want them to start their new lives with any bad associations.' He seemed unaware of the implied insult.

'No, neither do I, but I am an official journalist, given permission by the Party to be there. I want to write an article about the labour camp. I'm writing for a communist newspaper in the West and I want to surprise the readers in France with how well these camps are reforming people and helping families.'

'Only if you have the necessary papers. I don't want them to get into any trouble.' I couldn't help thinking, you mean you don't want to get into any trouble.

'I can assure you, comrade, my presence will only be an advantage to them,' I responded robustly.

There was another advantage to my plan. At this second orphanage, my translator, Vladimir, fell sick. He was an unimaginative but dutiful young man and I think he was tired of following me around and interviewing children and officials. He knew that I was recording only positive news about the orphanages and so he was not in any way worried when I suggested that he went home after he had fallen sick with a stomach bug.

As a result, it was that only me, with no translator, who entered one of the Khabarosvsk labour camps, accompanied by three children, who were very excited about seeing their mother again. Stalin might have replaced the family with the state, but these children were far more eager to see their mother than to stay with the state provision. Their parents might have been branded as 'enemies of the people', but, in their hearts, they saw them only as friends, whatever dogma they had been taught to express with their lips.

I was more excited about seeing the labour camp near Khabarosk than I had been about the prospect of seeing the orphanages. Before, I had no plan which excited me, only a resigned feeling of 'what else can I do?' But this was different. I felt instinctively that this was the key to my dilemma. I had also heard so much about the gulags when I was in Birobidzhan and we had even begun to hear about them in France. What were they really like? Who were these ghosts of people, who had been forgotten by society, who lived there? Were conditions as bad as I had been told? If so, how did anyone survive?

We left the railway station, an even smaller one than Birobidzhan, looking as if it was a mistaken addition tacked on to the long rails, in an open truck. The driver was indifferent as to who I was, even though I carried official papers. He was indifferent to the children too, not even bothering to help the two youngest up into the back of the truck. The older boy of 14 years and myself had to do that. The older brother was good at reassuring the younger ones about what was going to happen, even though he must have been afraid himself. Responsibility breeds maturity.

We arrived through the iron gates connected to the huge barbed wire fences, just as a huge clanging gong announced the end of the working day. It was 8pm and the workers streamed out of the factory and into the huts nearby. We were conducted to the commandant's office near the entrance.

I hung back not wanting to get in the way of the more important process of receiving the children. In addition, I had no interpreter, so I was relying on the magic of my papers to help me gain an entrance along with some elaborate mime work.

The commandant was a serious minded but conscientious man in his early fifties. His uniform was smart, and his shoes shone. I wondered how he maintained such standards in a labour camp. We waited while he examined the children's passports and he called an aide, presumably to get the mother. While we were waiting, he looked at my visa and at me.

'You have permission to look round for three days. I hope you write something good about what you see. We do our best.'

# Chapter Forty-Eight

To be honest in a strange way it was easy to write something good about what I was seeing. If you forgot the truth that labour camps shouldn't exist in any country, if you forgot that at least half the people there were innocent of any crime they might have been accused of, and, that, in a free country, the crime of subverting the party's policies should not lead to imprisonment, then there were a lot of good things to write about.

Mikhail, the commandant, had impressed me with his appearance on my arrival. Why should anyone bother about keeping up high standards of personal appearance, unless they had a sense of purpose and dignity, in a place which was poised between the Chinese border and the Pacific coast of Russia? He had to believe in what he was doing and think it was worth doing well.

I cannot begin to explain how touched I was by the reception of the children by their mother. I wondered whether my parents would have greeted me with such emotion if we had lost touch with each other for three years or more. The commandant and his aide averted their eyes while the reunion took place. The two youngest were happy but could hardly remember their mother. The fourteen-year old clung to his mother and seemed visibly relieved. It was as if all the responsibility for the last few years had been lifted from his shoulders.

'They are the lucky ones,' the commandant informed me in surprisingly good English. 'Most families even before the war didn't have a hope of seeing each other after being in a camp. With the lack of communication during the war and children often sent as far away as possible so they couldn't be contaminated by their parents' crimes, the chance of meeting up together, after all this time, has been nil.'

'So, how did this one happen then?'

'They have a mother who is not only very intelligent, a metallurgist, and useful to us here in the camp, but also a mother who doesn't give up easily when it comes to looking for her children. She posted over the whole of Russia to find them, and in the end, they were only further up the railway line.'

'But I thought they weren't allowed communication with the outside world when they were in the camps.'

'This is different. Yes, we have an inside camp, where the most serious political prisoners are sent. But people like Sofia only had a four-year sentence and we needed her skills here, so even during that four-year period she was placed in the outer camp. And now she's choosing to stay here.'

I was shocked. I imagined that everyone was desperate to leave the camp.

'Why doesn't she want to go and see the rest of her family and start a normal life?'

My question wasn't that of a journalist seeking to write an article. It was the question of a human being who was reaching far into the experience of another, one which was far removed from her own understanding.

Mikhail and I were still in the office where I had been received. The family had been taken away to their own quarters. This was a man seeking to explain himself and his country's system to a young outsider. I learnt as the days went on that it was an unusual moment in the life of a man, whose schedule was so tightly organised that he hardly had time to eat.

'As a foreigner visiting us, you might imagine, mademoiselle, that we conform to certain stereotypes. To you we are probably the embodiment of the evil system which invented work camps. But what makes you think that outside there' – he waved his arms at the fading light which never disappeared in the far east of Russia – 'life is any better? Stalingrad and Leningrad are in chaos after the privations of the war. There's not enough work and any 'enemy of the people' would be the last person to be welcomed there.'

'So, you're better off in a labour camp?' I queried, unable to take in what I was hearing.

'This camp works very efficiently. Everyone has their place here. It's always going to be hard in the labour camp itself. After all it's meant to be a punishment, but the outer camp is much easier than the other and I run it well.'

I paused and looked carefully at this man. He said these words without ostentation and without irony.

'And now, mademoiselle, we must find you something to eat and somewhere to sleep.'

I ate the leftovers of the beet soup in the kitchen along with the hunks of rye bread, but I had no complaints. It wasn't just my status as foreign visitor or even my limited pass which put me at ease. It was the sense that someone with basic human feelings and efficiency was in charge. I retired for the night on a bunk bed in the women's dormitory with one blanket covering me. I wondered whether the blanket rationing was increased in winter.

During the night I developed my strategy. I needed interviews with the guards, some of the workers in the outside camp, and if possible, I needed to see the school which the children attended.

The alarm sounded at 5am and I struggled out of my bunk with difficulty, even though the light in the far east had been glimmering for some time and seemed to be questioning why I took so long to be ready for a new day.

I started by visiting the school and spent most of the day there. I was surprised by the high standard of education, especially in maths and sciences.

'Of course,' replied the head teacher, a woman with her hair scraped back severely from her head in a bun. 'In Russia our children are provided with the very highest standards of education.'

'Even in a labour camp?' I queried.

'Yes, even in a labour camp. Our leader, Comrade Stalin, recognises that even children of enemies of the people need the very best at the start of their lives.'

Back to the old party line, I thought. I knew better than to question her view. Better to circumnavigate.

'And the people in this part of the camp are no longer enemies of the people. They have served their sentence.'

She narrowed her eyes, looking at me intently for any signs of criticism of the party. 'Once you have been an enemy of the people, you will always be. These children will always have a spoiled biography.'

I had heard that term 'spoiled biography' before in Birobidzhan. I couldn't help thinking of all the French people in Paris who had a 'spoiled biography' as a result of the war – people who had colluded with the Nazi occupiers – but we didn't consign them to the labour camps.

'It's very impressive what you do here, Comrade.' She nodded her head briefly in acknowledgement of my compliment.

I stayed all day at the school, and I was genuinely surprised by the high standard of teaching, especially in maths and science. I learnt that several of the teachers here had been classed as 'enemies of the people' and had chosen to continue their careers here at this camp. Why? I asked the Physics teacher. He was quiet and reluctant to speak, not surprisingly when any unguarded word could cause someone to report you and you could be sent back into the labour camp.

'Mademoiselle, it is my privilege to teach here. I was the son of enemies of the people. My parents were shot in the thirties. I was taken to an orphanage near Vladivostock, but managed to run away to Stalingrad, where I got false papers and went to the university to study Physics. Fortunately, everything was in chaos, so no one caught up with me. I heard from one of my teachers, who knew my background, that they needed science teachers here.'

'Weren't you called up to fight?'

'They didn't want enemies of the people for that.'

'Why ever not?'

'Because they thought that the fighting spirit might be tainted by them.'

'Sounds like you had a lucky escape to me.'

His eyes suddenly took on a nervous expression.

'Please, mademoiselle, don't say anything about me in your article. I am happy here. I help the children to learn important things. The camp commandant is a reasonable man, and I have even met a woman who is going to marry me.'

'Don't worry,' I reassured him. 'I won't put you in danger.'

What sort of country is this, I thought, where people are glad to work in the confines of a labour camp in Siberia because they feel safe here?

'I'm impressed by your school,' I said to Mikhail, when I found him later doing administrative jobs. 'It has a high standard of teaching.'

'I'm glad you approve, Mademoiselle.'

'Mikhail, could I go and see inside the real prison camp tomorrow?'

'It's not a pretty sight.'

'I'm sure it's not but I'd like to see it anyway.'

'You can see where they bring the iron ore up to the surface, not how they mine below the surface.'

'All right. That will do me.'

# Chapter Forty-Nine

I thought that I should get it over with as quickly as possible. I wanted to say that I had seen it, be able to write something about it to give my articles a sense of authenticity but – the whole emotional, moral part of me – didn't want to see it. I don't think I like suffering, which is not a good start for a journalist. I didn't want to empathise with the workers and pity them, because I didn't want to use up emotional energy worrying about it or being disgusted by it. I couldn't write about it critically because the regime would never welcome me again, but I couldn't also write lies for the sake of my own conscience. It was like going to the dentist. You had to get it over with.

I woke up with the rising alarm bell at 5am, had a thin hot drink which passed as coffee, and followed my assigned minder out of the outer camp buildings, through the barbed wire, past the sentries who stamped our papers, past the watch towers and onto the yard which was on the side of the entrance to the mine. Miners were filing up to go down the lifts into the mine. I hardly dared look at their faces but they seemed impassive. If I needed to be uninvolved emotionally in order to survive as a human being and as a journalist, they had to be twenty times more so if they were to survive as miners in a Siberian prison camp. If they asked themselves questions or felt the rising disgust and hatred of their fate and for the regime which had put them there, it could physically overwhelm them. Like the desire to vomit from an attacking infection, they could not keep it back. They would not survive. What amazed me when I looked at the figures, was not the percentage who died (about 20%) but the large percentage who survived. The human spirit of resilience and the desire to live appears to be very strong. I saw the iron ore being lifted by cranes

452

from the mouth of the mine onto the huge containers, where the men were engaged in separating the impurities from the iron ore. Later it would be sent by rail to Vladivostock.

I watched those men work for two hours. Why I stayed for two hours I have no idea, as they were doing identical jobs the whole time and I didn't learn anything new about their work. I can only say that I felt it would be disrespectful to stay for any less time. Who can imagine, if you have lived in a place of choice and done a job which gave you some satisfaction, even if not complete fulfilment, what it means to carry out the same back-breaking, monotonous work for twelve hours a day, with very little sustenance, no time off and often in sub-zero temperatures? And this was not the worst place. Underground were hundreds of men who for twelve hours never saw the light of day and faced injury through falling rock faces and tunnels. In that two hours as I watched the workers, and occasionally asked questions. I suffered boredom, lack of understanding, frustration, cold, thirst, anger, and it was only for two hours. These also were not dangerous men. That meant that they were political prisoners and likely to be intelligent with questioning minds. Mixed in amongst them would be a few hard-core criminals to report on their colleagues and stir up hatred and jealousy when they returned to their sleeping quarters.

During those two hours, I instructed my assigned translator to ask questions. I noted down a variety of answers. I sketched the way they looked, the facts of their occupation and the way the sky changed above them, and the glimpse of the mountains behind. I came away with all the facts that I needed to write a credible article for a Western newspaper, which would also pass the Russian censorship machine.

All the time I wanted to scream, 'How can you bear to be alive? Why don't you just kill someone near you, and leave for your death, fighting and angry? Why don't you fall into impossible despair and depression and never recover?' By the time I left, I found myself bowing to them in farewell. I was in awe of them and their indomitable human spirit.

Mikhail smiled gently at my reaction which I could not hide from him. It was a mark of my admiration for the man that I could even express my reactions. In response he managed to tow the party line, acknowledge the genuine nature of my reactions, and give reasonable answers and justification for the existence and success of the prison camp. He was constantly in demand from his staff and always choosing to go into the prison camp, the prisoners' living quarters, the school, the research department and every aspect of his domain. He held the place together. People, whether prisoners or staff, wanted to please him.

'You know, Mikhail,' I observed in a moment of unusual clarity. 'It's like you're the CEO of a huge 'entreprise' in France. If you were living there, you would get a huge salary, good living conditions and prestige.'

'But, Marie, I'm here to do my best for the Party and for my country.'

'I know, I know,' I ventured with a mixture of frustration at his 'correct' answers and a longing to find out what was underneath the surface in this man's mind. 'But, don't you ever feel really annoyed by it all and just … tired?'

He smiled gently. 'Yes, I do feel tired sometimes and yes, I am frustrated sometimes by the waste of human potential, but you know what? If I didn't do this, who would? Someone else – perhaps a former convict with ability but little love for the people.'

'And you have love for these people?'

'It would be unrealistic for me to feel love for the thousands of people here. I would never survive if I got too sentimental, but yes, I do care for them.'

'But why?'

'Because in no other country in the world has this great experiment of Bolshevism taken place and we must use all our energy to make it succeed.'

'And you believe that it will?'

'Yes, if we all help.'

'And will everyone help, or will they just feel rebellious?'

'I think that the Russian people have a great desire to succeed. Think about their self-sacrifice in the war. Was that all for nothing?'

'That was to get rid of the invader.'

'Yes, but it was also so that Bolshevism could continue.'

'I have to admire you, Mr. Director. Do you really go down the mines every week?' I had heard this story in the office but somehow, I couldn't picture the immaculate Mikhail down a mine, and certainly not in the company of criminals and political enemies.

He smiled again. 'Not in this uniform, if that's what you're thinking, but, yes, I do go down in the cage with the men once a week. It encourages them.'

'I thought they were being punished.'

'Yes, but even those who are being punished need some interest shown in them.'

'Then they are very lucky prisoners… at least to have you interested in them. I'm not sure that prisoners in the west get as much from the director of the prison.'

'Then remember to say that in your article, Mlle Marie. Remember that there are genuine places of correction in the USSR.'

I decided not to make any more comments or to pursue the discussion. Someone came to see if Mikhail could sort out a situation among the clerks in the metallurgy department, where there was an argument brewing about who should have the best sleeping quarters.

Suddenly I knew that I had to seize the moment offered.

'Mr. Mikhail, before I go tomorrow, could I have a talk with you about a friend of mine?'

He was immediately on his guard. 'In a socialist country we do not have favourites.'

'Of course not. I understand. But you can give advice based on your knowledge of the whole system.'

'If I can, without going against our party's ruling.'

'I would never ask you to do that on my behalf.'

'Good. And now, mademoiselle, if you will excuse me, I have work to do.'

# Chapter Fifty

Once I left the small branch line from the camp, the main train was hot and crowded and smelt of hundreds of sweaty bodies. It seemed somehow less pure than the Gulag and I marvelled that all these people on the main line seemed oblivious to the fate of their compatriots only a few hours away.

My visa allowed me to go to Vladivostock, even though it was a prohibited area for most Westerners, and I had very much hoped that Vladimir would not recover quickly enough to interpret for me as I went about my business in Vladivastock. When I arrived, I had to register with the police, I had to do an official tour of the town, but I also had to find out where the fishing trawlers came into port. I decided to do the official stuff first so that no one could enquire what I had been up to on the first days of my visit and I hoped that the tour would give me a better understanding of the geography of the city.

When the train entered the long descent towards Vladivostock, it felt as if I had already entered a different country. It is the presence of the Pacific Ocean down one side of the land, which created this impression. It shimmered under the mist with a promise of calm inscrutability. The USSR was no longer a vast prison continent without an exit. It was easy to forget that on the land side of the rail track, there was an unforgiving tundra with tigers roaming and huge mountain peaks pointing only to China where there was a civil war in progress between Chan Kai Chek and Mao Tse Tung with dreadful atrocities being committed. Russia felt almost safe by comparison though beneath it all, as I found out later, the Politburo was encouraging the emerging Communist state. Was the millpond of the Pacific a real link with another world or was it more likely to be an illusion and the reality was a deadly and long drawn out death by drowning?

Vladivostock felt different to the world of inland Russia, even on the Siberian side of the Urals, where I had been for the last three months. During the civil war of the late 20s, it had sheltered and supported the White Army, when they were fighting the Bolsheviks. It had received American ships and even volunteers who had come to fight for the Whites. Whereas in other areas of Russia both sides had committed atrocities, Vladivostock had been the centre of aspirations for the Whites. In the long term, as a result of their defeat, Lenin had shown no support for the town and Stalin had allowed it no resources. It was in a dilapidated state, but, just as for the first time for many months, I smelt the tang of the ocean brine, for the first time I also felt the intangible stirrings of freedom. Vladivostock had a different feel to it from the Russia I had encountered so far. Or was it just my imagination because I hoped that it would be entrance to freedom for those I loved?

The hostel where I stayed was at the top of a hill looking out over the ocean. With such a panorama, it should have been a luxury hotel, but, instead, it epitomized the second-rate status of a city despised by the Bolshevik leadership. Apart from being a port where some of Russia's iron ore was deported to China and Korea, there was no sense of it being developed as a cultural centre. When I left the hostel each morning with my Party minder alongside me, the hill was surrounded by mist. It gave me the feeling that I did not know where I was being taken, and that was my overriding feeling which persisted through the next few days of my visit.

I was shown the place where Russia had seen the last Japanese soldiers after they had left Manchuria and before Japan had allied herself with Germany in the Great Patriotic War. I was shown the place where the Whites had met defeat and where American capitalist supporters had fled back home. I was shown the port which seemed to rise up out of the mist at the bottom of the hill, where the minerals from the Gulag mines were taken from the trains, and placed into shipping containers, before they were taken off to China and Korea and Japan. All that was connected to the history of Vladivostock, according to my informant, was bad. All that was being exported from the Gulag in this era was good and contributed to the prosperity of modern-day Russia.

It was through the mist when we were visiting the port and the cargo ships that on the third day, I espied some small boats hugging the harbour wall.

'What are those?' I asked my minder.

'They belong to small-time fishermen,' he replied, dismissively. 'They catch and sell fish privately, but they are not part of the great Bolshevik enterprise.'

'What do you mean they sell fish privately? I thought that wasn't allowed in Russia.'

'They are not supposed to, but the Party allows some of this trade to go on.'

'You mean like Lenin allowed some private enterprise in the twenties?'

My minder was impressed by my grasp of history. In truth, I had learnt about Lenin's compromise with the black marketeers in the 20s from Dovid Bergelson in the café.

'Yes, comrade. The state allows a small amount of private fishing to go on.'

'And are there state trawlers?'

'Yes, there are but they are not as important as the ships which take the minerals.'

'Of course not. That is where your country's strength lies.'

I did not want to suggest he accompany me to the harbour side. That would be something I intended to do the next day by myself.

'But maybe it's a good place to go if I want some fresh fish. You know that I come from near the coast in France? Seeing those trawlers reminds me of home.'

'That is always pleasant, Mademoiselle, when you are in a foreign country.'

'Indeed, comrade. You have shown great understanding. Thank you for all the help you have given me. I have learnt so much about your great country and party from your tour.'

# Chapter Fifty-One

I had to choose an evening when no one would miss me or see me – a hard task when you are constantly monitored by the secret police. I had two nights left and I decided to choose the last night, as, if I was discovered, I would soon be back in Birobidzhan or at the worst put out of the country immediately. I had my story ready, in case I was interrogated. When I returned to Europe, I was planning to do research into the history of the war years in Russia, and especially what happened in Siberia.

Fortunately, the last night of my stay was particularly misty. I was discovering that mist from the sea was a characteristic of the town and of the whole peninsula, and one which made it especially evocative. Again, if questioned by the hotel, I would say that I liked it because it was an important reminder of the mists near the ocean in Mimizan.

My third day of tourism was dedicated to understanding the process of sending the raw material from the mines which was then moved onto the containers which would be taken to Korea, China and Japan by ship. Some of it would even be going to Europe.

With my levels of adrenalin heightened by my fear, and anticipation of my proposed adventure in the evening, I was especially dutiful in my attention to the subject of containers. I made a special point of asking how exports had operated in the war years and mentioned that, because of my admiration for the USSR, I had planned to write up the information I was being given back at the hotel in the evening. As the day wore on, I was so nervous that I wondered how ever I had worked so keenly for the Resistance in war time France. Perhaps at 17 years of age, I had been less fearful than at my present age of twenty-two.

I ate my dull potato stew in the grimy canteen next to the hostel where I was staying. Alongside me were workers from the container ships who lowered their gaze, as if they were afraid of looking at a woman from Europe.

It suited me if they were lacking in curiosity. I deliberately went into the kitchen to ask if I could have some bread for an early morning start the following day and, while there, noticed the exit at the far side of the kitchen. The kitchen staff were far too busy to take notice of my interest, though they were worried by my request for bread. I suppose it didn't fit into their quota for the day, but I reassured them, that as I was booked in for breakfast in the morning but didn't want to get up too early before my train left, I wasn't stealing from them. I promised to return and collect it in an hour's time.

My stratagem worked successfully. An hour later, clutching my small mound of bread and the bag, which was to contain it, I stepped out into the white, misty, light evening. It felt strange to be in the daylight but not to know which direction to take. Fortunately, Vladivostock was so hilly that the only way to go was down to the sea. I had deliberately worn the darkest and most muted colours, so that I would not easily be noticed.

Once down at sea level, I moved in the direction where I thought the harbour would be, but I became confused in the mist and spent half an hour longer than was necessary retracing my steps in some panic. I met one man, but I kept my head down and mumbled 'good evening' in Russian in a way which I hoped would not betray my foreign origins. There were plenty of Mongols and Koreans around, so being a stranger was not altogether unusual.

Eventually I came to the edge of the harbour and, as I worked my way round, I came to one boat after another attached to moorings. I couldn't see how many there were, nor identify the one I had visited with my minder two days previously. The first two seemed like ghost ships with no one present, but the third one had a light. I lay down flat on the harbour surface and called out quietly in case my voice alerted other people to my presence.

A Japanese face appeared from the outside cabin, inscrutable and showing no surprise at my presence. When I indicated that I wanted to come on board, he helped me negotiate the side of the boat. How I was going to get up again I had no idea, but I was emboldened by my success in achieving so much so far.

It was dirty and oily as you would expect from any working boat and the man indicated a small stool where I could sit, while he stood staring at me.

'Speak English?' I ventured, not knowing how else to start. Before this, the problem had only seemed to me about how I could get onto the boat. I had forgotten that, once there, I might not be able to communicate.

As an answer, the man went to the inside ladder and called down into the hold. Soon a younger man appeared.

'American?'

'No. French.'

Just in time I remembered that the Americans had been their implacable enemies during the war and that they might not want to communicate with any American. The two men talked between themselves and I had the impression that the older one was giving the younger one permission to continue.

'My friend wants to go to Japan,' I ventured.

'Friend – American or French?'

'No. Russian.'

'Difficult,' he replied screwing his eyes up tight as he tried to evaluate my request.

There was no answer to that. Taking a Russian on board away from their country could certainly cause them much trouble – even their lives or livelihood.

'How much?'

They talked together. The younger one held up his fingers. 'Three thousand roubles.'

'And for three people?' Further discussion 'Two of them are young,' I added.

'Children? We don't do children.'

'No. One of them is 13. The other two are adults.'

'10,000 roubles.'

An extraordinary sum of money! At that price it would be definitely worth their while.

'How much warning?' Lack of comprehension appeared on their faces. 'I mean, when do you need to know?'

'A week before.'

Apparently, they went back to Japan every two weeks in order to get their boat checked out and pick up supplies and take money to their families.

If Nicolai, quite apart from Daniel and Devorah, even made the journey to Vladivostock, how would he ever hide in secret in this town, while he negotiated the payment for the journey. And where would such a sum of money be found?

Impossible conditions! But you never know what you might do in those impossible conditions, unless you try. One thing is sure. You can't do anything if you don't even understand the possibilities.

I committed the name of the boat and its owners to memory. They were unfamiliar foreign names but my war time work in the resistance had taught me how to memorize without committing to paper.

I couldn't tell the Japanese when Nicolai would be in touch because I didn't know myself. But I had done my research and I had possibilities to offer him.

Which was just as well, because, back in the foyer of the hostel, I was met by my minder who was very angry.

I repeated my story about needing bread for the morning and added the part about needing a walk down by the sea in the mist. If my appearance had been reported by the sole man I had met, then there was no point in denying my walk there. During my walk I had got lost and had stopped to eat some of my morning supply of bread to give me courage. Yes, I had eventually arrived at the harbour which we had visited two days before, but it had been so misty that I had not been able to distinguish individual fishing boats. Keep as close as you can to the truth, Père Julien had advised me in the war years, and his advice proved effective.

My minder was angry and suspicious, but I had nothing on me which proved any guilt. He assured that he would be accompanying me to the station tomorrow morning. He would recommend that my visa be revoked. I had been trusted with a special entrance visa to Vladivostock and I had betrayed their trust. I had twenty-four hours back at Birobhidzan to gather my possessions, say my goodbyes and leave the country.

# BOOK THREE

# Chapter One

When you return from a journalistic assignment, your adrenaline does not know how to stop working. To begin with you are exhausted after the demands of the work in a foreign country, and you are glad to sleep and feel safe especially if you have been in a hostile environment. But after that initial reaction of relief, comes a time of restlessness and lack of purpose. Your personality misses the danger, the opportunity to meet special people in difficult circumstances. You need to get used to editorial meetings and agendas. In a war zone the most extraordinary people wash up in everyday life, and they are not the people who are the main protagonists in the crisis or even those who are most qualified as journalists.

They might be a local taxi driver who you find speaks six languages, or a man who lost his arm looking after his best friend, or a man who composes music under shell fire. Certainly not men only, though war seems to have a particular fascination for men. You meet women who gather children around them to give them an education in a place where there are no schools and no resources for teaching; women who look after their men when they return from fighting; women who provide love for their children when all around them are hatred and aggression and women who tend the sick with love, while endless numbers of people scream and bleed and die on the hospital floor around them.

Since that first overseas assignment in Birobidzhan in 1948, I had grown up both as a person and as a journalist. I had worked in Korea and Egypt and Vietnam. But each time I came back from an assignment, I felt empty and dissatisfied. I loved the thrill of the war zone or the new country which had thrown off its colonialist yoke. I liked the way you

465

could know people there without the trappings of civilisation. It was tough and basic, and you never had to pretend, and I loved the sense of living in the raw, of being with people where loyalties really mattered – of being with fellow journalists in a hotel where the lights flickered because of the bombs being dropped on the buildings around it and the way plentiful supplies of alcohol, which journalists always seem to find even in countries where religion has banned it, loosened our tongues and made us open up to strangers.

Meanwhile on home assignments in Paris, I found myself increasingly unable to be on a par with the French middle class and the niceties of bourgeois living.

On one occasion when, unusually, I returned to Les Landes to see my parents, I realised that my mother's silence on so many other topics was, because she was trying to draw me out, on the subject of potential marriage partners.

'So, you have a young man in Paris?' In the end she asked directly.

'Not really.'

As usual, I was giving nothing away to her. How to explain to my mother the reality of post-war life in Paris – about the journalists who wanted a quick fuck, but no attachment; of the bourgeois dinner parties, where I felt totally alienated? The old-fashioned middle-class male still wanted a trophy wife or a good mother for his children. But I was likely to be neither. I wasn't fashionable enough or beautiful enough or socially well-connected enough, to enter the ranks of the marriageable. And I wasn't respectable enough to be trusted with the sons of safe, caring families. Who would want a mother who had lived through the Suez crisis or the Palestinian riots or the attacks of the Viet Cong?

I mixed in the wrong circles. My mother, who had never imagined me marrying anyone who was not a farmer in Les Landes, could not understand the sort of person I met in Paris. I suppose she hoped I might meet a school-teacher or a 'fonctionnaire' – someone who was one step up from our family.

She could not have conceived of the left-wing journalists amongst whom I mixed in Paris. On the field, right-wing or left-wing did not make much difference. We were all witnessing people dying every day, and bombs did not distinguish between civilians and journalists or between those of different political persuasions. It was in Paris that we kept firmly to the political colours of our respective newspapers.

I worked for left-wing newspapers almost by accident. They had given me my first openings in my chosen career when I had first arrived in Paris, and I had stuck with Hervé and Ann-Marie and their associates for a long time. It was easier than moving anywhere else politically. As I became better known as a journalist, I mixed in wider circles, but I always came back to my original associates. I had continued to live above the offices of Libération for some years, though not as a cleaner for Mme Dubois. My flat had the advantages of a low rent and convenience and I was not interested in material prosperity.

I could have saved up to move to a better arrondissement, but somehow, living on the edge of war zones had given me no taste for bourgeois living. Instead, I spent my money on books, on the occasional holiday with whichever boyfriend I had at the time and I ate out in Parisian cafes almost every night. Earning money allowed me not to think about money and that was how I preferred it. When I returned to Les Landes, money was the last thing my parents appeared to need. They owned their own land. My father hunted and fished, and, if my mother wanted to do anything rather than work the land and keep the house, she did not make it known. They had lots of problems in their lives together, but lack of money was not one of them. Fortunately, neither of them suggested coming up to Paris to see me. I would not have known how to respond if they had.

After some time, I started to submit articles to l'Humanité, which came to be the most important left-wing paper after the war. It seemed to be a step up from Le Coq Enchainé and Libération which were struggling to survive.

I still did not see myself as a convinced communist, but it seemed too late to change into anything else and I certainly had no right-wing convictions. To be honest, I didn't have many convictions at all, especially of a political nature. I had met people of integrity from all political persuasions and I thought that the socialists were the ones who did the least harm. I think I was going back in my mind to the days of Patrice and

467

the trade unionists of Bordeaux. They had seemed to me decent people who had fought the Nazis more vigorously than anyone else. If socialism motivated them, then it was good enough for me. If you worked for a newspaper after the war in Paris, you had to connect with some political persuasion. A 'critical' socialist would have been my label of choice. Alain had taught me that you could not identify with any cause without being critical of it. Such a stance put you 'on the edge' looking in and that was where I liked to be.

Whatever the communists said, I admired General de Gaulle and the stance he had taken as leader of the 'Free French' during the war. Left to the communists, everyone would have argued amongst themselves and achieved nothing, but he had purpose and leadership.

I didn't like his associations with 'the right' after the war – the bourgeois who wanted to create a comfortable France for their own convenience, but I admired him. You knew where you stood with him and he seemed to have some sort of sense of the dignity of France and its place in the modern world. He could hold his own with the British and the Americans and make us proud to be French.

And what of Russia? The horrors of Stalinism had made me distrustful of the ideal communist state, but I had not forgotten the goodness of Matvey and Natasha. Since then, Kruschev had taken over and he seemed to be taking the Soviets on a path to liberal socialism. What had happened to my friends there I had no idea. My experiences in Birobidzhan had been swallowed up by my experiences in other parts of the world.

# Chapter Two

It was not only what was happening in other parts of the world which affected my job and my travels, but what France was doing in relation to other parts of the world.

Like everyone else in my generation, I had been brought up to believe that we had a civilising effect on the colonies which we ruled. It was the German occupation which first made me think about how other countries must feel about being taken over by a European power.

When Alain had discussed politics, in our private underground kingdom, he had made think about how it feels not to be in full control of your own land.

'Everyone wants their own homeland, Marie. That's why for us Jews it's always the ideal of our own land in Palestine.'

'Is that what you want too?'

'Of course. That's where I really belong.'

I found his attitude baffling. 'But you belong here. You're French,' I argued, upset that he saw a division between us.

He had laughed. 'That's not what my aunt and uncle tell me.'

'Well, they're wrong,' I had retorted, annoyed at their influence over him.

'I shall pass on your opinion to them, Marie,' he replied gravely.

So, I thought, some people feel at home in one country but not in another. There didn't seem to be much choice for me, though later I realised that part of me would always be a 'landaise', even though I now felt more at home in the city of Paris than in the land of my birth.

It was really the German Occupation which stirred up something else in me. It wasn't just that they had defeated the French in the war. It wasn't just that they represented the curse of Nazism. It was the sense that they had no right to be there. They didn't belong in our country. All the paper-checking and the military activities annoyed me rather than frightened me. The Germans were so different to the French in the way they did things. They were foreign and alien and 'other'.

It was only as I saw myself what was going in the Indo China war, and when I spoke to my fellow journalists in Paris that it occurred to me that other people might feel the same way about the French.

'But no one minds about them gradually ruling themselves,' I argued with my friend, Henri, who had gone on to be the special correspondent for l'Humanité in Vietnam. 'It's just the madness of this man, Ho Chi Minh. No one could want to be in a country governed by him.'

'Couldn't they?'

I was exasperated by the question.

'Of course, they couldn't, Henri! He's a communist like Stalin. From what I've seen in Russia, no one would want a lunatic like that in charge.'

'But that's your point of view, Marie. You're French. But what about the Russians? I bet most of them want it.'

'Do they?' I was not to be outdone by his questioning spirit. 'Or has it been forced upon them?'

'Don't tell me that there aren't any Bolsheviks who admire Stalin.'

I thought about Mikhail and Matvey and Natasha.

'Yes, of course there are, but no one in their right mind...'

Henri brought the ashtray crashing down onto the table in our café, making me and others around us jump. 'No, Marie. You think that anyone in their right mind must agree with you! You can't understand why they think like they do. But you've no right to impose your opinion on them. And neither has France the right to impose what they think is good on Indo China.'

'Even if it's going to bring them war and untold horrors?' I enquired, unconvinced by his argument.

'Yes, that's their choice. It's their country. It's no business of ours.'

'All right, Henri, tell me you're going to go out there and only report from the communist point of view!'

'Of course.'

470

'I hope you're right, Henri, but I'm not convinced.'

Henri lent back on his chair in the rather smart café we journalists sometimes frequented on the Place de la Concorde.

'I know I'm right, Marie.'

Henri made me think, especially as de Gaulle, the idol of the French people, whom we in the Socialist party were meant to disdain, had not been voted back to power. The communists were in an uneasy alliance with the socialists, and neither of the two parties knew what they truly wanted.

I suppose it was my friend, Brahim, who really affected me, when I came to think about colonialism. I had known him since my early days as a journalist. He had always so passionately expressed outrage on behalf of his people against the French politicians in power. Spending time with a man who feels passionately about his own country, would make anyone reflect more deeply and I was moved by his pain when he talked about his own country.

'You don't think that the Algerians are in any way grateful for what the French have done for them?'

'How can you be grateful to people who have taken away your freedom?'

'Because otherwise you might be living in the dark ages.'

'But North Africa has been one of the most civilised lands in the past. In Roman times they were far in advance of Gaul. Then it was you living in the backwater.'

'Alright,' I conceded, 'but when the French arrived in 1830, you had been backward for a long time.'

'Had we?'

'Yes, you'd had the Ottomans who didn't care about you and the Muslim armies who marched through you to get to Spain. They both left you fairly backwards.'

'That's what you learnt in a European school Marie. The Arabs were far in advance of the Christian empire in terms of Maths and Medicine. You learnt from us.'

'In which case, why didn't the ordinary peasants in Algeria get the advantage of all this great learning?'

'They would have done eventually.'

I snorted in derision. 'Oh, come on, Brahim. Things were pretty backward. Admit it.!'

'Maybe in some ways. But at least it was our backwardness, not anyone else's.'

This sense of belonging and possession again, I thought. I'd certainly come across it again in Indochina. As far as I was concerned, Ho Chi Minh was a nightmare, but I had to agree with Henri, he was their nightmare.

Brahim finished the discussion with me prophetically. 'You'll see when you get an assignment there, Marie. You'll see the Algerian people coming together and achieving something. And the people will recognise it, because it's their people achieving something and that makes all the difference.'

# Chapter Three

Algeria had been on and off the French news since 1945, when there had been a terrible massacre at a place called Sétif. Reports varied as to how many people had been killed. Le Figaro, that bastion of French journalistic civilisation, had said 100, but by 1958 there were reports that it had been many more. Of course, it was the Algerians who had started it, argued the right-wingers. If they hadn't murdered in the first place, there would have been no retaliation. This tit for tat argument had been going on for the last thirteen years.

Hervé was no longer the editor of Libération but I now had a good relationship with André, the present editor, and he called me that day in May 1958.

'So, Marie,' he said, getting to the point right away, 'things are brewing in Algérie.'

'Things are always brewing in Algérie,' I countered, matter-of-factly.

'No doubt but it's beginning to affect what's going on here too.'

There had been various marches recently by both the right wingers and the trade unions in response to the politics of Algeria.

'There's nothing new about that,' I said glumly. 'Everyone's been on a march just about every month for the last five years.'

It was true. There had been civil unrest going on in France for years, and it had not helped our economy. Arguments among political factions were inflated by poverty and widening rifts between the bourgeoisie and the working class.

'All grist to the mill for the talented left-wing journalist.'

André was half cynical and half admiring. As I had acquired a good reputation in my field, he needed my reports, but he could never quite rid himself of the feeling that I wasn't a whole-hearted communist, as he felt I should have been.

'This talented left-wing journalist likes to wait and see what is really going to happen. One more grève in a Parisian factory is not going to get anyone very excited,' I suggested smoothly.

'No,' he agreed, 'but a few reports from the point of view of the Communist Party in Algiers might get everyone going.'

'We never really hear about them, do we?' I agreed.

'Exactly.'

'But the revolutionaries in Algeria are a Marxist inspired group, aren't they?'

'Yes, so we have to ask ourselves why they aren't working together?'

'Perhaps you should be finding out, Marie.'

I sighed. I hadn't been back from Indo China for more than a few months and that had given me more than my fair share of death and destruction. Seeing tortured bodies in the French army and Vietnamese villages wiped out had haunted me. It was a surprise air lift out of Hanoi, which I had been put on by mistake, which had saved my sanity. Other people had lost their lives, but I almost lost my mind. It had taken me six months of talking to journalists in Paris, to soften my memories of hell. Since then, I had been quite satisfied with the petty arguments I had heard in the communist party in France. I didn't want any more adventure in a war-torn country.

'I think I'm quite happy running my patch in Paris, thank you, André. Everything seems quite chaotic here, more than enough for any communist journalist.'

'Mmmm' André considered me dispassionately, sizing up my ultimate use to his newspaper. I was no longer the protected protégé of Hervé. On the other hand, I was also a well-regarded, experienced journalist and my editor had need of such writers in a world of competitive left-wing journalism. He tipped his chair back and put his hand through his hair – a sign I knew from experience of a soon to emerge idea.

'How about a little trip to Bobigny?'

'I beg your pardon?'

I was taken aback. Bobigny was a deprived area of Paris, not the centre of the Algerian Communist Party.

'Bobigny,' he repeated, bringing his chair forward, as his mind gave birth to his idea. 'Lots of Algerians live in Bobigny. Go and find out what's going on.'

'But the Muslim Algerians there are not part of the Communist Party,' I objected.

'Some of them are.'

'OK, maybe here in France but they are notably silent about what is happening in Algeria.'

'Exactly.'

'You mean they know more than they're letting on?'

'Quite possibly. They're all fairly inscrutable. No one knows what they really think.'

'In that case they're fairly unlikely to confide in me, especially as I'm a woman.'

'Women always have ways,' said André, as if it was an absolute truth which no one disputed, at the same time challenging the gender equality policy of his chosen political party, 'Just be careful what you wear. Don't be too daring.'

'There are ways and ways of being daring,' I suggested, falling in with his talk about women's deviousness.

'Indeed, there are, Marie. Now just go and find them'

In this way, my relationship with Algérie Française began.

# Chapter Four

I had lived in Paris for ten years. I had been to Stalin's Russia and Ho Chi Min's Hanoi, but I realised that I did not have a single idea about how to go to the neighbouring suburb of Bobigny in Paris.

'How to go' sounds like getting a visa for a foreign country, and that is exactly how it felt. After the war I had cycled through the poorer Parisian suburbs north of the city to get to Philippe's house. I had often cycled through neighbouring arrondissements to meet up with fellow journalists but Bobigny felt like a foreign country.

The next day I cycled to the park which was the nearest area and I discovered that was where my notion of park or green stopped. Even the small amount of grass looked dirty and the river looked dank and unwholesome. When I gazed across the park and looked at the area, I thought was Bobigny, I couldn't quite take it in the fact that this was part of the same city, where I lived.

At that time there was none of the really high rise flats which were built in the 60s and 70s in Paris, but already in 1958 there were soulless, drab 'immeubles' of seven or eight storeys high, interspersed with the run down, traditional French houses and wide, empty expanses full of 'bidonvilles', which were hastily erected temporary housing, supposedly providing for the needs of the immigrant Algerian population, who had been needed to boost the manual work force in post-war France. I tried cycling through the maze of alleyways and very soon started feeling isolated and unsafe. There were no women outdoors and I received hostile stares from the men who were around. I also had the strange sensation of hidden eyes following me around as if the dwellings themselves were spies who were noting my movements. If I had had any hopes of starting

476

a conversation at a street corner or in a local boulangerie, I was quickly disillusioned. The few men who were standing still in the doorways of what looked like cellars or small storage areas stared at me directly in a hostile manner or deliberately turned their backs on me as I cycled past. I was not welcome, and there was no way I was going to get into casual conversation with any of them. My journalist's nose would be of no use, if I couldn't even get to talk to anyone.

I had a strong instinct that I needed to get out of the area as fast as possible, and, having been in danger on several occasions in my life, I obeyed my instinct. What made it strange for me was that the sense of danger came upon me in my own country in a time of peace.

I was relieved to get back to familiar territory in the 10th arrondissement. As I leant my bike up against the wall of the café where my colleagues congregated, I felt annoyed with myself. What could be so different in a place two miles across the city? Surely, I had been in war torn countries? What could be so scary about a few men dressed in djebellas and children playing outside in the mud? But, as I pushed open the door of the café, I felt everything familiar draw me in. I was at home here. Twenty minutes before I had been in a foreign country. Fellow journalists from l'Humanité and other papers were relaxing over their vermouth and aniseed and coffee.

'Anyone seen Brahim recently?' I asked as casually as I could. Surely my fellow journalist might interpret the situation in Bobigny for me accurately and give me advice? I didn't want to go back to my editor empty handed.

'Brahim?' Someone laughed in response to the name. 'who knows? He's probably gone back to Algeria by now. Probably joined the revolutionaries.'

I was shocked. Brahim had always been ready to argue about the current situation anywhere in the world. That's what journalists did. The idea of one of us disappearing off into a dangerous country simply because he belonged there was a new idea to me.

'More likely stirring up support for the FLN here in Paris,' suggested Anne-Marie, my old friend from Le Coq Enchainé.

'The FLN? You mean the Marxist revolutionaries? Here in Paris?'

Once again, I was astounded, and this time it showed on my face, which was not a fashionable look to present. Journalists need to be knowing and world weary and I was showing my naivety.

'Of course.' My colleague looked amused.

I fell silent. Now not only did I have a foreign country planted two kilometres away from my favourite café, but we were talking about war mongers in Paris. After the Occupation and the cold war and the war in Indo China, I was not prepared for this invasion of my comfort zone.

'Does anyone actually know where Brahim is?' I sounded business like and tried to stop my imagination going wild. Come on, Marie, I lectured myself. Do what André told you to do and find a way into the Algerian community. Once I had the possibility of a real story, I could run with that and stop all this fantasy crowding into my life.

'Does anyone know where Brahim lives?' I tried again.

'4, rue du Canal, when I last heard,' Gil, another friend informed me. 'But I've no idea whether he's still there.'

'Well, that's a start. Thanks Gil. Maybe I'll head out in a few minutes and look him up. It's only ten minutes from here.'

'You might as well stay and have another drink, Marie. He may still live there but he won't be back till late.'

'How do you know?'

'Because he spends more time with the PCF and with the Algerian community than ever before, and they always meet at night.'

I laughed, feeling reassured. 'Then I'll take your advice and enjoy another blanc sec with you!'

# Chapter Five

It wasn't until nearly midnight that I headed out to the Rue du Canal. Although I knew Brahim's views about his country in theory, I didn't really know what was at the heart of it or what his personal story was. Something in France had changed in recent years, but, more importantly for me, my excursion earlier in the day had changed me. I was not used to being nervous in my own country in peace time, but in Bobigny I had felt nervous and unsure. I had imagined that, with my experience as a journalist, I could handle any situation. I was blasé about my own self-sufficiency. But my twenty minutes of wandering the streets of Bobigny had taught me that in this environment, I didn't know how to look after myself. I was used to meeting women from Indo China, both communists and supporters of the French, and had had an easy relationship with several of them. But there were no women on the streets of Bobigny to have a relationship with. It was a parallel world which had chosen to ignore me.

I parked my bike under the stairs of the tenement building, wondering what sort of reception I would get. Eight years ago, Brahim had seemed like any other Frenchman with a serious view about how the post-war world could be made better. I had hardly considered him as an Algerian and different from myself. He was my colleague and a well-respected writer. As I climbed to the fourth storey, I wondered how much he might have changed.

The door was opened very cautiously at first and then, he was there and gestured for me to come in without speaking. He seemed cautious and didn't give me the customary 'bises' with which all French people greet each other, especially in the community of journalists.

He didn't quite say 'what do you want?' but he was clearly nervous about my presence. Without making the customary small talk, I told him that I wanted to find out more about the Algerian population of Paris.

'Why?' The dark eyes were guarded under the long lashes and his small body was pent up with nervous energy, which felt as though it might erupt out of him at any second.

'Because I want to know how they are reacting to what is going on in Algeria at the moment. We hear a lot about what is going on in the country itself, but it's as if the Algerians over here are a separate people.'

'So why do you want to speak to me?'

'Because I realise that I don't know anyone in their quartier, and as a woman it's hard to just start chatting.'

'I heard.'

'What?' I was startled. Surely, he couldn't already have heard about my wanderings in Bobigny that afternoon?

'Don't worry.' His face finally relaxed. 'I didn't know it was you, Marie, but my friends there said that there was a foreign woman snooping. They thought that it might be the police or a fonctionnaire.'

I snorted my disgust 'Do I look like the police or a fonctionnaire?'

'No, not to me. But my friends there don't know about such things. They're suspicious of anyone.'

'You mean they don't like outsiders.'

'Only an outsider they can't trust.'

Just like you, I thought. That was the quality about Brahim which had changed, I suddenly realised. He was suspicious.

'What do you want to write about?'

Something stopped me talking about the Communist Party.

'I just want to know what they think and feel.'

'That makes a refreshing change,' he remarked acidly.

'What do you mean?'

'Most people want to tell them what they should think and feel.'

'Ah well, that's always annoying.'

'Exactly.'

At last he held out a chair for me.

'Have a seat, Marie. I haven't got any alcohol, I'm afraid, but I've got a thisane.'

'That suits me fine. I've had enough at the Bar de la Poste tonight already. Thisane's a great nightcap, though I must say it's unusual for you Brahim. What I remember from a few years' back, is that you could drink us all under the table.'

'Yes, well I didn't have revolutionary principles in those days.'

'I seem to remember you had quite a few revolutionary ideas.'

'Ideas and principles are entirely different.'

'Fair enough. And, by the way, when I met the Vietcong, they didn't have a ban on alcohol. Rice wine is quite lethal, and, believe you me, they needed it in the jungles of Indochina.'

He returned from the little side kitchen which was attached to the main room with the tisane and I found that it was not the French version, but the real thing with peppermint in the bottom and lumps of sugar already dissolving in it. It tasted unexpectedly soothing after all the alcohol I had consumed earlier in the evening.

'You have to remember that we are Muslim revolutionaries.'

'There's a difference?' I queried in my ignorance.

'Certainly. We want a revolution, but we don't believe in the Marxist religion.'

'That's a bit of a contradiction, isn't it?' I pointed out, remembering many of the conversations I had had in Stalinist Russia. 'How can you have Marx without his atheism or his own all-consuming belief in his own socialist system?'

'You don't have to have anything you don't want, Marie, when you're talking about forming a new country. We Algerians have been reading and re-reading Marx and Mao. Lots of it is good but it's not all for us. We can't get rid of our religion. It's been around in our country since the 8th century. It's a really important part of our identity.'

'If you say so,' I answered obligingly. I hadn't come here to have a talk about religion, I thought. 'I don't really understand my own religion, never mind someone else's.'

'That's because you don't believe it passionately enough.'

'And you do?'

481

I was amazed. This was not the Brahim I remembered from a few years ago. From my discussions with the communists in Russia and Indo China, I remembered that they all had one thing in common – complete distrust of their country's religion and the way it had been used to manipulate their people in the past.

'I'm really fascinated by all this, Brahim, but you know that I work for a communist newspaper. I want to know how strong the communists are among the Algerian community in Paris.'

'Ah, now, that's a bit more complicated,' Brahim conceded, smiling a little and relaxing as we sipped our peppermint tea.

'What? More complicated than religion?' I risked saying, fearing that he might be too committed to his own cause to take a joke about it.

'May be not,' he grinned. 'But still complicated.'

'OK. I'm all ears. Tell me.'

'We are Marxist revolutionaries,' he stated clearly. I was longing to ask who 'we' referred to, but didn't want to arouse suspicion and stop him, just as he was beginning to talk to me as a friend, rather than as an outsider.

'So, you'd think we'd all be members of the Communist Party.'

'Seems logical,' I agreed.

'But there is another thread to this identity. Russia hasn't really backed us, and the Communist Party in Paris have backed the pied noir, not the Algerian people.'

'You're saying there's two types of communist?'

'Yes, I think so.'

'Actually, Brahim, from my experience, there's a lot more than two types in most countries.'

'Yes, that's what I meant by saying that we aren't just Marxists. We like some of it but not all of it."

'Good. I like that,' I said firmly. 'And who are the 'we' you are referring to?'

At this point in the conversation he was able to take the question in a much more relaxed way.

'The ALN or the FLN.'

'OK. I don't understand all the acronyms, but you're saying that they're not talking to the Parti Communiste in Algeria or in France. In that case, who are they talking to?'

482

'The Algerians who want to be free of the colons, the people who want their own country for themselves.'

'But I thought the Muslims were all supporting General de Gaulle?'

'Who told you that?'

'The newspapers.'

'That's because they're run by the French.'

'It's not true then?'

'Only partly. General de Gaulle is a lot better than the last lot.'

'Is that supposed to be a compliment?'

He looked at me without smiling. 'Why would I want to compliment a man who wants us to be integrated into the French system? He has the power to stop a civil war in France.'

'Are we in danger of having one?' I asked, startled by the idea.

'For a journalist, Marie, you're remarkably bad at reading the papers.' He paused. 'If you really want to know what's going on, you'd better come with me to Bobigny.'

# Chapter Six

I had agreed to meet up with Brahim two days later at 8pm.

'Leave your bike here, Marie. Muslim women don't go out on bikes. You'll be an oddity if you arrive on one.'

I now realised in the summer evening daylight that Brahim was gaunt and emaciated, but, now, instead of being combative as he had been at our previous meeting, he was focused and ready for action. This gave me hope. If he was ready for action, then there might be some and I would be part of it, and, if you're a journalist, you can't ask for more.

'Just stay behind me,' he advised. 'Keep your head down and wrap that shawl you brought round your hair and arms. I won't forget that you're there, but in Algerian society we can't be equals, and you won't get anywhere if you make out that we are.'

I accepted his advice without argument. I knew that it wasn't how he saw me as a fellow journalist, but how his fellow countrymen saw me as a woman. I knew some of my contemporaries who would have confronted this attitude head on. After all, we were in the Paris of Jean-Paul Sartre and Simone de Beauvoir, but instinctively I knew that this would be counter-productive. These people had lived like this for centuries. If I wanted to understand what was going on amongst them, then argument should not be my first line of enquiry.

Walking behind Brahim, I made my way through the park, as I had done three nights before. This time I had some idea of what I was going to see, but I also had a knowledgeable guide. We crossed the rough, disused land at the side of the park and found ourselves walking past the big granite and cement HLM – symbol of the brave new world of the post-war social services; on through the squats of the bidonvilles, which looked as though they were made of cardboard, but had naked, swinging lights at the front. We came to an open square of land, where children were playing football and young men sat on upturned oil barrels, smoking and exchanging short intense phrases of conversation, which sounded like the staccato of gunfire.

Brahim stopped at the entrance of what looked like the first of a series of horse boxes, which had been converted into a makeshift shop, with a curtain hooked to one side. The entrance was crowded out with men and I could hardly make out what was going on inside, but Brahim gestured roughly to me to stay outside and I meekly obeyed. I gazed at the backs of men, clad in burnous, with their hoods positioned half-way back from their heads and their curly black hair to the front. They stepped aside for Brahim to pass through, but this did not interrupt their fast-paced, passionate conversation.

I must have stood there for twenty to thirty minutes, trying not to feel stupid or ignored. Some of the children came over to stare at me for a short time, but most of the passers-by ignored me. Tonight, I seemed to be more acceptable as a hanger-on of a man than I was previously as a lone female visitor, and for that I was grateful. Through Brahim I had found a way to blend into the background.

I suddenly noticed that a whole crowd of men, dressed in long white robes, were coming out of one of the far-right 'horse boxes' whose entrances all backed onto this rough square. There were too many of them together to imagine that this was a coincidence, but again, they were far too engrossed in talking together, to take any notice of me. I was accustomed to passionate dialogue around the table in the bars frequented by journalists, but the average French group seemed silent and lacking in animation compared to these people. What did they have to talk about? I asked myself, especially as so many of them were living in poverty. In my experience in Les Landes and in the Far East, the poorer you are, the less you have to say.

Without any warning, the backs of the men in front of me parted and Brahim walked towards me. The summer evening had darkened so I could just make out the silhouettes of the boys playing in the square. The glare of the single light bulb in the horse box seemed garish in comparison. As the men parted, I could see bottles being produced from a crate in front and I guessed that this must be a make-shift bar.

'Come on,' relayed Brahim as he walked past. 'We've been invited to eat with a family I know.'

I was about to reply that I had already eaten hours ago, but it wasn't the sort of invitation that I could ignore. I was here on Brahim's terms, not on my own, and he was already walking ahead of me.

We had left the flats far behind. I now know that they were basic, soulless structures built as a post-war solution to housing needs right across Europe, regardless of nationality, but on the outside, they gave the illusion of Western civilisation. We left them behind and walked further on uneven gravel and across muddy potholes, which took me by surprise in the dark and made me stumble until we reached a great muddle of hastily constructed pre-fabs dropped in by cranes to help our biggest cities cope with immigrants and refugees and these were interspersed with temporary dwellings made from wood and cardboard. I was sure that it was against the law to live in dwellings like these, but the Algerian community appeared to disregard such irrelevancies. What I noticed was the way the life inside them seemed to spill over onto the ground outside even at ten o'clock at night. Children were squatting over games played with sticks; veiled women were pouring away huge pots of liquid; and men were playing what looked like basic games of backgammon. We stepped round and over many of them until Brahim stopped at a doorway.

'Habibi!' He threw his arms around the man who stepped out of a low entrance. I looked at the two of them nervously, suddenly seeing a new aspect of my fellow journalist, who had, up to now, always seemed as French as myself. Against the background of the bidonville, Brahim had shed his western skin and in the conflicting shadows of the light bulb swinging from the breeze, he was an alien figure whom I no longer recognized.

But to my surprise the introductions included me. It seemed that I was no longer to be ignored because of my gender and nationality.

'Habibi…Marie.' I didn't know how to greet this man, but he surprised me by holding out both his hands to me and saying in perfect French,

'Enchanté, Mademoiselle. You are welcome to my home.'

He made the last statement with such sincerity and dignity that I was both relieved and impressed – relieved that he saw me as an acceptable human being and impressed that he was not in any way embarrassed at calling this shack 'home'.

And, indeed, he had no need to be. If the outside looked like a builder's dump, the inside was covered with beautiful Algerian rugs and wall coverings. I was introduced with great affection and kindness to an attractive middle-aged woman, who was stirring a huge bowl on a cooker on the floor and several younger people between the ages of six and eighteen, who were sitting cross-legged on the floor round a little demountable table with folding wooden legs.

'Welcome to my family, Marie. This is our Ramadan meal and we are honoured to share it with you.'

# Chapter Seven

The meal consisted of couscous and vegetables, with some tender and succulent lamb. Later I found out that the family rarely ate meat. It was special because it was halfway through Ramadan. What humbled me was the way in which they willingly shared their meal with me, who was an uninvited guest, and not even a friend.

Throughout the meal, Brahim and Habibi chatted in Arabic with Brahim making the occasional, impatient translation for my benefit. It was all about what the French government had promised them in housing as immigrant workers. I didn't need a knowledge of Arabic to tell me that the French government had not honoured their promises of new housing. Sitting in one room of a hastily constructed wooden and metallic structure for a family of six, you could immediately grasp the problems.

'But de Gaulle will sort it out,' pronounced Habibi optimistically. Brahim reacted immediately and negatively.

'Don't put your trust in him, my friend. So far, he is only helping the French, not the Algerians. And from what I've heard, he's not really helping the pied noirs either. They want rid of him because they want Algérie Française.'

This phrase had been sounding as a bell right through the summer of 1958. It was the catch phrase of every French man and woman. Brahim, I knew, had other ideas, but I was interested in the fact that Habibi thought that de Gaulle could sort the chaos out.

None of the younger people or their mother, who was sitting behind them all with a scarf round her head and eating while stirring the floor pot containing the remains of the couscous, spoke. They were all too busy eating, which wasn't a surprise, when you considered that they had been fasting all day and that they rarely ate meat. The moment they finished, the boys went outside, and the girls picked up the large centre bowl and the spoons, and took them off behind, with a pot of water to wash them. I suddenly realised that, if I had still been living on the farm in Les Landes as an unmarried daughter, that would have been my lot too. Of course, my parents never had visitors, but the difference in culture as to what boys and girls had to do, was not so different after all, I thought. Maybe Simone de Beauvoir, our great feminist leader, had a point, I thought.

Black coffee full of sugar was served to the remaining men and it was assumed that I would share this too. I had made a special point of thanking Habibi's wife for the meal, but she just nodded her head shyly, served us coffee and disappeared in the same direction as the children. Later I saw her leading the younger ones further into the makeshift home, where everyone slept.

'So!' Brahim turned to me and, speaking directly in French, signalled that the time for more serious conversation had begun. 'Marie wants to know about the Communist Party and their work amongst Algerians and whether they support independence.'

'That's a complex question, my friend,' replied Habibi, smiling and speaking in educated and cultured French. 'The short answer is that the Communist Party supports the Algerian workers here, but it also supports the pied noirs in Algeria itself, so that is a conflict.'

'But,' I objected, 'I thought that the colons in Algeria were all wealthy and that was the heart of the problem. They won't let the Algerian workers have their own country and system of government.'

'No, no. There are lots of wealthy colons of course and they do want Algérie Française , because their work is tied up with the country. But there are lots of poor pied noirs in Algeria as well. They're the ones who belong to the Parti Communiste d'Algérie.'

'But I thought that it was the revolutionaries who are the Marxists.' I was struggling to get my head round the political divisions.

'They are but they aren't,' chimed in Brahim, confusing me even more.

'Perhaps you'd like to explain yourself,' I suggested.

'I'll try. The revolutionaries are greatly influenced partly by Marx but even more so by Mao.'

I nodded. 'That's the one the Viet Cong were always reading in Indo China.'

'Exactly. He's got loads of advice for revolutionaries on the ground, but it's what works best in your own country which matters.'

'Meaning?'

'Meaning that revolution in Russia in 1917 was different to revolution in Indo China in 1954 which is different to revolutionary tactics in the mountains of Kabylia in 1958.'

'So, who decides what the tactics are,' I queried practically. This was all a bit theoretical for me. I had thought that I had had the Stalinists in Russia worked out. Now everything was becoming blurred.

'The FLN leaders have all read Marx and Mao of course.'

'FLN?'

'Front de Libération Nationale. They're the armed side of the ALN, who are the political wing,' Brahim translated for me impatiently. 'Do wake up, Marie. You're supposed to be a journalist specialising in overseas affairs. Where have you been for the last two years?'

'Sorting out in my own head exactly what happened in Indo China,' I replied tartly. 'I don't live in neat rights and wrongs, like you do, Brahim. I don't want ever to see the bombings and murders which I saw there.'

Brahim looked at me dispassionately under his hooded eyes. 'You'd better get used to it, Marie, because there's going to be a lot more of it in Algeria, before we're done.'

'Don't frighten the girl so much, Brahim,' soothed Habibi, more affectionate and 'doux' than his friend. 'Marie, the FLN are the revolutionaries in Algeria, not the Parti Communiste.'

'Well, why don't they just work together?' I suggested reasonably.

'Because the Parti Communiste cares about the workers' rights, meaning the poor French, in Algeria. The FLN only care about their own people and setting their country free.'

'I thought the Communist party was supposed to be an international movement?'

'It is in principle, but it still gets caught up in the needs of its own particular part of the work. Think about Russia and Budapest.'

Everyone knew about the disaster of Russia invading Budapest in 1952.

'Actually,' chimed in Habibi, contributing to Brahim's history lesson, 'if we're looking at similarities with the Communist Party, one of the best role models is Tito in Yugoslavia.'

'Yes, he put down the rebels after the second world war.'

'And that's a problem for Algeria too, because a lot of Algerians, the tirailleurs and the veterans, fought for the French against the Nazis.'

'OK. OK. This is doing my head in a bit,' I moaned. 'Just tell me for the moment what the Communist Party in Paris is up to.'

As an answer, Brahim turned his head away, and spat towards the doorway.

'Traitors. On the one hand they claim they help the Algerian workers here; on the other hand, they come out in favour of de Gaulle.'

'You can understand why.' Habibi countered Brahim's suggestion with gentle reasonableness. 'The Communist Party in Paris don't want a civil war.'

I was shocked. Before Brahim had mentioned it the previous night, I had never conceived of such an event happening in post-war France. Maybe things had got a lot worse than I had realised, and I wasn't up to scratch.

'They want to support their fellow French communists in Algeria who are poor and badly treated by the rich colons, but most of the communist party in Paris is made up of Algerian workers like me. We're in a dilemma.'

I was intrigued. 'What are you going to do, and aren't you a fervent anti-Gaullist, like Brahim here?'

'No, not at all. I admire de Gaulle for the way he pulled France together in the war and for what he did afterwards. But I know too that he's a capitalist and a Catholic and all the other things communists are supposed to hate.'

'And so, Mademoiselle Marie,' Habibi asked, looking at me with shrewd eyes, 'do you count yourself as a communist?'

Brahim butted in quickly. 'Marie sits on the fence. She writes for the left-wing press, but she never really commits herself.'

Immediately, Habibi defended me. 'If you're a member of the press, that's a reasonable position to take, Brahim. She's an intellectual and a thinker.'

I bowed slightly towards him, delighted by this assessment of my ability.

Brahim was not impressed. 'Habibi, are you saying you can't be an intellectual or a thinker and be a member of the Communist Party or the FLN?'

'In a way yes, because an intellectual will always think for himself and be there to discern.'

'You don't count Ben Bella or Abbas as intellectuals?'

'Yes, they are. That's why they can't agree amongst themselves.'

'I'm really lost now,' I said. 'You're going to have to explain who Ben Bella and Abbas are. I've got what you said about the dilemma of the Communist Party. They're obviously going for peace at any price, unusual though that is for the communists. But this FLN – how do they affect what's going on here?'

Habibi and Brahim looked at each other, and Habibi summed it up for me.

'That is the nub of the problem. And, if you want to know about it, we're going to have to trust you for discretion.'

# Chapter Eight

The women and children had gone to bed. It was a hot night. Habibi, Brahim and I sat in the doorway of the little shack in the Parisian bidonville and we drank coffee after coffee, while Habibi explained the position of the FLN to me and how they operated in Paris.

To begin with I was amazed that they operated in Paris at all. 'I thought that the rebels were stuck in the mountains,' I queried.

'What made you think that?'

'Because that's what the newspapers are always telling us.'

'And Marie believes everything the papers tell us,' commented Brahim drily. 'You wouldn't guess that she's a journalist, would you?'

'Not so quick to judge, my friend, please.' Habibi again jumped in to defend me, which made me feel much more at ease. I found that I was always on the defensive with Brahim, who managed to make me feel like an evil capitalist defending the rich French, who had no care for the workers.

'Very little real news from Algeria reaches people here in Paris. Even half the Algerians here don't know what's happening back home, so no surprise that Mlle Marie here is in the dark.'

'Ever the charmer, Habibi,' commented Brahim acidly.

'Ever the realist, Brahim.'

I put down my coffee cup on the floor next to my small stool. I wouldn't drink it again until I felt I had a handle on this situation, which was beginning to assault my mind and my emotions.

'Whether I'm ignorant or stupid or whatever, could you two stop bickering and start to explain what is really going on here?'

Brahim made a quick hand gesture to give Habibi the right to explain.

'All right. Well the FLN fighters, who are the Algerian revolutionaries or nationalists or whatever you want to call them, aren't just stuck in the mountains of Kabylia or the Aurès fighting for their lives. Of course, they are there too, but they're fighting all over Algeria. The original political group was called the ALN, but the militants are always known as the FLN.'

'Even in the big cities like Oran and Algiers and Constantine?' I queried.

'Ever heard of the battle of Algiers?'

'No.'

Brahim sighed. 'That just shows you how the bourgeois press in France have stopped people from knowing what is going on.'

I was impatient with his moralising. 'OK. OK Brahim. I've got it. All the French in Paris are bourgeois capitalists and evil, but now, put me right. What's the battle of Algiers?'

'The battle of Algiers took place last year, all through the summer and into the autumn. The FLN blew up loads of places and people in Algiers. Algiers is one section of their offensive. The country and the militants are divided into wilayas.'

'What's a wilaya?'

'A section of the country like a department in France. Yes, they're administrative boroughs of the country but the FLN also use them for their organization. Last summer they planned their offensive big time in Algiers.'

'And presumably the French fought back?'

'Yes, but they were surprised by the strength of feeling amongst the Algerians. The FLN could no longer be cast as a few mad men in the mountains and the desert.'

'How did the French react?'

'Massu – he's the big army guy in charge in Algiers – brought in the paras.'

'They're the crack troops who are the heroes, right?'

'They're only the heroes if you're French.'

'Yes, well – they were the people who tried to sort things out in Indo China.'

'And didn't manage it,' concluded Brahim.

I turned to him. 'Remember, Brahim, I've heard it from their point of view too. And I spent a lot of time in Indo China. I'm not just the naïve French woman you're making me out to be.'

Silence. Even the cynical Brahim couldn't say anything to that. When it came to reports from the war front, I had won my colours in Indo China in 1954. It was not an experience I wanted to repeat, but it did mean I had lived in a war zone.

'According to the French paras, they were defeated more by the French politicians than by the fighting,' I added.

Habibi nodded. 'That's probably true, because the politicians and the generals didn't understand the way the revolutionaries fought.'

This man seemed to me to have some understanding of the situation on the ground, unlike Brahim, who I considered to be arrogant.

I explained further.

'That's true... But the paras did. They're not just fighting hunks you know. Some of them have got brains and they've read their Lenin and their Mao.'

'They just don't like what it tells them,' commented Brahim.

I turned on him aggressively. 'Of course, they don't because they don't want communism. And when you see what the Viet-Cong have been doing, you can understand why.'

'So how come you write for a communist newspaper then?'

'Because I have sympathy for the ideal of socialism and all they're trying to achieve for the poor but not the violence. It's ruthless and they kill their own people too.'

'You can't have victory for the masses unless you have some casualties too.'

I remembered more clearly than I wanted to some of the casualties of Indo China – the innocent girls raped and burned, the young soldiers mutilated, and the survivors traumatised.

'Maybe,' I answered Brahim, 'but when you've seen some of the casualties, it makes you wonder whether it's worth it.'

Some revellers from the Ramadan celebrations walked past us, saluting Habibi as they went. Under his shadow, I was invisible, which certainly suited me. I was beginning to like Habibi more and more.

'Anyway, the politics of socialism aren't getting us any nearer to understanding the situation in Algeria.'

'Fine. So, explain it all to me then. What happened when Massu brought in the paras?'

'As I'm sure you're aware, they're an elite fighting force. The casbah in Algiers didn't have a chance against them, but it didn't mean that the FLN didn't make progress.'

'How?'

'The more violent the French were, the more the Algerians turned to the FLN. The paras won the FLN loads of support. They appeared to be victorious, I mean, the French did, but the Algerians turned to the FLN instead.'

'And did the FLN win any actual victories in the fighting?'

'Sporadic ones and they put the fear of God into the pied noirs. They were constantly blowing places up – clubs, café bars, the lot. The pied noirs were afraid to go out onto the streets.'

'Were a lot of them injured?'

'Yes.'

'Including innocent civilians?'

Habibi hesitated as if nervous and he seemed unwilling to acknowledge the truth. Brahim was less squeamish.

'Marie, when it comes to freedom and getting rid of the colons, there's no such thing as an innocent.'

'If you say so, Brahim.'

'Of course, it was terrible that innocent people died,' agreed Habibi. 'But remember that the paras killed lots of innocents too. Neither side is without guilt.'

'But presumably the FLN were ultimately defeated?' I queried. I doubted very much that the revolutionaries would have enough fighters to hold out against crack French fighters.

'Yes and no. Yes, the FLN had to leave and regroup in the mountains outside the city. Their leader Yacef was captured but not before he'd caused a lot of trouble for the French, and he managed to get a lot of ordinary citizens to work for him.'

'Or he terrorised them so that they had to do it?' I suggested.

'Not completely, no. There were ordinary Muslim girls who offered to plant bombs for him.'

Judging from what I'd seen so far of the Muslim women in Paris, that was indeed amazing. Perhaps there was more to the position and character of women in Arab society than I had realised.

Habibi could almost read my mind. 'You've seen my wife, Marie. Maybe you just think she sits in the background and makes food? But she doesn't. She works in the factory too and helps us all financially. I might not always like it, but if we're ever going to leave this place,' – he gestured towards the opening and the little shack where his family of eight lived – 'we have to save some money.'

'I appreciate that life can't be easy for you here.'

'Life here is a lot easier than it would be in Algeria, I assure you.'

'How could it be harder than this?'

'The peasants in Algeria are the poorest of poor, Marie. If they work, their wages barely cover food and a roof over their heads and the French take what they can in taxes. They have very little land even in the villages and the earth is often poor and yields very little. It's a tough life.'

Silence again. I'd seen how some of the peasants lived in Indo China. To say that it was at subsistence level almost overstated the case.

Habibi continued, 'We try to send money back to our families of course but it's not so easy, now that the FLN are asking for our money too.'

I sat up straight on my stool in surprise.

'The FLN? Here?'

'Yes, of course. They're everywhere.'

'But how do they get into the country?'

'The main leaders are in Egypt and Malta. It's not the top people, who are all watched carefully by the French, but their underlings. They're sent over here to collect money.'

'For the people?'

Habibi laughed at my naivety. 'No, for their guns. You can't fight without guns and they're expensive. Also, you've got to feed the fighters who need to hole up in the mountains to defeat the French."

'And they come around here regularly?'

497

'Of course. Especially now it's Ramadan. We're supposed to give money to charity – it's our religious duty, so they make sure that we give it to the FLN.'

'Some charity!' I exclaimed.

'It depends on your point of view.'

'Would you like to meet one of the charity collectors?'

# Chapter Nine

I didn't have time to reply before a burly man hidden under his burnous appeared out of the crowd of men who were walking by. He went straight up to Habibi and Brahim and embraced them. As I might have expected, he ignored me completely but after an engrossing five minutes' conversation, Habibi turned in my direction and introduced me to the newcomer.

'Marie, this is Rahman, my brother-in-law. Rahman, Marie is Brahim's friend and a journalist.'

The eyes had what I learnt to be a characteristic Algerian look about them. How eyes can be warm, friendly, spontaneous and affectionate at the same time as being wary and distant, I don't know, but Rahman's managed it, and over the years I noticed it again and again in the Algerians I met. Somehow there was a battle going on between the law of hospitality, which was so important in Arab culture and the law of needing to be on the defensive and on guard against a possible enemy. Nowadays it reminds me of the terrain of Kabylia which I came to know so well – the warmth of the close-knit family behind the high-walled house and the prickly pear guardian of the village and the unforgiving, harsh terrain of the mountains against which the dwellings are set.

Rahman didn't even offer the habitual warm, first greeting.

'Journalist? Is this safe, Brahim?'

'Yes, Rahman. She's a friend. She can be trusted.'

Brahim's words appeared to be enough to satisfy him.

He held out both hands towards me. 'In that case, Marie, it is a pleasure to meet you.'

Again, I noticed the warmth of the gesture, but the wariness of the body behind it. I saw now that underneath the apparent chubbiness of Rahman's physique, there was a lean, action-hardened body.

'A pleasure for me too,' I said, rising from my stool. 'Yes, I am interested in what is happening to the Algerian community and how they relate to the situation in Algeria, but I'm not in the habit of betraying sources and being indiscreet. Besides,' I added, with half a smile, 'I've been schooled by Brahim here and I've heard all the arguments for independence.'

'No, Marie, you haven't. I need days to explain all those.' It was the first time I had heard Brahim laughing at himself.

'OK,' I replied, matching his tone, 'so I haven't heard them all, but I'm here to receive an education at Brahim's hands.'

'In that case,' replied Rahman genially, 'You're a very brave woman, because he doesn't let anyone go without first completely indoctrinating them.'

'I know. You wouldn't dare think anything else by the time he's finished with you and I've only heard him in the bars of the 10th.'

'Which newspaper do you work for, Marie?'

'Mainly it's Libération and its smaller satellites. But I'm a freelance so I also contribute to l'Humanité.'

'Well, they're mainly friendly to us, though they still don't really understand our position.'

'Does anyone?'

'Good point, Marie,' rejoined Habibi, laughing. 'Does anyone understand the Algerian mind?'

'Perhaps not.' Brahim responded in a more serious vein. 'But first and foremost, we need people to acknowledge that there is an Algerian mind.'

'Why?' I asked. 'Do some people doubt it?'

'Haven't you heard the famous saying by Abbas?'

'No. And who's Abbas?'

'The so-called moderate leader of the Algerians who said at one point after the Sétif massacre that there is no such thing as the Algerian nation.'

'Why would he say that?'

'Because he's the lackey of the French and wants to support integration.'

'And integration's not a possibility as far as you're concerned?' I asked innocently, aware that I would receive a torrent of words justifying national identity but wanting to hear them anyway.

Brahim did not disappoint me. 'Which nation on earth has ever wanted to remain under a different power? Did Gaul want to remain under the Romans or be part of Britain? Algeria wasn't a sophisticated nation state before the French came. They were part of the Ottoman empire for years, but that doesn't mean there weren't tribes of Kabyles and Arabs in the area for centuries and they ruled their own lives and destinies.'

'Fair enough. But you keep on referring to the Kabyles and Arabs as two separate peoples. Are there two separate nations there?' I had always been puzzled by these two names, and now was my opportunity to find the answer.

Habibi half smiled. 'Now you are on dangerous ground, Marie. If you start thinking that, you'll be further forward than any of us.'

I sensed that I had touched an important nerve here. 'So, tell me, what's the difference?'

'Who's going to answer her?' Habibi turned to the other two men, and, shrugging his shoulders, took on the task himself. 'You've got two Kabyles here, Marie, and one Arab, so it looks like I'm the spokesman. To sum it all up,' he grinned, as if anticipating a reaction, 'Kabyles are intelligent, strong, and great leaders. The Arabs are ignorant, followers, weaklings…' He didn't finish because he and Brahim were already scuffing on the ground, like excited schoolboys. They slowly got up, shaking the dust out of their clothes and laughing together.

'So, if you're so different,' I ventured slowly and more reflectively, 'how come you're working together?'

'We're working against the common enemy.'

'And is France always the common enemy?'

'Of course. They're the invaders.'

'OK. Got that. But are invaders always bad?'

'How could they not be?'

'You mentioned Gaul and the Romans before, but Rome gave a lot to Gaul. Civilised it.'

'Yes,' answered Rahman, suddenly coming back into the conversation, 'and that's part of the problem. France has done a lot of 'civilising' but that doesn't mean we couldn't have done the same for ourselves without them. It's also why France is so persuasive.'

'To whom?'

'To their own people of course, but to a lot of ours as well.'

'Ah, so you mean there are Algerians who support France?'

'Traitors,' interposed Brahim darkly.

'OK, traitors, my friend. But to be fair, reasonable traitors. They think de Gaulle can offer them a lot.'

'Ah now, de Gaulle!' Here I felt I was on safer territory. 'De Gaulle wants to offer freedom and equality to Algerians. Is that right?'

At this point Brahim muscled in on the discussion. I knew his views on de Gaulle already.

'He appears to be offering equality to everyone, but the reality is that it's an advantage to France, to the colons, especially the rich ones, and because that way he gets the Sahara too.'

'Sahara?' I was surprised. As far as I knew from watching films, the Sahara was all sand and Bedouins. 'Why would France be interested in the Sahara?'

'Because of the oil underneath it. It's potentially going to make Algeria a very rich country.'

'Do you think that's why de Gaulle wants to keep Algeria?'

'De Gaulle wants to keep Algeria because de Gaulle likes power and he resents anyone not wanting to have the benefits of his wonderful rule.'

I'd heard this point of view numerous times from all the left-wing côterie in Paris. Jean-Paul Sartre had famously said that he'd rather be under God's rule than de Gaulle's, which, as a convinced atheist, was quite an admission. My own private view was that, as we were facing endless strikes and changes of government in France, we needed someone who could sort us out. For some reason that I didn't understand, the working classes seemed to respond to Catholic, bourgeois, right-wing de Gaulle better than one of their own.

'The problem is,' added Brahim, somewhat more reflectively and less brashly than usual, 'that no one really knows what de Gaulle actually thinks. He tends to promise all things to all people. Also, he can't believe that all Algerians don't believe in the greatness of himself and of France. He has a sort of megalomania.'

'Better de Gaulle's megalomania than Stalin's or Ho Chi Min's,' I suggested.

'Better to have no one's megalomania.'

'You don't think there's such a character amongst the FLN revolutionaries?'

Habibi stopped for a moment before replying.

'The extraordinary thing is that it's a remarkably communal leadership and that's what makes it trustworthy.'

I didn't want to disillusion him. 'I hope you're right. But, back to what you're up to here in Paris.' The night was going on. Algerians never seemed to care about that especially in Ramadan, but I still liked my sleep.

I turned to Rahman. 'You're here to collect your dues. Is that right? You don't think that people here,' – my hand gestured to embrace the whole of the bidonville – 'are poor enough already?'

He returned my question with a look of complete assurance in the rightness of his view. 'No one's too poor to miss out on the privilege of supporting the revolution of their own country.'

'You mean to be squeezed to give even more money.'

'You don't think that that's better than paying taxes to your enemy?'

I didn't have an answer to that one.

# Chapter Ten

By 2am I was ready to faint from exhaustion and could not concentrate any longer on the complicated arguments, nor follow the switches from Arabic to French. Brahim walked me back to my rooms and then said 'goodnight'. I had a feeling that he had a whole other life, about which I knew nothing. After our visit to Bobigny, I could imagine him going back there night after night, exploring associations and political intrigues which were dark and dangerous. I was afraid of what I had unearthed in my visit with him, but it had also piqued my curiosity. For the first time, I had seen a judgment of my world – the world of France – about which I was completely ignorant.

Two days later, I went back to André with an article, about how the Communist Party in Paris didn't really understand anything about what was happening amongst their fellow communists in Algiers, and how neither group really understood what it was like to be a freedom fighter in Algeria. I wrote it from the perspective of 'Who is the true Marxist here?' and wrote about the many different points of view I had had suggested to me in Bobigny. I mentioned the revolutionary leaders in Egypt and what a different take on Marxism they had to the Russians and the Chinese and about how they were more interested in corporate leadership than any of the traditional Marxist countries were. As I had promised to Habibi and Rahman, I made it as positive a take as I could, and I gave away no guilty secrets. I wrote about how Algerian workers in Paris, despite their own poverty, wanted to support their brothers in the home country, and I spoke in a 'romantic' way about the David – the little man of Algeria – who was contending with the Goliath of France.

André seemed pleased. 'Good take, Marie. Well done. And I think there might be more coming out of this one?'

'You mean you want me to find out more?' To be honest, I had conflicting feelings about this. On the one hand my curiosity had been awakened, not just by the complexity of the political situation, but by the allure of this totally different civilisation. On the other hand, I sensed danger and suffering and I had had quite enough of that in Indo China.

André considered my question. 'Yes, but let's see how the situation develops.'

'You mean in Algeria?'

'Yes, but it's starting to affect us here too and I don't mean the FLN collecting their dues from the Algerian immigrants. There's more than that going on.'

'In what ways? You mean strikes?'

'No, I mean the whole de Gaulle thing. Now he's back in power, no one knows where he's going with it.'

It reminded me of what Brahim had said. No one really knows what de Gaulle wants, and he says different things to different people.

I was trying to find out what my editor wanted from me. 'How does that affect us here? I mean you seem to be implying that the average Parisian is likely to be affected too.'

'Well, they are already. There's a feeling of unrest. Haven't you noticed it, Marie?'

'Not really.' There's always unrest in the left-wing journalistic milieu, which makes it an edgy and exciting place to be, but I thought that the average Parisian just wanted to be left to get on with their lives.

André sighed. 'You're more out of touch than I realised, Marie.' Having recently heard a similar criticism from Brahim, I felt that my journalistic credentials were being challenged. 'Well, I don't want to be out of touch. In my experience, even in the German occupation, the average French man or woman wanted to be left alone. And actually, in any country, Vietnam included, the average citizen doesn't want extreme politics and revolution. They just want peace and a reasonable standard of living. I hate to say this to an ardent communist,' I added with some apology to André and his principles, 'but all my experience of life tells me that it's true.'

'It probably is,' admitted my editor, 'but that's only because the average member of the bourgeoisie doesn't know what's good for him and his country.'

'And you, the superior mortal, does?' I queried cynically. This sounded just like Brahim talking about Algeria.

'It's not about being superior. It's about being politically educated and having the whole picture – caring for the working classes and giving them freedom.'

'I suppose you're right,' I admitted reluctantly.

'There's no 'suppose', Marie,' replied my editor briskly. 'And I don't know why you're working for this paper, if you don't think that for yourself.'

Am I about to be sacked for my bourgeois views? I wondered. And do I really care? However, reality quickly took hold: I still needed to make a living.

'I admit that I have been a bit out of touch. So, what's happening on the streets then? Don't tell me that we're heading for revolution in Paris?'

'Who knows what will happen? On the face of it, it's the right-wing supporters of the colons, who are causing the trouble. On the other hand, any trouble brings ferment on the streets and makes people want a revolution.'

Perhaps, I thought to myself cynically. But the French are a lot better about talking about revolution than they are about doing it. Then, I thought, that wasn't true in 1789 or in 1871. Wake up, Marie This might be the greatest opportunity for your career to go forward.

'How about if I leave the Algerians alone for a while, and go and see the Parti Communiste in the Renault factory and get their take on the whole thing?' I shivered. The PC of France seemed likely to be more predictable than the Algerians in Bobigny.

'Excellent idea. You get what you can out of them, Marie. We need to be keeping up with opinion on the street.'

'Don't you think, Monsieur le Chef, we need to be creating opinion on the street?' I challenged tartly. We had a good enough relationship together for him to grin at my gibe.

'Touché. Get going, Marie.'

And so, off I went to the Communist party and trade union headquarters of Renault. I should have visited long ago, I told myself. The offices of the trade union were in chaos – people coming and going, talking about walkouts and wage increases and bubbling along under the surface with discontent. The Communist Party headquarters was an entirely different matter –disorganised but cold, not really 'engaged' with what was going on in the city, I judged.

It was when I was deciding which one to follow that I had an unexpectedly lucky break.

# Chapter Eleven

I waited for some time in the dusty, disorganised office of the Parti Communiste de France. I don't know if Lenin or Mao's offices were disorganised, and I know that tidiness does not have to be a hall mark of revolutionary greatness, but I couldn't help feeling, during the ten minutes when I stood in that office alone, that this was not the disorganisation of too much fervent action, but the disorganisation of people who were not prepared to put their lives at risk for what they were doing. As a visiting journalist I was not charmed or offered coffee, which I did not expect from the communist party headquarters, but neither was I elbowed to one side by those who had too many pressing engagements. I felt disillusioned and cynical. This place, I concluded, was not at the nerve centre of any important movement.

I was so deep in thought, that I hardly noticed when the door was pushed open and a man approached me.

'I can't believe it! Marie!' I looked up at this enthusiastic utterance of my name.

'Patrice? Oh Patrice!'

I forgot all my annoyance at the state of the office and rushed to embrace him.

'I can hardly believe it. I've heard of you of course – all the reporting you did from Indo China. You've become quite famous. But I never expected to see you here.'

I ignored all the compliments because I was so happy to see my fellow Resistance worker again.

'Patrice, fancy you, working in the party headquarters in Paris rather than in Bordeaux. You must have done well for yourself.'

'Yes, well.' He looked at me hesitantly. 'I do sometimes wonder whether it was a good move.'

'Surely it must have been a big promotion for you. I knew you were an ardent trade unionist of course, but not that you were any more than a member of the Communist Party.'

'Sometimes I think that I might have done more good staying in Bordeaux, and Cecile misses Les Landes.'

'Cecile!' I exclaimed, remembering the girl who sat next to me in school. 'How is she?'

'Fine and fully occupied with our three sons.'

'No! Three already?'

'It's been nine years since we were married, you know. Time enough to have three sons.'

Briefly I envied him. Nine years spent establishing a family and his future inheritance, while I had wandered round the world, reporting for obscure newspapers.'

'You must come and see us.'

'I'd love to.' If only to hear the news from Les Landes, I thought.

'And I assume you didn't come here just to see me.?'

'To be honest, no. I didn't even know that you were here.'

'So, why have you come?'

'As a journalist, I want the whole take on the French Communist Party's view of Algeria and the coming referendum.'

Patrice straightened up and laughed.

'Is that all?'

'I know, I know! I want it all bottled and distilled in a half hour's interview so I can get it back to my paper. Typical journalistic nerve!'

I was impressed. Patrice had always been sincere and brave. That had been proved in his war time work, but I still remembered him as the rather dogged and intellectually uncurious classmate in my school. Definitely not up to my high standards! But the quality of his humour and comments just now suggested that he had changed. Less tunnel vision, less assumption of only one point of view. Humour, I found, always shows what is going on in the mind underneath the talk.

Patrice looked at his watch. 'I have to admit that I'm expected at the Renault factory in half an hour. The strike's quite a serious one economically, as well as politically. How about if I pass you over to one of my assistants now? You'll get all the official Parti Communiste stuff and then how about coming over to eat at our place towards the end of the week?'

'I'd love that. But don't you have to check with Cecile first?'

He grinned. 'Cecile loves to cook for other people, and she doesn't get too many opportunities here in Paris to do the 'landaises' specialities.'

'Well, as the daughter of a true Landais small-holding farmer, I'm hardly going to say 'no' to those.'

'And it will be lovely to hear more of what you're up to at the moment,' he added with genuine friendliness.

'I hardly know what I'm up to myself at the moment,' I admitted. 'More like, just pushing against a few doors. But I would be interested to know what you have to say about the current situation as well.'

'Great. We'll make it Friday evening and, if Cecile wants to put it off to another date, I'll be in touch.'

And so, in a matter of ten minutes, I had my interview with Patrice's assistant, a Michel Ronson, sorted and the prospect of a social and political encounter for the end of the week.

Michel Ronson was young, earnest and dealt with facts, not imagination. The Communist Party in France was in league with its brothers and sisters all over the world, he assured me, and that meant the Algerian Communist Party too. The French government had oppressed and exploited workers who were French Algerians and the party in Paris supported their comrades' desire for better working conditions and equal pay against the Capitalist bullies.

'But how does that fit in with the FLN who are also Marxists but want to get rid of the French colons? Which part of the brotherhood do you support in that case?'

M. Ronson was having no such complications. We cannot support offshoots. 'We have to know what the official communist party in Algeria wants and go with that. Otherwise there would be chaos.'

Alright, I thought. We have two alternatives here. On the one hand you have individuality and chaos if you support the FLN against the

PCA. On the other hand, you have ignorance of what the real workers or peasants of the country need and want, if you ignore what the FLN are trying to do.

As I had so often discovered in Russia in the late 1940s, justice is never two straight alternatives. Justice is messy and I couldn't help thinking that, the more I heard about Algeria, the more it appeared to be a very messy situation.

I wasn't quite sure how much Patrice would be up for 'messiness', but I was pleasantly surprised by his much more nuanced understanding of the situation than the one held by his assistant.

I was both excited and apprehensive about meeting him and Cecile together in their home, but I was impressed by his growth of political understanding. He had managed to secure a pleasant house in a quiet arrondissement of Paris, which was neither fashionable nor very poor. Cecile was affectionate and straightforward. My guess was that she felt that she had done so much better out of life than I had, though I did wonder what had happened to her Catholic upbringing. She had a house, a husband and three children to show as products of her industry in the last ten years. In comparison, I had a few travels, a few articles and my personal freedom – not a whole load of booty as far as a traditional 'Landaise' was concerned.

She had been kind enough to produce a genuine 'repas landais', complete with foie de gras paté, and I enjoyed eating it in such a relaxed atmosphere. When I said the customary, 'J'ai très bien mangé, merci,' it was much more than a polite formula.

What I really wanted to know from Patrice was, what the Communist Party made of de Gaulle and his proposed referendum in the coming September of that year. He was quite clear in his response.

'We're not backing it.'

'Because you don't like it, or you don't like de Gaulle?'

'Both. De Gaulle is the puppet of the right wing.'

'I can't honestly see de Gaulle as the puppet of anyone.'

'I agree that he's his own man, but the right wingers are using him to get what they want in Algeria.'

'And is he going to give them what they want in Algeria?'

'Who knows? But they trust him.'

'Yes, but that might be a bad thing for them. He's a wily old bird.'

'Exactly… and wily old birds go off in unexpected directions.'

'OK. So, like most communists I've met, you don't like de Gaulle. But what about the referendum? Isn't that a good idea?'

'I don't know. The rich are the ones likely to be voting and getting their own way.'

'Possibly,' I agreed. 'It's always true that the rich tend to get their own way in politics.' But everyone, not just in Algeria, but all over French West Africa, have got a chance to have their say. And, if you don't back the idea of the referendum, all that will happen is that the poor definitely won't have a say.'

Cecile had come in from clearing the table and making sure that the boys were ready to sleep. 'All I can say, Marie, is that you haven't changed much from the days of being round the fire at the school in St. Paul.'

I laughed. 'I didn't know that I had a view on the Algerian situation in those days.'

'No, I didn't mean that. I mean that you were always so complicated. Always wanting to argue everything in every little detail.'

'How else do you get at the truth?' I asked, amused but also bemused by her observations.

'But why does the truth always have to be so uncomfortable?' she asked, pouring out the after-dinner coffee.

'Don't ask me. Ask God. That's how human beings seem to have been made.'

'Don't introduce the idea of God here' she warned me. 'I still go to church. I find it comforting but Patrice doesn't approve.'

'Well, that's the standard view of a communist,' I reasoned. 'But you know, Cecile, Patrice may not like God, but he likes you and will let you do anything that makes you happy.'

'I know. I'm lucky.'

'And,' added Patrice, 'Talking about religion, which, of course, you weren't, have you kept up with the Jews connected with your friend, Alain?'

'No. I've had no reason to.'

'They also have something to say about the Algerian situation.'

'How come? I thought they were all Muslims out there?'

'Not at all. There's a whole load of Jews in Algeria, just as there's a whole load of them in the communist party here in Paris.'

'Ah, well now,' I suggested carefully, 'if you're talking about making arguments complicated…'

'Yes,' joined in Cecile, unexpectedly. 'You and Alain were always the most complicated talkers in the world.'

'You know, Marie, you should really talk to some of them about it. And Germaine Tillion.'

'Tillion? Wasn't she in the Musée de l'Homme Resistance movement?'

'The very same. But she's also an expert on Algeria. She's an anthropologist and, she knows all about the politics there.'

'You have her address?'

'I can get it for you.'

# Chapter Twelve

Germaine Tillion! A heroine! A major player in the Resistance movement in Paris! I knew that she was an intellectual and professor – that was intimidating enough! No, not so much intimidating as totally beyond my reach. A woman in far-away space, part of another universe. Of course, she came from an intellectual family. Of course, she had money in her background and, more than money – aspirations and ambition. But that didn't negate the fact that most women of her background were bourgeois mamans in the suburbs, and, if they were single, they were mainly secretaries in family run firms. Germaine Tillion had had more courage than most in the days of the Occupation. She had worked with the famous Musée de l'Homme network. Alongside Agnès Humbert, she had been one of the few women in the group to help British airmen to escape and she had provided false identities for many people, including Jews, to escape the Nazis. The men who were on the staff of this prestigious Parisian institute were specialists in their own fields of study. People like Boris Vilde and Anatole Lewitsky were all executed by the Nazis in February 1942. Word had got through to the Resistance in Bordeaux about their stand. Agnès Humbert and Germaine Tillion had both been sent to the concentration camp at Ravensbruck, where they had suffered appalling conditions but had survived the war.

What I didn't know, because I had been so out of touch recently, was the part which Germaine Tillion had played in Algeria in the last two years. As I learnt more from asking around various journalist friends, it made me more and more in awe of her. Before the war, she had travelled to Algeria, a single woman in a conservative Muslim society and in a place, where the standard of living, was primitive to say the least. She had been living amongst the Chaoui, a minority people, even less numerous than the Kabyles, in the Aurès mountains. There she had chartered their way of life and championed the needs of the people with the French government. Even living there as a single European woman would have been an enormous challenge. Then came her work in the war. As a teenager I had played a small part in the Resistance on the west coast of France, but I was under no illusions that I in any way ran the same risks as a member of a prominent team of resistance workers in the capital right under the noses of the Nazis. Like so many other women of her social status, she could have got on quietly with her academic life and not drawn attention to herself. That she willingly sacrificed her family connections and her academic reputation to support the Free French in their unequal and seemingly hopeless battle against the enemy was an extraordinary act of individual courage.

Go to see Germaine Tillion and arrange an interview with her! What a nerve! But what an opportunity for a jobbing journalist without much formal education like myself. First, I needed the agreement of my editor.

'Yes, of course she's famous. But what exactly has this to do with the Communist Party and our readers?' he enquired in a matter of fact way, less full of nostalgic idealism than myself.

'To be honest, André, I'm not entirely sure,' I admitted. 'But Patrice at the Parti Communiste recommended me trying. I've got some good information from him but the whole thing is a lot more complicated than I expected.'

'It would be if you're after it, Marie.'

'Oh no, you're reminding me of Cecile,' I began. 'Never mind,' I added as my editor looked at me in a questioning way, 'It's just something it reminded me of from my childhood. But,' I countered robustly, 'we do have to assume that our readers have brains too. They don't just want to tow the party line.'

'Want a bet?'

'In that case, I'm working for the wrong newspaper.'

'OK. OK,' he conceded grudgingly, 'you want a journalist pass to see Mme Tillion? I'll sort it.'

And so it was, that I found myself approaching the rather elegant house, in the fashionable arrondissement, where the Tillion family lived. If Cecile lived here, I thought, she would know that she had arrived, and would probably never want to move again. Not so Mme Tillion.

André had done his preparatory work well and I found myself being led into a small study, covered with papers and maps. I felt extremely nervous.

'Ah yes Mlle Marie from Le Coq isn't it? Yes, do come in. You look surprised by all my papers. I chose the smallest room in the house for my study because once it's completely full, I have to tidy it.'

'I thought you might… perhaps you might have …' I stammered.

'A maid? That's for my parents, not for me. I prefer to rely on myself. Now do sit down, Mlle. I was surprised to have a request from le Coq, but, when I saw your name, I remembered the reports from Indo China.'

'You read them?'

'Of course. I always keep up with l'Humanité , and Le Coq and Libération from time to time, depending on who's writing. And, of course, le Figaro.'

'And the Echo d'Alger?' I added, trying to show my knowledge of the Algerian French newspapers.

'Mmm. Don't remind me. They unfortunately have more money than sense, though I do like Sévigny, despite him being like a dinosaur, unwilling to look at the twentieth century. But he does know his wines.'

'His wines?' I repeated, confused. 'What has that to do with an Algerian newspaper?'

'My dear, more than you can possibly imagine. I hope you're not just filled with the political nonsense of l'Humanité . No, of course you're not. I've read your articles from Indo China and I have to say that I liked their breadth of argument.'

I stumbled to reply, feeling deeply flattered, but aware that I was dealing with a shrewd and incisive brain here.

'Could I ask you, Mme Tillion to tell me all about your time in the Aurès after the war?'

'All about what? Are we talking living conditions or culture or religion or connecting with the revolutionaries?'

'I guess, any of them you'd like to tell me about. But really, if I'm honest, anything that's relevant to the present situation.'

We settled down with the tea she had ordered, brought in and served in a beautiful cup and saucer.

'If you ask an ethnologist to talk about 'anything you like', that's usually a dangerous carte blanche. But you're right to think that almost anything has to do with the present situation.'

'How did you survive all that time alone in the Aurès mountains?'

She let out a short, sharp bark of a laugh. 'Probably a whole load better than if I had been living with another French person to quarrel with.'

'Were you never afraid?'

'Never! Lonely? Yes. In total culture shock? Yes. Missing my creature comforts? Not often but sometimes. But afraid? No.'

'That's not what we're hearing at the moment about the wild regions of the Aurès and Kabylia.'

'To set you right here, the Aurès and Kabylia are actually very different. And just because it's wild and people live on subsistence farming in the villages and their religion is totally alien to ours, doesn't make the people 'wild' in the sense of being unpredictable or cruel.'

'So, the reports aren't true?'

'It rather depends who the reports are coming from. And if the people are seen as 'wild' it's a reaction to what has been done to them.'

'So, you're a supporter of the FLN?'

She paused before replying.

'I wouldn't say I'm a supporter of the FLN. I'd say I'm a sympathiser of the FLN.'

'So, why aren't you a supporter?'

'Because they've ditched the moderates, because they've divided opinion amongst the felllahins, the peasants and because they resort to unbelievable barbarity. I'm not talking against the French now. I'm talking about their own people.'

'In that case, why do you say you are a sympathiser?'

'Because the French have been so intransigent and stupid. Because they've refused to treat them like grown-up human beings, even though so many of them fought for France in the war. Because they're so damn selfish.'

'All of them?'

'Most of them. They can't see what's happening. Now the petits colons, fair enough, but the rich colons? They should have had more sense.'

'But they're the ones with the most to lose,' I suggested.

'That's right, my dear. They have a lot to lose, but they're going to lose it anyway, so they shouldn't be so stupid for their own sake, quite apart from the notion of helping the lot of their fellow human beings.'

'So, do you support the de Gaulle referendum?'

'Yes, of course I do and it's a reasonable one.'

'You don't think it's all an ego drive for de Gaulle?'

'Of course, it's an ego drive for de Gaulle, but that doesn't mean he's not making a good judgment.'

'How do you think the Algerians will respond?'

'It's not just about the Algerians you know. It's about the whole of French West Africa.'

'True, but most people care about the Algerian situation, not the Guinea situation.'

'Of course. Just as well, because Séchy is going to get everyone to say 'no' there.'

'And can't the FLN manoeuvre the same thing?'

'They wish. It would be easy if they could, but some Algerians want to be part of France and are not afraid to say so.'

'So, if it's a 'oui', will they be happy to be linked to France?'

'Very much so, especially if de Gaulle finally puts my recommendations in place.'

'Your recommendations?' I hadn't been aware that she was so influential politically.

'It's actually common sense for anyone who's lived in Algeria. They should have done it years ago. Unfortunately, it's probably now too late.'

'Too late for what?'

Mme Tillion looked at me seriously. 'Too late to avoid a civil war.'

'What? Here in France?'

'Yes. At the worst count. Hopefully not, but certainly a civil war in Algeria.'

'And how do you think the PCF will react to that?'

518

She scoffed. 'As they always do. Too rigidly and too late. They love the party line, not the people.'

'So, what would you advise them to do?'

'Stop being blinkered and meet real Algerians, not just the petits colons.'

'I have begun to meet a few of them in Paris,' I ventured cautiously.

'Good. But make sure you don't meet one sort only.'

'So how many sorts are there?'

'Let's see now.' Germaine held out the fingers of one hand. 'There's the Algerians who fought with France in the war and are still loyal to them; there's the intellectuals who have benefitted from French education and are like-minded; there's the independence people who are moderate and not Marxist; there's the people who support assimilation; there's the FLN diehards; there's the Jews who've been there for hundreds of years and support Muslim independence, there's the Jews who want to get back to France; there's the Algerians who don't care what it is as long as they are left in peace.

Is that enough sorts for you?'

# Chapter Thirteen

Enough differences to be going on with, I thought to myself, as I went over the categories in my mind. That's eight viewpoints on the subject and that doesn't include the differences between the Kabyles and the Arabs, which is an ongoing unease. Nor does it include the division of opinion among the pied noirs. Are there any pied noirs who support the FLN ? I had asked Germaine. Apparently, yes, a small minority. 'They tend to be thinkers and intellectuals,' she suggested.

'Like you?'

'Maybe like me, but of course I'm not a pied noir – never have been, thank God.'

'Why 'thank God'? Surely you love Algeria?'

'I do, but I'm only a respectful, admiring visitor, however many reports I might make for the government. And in the end, it won't need to be a choice between choosing my home or choosing my country.'

'Will it come to that do you think?' Despite the many arguments I'd heard from Rahman and Habibi, I was still shocked. No one in Paris could accept the fact that it wouldn't be Algérie Française for ever, however many U turns de Gaulle made.

'Of course, it will come to that.' Germaine Tillion was a decisive person who understood the world she lived in as few of her countrymen did in 1958. 'No question of it. The only question is 'how will it come?' and my prayer is 'as painlessly as possible.' She paused – 'especially for the Algerians.'

'You think they will suffer?'

'They're already suffering immeasurably.'

'So, it won't be solved by a 'oui' vote in the referendum?'

'No. In that case the suffering will be shelved, and the French will convince themselves that they have the answer.'

'But you don't think that they do?'

'Marie, look at what happened in Indo China. You were there. Is it solved even now with the Americans becoming involved as well as the French?'

I felt sick at heart. I had seen some of the suffering first-hand and the thought that it might continue and spread to another country was depressing.

Germaine Tillion had advised me to meet as many different representatives of the Algerian conundrum in France, as I could. She also told me that I needed to go over there and see for myself.

I felt that I was not quite ready to take that momentous step of leaving France for a war-torn colony, but I knew in my heart that she was right. If I was going to write truthful and challenging articles on this subject, then that journey would be necessary. In journalism it's impossible to stay on the side-lines.

However, I did take her first piece of advice, which was emotionally acceptable to me and financially acceptable to my editor. I kept in touch with Brahim, went back to visit Habibi and his family and was introduced to other FLN supporters in Paris. I continued to visit Patrice and Cecile, partly for the joy of being in touch with childhood friends, and partly because Patrice was so good at telling me what was happening in the Parti Communiste in Paris and the state of the strikes in France.

That summer of 1958 we lurched on rather ignorantly towards de Gaulle's referendum, which we were assured from on high would solve all the problems of Francophone Africa in one go. All of us in France wanted to believe it.

There was no point going to Algeria while there was such ferment in the air nearer home and while l'Humanité and le Figaro had its permanent reporters in Algeria. My papers were not sufficiently rich or important to justify an overseas assignment.

Often in my mind I went over the categories of Algerians which Germaine had suggested to me. Who had I not met? Whose point of view did I not understand! De Gaulle assured us that there were many who supported assimilation, but I could find no sign of them in Paris. And the Jews – what were they doing there? And what was their point of view?

One day in late August, I felt exhausted with the Parisian heat and realised that anyone who could, had left the city for their 'grandes vacances'. Don't bother brewing a revolution in Paris in August, I thought. No one would be here to support it. For all the talk of France's history of revolution, in the summer we are far too busy sunning ourselves on the Atlantic and Mediterranean coasts. And that thought sparked my next move. Why not go back home to Les Landes for a few days and see whether I could find the Jewish community in Bordeaux?

I have to admit that I never relished the thought of going home to see my parents. They didn't understand what I was doing and were puzzled and sad that their only daughter could not settle down and produce some grandchildren. I could see their point of view, but such a rôle had no appeal for me and, what was more, I knew of no one with whom I wanted to settle down. Whenever I returned to St. Paul that sort of discussion was avoided by myself at all costs. Even though we had little in common, they were still my parents and it upset me to see their lined and disappointed faces. My father kept out of the house more and more and found his escape in the forests of Les Landes as he had always done, but my mother battled on with the small holding, increasingly crippled by arthritis and with no other joys to make life worth living. It was a depressing place to be. I enjoyed seeing Thérèse and Mlle Tessier, but even these had become perfunctory meetings because our worlds did not touch each other.

Now, as a result of my conversation with Germaine Tillion, I went to Bordeaux and sought out the synagogue – an imposing building, which had amazingly been left intact by the Nazis, even though at that point, all of its life had been removed. Most of the Jewish population of Bordeaux had either escaped to safety over the border with Spain or had been destroyed by the terrible forced journeys to the concentration camps.

Nevertheless, on a Shabbat evening in 1958, the synagogue was open, and I found myself in the women's gallery. Up till then my own Jewish religious experience had been in Birobidzhan in Russia in the late 1940s, but this was entirely different. These were old people who were hanging on. There was no possible revival of their religion, not because it had been banned but because even their own people seemed apathetic. Younger people who had survived the Holocaust wanted to be 'assimilated' into main-stream French culture and society. That word 'assimilated' I thought. De Gaulle loves it. Is it going to work for the Algerians? Not if the experience of the Jews is anything to go by, I felt. It was in the war that assimilated French Jews were most in danger. They had never thought that anything bad could happen to them. They had taken no precautions against the Nazi evil.

One result of so few people being there was that it was easy to talk to them. Once I mentioned my connection with Alain and his aunt and uncle, smiles and handshakes broke out. It was truly lovely to meet people who remembered Alain when he had been at the lycée in the final year before the Occupation had driven everyone into hiding. The loss of Alain meant nothing to them personally apart from regret. Why should it, I reflected later. They had lost so many that one barely known teenager had not affected their lives. They were numbed by grief and an exhausted sense of horror as they recalled those terrible years of persecution.

'And other people are still benefitting from our persecution', one sad-faced lady told me.

'What do you mean? I asked intrigued. I had heard such accusations in Paris but not in my homeland.

'You mentioned your friend, Alain, and his family? Well, some of their betrayers got the farmhouse.'

'How do you know? Which betrayers?' This brought all sorts of confused emotions to my mind.

'You must have heard about Chanel and her seamstresses at The Woolsack!'

'Of course. Everyone knows they worked there with the aristocrats before the war.'

'But you probably didn't know that two of the seamstresses colluded with one of your men from Mimizan. They told the Germans about Alain's family and then inherited the farmhouse.'

523

I was angry and sad about this news. Sad to find out that one of the customers from the Hôtel du Centre might have done this; angry that two people had profited from the death of my friend's family: but aware too that revenge in Paris had done little good and was unlikely to do so here.

It didn't help me to hear such news. Nor did members of the synagogue have much to tell me about the Algerian Jews and they did not want to consider another place of conflict and possible persecution. They were just managing to survive where they were. However, they did point me in the direction of more information – Marseille. Why had I not thought of that before for myself? It was clearly the nearest point of mainland France to Algeria and the point of embarkation to Israel, as I had discovered several years before.

# Chapter Fourteen

As always, I enjoyed my journey down to Marseille. If you stop thinking that you have to get there in a hurry and settle down to enjoying the company of your fellow passengers and the changing scenery of France, the train journey south is a great means of collecting your thoughts professionally and of considering more broadly what you consider the purpose of your life to be.

The last time I had made the same journey, I was a very inexperienced journalist, trying to get in on the action of young socialist Jews going to Israel. I had no idea what had happened to my two protegées since then, but they had taken on Palestine and now had their own country. On that trip I had stayed at a little, evil smelling pension in the Vieux Port. Now my expense account allowed me something much better, but I wanted to relive the experience and I had a strange feeling that my earlier success in interviewing the Jews on that boat would bring me luck with my present assignment. Therefore, complete with my named contacts I had been given in Bordeaux, I set off for the schul on Friday evening. I anticipated that I would be the only person in the Vieux Port carrying out my religious duties, but I was wrong. There were some old women, dressed in black, climbing up to Notre Dame de la Garde and there were also some Muslims dressed in summer djebella heading towards a mosque in a converted garage a few streets away. Religious centres are the places you need to be at to get real information, I thought.

The schul in Marseille was much fuller than the one in Bordeaux and I remembered to dress modestly and as smartly as I knew how so that I would not look too out of place. There were young women in the gallery and we soon started chatting. When they found out that I knew Jews in Bordeaux, two of the girls invited me to join in their family shabbat meal.

Michelle and Yvonne were sisters of about 16 and 18 years old, who lived with their parents in Aubagne, just to the north of the main town. They seemed like typically carefree, modern girls but I knew that their parents must have a story to tell.

As I shook out the beautifully laundered napkin at the start of our meal later that evening, I ventured,

'Did you live here in Aubagne throughout the war, sir?'

Monsieur Tribier, the father of the two girls was cautious in his reply and I appreciated his hesitation. Ten years after the war, there were still currents of antisemitism in France, as well as guilt for what France had allowed to happen to the Jews. Ironically, this guilt had often led to further antagonism towards them, even though the Jews I had seen in Bordeaux were so cowed that they had not protested about obvious acts of betrayal like the seizing of Alain's family small holding. Here, on the sparse hills of Provence in the drought of early August, they seemed a particularly isolated people. As I posed the question as the mid-evening shadows of Shabbat lengthened, I could hear that familiar southern French sound, the cicadas chirping insistently through the open window. I explained how my contacts with the Jews in Bordeaux had come about and this made M. Tribier more at ease.

'We were fortunate, Mademoiselle. My parents lived in Algeria in the 'bled' for many years. It was where I was brought up, so, with our young family, we had somewhere to stay. Marseille, being part of the unoccupied territories, didn't suffer as badly as Bordeaux but, in the last few months of the war, there were terrible round ups here too. There is now only a skeleton of the Orthodox Jewish community left.'

In response, I explained about my contacts with Jewish young people in the camps at Gur.

'If you have rescued some of our people, Mademoiselle, you are doubly welcome here.'

On one side of the table, I could see Michelle and Yvonne looking impatient. They had been too young to remember the terrors and they wanted an ordinary life and fun with young people of their own age. M. Tribier looked lovingly at his fun-loving daughters.

'Michelle and Yvonne are bored by all the talk about the war, but we can never forget what happened to our co-religionists here.'

'Of course not,' I replied soothingly, 'but did you manage to escape before the Occupation?'

'Yes, it was relatively easy to do so because I was born and brought up in Algeria, not far from Constantine, and my parents still had a home for us to go to. I was doing well in the wine business and I had bought this house when it was a wreck of a place and very cheap, a couple of years before the Occupation.'

I looked around at the elegant open windows and beautiful furnishings and silver cutlery.

'It's anything but a wreck of a place now, Monsieur. It's beautiful. You must have worked hard to make it like this.'

'Thank you. We did, especially my dear wife.' He nodded affectionately towards the small and self-effacing woman who was busying herself bringing in the next course of the meal. 'Fortunately, I also had plenty of contacts in Algeria so, although we were limited in our exports, we could sell to the French in Algeria and even take it south to Dakar, as well as selling to the military of course. Churchill did us a favour by basing his troops in Algeria in order to retake France and Italy from the South.'

'But you still decided to come to France after the war?'

'Yes, we thought long and hard about it, but, after Sétif, we had our warning, and we are naturally very nervous about any sign of persecution.'

'Persecution?' I was fully alert now, the relaxed atmosphere of after-dinner chat suddenly receding. 'How could the Jews be persecuted in Algeria? Surely it's the French who are in trouble there?'

'Yes, but we're linked with the French colons in the minds of the Algerians.'

He paused while his wife placed some wonderful meringue desert on the table which looked light and soothing in this hot weather. The civilised exchange of opinions in this elegant room seemed far from the possibility of persecution. But I had heard Alain tell me long ago how the

527

Jews of Bordeaux had clung to their elegant, historic houses in that most sophisticated of French cities, while death waited for them.

'I fear, Mademoiselle, that after the war-years, Jews will never feel safe again. And Sétif was my wake-up call.'

'Yes, I've heard about Sétif, but I don't see how that affected the Jews.'

'It didn't affect them immediately especially as most of the Jews in the east of the country round Constantine, have supported the Algerian independence movement.'

'So, what's the problem?'

'The problem is, Mademoiselle, that where there is division and increasing hatred amongst people, Jews tend to get caught up in it and are hated by both sides.'

'You don't think that's all a bit neurotic on your part? Not persecution but a persecution complex?'

Michelle, his sixteen-year old daughter, nodded across the table. 'I completely agree with you, Marie. Papa's always looking on the bad side of things and worrying about how we might get treated at the lycée.'

'Being unpopular here in France is not part of your experience?'

In reply Michelle giggled and tossed her ponytail of brown curls. She had the beautiful young person's complete confidence in her own ability to succeed in life.

'Young people here accept us for who we are. We listen to the same music and follow the same fashion as they do.'

At the head of the table M Tribier grimaced a little.

'And it's not always to your father's approval?' I guessed out aloud.

'Papa is so old fashioned!' Her father smiled affectionately back at her. He might worry for their safety, but his daughters could do no wrong in his eyes.

'So why did Sétif make you nervous if you basically support the independence movement?'

'It wasn't what the Algerians did or didn't do. It was the French reaction. They went completely mad.'

'A hundred killed, I read in 'Figaro?'

'I think that was an understatement, Mademoiselle. Some people think it was several hundred. But the point is, it turned everything ugly. It turned the moderate nationalists into extremists.'

'You mean supporters of the FLN?'

'Yes, and it's not stopped since. I still go over to Algeria regularly for business and everyone is nervous, even the most complacent people, even the rich colons who are wine growers.'

'And how will this affect the Jews?'

'It will affect everyone, and the Jews are in the middle of it. As I said, many of them have always supported the rights of the Muslim population, but the Algerians are also jealous of the Jews.'

'I think I've heard that somewhere before in Europe,' I commented sarcastically.'

'Yes, I know. That's what they said in Germany before the war but in Algeria, the nationals have actually got a reason to be jealous.'

'Why? Prosperity? Success?'

'No, more than that. In 1873 there was something called the Cremieux decrees. They were made in Constantine. They said that Jews not Muslims could become full citizens of France. They didn't have to convert to be accepted as the Muslims did.'

'Oh, wow! That does sound pretty unfair.'

'Definitely. But it's not the fault of the Jews. There's trouble brewing now and I'd rather live over here or, probably, the best of all, Israel.'

'Oh Papa!' Michelle wrinkled up her nose. 'Please, oh please, don't take us there.'

A somewhat different reaction to that of the young people I had met at the end of the war, I thought.

'What's wrong with Israel?' I asked her. 'Most Jewish young people I've met want to go there.'

'How terrible! Imagine all those swamps and mosquitoes and fighting the Palestinians.'

M. Tribier laughed. 'You see, my daughters were not made for the pioneer life.'

Then he added more seriously,

'But if you want to know what's happening in Algeria, Mademoiselle, you need to go and see it first-hand and don't be fooled by the referendum. I fear that it's too late for such an easy solution.'

# Chapter Fifteen

I was beginning to feel excited and nervous about what was happening in Algeria, but I knew that M. Tribier was right. I had to go there and see for myself. Who to stay with? I was in touch with one of my colleagues from l'Humanité who was monitoring the situation, but I felt instinctively that staying in a hotel in Algiers with other journalists was not going to be the answer. I decided that I should stick with the people I knew best – the Jews – and now in Marseille I had been given an excellent link with M. Tribier's wine exporting business in the country just to the north of Constantine. Perhaps I would get a different perspective on the situation through the Jewish community there?

My editor was not so sure. 'Why go to all the expense of that journey, when there's a referendum about to take place and on our doorstep and any number of Algerians in Paris?' he asked reasonably.

'I know, I know, but somehow I've just got this feeling that this link is going to give me a handle on the situation. I can't explain why.'

'And why the Jews? Honestly, Marie, you're obsessed with them. What about all that stuff with the Paris Communist Party and Birobidzhan? Not exactly a hell-raiser was it? I never understood why Hervé let you do it.'

'Because he let me follow my nose. And it turned out very well for the paper at the time.'

There was some truth in this. Post-war Paris had had an entirely different take on the post-war Jewish and Communist situation as a result.

André grumbled, talked about the budget, went to his editor's meetings, raised more objections, but the whole of Paris was stifling, not just through the heat of summer but through the inertia of waiting for the referendum. De Gaulle was convinced he had the answer and Parisians wanted to believe him. Some of the right-wingers were uneasy about the vocabulary which de Gaulle was using – assimilation, equal status, new Muslim rights, but no one could really do anything until the referendum had taken place. De Gaulle clearly believed that all the Muslims were beguiled by his charm. The generals in Algiers were a bit more circumspect.

A week later I was summoned to the office. 'The management have said 'yes' but they want a 'workers' perspective' throughout.'

I was happy with this idea. You can interpret 'worker' in all sorts of ways and at least I didn't have to stick with the Parti Comuniste all the time. I had an expense account. I wired the Entreprise Gaullen where M. Tribier had contacts. I asked for opportunities to visit the workers in the vineyard and the surrounding villages. I booked my boat over to Algiers, and I left Paris, energised by the thought of reporting on a little-understood situation.

The boat over was beautiful, in pristine condition, French controlled but with areas reserved for Algerians (not citizens of France) and Europeanized Algerians, assimilated citizens, in separate parts of the boat. When not sleeping or eating, I wandered freely between the three areas. The French area was exactly how you would expect it to be. We might have been on a French cruise ship with dancing continuing far into the night. The non-citizen Algerian area didn't reveal very much. It was not French-speaking and I didn't have much of a feel for what was going on. It felt like the first time I had been in Bobigny. The second sector felt different to both. It was mainly reserved for the tirailleurs who had fought for the French against the Nazis. There was quite a large number of military personnel going home after the holidays and I felt that these people had been at one with me in fighting against the Occupation. I felt they should be my friends. Some of them had their families with them and I soon found it was not so easy to break into these close-knit groups.

On the second night I was drinking my apéritif, while standing at the rail on deck, for all the world like a fashionable society woman with her cocktail, rather than a jobbing journalist. I thought how much pleasanter this was than being in Indo China. Even getting there on the aircraft carriers had seemed like a military exercise as well as being doom-laden.

'Are you enjoying your trip, Mademoiselle?'

A man dressed in French military uniform came to stand next to me.

'Yes, I am,' I smiled out to sea, without looking at him. 'I didn't realise that it would be quite so relaxed here.'

'What brings you to Algeria?'

'My job. I'm a journalist.'

'Ah, so you are expecting excitement'

I turned to my interlocutor. 'I don't know what I'm expecting. At the moment, I'm just looking forward to seeing another country.'

'That's not how most of your compatriots see it.'

'Oh, you mean because they see it as their own country.'

'Exactly!'

'Ah well, I was brought up in rural West France and Algeria seems very exotic and different to me.'

He smiled and bowed slightly. 'May it always seem like that for you.'

'And what about you?' I returned the question. 'You're obviously part of the military but also Algerian. Doesn't that make you sympathetic to the French cause?'

'In a way, yes. By the way let me introduce myself. I'm Yussuf and I'm part of the third regiment Tirailleurs Francais.'

'And I'm Marie, a journalist writing for Libération and other left-wing papers.'

'Enchanté, Mlle Marie. Would you like another drink?'

'Yes, I'd love one.'

'And yes, before you ask, I do drink alcohol when I'm in Europe.'

'But not otherwise?'

'It's not hypocrisy if that's what you're wondering. There's always been plenty of drink available in the French military, and among the more Europeanised Algerians, but generally there's no alcohol in the villages. I'm not religious myself but I respect those who are, and I wouldn't want to offend them.'

'I don't mind what you drink,' I laughed, 'but I'd like something alcoholic myself and perhaps we could bring it out here again, because it's such a beautiful night.'

I liked being on deck in the cool air and I thought it would be easier to have a frank discussion when we weren't being surrounded by lots of French people.

'Sure. Great idea. Why don't you wait here while I go and get them? Then we can make ourselves comfortable.'

He appeared later with a lager and a beer and we settled ourselves between the lifeboats on the side of the ship. It seemed like the easiest thing in the world to be talking to this young man. We shared past experiences and I explained that I was going to stay at a vineyard not far from Constantine.

'I know it,' said Yussuf. 'They have a good record of employing Algerians and treating them well, but you still need to be careful.'

'In what way? I'm not going to be a threat to any FLN nationalists.'

'You're a threat just because you're French.' I was startled. I thought that I was going to an exotic new holiday destination, as well as being paid for interesting work.

'That's now the FLN policy. They're justified in killing any French person, whatever their gender or age.'

'Even children?'

'Even children. And yes, before you ask, that's partly my hesitation in joining in the nationalist movement.'

'I can certainly understand that. But surely other Algerians feel the same way.'

'They do. Of course, they do. The Algerian character is generally 'doux'. They love children and are respectful towards women. But often they don't have any choice.'

'Why not?'

'They are blackmailed. Their own women and children are threatened by the FLN. If they don't do as the bandits say, they will be killed. And, I assure you, they devise ways for them to die which are terrible.'

'But you've chosen to throw in your lot with the French?'

He hesitated. 'Yes, I have though I support the independence of Algeria. I just think they're going about it the wrong way.'

'What would you like them to do?'

'Put pressure on the French to build better facilities for them. Challe has already done that, and de Gaulle has promised more. Allow more moderate Algerians to have a say in their policies. I'd say to the revolutionaries – 'By all means fight the paratroopers, but not your own women and children.'

'And does that make you unpopular?'

'With some, but with not the villagers who know me and trust me. And anyway, I don't have close family so they can't threaten me in the same way.'

For the first time, he looked at me more directly.

'You're right, Marie, you need to go to Algeria to understand the complexity of the situation.'

# Chapter Sixteen

I started off in Algiers because that was where the boat docked. I could stay with some journalist colleagues and I wanted to have a feel for the capital before I moved further inland.

First of all, I went to the editorial office of l'Humanité, because I knew that I would be among friends there. I found their editor, Gervaise, serious minded and pessimistic.

'Don't expect anything very wonderful from the referendum, if that's what you've come to report on,' he advised. 'There's a huge amount of publicity for it in the casbah, but the FLN have an eye on it all and anyone likely to be persuaded to vote 'oui'.

'So, you don't think there's much chance of it succeeding?' I certainly wasn't hearing anything different here to what I had heard in Paris amongst the Algerian community.

'There's a chance of it appearing to succeed. All the Muslims might come out and vote like they're supposed to. If it's just a matter of going to the ballot box, of course they'll go, but that doesn't mean that it's going to turn out all right. The Algerians will do whatever you want them to do, but in the end the FLN will have their souls.'

'But the FLN want them to boycott the referendum!'

'Yes. They won't, because they want to please General de Gaulle, but what happens after the referendum is the really big question.'

'So, what will happen, in your opinion?'

'Everything will go back to normal. The Algerians won't get any better treatment from the French, despite what they've been promised. The FLN will move in and say, 'I told you so.' And then the fighting will begin all over again.'

'Has it been bad so far?'

Gervaise was quiet for a moment.

'There's something I never want to see in my life again. First was the scene of devastation when Yacer and his agents, who were mainly girls, went in and blew up the 'milk bar' near the centre.'

I'd seen a few explosions in Hanoi, so I could guess what the scene had been like.

'The youngsters in there, mainly lycéens and lycéenes, were just having a good evening out. Most of them were too young to know anything about the politics anyway. They were just having a fun time with boyfriends and a few drinks to celebrate the end of exams and they were dancing. Some of them were blown to bits. I held a girl in my arms who bled to death after she's had her leg blown off. They were screaming for their parents. The son of one of my journalists will never walk again and they will all be psychologically scarred for life.'

'Secondly,' he continued, 'I don't want to see the tail end of a ratonnade again.'

'What's that?'

'When the paras go on after they've been tipped off about explosives being held in a house, especially in the casbah. They get the kids of the household and they threaten them and hurt them, until they or their parents give out information. I accompanied the paras one evening and it's not pleasant.'

'I suppose they have to find out where the explosives are being made.'

'Of course, but it's the way they treat the kids. But the worst of all is the torture.'

'Torture?' I thought the France was signed up to the Bill of Human Rights?'

Gervaise laughed sarcastically. 'They may be, but it doesn't stop their soldiers from applying torture.'

'And you've seen it?' I had heard dark rumours of torture in the Algerian community in Bobigny, but this informant was a French citizen.

'I can take you to the prisons and the warehouses where it's happening. The screams you hear outside alone are enough to make you sick.'

So, no moral high ground for the French, I thought sadly.

'Have you challenged the military about it?'

'Of course, on numerous occasions. Soustelle denies that it's happening. Challe shrugs his shoulders and says, 'It's no worse than the Algerians are doing to us.'

'And the ordinary French soldiers?'

'Some of them are disgusted by it. But some of them are already addicted to it.'

'Addicted? That's a strange word to use.'

'Yes, but it's the right one. It's what happened to the SS in the war. Do you think that the people involved in murdering the Jews were any different to us?'

I thought back to how I'd helped my Jewish friends. 'I hope so.'

'Well, go on hoping, Marie, because it's not true. Once they've crossed the line of their own conscience and are doing it again and again and are getting information for their bosses as a result of the torture, they want to carry on. It becomes something which gives them a thrill.'

Silence before the enormity of what was happening here.

'So, there are bad things happening here?'

'It's getting worse all the time and that's the ordinary paras not the OAS.'

I had heard this title in France – the extremists who wanted Algeria to stay French at all costs.

'There's not many of them surely?'

'There's enough to cause trouble, and they're on the point of turning some of the big generals right under de Gaulle's nose.'

'You mean it's a three-way war?'

'That's only the start. I'd say it's a multi-faceted war. Why don't you speak to some of the journalists from other papers and see what they have to say?'

'That's exactly what I'd like to do.' I was relieved that this editor was broad-minded enough to recommend speaking to papers of different political persuasions to his own. 'Who do you recommend?'

'I don't recommend their papers, but it would be good for you to listen to the Echo d'Algérie.'

'That's fine by me. What's their take on the subject?'

'They support the pied noirs and the OAS.'

'You mean, against the Algerians and the army and de Gaulle?'

'Exactly. They're as hard as nails; but it's a point of view and you need to hear it.'

'Thanks. What's the best way of getting to the Echo?'

He grinned, suddenly more relaxed. 'Search me. You'll need every bit of influence you can find.'

To begin with, when I left Gervaise's office, I couldn't see how this was going to happen. I stayed for a few nights in the same hotel as some of the left-wing journalists and all of them raised their hands and shrugged their shoulders, when I mentioned the Echo.

'You have to be a hard bastard to get in there,' said Hubert from l'Humanité . He looked me up and down and his look said it all – you don't stand a chance.

But I was much more experienced and battle-hardened than someone like Hubert might imagine. I was getting nowhere with all my enquiries, when, quite by accident, I had a lucky break.

'No go,' judged one of the journalists from Figaro, who was a lot older and more experienced than the others in the hotel. 'Unless you happen to be a wine connoisseur and can bring him a '22 from Bordeaux.'

'Sorry?' I questioned confused. I imagined for a minute that he might be talking about expensive bribery.

'Didn't you know that Sérigny partly owns a vineyard in Algeria, inherited from his family?'

'Yes,' added another colleague in the bar in the hotel where we were staying, 'and they're all in league with the richest colons.'

Suddenly I remembered my contact with M. Tribier and the Entreprise Gaullen. I had been looking forward to my contact with them in west of the country, but now it occurred to me that the contact could be useful in Algiers too.

I had brought four bottles of vintage wine with me from M. Tribier's vineyard in Provence. It was supposed to establish a link with his former partner. But now without saying a word to my fellow journalists, I grabbed one bottle of the four and made my way to the offices of the Echo in the centre of Algiers.

'Tell the editor,' I said with disdainful confidence to the receptionist, 'that I bring a gift from his former business competitor in France, who wants to know how he is doing.'

The ruse worked, as journalistic introductions and questions about the current politics of Algiers, would not have done.

'Ah, a friend of Claude!' Sérigny rose to his feet to greet me. He was a charming, good-looking man with a grizzled curly hair cut. He was going grey in a way which increased his attractiveness.

After polite introductions, he asked, 'So why is Claude sending someone over here to find out about my vineyards, instead of coming himself?'

'I don't think he feels safe in Algeria at this point.'

Sérigny snorted in derision. 'Safe in Algeria? Of course not! When have we ever felt safe?'

'I thought that before the war, you had been?' I suggested naively.

He sat back at his desk, examining me quizzically. 'You thought that, did you? No colon has ever been safe in Algeria! Not surrounded by 5 million Arabs in the bled.'

'Then, why have you stayed here so long, monsieur?'

'Monsieur le Comte actually!' But he waved my apology aside. 'Because it's our home. And while it's never been really safe, it's been beautiful and exciting and our home country. Never forget that it's part of France.'

'And will it always be?' I dared such a challenging question to this defender of Algérie Française .

In answer he threw up his hands in despair. 'Who knows? Why not? It will, if I have anything to do with it.'

'Do you support de Gaulle in what he is doing?'

'I mademoiselle,' Sérigny leant back and poured a glass of M. Tribier's prize wine in a hospitable gesture, 'called for de Gaulle to come back.'

I almost laughed at his tone of complete confidence. Apparently, none of de Gaulle's other supporters, especially those in his mother country, counted. If M. le Comte Sérigny backed de Gaulle, then everyone else would follow his lead.

'Soustelle and I think he's the only hope; but what happens in the referendum and how de Gaulle leads the way as a result, is what will count.'

'And can he lead the way?'

'Against the filthy FLN with their evil tactics?'

'Yes.'

'I hope so, mademoiselle, because if he can't, then all is lost.'

# Chapter Seventeen

Comte Alain de Sérigny was an amazingly charismatic character. Later, when talking to other journalists in the capital, I had learnt more about his history – how he had been brought up in a privileged background in Algeria, but he had gone to fight with the French in the homeland at the beginning of the war, and had continued fighting as the Germans had taken over the Maginot Line, not running away before the advance of the German forces, as many Frenchmen had done. He had been captured by the Germans and taken as a prisoner of war. From there he had managed his own escape and that of three other officers and had managed to return not only to France but to Algeria, where he had eventually joined forces with General de Gaulle and the Free French and had gone back to the South of France and fought his way up through Germany as the war ended. I had to admire the man's courage and his devotion to his country. Now, as the editor of the Echo d'Alger and a member of the Association des Elues d'Algérie, which was an elite group of governors in the country, he had gained huge respect and influence among the pied noirs. He was a friend of the richest of all the pied noirs, Henri Bourgeaud, but he had also the respect of the poorest colons. He was a man who knew his own mind and I found myself listening carefully to what he had to say.

He, in his turn, took an interest in what I was doing in Algeria. He invited me for drinks at his home and listened courteously to my arguments. He also seemed devoted to his wife and family and not once tried to take advantage of me. Algeria, everyone felt, was on the brink of disaster, and it is often at such a time of tension and fear that many liasons are formed. I had seen it already in Indo China, and as I mixed with journalists and pied noirs and some of the Muslim left-

541

wing intellectuals, I felt the same atmosphere brewing. Journalists in a potential war zone are always waiting and half hoping for trouble to happen, even though they are afraid, because they are not natural warriors. The women amongst them were some of the only females around who were available sexually, and they prided themselves on their toughness and lack of emotional ties.

In that summer of 1958, before the referendum took place, there was a curious feeling of hiatus. No war was being fought by the Europeans, because they were waiting for de Gaulle to give the signal to advance. The French paras had seen some terrible action both in the interior of the country and in the casbah in the previous four years and they were waiting for permission to put the FLN down once and for all. The rich colons were hoping to be able to defend their land and houses for the future but were afraid that they would lose everything. The poor colons, if they were not allowed to stay, had nowhere else to go and no means of earning their living. The generals were rallying around first, Massu, and then Soustelle, but the military commanders of the country were being changed with frightening rapidity as none of them were sufficiently trusted by the French government to be a safe pair of hands. There was talk of a more extreme vigilante group, an Armée Secrete, being formed and tough terrorist hardened fighters, many of whom had been involved in torture in Algerian prisons, were looking expectantly at the generals and waiting for a signal. In contrast, there weren't many moderate Muslim anti – FLN men, but there were a few. They had all benefitted from a French university education and they were hoping that under de Gaulle's assimilation plans, they might prosper.

This was the heady mixture of people invited to one of Comte de Sérigny 's parties that summer. I hoped that I might have been invited because he liked me, but I knew also that I was one of the few French women available to the men in the capital.

'De Sérigny 's parties are legendary,' one of the female journalists from the Figaro had informed me the night before, as we journalists sat drinking into the early hours of the morning.

'He lives in a fantastic house near the beach. The food and drink are free, and he always makes sure that the single women get home safely.'

'Not that we always want to get home safely,' she added, grinning over her absinthe. 'But it's nice to know that the offer is there if you want it. I hear that he likes you, Marie.'

'Oh sure,' I said. I knew better than to admit to any possibility of being a favourite with a 'patron' of this society. To start with, it was too easy to fool yourself that you were 'special', and thus easily taken in by any sly plan the influential members of society might have for you. One of the worst conditions you can foster in a war zone, is jealousy. If other journalists start to be jealous of you, they are never going to help you when disaster strikes, and in a war, you need help more than anywhere, not just to get a good story, but even to stay alive. I had once seen a French journalist have an affair with an American captain in Vietnam. She collected the greatest information for her articles from her 'pillow talk', made everyone else feel under-informed as though they were a doing a bad job, but, when it came to being collected by her fellow journalists in danger, she was left severely alone. She had already demonstrated that she could 'manage alone', but in the end she died because she became so isolated. I might like my chats with de Sérigny, but I wasn't going to isolate myself.

'And I hear that he does everything with his wife, who will co-host the party.'

'That's what they say,' said my new colleague, grinning impishly at me, 'but you never know your luck. Anyway,' she added 'presumably you are coming.'

'Try and stop me,' I said laughing. 'There's going to be far too many interesting people there to stay away.'

Sérigny proved to be a charming host. He greeted me with what I found to be gratifying enthusiasm.

'You have a very beautiful home, Comte,' I looked round at the doors of salon opening out to the terrace, with the moon just starting to appear in the early summer's evening. 'I can see why you don't want to leave it.'

'Of course, no one would want to leave this, Marie. But that's not the real reason why I don't want to leave the country.'

'So, the real reason is altruistic, I suppose,' My tone and raised eyebrows indicated my sense of irony.

'Nothing is ever completely altruistic of course. But I like to think that I'm here for this country, whoever governs it. What do you think, Abdelkrim?'

He took hold of the dinner jacket of a young Algerian and brought him towards us.

'Marie, let me introduce you to Maître Abdelkrim, one of our most promising young lawyers. Abdelkrim practices here in Alger and also in Paris.'

I was impressed. 'You are very young, Maître, to have such an important clientèle.'

He laughed. 'Don't believe everything the Comte tells you, Mademoiselle Marie. I'm just starting out in practice and, when I do go to Paris, it's not to defend the rich, but my fellow countrymen, who are poor and in need.'

'Then I congratulate you, Maître. I've seen the situation of some of your countrymen in Bobigny. They need all the help they can get.'

I told Abdelkrim about my experiences there.

'So, you see, Krim' chimed in Alain, putting a hand on each of our shoulders, 'this isn't a journalist who just skims the surface. She does her research seriously. No, Marie,' The Comte patted me on the shoulder,' I'm not making fun. I admire your attitude to your job. I see that it is a vocation for you. From my own position as editor, I think it's important to have journalists who believe in what they're doing.'

'Even when they're working for a left-wing paper?' I queried.

'Of course. Even more important when they are working for a left-wing paper. No room for hypocrisy there. You may think that I'm an old stick in the mud capitalist and to a certain extent I am, but I have also been a visionary too in my time. It's just that I've come to a much more conservative position.'

Abdelkrim laughed at his host. I was amazed that, as a young man, he had the courage to do so, and even more amazed that Sérigny was laughing with him.

'I know. I know. It's typical talk of the middle aged but I do care about this country and what journalists write about it. Isn't that right, Krim?'

Krim bowed charmingly to his host. 'Of course, you care, Comte. Otherwise you wouldn't employ so many Algerians and people in the Casbah wouldn't be glad to be paid by you.'

'Is that right?' This was a new side to de Sérigny – not ardent right winger, but employer and defender of the people.

'You see, Mademoiselle Marie, you shouldn't believe everything that the Comte says about himself. He likes to present himself as the self-centred capitalist but underneath there's a socialist trying to get out.'

'A socialist? I find that difficult to believe. You're not much like any of the editors I work with in Paris.'

'Ask yourself,' said Krim, with his beautiful brown eyes lit up by thoughtfulness, 'If your left-wing editors look after their office staff when they are too scared to come to work because of the threats the terrorists are making against them.'

The question was left unanswered because I had another question for this young Algerian avocat, who seemed to be so acceptable to the pied noir community.

'You have no hesitation in calling some of your fellow Algerians terrorists?'

'That is what they are. They use terror to force people to support them, not argument.'

'And do you hope that argument will win?'

'That and any good I can do professionally in my job.'

'So, you support the referendum?'

'Without any doubt, mademoiselle. Who in their right mind would not?'

'The problem is, Krim, that there aren't many people in their right mind at the moment.'

A huge, burly figure in a double-breasted suit, had come up behind us and placed his arm round the young lawyer.

'Sérigny , is this your young wine-taster? Let me introduce myself, my dear.' The huge man abandoned Krim, grabbed my hand and kissed it. 'I'm Henri Bourgeaud. Delighted to meet you at last, Mademoiselle Marie.'

# Chapter Eighteen

I was intrigued by Abdelkrim, the young lawyer who I met at the Sérigny party. His views sounded rational. He had benefitted from the French system of education so he saw no reason why others of his countrymen and women could not also benefit, especially in a more liberal future promised by de Gaulle. He was in league with the pied noirs, the leading and most influential politicians of his day. Clearly Yacer and his associates had bombed innocent people and could, according to Abdelkrim, be justifiably classed as terrorists. All that made perfect sense to me. However, something was bothering me. He said that he had visited the poverty-stricken Algerians of Bobigny in order to help them. I had never heard of such support going on in Paris. Only recently I had spent a considerable amount of time with Habibi and his family and all of them supported the FLN. Habibi did this, despite being by nature a peace-loving man. I would have been surprised if he or any of his friends had ever been helped by a supporter of the French army. Perhaps there were aspects of the situation in Paris which I didn't know about, I thought, not for the first time in my dealings with Algerians.

Since coming to Algiers as a journalist, I had heard more and more about an FLN newspaper which had started up in 1956, mainly through the influence of Ramdane Abane, one of the main political thinkers of the FLN. Abane, apparently had had spent several years in a French prison, when he had been captured after the massacre of Philippeville and during that period of enforced inactivity, he had read the works of Marx, Lenin and Mao Tse Tung. This had allowed him to justify terrorism and, since his release, he was set, not just on practising it but encouraging others to do so as well. Once a potential leader becomes informed and convinced of the rightness of his actions, he acts as a fire-igniter to everyone else. I thought of how Matvey and Natasha had been totally convinced of the rightness of Stalin, despite their own basic good natures. Great thinkers have a lot to answer for, I thought.

The day after the party, I talked to one of my fellow journalists from l'Humanité. Like his colleagues, he appeared later in the day in the entrance hall of our hotel, having suffered the effects of a hangover earlier. Gilbert was a loner, and I guessed that he might have more inside information than others of his profession.

'Tell me, Gilbert, have you heard of El Moudjahid?'

Gilbert looked back at me, contemptuously and sullenly. 'Of course, Marie. Anyone who is sympathetic to the cause of the FLN has heard of it.'

'So how do they print it and get it into the hands of their readers?'

'Quite easily. They hide parts of the printing press in different parts of the Casbah and then, when the French are distracted by other things, they put it together and print off copies. The runners – the teenagers they use to do all their communications – distribute the copies all over the Casbah afterwards.'

'Do they ever get caught?'

'Yes, sometimes. But these kids – a lot of them, eleven or twelve-year olds – are incredibly hard to get information out of. The French try all sorts of things.'

'You mean the ratonnades?'

'Yes, except they're mainly used to find out where the explosives are hidden. Ratonnades are disgusting, but even the French don't take so much trouble for a newspaper.'

'Probably a mistake,' I remarked drily.

'So, you approve of torture in the French cause?' Gilbert challenged me directly.

'Of course, I don't, but I meant more of a mistake not to realise that the written word, highly politicised, can have as much influence as explosives.'

'Probably why we're both journalists,' he added in a more relaxed and friendly tone than he had used before. 'Sorry, Marie, I'm not feeling very communicative.'

'You must have partied too hard last night!'

'Certainly. But,' and he flashed me an unexpected grin at this point, 'it was worth it.'

'You scored?'

'What with all those well-brought up colon girls flirting away under their parents' eyes, it was hard not to.'

'In your case politics doesn't affect sex?'

'Not when the drink is a free gift from Sérigny.'

We seemed to be understanding each other better than at first, I thought, and decided to try my luck on a direct question.

'Gilbert, do you know when and where the printing press gets put together?'

'Sometimes. It changes every week, but you get to know, if you hang round the Casbah.'

'Could I hang round there with you?'

He eyed me solemnly. 'It's seriously risky, Marie, especially for a European woman.'

'But not for you?'

'I'm of Spanish origin and I've got the right colouring. But it's not so easy for you. And they don't really understand the position of a woman journalist.'

I wasn't convinced by his paternalistic attitudes. 'Well, it's about time they started to, isn't it? Especially if they're after a Marxist state.'

He liked that. 'Marie, I could almost wish that you worked full time for l'Humanité. You're a lot more of a risk taker than some of my colleagues here.'

'That's because they've got stuck in a French rut of communism where nothing happens. They haven't been part of the real thing in Indo China and Russia like I have. There women take real risks like the men. Besides,' I was suddenly seized by a new idea. 'All these veils, the white ones they wear, don't they hide who you really are? Isn't that why Yacer's girls were so successful at planting bombs?'

'Yes, that certainly was controversial. And they're called haiks, by the way. If you're really up for it, meet me down at the bar, the one nearest to the entrance of the Casbah tomorrow morning.'

'I'm up for it, but you'll have to find me a white veil.'

'And a white nose job to go with it.' He grinned. 'That's the easy part. Leave it to me.'

The rest of the day and that night I was nervous and excited. One of my main aims was to get to the wine growers in the east of the country and to find out what was happening amongst the workers, but I wanted to wire some reports to my paper before then. If I was going to report on the activities of the Echo d'Alger and the Depêche Algérienne, what better than to add observations about what the only Arab newspaper was doing in secret? I knew that El Moudjahid meant the religious freedom fighter and that brought another dimension to the struggle going on in Algeria. Religion had not been important in Russia or Indo China, but here it seemed to be another weapon of the freedom fighters, almost more important than the political one.

The following morning, I met up with Gilbert in the bar at 11am. He had already procured me a white haik and it was easy enough to drape it round unfixed to my hair and face. 'In the end I couldn't find you a handkerchief over your nose, but a lot of the young girls don't wear them anyway. One advantage of this sort of veil is that you can use it across as much or as little of your face as you want.'

I think I'll go for the 'as much' version, I thought to myself, as I modestly followed Gilbert across the street. Veil across my eyes and head down are the best possible ways of doing it.

It wasn't quite as easy to achieve this style as I had anticipated, because as well as shielding my face and hair, I had to concentrate on following Gilbert up the uneven steps and along the tiny alleyway, so tiny that I couldn't believe there was any room there for sellers of oil who seemed to be doing business there.

'All of the alleyways go for a different type of seller,' whispered Gilbert to me. 'Just keep going and don't bother to look at any of the stalls.'

I was so intent on not drawing attention to myself that I did exactly what he said. The cobbles were so uneven that I almost tripped several times. Suddenly, Gilbert dived through a smaller alleyway covered by dark, silky material which blocked any sunlight and led us deeper into the Casbah. I wondered how any French soldier managed to survive here, without being led by a guide. I later discovered that it was often well-paid guides who did escort them, sometimes because the guides were anti-FLN, but more often because the French army was being led into a trap. I decided that I wouldn't like to get trapped here as an enemy. No escape.

Unexpectedly, we came out onto a more open space where butchers' meat covered by swarms of flies was being sold. I forced myself not to retch into my haik as I passed by. The male customers were busy bartering over the price of, what looked like, sheep's heads and knuckles.

Suddenly, we turned up through an arch and up a narrow staircase. Gilbert gave three knocks at the door at the top. The door was opened, and several young boys stood there with knives at the ready, but they put them down quickly when they saw who it was.

'I haven't come to stop your work,' Gilbert reassured them, 'just to introduce you to a friend.'

Two of the younger boys smiled in a friendly way at me but the others looked suspicious and angry. There followed a whole rapid dialogue in Arabic, which Gilbert appeared to understand perfectly, and it was clearly about whether I was to be allowed to see what was happening. Eventually the dialogue faded away. They had accepted Gilbert's recommendation, and, besides, they didn't have time to argue, as well as putting together the printing press, which was being brought out of small cupboards, which were inset into the wall. With astonishing speed, the makeshift press, which was little more than a basic roller with ink, was producing copies which were being rolled off the press.

'The trouble is,' I commented to Gilbert, 'I can't understand what it says.'

'I can translate it for you,' said Gilbert helpfully. 'It's a fairly basic argument about why terror is necessary. Then there's the report on French use of torture in prison and finally about the new buildings which the FLN will fund for schooling, when they eventually come to power.'

'How come you're so proficient in Arabic?' My estimate of Gilbert had risen throughout the morning. I could see now that he was much more than just a token French communist reporter.

'As I told you, I'm Spanish, but I was also brought up in Morocco. I learnt Arabic there.'

'Very useful.'

He looked at me closely to check for any irony. 'Actually, it is. I can check up on what is really going on.'

As he spoke these words, the door was pushed open suddenly and the man standing there made an announcement.

'There's some soldiers on their way. Get the press back in the alcoves and, Mustapha, get these copies which are done downstairs and out amongst those carrying packets of meat. They will get copies to all the families near here. We will wait another two days until the next run is done.

Who is this?'

He turned to look at me, asking Gilbert the question at the same time. To my astonishment I recognised the man. It was the avocat who the night before had been supporting the French at Sérigny's party.

'Ah, our journalist friend, Marie. Gilbert, the two of you had better come with me straightaway. We'll get over to the goldsmiths in the other direction to where the soldiers are coming from.' Without waiting for my response, he pulled me down the stairs after him and I saw that Gilbert was following.

'Don't lose hold of your haik. Keep between me and Gilbert and don't look anyone in the face. If we pass any soldiers, keep your head down.'

I wanted to ask whether he might be recognised by any of the French but as he pulled the hood of his burnous over his face, I saw that it was unlikely.

I was so terrified of being found by the French and implicated in illegal activities, that I followed without a word, sometimes grabbing onto the man in front of me to steady myself. We seemed to half run between the alleys on the right and left, some of them hosting perfumers, some of them cloth merchants, and then up one staircase and down another, and out into an even darker concourse, where the gold merchants were plying their trade, through a curtain and then into a back room.

'So,' said Abdelkrim, turning me round suddenly to face him, 'What exactly are you doing here?' I was frightened and angry as I tore my haik off and looked him in the face.

'I could ask you the same question, Maître. What exactly are you doing in the Casbah?'

# Chapter Nineteen

That was the moment that I grew up in Algerian politics. Before that, my visit to Algeria had been an extension of the malaise I had experienced coming back from Indo China. The beautiful boat trip, the prospect of a visit to the vineyards, the link with the Jewish community, the society parties, had all given me the feeling that this was pleasurable half-work and half-vacation assignment. It was foreign enough to be alluring and domestic enough to be safe.

As I stared back into Abdelkrim's eyes, I knew that what I was doing was neither romantic nor safe.

'This is my country and my people, Mademoiselle, and I will do what I like here.'

'Yes, you can do what you like here, Maître Abdelkrim,' I replied with the same tone of assurance he had offered me, 'but I am here to investigate integrity and honour and good intentions, and, as far as I can see, you are not demonstrating any of them.'

He sneered at me derisively. 'And you think that your compatriots are?'

'Some of them, yes. Some of them may be mistaken, but at least they are not hypocrites.'

'I can assure you that I am not a hypocrite.' He pushed the hood of his burnous back from his face as he spoke, as if proud to reveal his full character. 'I am living in a war zone, and I do what is necessary to fight the oppressor.'

'And I can assure you,' I responded with defiance, 'that I understand just what it means to fight in a war zone. I fought the Nazis in the Resistance.'

'In that case you will understand.'

I hesitated. The question shook me. I had been revolted by the thought that this man attended French parties and pretended to be the friend of the pied noirs, when he was in reality part of a terrorist group plotting their demise. But was that in truth any different from what the French spies had done under the occupation? I asked myself.

'That was under a Nazi regime,' I retorted quickly in case my hesitation appeared to give justification for anything he was doing.

'And who decides who the Nazi regime is?'

'Maybe you don't like the regime here but there are ways of opposing it without violence and you have a chance to vote in a referendum about your country's future. Nazi Germany never gave the French people a vote.'

He laughed bitterly. 'Sure, a vote to become slaves of the French.'

'No, a vote to gradually experience more freedom and the ability to be educated to exercise that freedom wisely.'

'You have been swallowing the lies of the pied noirs and of General de Gaulle.'

'And you are spreading the lies of terrorists.'

Suddenly he lunged forward at me and forced my hands behind my back and my whole body against the wall of the small room in the upper chamber of this house in the Casbah. I was more afraid of Abdelkrim's physical proximity and eyes lowered to within an inch of mine that I had ever been of guns and bombs going off around me in other war zones.

'This is not a time to talk politics. Your liberating French army is at this moment spreading through the Casbah and if they find me, I can assure you that I will take you down with me.'

'What do you intend to do – kill me as they arrive?'

'I wouldn't hesitate to do that, Madam journalist.'

'Oh, I know.' My words sounded much more assured than my shaking body and my knees buckling under his weight, felt. I was not going to let my voice betray the fear I felt of this man. 'I've read about your tactics of killing any French person, woman or child who gets in your way.'

'Not just in the way. Any French person for any reason at all.'

'You mean just because they're another human being of a different nationality.'

'Another human being who is part of the force of oppression.'

At this, he relaxed his hold a little and I almost slumped to the floor in reaction. As I looked up at him, he didn't appear to have a knife, but I knew that he was capable of strangling me without a second thought. I fought back with the only weapon of aggression I knew – words.

'But don't forget the effect of your murder. I am a journalist who writes for the international press as well as for French newspapers. If you murder me, the UN will know through my editor at home and you need the UN vote to gain independence and international goodwill.'

'We already have it as well as the backing of America.'

'But you haven't had the referendum yet. And remember that you still need to convince your fellow Algerians.'

'You needn't worry about that. They are already convinced.'

'To your face they are, when cowed by violence and threats. But in a free vote? I don't think it's so obvious, Maître.'

My use of his professional title seemed to bring an element of civilisation to the argument. Slowly, he backed away from me.

'I haven't the time for academic arguments.' Then, as if making a concession in order to save his pride, he continued, 'I won't kill you this time because, as you were with Gilbert, I assume that you were wanting to see how our paper worked.'

El Moudjahid! I had forgotten all about it. It now seemed like a very tame project, compared with Abedelkrim's threats to my life. He read my thoughts immediately.

'Don't think it has no effect. It is the tool of the party and, as you should know from your métier, it has an effect on its readership. That's why the French are trying to stop its publication.'

I decided that this was a good time to affirm my neutrality and objectivity as a reporter.

'Indeed, you are right. And I would not object to freedom of the press. My job depends on it.'

'It's Abane's idea of course. He thinks it's as important as the bomb. And, while I don't quite see it like that, I admit that it's important.'

I pushed ahead with a point of view we might agree on. 'Especially in the days leading up to the referendum when violence might be less effective as a means of persuasion.'

554

'Perhaps.' He turned away impatiently from what he saw as an argument about ideas to the more immediate and important things on his mind. I could see that what to do with me was only a moment of intermission as he again focused on his beliefs and actions.

'As a journalist, you may report on the production of El Moudjahid, and the French attempt to stop its production, especially if you write sympathetically about our cause for the international press.'

'You should know that as a journalist of integrity, I always write to make readers consider the views of others.' This sounded rather self-righteous, so I continued quickly, 'Do I sense that there is a 'but' there, Maître?'

'If you ever give information to the French about where you have been today, the identity of the workers or a description of their house or anything about my role and loyalties, I or my supporters will find you and kill you, have no doubt about it. Because you are a woman, or because I met you at a party, or because you are a newcomer to Algérie, will not protect you. And I don't care what the backlash is in the international press. I don't like informers.'

'No one likes informers. I also don't like hypocrites who are playing both sides. But I won't give you away, Abdelkrim. Not only do I believe all your threats, but I'm not in the habit of betraying one side to the other. I've not only fought in a war, but I've reported on too many wars and crises, and I know what goes on with both sides. When it comes to atrocities, usually, neither side is blameless.'

He nodded cursorily. 'Now you need to get out. One of the boys will take you. If I see you again, remember that the last time I saw you was at Sérigny's party. And don't forget what power I wield.'

'I shan't forget, Maître. But don't you forget that I am a journalist who is capable of writing sympathetically or unsympathetically about your cause.'

# Chapter Twenty

It took me a couple of days to recover psychologically from my experience in the Casbah. I needed time to decide what to do and to think more clearly about the situation. I had met turncoats and spies both in Vichy France and in Indo China and in Russia, but none who were accepted in the social circle of the side they were fighting against quite so seamlessly as Maître Abdelkrim. The thought that he was pretending to be friends with the people he was helping to blow up sickened me. It was also a war which had never been declared openly, and the violence here counted as terrorism. Was it my duty to report him to the French authorities? What if he caused more bloodshed? Would I be guilty of colluding with it?

As I considered this dilemma through the next humid twenty-four hours in my hotel, I decided that, as a journalist, I did not support either side. My job was to report on what was happening in the country, not to consider either side to be traitors. I felt that I wanted to be able to report on the torture carried out by the French soldiers, I argued to myself. This was an illegal activity carried out by a power, who said that they did not practice torture. In war there have always been spies. Just because I had detected one, did not mean that I should betray him to his enemy. That would be to take sides. But what if there was another bomb, similar to the ones of the previous year? Would I not be guilty of allowing tens of young French colons to be killed or injured? I agonised over this problem of conscience in my cheap little hotel room, the sweat pouring down my back, as I sat near the open window in the middle of the night.

I had not seen Gilbert since we had been separated in the Casbah. It occurred to me now that he must know more about Abdelkrim's association with the FLN than I had realised. Yet he too had been at Sérigny's party, so he must have been aware of the deliberate deception.

In the middle of the night I decided that I would seek him out the next day. With that decision made, I had some sort of rest. I went to bed in the deadly humid heat which hits Algiers in the summer and slept for five hours.

In the morning I went downstairs to the entrance hall of the hotel to see if I could locate Gilbert. I found him about 11am looking tired and dipping his croissants in his coffee.

'Could we talk sometime?' I asked without launching into the commonplace small talk. He looked less than delighted.

'Maybe. But not here.'

'In a café?'

'Not even in a café. There are too many watchful eyes.'

'How about in my room?'

'Alright. This afternoon, after the sièste and before l'heure de l'apéritif.'

'Sounds perfect. I shall expect you about 4pm.'

I spent the intervening time wandering around the city. Everything seemed so normal. Outside the 'other world' of the Casbah, it seemed like a typical French city – pavement cafes, people congregating in the middle of the day for their déjeuner, offices full of avocats and comptables, the main square where the civil service offices were situated, and, added in as an extra, the brilliant sunshine, and the view at some angles over towards the port with the shimmering sea beyond. That summer of 1958, with a lull in the violence, Algiers seemed like the most beautiful city in the world.

I returned to the hotel after lunch, agreed on an apéritif appointment later in the day with two of my female colleagues and determined to have a sièste to make up for my lack of sleep the night before.

I was in the process of rousing myself from my afternoon sleep, at the point when the temptation to sink back effortlessly into more sleep is at its strongest, when I heard a knock and forced myself out of bed.

'Sorry, I didn't sleep much last night,' I muttered as I opened the door, as if justifying my confused state and sweaty appearance.

'It's OK,' replied Gilbert, less than enthusiastically, 'You got out all right from the Casbah, without meeting any soldiers?'

557

'Yes. I assume that you knew about the loyalties of Abdelkrim well before this?' I asked him in a rather belligerent way as he sat down on the one upright chair and I perched back on the pillows of the bed where I had slept.

'Knew that he was coming yesterday morning? No, not at all. Knew who he was? Of course.'

'But you were at Sérigny's party the night before,' I stated in an accusatory tone.

'Yes, but you have to learn to keep your mouth shut in this place, Marie. If you want to be a good journalist, you must not take sides.'

'Even when there are innocent people being killed?'

'There are innocent people being killed on both sides. It's part of a civil war.'

'A civil war?' I queried. 'I've only heard it called that once before. At least it makes both sides equal.'

'They're only equal because the French lay claim to this country too.'

'Do you think they have any right to?'

He considered the question carefully. 'To be honest, I don't know. They have a right to something. But they were always guests here.'

'Guests? Even when their country was in charge?'

'In charge according to their decision. Not as far as the host country was concerned.'

'But the host country was not going anywhere before they came.'

'Who says? Who knows how they might have developed after the Ottoman Empire collapsed, if they had been allowed to get on with it?'

I decided to change tack. 'So, you don't feel guilty about not informing the authorities about Abdelkrim?'

'Marie, Abdelkrim is fighting for his country. If the pied noirs are stupid enough to believe everything he says when he is dressed up as an avocat and supporting the party line, then more fool them.'

'Are there many other people like him?'

'Of course, there are. They are the future leaders of Algeria.'

'Yet they are the ones who've been educated by France.'

'They would have been educated by anyone. They are intelligent enough to be educated on their own without the help of a colonial power.

558

Maybe differently, but cleverness doesn't depend on education. Look at some of the leaders of the wilayas.'

'Have they been educated without the help of the French?'

'Several of them. Look at Abane in prison. He's got more political acumen than most French men.'

'So, you don't tell the French what you know?'

'Marie, I'm a journalist for a communist newspaper. Why would I betray the Algerians? And, if you've got any sense, you won't either.'

'I thought the communists were backing the unions and the poorer pied noirs?'

'True, but back in Paris, they've misunderstood the situation. It's the Algerian worker who needs help here, not the French.'

'That's your point of view,' I remarked cynically, but I continued. 'I'm not intending to betray anyone, and I don't want to stay in Algiers anyway. I want a wider view of what's going on.'

'Fine, but don't expect to go into the bled and stay the same.'

'Have you been yourself?'

'No. I've been mainly to Oran to interview the French supporters of the FLN.'

'French supporters? Who are they?'

'A doctor and his wife. They can see what is happening from the Algerian point of view.'

'Sounds unusual.'

'It is and the readers of Humanité are enjoying hearing about them.'

Gilbert picked up the empty glasses which had been left on the tops as he walked round my room.

'Go to the bled, Marie and get a different angle on the whole thing. Nothing's really happening in Algiers at the moment anyway.'

'Apart from the newspapers being delivered.'

'I'm not saying that's not important. It is. It keeps everyone in the Casbah informed about what is really happening. But everyone's waiting for the referendum.'

'And then?'

'Who knows?'

'I think it could be bad.'

'Oh great,' I said sarcastically, 'Wonderful having you around, full of comfort and cheer.'

'Marie, if you just want to be around comfort and cheer, go and talk to the Figaro journalist or the Depêche d'Algérie – the people who believe in the status quo. Actually,' he corrected himself, 'The Figaro guys aren't that stupid. They're conservative and supporters of de Gaulle but they are aware of some of the problems.'

I reflected for a moment about my situation, before concluding, 'I think the best thing I can do is, I should get out to some of my contacts near Constantine. I've got links with wine growers there.'

'It sounds like Bourgeaud country.'

'Is that the man I met at Sérigny's party?'

'Yes, he's everywhere and very anti-independence.'

'He said to come and see him at his office.'

'He would do. He's always trying to influence French journalists.'

'Maybe, but actually Gilbert, I do have a brain.'

'From my experience here, you need a brain and very little heart.'

'I've got you. Thanks for your advice and for taking me to the Casbah. I think the Moudjhadin effort is fascinating. Do you have any recent copies? Could you translate some of it for me?'

'Sure,' he answered helpfully, 'Come to my room now. I don't allow copies out of there.'

And so, in the next couple of days, I took down some facts from the Moudjhadin and made my appointment with Bourgeaud, who made me an offer straightaway.

'You come down to my vineyards, Mademoiselle Marie. I'm going tomorrow. You can stay with my family and then go on further to meet Claude Tribier's cousin. It's a whole lot healthier in the bled compared to here in Algiers at this time of year.'

# Chapter Twenty-One

M. Henri Bourgeaud came for me the next morning, as I waited in the hotel. I suppose that it proclaimed to all observers that I was a friend of the richest pied noir in the country and the foremost supporter of Algérie Française; but I didn't care what anyone thought. Nor, as the car drew up in front of the second-rate hotel where I had been staying, did I care that my appearance did not match the style of my patron. I was just enjoying the fact that I was being picked up in a gleaming, luxurious Citroen car with a chauffeur and being invited to sit next to an urbane, confident and rich man. There had not been much contact with this species in my life, and I found it soothing and relaxing. For a few hours I was leaving the world of grubby hotels where washing facilities were inadequate, the world of discussion with highly principled left-wing journalists, and the world of unexpected terror. Luxury! I had the door held graciously open for me by the chauffeur and I found myself cocooned by the rich burgundy leather seats. I did not have anything to do but to enjoy myself.

'Now then, Marie,' enthused my fellow traveller, 'you are about to see the real Algeria. Sit back and enjoy it. It is the most beautiful country in the world.'

'So, in your opinion, it's not the same world as that of Algiers?' I enquired, intrigued.

'Algiers? Psst!' Monsieur Bourgeaud flicked his hand away contemptuously. 'Algiers is alright in its own way. It has a wonderful prospect over the sea. The parties are sophisticated, and all the educated Algerians speak the most beautiful French. Parliament meets regularly and is increasingly making good laws. But, apart from that, it's crowded, noisy, full of health hazards and the climate in summer is unbearable. I can hardly ever get my wife to come out here. She loves it in the mitjda and says there is no comparison. That is why I have to keep on going back home.'

'I thought you had business interests in Algiers. Even I have heard of the Bastos cigarettes.'

'Of course, of course and in these days of political debate, I have to keep on coming back here. But really, there is no comparison between the two places.

Sit back and enjoy, my dear Mademoiselle Marie. When we start getting into the hills, we will stop for a picnic en route.'

'Isn't that dangerous with so many bandits around?'

'Not if you know which village to stop in. I know those who I can trust in these places. So, while you are with me, Mademoiselle, you have nothing to be afraid of.'

And that's exactly how it felt – a sort of fairy tale existence, where I was under the protection of the King, who always knew best! I later discovered that that was indeed the nickname of Henri Bourgeaud. If you spoke to the nationalists, the term denoted privilege, riches, a sense of entitlement. If you spoke to his colleagues and admirers, it meant someone who was dignified, who knew his place and who treated his subjects in the best possible way.

We passed through the bidonvilles of Alger on our way out of the city. Some of the slums I had seen in Paris were bad. These were worse in terms of poverty – made of cardboard, no protection against the sun or rain and no sanitation. But in terms of freedom they were far better. They didn't have the grim odour of desperate, civilized poverty. Children could play where they wanted. People could share because there were no barriers between them. But I looked out on them through the windows of a luxury car and I knew that I didn't understand them at all. I could point at them as being how 'others' lived but their health problems, their lack of sustenance was nothing to me. Henri caught my look of curiosity as I gazed out.

'Poverty is at its worst near a big city because it cannot compete with its demands. You will see later, Marie, that the poor are much off in the bled.'

'Then, why do they come here?' I asked reasonably.

'Part of the allure of the big city and the illusion that they will make money here. It happens in every civilisation.' He paused. 'But naturally, there are more particular reasons here.'

'Meaning?'

'They come to escape the terror and the blackmail of the small villages.'

'But surely they find the same thing here?' I suggested, remembering my encounter in the Casbah.

'For some reason it's easier to avoid it in the big city. Yes, the terrorists have an effect here, especially in the Casbah. But that's more about the help they need in placing the bombs. Out here in the slums, there are so many of them, that if they're lucky, they can escape the attention of the bomb makers.'

'Don't any of them especially the young people want to be involved?'

'Mademoiselle Marie, the average Algerian wants to till his own soil or open his own shop and get his children educated. He doesn't care about politics.'

Try telling that to Abdelkrim, I thought.

'There are other reasons they come here too Many of them have been moved out of their villages by the FLN and the French.'

'You think both are at fault?'

'Yes, I admit both of them, but for different reasons. The FLN start the process by forcing a village to support them. If they don't agree, they kill some of them and then force the weakened community out of the village where they have always earned their living, even if they are dirt poor. They come to these bidonvilles, places of dirt and squalor and no hope, and they lose the will to live. They can't fight the FLN any longer, but they don't see any future for themselves under anyone's rule.'

'So how do the French force them?' I asked intrigued. 'And, surely, you, M Bourgeaud...'

'Henri,' he corrected me smiling.

'Henri, you have a part in this. You have been their representative in the French parliament for the last six years. You must have agreed to the tactics of the French.'

I expected his to argue against me, but, instead, he nodded thoughtfully.

563

'You're right, Marie. I have allowed the army to act in this way, but, sometimes, it seems as if I've had no choice.'

'That's what all tyrants say,' I responded tartly.

'Not tyrants, Marie – rather, those who've always tried to pacify both sides.'

'Like Pétain?' I suggested, aware of the harm that Pétain had done to his country, by capitulating to the Nazis.

'Yes, like Pétain. And I understood Pétain, even though he brought shame on his country.'

'But you've always supported de Gaulle?' I queried, perplexed by this ambivalence.

'Yes, I have, and de Gaulle was right, but it didn't mean that I didn't have any sympathy for Pétain, and, with a different outcome in the war, he might have been a hero.'

Considering all the blame which had been heaped on Pétain in the years after the war in France, I was surprised by the great man's reaction.

'Anyway,' I added briskly, more interested in the present situation than revisiting the past, 'What exactly have the French been doing in these villages?'

He sighed. 'You must understand, Marie, it's hard for me to talk about it. The French army have been fighting a war against terrorism in the past few years. For them, it's just a tactic. But for me, these villages – the felllahin – are people I've come to love.'

Not a reaction or vocabulary I expected to hear from the richest colon in the country.

'You'll understand what I mean when you see where I live and work. But the French army have needed a tactic to get rid of terrorists. So, in all the mountainous areas and in some parts of the plain, what we call the mitjda, where Algerians have villages without French influence, there have been three ways of isolating terrorists.'

'So not just following them up and capturing them?'

'That's too simple. They know the mountains better than anyone and it's easy for them to disappear into them; so, if you want to find them, you have to take a step back and find a strategy.'

'So, what has this strategy been?'

'You divide every area into three parts. You have parts, like where my businesses are, which are zones de pacification. That means you leave them as they are, because of their economic importance.'

'That's rather convenient for you,' I observed.

'Of course. But if you harm those areas, you not only harm the economy for the colons, but also for the felllahin.'

'So basically, you're saying that the army didn't do anything there.'

'Not quite. André Beaufré did. He's the general in charge of the whole Constantine area,' he added, seeing my lack of recognition of the name. 'They built more schools and gave the felllahin better facilities there.'

'They didn't want the French to leave?' I queried. 'A sort of blackmail or bribery.'

'Yes, but a bribery which benefitted the average Algerian.'

'OK, go on,' I asked him, fascinated by all that I was learning.

'Then you had the zones interdites. You settled all the villagers in this area and made sure they were guarded well and couldn't be in contact with the FLN.'

'I bet some of them managed it.'

'Undoubtedly. No question. But it's not been to their advantage to manage it.'

'You work very much on the idea of 'advantage' don't you, Henri?'

'Of course. It's realistic. Every regime does it. Lenin gave more corn to those who accepted his principles. It's human nature to follow things up to your advantage.'

'OK. What about the third area?'

'That's the Zones d'opérations. These were realistically the only areas left for the FLN to operate in and, because they were much smaller than the others, the army could pursue the terrorists more effectively, without the villagers hiding them.'

'Mmm. Sounds efficient. But you seemed to suggest before, that, although you were obliged to agree with them, perhaps in your heart of hearts you didn't really approve?'

The car had now left the outskirts of the city and was following a clearly marked road up through the hills. They became stony and inhospitable quite quickly but there were still outcrops of wood lower down. The chauffeur was driving quite carefully over the increasingly rough surface of the stony road – not particularly good for the chassis of a deluxe Citroen, I thought.

'Don't worry about the Citroen,' smiled Henri, reading my thoughts. 'They're built to withstand any terrain. Just admire the scenery and I hope you didn't have too much to eat this morning.'

'I don't often do breakfast. Why?'

'Because the bends start to get very twisty and Kaid doesn't slow down.'

'I'll make sure I concentrate on the view,' I conceded. 'But, to make my mind off those bends, tell me your real thought about the French army tactics.'

'I admit they're necessary and clever tactics. But unfortunately, when they moved the villagers out, they didn't just allow some of them to go to the bidonvilles of Alger and Constantine. They sent some of them to camps.'

I sat up straight and hung on to the front seat as the car lurched round the bend at speed.

'Camps? What sort of camps? Surely not concentration camps?'

The very name brought Nazi cruelty racing into my mind.

Henri sought to reassure me. 'Not in the Nazi sense, no. But sometimes there's not enough shelter and not enough food and water. And they can be hell on earth.'

'Apart from the horror which you are describing, surely that's not a way to make friends with the felllahin?'

'I agree, it's not; and that's what I keep on telling Beaufré, but he's too busy fighting the FLN and the military often don't see the bigger picture.'

'Which is?'

'What's going to happen when they've won.'

'Are they going to? Win, I mean?'

'They've got superior tactics and manpower and firearms. I don't see why not. But, unfortunately, it's not enough.'

'Why not?'

The car was now purring along the crest of the first hill.

'Because you've got to win men's hearts too, Marie, and unfortunately the French aren't very good at that.'

There was a pause. Instead of explaining further, Henri looked out of the window at the freshness of the morning. 'We're going to stop at the next village and get breakfast. The next part of the journey is breath taking and I want you to appreciate it on a full stomach.'

# Chapter Twenty-Two

I wondered what 'stop at the next village for breakfast' might mean. Was there a café there? Were we talking about the boulangerie in the French tradition? Did Henri have friends who would welcome him and his guest early in the morning? I couldn't see anywhere which looked inhabited, but I needn't have worried. Later, when I had visited Algeria many times, I discovered that in a completely empty landscape people miraculously appear from nowhere. Especially when it is in a desert scenario, it appears that there is nowhere to hide. But people blend into the background so effortlessly that they seem to appear by magic from nowhere and nothing. The other thing that I soon learnt was that Algerians are big on hospitality, and they can make you feel welcome in the middle of a wilderness.

As it turned out, it was neither a roadside café nor a friend's house. It was a picnic delivered from nowhere which arrived next to the Citroen.

A man in the traditional dress of the burnous, with a gun over his shoulder appeared next to the car as it travelled slowly over the atrocious road surface. Henri wound down the window to talk to him. I thought there was something familiar in the man's face, but I wasn't sure what and he ignored me completely. There was also a conversation between Henri and the chauffeur.

'We're just finding the right place,' Henri reported cheerfully.

I waited as the car slowed down ever further and pulled into the shelter of some olive trees by the side of the road.

'Perfect,' enthused Henri as if had just discovered the ideal picnic ground for his family on holiday.

'We'll have our mid-morning refreshments here, Marie.'

'It looks lovely,' I agreed. And, indeed, it did. The shade of the overhanging olive branches protected us from the rising heat on one side and over the other side of the road we could see the range of smaller hills going down to a plain in front of us and further in the distance a much higher range of mountains.

'But where's the café?' I asked innocently.

Henri laughed, an enormous, bellowing laugh, which seemed to rock his whole frame. It was one of the characteristics which I grew to appreciate about him – the capacity to laugh in a totally unselfconscious way, as if he spontaneously saw the potential for comedy in every situation. He said something to the chauffeur, as he got out of the car and Kaid enjoyed the joke too.

'The great thing about Algeria, Marie, is that you don't have to wait for a sign to go up announcing opening hours. Where there are people, there is hospitality.'

'Except your hosts have got guns,' I suggested cautiously.

'Ah, true. But that's only the ennui of the times. At the moment guns have to accompany coffee, but, please God, it won't always be like that.'

'That's a nice thought,' I responded, remembering the gloomy talks I had had with Gilbert in Algiers. 'I just hope you're right.'

He held the door open for me on my side, and when we went around the car, I saw that beautiful rugs, covers and cushions had been set up against the side of the car and in the shade of the olive trees.

'Now, Marie, it doesn't do to talk politics all the time, especially when you're about to enjoy the local hospitality.'

I laughed. 'No, I see your point. I have to say that this,' – I took in the sumptuous ground covering with my hand as I spoke – 'is looking promising.'

'And you haven't seen the main part yet,' said Henri, almost like a pleased parent looking forward to his offspring being delighted with his gift.

As he spoke, two men appeared from nowhere and placed a small silver coffee table in front of us, supported by separate, fold-up wooden legs.

Henri helped me to settle on the cushions though I couldn't help thinking that, with his bulky frame, he was the one needing help, but he was remarkably agile for a man of his size and in a moment he was presiding over the small cups, which were placed before us on the table. One of the men who was attending us held in his hand a beautifully ornate pewter coffee jug, the shape of which was so distinctive and artistically formed that I could have been content just to gaze at its exterior without the benefit of the hot liquid which was being poured out. Behind this server was another man who unfolded a cloth and placed it on the table. Uncovered, it revealed the beautiful sweet pastries made with honey and nuts which are so common in Algerian cafes. But these were not the average 'café fare' of the city. They were fresh from the oven and their surface seemed to sparkle with rays of the sun caught through the olive tree branches above us.

For me it was like an 'Alice in Wonderland' experience. I asked no more questions but submitted to being waited on and my material needs seen to.

I was amazed at how hungry and thirsty I was. I had left the hotel early in the morning without a drink, had felt sick on the winding road, and now was fully ready for the hot drink and food on offer.

When I stood up again, I noticed how many men there were standing at discreet distances with guns at the ready.

'You don't leave anything to chance in the countryside,' I observed. It was obviously not the idyllic pastoral scene I had been imagining in the last half hour.

'I didn't ask for them, I assure you. Of course, I asked for the coffee and cakes, but they provide the guards quite spontaneously.'

'Is that because they're worried that someone is going to attack you?'

'They are, yes. They know what it would mean for the villages where I own land, if I disappeared.'

'What would it mean?'

'To understand that, my dear, you will have to do the full journey and come home with me.'

'Yes, of course.' I suddenly felt embarrassed by my apparent rudeness and lack of appreciation. 'If that was the first part, then I'm looking forward to the second part of the journey. Thank you for the refreshments. They were wonderful and just what I needed.'

'You are welcome. And I can assure you that's it's the families of these men here who go to all the trouble.'

'Please thank them from me.'

'You can speak to them in French if you like.'

I did so, and they bowed courteously, whispering something to me, without catching my eyes directly.

I turned to Henri. 'What are they saying?'

'May God bless you and your husband, keep you safe and give you many children.'

I smiled. 'I don't have many prospects in that direction but thank you all the same.'

Henri moved to stand next to me. The covers and cushions were whisked away into the back of the car and we were off again, this time downhill. At a fork in the road, another track turned off up to further mountains, but we ignored it.

'That's up to Greater and Lesser Kabylia,' Henri informed me.

'Is that where there has been so much trouble?'

'There's trouble everywhere, but, yes, it's a good place for the FLN to hide, and there's some particularly tough customers up in those places.'

'Meaning?'

'Men who torture the people and their families, when they don't do what they want.'

'Worse than elsewhere?'

'There's a character there called Amirouche. He's one of the leaders of the Wilaya. He's ruthless. He even disgusts the most hardened fighters. You don't want to know what he does.'

'M. Henri, I am an experienced journalist you know.' I reminded him gently.

'You're also a delightful young lady,' he replied gallantly.

Elsewhere that sort of attitude might have annoyed me, implying that women such as myself could not cope with the real world. With my experience of the Second World War and overseas wars, it didn't seem to be a very relevant attitude. However, sitting in Henri Bourgeaud's limousine, it felt as though I was protected inside a charming and reassuring cocoon. What nicer idea than to be taken away from the mountains of Kabylia, where all the terror was happening, and speed down to the plains, where the great white King held court?

To begin with, as we descended into the plain, the soil seemed hard and infertile, but as we turned east, the countryside changed.

'We've channelled the water coming down from the side of the mountains,' my host explained.

'We've channelled? What does that mean exactly?'

'What it says. My family and our workers have channelled the mountain streams to irrigate this area.'

'So, it didn't happen naturally before you came?'

'Not at all. The soil on this plain was poor; it was fit only for herding the goats. Now, you will see, all of that has changed completely. Before we came, it was like the land to the West and the South of here, the Hodna.'

The car descended into the plain. We were surrounded by vines and cornfields. It was the sort of countryside you expect to see in the South of France before the rocky coastline takes over, but here, after the mountains to the north, it was a surprising view.'

'Welcome Mademoiselle, to the farms and lands of La Trappe. May you be very happy as you stay with us here.'

# Chapter Twenty-Three

If Henri Bourgeaud was a king, then his kingdom was magnificent. The vines were due to be harvested soon and there were scores of men out under the burning summer sun, testing them, and feeling them, watering them, making sure that they were just right for the autumn harvest.

'This is a very important moment before the récolte,' Henri informed me, full of pride in his own harvest success. 'If we get this wrong, then everything fails, and many people's income will fail.'

'Including yours presumably,' I dared to add rather cheekily.

'Yes, mine too. In one way that's not important at all. I have other sources of income like my cigarettes and the corn. But in other ways it's very important for the region. If my business goes down, I take my workers down with me.'

I couldn't argue with that. Having come from a region of independent small-holders, I had no understanding of big business. When I had investigated businesses in Paris, it was always from the point of view of the unions and the workers.

Suddenly we turned a corner and entered between huge gates which opened up to a gravel drive and then we went around the side to a huge terrace of a house or rather a mansion.

The first thing I saw nearest to me as I looked through the windows of the car, was the statues. In the middle of the terrace, leading up to the front door on every level were statues which were completely out of keeping with the style of the house, which was of a type you might imagine in a film about sub-Saharan Africa or the Southern states of America, where the mansion belongs to a plantation owner.

'Do you like my statues?' asked Henri impishly, as if he already knew the answer.

'Well, they're different,' I answered cautiously, not really knowing what to say. I'd never really liked the religious figures which were part of the wayside shrines which were common in Les Landes, and to see them under the African sun, seemed inappropriate to say the least.

'Come and look at them a bit more closely, as we go up to the house. There is a story behind them.'

'I thought there might be,' I remarked. I had no doubt that I was going to be 'regalé' with the full story sometime soon.

'Come and meet my wife, Denise. She'll have lunch ready for us.'

The chauffeur had gone ahead with our bags and Henri led me up the steps of the terrace, as an older lady in her early sixties, slim and well-kept and beautifully but modestly dressed, appeared above us.

'Bonjour, mademoiselle.' Madame Bourgeaud held me by my shoulders and kissed me affectionately. 'Henri told me how well you had reported on the situation of the Algerians in Paris and that you were listening to what was going on here – even if you are writing for a left-wing newspaper,' she added, with a twinkle in her eye.

'I hope Henri hasn't worn you out with the car swerving round those bends in the road at top speed.'

'Thank you, Madame. I survived.'

'Oh! please call me Denise.'

She was so genuinely welcoming that it didn't seem patronising or an attempt to be sycophantic, but entirely natural – one equal speaking to another.

'Thank you, Denise. I hardly noticed the road. Your husband kept me entertained all the way.'

'You mean he never stopped talking to you about the wonders of Algeria.'

'Something like that,' I laughed. 'But it wasn't boring, and I'm totally converted to the wonders of Algeria. What amazing vineyards you have here!'

'And even better wine I assure you. You must taste some of it while you are here. Do come into the house now and I will show you your room.

After you've felt a bit rested, I'll be serving a simple lunch. I know how your stomach feels after all those twists and turns with Kaid at the wheel. Later you can rest and make up for the simple fare with a proper meal in the evening.'

She quite unostentatiously went up to Henri and put her arms round him and kissed him. 'Lovely to have you back again, dear. I hope all that foolish political manoeuvring in Algiers hasn't worn you out.'

'Of course, it's worn me out. You know what I'm like, Denise, but the moment I saw our vineyards, my spirits revived.'

'Quite right too. They're doing so well this year, aren't they?' They fussed over each other like a pair of elderly housewives, but it was clearly a close and loving relationship. It occurred to me that it was one of the first examples I had seen of long-term married love. Whatever my journalistic purpose in coming here, I found that I had begun to relax and enjoy myself.

The house was built on one floor, but it was raised high on stilts and the terrace completely encased the stilts on one side. Apparently, the reason for the architecture was a practical one. When the Bourgeaud family first came here, there were many mosquitoes, because the land hadn't been drained properly, so the idea was to build the house away from such contagion.

When left to myself, I was able to unpack the few things I had brought with me – only one socially acceptable cocktail dress, which I had already worn at the Sérigny party and for the rest, a typically highly utilitarian wardrobe for a jobbing female journalist. But I wasn't worried. I had a feeling that the Bourgeauds were at ease with each other and with their guests. The sanitation was of the highest order, running water, showers and my own en suite toilet. Physical surroundings for this work placement were a lot superior to those in Indo China or Russia, I thought. There it had only been the awareness of my own body odour, which had persuaded me to go anywhere near water and the latrine pits had been a constant hazard. There were all sorts of non-professional reasons which made an assignment in Algeria a very pleasant surprise. At this moment, I didn't really care about the politics of the Bourgeauds. Their home felt like heaven.

After lunch I was shown round the house – a combination of gracious living and relaxation was my immediate impression of it.

'You must be exhausted after rushing round Algiers for the last few days, finding out about all the political shenanigans going on,' ventured Denise, sympathetically. 'No,' she held up her hand. 'Don't tell me that it's not a bear garden. I've spent enough time there myself to know about the 101 different political views on sale. And that's without the terrible violence and generals vying with each other to take power.'

'I take it you don't approve?' I suggested.

'I'm a simple person, Marie and I know how people get on. Here we concentrate on the important things and it's not constant argument and power politics.'

'And does Henri agree with you?'

'He does when he uses his common sense, don't you darling?' She appealed to her husband as he appeared around the corner of the terrace.

'She means I do when I follow my wife's opinion,' he laughed.

'You don't strike me as a hen-pecked husband.'

'Ah, Marie, there's more than one way of being worn down by your wife.'

'I can't say you look very worn down either.' The two of them were playing a delightful game together and, I sensed, would have been whether I was there or not.

'Henri does get drawn into politics sometimes, but it only makes him cross and uncomfortable,' was Denise's conclusion.

'And so, not very nice for my wife.'

'Not very nice for yourself, never mind for your wife.' She pinched him gently on the cheek, laughing.

'But no politics now, at least not until after the after-dinner sièste. Marie, feel free to rest in your room or relax out here on the terrace. I'll leave jugs of fruit juice and glasses in the kitchen and you can come and help yourself any time.'

'Thank you, Denise. I might go back to my room and have a sleep. I haven't slept well for the last couple of nights.'

'If you've been in Algiers, I'm not surprised,' she said sympathetically. 'Terrible place with the heat and the mosquitoes.'

She might almost have been talking about another country, I reflected. Clearly in her view – Algiers – bad; Mitdja- good. As I lay down on my comfortable bed with the shutters closed against the heat, I could see what she meant.

I woke up a couple of hours later, refreshed but confused. Had I really been transported to this haven of peace? Was it only two days ago that I had been wearing a haik and been held up and threatened by Abdelkrim? And was this part of the world one which Gilbert had seen or was he inhabiting an entirely different country? My head could not cope with the reality of where I was, but reluctantly I got out of bed, looked at the time and started to get ready for dinner.

I found Denise arranging plates and preparing entrées.

'Can I help at all?' It felt like asking my mother without the expected rebuff.

'You can take the olives and apéritifs through to the terrace. You'll find Henri there, pretending to read the paper, but really sleeping.'

'Do you not have any help preparing the meals?' I asked, surprised that a woman from her background, did not have servants to do the work.

'Yes, I have some for the general maintenance of the house and to help me in the kitchen when we have an overflow of visitors. But when it's just Henri and myself plus a guest or two, I like to do it myself. I enjoy looking after people.'

'Sounds good to me,' I said, happily as I helped take things to the table.

'And to me too,' added Henri, as he came into the salon. 'I'm just going to put on my other jacket for dinner, dear,' he told his wife comfortably, as if waiting for her approval.

'I should hope so, Henri. I don't want a man with a rumpled shirt and travel-stained jacket at my dinner table.'

'So, you like our place, Marie?' he asked, later, changed and ready to carve the lamb at the table.

'It's magnificent,' I assured him. 'but tell me about the statues. What are they doing there?'

'You've got him started now, Marie. Just let him serve the lamb first,' said Denise happily. 'He won't be satisfied until he's told you the whole story.'

'Good. I like a story,' I replied, intrigued.

'It all started in 1904.'

'Actually, it started long before in 1870,' Denise corrected him.

'You're right, my dear. It all started in 1870, when the first Trappist monks arrived with the French.'

'Monks? Here?' I was astonished.

'I know, I know. You don't quite connect them with the place as it is now, but they were here all the same.'

# Chapter Twenty-Four

We had such a wonderful time with the lamb and the cheese and Denise's home-made crème caramel that we didn't have the emotional energy or space for further conversation until coffee time on the veranda. Despite being French, I can recall very few such wonderful meals, and this one has become part of my emotional hinterland. For the last eight years I had been a journalist always on the go, and my life had been focused on my job. All domestic fripperies had been discarded in my effort to establish my professional reputation. It was true that I had had a really good meal in a restaurant with friends, but nothing like this. Beautiful food, the whole experience nourishing, not just the body but the soul, an aesthetic experience – the cut-glass wine glasses, the beautiful porcelain, the solid silver cutlery and the wider beauty of the scene, the terrace beyond the huge glass windows, the vineyards and the awareness of the distant mountains far beyond. It felt like the most beautiful, relaxing experience on the earth. My whole being was taken up in absorbing it. It wasn't until an hour later, totally satisfied and ready for a small black coffee to finish the evening that my mind had time for questions. For the Bourgeauds, eating like this must have been an everyday experience, but even they were relaxed as they answered my questions.

'So, tell me about the Trappists being here?' I managed to say.

'How much do you know about their history?' asked Henri

'Nothing at all apart from a vague idea about them being some sort of religious sect.'

Henri laughed at my ignorance. 'They started in the seventeenth century and were the Cistercians who had already been going since the twelfth century, so I don't think you could classify them as a minor sect.

They were part of the great French monastic tradition begun by St. Bernard.'

I was silent, afraid to reveal any more of my woeful lack of education in such matters.

'Don't worry, Marie.' Henri leant forward to pat my hand reassuringly. 'I'm not religious either so, if wasn't for the history of this place which belongs to my family, I wouldn't know anything about them either. The Trappist tradition started in the eighteenth century created by monks who thought the Cistercians weren't being spiritual enough.'

'You mean they were competing for being known as ultra-religious? Sounds familiar,' I commented cynically.

'Yes, I know what you mean, but the Trappists did put their spirituality into practice. They combined practical work, usually in farming or making alcohol, with contemplation and prayer.'

'The alcohol sounds alright.' I tried to make my tone as flippant as possible.

'As a seller of wine, I would tend to agree but the Muslims here would say that it was the prayer which was important.'

'Muslims?' There was genuine surprise in my reaction. 'Surely it was the wrong religion for them.'

'Mmmm. That's what you would think if you came from Europe. But, actually, the Muslims had a huge regard for the Trappists and their religion. There's another Trappist monastery near Tlcemcen, which is still going, and the brothers are highly respected.'

'Yes.' Denise came into the conversation at this point. 'They didn't like the Trappists leaving here. They much preferred them to the secular French government. They recognise and respect true spirituality when they see it.'

'If you say so,' I commented doubtfully, not anxious to get into a conversation about religion at this point.

'Anyway,' agreed Henri adroitly moving away from the subject of religion, 'because the Trappists were part of the French Catholic tradition – they originally came from Normandy – when the French occupied Algeria, they came here too.'

'What was it like here then?'

'When the Trappists arrived, it was a desolate wilderness. A few herdsmen with goats, a place overtaken by mosquito-ridden swamps, with nothing growing here. A wasteland, but little by little they started to change it. A lot of hard work.'

'And prayer,' I interjected piously.

'Indeed,' Henri replied seriously to my facetious comment. 'Prayer certainly made a difference. Within thirty years the place was transformed – the beginning of vineyards being grown and the start of the corn and orange trees.'

'I've seen the corn and the vines, but not the orange trees.'

'You will tomorrow when we show you round,' broke in Denise. 'The orange trees are the most beautiful of all. The scent of the blossom in spring is amazing and even now, seeing the fruit hanging from the branches, is to feel the succulence and bounty of the whole tree.'

Henri took over from his wife using less poetic language. 'The Trappists saw the potential for the whole place. They had some of the villagers working with them, but nothing like the manpower they really needed.'

'What happened to change that?'

'My father, Lucien, turned up in 1904.'

'Wow! What did he think of the place?'

'He was a financier and he was looking for somewhere to put his money before any more trouble happened in Europe.'

'You mean he saw the First World War coming?'

'Yes, he saw how things were going. He was a Swiss banker.'

I sat up and leaned forward away from the reclining back of my chair. This was an unexpected twist in the story.

'But I thought you were a French pied noir, M. Henri?'

'Oh! I am, but a naturalized one. My darling wife, Denise, is a true pied noir. I'll give you the full story of that later.'

His wife sighed smiling.

'Now look what you've done, Marie. You'll never get to bed. We'll be here for ever.'

'Well, I had a long sleep this afternoon. I'm ready to stay up.'

'Don't encourage him my dear. He will make the most of any excuse to get him going.'

'Can't you see, my darling, that she really wants to know?' Henri smiled triumphantly. He couldn't imagine anyone not wanting to know the full story of his family.

'My father, Lucien, was Swiss and he came here in 1904, when the Trappists had already started something good, but hadn't been able to expand because of lack of investment and manpower. I came here then.'

'What? In 1904? But surely you can't have been born by then?'

Like a woman, complimented on her youthful looking appearance in old age, Henri looked gratified. 'I was actually nine years of age.'

'So, this house wasn't built then?'

'No, but the stone masonry of the monastery was. And, yes, you can still see some of it. We've kept the chapel but most of the accommodation for the brothers was too rough and we couldn't use it.'

'And the statues?'

'Yes, we'll come to those later. They were originally part of the chapel and outside its entrance.'

'But you moved them in front of your house? Why?'

'We loved them. They were beautiful. But we're Swiss Protestants by origin, so they wouldn't have had religious significance for us.'

'But still some significance?'

'Yes, the history of this place, a reminder of the Trappists and what they achieved. I love them.'

'Alright. So, your father wanted an investment? But I can think of easier places to choose.'

'Of course, but France already had rich wine merchants as did Switzerland. My father wanted to start something different. And he wanted to pass on something worthwhile to his son.'

'Not all sons want to inherit their fathers' dreams.'

'True, but my father was much more practical than that. He came to live here himself, became French and made sure I was educated on the land.'

'How?'

'I got sent to the l'Institut Agronomique de Paris.'

'The top French place.'

'Exactly but he also brought me up here on this land. At 9 years of age, I fell in love with this place.

'Even though it didn't look like it does now,' he added.

'You must have really loved the land.'

'I did. I loved the chapel and the statues and the mountains beyond. It was like a huge adventure. Like the Americans going West.'

'And he's never fallen out of love with the dream,' added Denise, laughing.

'You've stayed here ever since you were a child?'

'Not quite, as well university in Paris, I was educated at the lycée in Algiers, but also there was the first world war.'

'Surely you were cut off from all that?'

'I could have been, but I felt an intense loyalty to my newly adopted country, so I went back to Europe and fought in it.'

'Amazing!' I thought back to my village and the hundreds of names on the war memorial. 'You could have got out of it so easily, but you didn't.'

'Probably, just part of being an idealistic young man, I guess, but I wanted to earn the right to do what I was doing.'

'To be honest, it's more amazing that you came out of the war unscathed.'

He suddenly turned serious. 'Marie, no one came out of that war unscathed. But if you mean physically, I had a bullet in my shoulder, which now aches when the Sahel blows too strongly.'

'And he was awarded the Légion d'Honneur for bravery,' added Denise proudly. 'That was part of the attraction when I met him at a party in Constantine.'

'When was that?'

'After the war. I was brought up in Constantine and the First World War didn't touch us too closely. Unlike many of the young men I knew who were glad to avoid being called up, Henri here was a hero! Once I had met him, I never wanted anyone else.'

'She has some sense you see, Marie.'

'I can certainly see that.' You couldn't really argue with two people who were so obviously passionately in love. 'I just wish it was like that for all of us,' I added wistfully.

'It will be one day, don't you worry,' said Henri knowingly.

583

'Well, I'm 29 and no sign of it yet. I've loved of course, two or three times quite passionately, but, apart from the first one, I've never had a sense of what people say is, "I know this is the one".'

'What happened to the first one?'

'He was shot by the Nazis before his family was sent to a concentration camp.'

No answer to that. We sat in silence over the remains of our coffee and against the enormous sky outside, I felt the bitter-sweet regret for what might have been.

# Chapter Twenty-Five

The next day I had a conducted tour of the estate. I had already told Henri that I wanted to write about the workers' lives in Algeria-both the workers, who were the felllahin and the workers, who were the pied noirs – and their opinions. Any clear-thinking communist newspaper had to be interested in both. The Communist Party supported the French workers in the Bourgeaud cigarette factory. They were interested in their rights and their future. I also wanted to know what an Algerian worker in the fields thought about the future of his country.

'That will be more difficult to gauge,' commented Henri over breakfast.

'Why?'

'Because the Algerian worker here is fairly inscrutable. He will tell you exactly what he thinks you want him to say.'

'But surely he must have a point of view.'

'Does he? If he earns enough money to buy his family food and clothes; if he feels secure; if he laughs and enjoys the festivals and practices his religion even at a basic level and isn't threatened and blackmailed, then he's happy.'

'You're saying he doesn't care who his country belongs to?'

'His country has belonged to so many different people – the Romans, the Ottoman Empire, the French.'

'I thought there was an Algerian freedom fighter here before the French took over?'

'Abd al Qadir? Yes, but he was an Arab and most of the workers here are Kabyles.'

'Does that matter?'

585

'My dear, they are two different races. They work side by side in an uneasy alliance, but, given the chance, they will always fight each other.'

'So, you don't think I'm going to get any answers out of your workers?' I was disappointed. This was after all why I was in Algeria.

'Oh, don't worry,' he replied laughing, 'You'll get plenty of answers. It's just that you'll never know which one is the truth. Look, Marie. The papers are always looking for an article which supports their political point of view. So, that's what you need to write. But don't just write about what the workers say. Write about what they do.'

'How will that help? Surely all workers 'do' the same.'

'It's the way they do it that matters. You must look at the way my workers work. Draw your own conclusions and write about that.'

I had no choice except to follow his advice. I was put under the direction of the Algerian manager of the vineyard. Henri had other business to attend to and, 'Besides,' he added with a smile, 'You don't want me bearing down on you all the time. You want to make sure that the workers are free to make their own comments without the boss looking at them all the time.' Then he added practically, 'If you come home at dinner time after the sièste, Denise will take you to the school.'

'Where's that?'

'About half a kilometre from here near where the workers' families live. Denise often goes there to help. She'll be your expert guide.'

I met the manager outside the main house, charming, attentive and polite as I had found many Algerians to be. The grapes were at their full ripeness and lots of the workers were engaged in filling the vats ready to be taken to the fermenting shed.

'It must be strange for Muslims to be engaged in making something which is against their religion,' I suggested.

'They don't have any difficulty in accepting that Europeans have different rules for their religion,' answered the manager.

'In that case, they must be the only religious people who accept others' views so easily,' I observed sardonically, and he smiled.

'Actually, in the towns they see Europeans behaving badly under the influence of drink, so they don't envy them. And, more than that, here they appreciate their work and what the boss gives them.'

'What does the boss give them?'

'A better wage than what they would have got elsewhere in the country.'

'More than their own bosses would have given them?'

Ali snorted in disgust. 'Here they get the top wage in the country, more than any other boss, whatever their background, would give them.'

'Are there French workers here too?'

'Yes, in the cooling sheds where the vats are. M. Bourgeaud always brings some specialists over from Europe at this time of year.'

'And do they get more than the Algerians?'

'If they are experts, yes. If they're labourers, no. If they're French, they get free wine as a gift, but M. Bourgeaud makes it up to the Muslims by giving them more oranges.'

'Oranges? Yes, of course, I'd forgotten about them for the moment.'

'That's our next stop. Do you want to get in the truck, Mademoiselle, and we'll go there now?' As he drove the truck, he continued to give me information.

'To get orange trees of this quality, M. Bourgeaud had to drain the swamps first years ago. When he first took over the land from the monks, he concentrated on the récolte de raisins. But then he gradually moved to corn and then to oranges.'

'How long have you been working here, Ali?'

'About fifteen years. I started here as one of the grape pickers, but gradually moved to become the manager of the vineyard.'

'Have you never wanted to move anywhere else?'

'Like where?'

'Algiers? Constantine? A big city?'

He shook his head emphatically. 'Never. I was raised in the mountains to the north of here.'

'The mountains of Kabylia?' I was gradually getting my geography sorted out.

'Exactly. My father was a poor herdsman. We were ten children and most of the time we were hungry. I had heard about this place and how the workers were treated. My father didn't want me to go. He knew nothing else but the village and the herd and he thought it would bring trouble if I came down here. But my mother wanted me to come.'

'Why?'

'She wanted something better for her children than the cold and starvation. She'd heard that there was a European who provided for his workers.'

'And does he?'

'Mademoiselle, you cannot believe the difference between what the workers have here and their existence in the mountains. It's not just the wages. There, they have to pay money they haven't got to the caid and the garde-champetre.'

'Who's that?'

'The guard, like a policeman in the towns. He reports to the French and he fleeces the villagers as well as reporting them to the authorities for things they haven't done.'

'And you escaped all that?'

'Luckily, Mademoiselle. I thank Allah every day that I came to work here.'

Later we passed the cornfields where the cobs were piercing through the reddish webs surrounding them. When we first rounded the next corner, I could hardly believe the miles and miles of orange trees, which were now planted and the irrigation channels on the side of the orchards. The scent, as we got out of the truck, was overpowering.

'How difficult is it to grow oranges here?' I asked Ali. I had always associated oranges with South Africa.

'It was very difficult for the boss to begin with, making sure that the soil was rich enough and watering it.'

'Did he know what he was doing?'

'Not at first, I think. But he brought over experts each year and learnt from them.'

'You're saying he did all the work himself?'

'More or less. M. Borgeaud isn't afraid of hard work, Mademoiselle. That's why the workers respect him so much. He leads by example.'

'And he pays more than most European bosses would you say?'

'Much more, and he provides clinics and schools too. Madame Bourgeaud will show you later this afternoon.'

If I thought I had something to write about after that morning's visit, it was nothing to what I saw in the afternoon with Denise.

Later, after we had avoided the pounding sun of the early afternoon, we walked the kilometre to the area where the workers had their quarters.

'Come and see what some of these ladies are doing.'

We knocked on the door of one of the squat houses, made of baked bricks. The door was opened by an eight-year old.

'Hamid, you should be away to afternoon school by now,' Denise scolded. She explained that often the boys of the family opened the outside door so that the women were not in danger of being seen unveiled by anyone outside.

'But that's mainly the Arabs,' she went on to explain. 'The Kabyle women are much freer, at least in the way they dress. If you stay around, you'll get to recognise the difference.'

We went through into the front room, used by the men in the evening, through a courtyard and then into a room, where a young woman was seated on a low stool in front of a loom.

'Es…sabel …her.' Denise greeted her in colloquial Arabic, which is so much more straightforward than classical Arabic. The young girl, clearly the mother of Hamid, returned Denise's greeting but kept on with her activity. Not far from her, an old woman, her mother-in-law apparently, was carding the sheep's wool and making it into a long twine.

'Just look at this beautiful pattern.' The pattern forming itself on the loom's surface onto the woollen material was indeed complex and beautifully designed.

'They have a natural talent for this, going back centuries,' explained Denise, 'but the nuns also have been great teachers.'

'Nuns?'

'Oh yes, in Kabylia, under Archbishop Lavigerie, lot of the White Fathers and Sisters came to Algeria and taught people these skills.'

'Can they make money out of this?'

'Of course. It will be packed off to Algiers and Bougie and Constantine and sold to French tourists.'

After the customary refreshments were offered and accepted, we left the house and walked past what looked like a more modern building.

589

'This is the clinic where the workers come for inoculations, and to see the nurse.'

'Who provides that?'

'We do. It's quite simple. Look after your workers well and they will be better workers and loyal. We don't wait for the French government to provide medical aid. It would be too far away for them anyway, and if you have seven or eight children, you could never keep up with the inoculations. Besides, they like the personal touch.'

'The personal touch?'

'Yes, the fact that we, their employers, find the nurse and make sure she does her job properly. They like it, even though they could go to the town and get the same inoculations there.'

'You mean they wouldn't bother?'

'It's difficult to explain. It's not just the distance. Again, it's the personal touch. That's what they like. It's like with the missionaries.'

'You mean the White Fathers?'

'No, I mean the Protestant missionaries. Some of them are medical workers too. The Kabyles would far rather go and see them, than the government workers in the official clinics, because they trust them, and they pray for the patients.'

'Even though they have a different religion?'

'It doesn't matter. It's a sense of the spiritual. They like it. They feel blessed by their attentions, and that's far more important than the pills and the injections.'

This was, for me, a surprising revelation and gave me something to think about as we walked from the clinic to the school room, where we could hear lessons being repeated.

'Do they learn in Arabic?'

'Yes, but as they get older in French too, because this will help the ones who want to go further with their education and anyway, for the Kabyles, even Arabic is a foreign language.

Before you leave us, Marie, you'll have to come to the prize giving and you'll see how proud the children are of their education here.

We haven't got time to stop now. I have to prepare dinner for tonight. We have an extra guest with us.'

# Chapter Twenty-Six

To say that I helped Denise prepare dinner would not be accurate, because she knew exactly what she wanted to do. But I did hang round the kitchen with her, cutting up vegetables and marinating cuts of meat which she had ordered. It was a relaxed companionship in domestic work, which I had never really experienced before. She was the easiest person to be with – the ambitions of her life seemed to be small, but she did whatever she undertook with considerable skill.

'Have you never regretted coming to this out of the way place?' I ventured, as I saw her prepare dishes which would have been acceptable to many professional chefs.

'Never,' she replied resolutely. 'And what would I have done with my life anyway?'

'A career?'

'Women in my day didn't have careers. They were stuck in offices, serving bad-tempered men, until their time came, and they found someone who would marry them.'

'Thereafter they served bad-tempered men in a different way.'

She laughed. 'Maybe. But at least they loved them.'

'Or so we imagine.'

'Don't be so cynical, Marie. Most marriages that I have come across have been happy when there has been determination to make them succeed.'

'It sounds like a lot of effort to me. And what do you get out of it in the end?'

'Children, grandchildren, friends and a companion.'

'So, is it worth it?'

She paused for a moment before answering. 'Yes, I think it is. If I had continued as a single girl, I would have carried on going to dances and concerts but in the end, I would have been bored by it. And Henri has given me so much.'

'It must have been a risk.'

'Love is always a risk,' she said simply. 'You can never be sure how it's going to work out.'

'So, is it worth the risk, when there are so many bad marriages?'

'The really bad ones I couldn't comment on. Fortunately, nowadays there are ways out with divorce. You don't have to be stuck there for ever.'

'The problem is,' she reflected with her knife in her hand before she dissected the salad and tomatoes, 'that, if you reject love, you end up bitter and isolated, and turned in on yourself, and that is a sort of hell, not freedom.'

'All I can say is, I hope I will know when it's worth taking the risk, as you claim.'

'You'll know. And then you must jump.'

'It hurt a lot last time when I lost a person I loved. The others didn't hurt as much, even though I was sad, because I didn't love them as much.'

'Love always hurts. It's part of the risk. When you lose the person you love through death, it's going to hurt like hell.'

'Do you ever think about it, Denise – I mean losing your husband?'

'Of course. Every time he goes to Algiers, I wonder whether he will ever come back again.'

'It's that risky?' I asked, shocked.

'It's that risky, especially for a man like Henri, who has openly supported the French government.'

'But what would anyone gain by destroying him?'

'Absolutely nothing.' She stood in the middle of her kitchen, with her beautifully manicured hand sweeping aside her bobbed, white hair. 'But you see, they don't do things to gain; they do things to lose.'

'What do you mean?'

'If they can't get a gain out of it, they would rather other people lost.'

'You mean they do it deliberately to cause other people pain? And,' I added, before she had chance to answer, 'are you saying they don't have any ideals – because if you are, I don't think that can be true. The FLN do have ideals – they might be misguided but they do have ideals.'

'Yes, they had ideals at the start. But the ideals became more important, than the people they are supposed to help. The more they rely on the ideals, the more they forget about the people.'

'You think they don't care about the people?'

'I don't think. I know they don't care about the people.'

I was surprised by the vehemence of her judgements. I had thought her to be a charming addition to her husband, a homemaker, who enjoyed the high life in the bled. I saw now that I was wrong. This was a woman with a carefully worked out philosophy of her own. 'If they cared about people, they would not torture an old man in the village to find out about the movements of his son. Yes,' she replied to my unspoken question. 'That's what they did to Ali's father. They raped his wife and daughters and cut off his testicles because they couldn't get the information they wanted. Hatred of one manager who worked for Europeans and had done well for himself was more important to them than honouring a family of their own people in the mountains.'

'How did Ali react?'

'You won't see a reaction on any of these men's faces, but he will bide his time and enact revenge.'

'That's no better than the original act.'

'It's the only weapon he has to fight against the hatred that is ripping his country apart.'

'From what I've heard the French soldiers do that as well in order to win the country for themselves.'

'Granted that the French have done terrible things, but if they don't win the war, chaos and hatred will take over. There will be no agriculture, no future, no prosperity.'

'Isn't that a bit extreme?' I reasoned. 'I thought the FLN had their own goals for the economy and education.'

'Maybe they have. But it will take years to come to fruition and by then most of the people will be dead.'

'But free?'

'What sort of freedom is it just to know misery? And it's not as if there isn't an alternative.'

'Which is?'

'If the people vote 'oui' in the referendum, then we can gradually hand over the country to the Algerians. Yes, it will be hard for us because we have always lived here, but it is right that they should become independent.'

'I thought that most of the French here don't agree with that?'

'Some of the French don't see that, but the intelligent ones do, and they will support de Gaulle.'

'What will you and Henri do?'

'We will gradually give up our ownership of this place. We will gradually sell it at a knock-down price to Algerians who will know how to manage it for their people. We will train them. There is no doubt about it. We love this country. We don't want it to go back to chaos and poverty.'

'And what will you do?'

'When we feel as though we have done a good job, we will go back to France. And we will live well, of course, because we are rich enough to do that. This place will always be in our hearts. But we want to leave it to the people of this country, for the children who have attended our school.'

I noticed with a shock that there were tears in her eyes as she spoke. 'You see, Marie, I talked about the risk of loving and we were talking about falling in love with a man, but love can take many forms and Henri and I have fallen in love with this country. We know that we will have to leave eventually, but that doesn't mean it wasn't worth loving in the first place.'

She caught herself up suddenly and raised her eyebrows at me. 'And now you've got me all sentimental and unable to concentrate on what I'm doing. Our guests will be arriving soon, and they will be hungry.'

'Guests?' I had forgotten that she had mentioned this before.

'And I thought you were preparing this feast just for me,' I quipped, adopting her own lighter tone.

'Don't worry, my dear, you can be part of it too, and I always cook special things for Henri, even when we're alone.'

'Lucky Henri.'

'Indeed, and lucky me that I have someone who I love to cook for.' Then she turned to practicalities.

'Marie, you'll find the silver cutlery in the drawer of the sideboard. And you'll find the linen napkins and the candles in the drawer next to them.'

I hardly knew how a table should be laid out in the correct manner, but I tried to remember back to the occasional formal dinner party which I had attended in France.

I had just lit the candle in the centre of the table and was deciding on the best setting for the dessert spoons, when a voice spoke behind me.

'Mademoiselle Marie, now you've surprised me again. I didn't expect you to be the expert on table settings.'

I turned around, with dessert spoons in hand, recognising again the timbre of the voice and then the features of the man who was speaking to me.

'It's Yussuf, isn't it?'

'Indeed, it is.'

Instead of taking my proffered hand, he kissed it and it had the effect of being formal and respectful.

'Marie, let me introduce you to my friend and colleague, Christophe Bourgeaud.'

'Welcome to our house, Mademoiselle Marie. Yussef has already told me all about you.'

# Chapter Twenty-Seven

I was taken aback by seeing Yussuf in such different surroundings. On board ship coming over to Algeria, he had seemed like a romantic figure, dressed smartly in his military uniform, with dance music in the background and someone who could find the right time and place for private conversation up against the lifeboats. I would not have called him 'good-looking' in the conventional sense, but he had intense, intelligent eyes and a slightly disjointed nose and was of medium height but very muscular – not a spare inch of fat. There was a restless energy moving within his frame. On board he had seemed to me to have a very suave appearance. Here in this house he was dressed as a local farmer with clean clothes, wide pantaloons and an overshirt. In this European environment and inside a sumptuous house, he seemed an alien figure.

However, he seemed completely at ease now as he introduced me to the young man who was standing behind him.

'This is my friend, Christophe Bourgeaud. And, yes, in case you're wondering, he's part of this household.'

'Delighted to meet you, Marie.' Christophe came forward and kissed me on both cheeks, as if we were already comfortable together. 'Not only Yussuf, but my father has been talking to me about you, and he obviously holds you in high regard.'

'That's very kind of him, but I don't really know why he should. He's the one who's been doing all the giving and the informing so far, and I've just sat back and let him do it.'

Christophe looked at me with amusement. 'Ah, well, that just shows your wisdom. You've allowed my father to do exactly what he likes doing and that is bound to put him in a good humour.'

'You should always trust your father's good humour and his good character judgement, Christophe,' said Denise, appearing out of the kitchen with salad and endives and tomatoes in her hand, ready for the entrée.'I've also enjoyed having Marie with us, so it's not just your father's bias.'

Christophe hugged his mother affectionately.'Now that tells me far more. You'd get into my father's good books just by humouring him at the right moment. But, maman – that's different altogether. You never let bad people through the sieve, do you?' He hugged her again, laughing affectionately.

'I should hope not. I've been making good judgements ever since I met your father. And I always know the people who work here. And, Yussuf,' She had now placed the serving plates down on the table.'How delightful to see you! And, though I like seeing you in your military uniform, you still look quite delightful as the local farmer's lad, from the bled.' With that, she kissed him three times, according to the Algerian fashion, and with evident warmth and sincerity. I was intrigued. How come a local peasant, as I assumed Yussef's origins to be, could not only visit the Bourgeaud empire, but be completely accepted as an equal in their mansion?

As if answering my unasked question, Denise informed me, 'Yussuf has always been part of this household. He grew up here and was Christophe's best friend.'

'Not 'was',' chimed in her son,'is my best friend.'

'So how come you two got so close together?' I asked them intrigued.

'You mean, considering we came from opposite sides of the line and opposing cultures?' Yussuf suggested bluntly.

'Ah, now, you three young people have met,' came the booming voice of Henri Bourgeaud, as he moved triumphantly from his own study in another part of the house to the dining area.

'I assume you've made your introductions. Shall we sit down, my dear?' he asked his wife who was in charge of the food.

'Yes, Henri, let's get going with the entrée.'

'And shall we have some 45 to celebrate?' he enquired as he drew back his heavy oak chair.

'What's that?' I asked, intrigued.

'It happens to be the prize wine of the vineyard. We keep a few each year for celebrations.'

'That sounds wonderful,' I enthused. 'And what exactly are we celebrating?'

'Lots of things,' confirmed Henri contentedly, as he uncorked one of the chosen bottles.

'Christophe being on leave. Seeing Yussuf look like a normal human being rather than a bandit. The fact that things seemed to have calmed down in Algiers for the time being. Even Soustelle is being sensible. And having the beautiful Marie with us.'

I bowed in acknowledgment of the compliment. 'Let's hope my editor in France thinks I'm using my time well.'

'He's bound to,' said Henri modestly. 'How could it not be time well spent talking to the richest French citizen of the country?'

'The only trouble is,' I said, happily receiving my glass of celebratory vintage wine, 'I do actually work for the left-wing press and I'm supposed to be reporting on the state of the workers in Algeria.'

'Nonsense,' answered Henri robustly, as if he could solve all the problems of left-wing editors just like that, 'You've spent all day with Ali and heard all about what the workers do here. Then you spent all afternoon with Denise, and she told you all about the workers' wives and children here. What more does this man want?'

'Papa, you know perfectly well what she means,' remonstrated his son. 'Writing about the workers on this estate here, does not justify the working conditions of all the Algerians or the pied noirs in the rest of the country.'

'No, it doesn't, but it tells you the truth about some of them. And they shouldn't ignore these ones here. And Marie can include them in her report. And what's more she's going on to Gaullen's empire near Constantine so she can write about the workers there too.'

'You're going to Constantine?' Yussuf suddenly looked more serious.

'Yes, I've got an invitation there through a contact in Marseille. Is there any reason I shouldn't go there?'

'You need to be careful. There's been quite a lot of unrest there recently.'

'Nonsense, Yussuf.' Henri dismissed his objection airily. 'There's always unrest in Constantine. If it's not Beaufré,, then it's Challe. And if it's not those two, then it's Amirouche and all his brigands. We can't just refuse to go about our business because of people like them. Let the girl get about. The French papers need to know what's going on.'

'My father dismisses all the fighters on both sides as naughty school children,' his son informed me. 'He doesn't see why he should let them stop him doing anything he likes.'

'I can't imagine your father letting anyone stop him doing what he wants,' I agreed. 'He's really unstoppable.'

'But one day, you are going to be stopped, sir,' said Yussuf more seriously, 'And I don't want you to be here when that happens.'

'Stop being so morbid, Yussuf. Get the 45 down you. We don't know what miracles de Gaulle is going to bring about.'

'The problem is that everyone will think he is bringing about a miracle and they will all be thrilled. But I'm afraid that the miracle will vanish into thin air.'

'So, you think that the French will be defeated?' I asked, sensing that some serious points were being made.

'If you mean in a military sense, not at all. Challe's got the upper hand. He's chasing away the opposition all the time.'

'But surely in a war, victory must mean a military victory?'

Yussuf looked serious. 'You can win battles, but you can lose a war.'

'How do you mean?'

'If you lose people's hearts, you will lose the war.'

'And have the French done that?'

'Yes.' 'No.' Both answers came at once from different ends of the table. The 'no' came from Henri. He could not believe that all he had given his Algerian workers and the huge boost he had given to the country's economy through his businesses, had not been appreciated. The 'yes' came from his son, Christophe. He could see what was happening on the ground. Brought up in the bled, fluent in Kabyle and Arabic, he saw clearly that the FLN were winning hearts and minds.

'Papa, you have to accept that the French are finished in Algeria.'

'Christophe, I have no intention of being finished in Algeria.'

'And what about you, Denise?' I enquired of his wife, who had been silent so far. 'What do you think?'

'I will stay with Henri, whatever,' she replied simply, not because she had to, but out of loyalty to the man she loved.

'That is a beautiful statement,' I observed, 'but not quite the same as an answer to the question.' I couldn't quite decide whether the look she gave me was one of sadness or irritation, as if she was annoyed that I had not sufficiently understood her position.

'It is the only answer which is worth giving. I want to stay with Henri because I love him. I want to stay in Algeria because I have always loved its people and I want to be part of them.'

'But it's not enough, Maman,' observed her son seriously.

'How can it not be enough, Christophe?' she answered him. 'Surely, love is the best answer of all.'

'It's not enough because the people who want to change things have the upper hand.'

'I can only hope that the people who want to change things have the same love as I do.'

Yussuf came into the discussion at this point. 'Some of them do. Of that I have no doubt.'

'So why are you fighting them?' I asked reasonably.

He turned to me as he answered. 'Because not all of them do. Some of them love ideas more than the people. They will follow their ideas through to the end, even if it means hatred and carnage.'

'But surely only because they think that the ideas are good for the people?'

'Maybe, but it depends whether you can stand all the hatred going on meanwhile.'

'And you can't?'

'I can't stand to see all the good things,' he swept his hand around to include all the lands of the mitjda, 'disappear, for the sake of people who are perhaps more personally ambitious than they are filled with love for their fellow countrymen.'

'You must be in the minority.'

'I am, in that I'm prepared to say it. I'm not, in that many ordinary people privately feel it. The ordinary person here wants prosperity and freedom to give to his family what he has not had.'

'As far as I can see the French haven't been very good at doing that.'

'No, you're right. They haven't and that's the trouble.'

'How many people think like you?' I asked, intrigued.

'Apart from the village people, who just want to live the way they've always lived, you mean?' I nodded my head. 'There are educated Algerians who have gained from the French system. They are the moderates. And then there are the harkis like me.'

'Harkis?'

'Yes, those of us who fought in the war for the French battalions. We fought for the freedom of France and Algeria. I just can't turn my back on them now.'

'So, you prefer to fight against your own countrymen?'

'Only against those who threaten and kill their own for the sake of their political ideals. Generally, I'm a scout not a soldier.'

'Yussuf is one of the harki scouts,' explained Christophe. 'It means he finds out where the most extreme bandits are and tells the French.'

'That's why it's so delightful seeing him tonight dressed as a normal person,' chimed in Henri. 'Normally he's clambering up mountains relying on his wits.'

'And you do this out of loyalty to the French?'

'I do this because I want to protect my people, allow them to keep the good things they have and to protect them from the extremes of communism.'

I was silent. I had seen this situation in too many other places to know that there was no easy answer.

'If you want to see how the ordinary people live, Marie, you'll have to come with me to see how they are living.'

'You want Marie to climb up the mountains of Kabylia after you?' asked Henri, sounding horrified and incredulous.

'If she really wants to see how the Algerian people live and what they want, yes.'

601

He had ignored the comments of those around the table and was staring directly at me. I held the gaze of those intense eyes. The idea of clambering up mountains at a reckless pace rather than staying in the luxury of Henri and Denise's beautiful estate was not tempting. But here before me was a challenge for a journalist from a vibrant man, full of integrity, with questions, which had no easy answers.

'Sure. I'll do it. This place is beautiful, but I'd be a fool if I thought this was the real world for everyone. When do we start?'

# Chapter Twenty-Eight

I waited for another day because Denise wanted to show me her school and introduce me to some of the pupils who were working in the vineyards and fields of the estate during the summer holidays. They answered all my questions about their education, and I thought that the appreciation shown by the families for all they received from their employers was genuine. Schooling was free for the children of the estate; they could speak in Kabyle or Arabic as they wished in the playground, but they learnt to read and write in French. If they wanted to read the Qu'ran in Arabic, then they attended a special madrassa in the mosque on Saturday mornings. After the age of fourteen, if they were especially able, they attended the French lycée in Tizi Ouzou or Sétif, , especially if they were able to board with relatives. It reminded me of my own elementary education in Les Landes. Most of the families regarded further education as an unnecessary luxury, especially for the girls, who only needed, in their opinion, to be able to sew and knit. However, Monsieur and Madame Bourgeaud insisted that the girls had to read and write and do arithmetic as well. 'Apart from anything else, some of them may be involved in their husbands' 'commerces' as book-keepers later on,' explained Denise practically. 'And then some basic maths will be helpful. Some families are able to look to the future and want more for their girls, but most of them do not. We had a very clever girl here a couple of years ago and we tried to persuade her to do the science course at Tizi Ouzou, but the parents didn't see it that way.'

'That sounds like a lot of parents of girls in Les Landes,' I observed drily. 'However, some of us were lucky enough to have teachers who really cared and inspired us.'

'Oh! I know. It's the same story the world over, both for the boys who are encouraged only to do traditional farming and certainly for the girls, who can get married from the age of 13 onwards.'

'Are they allowed to do that under French law?' I asked, shocked.

'Of course not. But they do. Tradition is stronger than the law in these parts. And you're right about the inspiration of teachers. I'd love to have been one.'

'It sounds as if you are one anyway.' I had heard enough now to know how much Denise took an interest in the school and inspired the children.

She smiled. 'Only unofficially, but I do care about the children, it's true.'

Every autumn on the estate, each child was presented with a new school uniform, free of charge. 'That way everyone is equal,' Denise informed me. 'No child will be different because their parents don't approve of education.' And each December, the children received gifts for Christmas.

'They don't care about it being a religious festival.' Denise answered my unspoken question. 'It's just a time of celebration and fun for our school.'

'Do your freedom fighters object to Christmas being celebrated?' I asked Yussuf later.

'Yes, of course, because it's part of the colonialists' religion.'

'You can see their point of view.'

'I would agree if they didn't object to fun anywhere for anyone. Believe you me, they're far too busy making sure everyone uses the right revolutionary tactics, to have fun themselves.'

'I suppose then they object to Eid El Kbir and other festivals?'

'Strangely enough, no.'

I was surprised. In my experience, all Marxist regimes objected to religious observance.

'No, they are different.' Yussuf explained. 'They pride themselves on being unique.'

'Well, good for them. Perhaps they will bring about something great for their country.'

'Perhaps, but I don't trust them.'

'Why not?'

'Because they kill too many of their own people.'

'All partisans have done that, even in the last war.'

He sighed. 'True. War is a hellish business. I don't know, Marie. There are no simple answers.'

I admired him for saying that. I have met many passionate men and women who are completely committed to their political views. I have not met many who can get inside the skin of their enemy. With Habibi in Paris and Yussuf, I met educated and thinking men who could see the point of view of others.

Yussuf came for me early next morning. He had been staying with cousins on the estate for three nights – apparently an unusual break in his routine as a harki scout.

'Do they agree with what you are doing?' I asked him.

'They understand what I'm doing. All the families here do. They've been the recipients of the Bourgeads' generosity for years.'

'Maybe they don't want colonialists being patronising to them?' I suggested.

He laughed. 'Just wait till you see how some of the villagers live in the mountains, Marie. Never mind being patronising, everyone envies the families here. They have enough to eat, and they work hard for their food.'

We were driving in an old covered waggon from the estate, taking melons up for sale in the villages.

'Is this part of your work?'

'Yes, in a way. I might as well make myself useful while I'm here. And doing genuine business makes me useful as eyes and ears for the authorities.'

With the huge yellowy green melons and dark green watermelons bouncing in the back behind us, we drove up through the mountains, stopping off at village markets on the way.

'You don't need to get out at every market stall,' he reassured me. 'But if you do get out, make sure you stay in the background and observe.'

'Do I need a head covering?'

'No, not here. Most of these are Kabyle villages and the women don't veil.'

'Does that mean they have freer lives?'

He snorted and looked at me askance. 'Don't confuse the two ideas. In some ways the Kabyle women are more under their husbands' thumb than the Arab women. They have to do exactly what their husbands say inside, not to mention their mothers-in-law.'

'It sounds awful.'

He grinned at me. 'It's a woman's lot.'

'Not as far as I'm concerned,' I retorted hotly. 'If the Marxists change that, they'll be doing everyone a great service.'

For a moment he looked serious. 'If they do manage to do that, I'd agree. But somehow, I rather doubt it. Tradition here is very strong.'

'They've managed it in Russia and Indo China,' I pointed out. 'The women are equal to the men in revolutionary terms.'

'But the revolution's come out of different religious traditions,' he replied. 'No one really knows what an Islamic Marxist state will look like.'

'So, we wait to see what will happen?'

'When it happens, I won't be there,' he observed simply.

'Why not?'

'I'll either be dead or in a different country. It's only my family who would keep me here.'

'You'd stay for that reason, even if that means you'd lose your freedom?'

'What's the point of being free if all your family have been killed or are being threatened? I could never do it.'

Like Alain, I thought.

We came to a lower ridge on the West side of a mountain range.

'See those mountains up there?' He pointed to a huge dark mountain range ahead.

'That's where we're going tomorrow. But for now, we're going through Souman.'

'Where's that?'

'Between the two mountain ranges of Greater and Lesser Kabylia.'

I sensed immediately that it was somewhere important for him. 'What goes on in Souman then?'

'It's already happened. The great conference.'

'What conference?'

'The first great ALN/FLN conference on Algerian soil.'

'You mean there's been others not in this country?'

'Yes, of course. Most of the revolutionaries are in Egypt.'

'Yes. I've heard that. Why?'

'Because they know they will be captured here. It's not safe for them.'

'Because of the French army?'

'Exactly. But also, it's easier to formulate theories, when you're out of the country.'

'You're very cynical.'

'True. That's what life has taught me.' Then he added, 'Actually, we're going to a little place called Iqbal. We're staying the night there.'

I didn't argue, although I had no idea what that would mean practically. Would we both be staying with one family? Would we pretend to be related or even engaged? I had no idea what the protocol was in these circumstances. I was completely unprepared for Yussuf's solution to the problem.

'You're going to stay with the lady missionaries for a couple of days.'

'Sorry?' I could hardly take in what he had just said. 'You mean the nuns?'

'No. The missionaries. Protestant missionaries from England.'

'You've got to be joking. What am I going to be saying to them?'

'I've no idea. But you'll find something to say, I've no doubt. Journalists normally do.'

'But who shall I say I am?'

'Tell them you're a journalist. Don't worry. They're prepared for all sorts.'

'But what exactly are they doing here?'

'Being nurses, being missionaries, helping girls learn how to knit, being kind to everyone; preaching their religion.'

I couldn't imagine anything more alien in the Algeria I had seen so far.

'But doesn't everyone hate them?' I objected.

'Not at all. They love them and trust them.' After a pause he continued, 'I'm not saying they want to convert to their religion, though a few have done. But they are highly respected. In fact,' he added, 'more people will go to their clinic than the one run by the French government, even though it's free.'

'Why?'

'I don't know. Maybe the love and care they show. Maybe the fact that they pray over every single patient.'

'But surely that's seen as a means of converting them?' I asked, puzzled.

'Not at all. It's a way of inviting God into the business of their everyday life.'

'You sound as though you could be converted to their religion yourself.'

'I've no interest in being converted to any religion,' Yussuf assured me. 'but I admire them. You've got to. Before they came down to Iqbal, they lived in a village high up in the mountains, which took two days to get to by donkey. And they stayed there for ten years.'

'Why did they come to Iqbal?'

'Nowadays, it's very dangerous to be high up in the mountains. And their mission wouldn't let them stay by themselves.'

'And is it any safer down here?'

'Probably not, but they don't worry about danger. You'll understand when you meet them.'

# Chapter Twenty-Nine

The Misses Lambert were two ladies in their early forties with the most beautiful blond hair. This was what made the greatest impression on me and the way they greeted Yussuf, as if they knew him and cared for him.

'Hello, Marie. Very nice to meet you. Yussuf, come around to the clinic entrance on the other side of the house, please. You know how people talk.'

'Of course, Jeanne. We'll be there in a minute.'

The next moment we were being ushered into a large room with bordered off compartments for bed, weighing scales with thermometers on the tops and the means to sterilise instruments.

'Now don't compare us with a modern French clinic, Marie. Unfortunately, we don't have the means to compete with them.'

'You do very well,' responded Yussuf reassuringly and without being patronising. 'I know how appreciative the villagers of Iqbal are that you have come here to work with them.'

'Most of it is a case of basic hygiene, not anything very sophisticated. Marie, this is my sister, Stephanie. We work together here, taking it in turns to nurse and present the pictures of the Gospel and pray.'

'That must be quite discouraging if you don't see any response,' I suggested.

'Ah, you'd be surprised. They all want us to pray for them and often say afterwards that God has healed them. You never know what effect it has had.'

There was no adequate response to such a statement in my view. I looked round the big, sparsely furnished clinic and thought I'd hate to spend years of my life in this place. Yet, these two ladies seemed happy and even full of contentment.

'Yussuf, come and have a cup of tea with us before you go any further. It's such a long time since we've seen you and we want to know what is happening in the big wide world.'

Then, turning to me, she explained. 'He is our carrier pigeon, you know, our source of news. The French don't talk to us; the FLN watch but don't say anything, in case we betray them, though we wouldn't. But we know we can trust Yussuf.' She patted his hand as she led us both into a front room. There was some European furniture, but it was old and not in a good state of repair. There was a small Algerian coffee table with some stools placed around it and an old horse-hair sofa on one side, which looked even more uncomfortable than the stools. On one side of the wall was a huge picture of embroidery with the words 'Dieu est Amour' depicted.

'Now then, tell us what is going on in Algiers,' said Jeanne, in excited anticipation, as she poured out the mint tea and Stephanie found sugar lumps to bring over from the rickety sideboard.

'The answer is – not much – I'm afraid,' replied Yussuf. 'There are no more attacks going on in the bars at the moment.'

'Good. A good sign.'

'Yes, I agree. It's always a good sign if people are not being killed. But it's a waiting game. The whole political thing is picking up momentum.'

'Well, let's hope that de Gaulle manages to diffuse the momentum,' said Stephanie. They both seemed surprisingly knowledgeable about the situation.

'Let's hope so,' agreed Yussuf. 'But you probably have more real news here. Are there people moving?'

'Yes, up to the mountains, all the time. But we don't concern ourselves too much and we mustn't tell you too much. Otherwise people don't trust us.'

Yussuf turned to me. 'The villagers here trust the Miss Lamberts with their lives. If they thought for a moment that they were spying for the French, that would be the end of their work here.'

'But do you ever have to take sides?' I enquired, curious as to what these two gentle women, committed to sharing the love of God, were doing in this bleak environment, where people were killing each other.

'We treat both sides the same and we make that very obvious. We have been asked to treat, what Yussuf here would call, the bandits and also the harkis. We always do it without question. We're not involved in the political situation. Actually, it's quite easy for us not to be, because we're English, not French.'

'And everyone knows that, and respects it,' added Yussuf as he stirred in his third sugar lump. 'My nieces have attended the club the Miss Lamberts run. They've learnt to knit. My uncle and aunt really appreciate the skills the girls have been taught.'

'What do your parents back in England think about you being here?' I asked intrigued.

'Fortunately, they're believers, so they understand. They trust to God's protection.'

'But don't they worry about two single women being on their own in the midst of such madness?'

'Women or men, it doesn't make any difference,' affirmed Jeanne cheerfully. 'We're all equal in God's sight.'

'Now that is really a modern European thought for this country,' said Yussuf laughing.

'How long are you staying in Iqbal, Yussuf?' asked Stephanie.

'A couple of days, I think. Time to speak to my aunt and uncle. Time to see how many bandits have been through the village and whether they're expected back again. We're also tracking Amirouche.'

'Oh dear, that terrible man! They're all terrified of him. If you got rid of him, things might be better. Oh, alright, I know, I know.' Stephanie looked at Yussuf's raised eyebrows in mock penitence. 'I know I'm not supposed to be on one side or the other. But that man is responsible for some terrible things.'

'Don't worry. He won't get away with it for ever.'

'Everyone got excited last year when all the important people in the FLN turned up in our little town. But some of them looked very fierce. And in truth, the mayor here, who is a supporter, was very uncomfortable while they were here.'

'They're not exactly comfortable people to have around, especially those from Wilaya 2.'

'Which one is that?' I'd heard that number before but wasn't sure what it meant.

'It's the district on the outskirts of Constantine. It's the nearest main town to us and they're Kabyles there. That means there's trouble.'

'I love them,' said Jeanne cheerfully, 'but they are the biggest trouble-makers ever.'

'Thanks, Jeanne,' said Yussuf, smiling. 'It's nice to know that you think we're all trouble-makers.'

'Sorry Yussuf. Now, what do you want me to do with Marie? We have our clinic here tomorrow morning.'

'And I know nothing can interrupt that. Marie can watch or even help with the practical things. I expect she can hold babies in scales as well as anyone else.'

'No, I can't. It sounds awful.'

'Are you any good at knitting, my dear? We have our girls' knitting class in the afternoon.'

'No. I've always been terrible at it. Ask my mother.'

'Well, you're never going to be an ideal bride, are you?'

'Exactly my own thoughts. I'm not intending to be.'

'You can come along to our class tomorrow afternoon, Marie, and see what you can learn.'

'Thank you.'

And strangely enough, I did learn. About kindness. All the children received a drink and home-made biscuit, which they treated like gourmet food, giggling at each other when they bit into it. They had very little sugar these days, Stephanie explained to me, because of the war cutting off supplies. Despite that, the children still had more luxuries in coming here, than they ever had at home. Then the business of the day – learning to unravel the carded wool correctly and using the needles. The way some of the girls looked after their knitting was amazing to me. I watched them with admiration, just as I had watched my peers at school in France.

'Now we have time for our story,' explained Jeanne, as an old flannelgraph was brought in with illustrations of the story of the lost sheep. She made the story dramatic and exciting, I could tell, even though I couldn't understand the Kabyle language. The children were all listening

612

intently, and it wasn't hard to link the precipitous situation of the lost sheep on the rock with what they were going through in their daily lives. The crags of the mountains of Kabylia came to life in that story. Their imagination was being ignited, I thought, even if it had no effect on their religious beliefs. And the prayer! The atmosphere of that prayer made us feel that, despite the wild country round about and the evil men fighting on both sides, God was gathering us together for protection and He would not let us go. Afterwards I felt much better myself, especially when I contemplated that, in the next few days I would be travelling up in the mountains with Yussuf.

As the last of the girls left, Yussuf arrived at the side gate of the clinic. 'Tomorrow morning. 5am. Be ready!'

# Chapter Thirty

It was a cold morning with the mist still shrouding the mountains, when I crept out of the house in Iqbal. I had said my 'goodbyes' to the two lady missionaries the night before. They seemed quite unperturbed by my visit but made sure that I heard a reading from the Bible before we all went to bed. They assured me that they always had a little service together last thing at night, but I thought that there was extra meaning in the way they read their French Bible out aloud when I was listening. I was amused but also respectful of their energy and courage in staying in this remote and dangerous place on their own.

'Don't you ever meet up with other missionaries?' I asked, amazed at their resilience and ability to live together peacefully.

'We see one or two other adults when we go down to Tizi Ouzou once a month,' they explained. 'But families with children have all left now. It's far too dangerous.'

'Aren't you frightened?'

'Actually, the villagers look after us a lot and give the FLN favourable reports about us. And it helps that we're not French. We just trust our Heavenly Father,' she added as if it was the most natural statement in the world.

I wasn't feeling like trusting anyone, as I waited for Yussuf in the morning cold. Two minutes later he came by driving the empty melon truck of the day before.

'We'll stop for breakfast in the next village up the road. They have a good café there and I want to get going.'

We were silent as we climbed up the steep hill to the next village. I kept hoping that the clutch and the brake would not give way. We passed the entrance to the next village, which was marked, as I found all the Kabylie villages were, with a hedge of prickly pear as a barrier. It was a really excellent deterrent. Barbed wire was nothing compared to those huge cactus-like spikes. The surface of the road became a little better as we went through the village early in the morning, the jeep raking up clouds of dust. We stopped outside a shop, where men sat on upturned wooden chests, and there were one or two chairs and even a table.

Yussuf left me in the truck, while he went through the beaded entrance of the shop to call on his cousin.

He came out five minutes later, carrying big bowls of steaming café au lait.

'Come on. You can sit out here with me if you like.'

I bundled myself out of the car feeling stiff from the cold even in the last half hour and shaky from lack of food and drink.

'Yasmina's even made us pastries,' he said, as his cousin appeared with a chipped plastic tray.

'I suppose she won't come out here and join us?' I suggested hopefully.

'What and be named as a scarlet woman throughout the village? Not likely! She cares too much for her family's reputation.'

'You don't seem to worry about mine,' I retorted.

'Of course not. That's different. You're European. And everyone knows that French women live sinful and immoral lives!'

He grinned happily at me, as I aimed a mock blow at his face.

'But if you hit me, I will have to avenge my honour. I can't have a woman hitting me in public. It would be too shameful.'

'Remind me to do it in private instead.' I took on the same light tone as his in my answer. Our relationship had changed as we went further up into the mountains and away from civilisation. Before we had been polite and very careful. Now we felt relaxed together and ready to joke. Perhaps it was a reaction to the danger which we knew was all around us. Journalists, I knew from experience, are the most flippant and jokey of people, especially when death is lurking in the background. It is the only way to survive emotionally. We need a 'front' because none of us ever admits to being afraid.

Yussuf's cousin sat opposite us on one of the packing cases. He chatted away to Yussuf in Kabyle and they both brought out the inevitable cigarettes, the black smoke curling up through the cold, clean mountain air. The sun was beginning to rise between the peaks of the mountains in the distance or rather the glory of the sun was gradually being revealed as the morning mist lifted.

'If you'd like to meet Yasmina, Mohammed will take you through to the back.'

I wanted to go and say 'thank you' for the delicious pastries filled with honey and nuts which had been made for us so early in the morning, so I followed Mohammed through the shop where crates of fizzy drinks were stored and we went past the outer wall of the house and through into the inner wall door and in the darkness I made out a young woman, bent over a floor stove with a couple of children round her. All three held back shyly when I appeared, but Mohammed said something to her, and she very carefully got up with the children hiding in her skirts. She couldn't have been more than twenty years of age, and I knew that she would stay in that house for the rest of her life, unless she was thrown out through divorce. She was clean and presentable, even at that time of the morning, with kohl highlighting her beautiful eyes.

'Shukran,' I said in the Arabic, which is used to the Middle East, and then added in French, 'The pastries were lovely,' as I put my fingers to my lips, mimicking their sweetness.

She smiled and half bowed towards me. Mohammed translated what I had said, and she replied.

'She says that she is glad you liked them, and it is an honour for her to make them for you.'

With the extraordinary courtesy of the mountain people, I knew that this would be a genuine statement, though how anyone could think that it was an honour to make pastries at five in the morning, I could not imagine.

'She's doing it for her husband's family, of course,' explained Yussuf, as we made our way up the mountain road afterwards. 'She knows that she is bringing them honour by doing it, and then his whole family will be pleased. Amazingly she hasn't got a mother-in-law, because Mohammed's mother died a few years ago, but the aunts will hear about it and she will have done well.

'Why is that so important?' I asked curiously.

'It just is. It's the tradition here. Normally the mother-in-law is the most powerful person in the family, and she can make the girl's life hell on earth.'

'Do they always live together?'

'Yes, unfortunately. If I loved a woman, I wouldn't want her to be subject to such pressure, but, of course, I've seen a different way of living abroad.'

'Did you like the European way of living then?' I asked intrigued.

'Yes. I saw it of course when everyone was under pressure in the war, but I see it here among the colons. It's got to be a better way of enjoying your married life than having your mother poking her nose into everything. There are some women in the villages who have endured such an awful life themselves that they are determined to make their daughters-in-law suffer as much as possible. It's terrible and it's worse when there's more than one wife.'

'Does that still happen?' I was shocked. 'I thought that sort of thing was for medieval times.'

'If it is, then medieval times are still very much with us in Algeria. A man here can divorce his wife with just a sentence and then she has nowhere to go and the children are usually taken off her.'

I shivered. 'It sounds barbaric. Would you like to live like that?'

'Certainly not. It's no way to treat a woman. I've seen that clearly in Europe and the French have much to teach us about civilised marriage.'

I thought about my own parents in Les Landes. 'Not always.'

'I know they're not perfect and there are bad French marriages. I've seen those too. But nothing can be as bad as multiple marriages in a Kabylie village.'

We climbed higher and higher, round impossible bends, past dirty villages where all the hens in the world seemed to be on the rampage round our truck, others where we narrowly missed children playing in the dirt. I suppose children the world over play, but what these children found to play with I have no idea – mainly sticks and stones which were being thrown into the nearby stream, and there were little girls of about six years old, mothering a couple of little tots.

Finally, we came out onto a plateau and the truck came to a halt.

'Like the view?'

We leaned over the bonnet and looked down over the villages we had passed. More villages were hidden in those valleys and ravines than I could possibly imagine.

'We've seen lots of villages so far today,' I suggested,' But no bandits, as far as I know.'

'That's because you haven't known where to look. They're mainly hiding in caves but here it's too low down.'

'Too low down?' I repeated with lack of belief in my voice. 'You mean we're going higher?'

'If you really want to see what's happening, I've got a few things to show you, some of them not very nice. But you said you wanted to know what it's really like.'

'I do. I'm a journalist and I've seen a few horrible things in my time. But,' I squinted up against the sun in the bright blue sky, 'where else is there to go?'

'A long way further to go, I assure you! You just can't hack it, Mademoiselle Marie, can you?' He laughed. 'You think you can but you're not a Kabyle.'

'No, I'm not a Kabyle, but I can keep up. You just watch me, Monsieur Yussuf,' I replied with spirit. 'The only thing is, I can't see a road.'

'That's because there isn't one. Get what you need for the night and follow me!'

# Chapter Thirty-One

I thought being a journalist meant running through bombed out buildings and reporting about people who had no hospital to go to for their wounds. I now found out that it meant being really fit and that I wasn't. Yussuf's pace up the mountain side was punishing. He was kind, took my bag for me, hauled me up the tougher stretches of rock, but, after an hour, I was exhausted. We stopped in the shelter of a couple of bushes perched precariously on the side of the mountain.

'I don't think that I can cope with this pace all the time,' I admitted.

'That's why we started with breakfast and I brought some goûter as well.'

We munched on figs, raisins and pomegranate pieces which he had carefully wrapped in his bag.

'I want to get to our first village within an hour, because after that the heat becomes impossible to cope with.'

'Even at this altitude?' I queried.

'Even at this altitude. In a moment when we round the bend up there, you'll see the desert stretched out on the other side in front of us. Up here it won't be 45 degrees like it is there, but the Sahara winds blow straight across and it's difficult walking in that heat.'

'I believe you.' I couldn't manage even now, never mind in an increasing heat. 'Yussuf, do you really climb these mountains all the time? And how do the French soldiers manage?'

'I was partly brought up here and I'm used to it, so, yes, I climb here all the time. Some of the French find it hard, especially if they have heavy equipment, except they're trained for it. You get used to it after a while. But it's also part of the reason the French don't send many of their platoons up here. They're sitting targets for the villages and revolutionaries hiding in caves. They send us instead.'

'Us?'

'The Harki scouts, especially those of us who are Kabyle born and bred. We know the terrain, but, more importantly, we know the people and speak their language. They use us to follow up the FLN and hunt them out of their hiding places.'

'Where do they hide?'

'In the caves. That's fairly straightforward. It's hand to hand fighting.'

'It sounds anything but straightforward.'

'It's skilful fighting but if you isolate one or two at the right time and know how to do it, you're OK.'

'Does 'how to do it' mean how to kill them?'

He looked away from me across the further mountain peaks. 'Of course. That's what we're trained to do. You can't fight a war without killing people.'

'But they're your own people.'

'Yes, but they set themselves up as leaders and threaten and kill everyone else. When you see what they do, you'll understand why we need to fight back.'

'But it's on behalf of the French.'

'No, I don't do it on behalf of the French. I do it on behalf of civilisation. I'm part of the third force in Algeria. I want my country to be independent, but I don't want these mad men to be in charge. I want moderation and democratic movement. Unfortunately, you can't have a third force fighting the other two. So, I have to back the best of the other two, for the time being at least.'

'You sound as though you think that might change.'

'I'll never fight against the French. They watched my back too many times in the Second World War for me to do that. But I'll happily see the French gradually leave Algeria. Colonization isn't the way forward for the twentieth century.'

He handed me another fig. 'Last one for now. Come on. Only another hour till our next village. You can do it.'

I was amazed how revived I felt after our brief stop. For the first twenty minutes I had much more energy but then the heat and the steepness of the ascent took its toll again. My shirt was covered in sweat and I had to stop every ten minutes. Yussuf looked as though he was just running up a hill for exercise before breakfast, but he waited patiently for me to get my breath back each time.

It didn't seem possible that there was a village at this altitude but suddenly I saw the familiar barrier of the prickly pear and the stream running down the mountain side opposite the dilapidated-looking squat houses. In this part of the world the houses seemed to have sloping roofs instead of the familiar flat roofed compounds of lower down. 'It's to take the snow off the houses in the winter,' explained Yussuf. 'It's hard to imagine what the place looks like in mid-winter.'

The dogs were barking, and two mangy looking hounds appeared near the houses but Yussuf spoke to them and they backed away. He led me past the mandatory outer walls and into the main reception room of the house, with poor cement and wattle walls, a few cushions and a couple of old mattresses on the floor to sit on – the men's room, as I discovered. We hadn't sat down for very long before an older man appeared – droopy moustache, turbaned head and ragged over shirt. He embraced Yussuf and gave me a quick glance. Almost by magic hands appeared round the door and a tray with a pot of hot liquid appeared. It wasn't coffee, but some sort of herbal tea, which was refreshing.

'My uncle says he is sorry he cannot offer the French lady coffee. They have no such luxuries here because of the bad times we are living in.'

'Please tell him not to worry. And this drink is very refreshing.'

I nodded and smiled in an encouraging way at the old man.

'Just take your time. I want to ask him what's been happening in the village. I'll tell you later what he said. We're only staying here for a short time, because I don't want them to have to offer us food. There's not enough for them as it is.'

'Go ahead. I'm happy to do nothing.'

The old mattress could have been a cushioned armchair in the Ritz Hotel, as far as I was concerned. I was just relieved not be doing that dreadful ascent.

An hour later we made our way out of the village, accompanied by one or two dogs and a couple of twelve-year old boys, who reluctantly said 'goodbye' to Yussuf as we passed the limit of the prickly pear.

'Our next stop is a cave about two hours from here. I hope you've got your breath back.'

I ignored the last comment. I knew that my feelings of relief would not last for more than thirty minutes, but we needed to keep going if we were going to avoid the worst of the sun, and my pride stopped me from moaning about another two hours of climbing.

'I hope this cave isn't going to produce your bandits ready for hand to hand fighting.'

He grinned. 'Don't worry. I'll look after you. But no,' he continued, seeing my expression of horror, 'I'm not looking for the FLN at the moment. I've got one or two of my colleagues holed up in the caves, keeping a look out at what is going on there.'

'They might be a bit surprised if I turn up.'

'Perhaps, but they won't say anything. Also, they know that a war is fought on publicity as well as arms, so a sympathetic journalist isn't such a bad thing.'

We carried on climbing. On one side of the mountain range overlooking the desert, the vegetation was down to low scrub, and there was nothing to hold onto apart from overhanging rocks and nowhere to shelter from the sun. At one or two points I felt sick looking down from the dizzying heights.

'Don't look down,' warned Yussuf. 'Keep looking at me and the path ahead. And don't worry. If a donkey can get up here, so can you.'

'A donkey?' I couldn't imagine how anything wider than one human being could manage such a track.'

'And if a missionary medic can get up here, then so can you.'

'You mean the Misses Lambert?'

'I wouldn't put it past them, but, no, there's a male missionary in Tizi Ouzou who used to come up here before the war to visit the villages.'

'Brave man,' was all I had breath to say.

'Indeed,' agreed Yussuf.

Later the terrain flattened out a bit and there were huge boulders.

'Wait here,' whispered Yussuf. 'I'm going to gradually make my way to the cave, watching and giving signals. Don't move. I'll be back for you, but if I'm not back in thirty minutes, start to make your way back very quietly and quickly to the village we were at before. They'll look after you.'

I didn't find his assurances very helpful. I didn't want to think about what would be happening to him if he didn't return and I refused to think about finding my way back to the village with those dizzying heights and some murderers behind me. Yussuf didn't wait for my response. He was gone.

There were some cicadas in the background, though I couldn't see any grass where they might feed. I saw lizards warily sheltering underneath the boulders and keeping a careful watch on their human intruder. I thought I saw a snake slithering away in the haze of heat and I hoped that I wouldn't scream if it came nearer. I felt a most extraordinary sense of unreality, as if I had landed temporarily on another planet and didn't know whether I was still a human being.

After about fifteen minutes there was a soft whistle and Yussuf was beside me again.

'Come on. It's safe.'

We crept up to the mouth of the cave. One man was on duty with his gun, looking out over the landscape as we approached. Yussuf helped me up the outer ledge and into the darkness, where I was violently sick.

I had just seen at the side of the entrance a pile of corpses which were disintegrating in the sun.

# Chapter Thirty-Two

I held back, trembling with the exertion of the climb, the after-effects of vomiting and terrible sight of the bones, half covered with mouldering flesh.

Yussuf was speaking to two other men, even while one of them was keeping watch from the front of the cave, which, while partially hidden by thorn trees, commanded a wide view over the surrounding countryside. You could watch your enemy approaching, except that this hadn't helped the people who had been slaughtered here.

Yussuf came over to me, where I stood half-supported by the side of the cave.

'Are you alright?'

I nodded dumbly.

'I wasn't expecting this myself here and I didn't stop to talk to the other harkis before; otherwise I would have warned you.'

'I'm not sure a warning would have made it any better.'

'I agree. Nothing can prepare you for such a sight. I've seen it hundreds of times, but it doesn't make it any better.'

'Who were they?'

'Some of the people from the village we have just been in.'

I thought about the little household we had visited two hours previously. Were they friends? Family? Did they know what had happened? If I'd know what they had risked, I'd have handled the herbal drink with more reverence.

'What had they done?'

'They probably hadn't done anything. Just hadn't turned some of the harkis over to the enemy or gave us food.'

624

I was alarmed. What problems had I caused by just going to the village?

'Don't worry. This happened at least ten days ago. Everyone knows you're a journalist. They won't kill anyone because of you. They value their reputation in the foreign press too much.'

'But there are children there amongst them.' My quick glance at the decomposing bodies had identified three children with the adults.'

'They don't distinguish between children and adults. It was two parents, three children and one grandmother.'

'You knew them?'

'Yes. I know all the villagers. They might even have selected this family at random to make them an example to everyone else. They do it all the time,' he added, seeing my horrified expression.

'Their enemies, I can understand though why children should be involved is beyond me. But why their own countrymen and their children?'

'I told you before – their idealism has become more important than their humanity.'

'But how can it be stopped?' I asked hopelessly, seeing it as a disease which was spreading remorselessly through these mountain ranges.

'Unfortunately, it can only be stopped by fighting.'

'What would happen if the French just left and allowed them to get on with it?'

'Slaughter; starvation; destruction.'

Then there was no answer.

'Marie, I'm just telling you what we're going to do now. Take your time. You don't have to be involved in anything you don't want to be.'

'I already am.'

'We're moving the bodies onto the land out there and burying them. It's important that Muslims are buried as soon as possible after death. We'd stay in the cave but the earth here isn't deep enough to cover them. There's a real risk that wild animals will get to them out there, but it's still the only choice as far as we can see. We'll wait until it's early evening and we're less likely to be targeted. I've got some water here for you which will help settle your stomach.'

'Thank you,' I replied listlessly. I leant against the side of the cave, trying not to look at the heap of corpses at the entrance, though the smell was beginning to pervade the whole cave. During the afternoon, I offered to go outside and pick up firewood, but the men declined. They obviously did not trust me to know what I was doing. I hardly cared that I crouched at the side of the cave with nothing to do. I used that time to let the horror of what had happened to those people take hold of me.

I continued in that position all afternoon, unable to take in the enormity of what I had seen. I envied the three men that they had a purpose and a task which involved great physical energy. Later, when they had finished, and the rocks lay over the graves both as a protection from animals and also as a marker and a memorial, Yusuf came to help me down the ledge again.

'None of us are great believers here,' he said pointing to the other men. 'One of us can say the shahada, which all Moslems have to say before their death. Do you know any prayers to say?'

It didn't seem worth arguing that they were of a different faith and that my own religious background was sketchy in the extreme. Something more needed to be said to give this occasion solemnity and meaning and all three men were looking at me.

'OK,' I said reluctantly, 'I've got a prayer which will do.' Everyone held out their hands to heaven as Muslims always do when they pray, and I said the 'Our Father' prayer. To my surprise Yussuf joined in. He said that he'd learnt it in the French army and liked it. Wanting to subscribe to a different kingdom of justice and love seemed particularly relevant to a situation like this.

'Am I allowed to ask what these men are doing next?' I asked a little later.

I was beginning to understand the dangers of these fighters and how easily I might give away a scout's position and cause him danger.

'You can ask what you and I are doing next,' Yussuf informed me. 'Everything you do will be known anyway and you have the freedom to write about it.'

'How will it be known?'

'Because they have spies all over the place, the ones who are genuinely loyal to the cause and the ones who are forced to give information through blackmail.'

It was a sobering thought that the men who had perpetrated these murders a day or two ago, knew exactly where I was.

'Doesn't that put you in danger?'

'While I'm with you, not at all. Afterwards, yes, but I am anyway and all of us here face constant danger. It's a war.'

As I looked at the faces of these men, this fact seemed to draw no emotion from them.

We moved away from the makeshift grave and back into the shelter of the cave. As the uncomfortable business was finished, I was now introduced to Mustafa and Yannis, Yussuf's fellow scouts. They didn't speak much French or Arabic so Yussuf had to translate whatever they said. They were respectful and courteous to me, but their eyes were guarded. They looked out for each other and any stranger could bring danger.

'We're going to make a fire at the back of the cave, and we've got some food here which we can all share.'

The scouts had killed some birds earlier and they set about disjointing them and putting their flesh over the hot coals. They also had collected bitter herbs to accompany the meat and that, and the water, was enough for us all. I was surprised at how this meal satisfied my hunger.

Over the meal there wasn't much talk. I think that all three men, however used to the ravages of war they were, felt overawed by the brutal deaths of the family and any superficial chat seemed inappropriate.

The fire was surprisingly welcome because it had become quite dank and cold in the cave. Like all men who lived in the outdoors, they were experts at creating it.

'Can either of them tell me what they were doing before this war and how they came to be involved?'

It was a familiar story. Yannis, like Yussef, had fought for the Tirailleurs in the Second World War. Many of the troops had remained loyal to the French as a result, though some had since changed sides.

'The French have not helped the situation.' Yussuf translated what Yannis was saying.

'How do you mean?'

'They have carried out their own massacres and the first one at Sétif, shocked everyone.'

'There was no real accountability,' continued Yussuf. 'No European journalist reported it properly. The Figaro said 'tens of people' had been killed when it was more likely to have been hundreds and no one took it seriously. They were only Algerians in their eyes, so didn't count.'

I was quiet. The jibe was true; that's how colonial powers often saw people in their territories; and I knew that such disdain for fellow human beings always brought about consequences.

'It started the whole thing off and won many supporters for the FLN, especially the well-educated. They had benefitted from the French education system themselves, but now they understood the rhetoric of the fledgling nationalist movement.'

'Even then the extremists harassed the moderates,' chimed in Moustafa. 'Abbas' nephew was killed because he was a deputy mayor in the French system. Abbas got the message – do what we want or else!'

# Chapter Thirty-Three

I drifted to sleep, conjuring up the image of the Bourgeauds' estate and then I dreamt about their decline. An image of the beautiful, succulent orange trees, all fading and dying stayed with me throughout the night. I found myself crying inwardly for beauty disintegrating, for innocent people dying needlessly and for people being caught in the two-power struggle between the French and the revolutionaries. I found myself weeping for the lack of kindness and reasonableness on the part of human beings. I stayed cocooned in my sleeping bag unable to sleep on the hard rock until I drifted off to sleep and was awoken by the realisation that the journey had to continue.

I had no idea where Mustapha and Yannis were going, if indeed they were going anywhere at all. For all I knew, they might use this cave as a look out for days on end.

I woke to the drip -drip of the water at the back wall of the cave and Yussuf softly calling me awake. I was sleeping in my day clothes, because it was far too cold and uncomfortable to do anything else, so it only took five minutes to make sure everything was in my bag and I was ready to follow Yussuf.

We made our way out of the cave as the dark shadows were shortening and the stars just receding in the sky, and we passed the graves which had been dug the previous day and which now seemed to belong to the world we were leaving.

I realised that we were positioned on a high ridge of the mountain range and we were moving across huge boulders and outcrops of stone. It was a less arduous journey than the one we had taken the previous day, but I still needed to concentrate hard to keep my footing steady.

Round a bend we saw a village laid out before us.

'How the hell does anyone know what is going on here?' I asked, amazed at the unlikely appearance of human dwellings in this desolate place.

Yussuf grinned. 'The same way that you do – by being a mountain goat.'

'I'm not a mountain goat,' I objected 'I'm more like one of Hannibal's elephants.'

'You'd be surprised how much you've changed over the last two days – much more sure-footed than you were. Anyway, even Hannibal trained his elephants to go up through the mountains.'

I stared down at the red roofs which appeared to have been there for ever, though only just discovered by me. 'So, what happens here?'

'Everything happens here,' replied Yussuf with calm assurance. 'This is a strategically placed village for both sides, but up to now the ALN have avoided it as much as possible.'

'Why?'

'Because they are loyal to the French here. They've always had a caid.'

'Caid? Does that mean judge?'

'Literally, yes, but it's come to mean the overseer of the village placed here by the French.'

'Sounds like a dangerous position to be in.'

'It is, and lots of caids and champetres (military garrison leaders) have been killed. Often no one minded because they were corrupt. They took more than the taxes from the people and the French turned a blind eye to it.

And, yes, before you say it, there has been a whole lot wrong with the French system. Anyway, the caid here is different. He's strongly in favour of order and has always looked after his own people.'

'And can he succeed in doing that?'

'So far, so good. He won't be immune from the possibility of slaughter of course, but, although the village is so strategically placed, before the mountains start descending to the desert, it doesn't have much influence over any other villages, simply because there aren't any more on this side.'

'How does he manage to protect his people?'

'By ensuring he knows exactly what is going on. The people trust him and tell him everything. By using money to buy weapons, having his own lookouts, and by keeping in touch with the harkis like me. We always call here when we're on this track. It's nice to have a friendly reception and we tell him what's going on in the wider area.'

'So, you're going to call on him now?'

'Exactly.'

'Well, I hope there's some sort of breakfast around and a ladies' room. There's only so much lack of civilisation a girl can put up with.'

Yussuf replied with a mocking bow. 'Madam, your wish is my command.'

As usual, the dogs announced our approach and two small boys were on the alert behind the boulders, as we descended the steep path to the village.

The caid was already up and looked as though he had been expecting us. I had both my wishes granted – time in one of the women's rooms, which even boasted a small mirror, and steaming herbal tea and fresh baked bread to dip.

When I joined the men, it was obvious that Yussuf had used the time to explain what had been going on up the mountain in the cave and the caid looked sombre, though his old, gnarled face did not reveal much emotion. I sat down on a mattress covered with bright red satiny material and crocheted cushions and let the conversation roll over me, while I enjoyed the refreshments.

At last Yussuf turned to me. 'The caid hopes that you have had all you need, and afterwards, his wife, who is busy at the moment with household duties, would like to help you.'

'Thank you.' I bowed in the direction of my host, smiling to indicate my appreciation of his courtesy. 'I would be delighted to accept.' Pause. 'What does he think about what has happened?'

'He doesn't allow himself too much emotion. We've all got used to these atrocities. He uses his energy to plan how he can protect his own village better.'

'He seems to be doing a good job.'

'Yes, though whether that can last I don't know. There's a stream of harkis passing through at the moment and that helps.'

'Why specially at the moment?'

'Because the French are chasing the FLN down into the Hodna. It's easier to corner them there.'

'Is that the Sahara?'

'Sort of. It's at the edge of the main desert and it's formed from vast former salt lakes which are below sea level.'

'If the French come by here, surely the FLN do too?'

'They tend to go around a different way, because they know the caid won't give them shelter. On the other hand, he won't betray them either.'

'Isn't that a bit contradictory when you're fighting a war?'

'No. It's a matter of honour, not betraying his own countrymen. The bandits might be near, but they won't touch the caid's village. The FLN don't waste their time on well-guarded villages who know what they're doing, just weak ones.'

'Like the one we were at before?'

'Exactly. You don't save yourself by dithering, or by supporting whichever side turns up on the day.'

'I can't blame them if they do. It's a terrible position to be in.'

'Indeed, it is. It's called a civil war. They are always the worst.'

After listening to more conversation, I was directed back to the women's quarters. A young lady, only in her teens I would guess, had a bowl of water and sponge. Even in a Western spa, I have rarely had such a refreshing or relaxing experience as that one in an isolated Algerian village at the top of the world. I was washed, anointed with oil, given some shoulder and neck massage, had my nails attended to and my hands henna-d.

'It's not normally something which happens to a war correspondent,' I observed later to Yussuf, who also looked more relaxed after a long conversation with the caid. He told me later that it was a wonderful experience to have this conversation, and to hear the views from one of his countrymen, who had proved himself to be utterly reliable. 'There's a lot of things we wouldn't agree on,' he explained, 'but at least you know where you are with him. He's not two faced like a lot of people are.'

'We're going to the Hodna next,' he informed me. 'By the way its name on the map is the Hodna depression. You'll see why it's so apt when we get there. I want you to see what some of the French military forces are up to.'

'Alright with me. Are we doing lots more walking?'

'No. I thought we'd try donkey travel this time.'

'A donkey? You're joking! I think I'd rather be on my feet.'

'The trouble is, Marie, you're so ungrateful. Here's the caid offering you first class travel and you don't appreciate it.'

'From what I remember of my childhood, donkeys are stubborn and difficult to control.'

'But not if they have a donkey driver with them. This one's the best – a nephew of the Caid, and he has a miraculous touch with donkeys. He helps keep them in order and then drives them back up to the village after we've reached our destination.'

'If you really think so,' I said doubtfully.

'I do really think so. And remember the Misses Lambert used to use them every month when they lived up here.'

'The Misses Lambert are made of sterner stuff than me. And they've got God on their side. No donkey would dare disobey them.'

'Quite right. That's why they're so admired in these parts.'

'I'm not aspiring to be admired. I'd just like to stay in one piece.'

'That, Marie, will be my goal over the next few days. And, by the way, the Caid and his wife are bringing us dinner.'

'Now that is good news. I've got a very high opinion of the Caid's wife.'

'I'll tell the Caid. Unusually, he also has a high opinion of his wife.'

'So, he should. So, should lots of Algerian men, considering how much their wives suffer.'

'Mere chattels,' rejoined Youssuf, laughing, as he avoided my bag which I flung at him. 'but good, when they bring in food like this.'

Into the room came one hot plate of steaming couscous with a vegetable stew and a few pieces of bone with scraps of meat on it.'

'We're all sharing this, the common plate, and even you, inferior woman that you are, are allowed to take part. Get your stomach full, have a short sièste; then be ready for the donkey ride of your life.'

# Chapter Thirty-Four

Yussuf seemed to manage his donkey alright. I guess he could talk to it in a familiar language, even though his long legs reached almost to the ground. I felt my own experience would have been a disaster, if it hadn't been for the ministrations of the Caid's nephew, a boy of about twelve years old, who walked alongside its head and when not talking to it in a persuasive tone, made his point with a vicious looking whip. I've never had any great liking for donkeys, but I have to say that I felt sorry for this one, when he received such disciplinary measures. To begin with I thought that we might have walked more quickly, but I soon realised that the animals were so sure-footed, and knew the winding, precipitous path so well, that we descended at a very fast rate.

As we came to a riverbed at the bottom of the mountain, I realised that it was dry, and it widened out until it became part of the scrubland which became more and more sparse of vegetation. Trees had become low in height and then gradually disappeared altogether.

'I don't exactly see where we're going to,' I observed to Yussuf, after we'd crossed the wide, dry bed, known as a wadi.

'No. It's a strange thing but it's almost easier to hide in this vast flat land than it is in the mountains, where there are holes and caves all over the place. People who know what they're doing disappear in the desert.'

'What's that over there?' I suddenly pointed to some moving figures which appeared to be about three kilometres away.

'They're a string of camels and they're actually about fifteen kilometres away. Perspective is a very strange thing in the desert, and you nearly always judge distances wrongly, especially when you first go there.'

'Don't tell me that we're going to travel by camel,' I pleaded, unable to hide my suspicions.

'They're not as uncomfortable as you imagine, though, if you think a donkey is stubborn, you haven't met a camel. But, no,' looking at the expression on my face and laughing, 'we're keeping to the humble donkey for another hour or so, until we reach the French camp. Then our transport will return back home. And later on, we'll have a truck.'

'A truck? That sounds very luxurious!'

'You haven't seen the suspension on these trucks. Soon you'll be wishing you were back on the donkey.'

'At least jeeps don't need whipping.'

'No. They just break down and refuse to go any further. Come on. Let's get a move on and we should be there for dinner.'

'Sounds good to me.'

In another hour we were approaching the French camp with guards acting as outposts to check on us. They clearly knew Yussuf and were polite and friendly to me. It was great to understand what everyone was saying as they spoke French.

'I'll take you over to your tent and then introduce you to the lieutenant who is aide to General Beaufré,. He'll want to know who you write for. He always wants to make a good impression on journalists.'

'He can try to if he likes, but I don't believe everything I'm told. What about you? Where will you be staying?'

'Part of the encampment is reserved for the harkis.'

'You mean you're kept separate from the French?'

'Yes, it's easier that way. We all come from the same background. When we're out on the job we all mix in together. And the harki officers have different tents to the squaddies.'

'Do you mind?'

'No, of course not. That's life and army life. When it comes to real friendship, with people like Christophe, there's no barrier whatsoever.'

I wasn't sure whether he was hiding his real feelings or not, but I decided not to pursue it. This man was risking his life every day for being part of the occupation forces. Who was I to question whether he was being treated acceptably by them?

I was shown to my tent with a camp bed and an orderly was on hand to bring me hot water and drinks. It seemed to me a bit like being on safari in sub-Saharan Africa. Later I was escorted to the General's tent.

General Beaufré, was a man in his early 50s, grizzled but still good-looking, fit and able to keep up with his men in tough territory.

'Except of course, the harkis,' he added. 'No one can really keep up with them.'

'I can imagine. I've been with one of them for the last five days.'

'He's the best. Tough, always on the move. He can survive behind enemy lines for days without food and drink.'

'I suppose I should be thankful that he didn't expect me to do that. I've been the recipient of quite a bit of Algerian hospitality.'

'I'm glad to hear that, Mademoiselle. It's always a joy to receive their hospitality. I've spent most of my life in the area of Constantine. It's good there too but in the mountains of Kabylia it's amazing.'

'Are things difficult in Constantine?' I wanted to know. An angle on Constantine would be good for my paper.

'I think 'difficult' would be an understatement. 'Impossible' would be a better description.'

'Can you tell me a bit more about that, General?'

'Certainly. It's not been made easier by the fact that two thirds of the population are Muslim, but the political power is all in the hands of the French who are vastly outnumbered. General de Gaulle needs to come and speak to the population there.'

'And will he?'

'I'm hoping so. He has a good way with words so I'm hoping he'll be able to calm things down. And another thing – we've got the Jews in Constantine too.'

The Jews! I'd forgotten all about them! How stupid of me, when all along I'd been hoping to visit the Gaullen vineyards. How much did General Beaufré, know about them, I wondered.

He gazed at me silently for a moment. 'It's complicated.'

'It always is. I had Jewish friends who ended up in the concentration camps.'

'Well, thank God there aren't any concentration camps here.'

636

I didn't want to reply to that statement. I'd heard what Henri Bourgeaud had had to say about the French treatment of the local population around Constantine, but for the time being I wanted to ask him more about the Jews.

'In your opinion, General, are the Jews supporters of the French or of the ALN?'

'Both.'

'Surprising. They've usually got strong views about things and they tend to stick together.'

'I don't mean they change sides, like a lot of villages in the area.'

'Maybe they only change sides because they're being threatened all the time. It's understandable.'

'True, but it doesn't help us sort out the situation.' General Beaufré, suddenly stood up and paced round his headquarters' tent, straightening up the maps on the notice board which weren't quite to his satisfaction, as if he was trying to regulate the whole situation in Constantine.

'Fairly early on in the conflict, the Jews in Constantine produced an open letter, which they published in the local newspaper. It said that, unlike the French, they had been in the country for one thousand years.'

'As long as that?' I was surprised.

'Yes, though most of them came over later as a result of the persecution under the Spanish Inquisition. Over the years more of them arrived and of course quite a few more came when the Nazis came to power in Europe.

The letter said that they were natural allies of the nationalists and therefore they shouldn't be lumped with the French in the Algerian mind set.'

'And were they?'

'Not to begin with. The ALN were grateful for any allies, but since then, things have deteriorated.'

'In what ways?'

'They've received threatening letters from the revolutionaries, demanding money, even threatening the welfare of their families if they don't comply.'

'And they did comply,' I stated matter of factly.

'Of course. If you are told that if you don't cough up with the goods, your daughter will be kidnapped and gang raped by the local bandits, then you tend to comply. After that, the rabbi in Medea was killed on the steps of his own synagogue.'

'What was the purpose of that?'

General Beaufré, came over from his notice board to stand over me. 'Mademoiselle, if we could only call it a purpose, if we could indulge in logical thinking about cause and effect…'

'And in your view, there isn't?'

'A general strategy, yes, but this is just part of spreading fear everywhere.'

'But surely that will just alienate the Jewish population?'

'Yes, although some of the intellectuals, the liberal thinking Jews have always been supporters of independence.'

'Yes. They've got a very strong instinct for freedom. Not surprising really, when you consider how much they've suffered.'

He looked surprised at my response. 'You sound very sympathetic.'

'Of course, I am, General. I've seen first-hand how much they've suffered.'

'The problem is,' Beaufré continued, 'It's not that simple. It's not just, should they join the goodies or the baddies.'

'Presumably, it's not that simple for you either.'

'Mlle Marie, I'm a soldier. I don't deal in shades of grey. I do what I'm told and what I have to do.'

'Even if you don't approve personally?'

'That's the discipline of the army, and, generally speaking, I think that the French army is trying to establish order here and that in the end will help everyone.'

I ignored his stock military reply. It was a journalist's job to deal with the greys and I intended to do so. In fact, I was intrigued by the fact that this high-ranking military officer thought the situation in Algérie Française might not be that simple.

'So, what do you think is the root of the problem here then?'

'It's jealousy and a feeling of injustice.'

Where had I heard this one before?

'Why should the nationalists feel jealous of the Jews?'

'Because of the Cremieux decrees.'

'Yes, I've heard about those and the sense of injustice felt by the Muslims. But surely against the French?'

'Yes, I agree. If anyone was unjust it was the French. But it's like the favoured child in the classroom, Mlle. He attracts jealousy and the favouritism becomes part of his fault.'

I ignored the parallel though later I came to realise that it was an accurate one. 'Of course, it's unjust. Why the difference? What was the motivation behind it? Why did the Muslims have to change their religion?'

'I have no idea. I think it's a sense of what it meant to be a European. The Jews have been round Europe for centuries. The Muslims haven't.'

I couldn't really grasp all of this. I turned to more practical matters. 'So, there's a lot of injustice for you to sort out, General.'

He sighed. 'I haven't been trained to sort out injustice. That's what politicians are for.'

'When you look at the French ones, they don't seem to be very good at it.'

It was a statement on my part and we both knew that I was right. The politicians were answerable to the French at home.

Later on, I was invited to the officers' mess for dinner. It was amazing to me that here on the outer rim of the desert in the middle of a guerrilla war, there was so much good food and alcohol. They say that an army marches on its stomach and that evening proved to me that it was true. I was placed among the mainstream French officers, though I saw the group of Harkis, Yussuf included, at the far end of the table. I would far rather have been placed with them, because Yussuf now felt like a friend, but I could hardly object to my placement. My dinner companions were educated and polite, came up with all the right questions and answers, but they left me unmoved. Even in Paris I had seldom dined with such uninteresting socialites. I knew that these men were courageous, otherwise they would not have been there, but, apart from that, they held only fleeting interest for me.

After the meal, one of them gallantly escorted me back to my tent, but it was only a gesture of courtesy, or perhaps the protection afforded to all visitors to the camp. No one could be sure that there was not an enemy marksman near and ready to pounce. I had already witnessed how a lone figure could disappear into the desert.

'Marie!'

I was just getting ready for bed when Yussuf's voice came from outside.

'Can I come in?'

'Yes.'

'Sorry to disturb you like this.'

'It's alright.' I found myself hastily buttoning up my shirt and uncharacteristically blushing as he stood near the entrance flap of the tent.

'Sure. No problem.' I tried to sound unconcerned.

'I thought you might like to know about our plans for the next few days.'

'Yes, I did wonder what was supposed to happen now.'

'I think a day off is called for. You've done a lot over the last few days.'

'And you haven't?'

'I'm used to it. But then we'll take an army truck and go the long way around to Constantine.'

'The long way?'

'Yes, round the Hodna and the Aurès and that way. There's more roads there than in Kabylia and it's easier to keep a look out for the enemy.'

He had come forward, and, in his attempt to engage me in his plans, placed his hand on my arm. Immediately I felt the characteristic tension and connection which I had felt before with Nikolai, but, multiplied by a force of about a hundred.

Candlelight is a great medium for a romantic liaison, but suddenly our tentative touching evaporated, as a massive explosion threw us both up in the air and then onto the floor. I clung onto Yussuf as we lay there, but it was only for a moment, as he sprung up and reached for his gun.

'Stay here, Marie. Don't move. I'll come and get you if it's safe, but I have to go and see what's happened.'

'Be careful, Yussuf. Maybe they're waiting for others to appear before attacking again.'

'Without doubt,' he agreed grimly, 'but I have to go and see what's happened to my colleagues.'

# Chapter Thirty-Five

I found out later that evening that the bomb had been detonated in the French officers' tent which was nearest to where the Harkis were placed. As predicted, the Harkis had come running to the aid of their colleagues and they had been gunned down by snipers. Immediately the other French soldiers had gone into action to locate them, but it was too late. They had disappeared into the desert and fast-moving sunset and the encroaching dust of the Sahara had quickly obliterated any possible signs of who and where they were. If Yussuf had not been with me at the time and therefore had had a greater distance to run to the explosion, he would have been gunned down with the rest. Four of his fellow scouts had been killed, including Mustafa who had been with us in the cave. Yannis had been badly injured, and the medics were trying to save his leg.

At about midnight Yussuf crept back to my tent. His face was completely expressionless and immobile. Only his shaking hands betrayed his agony.

He didn't even apologise for his request. 'Marie, can I stay here for the night?'

'Don't worry. I won't bother you with my attentions. That's the last thing on my mind at the moment. I just need to be with another human being who isn't embroiled in the violence.'

'Of course, you can stay. But won't the army think that it strange?'

'The Harkis are the only ones I would have stayed with in these circumstances and they're all dead. Yannis who is injured is out for the count. I was with him when the doctor was trying to sort his leg in the hospital tent. But now he's been morphined up and he doesn't know what's going on.'

He started unrolling a mattress which he had salvaged from the remains of his own tent.

'I'll just lie here. Even hearing your breathing will help me.'

'How?'

'Your breathing is softer than a man's. It will remind me that there's some goodness in the world.'

We were both silent as we lay on our separate beds. The magnitude of the attack did not invite easy comments, but neither of us wanted to sleep, and we were in our own separate ways, thinking about the men who had been killed in such a cowardly way.

'That's what I hate,' broke out Yussuf suddenly, as if he was continuing a conversation which had been progressing without my participation. 'If it was hand to hand fighting, all right. You know who your enemy is, and you just get on with it. But this bombing and sniping from nowhere – it seems so unjust.'

'It was,' I agreed. 'The worst war of all is a civil war.'

'Yea. It just makes me want to leave.'

'Then, why don't you?'

'I've considered it time and again, especially when I was in France this summer. Why don't I just stay there, and get myself an ordinary life, I asked myself?'

'And what answer did you come up with?'

'If I just think about the French army and the FLN, then I have no problem. Let them fight it out among themselves. I don't belong to the French and I don't support the FLN, so why get involved? And then, I think about all my innocent fellow countrymen, and the people who don't have any choice about staying like the Caid and my cousins. And I think – how can I just leave them to their fate?'

'But, you staying here won't make any difference to them in the end.'

'It won't make any difference to the outcome of the war, I agree. But it will make a difference as to whether they feel anyone cares about them or not.'

Brave words, I thought silently. How many people stay because they care more for their friends and family than about their own safety? Alain was the only one I could remember doing that.

For a long time, we remained awake but silent.

'Yussuf?'

'Yes?'

'Can you come here?'

'I could, but why?'

'The world is a cruel place. You wanted to hear my breathing tonight. Maybe I can give you touch as well. I want to hold you and be held by you.'

'Are you sure?'

'Yes.'

Almost immediately, he was leaning over towards my bed.

'There's not a lot of room,' I conceded, 'but sometimes being close to another human being is more important than being comfortable.'

Neither of us said any more. I shifted onto my side and he held me from behind. He was trembling ever so slightly from the shock of seeing his colleagues maimed and killed and from realising what a near escape he had experienced. I pushed my head into the side of his neck, and he put his face to mine and ever so gently nuzzled me. It was like one animal comforting another. Whatever our human instincts, neither of us had the emotional energy for anything else. All of our strength was taken up in absorbing the horror of what had happened.

In the morning I woke up alone. By the time of breakfast in the mess, he was with his injured colleague, who was waking up in the hospital tent.

'Mademoiselle Marie.'

I turned around from my coffee and bread to face one of Beaufré's lieutenants.

'I'm sorry about all the commotion of last night. It's most unusual that none of our look-outs spotted what was happening before the attack.'

'If you're saying it's unusual, Lieutenant, I must say I'm surprised. You must be a sitting target in the desert, and I've already seen how quickly anyone can disappear out here.'

'Very true, but, as I say, it's unusual because we always post good look-outs.'

'So, what happened to them this time?'

'We're still investigating but it seems like they were called round to the other side of the encampment.'

'So, there you are. Your enemy knew what they were doing.'

'So, it seems. Can I ask you, Mademoiselle, what is the nature of your relationship with Corporal Yussuf?'

I was immediately on the defensive.

'What do you mean?'

'How do you know him in the first place?'

'I met him at the Bourgeauds' estate. He's a very good friend of their son, Christophe, and he was brought up there. I'm investigating all aspects of Algerian society, especially the workers. It was a great chance for me to find out how Yussuf was brought up and the advantages he had.'

'How did the two of you get through the mountains?'

I explained about our journey and who we had stayed with.

'So, you didn't see him doing business with any unusual characters?'

'They're all unusual characters in the mountains, but no, I saw people who had been attacked by the FLN.' I recounted the story of the family who had been tortured and killed in the cave. 'We met up with the Harki scouts there, Mustapha and Yannis, who were killed and injured in the attack last night.'

'Quite so. The two of you are planning to go to Constantine. Is that right?'

'I'm not sure we've planned anything at all together,' I said carefully, cautious about the possible innuendos in his conversation. 'There are some contacts I have in Constantine, whom I want to interview for my paper and M. Bourgeaud thought Yussuf could take me there. But you're in charge,' I added, almost as an accusation. 'Can you spare one of your soldiers to drive to Constantine?'

'As it happens, General Beaufré needs someone to go to Constantine – someone to take messages and papers to the colonel deputising for General Beaufré there. He has his work cut out being in charge of the Constantine area. The wilaya there is very active with FLN supporters.'

'And,' added the Lieutenant, 'it's not just that. The soldier who was injured last night, Yannis – he needs his leg assessed for gangrene and proper care in a hospital. It would be great if you could take him too.'

'Good idea.'

The lieutenant didn't move. He obviously had something more to say.

'Mademoiselle Marie?'

'Yes, Lieutenant.'

'You are a French woman and loyal to Algérie Française.'.

I hesitated. What was my own view of the situation? I wasn't at all sure.

'I'm loyal to my own country of course but that doesn't mean I'm not interested in the point of view of the Algerians.'

'Journalists!' the Lieutenant exclaimed disdainfully. 'You never know whether you can trust them!'

'You can trust me never to do anything which would be harmful to my own countrymen.'

'What about withholding information?'

'What do you mean?' I was cautious. In some indefinable way, I felt he wanted to catch me out, to prove that I was a danger.

'What would happen if you knew someone was a traitor to our cause? Would you tell me?'

'If I thought they were about to harm one of our people. Yes, of course.'

'But not because they belonged to the revolutionaries?'

'I want to be more neutral than that. I am a journalist and I need to be able to listen to both sides.'

'But if people were traitors to the cause?'

'Who exactly are you thinking of, Lieutenant?'

'It's just that it's very unusual, what happened last night.'

'I would have thought it must be fairly common in this sort of conflict.'

'Lots of attacks and counter-attacks, yes. But an attack aimed at one small group only when one of their number was elsewhere and the lookouts given advice to change their position just before, no.'

'I don't know what you're suggesting but I've seen no evidence of disloyalty among the Harkis.' I was careful not to mention names. 'Changing sides is normally seen as unacceptable and runs very big risks.'

'It's much more common here than you would imagine, Mademoiselle. There are double agents all over the place.'

I went cold. His words brought me fear. I remembered Krim in Algiers, living the double life and leaving no trace of his disloyalty amongst the colons.

'Treachery is a terrible thing, Lieutenant. I can assure you that I will have my eyes open and be on the lookout for it.'

'That's all I ask for, Mademoiselle.'

# Chapter Thirty-Six

In the next few hours I had no time to think about the implications of the conversation because I was so busy helping to get Yannis loaded onto the truck. It was a land rover with a tarpaulin cover over the back.

'I think I should be with him in the back,' I suggested. It was clear that he was going to need help with morphine shots in order to manage the pain.

Yussuf was firm in his disagreement. 'You need to be in the front with me. He's conscious enough to be able to take water if he needs it. We'll give him a morphine shot before we start, and we'll have to stop at midday anyway.'

'I agree.' One of the French soldiers was helping to load up provisions into the jeep. 'You'd be far too exposed in the event of an attack. Better to be in the cab with Yussuf.'

'And Yannis?'

'Sure. That's the risk all combatants take. And he can't stretch his leg out in the front anyway.'

I can't pretend I was unhappy about being better protected. I found that last night's attack had unnerved me and, much as I cared for the harkis, I found that I didn't want to die alongside them for the sake of their cause.

'Or for any cause,' I thought privately. 'I'm not brave enough or idealistic enough for that.'

I found myself explaining my reactions in an embarrassing way later on in the journey.

'From what you've told me, you were prepared to die in the Resistance.'

'Actually, I'm not sure I was,' I confessed. 'I was so young that I didn't think about the consequences of what I was doing. And I was inspired by a friend who I admired very much.'

'You still took the risk though.'

'True. But somehow it seemed like a noble cause – freeing my country from the Nazis and saving innocent people, especially children.'

'That's exactly how the FLN see what they're doing – a noble cause. And the French too to a certain extent though they're also motivated by what they would lose.'

'You mean all sides are equal?'

'Yes, in a way.'

I thought back to my early morning conversation with the Lieutenant.

'So, it's alright to do whatever you want, if you believe in the cause badly enough?'

'No. I'm not personally saying you can do whatever you want. But the real idealists think that the end justifies the means.'

'But you don't?'

'No, of course I don't, Marie. That's why I'm a harki. But it's not black and white. There are brave and good men who are fighting for the ALN out of conviction.'

I was silent. Could he be one of them, or a spy? Someone who was turned, so that all this time he was really fighting for the ALN? Or might he always have been one of their number and was just a plant in the French army, because he had the right background?

The landscape did not help my gloomy suspicions and lack of clarity. The Hodna depression was different from the Sahara, though, as I found out later, even the Sahara is so changeable that it is difficult to define the characteristics of the desert. The Hodna landscape was under sea level and so flat that it seemed to go under at the edges like a crêpe when it is lifted out of the pan. The horizon shimmered in the distance as the sun came up. There were mirages at every point on the landscape. We passed huge blocks of dried salt and what must have been salt lakes a hundred years ago. On a couple of occasions, we encountered camel trains, one of the them led by a single man with no baggage. We stopped to talk to him.

'He's going to Mali to sell camels,' observed Yussuf.

'Mali?' I had hardly heard of it. 'Isn't that hundreds of miles away? His camels must be worth a lot for him to do that.'

'They are. And, besides, you get a better price in a country which is not at war.'

As we had stopped to speak to this man, we spent time with Yannis in the back of the truck, making sure that his needs were cared for, though he was so drug fuelled, that he hardly knew what was happening.

'You check everything. I'll stand watch,' said Yussuf.

'But there isn't anyone here,' I objected. 'And you can see someone approaching from hundreds of miles away.'

'Just do as I say,' he responded curtly.

That was a Yussuf I hadn't encountered before – neither giving arguments or explanations. I wondered if I really knew him. It seemed a very lonely place to be on the edge of a saltlake, hundreds of miles across, with one man in desperate pain and another, whom I scarcely knew, in control of a shot gun. If it hadn't been for the practical medical needs of our passenger, I had started to feel a sense of disassociation, which I knew from past experience, was a symptom of panic and anxiety.

'Sorry to boss you around, Marie.' His tone became more conciliatory as we were on our way again. 'Being here is a very dangerous situation anyway, and always would be, but it's made worse by the fact that four of my colleagues were murdered last night. And Yannis, who I've known for years from the Cadi's village is seriously injured. He'll probably lose his leg.'

'At least that will take him out of the war,' I responded practically.

'No, it doesn't. It takes him away from his ability to defend himself. He'll be even more vulnerable than before. They search out any known supporters of the French regime. To be honest it might have been better if he had died in the attack. I know I'd feel that it was me.'

'That's depressing.'

We continued along the empty landscape. Suddenly a boy herding goats came into view. What they were eating was not obvious. I couldn't see one sign of anything green. Yussuf understood what I was thinking.

'It is actually there, more or less underground. You can't see it, but the goats can sense its presence.'

'But where did they come from?' I asked, amazed once again that anyone could inhabit this bleak landscape.

'You should know by now, Marie. People just appear by magic.' My companion's mood had changed again from bleak pessimism to gentle teasing.

I took advantage of the change to ask him a serious question.

'There's too much magic in this place to my way of thinking,' I observed.

'What do you mean?'

I hesitated, not knowing quite how to broach the subject.

'People come from nowhere; and attacks come from nowhere. And yet they don't. I'm a secular French humanist and I don't believe in magic.'

He laughed. 'In that case, you won't fit into Algeria. There's magic all over the place. The place is inundated with superstition.'

'What do you mean? I thought the people here were good Muslims.'

'It depends what you mean by 'good Muslims'. Yes, they're all religious, but part of that for them means superstition – saints' graves, offerings and sacrifices.'

'It sounds like wayside crosses in Brittany or the offerings in Notre Dame de la Garde in Marseille.'

'Of course. No one can resist bargaining with God. You would as well if you had impossible diseases to endure and no medical services.'

'And impossible mothers-in-law?' I ventured.

He laughed. 'Absolutely. You need a hundred sacrifices at the saint's grave to cope with her.'

I took advantage of his relaxed banter.

'So, if I don't believe in magic, how did those people know when to attack last night?'

He frowned. 'I have no idea. But there's plot and counterplot, people changing sides, people concealing their true loyalties all the time.'

'That's what the lieutenant said.'

'Did he?' His hands on the steering wheel, which were already fully used in getting the land rover over the ridges of hard, fine sand without a road to guide him, tightened.

'And what do you think?'

'I can see why he's worried.'

'Yes, he's right to be worried. There were several things in that attack which didn't add up.'

Silence.

'So, do you still trust me, Marie?'

'Yes, I trust you as a human being.'

'That's a dangerous position to take.'

'Why?'

'Because in a war you shouldn't trust anyone. Even your own instincts.'

'But I'm not in the war. I'm not on one side or the other.'

'Yes, you are. You're French.'

'That doesn't mean that I approve of what the French are doing.'

'It doesn't matter. The FLN still see you as the enemy. They kill French citizens indiscriminately. It doesn't matter how much good they've done for this country.'

'That seems unfair.'

'Exactly. They're biting the hand that feeds them, as the English say. But it's the truth. And you'd better realise that, Marie; otherwise you're going to be in trouble.'

'I already am. I'm a journalist, remember. And, actually, I do trust my instincts. I've had to rely on them a lot in the past, and they're not often wrong.'

'Because of last night?'

'Not just because of last night. You don't feel like a traitor.'

'That doesn't stop me being one. But just for the record, I'm not a traitor. If I changed sides, I'd do it openly. I'd go and join the maquis in the mountains.'

'Wouldn't they kill you?'

'It depends what I brought them.'

'As a spy you could give them lots of information.'

'True, but I wouldn't allow my former colleagues to be betrayed. Remember I fought with them in the war.'

'I believe you.'

'Thank you. But the probable truth is that someone did betray us last night.'

'No idea who?'

'Not at all. I could be suspicious of every single person, including those who died last night, but I have no real idea.'

'It must make it a terrible war of nerves.'

'It is. And no one knows where it's going to lead or end. It could all be an "impasse".'

We both fell into our own moods of gloom. As the landscape changed before us and gradually became greener, the land rose slightly on either side, but more towards a plateau rather than high mountains. We were traversing a deep ravine between.

'Not far till Batna now. We're stopping there for the night. The Aurès are really beautiful, far less forbidding than the ranges in Kabylia.'

At that moment, as the dusk settled above us, two men jumped into the road, behind us, carrying Kalashnikovs and balaclavas covering their faces.

'Get down, Marie.'

I didn't need telling. The land-rover picked up speed and shots were fired at the back of the truck. One of them punctured a wheel and we careered along the unmade road with the truck struggling on like a wounded animal trying to find shelter.

I stayed under the dashboard, far too terrified to sit down again, with my eyes closed, just willing the jeep to go further.

To my horror, it stopped abruptly.

Yussuf looked down at me, seemingly quite unfazed by the attack.

'Are you intending to stay down there all night?'

'If need be. I feel safer here.'

He smiled kindly. 'We're among friends now.'

'How can you possibly know that?'

'Because I know a lot of people in Batna.'

'Well, you didn't appear to know those two in the road and they certainly weren't your friends.'

'No, that's true but that's more of a village on the outskirts and they've always been changeable in their loyalty.'

'Thanks for telling me in advance.'

He grinned. 'It would only have worried you.'

'You bet.'

'The danger's past, I assure you, Marie. Here we are among friends.'

We had both completely forgotten our injured passenger in the back. As I disengaged myself from my cramped position on the floor, Yussuf got out.

He was back in a moment. 'Sorry, Marie. He's gone.' I thought for a moment that it had been another magical disappearance. 'I mean, he's been shot. He's dead.'

'Oh no! The one survivor of last night. I'm sorry.'

'I am too because he was my friend. We've been together in the mountains for the last five years. And we were tirailleurs before that.'

I looked down at the ground, silent with respect.

'But I have to say, I'm glad too. This is a harsh country and a harsh war, and he'd never have survived without a leg.

I'll have to tell his family. That will be the worst part. A young man who has supported them financially through his army pay, suddenly taken.

I'll get the men here to take his body into a back room. Come on! I'll take you into the house before I do that.'

# Chapter Thirty-Seven

I was pleased that the next two days passed without incident. Batna was a beautiful place surrounded by palm trees and the buildings were low and white, which gave the illusion of glamour. The skies were not as extraordinary as they were in the desert, but I still enjoyed the vast canopy of different cloud formations as they passed from the high mountains in the distance, over the Aurès and then over us and then floated off into the desert. Despite the attack on the outskirts of the town, everything seemed very calm here. Yussuf was preoccupied with talking to various groups of people in the town and he did not have time for me. I was quite happy to be on my own with limited communication with the women of the house where I was staying. I had time to write articles about my experiences in the last week, which I would send to Europe from Constantine. There was no sense that any intimate relationship between Yussuf and me would continue. Had it just been a temporary human need for closeness or a deliberate ruse to keep himself safe from the attack? Both possibilities disappointed me, but I had enough experience in life to shrug it off. More emotional attachment complicated life and life in Algeria was complicated enough without romantic liasons.

Two days later we were approaching Constantine in our army truck. It was some time since I had been in such a big city and it seemed strange – both reassuring and alien. Yussuf understood immediately how I felt. We had stopped in the suburbs to take coffee with some of his friends before moving on to our destination.

'You're right. It is strange. It is as though the world has been continuing without you. They've shown that they don't need you and it's hard to adjust to that idea.' He had had similar feelings after he had been on duty for weeks in the mountains, he explained.

'It reminds me of going back to Paris after being in Indo China,' I told him.

'That would have been a big change. How did you feel?'

'Just like you've said. But also, there was the sense that this terrible war had been going on abroad on behalf of France and no one in France really cared. I mean they all had opinions about what should or should not have been done, but it didn't affect their comfortable lives. And I had seen all these young people, soldiers and civilians burnt, made homeless, tortured and it was like they didn't exist anymore. Every time I tried to reintegrate into Parisian life, all these people who had suffered would float in front of my mind, and I couldn't forget them.'

'So, you're not such a neutral journalist after all?'

'No,' I admitted. 'I think neutral in terms of reporting lots of different viewpoints, but you can't be emotionally neutral.'

'I agree. I feel the same thing. It's emotion which drives me to take part in the way I do.'

'In what ways?'

I was intrigued by this admission. This man had seemed entirely emotionless in the way he went about his job, even disposing of the body of Yannis and not even mentioning him again.

'In my head I know that the ALN are going to be victorious. If I had any sense of my own welfare in the future, I would join them now.'

'Surely it must be dangerous being a revolutionary?'

'Of course,' he scoffed, and I realised that I had just insulted his manhood by implying that he would in any way retreat from danger. 'The truth is that it's dangerous whatever you do, and, when you choose to be a harki, the danger is worst of all, because you're an outsider for everyone.'

'So why do you do it, especially if there's no future for you here?'

'There are reasons. I just can't see that the country is going to prosper under them. It would be much better if there was a good range of politics and opinions, and, however much we hate colonialism, we still need the French at the moment.'

'Wouldn't a clean break be better?'

'Are you crazy? How are we going to manage the vineyards and the 'mais', and the orange trees without expert tuition? With a hand over period of three or four years, yes. But, without that, there'll be no exports, no money and people will die of starvation.'

'Sounds bleak,' I admitted. 'But surely your ALN, don't they have an inside committee or governing group?'

'Yes. The CNRG – it's like a fledgling parliament in Algiers. Yes, they do have political ideas, and there's some astute political brains amongst them too.'

'In that case, they'll eventually get it sorted out, won't they?'

'Eventually is the key word. And that's fine to have for an interim period. You can't expect to know everything immediately. But they rely on things like oil far too much. That's why the French want a share in it as well. And no,' he replied, grinning. 'they certainly won't be given a share of it. I don't have a problem with that. The French are just being greedy colonialists. Why shouldn't Algeria keep its own oil supplies? But money is not enough.'

'It's not bad for a start. It can buy you quite a lot of resources.'

'Yes, but it can't buy you skills which take twenty years to learn. Go at it more slowly, and you will get rid of the French eventually, but, meanwhile, you will have profited from their expertise.'

'But you don't think there's any way that's going to happen?'

'Of course not. The CNRE have already said that there won't be any cessation of violence until independence is declared and the pied noirs can only stay if they renounce their French citizenship.'

'Fair enough. They will at least know who's serious about loving Algeria.'

'They might want to stay, and they might love the country, but they will be afraid.'

'Will you be afraid?' I didn't know how he was going to take such a direct question, but he answered calmly enough.

'What, if the ALN are in charge and I've fought against them? Of course. You bet! I'd be a fool not to be.'

'So, will you leave?'

'That will depend on what they offer my family. I can't just leave them defenceless.'

Where had I heard that before? Surely the French would allow this man to live in France, when he had fought for them?

I had lost too many people who I had loved through wars. Perhaps that was why I was drawing back from an involvement with him.

'Yussuf, when the time comes, you'll have to leave with me.'

He shook his head and laughed, a bitter, hopeless laugh.

'And are you going to stay till independence?'

'No, of course I'm not. I have to report to my papers in Paris and they won't fund me to be here for ever, but I'll be back.'

'Will you?'

'Yussuf, let's quit acting like children. You know how I feel.'

'You're very direct. Are all French women like that?'

'Probably not, but not all French women have lost men who they love through war and oppression like I have.'

I told him about the men in Indo China and Russia who I had loved and lost finally I told him about Alain.

'I guess you might be shocked that I have had affairs with all these men, but Alain was when I was very young. I didn't have an affair with him. I was too young to understand, and he wouldn't have put me in that position, but I truly loved him.'

'To be honest, I don't think I understand, what love is all about. I've held my emotions in check for too long.'

'But you said you took the position you have here in your country, because of feelings, not because your head was telling you to.'

He sighed. We were perched on rickety plastic chairs which were garish and hideous on a pavement in the suburbs of the city and here was I having the frankest conversation of my life about intimacy and relationships with a Muslim man, who came from an entirely different world from mine.

'Marie, do you always bombard your lovers with argument, before they can even get near you?'

I grinned in response. 'Yes, it's my normal way of starting to make love.'

'I should tell you that it's having the desired effect. I've no idea what to say to you, except that it doesn't seem fair on you, when you've no idea what is going to happen in the future.'

'Know what's going to happen in the future? Don't make me laugh!' I leant forward as I spoke these words with a little too much passion.

657

An old man across the road was eying us with considerable interest and I realised that I should try to be more subdued in the way I expressed myself. 'I've been in four war zones and I've never known what's going to happen in the future. Who the hell does anyway, even in the most peaceful environment?'

'You might be right. Sure, I never imagined as a little boy, being brought up in the Bourgeaud farm and vineyards that one day I would be fighting in a world war up through France and Germany. Or that I'd be fighting my fellow countrymen in the mountains near me.'

'It sounds like life has turned out to be a disappointment!'

'Only recently.'

'Thanks a lot!'

'You could change that perspective.'

'Only if that's what you want too.'

'Marie, of course I want you. Any man would. But where it's all going to lead, I don't know.'

'Maybe you've just got to trust to Lady Luck.'

'That's sounding an awful lot like a religious fate. 'Mktub' as the Arabs say.'

'Nothing quite as intense as that,' I ventured. 'How about enjoy what's looking good and maybe something good will happen as a result? Trust your instincts.'

'My instincts are in fine form.'

The man across the road had not stopped staring at us. Yussuf saw my embarrassment and laughed.

'Don't worry. He's just staring at a European woman in trousers and without a veil. He's intrigued.'

'Does he have to make it so obvious?'

'No one's told him that it's impolite to stare. But, come on, I want you to meet my friends in the city.'

We approached the city slowly and I was impressed by its beautiful buildings and the bridge over the gorge.

'Right up there you can see the Roman Catholic cathedral. It's one of the oldest in North Africa.'

'How do the 'Constantinois' feel about that?'

658

'They love it. You can see that it dominates the whole city. And then further down the hill is the synagogue and the Jewish quarter.'

'Don't tell me that they love that too.'

'Of course. The Algerian people are the most easy-going folk imaginable. They've always accepted the Jews.'

'But not any longer?'

'They're being forced into being their enemies. Come on. I'm going to introduce you to my friends there. We'll eat with them and then spend the night there.'

# Chapter Thirty-Eight

It was like a smaller version of the Casbah in Alger on the side of the hill with a main road lying across it. On one side of the road were lots of bars and further up merging with the houses were gold merchants and cloth merchants and then, about half-way up, a synagogue with beautiful wrought iron gates. There was a Hebrew inscription on the front with gold inlaid lettering which shone in the setting sun. I was impressed.

'It's so beautiful. I've never seen one quite as decorative as this one.'

'Yes. I agree. But there are synagogues like this all over Algeria. Come on now. Let me introduce you to my friends.'

We went through the back of the gold merchants, who were serving some last-minute customers of the day. We pushed through a curtain at the back of the shop and found ourselves in a small courtyard, with delicate blue and white porcelain tile decoration. On one side grew a lemon tree, the yellow of the fruit contrasting with the light blue of the tiles and making the whole space glow with vibrancy against the background of the gradually darkening sky.

'Yussuf! How wonderful to see you!' A small elderly lady came through one of the courtyard doors, holding out her hands to his and then cupping them round his face, as if he was a child or a favourite nephew whom she had not seen for some time. He did not seem the slightest bit embarrassed by her attentions as he bent down to kiss her on both cheeks.

'Maia, it's more than wonderful to be here. It always feels like a home-coming in this courtyard.'

'In that case, why aren't you here more often?' she scolded him. 'I know, I know. There's a war and you're doing terribly dangerous things and keeping us all safe!' This was said without the slightest sense of irony. She smiled and smiled, one of the most enchanting smiles I have ever seen. In that smile she reassured a young man that she trusted him completely and believed totally in his ability to banish all danger. It was a moment when I observed the ability of an older woman to keep a young man full of hope and I was so grateful to her for the energy and purpose she conveyed. In our recent conversations Yussuf had veered from a position of doom and desperation to one of duty and discipline, without any true feeling appearing between the two extremes. Maia's expression and her gesture appeared to bring out happiness in his face and I was grateful to her.

'And, my dear, who is this lovely young woman? I feel quite jealous of her, distracting you from me, but I perceive her ability to do you good.'

She turned her attention from Yussuf to me with equal enthusiasm and I also felt affirmed and understood by her greeting.

'Maia, this is Marie, a journalist from l'Humanité in Paris.'

'But how wonderful!' exclaimed Maia, as if I had made her day, rather than my turning up at the end of the day as an inconvenient and unexpected visitor.

'A journalist from Paris! I hope you're putting us on the map, Marie. Paris needs to hear all that is happening in Constantine from someone who is properly informed.'

'That is part of the reason for my being here,' I reassured her. 'I want to really understand what is going on here.'

'I like that – 'understand' before writing. Not many journalists are good at that!'

Yussuf continued to enhance my status. 'She's been everywhere in Algeria has Marie over the last two weeks, with the Bourgeauds, in the Kabylian hide-outs, the army barracks, the Aurès and now here.'

Maia's eyes widened. 'How terrifying! You. must be very brave, my dear!'

'Not at all,' I assured her. 'I've had a very good guide, and sometimes I've been terrified.'

'I'm not surprised. All those ravenous dogs in the villages!' She wrinkled up her nose, as if dogs were the worst sort of enemy you could meet in an Algerian village in the middle of a war.

Yussuf laughed. 'And now she's come to experience the Jewish quarter in Constantine. I left the best till last.'

'Of course, you did.'

'It is a truly wonderful and unexpectedly beautiful place,' I told her. 'I've never seen anything quite like this before.'

'Well, come and see the rest of it, my dear, before you have a cup of mint tea to refresh you before dinner.'

'Just what we need after battling along that road from Batna,' agreed Yussuf. 'We're completely covered with dust from every passing truck and donkey.'

'How thoughtless of me!' our host exclaimed. 'Would you like a shower before dinner, Marie?'

'I would love one but I'm afraid my only dress has been rather crushed on its passage through the mountains.'

'You could borrow one of our daughter's dresses if you like. She always leaves plenty in the cupboard and she's about the same size as you.'

'That would be wonderful. Thank you.'

We were swept up in a tour of the house, which was much bigger than you would expect from entering the courtyard through the shop. The rooms were rather dark compared to the luminous courtyard, but I could see that the heavy oak furniture was of excellent quality.

'There are a couple of rooms made up for you.' She led me into two adjoining bedrooms.

'You were expecting us?' I asked surprised.

'I always have a room ready for Yussuf when he comes through and the other room is my daughter's. She works in Bône – (Annaba the Algerians call it) and she never knows when she is going to get a lift from the coast, so again we always have a room ready for her.'

The shower was on the opposite side of the corridor and, after the first proper wash I had had for days, I felt wonderful. It did indeed seem as if all the dust of the paths and roads we had travelled had stuck to me and had just been miraculously wiped away. In the cupboard of my room I found a long, flowing day dress, which I recognised as typically Algerian and yet had tucks and gatherings in the bodice which gave it a sense of style which was European. Whereas wearing a full-length dress would have felt like over dressing in France, here it seemed to be a convention of modesty which everyone adhered to. Even Maia had been wearing a full-length dress when she first greeted us.

I was satisfied with my contours as I gazed at myself in the half-darkened mirror. I went downstairs to the dining room which was now lit by several candles which gave the dark furniture, indeed the whole room, allure.

Without intending to, I effected an entrance which made everyone turn around and stare, including my travelling companion.

'You didn't tell us that you knew such a beautiful young lady, Yussuf,' laughed Maia. 'Actually, my dear, despite the disciplined military look, he can be quite dashing himself.'

'I know. I first met him coming over on a boat from France.'

'How romantic! And how wise of you to spot her and pursue her, Yussuf.'

Yussuf smiled charmingly. He seemed to know how to answer his hostess with exactly the right mixture of banter and diplomacy.

'How could I do anything else? To be honest, I didn't pursue her. She turned out to make a conquest of M. Bourgeaud and I, of course, was an extra in the household.'

'In that case,' came a deep voice from the end of the table, 'she not only has beauty but lots of worldly know-how. If you want something doing in Algeria, you have to be on the right side of M. Bourgeaud. How do you do, Marie? My name is Emile and I'm the one who tries to keep this household together and functioning.'

'You seem to manage that very well, Emile,' I said as I went forward to shake his hand. 'I love your home, hidden here behind the shop front and half in the Casbah.'

'Do you? We like it too, near my shop and a few steps from the schul as well.'

'Typical Jewish!' agreed his wife. 'In between money and religion. An essential combination!'

'I've never really known how the Jews manage to do both so successfully,' observed Yussuf. 'Moslems seem to specialise in poverty and religion.'

'Maybe the ordinary people do,' I suggested. 'But, if you look at the Catholic church, they appear to preach poverty but the church itself is very rich.'

'Of course. That's true for all religions,' added Emile tactfully. 'The only difference is that the Jews are up front about the link between money and religion.'

I was intrigued. 'Why is that, do you think?'

'It's all to do with the Patriarchs being blessed with money themselves as well as giving it to others.'

'I've got to say that I've always loved the fact that my Jewish friends in France were never ashamed of their money.'

'I should think not!' exclaimed Emile almost piously. 'Shall we sit down to dinner?'

'No, let's take our drinks out to the courtyard before the darkness really closes in,' suggested Maia. 'I don't think dinner is quite ready and I promised Marie a drink in the courtyard first. Yes, I know it was tea I offered you, but I think it's time for a little apéritif instead.'

'Sounds good to me,' grinned Yussuf happily. 'I also like religions which combine alcohol and piety.'

We sat in silence as the courtyard darkened completely and the brightness of the lemons were taken up by the lights on the inside of the house shining through them.

'Marie, we never tire of seeing night fall in this beautiful place. But tell me about your connection with the Jews in France? Yussuf has been telling us that you have several links.'

As we sat down to our dinner, I explained about Alain and Les Landes, Bordeaux, Russia and Marseille. There was so much to say that we were almost finished with our plat de resistance in the form of boeuf bourguignon, richly flavoured with wine, which was absolutely delicious, when my story came to an end.

'In that case, you will compare what you see here in Algeria with all the other Jewish communities you have known.'

'Yes, indeed, I find it fascinating, especially the fact that you have been in this country for so long.'

'Yes, my family have been here for 400 years.'

"400!' I repeated with amazement. 'Why so long?'

'My ancestors came out of the Spanish Inquisition. They were banished by Isabella and Ferdinand, because they wouldn't convert. They went first to Morocco, but somehow never settled there, and so decided to take a ship to Malta, but got shipwrecked on the way and ended up in Algeria.'

'And that turned out to be a lucky shipwreck?' I suggested, before Emile continued his story.

'Of course. They loved the coast and mountains here and eventually came to be part of Constantine.'

'So, you really don't want to leave?' I said bringing it up to the present day.

'Leave? Of course not! Why ever would we want to do that?'

I hesitated, not wanting to be brutal about the reality of the situation. 'Because of the escalating violence here?'

Maia shuddered. 'It's true, Marie. There have been some awful things happening here, even in the Jewish community.'

Emile remonstrated. 'In Medea, yes, but not really in Constantine.'

'I heard about that from General Beaufré. What had the rabbi done to deserve that?'

'Absolutely nothing,' interrupted Yussuf. 'But that's what it's like. Someone had told the mob that he had given money to the French authorities to help hunt down revolutionaries. It was all a lie of course but they don't wait to find out the truth.'

I thought about some of the Parisians who had been murdered by some of their fellow countrymen after the war, because somehow the rumour had gone around that they had been collaborators. Many of them were innocent but that had not stopped the mob going crazy.

'But some of the Jewish community in Medea had changed their support,' explained Emile. 'Some of them were acting as double agents.'

'But not the young rabbi.'

'No indeed. That was so terribly sad.'

'More boeuf, Marie?' offered my hostess.

'I really couldn't, Maia. It was gorgeous but I haven't eaten so much in the last week and it's just as well, otherwise I would have never got up those mountains.'

'Yes, well I can't say we get a lot of exercise,' added Maia. Both she and Emile were a little plump.

'And I gather you're hoping to visit the Gaullen vineyards?' enquired Emile.

'Yes. I'd really like to. I'd heard a lot about them from M. Tribier in Marseille.'

'Ah, yes, the Tribiers. I remember them when they used to visit Constantine before the war. How long ago that seems!' He sighed, somehow seeming suddenly like an old man.

'Yussuf, how are you taking her to Gaullen's vineyard? It's dangerous out there these days.'

'I know a safe route.'

'You'd better had. I don't want this young lady in danger.'

'Nor do I.' Yussuf turned gallantly to me. 'Don't worry. I'm committed to keeping you safe.'

Before the night was out, I did feel safe with him. The adjoining bedrooms were the only excuse we needed to get to know each other more intimately.

'That's the Jews again for you,' remarked Yussuf, as we smoked in bed after we'd made love. 'Much more practical and realistic than anyone else.'

'Must be why I like them so much,' I agreed happily.

# Chapter Thirty-Nine

The next morning Maia insisted on a visit to the synagogue next door, and, even though I had made several similar visits in my life, I had to admit that it was beautiful – nineteenth century wood panelling and carved desks for the reading of the Torah and the Cantor's part.

'When we see how many synagogues have been destroyed in Europe, we hold onto this as our precious possession,' she remarked.

'Did you have family in Europe during the war?' I asked, afraid of what the answer might be.

'Fortunately, our immediate family were all here and they were safe. That's why we cherish Algeria so much.' She sighed and I understood her unspoken fears. 'But even though they were not our family, all Jews are our family. I could not believe the horror of what I heard after the war.'

'No one could believe it and we were in Europe and knew about the transports. In France we knew many of them were being sent to Germany, but no one really knew what was happening there.'

There was silence as we each thought with respect and sorrow about those who had been lost.

'Some were actually saved by coming here at the right time,' Maia added.

'Yes. The Tribiers told me about that. But now they are choosing to stay in France.'

'I can understand that even though I have chosen differently. I am afraid too, Marie, about what is going to happen. Emile doesn't want to think about it, but I do.'

I tried to reassure her. 'But this time it's not the Jews who are the targets.'

'Not primarily them of course, but they are targets when they are perceived to be supporting the French.'

'And you are?'

'Of course. We just want the best future for this country, and we think that a gradual withdrawal is the best way.'

'Like Yussuf then?'

'Yes, like Yussuf.' She paused. 'I worry for Yussuf. He is such a lovely boy and he has taken such a dangerous position.'

'He knows what he is doing.'

'He knows what he thinks is right and the possible consequences. But he doesn't know how it could kill his future.'

'Maybe you should try telling him.'

'He won't listen to an old woman like me.'

I laughed. 'You don't strike me as old, Maia.'

'You know how to flatter.'

'I know how to speak the truth. But seriously. Yussuf trusts you. You must talk to him.'

'I have on several occasions, but the problem is – what is the way forward? If he's not for the French, he's for the ALN, and, however much he sympathises with them, he won't turn against the people he fought with in the war.'

We examined the beautiful oak handles of the Torah scrolls.

'Yes, they're wonderful, aren't they? They were brought over from Russia in the nineteenth century, when a family came to escape the pogroms.'

'They're so reassuring, aren't they?' I commented, tracing the carved branches.

'How do you mean?'

'Not only have they been here for one hundred years, but they hold together a book which has been here for thousands of years. It's not easy to get rid of it. It's wonderful.'

'My dear, you're beginning to sound like a "yid".'

'That sounds like a compliment to me,' I said, remembering Alain and his family.

Maia turned to show me some of the beautiful glass in the doorway.

'It's not stained glass of course and it can never portray figures, but it's still a work of art.'

I agreed as I tenderly touched the yellow and purple patterns in the glass.

'Marie, perhaps you could help Yussuf.'

'How?'

'Persuade him that he has to leave the country with you now, while there's still time.'

'I don't think he'll go. He would see it as a cowardly act of withdrawal'

'I don't want someone so good to die.'

I shivered. 'I don't either. I can try, Maia, but he cares too much about his family and friends like the Bourgeauds to leave.'

'Family, yes, I can understand but the Bourgeauds? Yes, they've done great things for this country, but they'll always have money. They'll always be able to buy their way out of catastrophe.'

I was surprised by her sharp tone. 'You sound very cynical.'

'I don't mean to be and they're not bad people. It's just that it's always the good and the poor who get left behind.'

'You're right,' I agreed sadly. 'All my life experiences teach me that.' I thought of the Vietnamese who were left to face the Viet Cong when the French left – lovely, peace-loving and good people, destroyed by hatred.

'I'll try to take him with me when I leave, Maia, but I'm not hopeful.'

'You love each other so it might work.'

I was startled. 'Is it that obvious?'

She laughed, changing the atmosphere immediately, so that it became lighter and more playful.

'Yes, it is, especially to old lovers like Emile and me.'

I couldn't imagine Emile with the white beard and skull cap as a lover. Maia saw immediately what I was thinking. 'No, Marie,' she said mischievously. 'You mustn't imagine that us oldies can't be lovers too. I know that it doesn't seem likely but you're wrong, you know. I'm still as much in love with Emile as I was when I was twenty. Don't ask me why. That's just how it is.'

I was struck by the truth of her words. 'You're right about the 'don't ask me why' bit. I have absolutely no idea why Yussuf and I love each other. All my experience and teaching were against it. Wrong culture and religion. Not a fashionable political viewpoint. Dogged and determined and not often very romantic. But there it is. We love each other.'

'Wonderful, my dear.' Her eyes were sparkling with delight. 'A love story! Just what I need to cheer me up. Now, shall we go and see these men of ours and find out what's happening for the rest of the day?'

We had our lunch with Emile but Yussuf had disappeared into the Casbah, ready to find out more information about the latest movement of the ALN, I had no doubt. He seemed to spend more time and had more success in listening to people over coffee than any spy I had ever heard of.

I profited from his absence by enjoying a wonderful 'sièste' in the cool bedroom, shut off from the midday heat by the shutters and the inside courtyard. And then just as suddenly, he was there lying next to me in the bed.

'Been missing out on sleep or something?' he asked carefully, tracing the contours of my throat with his fingers.

'Definitely,' I murmured back, lulled into semi-consciousness by the heat and my own fatigue. 'Too much climbing mountains and escaping in uncomfortable trucks in very dubious company.'

For once, he did not respond to my whispered, playful tone.

'You did escape in an uncomfortable truck and so did I. I've been worrying what that was all about for the last two days.'

'What do you mean?' My mind was beginning to rally in response to the seriousness of his tone.

'Obviously the attack on the French camp had to come from somewhere. It was too knowing, too organized to be chance. Someone knew too much.'

'You mean, you were betrayed.'

'Yes, but I couldn't work out by whom. Was it some of the French who had been careless and had been followed when they went out of the camp?'

'Would they behave like that?' I asked surprised, 'the French, I mean.'

'Yes, there are girls in the villages nearby and they're only human. They can easily give away too much information.'

'You mean it's a deliberate seduction to make them reveal the camp's whereabouts?'

'Not always. Sometimes it's just sex, even love,' he added, for a moment playfully, as he looked at my outline half covered by the sheet. Then he continued more seriously, 'It could have been that. But the attack which led to the 'harkis' being killed was too deliberate. It made me suspicious.'

'But who would you be suspicious of?'

'Everyone. You get like that. They would have been suspicious of me too, and the lieutenant certainly was.'

'I know. He asked me to watch out for you.'

'Did he indeed? Well, I can understand it. Just at the critical time of the attack, I was with you and missed the onslaught.'

'You don't have to feel guilty about that.'

'Well, I do. I evaded the gun fire which mowed down my friends.'

'I'm just glad that you're alive.'

'It's not much fun being alive when all your friends are dead.'

'Not all of them, Yussuf.'

'No. You're right. But anyway, I've been doing my usual listening job in the casbah. It turns out that there was a traitor.'

'Who?'

'Yannis.'

'Yannis?' I shot up in the bed to a seating position. 'But Yannis was the scout in the cave who first found the murdered family. And he's just been killed himself. It can't be him.'

'Oh yes, it can. Sadly, they don't always leave their informants alive. They might have let him escape the massacre, but they finished him off as we were coming along because they didn't want him to talk.'

'Would he have done?'

'Most probably if the French got hold of him in the hospital.'

'Is there anyone who doesn't get destroyed by this evil?' I asked hopelessly, not even hoping for an answer.

He sat next to me on the bed and put his arms around me.

'One day it's got to end, Marie.'

'I want it to end now.'

'Me too.'

'Why don't you let it end for you? You can't make it better so you're not doing any good here. Come back to France with me, Yussuf.'

671

'What? And marry you?'

'I don't care whether you do or not. It doesn't matter to me as long as you're with me and as long as you're safe.'

I sensed the muscles of his face smiling behind me.

'You won't make a good Algerian girl, my dear. You must be married to defend your honour.'

'You can defend my honour as much as you like, but, come away, Yussuf, and be safe.'

Silence. Then surprisingly, 'If you insist enough, I might just do that.'

I turned to him suddenly, knocking his chin and causing him to rub it. 'You don't have to injure me in the process.'

'Really? You will? O Yussuf, that would be fantastic.'

'Nothing would be fantastic here, but, yes, for you and me, that would be fantastic.'

'Maia wants you to do it and I want you to do it.'

'Oh well, that's it, isn't it – if that's what you two want.'

I pushed against him with my arm and he caught it firmly. We struggled, giggling against each other, until we fell in a heap onto the floor.

'It's too late to go over to the Gaullen vineyards now but tomorrow, even though I am taking you, I'm asking for a French army backup.'

'Really?' I got off the floor quickly.

'Really. I don't trust myself to protect you any longer.'

'But you trust yourself to be safe. Why?'

'Because when I'm by myself, I can hide easily. I can run fast. I can keep going for days with very little food. It's not that you're not up to these things, Marie. It's just that I've lived like this for years.'

'How ever will you settle into a normal life again?' I questioned instinctively and then regretted my words.

'Perhaps I can't and that's part of the problem about the future.'

'Anyway,' I said, firmly and practically, not wanting to get too morbid and make him go back on his agreement to escape the country. 'I think we need to get ready for Maia's soirée. It promises to be a good one and she won't want to be kept waiting.'

He smiled up at me. 'I want you to look as beautiful as you did last night in that dress.'

'Fine. I need some time to make myself beautiful.'
'Then let me leave you the time to do it.'

# Chapter Forty

The French army truck came early in the morning. Not many people were out in the streets at that time, but I had the uncanny feeling that people were watching. Emile and Maia had sided with the French by hosting Yussuf and myself and I couldn't help feeling that they were the ones who now needed protecting. The night before they had assured me that the Jewish community always banded together at times like this, but Yussuf was not so sure.

'Be careful,' he warned them. 'Some of the more educated Jews are casting their lot in with the nationalists.'

'But Yussuf darling,' Maia looked at him imploringly. 'No Jew will turn against another of his own.'

'Maybe not. But they will spy for the FLN – in fact in many cases be forced to – and, then, they will give away information almost by accident and the FLN will use that information against the others.'

'But why should they fight us, when we have always supported their right to vote and be educated?'

'Maia, they're not logical. Don't get involved. Be careful who you're seen with. In fact, it's good that we're going.'

'How could that be?' she asked seductively.

We sped away from the shop and the synagogue in the early light.

'Yussuf, you must not go back there,' I said firmly. 'It's not safe for them.'

'I know.'

We both felt so gloomy that we had little to say to each other on the journey. I don't know whether there was any threat, but we didn't encounter anything obvious. There were several roadblocks, but being in a French army vehicle, we were waved through very quickly.

'Working on a roadblock is a dangerous place to be,' observed Yussuf.

'More dangerous than being in a camp or on foot in the mountains?'

'Yes. You're a sitting target both from the mountains above and, also, the enemy can fool you with their own vehicles which are disguised. They can throw a grenade at you and kill you very quickly. Then the rest of the unit has the choice of defending the roadblock or escaping.'

'And what do they normally do?'

'Escape, if they have any sense. You can't win a skirmish against guerrillas. They're too good at it.'

'How often are you placed on a roadblock?'

'Not very often, I'm glad to say. We're much better at blending into the mountain scenery and then we have a good chance of evading the enemy.'

The road was now very dusty, and the wheels of the jeep were churning up huge clouds of dirt. We could hardly see the mountains on one side of us, even though it was now full daylight.

'Are all the 'harkis' Kabyles?'

'No. But a lot are. There were more Kabyles than Arabs who fought in the war.'

'Why was that?'

'Because we're braver than they are.' He grinned. 'No, No. Ok. Ok,' as I threw the book I was trying to read at his face. 'It was just in our regiment. And there are lots of Kabyles in the FLN, especially in Wilaya 2. Centred round Constantine. Even the FLN are divided between the Arabs and the Kabyles.'

'That doesn't sound very promising for the future,' I observed.

'Nothing's very promising for the future,' he said darkly, and that was the end of the conversation. I returned to reading my book on the rutted, twisting road.

Before long the road straightened up again and we were starting to see first olive groves and then vines.

'This is the start of the Gaullen empire,' explained Yussuf. 'But it's nothing like as extensive as the Bourgeauds. They don't have the same defence system either.'

'I didn't know that the Bourgeauds had one.'

'Of course, they do. All the men on the estate would defend it with their lives and M. Bourgeaud makes sure that he keeps hold of men like me as well – people who support the French army. Not that I object to doing it. He supported my family and gave me an education. But not all the colons are as rich as Henri Bourgeaud. Gaullen has got workers but he hires them rather than keeps them. And hired workers will always go for the highest bidder.'

'According to M. Trimbier, it's got a great export business.'

'Yes, but how long is since M. Trimbier was here?'

I hazarded a guess. 'Five or six years.'

'Exactly. A lot has changed in that time. Here we are now, at the Entreprise Gaullen.'

The truck swerved round in front of the offices and the wine tasting 'cave'. An inquisitive, teenaged Algerian face looked out from the doorway, then quickly withdrew to report on our arrival.

Soon a stout, middle-aged figure came up the few steps and crossed the front square. He was clearly reassured by the sight of the French truck.

'Good morning. How can I help you, gentlemen? Have you come to sample a particular vintage?'

The driver laughed. 'We'd like to, sir, but we're on duty.'

'Don't tell me a Frenchman is not allowed to have a 'verre' before dinner even when working?'

'Sorry, sir. General's orders.'

The man shook his head in mock horror. 'What's the world coming to?' And then, on seeing me, he added, 'And who's this in the back? Are the French army employing front-line women now?'

I felt his eyes on me, sizing me up in a rather distasteful way. All Frenchmen size up the women they meet in bold, physical terms, but most manage to disguise it. Monsieur Gaullen didn't. I felt uncomfortable under his stare. Yussuf saw the problem immediately.

'Let me introduce you to Mlle Marie, from Libèration and l'Humanité.'

'Ah! A communist hack!'

'No.' I corrected him, 'a hack from a communist newspaper – rather different.'

He bowed his acceptance of my explanation. 'A quick-thinking one anyway. And you?'. His eyes narrowed as he took in Yussuf's appearance.

'I'm a scout for the French army and I'm just delivering our journalist friend here. She knows your cousin, Monsieur Gaullen.'

'Ah! You mean the man who is the French coward in our family?'

I was angry at such an insult. 'I haven't found him to be a coward at all. He just looks ahead to what is happening in the world.'

'Nonsense, a coward. But,' he added more good-humouredly, 'a good wine grower who is helping the company in France.'

Monsieur Gaullen suddenly seemed more relaxed and friendly. 'We don't often get visitors from the home country, especially ones who know my family. Please come to the house and eat with us.'

Suddenly I wanted Yussuf to stay with me.

'Thank you, M. Gaullen. I was hoping to see round your vineyard, and also to find out how your workers are faring in these difficult times. I'm trying to get the colon view for my newspaper.'

He laughed, a short, sharp bark as if dismissing any such thought out of hand.

'That will be the day, when a French leftist newspaper really wants to know what the colons think.'

'Well this one does, I assure you.'

'I'll believe it when I read it.'

He turned to Yussuf. 'So, what are you doing here, Corporal?'

He was trying to judge Yussuf's rank, deciding whether he wanted him in his house or not.

'Yussuf has been showing me round the Algerian and French scene in Constantine.'

'I bet he has.'

I could feel Yussuf stiffening near me. 'Monsieur Gaullen, I work for the French army. We've been assuring Mlle Marie's safety while she's been on her travels. If we leave her here for the next 24 hours, can you guarantee her safety? I need to go north to Annaba on army business.'

'Of course, I can't guarantee her safety, not with all the barbarian bandits out in full force. But I can assure you that they won't get to her without a fight. If you want to abandon Mlle Marie here to her fate, I'll do my best.'

Yussuf bowed his head slightly, almost dismissively.

'That's all we can ask for. We know that the situation is difficult.'

'Difficult? It's bloody impossible. How are we supposed to survive with de Gaulle changing his mind all the time and the army never being here to protect us? I don't know what will happen at the best of times, but we'll do our best.'

He turned around to face the office. 'Give me her bag. My wife and I will make her as comfortable as possible.'

I felt awkward but determined to make the best of this half-hearted welcome.

'When will you be back, Yussuf?'

'In two days-time.'

'Be careful in Annaba, won't you?'

M. Gaullen turned around from the doorway.

'Since when has being careful made any difference? If they get you, they get you – the bloody wogs!'

I didn't bother to apologise as I turned to face Yussuf. 'I think he's expecting me to follow.'

'See you in two days' time.'

# Chapter Forty-One

I had come to expect the high standard of housing which the richer pied noir aspired to and, in the Gaullens' house, I was not disappointed. I had also come to expect humanity, bonhomie and a concern for employees. Immediately I stepped into the Gaullen house, I sensed a different way of living.

I was introduced to Mathilde Gaullen, a tall, willowy lady, who, when she was younger, must have been a great beauty. She had slanting grey eyes, which looked out at her world with little expectation. Although she greeted me courteously enough and invited me to join her and her husband at their midday meal, there was no enthusiasm for my company.

'You'll have to put up with what we have, I'm afraid,' she said in a restrained, sad voice, accompanied by a sigh. 'We don't often get supplies from Constantine or Bône now, and anyway, the only girl who is up to working in the kitchen here doesn't go out of her way to produce variety.'

'Stop whining, Mathilde. The girl does the best she can under the circumstances.'

I was puzzled by the tone of his reply. Not only was he rude to his wife, but there was no attempt to criticise the cook, only to defend her.

'I've already spent two days in the mountains with very basic provisions and, anyway, I'm not very fussy about food. I don't think that anyone who has lived through the war with rationing in an enemy occupied country finds cause to complain. So please don't worry on my account.'

I was shown where to leave my bag and refresh myself and then I joined my hosts at the table. The door opened and a young girl came in with salad and a bowl of couscous. It was basic North African food, not of a gourmet variety, but fresh and tasty and filling. After my early start I enjoyed every mouthful and I was able to concentrate on it, because there was not very much conversation at the table. Having been in a vibrant Jewish house for the last two days, the contrast was marked. I had almost forgotten that this was a Jewish household too and I wanted to mention his relatives, the Tribier family, who had recommended this visit.

'Stephane knows a good thing when he sees one,' commented Jules Gaullen. 'Better to stay in France where it's safe.'

'My husband knows that it's safe there,' interrupted Mathilde unexpectedly, 'but he doesn't want to go there himself. He has too many things making him stay here in this g-d forsaken country.'

I tried to dispel the tension between them. 'I'm not surprised you don't want to leave, Monsieur Gaullen. It's such a beautiful place you have here.'

He scoffed in answer to my comment. 'I assure you, Mademoiselle, the beauty of the place, as you call it, is the least of my concerns.'

'So, what's the attraction then?'

'Money, having enough of it. And don't tell me it's not important. You're still young and you don't need to know that yet.'

I was irritated by his assumption about my lack of experience in life. 'Everyone needs enough money to live on, but surely you have enough contacts in the wine-growing business in France to be able to transfer there and make a success of it.'

'Mademoiselle, I'm nearly sixty. I have put all my life's work into developing this place. I do not want to start again somewhere else.'

'Even if that meant you would be safe?'

'Safe? Who knows where is safe?' I felt instinctively that he was rehearsing a well-known speech. 'Will we be safe in de Gaulle's France with all the communists and the foreigners and the army on the point of revolt?'

'It's not as bad as all that,' I countered reasonably. 'If you are a French citizen there would be a place for you.'

He smiled condescendingly. 'Very nice of you to think that. Something tells me that it won't be so easy to start from scratch in France with no money.'

There didn't seem much point in pursuing this line of argument.

'And what about you, Madame? Where would you like to be?'

Jules laughed in response on her behalf.

'Believe you me, Marie. She would like to be where the money is.'

She flushed under his accusation. 'It is true that it is difficult to restart life at our age in a country you hardly know.'

'Were you born here?'

'No. In France. I only came out here when we got married.'

'That must have been difficult for you.'

She replied remarkably directly. 'It was, especially as I married into a Jewish family, who didn't want a Gentile amongst them.'

'Here we go again,' lamented her husband. 'Mathilde has been repeating this like a long worn-out record for the last forty years.'

I tried to help her as much as possible. 'It's always difficult adapting to a different religious community.'

'Religious?' Jules laughed at the idea. 'I don't think that I count as being religious, Mademoiselle. There wasn't much for her to adapt to in that area.'

I had already discovered that this couple had no children. Living in a foreign country with a man who was as self-seeking, cynical and unromantic as Jules Gaullen must have been soul-destroying, I thought.

'But, seriously, Madame, perhaps you would enjoy connecting with your home culture again.'

She looked at me searchingly. It occurred to me that no one had considered what she wanted for a long time.

'You are probably right. It would take a lot of effort to readapt, but it might be worth it.'

Monsieur Gaullen took up the argument again. 'You know, Marie, we're not like the Bourgeauds.'

'In what way?'

'Everyone talks about how much they give to their Algerian employees, but they forget that, even if they left, they have so many business connections in France, that they would always have enough.'

A speech, I thought, which being translated meant – some people are always lucky: we are not like that.

After a meal and the chance of a 'sièste', M. Gaullen offered to take me round the vineyard. It seemed well-run, but no one here appeared to have the alacrity to please which had been so evident among the employees in the mitdja.

'They are afraid,' commented the head of the Gaullen entreprise, as if he sensed the comparison I was making.

'What of?' I thought I knew the answer, but I wanted to know how Jules Gaullen saw it.

'They're afraid for their livelihoods and their lives and unfortunately the two are in direct opposition to each other.'

'How do you mean?'

'If they stop working here, they will earn no money. If they continue working here, they will be killed by the nationalists.' It was a gloomy outlook.

'So, what's the solution?'

We were sitting in a small, open-sided jeep, looking out over rows of beautifully tended vines. How could death be lurking here? I thought. But I knew it was.

'The only solution is for Challe and his company to totally get rid of the revolutionaries.'

'And could they?'

'Of course, they could, if they put their minds to it, instead of worrying about their scruples and the French electorate, who don't know a damn thing about this country anyway.'

'I can't help thinking that if there are people who want freedom for their country, you will never get rid of them. Freedom is an intoxicating idea.'

'Whose side are you on?' he asked accusingly.

'I'm not on anyone's side. I'm just a journalist. But what I've seen in other parts of the world tells me is that you ignore freedom fighters at your peril.'

'Jumped up little wogs who think they know more than people who've been here 130 years.'

'Maybe in your view, but they're educated people who are leaders. And they're prepared to sacrifice their lives for their country.'

'If I had my way, they'd all be made to sacrifice their lives.'

'And their families?'

'It's their choice.'

I didn't argue anymore. He was determined to retain his point of view, but I had the impression that it was more about bitterness and lack of fulfilment than any thought-through philosophy.

When I went in, to rest and prepare myself for dinner, I was surprised to find the girl who had prepared our meal in my room.

'What are you doing here?' I asked suspiciously.

'Just making your bed and room ready for you as Madame Mathilde asked me to.' She answered swiftly, giving me a disdainful look from under her beautifully curved eyelashes.

'Fine. Well, it's ready now. Please don't enter again without my permission.' I felt annoyed by her intrusion but added, 'Thank you,' not wanting to sound ungrateful for any of her services.

'Je vous en prie,' she replied with perfect etiquette, but, beneath the correctness of the phrase, I thought there was an attitude of contempt.

The rest of the evening passed pleasantly enough. We talked about France and the army movements and Mathilde's childhood and adolescence in the Gard. I found that she had been unusual in her generation in that her parents had encouraged her to go to university. She had been part of an elite group at the Sorbonne when she had met a group of wine growers during a placement connected with her degree in economics. Academically she had been advanced, but in relation to men she had been very naïve. Jules had overwhelmed her with his sophistication and knowledge of the world. The idea of going to live in an exotic country, like Algeria, was too much of a temptation.

'What did you think when you arrived here?' I asked, curious to know how hard a blow it had felt at the beginning. I could not imagine the start of married life in this isolated place as an eighteen-year old.

'Actually, we went to Algiers for the first five years and it was very exciting. I had a wonderful social life and I even wanted to use my economics training for the good of the country.

'And did you?'

'There's only one sort of economics which is good here.' Jules interrupted the story sourly. 'Hard work; low wages and exports to Europe.'

I turned to Mathilde again. 'Could you not have used your ability in the export side of the business?'

683

She shrugged her shoulders. 'I didn't think far enough ahead and, after a few years of trying for a baby, I had a miscarriage.'

'I'm so sorry.' There was nothing else to say after this exchange about the past and, after the meal was cleared away, and after we had a enjoyed a digestif together, I went to bed.

The next morning, Jules had already disappeared for work and I sat with Mathilde over a late breakfast, which she had made herself.

'Yamina doesn't come in till lunch time.'

'So at least you get the house to yourself in the morning,' I commented, suspecting that having the Algerian girl round was no help for her own very real loneliness.

'Yes. You're right. I like that.'

A pause as we slurped our café au lait.

'Marie, have you noticed anything about her?'

'Yamina, you mean? No, not particularly. I thought she was a bit over-zealous about sorting my room out yesterday, but no doubt she does that for all your guests.'

'We don't get many.' It seemed like an admission of failure rather than a fact. 'That's why it's nice having you.'

I was surprised by her appreciation. 'Thank you, Mathilde.'

'She's very pretty, isn't she?'

'Yes, of course. Lots of Algerian girls are before they get married.'

'You mean before marriage wears them down? I think I know how they feel.'

'However awful it is here alone it can't be as bad as having ten children…' I was going to go on and say, 'and no money', but faltered, as I suddenly remembered her miscarriage.

'No. You don't need to be embarrassed. They do struggle with so many children, but even more so when it's a loveless marriage and there are several wives.'

I agreed. 'It sounds like a nightmare for any woman.'

'Especially the loveless marriage. It must be obvious to you as a guest, but Jules and I have very little affection for one another.'

'It's difficult to tell when you're a newcomer. Different married couples behave differently.'

'No doubt but the truth is that ours is a loveless marriage and Jules is having an affair with Yamina.'

"Mathilde!' I was genuinely shocked. 'In the same house?'

'No. At least he's civilised enough to go somewhere else, usually to her house.'

'I'm surprised her parents allow it.'

'They will if there's money involved.'

'You sound cynical. In that case, you don't think it's a case of true love?'

She buried her head in her napkin for a moment.

'I only know that it's the most humiliating experience of my life. I'm stuck here, at least 100 kms from civilisation, with a man who despises me, and his lover is in the house with me all the time.'

'So, why don't you leave?'

'Where is there to go to? I didn't pursue economics. I didn't have children, but I did help build the vineyard up. It's the only thing I know. If I leave, I lose my interest, my money and all the love life I've ever known.'

'Are there none of your family left in France?'

'I don't know. I lost touch with them years ago. And Jules' family rejected us completely because I'm not a Jew.' Quickly she added, 'Please don't say anything, Marie, because there is nothing to say.'

And what can you say in the face of one woman's utter misery? There was only deep within me a desire to help.

'If you like, if it would give you courage, you could come back to France with me. I know I'm not family, but at least it would be someone to travel with.'

She laughed, a hopeless, mirthless laugh. 'Then what would happen? I don't have a job. I don't have any money. I don't have a family. I'm non-existent.'

The future did indeed look bleak for her. 'But, Mathilde, you will have your dignity, and, you will have made a decision for yourself, which preserves who you are. And you can never tell about the future. As you've said, it can't get any worse than it is at the moment, so the future can only be better.'

'Thank you, my dear. I'm feeling better just listening to you.'

'Well, don't let it be a nice moment to look back on. You could decide to come with me in the next twenty-four hours. I'm going up to Annaba with Yussuf and then we're going to France.'

'Together?'

'I'm hoping so. That's a risk too. Why not join us in the risk taking? You've got nothing to lose.'

# Chapter Forty-Two

We didn't have any more time for conversation because I had to spend time composing and editing some more of my articles about the workplace in Algeria for the 'pied noirs', and for Algerian nationals. I needed to mix in comments about the political situation and how the current unrest made it harder for everyone – the impossibility of quick, superficial judgements and the hiatus which had descended on the country as they waited for de Gaulle's referendum. At the same time, I tried to find out a little more about Yamina. I found her to be charming to my face, but it was impossible to penetrate her real thoughts and feelings. I saw no sign of her relationship with Jules, but I had no trouble in believing that what Mathilde had told me, was true.

To my amazement, Mathilde was ready and packed when Yussuf arrived in the morning to take me to Annaba. Her husband was not there to say goodbye.

'I told him that I was going to Annaba for a few days with you,' she informed me tersely as we got into the car. 'I couldn't pack any more in the time, but I've spent most of the time thinking about what you said, mainly that my life didn't have to be over just yet.'

'Well done!' I smiled, trying to stop my own panic about what this would mean for my arrangements. Yussuf was accompanied by three French soldiers, so there was no opportunity for personal conversation.

'We need all the help we can get on the journey,' Yussuf explained, pointing to his colleagues. 'The mood in the Constantine wilaya is inflammatory and even with three men riding shotgun, it's not without its risks.'

As it turned out, the journey was without incident but the atmosphere in the army truck was a tense and brooding one. The soldiers were concentrating on driving and their look out positions. Yussuf was thinking about the situations he had encountered in the last few days and about Yannis's death. Mathilde was thinking about the end of her life in Algeria and the yawning chasm in front of her. I was thinking about my return to France and what would happen to my relationship with Yussuf.

We climbed up another smaller range of mountains to the east of Constantine, but at least this time there were reasonable roads. Then at the ridge before we finally descended to the coastal plain, the truck stopped, and the windows were wound down.

'Don't get out,' warned Yussuf. 'It's too risky, because everyone knows that tourists stop here, but take this opportunity to look at the view.'

The skies over the mountains were still misty and there was a suggestion of drizzly rain but in front of us, the sky phased out of its greyness to become an electric blue. The mountain road pass snaked through the boulders and the waterfalls, and at the far end of the coastal plain was a small mirage of a city perched on the end of a promontory and almost falling into the sea, which glimmered in the distance. Mathilde made a little moan next to me.

'I'd forgotten how beautiful it is. I've spent too long next to those damn vineyards, looking over the desert.'

It seemed to me that the scene before us awoke in her all the possibilities of the future.

'Look long and hard, because that's where we're going. And from there you can sail to France. Well, not quite, possibly Italy first and then up to France.'

'I hope I can make it.'

'Of course, you can make it,' I said with all the impatience of a young woman, who doesn't really understand what it is to have failed and be overburdened with the emptiness of years. 'All you need to do is cross that water and you'll be a free woman.'

'Easy for you to say, Marie. What happens if I find I don't want to be free?'

'Then, you can choose again, can't you? But at least you've given yourself a chance.'

'What happens if I change my mind and he doesn't want me back?'

'That means he's a stupid man and not worth worrying about.'

She was quiet for a moment.

'It certainly looks beautiful from here.'

'Let's find out if it is,' I challenged, full of optimism that I might be going over that sea with Yussuf and Mathilde. She had become a talisman of my own good fortune.

The car started and we were off down the mountain road with energy and laughter. Even the soldiers were glad to be turning their backs on the dangers of the mountains and to be entering a relatively safe area.

Of course, it wasn't really safe. It's easy to be under the illusion that a small town, clearly under French influence, was safe, but it was a compact town, the main town square being almost like a French provincial town and the only large hill being covered with woods, where families went on a Sunday afternoon to relax and at the top was a magnificent Roman Catholic Church.

Yussuf disappeared off with the French soldiers to their barracks and Mathilde and I stayed in a small French run pension, near the town square. We could easily walk from there to the beach, where in better times there had been beach-front hotels open for pied noir families holidaying in the summer. The hotels were now deserted and had a neglected look. Clearly the French economy in Algeria was suffering.

On our first night, Mathilde made an unexpected suggestion.

'Marie, I'd like to go up to the church at the top of the hill.'

'Sure. I didn't know you were religious.'

'I never have been, but it reminds me of the church of my childhood, only it's much grander. I feel rather nervous about leaving Algeria. It was such a sudden decision.'

'Those are often the best. Anyway, although it was sudden, it was the culmination of years of feeling dissatisfied and frustrated. It was just that before I came, you didn't have the possibility of leaving with someone. What you've done is incredibly hard, but it will be worth it in the end.'

'I know that's what you think, and I am grateful for you giving me the opportunity and the energy to do it. But I just want to go up to the church and light a candle.'

'Sure. Do you want me to come too? I think we can get there and back before it becomes properly dark.'

'Yes, Marie, that would be nice, especially for the coming back bit.'

We climbed the hill, which, even in the early evening, when it was cooler, took more out of us than expected. The church was incredibly ornate, and its doors were huge. I might have found it rather overpowering, except, by contrast, the inside was unusually plain and calm. At least that was my first impression. Then I looked at the floor. It was made of tiny mosaic pieces of beautiful varieties of blue and yellow stone, with stories of the saints' lives appearing in circles in some places.

Mathilde went off to light her candle and to seek guidance and I found that the vestry door had opened, and a small, old priest hobbled out.

'I had no idea that there were such large churches here in Algeria,' I began conversationally.

'There are a few in the country built by the French over the years.'

It was his naming of 'the French' which made me look at him more closely and then I realised that he was an Algerian.

He responded to my scrutiny. 'Yes, there are a few of us Algerian brothers.'

'Are you a monk then?' I asked surprised.

'Yes, I'm part of the White Fathers, started by Archbishop Lavigerie in the nineteenth century.'

'And you don't feel that you turned your back on your own religion by becoming a monk? I'm sorry to be so direct but I'm interested.'

He smiled gently. 'The brothers rescued me and my mother when we were thrown out of my father's home. My mother became a housekeeper for the monks, and it felt the most natural thing in the world for me to become a brother.'

'Besides,' he added,' you're wrong about the automatic religious affiliation of our country. In Roman times Algeria was Christian. You can go along the coast, almost into Tunisia, and see the ruins of Hippo, where St. Augustine was brought up.'

'I'm not very knowledgeable about religious history I'm afraid.'

'That's alright. Very few people are. Your friend has gone to pray. I'll leave you in peace too.'

'I'm not someone who prays. I'm too down to earth for that.'

'Maybe but you never know when you're going to need it.'

He turned away from me, but I was curious.

'Father?'

'Yes, my child?'

'With all that's happening in Algeria at the moment aren't you afraid?'

He stopped and considered my point carefully.

'I'm very lucky. My mother is no longer alive and I'm the only one left in my family. The brothers have taught me how to remain calm and trust in God.'

It seemed a much more peaceful response than anything I had heard from anyone else so far in Algeria.

Mathilde joined me as we walked the paths through the woods. Neither of us were in the mood for conversation. I was embarrassed to ask her about what she had done or decided in the church and whether it had made a difference, and the response of the White Father had made me turn again to the simple things of life, like enjoying the wind gradually getting up strength through the trees and following the movements of the moths and dragonflies which were careering in the dusk all around me.

'Shall we have a café in the square before going to bed?'

'Is Yussuf really going to go with you to France?' she asked as we settled at the table.

'I'm hoping so. He's due some leave anyway, and he does do errands for the army in France from time to time. But I'll know definitely tomorrow morning.'

'And do you love him? I mean enough to stay with him?'

I considered the question carefully as the garçon served us our digestifs.

'I know I love him. I'm not sure how long that will last. But it's enough for me for the time being. No one knows what the future holds, but I care for him very deeply and I want to keep him safe. I've lost too many other people I love so far in my life. I'm going to try and hang on to this one and see what happens.'

'Do you think he'll come?'

'I can't be sure. He's not stupid. He's fairly pessimistic about the situation here, and, yes, he does have family, but no wife and children. I think he's better to make a clean break while the going is good and he's young enough to forge a new future for himself.'

'You're both very brave.'

'Yes. Well, it's worth it sometimes. How about you, Mathilde? Are you feeling brave?'

'I asked God for guidance. It's the first time I've ever done that. I was never religious in my childhood and it didn't cost me anything to give up my religion to marry Jules.'

'And did God answer?'

'I felt God saying that I had to be myself and I didn't deserve to be ground down for ever.

Je suis en route, Marie.'

'Moi aussi, Mathilde.'

# Chapter Forty-Three

I returned to Paris with two more people than I left with and I felt strangely responsible for both of them. Mathilde, who was a silent companion throughout our boat journey to Italy and on the train to France, and who I felt was calmly observing the relationship between Yussuf and myself, came to life with an amazingly practical attitude to the demands of life once we were in Paris. I had already thought ahead to the offices of the newspaper I worked for. I reckoned that, although she didn't have any professional qualifications, she had kept the offices at the Gaullen vineyards in order for many years, as well as making sure that the bills were paid, and the workers looked after. Most newspapers are full of opinionated people and the editors manage to be both creative and cut-throat. There are not many people who like organising offices. No one wanted to pay for that to happen, although everyone felt the lack of organisation keenly. On my recommendation, I landed Mathilde a job as office manager at l'Humanité .

'Ignore the politics,' I warned her. Mathilde didn't look like someone to be in sympathy with the communist agenda. 'You're there to organise things, not to agree with the editor. They have their own left-wing agenda, but secretly they want someone to bring order to their lives. You can do it!'

I thought she might be a whingeing, spoilt society lady, who wouldn't dirty her hands or shut up about her strongly held opinions, but I was wrong. She was not only efficient but launched herself into her new life without complaining.

'It's wonderful to feel useful,' she confided to me a few days after she had started the job. 'Every time someone is surprised that I can find something, or a bill gets paid on time, I feel gratified. I did all this sort of thing free at the vineyard, because my husband was the boss. No one even said, 'thank you'. Here I even get paid for it.'

It was the first time in her life that she had been paid for work and she felt the thrill of it, almost as if she was an eighteen-year old. After a couple of weeks sharing my flat, she insisted on finding a place of her own to live.

'You and Yussuf need time on your own together,' she stated in a determined way. 'I've got to find my own way of doing things and you've been more than generous to me as it is.'

'I've enjoyed having you around,' I answered, not as a polite rejoinder, but as an honest reply. She was different from my usual journalist friends. I knew hardly anyone in Paris who was my mother's age, and Mathilde was far more consistent as a personality than many of my contemporaries. I liked her too, because, despite the high-class veneer, she was gutsy and didn't expect everyone to look after her.

However, it was true that I enjoyed having Yussuf to myself in the flat. Having an older European woman living with us had made him restrained and cautious. Left to ourselves, we felt much more relaxed and enjoyed each other's company. He was not someone who showed his physical feelings in public and it took him time to feel at home with me, but once he realised that he was fully accepted as an equal, our relationship flourished. I found him far more open to exploring French culture than I had expected. For someone who had lived by his wits in the wilds of the Algerian mountains, he adapted surprisingly quickly to the finer parts of civilisation.

'You know, it's true,' he admitted one evening to me. 'I haven't had an education to speak of. I know I was sent to the lycée in Constantine, and I prospered there academically, mainly in the maths department, but I hardly had time to finish school, before the war broke out and I signed up with the tirailleurs.'

'Presumably you didn't fight in northern France near the Maginot Line?'

'No. There was no time to get us there from North Africa and it was just as well really. Either I wouldn't have survived, or I would have become part of the defeated French army who fled before the German invasion and then had the misery of being left behind when the British left Dunkirk.'

'Some of them did go to join the Free French with General de Gaulle,' I reminded him.

'Yes, but comparatively few and it would have been unlikely as an Algerian that I would have had the chance, exciting though it was. No. I did better, staying in North Africa and then being picked up later by the Free French and the invasion of the liberated zone. It was wonderful. It was the headiest most exciting thing I have ever done.'

'Even though you were missing out on the advantages of an education and what you could have achieved in the French administration? You would have been one of the favoured ones in a place like Algiers.'

'Yes. But it was even better fighting alongside my compatriots with the French for freedom. It was an amazing feeling, landing in Nice and fighting all the way up through Northern France, seeing places like Lyons being liberated and fighting alongside the 'Maquis' and seeing off the last of the Nazis.'

'You must have been terrified you were going to die.'

'No. I know it sounds strange, but I didn't even think about it. We were permanently drunk with a self-righteous honour which meant we couldn't give up.'

'Oh wow! It shows how different we are. I was proud to be part of the Resistance and I cared a lot about the people we rescued but there was never a time I wasn't frightened of the Germans, especially at the end when they turned up in so many of the villages. They did some terrible things and we were just lucky in St. Paul and some of the other villages in Les Landes that nothing similar happened. We were just a bit out of the main retreat line, I think. But because I had regularly visited in the Pyrenées, I knew about Oradour and what they had done there, massacring innocent people.'

'Maybe it was because you had lived under the occupation for three years and you just got used to it. And were used to feeling impotent. I'd never been in that situation. I was just heady with the idea that we were winning, and Europe was going to be free.'

'Perhaps it's just that you're a man and see war differently.'

He didn't respond to the jibe which could have led to flirtation and sex as we sat over our coffee at the end of the day.

Yussuf pondered over my statement. 'Actually, I think it just shows that I was a very young man who didn't understand the complexities of war.'

'And now you do?' I questioned.

'I don't think I understand them any better. In fact, I think I understand them worse; but at least now I realise that they exist.'

'And does that make it easier or harder to act?'

'It both makes it impossible to act and impossible not to act. That's the hell of it. I don't know why life has to be so unjust.'

We'd both seen a fair amount of injustice in our lives and there was no easy answer, no simple way to be on the 'right side.'

I put my arm round him, like an old married woman. 'I'm so glad you're away from it now. I can't bear the thought of you being embroiled in all that misery.'

We moved easily into each other's arms on my sofa, which was not especially suitable for such a move. It had angles all over the place which seemed to jut into our bodies. Over the nights in the flat we had often moved swiftly from my rather uncomfortable sofa to my bed which was fortunately a double one, part of the furniture in a rented flat. Yussuf used to remark about how inappropriate my flat was for a good romantic liaison.

'Oh, so you mean an Algerian house is better in that department, do you?' I teased him. 'No sofas and very little furniture at all and not even inhabiting the same room as your spouse half the time.'

He laughed. 'Marie, you don't know how romantic an Algerian house can be. Mattresses and cushions give you all the freedom you want and there's always space in the forests and the hills.'

'Sounds uncomfortable to me!'

'That's because you're such a hopelessly spoilt little indoor girl.'

'I am not,' I protested. 'I spent half my life in the forests of Les Landes.'

'Oh, European forests!' he mocked. 'Just man-made. Nothing like as exciting as the forests of Kabylia.'

'Yes, sure – where you can get shot at any moment.'

'You just don't like excitement, that's your trouble.'

'Try me!' And as usual our conversation dissolved into the passion of lovemaking.

Later we would be sitting in bed smoking and continuing the endless discussion about who was right and who was wrong in Algerian political life. It was a comfortable almost domestic rehearsal of ideas, which could never reach any conclusion.

'Yussuf, I'm really glad that you're here discussing it in my bed in Paris. As it's an impossible subject for anyone normal to understand, I'd rather talk about it here than have you killed over there.'

'I agree with you. It feels wonderful here. You're a fantastic girl to be with, Marie. I could never have this conversation with an Algerian girl.'

'I hope I'm not just good for conversation?'

He laughed. 'Haven't I proved that to you already?'

'Not to my satisfaction,' I answered in a similarly flippant tone.

Later, emerging from our sheets and showering and making more coffee, he turned serious again.

'It's wonderful being here, Marie, but I don't know how long this enchanted life is going to last.'

'As long as you want it to.'

'I've got to earn my living as a soldier. It's the only profession I know.'

'It doesn't have to be,' I answered reasonably. 'What would you like to have done, if you hadn't become a soldier?'

'Be a Maths teacher, I think. I always thought that it was a worthwhile job, influencing the young.'

'I quite agree with you about it being worthwhile. I've been greatly influenced by my first and only teacher and that's without even going to a lycée. It's not too hard you know, Yussuf. You have your bac, and you could easily go to university here.'

'And how would I earn my living?'

'That's easy. We're together and I'm earning.'

'That does not sit easily for an Algerian man.'

'It's common sense and that should triumph over your male pride. I'm already doing job I love and I'm earning enough for us both to live on. You can always do some teaching to help you on your way, if that makes you feel better. There'll be plenty of families in the Algerian community who will want to give their kids extra maths.'

'That brings us to another problem. How am I going to be part of the Algerian community and which side of it am I going to support?'

'You're already helping those who are pro-French.'

I knew that he went out on behalf of the French army to try and dissuade people from supporting the ALN.

'Yes, but the divisions are going to get bigger even here, especially if any of the French military decide to take things into their own hands.'

'How do you mean?'

'In Algeria there are some parts of the French army who feel that the army isn't doing enough to protect the pied noirs. They're scared they're going to be betrayed by de Gaulle. They're already planning things.'

'What sort of things?'

'Atrocities against the Algerians.'

'Oh, my God!' I exclaimed, disgusted. 'Haven't we had enough atrocities already?'

'Not according to them, because de Gaulle isn't determined enough to keep Algeria French. They're going to try and force his hand.'

'You mean that there's more fanatics on the rise wanting more deaths?'

'Exactly. That's why being in France isn't going to be an easy ride either.'

'At least you don't have to escape across mountain ranges here and discover the mutilated bodies of your fellow countrymen.'

'True.'

We were silent, as we thought about the madness of civil war.

'Yussuf?'

'Mmmm?'

'I've got an idea.'

'You've always got ideas.'

'I know, but this one's really good.'

'OK. Looks like you're going to tell me anyway.'

I turned eagerly to his side of the bed, with my knees drawn up beside me.

'If you live in Paris with me, you don't need to have anything to do with Algerian society.'

'But that's why the army are allowing me to be here at the moment.'

'Yes, while you're working for them. But you don't have to carry on doing that. Resign your commission, go to the Sorbonne, mix with my friends who are journalists.'

'I thought you said that one of them was an Algerian and a Marxist?'

'Yes, true, but we can keep out of his way. Anyway, he's such a crazy character, I can't imagine him having anything to do with the revolution in practice.'

'Don't you believe it. If he's a Marxist, he'll be in with the leadership of the ALN.'

'OK. Well, leave him out of it. I get a job with another newspaper in Lyons or up north in Lille or even in Bordeaux. We get out of the whole Algerian thing.'

'Except I'm Algerian.'

'I know but you're clever enough to be able to mix with Europeans on their own terms… and Yussuf?'

'Yes?'

'We could get married!'

He laughed, a huge uproarious belch of laughter. 'What? You're such an emancipated European woman that now you are proposing marriage to me?'

I was hurt by his reaction. 'I thought you might even like the idea.'

'Marie, I think it's a wonderful idea. All by itself, but not as an escape route from my Algerian identity.'

# Chapter Forty-Four

We never did get married. It didn't make any difference to the passion or the tenderness or the fun of our relationship. It did make a difference to the sense of our stability and the way we could plan our future.

'Marriage is not all it's cracked up to be,' Mathilde reminded me gently, as we met regularly after work for chat and companionship. She seemed to have moved seamlessly from a thirty-year married status to being single. She had not even heard from Jules in the intervening months.

'I could have left ten years ago, and he wouldn't have cared. I could have established a new life for myself or even a new relationship,' she remarked bitterly.

'The important thing,' I reminded her, 'is that you've done it now and it's not too late. Are you happy, Mathilde?'

'Happy?' She considered the question carefully, as if it was an alien concept. 'In every-day life, certainly. I love my job and feel appreciated at the office. I love coming home and deciding what to cook and who I want to see. I love the fact that the city is on my doorstep, and I can be with people whenever I want to. But happy? I don't know. I'm not sure that I have a right to know.'

'What do you mean?'

In my own happiness, I felt impatient at someone being unsure of what they wanted.

'I'm not sure you can define happiness that easily, or that human beings deserve it. If I ever started to look at the future, I might see a lack of security, inability to work and loneliness. Most of the time I don't let myself do that. I just concentrate on the satisfaction of the every day. And, as for Algeria, if I ever thought about the politics there for a moment, I'd panic.'

'That's true for us all,' I agreed gloomily. 'In the end for you and me, however much we'd like a good solution, if there isn't one, we're still safe in Paris. We can shut it out. For someone like Yussuf, it's a nightmare that's not going to go away.'

It seemed to me in those last months of 1958 that our personal happiness all relied on politicians and generals and, as we wanted nothing to do with them and didn't trust them, that seemed very unfair.

The promised referendum happened right across France's colonies and Algeria (which was not a colony) in 1958. Only Guinea had the courage to say 'non' and was immediately denied all help from France both in terms of finance and human resources. It was an extraordinary decision – not only that they thought they could manage by themselves, but that their leader, Ahmed Sekou Touré, managed to persuade his people that they could achieve a modern independent country by themselves. Foolhardy, French people said, and I thought, 'it probably is, but at least it's clear. They're not pretending like everyone else is.'

Why did so many other countries say 'yes'? Only to get money to help their fledgling governments, I thought. Only to appease General de Gaulle's pride. Only to fawn.

And in the case of Algeria, it achieved absolutely nothing. There was a huge turnout for the vote, and most of the indigenous population said 'oui'. France breathed again and the pied noirs said that everything was going to be alright, but Yussuf kept telling me that it was all an illusion and I trusted his judgement. The ALN stood back and let people please the French by voting 'oui' and allowed the country to gain financial resources which they needed, but it was merely time gained. All the real work was going on in the background. The ALN had advised the populace to vote 'non' but, even though they had disobeyed, it didn't make any difference to the will of the revolutionaries. They had already said that there would be no cease-fire until independence took place. When General de Gaulle made his famous speech about 'la paix des braves,' you could hear the ALN laughing in the background. The white flag which they were offered, only meant surrender as far as they were concerned, and they had no intention of surrendering.

To have one group of people who were implacable in their violence was bad enough. Even if you had voted 'oui' on the day of the referendum, maybe in some idealistic way, or with a view to pleasing the French who had always been there, or even if you seriously thought, as Yussuf did, that a gradual change-over of power was a better idea, the truth remained that, underneath all the happy turning up for the vote and agreeing to General de Gaulle's proposals, there was a deep understanding that France would be booted out of Algeria in a violent way. Maybe it was the tide of history – the end of colonialism, the end of European domination, the inevitable rise of world Marxism, which was making it happen. But it was as if the sensible and nice people in European countries were playing a game and assuming that the 'children' who they were responsible for, wanted to play nicely. They didn't. And they had already decided that they would win, no matter how much violence it cost.

What made the referendum such a disaster was that it also awoke the implacable hatred of a different group of people – not the French army, or the pied noirs, but the extremists who were committed to keeping Algeria French, no matter what the government said. They were also committed to violence and they did not care who suffered. They were the bullies, who had been denied their point of view, and they were going to fight back. They represented a new player in the game and most reasonable people in Algeria were caught between the two extremes. For the first time, France itself was disturbed. Before the referendum of 1958, if you were French, you could retreat to the mainland and forget about the troublesome situation of Algeria. Once the OAS came into being, you couldn't. They brought violence onto the streets of Paris and threatened the existence of de Gaulle's government. The ALN must have been laughing, not because of having to fight even more dangerous battles for survival, but because the actions of the OAS made the French very unpopular amongst ordinary Algerian people. No other organisation acted as a better recruiting officer for the FLN. In France everyone was sickened by their actions.

I wanted Yussuf to gradually fade out of the turmoil, which was taking place in his own country, and settle down to a useful and fulfilling life with me. The acts carried out by the OAS in France prevented that happening and made me feel angry. Yussuf was continually being reminded of the war in Algeria and of the suffering of his own people.

'I really can't see how your suffering over there is going to contribute to their good,' I argued with what seemed to me incontrovertible logic.

'It's not. But I can't just turn my back on my own people.'

'No one could ever accuse you of that,' I retorted, frustrated by his lack of acceptance of the good life. 'You've been suffering with them for the last four years.'

'But they're my family. I can't abandon them.'

'Look Yussuf. If it was your wife and children, I could understand. But you're a free man. The rest of your family need to sort themselves out. If you get a good job here, then when the time comes, you'll be able to help them financially. Thousands of Algerians in Paris already do that. If it's true, as you say, that economically, sudden independence is going to be a disaster, then they will be very grateful to you for helping them.'

'I know.'

At the end of each argument, he seemed to agree with me, but I knew that deep within himself he wasn't convinced.

There were several OAS attacks in Paris. Some people were even talking about a coup against the General. The left wing, who would normally not have supported de Gaulle, were even more angry than the moderates about the actions of the OAS. My papers sent me to various French cities to do reports on their activities and the union reactions to them. It made a change for me to do so much 'home' journalism, but it was always against the background of my worries about Yussuf. I became scared that one day, I might come home, and he would be gone.

On one trip I was in Marseille, interviewing some of the pied noirs arrivals from Algeria. These people had enough money to settle themselves in France, but not so much money invested in Algeria, that they could not bear to lose it. They were gloomy but determined. On the same trip I went to visit the Tribiers, partly out of friendship, and partly to tell them about my visit to their family vineyards. I was a little worried that they might have heard about the Gaullen marriage break-up and might even hold me responsible. But there were no problems. They were delighted to see me and hear about my assessment of the financial viability of the Algerian vineyards.

'They're doing alright, Monsieur Tribier,' I assured him. 'But I think you're better off here.'

'That's what I feel too, Marie. We're not doing so well here in comparison to them, but peace of mind can't be overestimated. I worry for my cousin.'

'He seems very well set up there,' I suggested cautiously. 'But the future generally is not looking good for the pied noirs. Let's hope he'll know when to go and hand the business over to the Algerian workers.'

'Oh, that would be far too forward looking for my cousin,' commented Monsieur Tribier with remarkable sharpness. I hadn't expected him to understand Jules' character so well.

That year I worked hard at keeping Yussuf happy in Paris and he seemed to be. After much heart searching, he gave up his commission with the army. 'Whatever I do in the future,' he decided, 'working with the army is not an option. I'm fed up with being regarded as a traitor by my compatriots and I neither want to join the OAS or fight against them. There are just too many crazy factions in Algeria and I just prefer to be me, without working out the precise rightness or wrongness of all of them.'

That was alright as far as I was concerned. I increasingly liked the personal 'me' of who Yussuf was, and I wanted to engage with him more seriously. Perhaps we should have moved to another city, but I had lots of assignments in the capital, and Yussuf was unexpectedly offered a scholarship as an ex-army man to study maths at the Sorbonne. It gave him at least a modicum of dignity. We needed my salary to live on, but he had financial help for buying textbooks and travel. We were secure.

Most of the news about the Algerian situation was about the activities of the OAS. They seemed to be the latest scapegoats, and this distanced us Parisians from the real protagonists in the country. It even made Yussuf more supportive of the FLN, because he heard more about OAS violence than he did about the activities of the FLN. Being overseas gave us an emotional barrier and we gladly hid behind it.

By the end of 1959, I felt so secure in our relationship that, when the editor of my paper, asked me to return to Algeria to explore the situation I felt cautiously interested. News had been coming through over the last few months about the existence of concentration camps there.

'What do you mean?' I asked puzzled. 'Do you mean Beaufré's policy of putting the inhabitants of enemy territory into one place? It's being going on for some time. It's just a practical measure to ensure that they don't attack women and children when they're trying to flush out terrorists. I know it must be difficult for them, being moved from their homes, but in the end, it saves their lives and helps end the war more quickly.'

My editor looked at me with some amusement. 'It's not like you, Marie, to believe everything you're told and roll out the party line.'

'I don't,' I replied, annoyed at his accusation. 'I've seen what happens when women and children are on the front line in guerrilla tactics. I won't easily forget a family of six, all with their throats cut and mutilated at the entry to a cave. Also, I've had the whole division of territory theory explained to me by the French army.'

'That might have been true when it was carried out with good motives two years ago. I'm hearing different rumours now.'

Look, Marie,' he continued, 'I know l'Humanité are onto it and even the Figaro. I want you to find out what's really going on. I know you've got some good contacts there.'

I was always up for a challenge. 'All right. How do you want me to get there?'

'Sail to Bejaia at the end of this week.'

'And from there to French army headquarters in Constantine?' I suggested.

'Exactly. You'll have done it in five days. The French public have had enough of the war. We know independence is coming. We want the report to coincide with the trial of the OAS generals.'

'To be fair, this doesn't sound like the policy of the OAS generals. It's French army policy.'

'Yes, but the man who's been the main protagonist in this is Beaufré, and he's one of the generals who has supported the Putsch and the OAS.'

'All right. I can see your point.'

It promised to be good journalism and maybe I was a bit tired of having tame assignments in France. I would return to Algeria on my own.

# Chapter Forty-Five

Bejaia is a little jewel of a town, perched on a rocky promontory, as if it is about to fall into the Mediterranean Sea. Rising behind is the start of the mountains. The sun was shining when I arrived there, and it felt like the most romantic place in the world. I only wished that Yussuf had been with me, but we had agreed that it was not a good time for him to be back in his home country, now that he no longer belonged to the army. I spent two nights in a French pension in Bejaia, going onto the streets at night to find somewhere to eat and feeling so free as a European, that I even drank in the bars after night fall. It was like a smaller, old fashioned France. I had a five-day assignment and then I would be back in Paris with Yussuf. The Europeans I spoke to were hopeful about the future. The Generals' Putsch had destabilised the whole peace process, but no one thought that it was worth challenging de Gaulle's plan. Algeria would become independent and the Europeans were enjoying their last days in this beautiful country. They thought that the French army might protect their property for them when they were gone, so they could sell it later. They weren't sure. But everyone was breathing freely again. It felt as though there was a future.

I arrived armed with an official press pass to get to the army headquarters in Constantine and, consequently, I was due for an official escort two days after I arrived there. After all the drama I had experienced in the mountains the year before, I was glad of the offer. Things seemed to be much more in a state of equilibrium than they had been previously, but I still had bad memories of the violence of my previous journeys in the country.

I was pleased when a French patrol jeep with a driver and two armed guards collected me from my pension. The journey was testing from the point of view of the condition of the roads, but otherwise the soldiers were pleasant and relaxed because they were looking forward to leaving the country soon.

'Did the Generals' pusch cause you any problems?' I asked them.

'Of course, Mademoiselle. We were put in a very difficult position. Some of us wanted to follow Beaufré. After all, we had been committed to protecting the pied noirs and we didn't see why they had to be deprived of their country, all because of de Gaulle's referendum, but it was too much of a risk. Most of us decided not to support Beaufré.'

'It was an idiotic idea, anyway,' added the other soldier. 'You can't just have a coup against the president of the French Republic and think you'll win. And no one in France really cares that much about what happens in Algeria.'

'I don't think that's true,' I answered. 'To begin with there are loads of Algerians in France and they care. And what's more lots of French people are used to thinking of Algeria as theirs, even if they don't live there.'

'No, but did they want the whole government to be brought down because of it?'

'Probably not,' I admitted. 'but there's definitely been some support for the generals. But I admit that a take-over in the middle of the night in Paris was rather dramatic and improbable.'

'Anyway,' concluded my driver cheerfully, with a cigarette casually hanging out of his mouth, 'We're glad we didn't get involved. A few of our comrades did and now they're in a very difficult position.'

'Sure, but they did get sent back to France, lucky things,' the man in the front seat added mournfully, obviously feeling envious of their position.

'I think we'll get back within six months anyway, André. And good riddance, I say.'

'You don't like Algeria?' I suggested.

They immediately lost their relaxed attitude. 'Like it? You've got to be joking. It's hell. Maybe if you were here as a tourist it would be beautiful, but for a French soldier it's been hell. You never know when your enemy's going to strike next. We've lost mates here, and it wasn't a nice way to die.'

'Are there any nice ways to die?'

'Yes, in your bed, if you're old, but at least shot with a clean bullet in a war.'

I remembered some of the hellish ways people had died in Vietnam.

'I think the days of honourable death in battle have long gone.'

My escorts did not want to discuss the philosophy of dying. 'Yeh, well the sooner we're out of here the better.'

We drew close to the French camp and after all the security checks we were allowed inside, and I was taken to report to the commander's office as a member of the press.

Lieutenant Dupré was polite but cynical about my presence here.

'I've helped some of your colleagues here before, but their reports in the French press weren't very flattering. As usual, if you arrive here suddenly, you don't understand the real situation.'

'Maybe they said it as they saw it?' I suggested, wondering what sort of message the French army had tried to give them.

Lieutenant Dupré replied without emotion. 'Maybe they said it because they hadn't been here for the last six years and seen the things we've seen.'

'You mean the atrocities from the FLN?'

'Mademoiselle, you cannot imagine the state of the bodies we have retrieved. When you have seen some of your men tortured like that, and you know that the mutilation was done before they died, it does not make you feel well-disposed towards the enemy.'

'But perhaps if you had heard the accounts of how some of the Algerians were treated by the French army when they were captured, you might feel differently. They were not treated humanely either.'

'That is more hearsay than anything else, Mademoiselle.'

'Hearsay doesn't just arrive. There is usually some truth behind it.'

'Maybe. But it was the quickest way to get information out of them. That way the war was being shortened.'

'I think, Lieutenant, that in using torture, you lowered the reputation of French justice to such an extent that people were willing to change sides. You also brought shame to lots of French soldiers who didn't want to behave like that.'

'It was a war, Mademoiselle.'

708

'Indeed. And all wars are horrible but some of them have been fought more honourably than this one.'

'So, have you come here just to lecture me about the morality of war?'

'No, Lieutenant, I've come to see the scorched-earth policy at work.'

He pointed to the chair behind his office desk and sat down with the air of someone who wants to do his best to explain but is not expecting much.

'All right. But first, you must understand the thinking behind the policy. To see that the only way to let us get to the insurgents was to make a clean sweep, and to get all the families out of the way so that they couldn't be blackmailed.'

'I understand that, but how long does that policy continue? Surely the guerrilla war is now drawing to a close. Why are they still here and when are they going to be allowed home?'

'I think that you're under a slight misapprehension when you say that the guerrilla war is over. To begin with the FLN themselves say that they are not stopping the fighting until the French have left and they are in charge. As you know de Gaulle wants to leave in an orderly fashion, protecting the pied noirs as far as we are able. We can have no let up. We still need to know where our enemy is and so we need these camps to prevent more blackmail and more bloodshed.'

'But when you eventually leave, will these people be able to return home unharmed or will they be made to pay for your protection by being treated as traitors?'

'That's not our problem. If the FLN want to murder their own people, then that's their decision.'

'Even if your policy makes it more likely that there will be retaliation against them later?'

He shrugged his shoulders. 'Our job has been to win the war. We have also been protecting these people. We can't go on doing that for ever, especially as our own government has ordered our withdrawal.'

I felt cold. I had a sickening feeling that there was a large group of women and children and old men who were being used as pawns in the game. No one really cared about what was happening to them, while they were part of the shield protecting each side.

'Lieutenant, I would like to be taken to see these camps.'

'Very well, Mademoiselle. I will get two of my men to take you. But before you pillory us in the press, let me tell you , that left to their own countrymen, they would have been starved and forced to join in the fight and give up their men, whatever side they chose to fight on, and many of them chose to be on the French side.'

'And which side are they are on now?' I wanted to ask but I could see that the Lieutenant was not going to continue a discussion about right and wrong. He looked like a man who did what he was told and perhaps justified it to himself.

I was driven back through the gates of the army camp back down to the town of Constantine and onto the other side of the town, where the country flattened towards the plain on the east side of Algeria as it continued to the border with Tunisia. The wheels of the truck were throwing up such large clots of sand onto the windows of the truck, so as to make it almost impossible to see the scenery on either side of the road.

I was concentrating on willing the truck through the chaos of the sand and almost missed the posts which were the same as that of an army encampment but with barbed wire fences enclosing them. We showed our papers at the gate and then drove towards the first prefabricated buildings at one end. Away from them, stretched what seemed like miles of white tents.

'This is the headquarters of the medical centre, and where the wells are dug. If you want to meet the Médicins sans Frontières personnel and the Red Cross people, they are here. We'll pick you up later tonight.'

'Thank you.'

I got out of the truck and entered one of the prefabricated huts. Immediately a nurse came to meet me. She was Swiss and worked for the Red Cross. We introduced ourselves and she invited me to enter the adjoining building where there were rows and rows of beds.

'This is the infirmary.'

'There seem to be an awful lot of ill people,' I commented. 'How come you have so many?'

The nurse was an older lady with white hair held back by her scarf and a lined face, and she clearly had no illusions about what she was doing and how much she was achieving.

'It's a miracle that there aren't more ill people. These here are the worse cases of dysentery. We've tried to isolate the cholera patients at the far end.'

'What sort of medicines do you have?'

'The most basic, and that is courtesy of the Médicins sans Frontières charity, not the French government.'

'Why don't the French government give anything?'

'Because half the time they don't know what is happening here. This camp forms part of the army strategy, so the money comes from the government and the army doesn't have any surplus money. The government doesn't make any effort to supply the deficit.'

'That's dreadful,' I said. 'You must be at your wits' end.'

She replied without emotion. 'We're so used to being at our wits' end, it's become the norm. But if you can write some articles and stir up public indignation in France, that would really help.'

She looked as though she had already tried to take on the whole world and had refused to give up. Just then a young woman called out to her and she went over to adjust the drip in her arm.

I followed her over. 'Does this woman have dysentery?'

'Yes, and we only have a few antibiotics, so we are always having to make a choice of who to give them to. This young lady, Farida, has been one of the lucky ones. She has six young children in her tent. If we let her die, the children will be orphans and they are likely to die themselves.'

'Isn't there enough food for them?'

'Technically, yes. We get food supplies; but without the mother there, there will be no one to cook it and no one to make sure that basic hygiene is carried out. It's like a series of funerals which are waiting to happen.'

# Chapter Forty-Six

'Funeral' is the word which stayed with me long after the end of that day's visit. The funerals I saw were short and practical. Muslim funerals are always carried out within a day of death for religious reasons, but these fast-track funerals were not only due to the need for religious ritual, or even hygiene, but they were the result of hopelessness. I have found the 'ululay' sound which the women make at funerals in Moslem villages heart-breaking but at least they have to do with an expression of grief for people who were known and loved. By contrast, the funerals I saw at the camp were almost a relief – one less person to feed, one less person to suffer. I even found an empty room full of cheap coffins which were being stored for the inevitable events to come, like the supplies of coffins which were delivered regularly to the front line in World War 1 in anticipation of the bodies who were cannon fodder.

Perhaps most distressing, as I wandered later among the rows of tents, accompanied by a Red Cross official and translator from the camp, was the lack of children playing. In war zones I have found that, even though the surrounding area may have been bombed the night before, children always find a way to bring normal life back almost immediately. Here there was none, as if there was no imaginative escape from the terrible conditions people were suffering. When there is bombing, there is always hope that the next bombs may be concentrated in a different area of the town but, here there was no escape from the grim conditions of everyday life. The older children sat listlessly near their mothers ready to help, when grain needed pounding or water fetching or they were sometimes carrying a young toddler round who would otherwise have been annoying everyone else with their wails. There were no young men, because they were either supporting the French forces, though that was less and less the case in these last days of the war, or out in the mountains fighting for their country's independence. There was a clear lack of young babies around because the men had not been there for so long. In a way that was a blessing because babies succumb quickly to bad conditions and births weaken the mothers and provide more mouths to feed. The young women had quite enough to cope with as it was. I saw old men and women – most of them sitting in the entrance to the tents looking confused and frail. There was none of the rivalry that you often observe in North African households, where the latest and youngest wife is being manipulated by the oldest one and jealousy pervades the whole atmosphere. There were enough chores to do here, but there was very little sense of purpose or joy.

'Is there nothing for the older children to do? No school?' I asked, trying to find at least a glimmer of a solution to everyone's boredom.

The translator looked askance.

'Most of these children here are from the villages and they've never been to school. It's not something which is a priority,' he answered, before even bothering to consult the official.

I fought against his gloomy reasoning. 'I'd say it was a priority to give the children something to do. It could be one good thing which the camps could give them – the start of an education.'

The translator looked incredulous at my suggestion. The Red Cross official tried to explain the reality of the situation they had to cope with.

'To give them an education, you need personnel and resources. We simply don't have them.'

Never one to back down on an argument, I continued. 'I'm not talking about a school room, with writing equipment and books. All you need is one room or even a tent with slates and chalk. Would that be too much for the French to supply?'

'Mademoiselle,' he explained patiently, as if I was a naïve child, 'we hardly have enough people to distribute the grain and milk for the children. You've seen the main building. Those who are in beds there are being looked after, but they are a tiny proportion of those who are ill. We try to isolate the worst cases of cholera, so that we can stop an epidemic. Even that feels like a hopeless task. Most people who are ill stay untended in their tents. Anything more than the basics, and you are asking for the impossible.'

It seemed to me that those who were working in the camp had been infected themselves with the epidemic of hopelessness. I had all sorts of ideas in my head about how those who had even a rudimentary education could help those who didn't, how it could provide a distraction from the endless boredom of living in these tents; how the younger ones could learn to play again; how they might learn to sing. But I squashed down those ideas because I realised that no one wanted to hear them.

When I saw the conditions inside some of the tents, I could understand why my ideas seemed hopelessly idealistic. It was already October and the worst of the heat was over, but the atmosphere inside the tents was still stifling. I was told that the in mid-August the temperature reached over 40 degrees and there was a choice between the stifling, fetid atmosphere of the tents and the burning heat of the sun outside, with no other shelter available. Because the camp was situated on the edge of the plain, where previously wheat had been planted, there were no trees. The farming had been disrupted and the tents supplanted the grain, and there was no shelter from the wind or sun. I couldn't help thinking that, if this refugee camp was ever disbanded and the people sent back to their villages, the ground would have become useless for agriculture. It was a symbol of what was happening as the French imposed their resettlement projects – uselessness and poverty.

I was taken into another tent nearby, where two old people had contracted cholera. They were not considered to be worthy of saving at the hospital. They were useless. Their deaths would help the family – it meant two less mouths to feed.

'Cover your nose and mouth with your scarf,' the official warned me as we entered the tent. 'Cholera isn't usually carried through the air, but better to be sure. And don't touch anything.'

This visit left a deep impression on me. The two old people had been given the only available mattresses to lie on and, the red cross official informed me, it was vital that they should be fumigated later before anyone else used them. The flies were already attacking their faces and were also gathering round the bowls of sick which were next to them. There was a terrible stench of defaecation because cholera attacks so quickly that there is no way that ongoing diarrhoea can be stemmed. It seemed to me to be almost obscene to be looking at these people in their desolation. In fact, the old woman just had the strength to turn on her side when we entered. She seemed by this gesture to be saying, 'Go away. Leave us to die. We don't want you and your pity and your fine words.'

There was a bidon of water outside the entrance flap. It was the job of the older children to fill it each morning and a little girl of about six years old was scooping some of it into a plastic cup and taking it to place on one side of her grandmother's mattress. She was also wafting the flies away from her grandmother's face. She looked with such earnestness and love at her grandparents that I was overcome with emotion as I saw beauty being demonstrated in the life of a little girl with enormous brown eyes who quietly got on with the job of loving, when everyone else around her had stopped.

'Where's the mother?' I asked.

'She's trying to cook outside away from the tent, so the food won't get contaminated by the cholera.'

'Is that a hopeless task?'

'At least she's got the will to try. Cholera is generally spread through faeces and you can see how hard it is to contain them.'

'Will anyone clean up after them?'

'The Red Cross will go in and clean out the tent after they've died. But we can't do it all the time while they're ill. There's too many people in the same situation.'

'And no latrines?'

'There are pits dug away from the tents but lots of people can't get there in time so there's always a danger of reinfection.'

I had nothing to offer this family. By contrast, I was ashamed because I had taken away their dignity by even coming to look at them. As the child came out of the tent, I caught her eye and gave her a big smile. 'Shukran,' I said to her, as if she had been serving me.

'Tell her that she is doing a wonderful job for her grandparents,' I told the translator. When she heard these words, I was rewarded with a beaming smile. It was the only good thing which the visit gave me.

After I had seen the way the millet and corn and milk were brought into the camp and distributed among the refugees, I returned to the French army camp with my escorts. I had plenty to write about in my reports for Libération and for l'Humanité and any other newspaper who would accept my findings. I hoped that I would be able to write something in English for the American press. They had always been so supportive of the Algerians. The new young president Kennedy had actively backed the demand for independence on the part of the Algerians. Seeing what the French were doing in these refugee camps, I was starting to feel the same way.

The next morning, I went to see the Lieutenant.

'So, what did you make of your visit, Mademoiselle Marie?'

'It was dreadful. It made me ashamed to be French.'

'Oh really?' he sneered. 'Despite all the food we are giving them rather than leaving them to starve in the villages?'

'What's the point of food when the conditions are so bad that hundreds of them are dying of cholera and dysentery?'

The lieutenant was unimpressed by my criticisms.

'Those are diseases connected with lack of hygiene. People there are not used to high standards whether it's at home or in the camp.'

'No one can have high standards when they are living in those temperatures and they have to use latrines so close to the tents.'

He shrugged his shoulders. His eyes were amused and showed no interest in what I was saying.

'I don't think that you realise that we are trying to help them.'

'You mean that you're helping yourselves to win a war.'

'Without winning the war, mademoiselle, there is no way we can help them.'

'Maybe that is why General de Gaulle is encouraging you all to leave.'

'Whatever the politicians say, I can assure you that the ordinary people will be worse off when we go.'

'Oh? Does that include the people who are dying of cholera far away from their own homes?'

'You make it sound as if the villages were some sort of ideal home place. The reality was that there was disease, poverty and death there too.'

'Maybe but at least they were dying amongst their loved ones in a familiar place.'

'They were dying tormented by terrorists who blackmailed them and forced them to sacrifice their families. You shouldn't be so naïve, Mademoiselle. I can assure you I've seen what it was really like in those villages.'

'And I've seen those villages too,' I replied unwilling to be defeated by his argument. 'However bad it may have been, give me the choice of the village or that internment camp, I know what any decent human being would choose.'

He remained indifferent to my passionate outburst. 'It's a war and we do our best.'

'And you're leaving anyway so it doesn't really matter to you.'

He sighed. 'No, not really. I'll be more than happy to leave this god-forsaken place.'

'And what about the children, Lieutenant?' I had not finished my argument with him yet.

'What about the children? There are more than enough of them. They all need to learn about contraception.'

'What about what you are teaching the children by your actions? You're teaching them to hate you.'

'They hate us anyway.'

'And I can understand why. Nowhere to play. Nothing to do. No school provided for them.'

'There was no school in their village anyway. Only what the French provided in the town.'

'The very least you could do would be to provide some elementary education for them.'

'You give me the funds for it, and I'll be happy to oblige.'

And so, we ended our argument where it had begun, going around in circles. Underneath my accusations, I was continually reminded of the challenge of the Red Cross worker – 'if you care so much, come and teach the children yourself.'

But I was not a teacher. I was a journalist, and my job was, to tell the world what was happening out here. Besides, I needed to get back to Paris and see Yussuf again and encourage him in our new life together.

717

With this as my aim and burning with indignation against the French army, I arrived back at my flat in Paris. On the front door was pinned a note.

'Your lover has to return home to finish his unfinished business.'

# Chapter Forty-Seven

I stared at the note for a full five minutes. I knocked on the other two doors on our landing, trying to find out if my neighbours had seen someone pin the note or drag Yussuf out. I reasoned that he could not have gone of his own free will and that dragging a large male from a third – floor apartment must have caused a commotion. Neither of the neighbours had seen or heard anything. One of them was old and deaf, the other a middle-aged woman who was out at work throughout the day. I let myself into my flat and tried to make myself think like a trained investigator rather than the panic ridden person I felt myself to be. I looked for signs of disturbance. There were none, but also no sign of communication from Yussuf. There was a drawer containing a few pieces of personal jewellery and we had sometimes left notes for each other in a kind of private, romantic ritual. There was only one anomaly. Yussuf had recently bought me with the first money of his university scholarship, a pair of pearl earrings. One of them was gone. Had they been stolen? In which case why not the pair? Or was Yussuf himself trying to send me a private message, when writing was not possible?

I rang the police to report a missing person. An officer dutifully arrived to take notes, but he had little motivation to do anything dynamic. Yussuf was a French citizen (he had that privilege because of his service with the French army) but a stray Algerian was of very little interest to the authorities.

'I don't suppose he could have been part of the plot against de Gaulle?' suggested the officer hopefully.

'You mean an abducted man is only of interest if he's involved in current politics?' I asked despairingly.

There was no answer to my question, but I understood that that was the reality of the matter.

'There is even the suggestion that he has returned of his own volition,' the policeman suggested, clearly eager to be rid of an annoying and unsolvable case.

'Why?' I demanded.

'Has to return and unfinished business?' he queried.

'Nonsense! If he had to return, he would have discussed it with me first. He knew I was coming back in a few days' time. And what's more he didn't have "unfinished business." He had no immediate family out there at all.'

'As far as you know.' The police officer was annoying me. If he didn't have the brains to investigate the case, then he should have acted as the stupid, inactive drone of the state security service, which he clearly was, not a questioner who doubted the integrity of my fiancé. He duly took details, but he had no intention of doing anything more. Algerians of doubtful origins were two a penny in Paris at the time. Why waste any more police money on a ridiculous case?

'One thing you could do,' he said, as he stood up to go, 'is to check things like food and milk in the fridge and how long it's been there. You might find out more about when he went.'

As he went out of the door, I dismissed his suggestion with scorn. How could I bear to check out milk bottles when the anchor of my life had disappeared? It was only later, when I was about to make myself a cup of coffee, that I thought it might be worth doing. Yussuf, like most Algerians, never used milk with coffee, and probably would not have eaten much when I was away. His habits of surviving for days as a harki in the mountains had led him to despise the regular meals of a normal citizen. But for some reason he had taken a liking in his few months in France to the English habit of eating cereal. It was just then in the early sixties that cereal packets were starting to be on sale in some shops in Paris. Most French people despised English eating habits but Yussuf had liked breakfast cereal. It was the ultimate 'fast food' and he would often grab some before he left in the morning or even eat it last thing at night, if he had missed a main meal in the evening. My own domestic habits were extraordinarily irregular. Most journalists avoid routines. If I had had too many coffees and alcohol at night and could not be bothered to cook, I often ate it too. I looked at the packet in the cupboard. I had bought it for him just before I left and normally it would have been empty by now. It was unopened. That meant he must have been taken almost immediately after I had left myself.

The police were gone. I couldn't just sit there and do nothing. All journalists have contacts. I had to use them and the most obvious one was my old colleague, Brahim. Since living with Yussuf, I had almost lost contact with him. He was after all a dedicated Marxist believer but maybe he would have the information I needed. Despite his absolutist beliefs, I thought he would still retain a modicum of human understanding.

I found him late at night in the Café des Quais. I couldn't help thinking back to the days when we had all met here regularly and discussed the current issues of the day with passion. Well, we had all grown up and we had moved away from idealism to practicalities. Except I soon discovered that Brahim had not made that journey.

'Wasn't your boyfriend a supporter of the French?' he asked in a way which I thought was not encouraging. He was still more interested in the person's beliefs than in his attitudes.

'Only because he had fought with them during the war and wanted to be loyal. He saw the mistakes of the French, but he also wanted a more moderate solution than the one offered by the FLN.'

'Oh, a moderate!' he exclaimed sighing. 'Will they never learn?'

'What is there to learn?' I asked icily.

'That real change is never effected by moderates. There is no solution for Algeria apart from Marxism.'

'Great, Brahim! Here you are sitting in your nice cosy café in Paris, pontificating. Other people live in the real world. And the real world of the FLN is a rather horrible one.'

'The real world of the French army and their colonialist masters is rather a horrible one too.'

I couldn't argue with that, not after my experience of the displacement camps and the interrogation centres.

721

But such an argument was not getting me anywhere in my search for Yussuf. 'Look, Brahim. I'm not here to argue politics. I know all the rights and wrongs of Algeria and, believe me, I have considerable sympathy for the FLN but I'm talking about the fate of one human being here.'

'You mean, your lover?'

I flinched as the word seemed to come out as an accusation. 'Yes, he is my fiancé, but, more than that, I object to someone being abducted against their will, whoever they are.'

'How do you know that it was against his will?'

The same question which had angered me so much before!

'Because if he had gone of his own free will, he would have waited to tell me.'

'Would he?'

I forced myself to wait before I answered.

'Yes, because he wasn't a coward. It was hard for him to leave his country, but we had agreed that there was nothing more that he could do there. Also, Yussuf is very straight.'

Brahim tipped back his chair and laughed derisively.

'Marie, you don't know anything. You don't know anything about Algerians.'

I flushed. 'I don't know whether that's supposed to make me a naïve fool or make all Algerians deceivers, but, either way, it's an insult, Brahim.'

'Sure, Marie. Go away and feel insulted. It might make you feel better, but both are true.'

I fought my rising anger, incredulity and panic, which seemed to overwhelm me, as if it was altitude sickness taking hold.

'Brahim, all your accusations and counter-accusations may be true, but the fact is that Yussuf has disappeared and I want to know how and why.'

'Perhaps you do,' he answered, swinging back on his chair, laconically, 'but why is your man more important than all the thousands of Algerians who have disappeared in their own country?'

'He's not more important.'

'Well then?'

'He's not objectively more important, but he is more important to me.'

'Ah well then, Marie, I can't help you. I'm not here to comfort your emotional distress. As far as I'm concerned, he's a traitor to his country. Good riddance, I say and, if you want a nice life, which I guess you do, you'll say the same thing.'

It was true, I had to admit to myself later, as I lay on the bed, which now seemed strangely empty. I did want a nice life. But nice lives only make sense when there's love and I wasn't prepared to sacrifice that rarely experienced but vital emotion.

I would have to go hunting further. In the middle of the night, when I had thought of every possibility, I remembered Habibi in Bobigny. His politics might be similar to those of Brahim, but, as far as I could remember, his humanity was a lot more advanced.

It was more than two years since I had first visited Bobigny and I was surprised by how much the area had changed. I realised that I also had changed. I understood much more about the complexities of the situation than I had on my first visit.

The bidonvilles had been largely dismantled and two high-rise blocks had been built in their place. To me they looked forbidding and ugly, but I had to admit that the facilities were far better.

'Yes, of course,' Habibi agreed with me. He and his wife appeared to be very welcoming but how wary they were about the reasons for my appearance, I was not sure. Algerians in Paris are used to the idea that when French people visit them, they usually want something. I have often heard Algerians being called 'duplicitous' and that may be true, but so are the French. They just play by different rules.

'I'm so glad that you've got a different housing arrangement at last,' I told them, genuinely delighted about their better material prospects, as we sat down to eat together.

'Yes, it's great. Though, I admit, we do sometimes miss the bidonvilles.'
'Why?'
'It's true the facilities were awful – colder in winter, muddier, but much easier relationships with our neighbours.'
'How do you mean? Surely they're the same as before?'
'Yes, but when you're on the same level, you're always wandering into each other's houses and the children play together near you. Here it's

much easier to be cut off and the children don't have anywhere to play except outside a few floors down, where you can't keep an eye on them.'

I looked out of the window of their sixteenth-floor apartment. The view over Paris was wonderful but anyone on the ground was a little dot. You couldn't just call a child in to eat or remind them that it was bedtime.

'But I think that the situation has been made worse by the war. Everyone is suspicious of everyone.'

'And you?' I asked them, hoping for a genuine response, 'do you still feel the same way about supporting the FLN?'

Habibi hesitated, looking uncharacteristically at his wife, for confirmation. She inclined her head slightly as if giving him permission to talk as she cleared the plates. 'Those two confer together,' I suddenly realised. This was a marriage of companionship, not just duty. I envied them their relationship.

'Yes, we do. They're not perfect of course. There is intimidation and harassment and it's difficult for people to avoid them if they disagree. But they do want a free Algeria and they will provide good things for their people.'

'Would the FLN abduct anyone do you think?' I explained my crisis over the whereabouts of Yussuf. His wife was now back in the room, the children had been shooed back to the bedroom. Habibi hesitated.

'It happens of course, but I think more often in Algeria itself.'

'Could they be using stories about his relatives to get him back?'

'It's possible. But it takes a lot of work to get one man back over there.'

'Could it be revenge?'

'Possibly. But then they could kill him here quite easily.'

I shivered.

'Except there would be a police investigation here.'

'No, no. Sorry, Marie. You have too much faith in the police. They have no interest in another dead Algerian. It's easy to hide and dispose of a body in this warren, I'm afraid. Look, Marie, I know you don't want to hear this, but it's far more likely that he went of his own volition.'

# Chapter Forty-Eight

I now had two Algerians and the French police telling me that my fiancé had left of his own volition. I was furious. I was furious with them that they had such a low view of our relationship. I was furious with Yussuf that he could have done this to me and left me in such confusion. I was furious with the writer of the note on my door that he had sown such mistrust and fear in me. I was furious with myself that I was reacting with such panic, felt so confused and had become indecisive.

By the next morning I had to go and see my editor. I had already sent him the copy of my article on the internment camp and he was pleased with it.

'This is excellent. It's really going to stir up a stink in France.'

'Good. It needs to. The New York Herald Tribune are interested in it too. Are you OK with me something for them in English?'

'Why not? Especially if you manage to get our name in there somewhere.'

I hesitated.

'It could be tricky, André. The Tribune aren't exactly commie lovers.'

'No, but they hate the French establishment even more, especially de Gaulle.'

The antipathy between de Gaulle and the Americans was well known throughout France. De Gaulle thought the Americans had too much influence in Europe. He wanted to be the king pin.

'I guess I could get the angle about Kennedy supporting the nationalists.'

'You'll work it somehow, Marie. I have every confidence in you.'

A compliment from André was rare. I wished I could relax and enjoy the moment of triumph more.

'You seem a bit edgy,' he remarked. 'Are you all right?'

'Yes, yes, just disturbed by what I've seen of the French at work.'

'Ah! So, you're beginning to come around to the Marxist way of thinking?' he teased me. André was a true believer and sensed a conversion in the air.

'I don't think I can ever be a true ideologue, André, I'm afraid, but I've got to admit that the French haven't done well here. And as for the lieutenant at the French army camp in Constantine... words cannot describe what I think about him.'

'He was an arrogant bastard, was he?'

'I'll say.'

'You know, Marie, there are lots of people in Paris at the moment leaving the army. Most of them have been in Algeria and are disillusioned. You could get a good angle on them for us.'

'Sorry, André. I've got other things to do.'

'Meaning what?'

'I'm going back to Algeria.'

He stopped stacking his papers and put them down suddenly on the desktop.

'Have you gone mad or something?'

'Probably.'

'What are you talking about, Marie? The whole place is going crazy, didn't you know? No one knows how long the pied noirs can hold it together. The army will leave. It doesn't matter what terrible things they've done. They'll be out of it and leave the chaos to someone else.'

'I know. I know. In six months-time they'll be drinking champagne at home and abandoning the mess they've created. But I've decided I'm going back.'

'OK. I can see some brilliant reports in the offing, but surely, Marie, you only just got out of Vietnam alive. Are you sure you want to do this?'

'Quite sure.' Suddenly I knew that this was the only way I was going to sort out the mystery of Yussuf and I couldn't just abandon him or keep going over the unresolved rumours in my head and heart.

'Look, André. I know this is going to sound crazy. And I will send some reports of course. But it's not really about my job.'

He looked at me suspiciously.

'Well, what is it about then?'

'That day at the camp near Constantine. It was one of the most horrible experiences of my life. Indo China was disgusting, so were the camps in Siberia, not to mention the concentration camps for the Jews. But it was always the enemy who did it, the 'other'. This was the first time I'd seen my countrymen callously cause the destruction of innocent people.'

'What can you do about that?'

'Not much, it's true. I can't bring money. I'm not a nurse. But one thing I can do. Those kids are dying of desolation and boredom and I challenged the lieutenant about giving them a schooling, a leg-up. I was scoffed at. Well, I'm going to do something. Yes, I know it will only be for a short time, but it will be something. And meanwhile I'll send you reports and see what else I can find. I'll do the angle of 'What hope for Algeria in the future?'

At the possibility of Libération getting a roving reporter at a time of crisis, André became instantly interested. His hands left his papers on the desk and went all over the place in his excitement.

'Tell you what, Marie. If you do this, we'll get resources for you, boards and slates, even an extra prefab to teach them in. Fantastic idea! The ALN will see that the communist party in France are helping their people.'

'I'm OK with left wing papers helping financially, André, but I'm not sure I want to represent the Communist Party. Couldn't I just be myself and I will be seconded by your paper?'

'Sure, you could, Marie. We'll work it somehow without you turning into a fully signed up Marxist.' He paused. 'You haven't got any other motivation for this, have you?'

'Such as?'

'Did I hear about a friendship with some mad Algerian here in Paris?'

'I've had a few mad friendships in my time, André. No, this is about my anger at the French army.'

'Great stuff, Marie.' Fortunately, he seemed to be quickly distracted. 'Get it organised. I'll set your new woman to track down resources.'

'You mean Mathilde?'

'Yes, she's fantastic once she gets started. Besides, now she's come, I can't find anything in the office. It would give me some space.'

'I can't think of anyone better to do the job.'

# Chapter Forty-Nine

As far as I was concerned, Mathilde was the best person to work with, mainly because she was such an efficient and motivated worker. When she put her mind to organising lorry loads of slates and chalk and blackboards and books, she did it in double fast time. She also seemed to know how to get lorry loads of stuff packed onto a boat in Marseille and how to get it sent to Bejaia. She had other advantages too. She knew how the French army worked and she completely believed me when I told her about the conditions which the French army had created in the camps.

'I had a fair idea of what was happening when I lived there,' she admitted. 'I didn't want to face up to it, but I knew.'

She explained that a malaise had come over her in Algeria in the last few years. She had been unable to think decisively or face up to responsibility.

'I was just overcome with misery about my own personal situation. I am ashamed now. I could have done so much more.'

'You were overwhelmed with the misery of your own marriage and the betrayal of your husband,' I reassured her. 'Nobody would have blamed you.'

'I blame myself. I can't believe that I was so blind about him and I let that blindness stop me from seeing so much injustice.'

She felt remorse not only about her own domestic situation but about the events within the whole country.

'Never mind, Mathilde,' I said practically. 'You're making up for it now.'

There was another reason that Mathilde was good for me at this point. She knew Yussuf – not merely guessing about his existence, as my editor and a few fellow journalists had.

729

'Marie,' she said, looking worried as we were deep into ordering educational material, 'you've gone slightly crazy here.'

'You mean with all this teaching stuff and the camps?'

'No, with your desire to find Yussuf again.'

'I know, Mathilde, that's what a lot of people would think.'

'But,' she stopped what she was doing and came around to look me in the eye. 'I'm not "a lot of people", Marie, you know that. Love makes people do crazy things. And,' she added, with a wry smile, 'in case you're wondering, I do know from experience what love feels like, as well as the disillusionment when it doesn't work out.'

She understood the extremes of emotion I was feeling, and I was glad to be able to talk honestly with her.

'Mathilde, I may be crazy, but I don't believe he left of his own volition. Got tired of me? Possible. Felt he was betraying his country? Possible again. But just walk out on me like that? No.'

She sighed. 'I know what you mean. He was full of integrity, too much so for his own good. But kidnap him? There's no evidence for it.'

'But surely that's what happens when you kidnap someone. No one sees what has gone on.'

'There are other possibilities of course,' she suggested carefully, waiting for my reaction.

'Such as?'

'He was blackmailed into going by saying they would hurt his family if he didn't go.'

'But he didn't have any close family.'

'No, but I'm talking about cousins' families who had young girls and children, as well as elderly parents. They could have made him feel guilty about what they might do to them.'

'I guess so. We'd talked before about who he was leaving behind. But, Mathilde, I've got to find out.'

'I know you have but, to be honest, I'm feeling very fearful for you, Marie.'

'I'll be careful, I promise, and I do genuinely want to help those families in the camp. Maybe it's me trying to help ordinary Algerian families like Yussuf's.'

'I can understand that. I just hate seeing you go off into the maelstrom of civil war.'

'I'll be as careful as I can, I promise. But, Mathilde, there's something else.'

'What?'

'I don't know why, but I do actually love him. I didn't know him very well when we first came to Paris and I did wonder whether it would last or whether it was just an impulse and the desire to save someone. But it did last. I've loved him more in the day to day stuff here than I did in all the high drama. And that's pretty amazing for me. Normally I get turned on by all the excitement and adventure but when any relationship descends to the day to day, I get bored. That didn't happen with Yussuf.'

'Yes, I saw that myself and I was glad for you.'

'And, Mathilde, I feel like it's my last chance. I've had a few different affairs but for ages they've all been lived in the shadow of Alain. He was my hero for years. None of the others could live up to him, not even Nicolai. He came near. He was a really great friend as well as a lover and I felt bereft when I left him in Russia. But Yussuf's different. I really think he's my soul mate.'

'Then I guess you'd better find him.'

'Thanks, Mathilde.'

'What for?'

'For believing me, even though I sound like a mad woman.'

'Marie, I'm only returning the compliment. I thought I couldn't have any future on my own. I thought it was too late to retrieve my life, but you showed me something different and gave me the energy to make my own decisions.'

We hugged long and hard. I was shaking and crying with the fears I had for myself and Yussuf. She pulled away from me and held my head, stroking my hair back from my forehead.

'No more tears, Marie. It's action you need. I've got to get these damned orders in now and you've got to catch the same boat. Otherwise it will all get siphoned off somewhere else.'

'What? How?' My emotions receded into the background. I hadn't anticipated the need to do something so practical.

'You have to go across with the supplies. Without you there to see it through, there'll be delays and excuses and corruption. I know. I've seen it all before. You want to get these children helped?'

'Yes, I do.'

'Well, you've got to be strong. No more mooning about.'

She was right. I channelled all my fears and anger into accompanying the lorries down south onto the boat in Marseille with all the paperwork. No one can feel sentimental when they are dealing with French paperwork.

I stayed the night before we embarked with the Tribier family.

'It's not a good time to be going over to Algeria,' warned M. Tribier, who looked worried when I explained my plan as we sat together with the family having dinner.

'Not if you want a future in Algeria,' I agreed. 'But I just want to help the children there in that camp. It's not a long-term project. I know the camp won't last for ever. I just hope the revolutionaries won't take it out on those families because they've been held by the French.'

'You think they could?'

'Frankly, anything could happen. The whole country's gone crazy.'

'Then not a good time for you to be going, Mademoiselle Marie.'

'It's the last time anyone can do anything good there, at least anyone who's French.'

'You don't think the Pied Noir community will survive it all?'

'I'd be very surprised. It's not looking good.'

'So, my cousin, Jules? What do you think will happen to him?'

I hesitated, not knowing how much he knew about the situation.

'Yes, yes,' said M. Tribier, sounding surprisingly matter of fact for such an old-fashioned gentleman. 'I've heard already about Mathilde and how you helped her.'

'I only did it because she was desperate to escape. The marriage had finished long ago. He was having an affair with a local Algerian girl,' I added.

'Oh, don't worry. I don't blame you. He was always obstinate. And it sounds like he's been totally taken in by the girl.'

'I fear so. I just hope he doesn't try to stay with her. He can't survive out there by himself.'

'Hopefully he'll see the truth before it's too late. Actually, he's not the person I'm most worried about.'

'No? Who is it then?'

'People like Emile and Maia.'

'Why them? I didn't even realise you knew them.'

'It's not just them, but they've been in Algeria for at least three generations and they don't know anything else. If they leave, they lose everything.'

'But why should they leave? The Jews have always supported the Algerian nationalists, even if Emile and Maia thought the French should stay.'

'Yes, in theory, but not always, especially when there's been violence. In the last six months the Jews in the Casbah in Algiers have been attacked. I don't think they should wait to find out if they're the next on the list.'

'Of course not.' I couldn't imagine why two such beautiful and generous people should be attacked. 'Why would anyone have anything against Emile and Maia?'

'No one could. But once violence starts it doesn't stop. It's a sort of madness which takes hold. I've seen it all before.'

'I have too,' I agreed sadly. Too many of my dearest friends had been destroyed by mob violence.

'But,' said M. Trebier, as he poured me more wine,' you are going to do something good and that will counteract the violence.'

I felt guilty because he didn't know about my motivation for going back. But it made me determined to at least do the job in the camp properly. In the next few days I was preoccupied with checking papers, insulting bureaucrats, and insisting that the drivers from France came all the way with me to the French army camp. Naturally they had heard the worst about what was happening in the country and were wary of my request. But they had been well paid by my paper and I assured them that the sooner they offloaded their cargo, the sooner they could return home to safety. The French army too was reassured by my French drivers and gave them no problem in gaining access.

The French lieutenant was cynical about my presence.

'So, you've come back?'

'Yes, I want to do some good, now I'm here.'

'It won't be appreciated. They couldn't care less about the children's education.'

'No, of course not,' I replied in spirited fashion. 'That's because the only thing they've been able to worry about is survival. But, believe me, Lieutenant, those children are going to be happy about it.'

'I've never known children in any part of the world to love education.'

'You wait and see. They will love being occupied and being drawn away from the misery and boredom of everyday life.'

'They've got used to the boredom. It would just be as boring for them if they were still in their villages.'

'All right. Just you wait, Lieutenant. You'll see a difference soon.'

Despite his pessimism, I was determined. I asked the Red Cross for advice about who were the young people who might already know how to read and write and who had the leadership skills to organise the younger children. It's always amazing to me that in any situation, without any prior training, there are young people who have the instinct to lead others. Before long we had chosen five girls and five boys who could be trusted. The Red Cross volunteered to teach the basic hygiene skills and bandaging. Two of the Médicins sans Frontières nurses turned out to know a lot about children's games. I started on some general geography and history and basic French language lessons and one of the orderlies started on Mathematics. In two weeks, we had a timetable drawn up with foundation courses being given to ten young people. As the chosen ten organised themselves to teach the younger ones, I restarted the whole process with the next ten teenagers. I was humbled by their enthusiasm and excitement. I had never had much experience with children and would have been happy to finish in the afternoon and later to mix only with the adults, but I was not allowed to do so. I was mobbed by the children at all hours and I found myself having to go around and visit the families in the evenings and be introduced to their parents.

I was soon exhausted but felt incredibly satisfied.

'If this had happened years ago in the villages, never mind in these camps, things might have been different,' remarked one of the Algerian Red Cross nurses.

'Well, you managed to get educated,' I remarked to her.

'I was one of the lucky ones. I got taken over to France by an uncle who was a Caid. Most of my village was not so lucky.'

'Well, let's get on with it now,' I replied enthusiastically.

But I had to admit to myself later that I was throwing myself into the job with such enthusiasm, because I didn't want to think about my own future without Yussuf.

# Chapter Fifty

After two months of being involved in this education project, I knew that I needed to have a weekend off. Even the Red Cross nurses had some time to themselves and I knew that time was running out for the French in this country. I had to apply to the Colonel at the French army headquarters. Colonel Lemarle was much more practical and less officious than Lieutenant Dupré, who had succeeded in annoying me so much, when I had first approached the camp.

'I'll gladly give you a pass, Marie. I've heard a lot about your work with the children and I'm impressed.'

'Thank you, but the reality is that it's probably far too late to do any good.'

He looked thoughtful, not a look which I often noticed among the army personnel. 'Yes, it is late of course, and we'll all be out in a few months, but that doesn't mean it's all pointless.'

'No?' I looked at him suspiciously to see whether he was just being flattering. 'So, what good will it do?'

'Some of them will remember the good time they had with you. They might not remember the learning, but they will always know that a French woman cared about them.'

'I guess that can't be bad,' I agreed.

'And you might even give some of them a taste for learning. Most of them won't be able to do anything about that, but one or two of them will have the opportunity to go to school in the future.'

'You think so?' I could hardly believe that a French army officer was feeling so positive about the future of this country. Most of the army personnel had just given up.

'Alright. I know that the fashionable thing to say among ourselves is that the whole country is going to be in permanent chaos, but I don't think that's necessarily true.'

'Really? What gives you such cause for optimism?'

'In fighting them, I've come to have great respect for the ALN leadership. Yes, they fight hard and dirty, but then so have we. But there's some great brains amongst them too. They'll get a plan together when we've gone, of that I'm sure.'

I looked at this man with respect. 'Wow! That's the first time I've heard the French army talk about the Algerians so positively.'

'Isn't it about time we treated them with respect?'

'Certainly.'

I hesitated but with some new-found confidence decided to ask for advice.

'I know I've got a pass for a couple of days, Colonel. But I don't really want to go to Bejaia, even though it's so lovely.'

'Where do you want to go?'

'To the mitjda – the Bourgeaud estate.'

'That, Marie, is quite a way and across dangerous country too.'

'I know.'

'Would you mind my asking why?'

I took a deep breath and took my chance.

'I stayed with them before when I was in Algeria and they've done an awful lot of good here. They're not just rich wine growers. I got to know some of their workers too and one of them has been in France recently. He's planning to come back here but I don't know whether it's a good idea. I want to ask the Bourgeads what they think.'

He eyed me shrewdly. 'That's a lot of trouble to go to for a vineyard worker.'

'True,' I replied boldly, continuing with my half-truth. 'But he's a special friend of their son and they'd hate him to be killed at independence. I want to know what to advise him.'

The colonel decided not to follow up his suspicions. He must have had so much experience in his posting, of relationships between the two groups of people, that he was not surprised by anything.

'It's a long way. You can't possibly go for a weekend. Why don't you have a night in Bône to revive yourself and then in a month's time take four or five days to get over to the mitjda with a proper escort of my men? I want to know how the Bourgeauds are getting on myself. They've always been very independent and sure of themselves, but no one should assume that they're going to be alright. At the moment there are mutinies happening all over the country and when the fuse is lit, there will be all hell let loose.'

'But surely the government will have seen the pied noirs back safely to France by then?'

He nodded gravely. 'That's what everyone hopes but, in my experience, gunpowder is a rather unpredictable substance.'

'Thank-you, Lieutenant. I'll take up your offer.'

I felt reassured by his calm professionalism and good judgment. I went off to Bône for my night away with a lighter heart remembering the time when Mathilde and Yussuf and I had been on the edge of a new life there. Had we been naïve? Did I regret persuading Yussuf to come to France with me?'

At least Mathilde had found peace, I thought, as I also wondered what had happened to Jules, her husband, and whether he was still managing the vineyard and whether he missed his wife. Would he even stay in Algeria with his mistress after independence? I wondered. And, even if I blamed myself for leading Yussuf into more trouble, I knew that he would have been in an equally dangerous position, if he had remained in his own country. It seemed that someone like Yussuf was doomed to be in trouble.

I stayed at the same pension as before. I felt lonely without Mathilde but strangely reassured that I had a useful educational project to complete and a plan to visit the Mitjda in the coming weeks.

I had been intending to go to bed early because I did not want to seek out convivial company, but, as I turned back to the pension after an early evening walk along the beach, on a sudden whim, I passed the entrance and climbed the hill to the cathedral perched above it. The autumn nights were closing in and the woods were dark, stark and ghostly without the comfort of the leaves to offer protection. Although it was very dark, I saw the comforting beacon of the light in the cathedral porch and I climbed up.

Following Mathilde's example, I found a candle and lit one. Who do you light a candle for? Someone, who has died? For yourself? For guidance? I hardly knew but I felt that I wanted to do something, not just hover at the door, as I had done the last time I was here. I knelt in front of the candles, closed my eyes but didn't say a word even silently. If there was a deity, he would have to understand what was in my heart without having to utter a word. There was no logic to it, but I knew that I had done the right thing in following Mathilde's example.

'Ah, Mademoiselle!'

It was the same Algerian priest as before.

'It is good to see you again.'

I felt welcomed and affirmed by this solid, dignified figure who didn't feel the need to ask personal questions.

'And your friend who was here with you before? Did she find the way she was seeking?'

Suddenly I knew the answer to his question.

'Yes, she did. She is very happy, Father.'

'Of course, she is, if she committed her way to God.'

I had no idea if that was true or not, but I was heartened by the idea that Mathilde had lit a candle in this church months ago and now she had found a way forward in life. That was why I wanted too.

'Thank you, Father.'

'You don't need to thank me, my child. I am just there to open the door for those who come to seek God.'

'In that case, opening the door is a very important task.'

He smiled with tremendous humility and kindness.

'I like to think that it is and it's always a privilege to open the door for someone else.'

I ran down the hill as fast as I could to avoid the straggling branches which seemed to hold onto me. Just as I got near the bottom and my heart was beating furiously, I saw a figure move from behind one of the trunks. For a moment I was reassured that it was a woman, but there was something in the movement, a raising of the neck and a slightly uneven pace that I recognized. Where had I seen that before?

It wasn't until I was safely in the pension and getting ready for bed that I recalled where I had seen that walk before. It had belonged to a young girl who had been caught in my room at the Gaullen's house. It was the way her neck had arched in disdain, and she had been hampered by a very slight limp in her walk, which made it hard for her to be completely superior in her approach to me.

What was Yamina doing in Bône, and where was her lover, M. Jules Gaullen?

# Chapter Fifty-One

A month later I arrived in the mitjda. Last time I had been there the vineyards and orange orchards had been ready for the harvest. I had just started getting to know Yussuf, and I had been charmed by the generous personalities of Henri and Denise Bourgeaud.

This time everything felt different. The weather was now very cold at night; there were few workers on the farm, and no one was expecting me. Even the dogs were half-hearted in their welcome. I didn't care about the lack of reception. I did care about the lack of information.

'Are you sure you want us to leave you here, Mademoiselle?' The army driver turned around to me, looking unsure about what he should do.

'Yes.'

If I didn't get help here, there was nowhere else to go.

'I'm sure the workers on the estate will help me, if the family is not here.'

'I think you need to check that before we go. Algerian workers aren't quite so open and hospitable now, as they once were. They're fearful about the future too.'

The truck driver took me round to the houses nearest to the school and one of the workers recognized me.

'It's the lady who visited the school with Madame Bourgeaud, isn't it?'

'Yes, that's right.' It was great to see one familiar face. 'Do you know where Madame Bourgeaud is?'

The girl went to the front door of the house and shouted inside. A man, probably her father, appeared at the door, looking wary.

'The master and mistress have gone back to France. All their things are packed up, but Monsieur Christophe is here. He's supervising the removal.'

'Is Christophe here now?'

'Yes, he's here for another couple of nights.'

'Thank you.'

I returned quickly to the army driver to tell him the news.

'Let's go back to the house. If the door is open, I know it will be alright to stay and wait.'

'Are you sure, Mademoiselle?'

'Yes. I know the Bourgeauds would be happy for me to be in their house and it sounds like Christophe will be around soon.'

'Yes, but how are you going to get back to Constantine?'

The driver was taking his responsibilities seriously.

'I'm sure I'll be able to; but, if not, give me the lieutenant's phone number and I'll be in touch. I want to be back in five days' time anyway, because I must get back to the school.'

'I'm more worried about your safety, Mademoiselle, than the school.'

'I'm sure I'll be fine, but I will let the Lieutenant know if I need help.'

We found the front door open and signs that someone had been eating there recently. I assured the army escort once again that I would be alright and waved to them as they left.

The estate suddenly felt more isolated than I had realised, and I felt afraid. Would I survive these four days on my own and how would this stay give me any more information about Yussuf?

I was just thinking about making myself a meal with the ingredients which I discovered in the kitchen, when I heard the noise of a car and footsteps on the veranda outside.

The footsteps stopped abruptly; the door swung open and I found a gun trained on me. Immediately it was returned to its holster and Christophe grinned at me.

'Sorry about that but you gave me a fright.'

'That was nothing to what it gave me! Who did you think it was?'

'Anyone! The revolutionaries from the mountains coming to take over now they know my parents have gone; people looting the house; a whole load of undesirables lurking around.'

'So, what are you doing here? Is it true that your parents have gone back to France?

'Yes, it was time for them to face reality about the future. I'm still with my unit here in Kabylia. There's a lorry coming to pick up their stuff and take it to Algiers the day after tomorrow. Then the house will be shut up.'

'It's such a shame to close this beautiful house up.'

'True, but no one dares live in it. When the pied noirs go, the workers here don't want to be accused of profiting from the enemy.'

'What will happen to the workers here?'

'No one knows. The managers here have the know-how to continue the business and make it prosperous, but whether they will be seen as traitors, they don't know. But they're getting prepared.'

'How?'

'They mostly have relatives in the mountains. They'll go to stay for two or three months with them until the danger is passed. And what about you, Marie? I don't want to be rude, but what are you doing here? I assume it's not just a social call?'

'No, indeed.' I explained about my work in the internment camp.' Christophe nodded. 'Great. That needed doing a long time ago. Short sighted strategy on the part of the French. Now you're here, shall we go and make ourselves comfortable? Fortunately, my parents have left a few bottles around, which don't need to go back to France.'

I relaxed for the first time that day.

'After three months in a Muslim camp, I'm glad to hear that. I can certainly help you empty one or two.'

We made ourselves comfortable in the sitting room and Christophe lit a fire against the cold.

'Christophe?' I suddenly needed to talk about what was important to me. 'Christophe, I've really come to find out whether you know anything about Yussuf.'

'Yussuf?' He sounded surprised. 'I thought he was in Paris with you.'

'So did I.' I explained about his sudden disappearance and my hopes of finding out more information here in Algeria.

Christophe looked serious. 'No, I don't know anything, but, knowing Yussuf as I do, my guess is that someone has put pressure on him by telling him that someone in his family was in danger here.'

'But he doesn't have any close relatives,' I objected.

743

'True in the sense of wife or children but there are other obligations.'

'What sort?'

'One of his cousins is a young widow. Her husband was killed by the FLN a couple of years ago. She has two young children. I know Yussuf has given her money sometimes. They might have used her to get him back.'

'But they can't just drag up endless relatives to make him feel guilty about.'

'Can't they? Also, there's the complicated matter of personal vendetta.'

'What do you mean?'

The word 'vendetta' which spoke to me of Italian mafia or Medieval cruelty seemed totally out of place in a beautiful dining room with lovely before-dinner drinks, even if there were crates of belongings behind us ready for moving.

'The idea of vendetta – paying back your enemies – still exists for people in the mountains.'

'You mean them paying back Yussuf for belonging to the French army.'

'Yes, but more than that – that innocent people's blood needs to be avenged and Yussuf is the one who should be doing it.'

'Surely it's up to Yussuf to decide that?'

'For the Western mind, yes, but if there are defenceless people in his village, then his moral obligation might be to protect them against any more attacks.'

'But why wouldn't he talk to me about that first?'

'Possibly because he'd think you wouldn't want him to do it, and also, he'd be afraid that you'd persuade him not to.'

'Too right I'd persuade him,' I answered indignantly. 'I've never heard such a load of medieval claptrap in my life.'

'I think 'medieval' would be far too late in history. We're talking about 1500 years ago or earlier.'

'But this is a man who chose to fight in a modern French army and who's doing a degree in Maths at the Sorbonne.'

'I'm sorry, Marie. I can see how hard it must be for you. Actually, it's hard for me too.'

'Even though you understand the culture?'

'Yes, because Yussuf was my best friend growing up and I don't want anything to happen to him.'

There was the silence of misery between us as we sipped the last of our drinks. What was there to be done about this situation?

Absolutely nothing.

With this unspoken agreement between us, we moved to the kitchen to see what we could salvage for our dinner. Denise must have deliberately left food for her son to eat as he was packing up the house.

Much later, when we were eating up some left-over fruit compote, Christophe returned to the problem of Yussuf.

'The only thing I could do would be to take you to the village of Iqbal.'

'What? The village where those two lady missionaries live? Don't tell me they're still there? Surely they'll be going home?'

Christophe laughed. It was the first spontaneous, relaxed sound we had heard all evening.

'They don't scare easily those two, I can assure you. I'd heard they were thinking of going to Algiers for a time to stay with friends. But the reason I suggest them is that their village is on the crossroads between Lesser and Greater Kabylia, and if Yussuf has been taken anywhere against his will, they'll know about it.'

'Amazing!'

Christophe grinned at me. 'I know what you're thinking – what would two Protestant missionaries know about what terrorists are up to? It sounds unlikely but the truth is – everyone trusts them, so people tell them things.'

'And you'd really be willing to take me there?'

'Yes. Give me another day to get all these crates finally ready for the lorries and then I'll take you on the way back to my posting. It's a better bet than going up to the higher mountain villages where the remains of his family are. I don't think they'll talk to us as Europeans and we can't get up there on the truck.'

I remembered our scramble up the cliff face. There was no way I could do that again.

'That would be fantastic, Christophe. I haven't got more than two or three days free anyway, because I've got to get back to the resettlement camp.'

I didn't know why I felt so certain about what Christophe proposed, but I think that I was secretly relieved that I didn't have to go up to one of the villages and stay with people I didn't know or understand. It was different when Yussuf had been with me but now that country was on the verge of independence and he had enemies who were pursuing him, it felt different. The next day felt lazy. Christophe was waiting for the lorry. Most of the work was done and I had a chance to get to know him better.

'You and your parents must be incredibly sorry to leave all this,' I remarked after he had spent a morning marking the crates to make sure they went to the right destination.

'Of course. It's been our life. But, hey, we have to face reality and it would be suicidal to stay here.'

'I've heard some of the pied noirs are.'

'A few. Those who have positively worked for the revolutionaries, especially in the cities of the West, like Oran. But here we've supported the French, and there's no way we would come out of it with our lives intact.

And yes, my parents will cope if that's what you're thinking. They're brave and resilient and they've got money.'

'But they must be losing millions by leaving all this.'

We were looking out of the big picture windows at the edge of the vineyards and fields. Ironically it still looked perfect and there were workers hurrying to their places of work early in the morning.

'They are, but it's nothing to what they're losing emotionally. My mother wept all night when she knew that she had to go.'

I could hardly imagine what it must mean to Denise Bourgeaud, who had been so resourceful and hard-working in this country.

'Will the management be able to carry on here without them?'

Christophe shrugged his shoulders. 'Who knows? They have the experience and Abdul, who's the manager, is very solid. But you need all the other resources like irrigation and electricity to back it up.'

'And how will they be treated by their new political masters?'

Christophe looked serious, as if his natural optimism was being suppressed.

'No one knows. I wouldn't be sure of anything.'

And it was that gloomy forecast which went with me all the way to the village of Iqbal and the house of the Misses Lamberts.

When we knocked at the door, a strange man opened it. He was a European and a fellow missionary.

'The Miss Lamberts have gone to Algiers,' he informed us. 'My wife and I have always lived further up in the mountains but we're moving temporarily to Bejaia.'

Christophe and I explained the reason for our visit. The man introduced himself as Bill, which sounded incredibly English and friendly, but we discovered that Bill and his wife, Alice, had been in Algeria for 42 years and spoke three languages fluently as well as their own native English – Kabyle, Arabic and French.

'Don't you just want to leave the country?' I asked them over a cup of coffee. Alice looked at me with mournful eyes. 'Mademoiselle, I was born and brought up in this country. It is my homeland.'

'Even though you're English?' I asked surprised.

'That's just an accident of birth. I belong here. There's no way I'm going to leave. My parents were missionaries here before me. This country means everything to me.'

I couldn't imagine the loneliness of an upbringing here without other European children to play with.

'The only time I spent away from Algeria was when I was sent to an English boarding school. It was the worst experience of my life.'

'I'm sorry. I expect your parents thought they were helping you.'

'They did but I was isolated with no one who understood me and forced to spend holidays with relatives who didn't really want me.'

I was so wrapped up in my imaginative understanding of the misery of the little girl fifty years ago, that I almost forgot to ask about Yussuf. Christophe reminded me gently of my quest.

'There's a lot of revolutionaries who pass through here,' Bill informed us. 'Sometimes it's difficult to know which ones are prisoners, and which ones are informants. Generally, they give nothing away. But I'll do my best.'

'Wait a minute.'

As if by magic, a small boy appeared at the door.

'If you promise him enough money as a reward, he'll find out for you.'

# Chapter Fifty-Two

It turned out that Yussuf had passed through the village to go further up into the mountains. The boy came back with the news that he was an informer for the FLN, but I doubted it. I believed that he had been made to go. What surprised me more was the report that he was now in Algiers.

'But Yussuf never had anything to do with Algiers. He told me that he had only been there a couple of times in his life when he was passing through on his way to France.'

Christophe agreed with me.

'Yussuf always stuck to his own area even when he was working with the French army. He always said that he was more at home in the mountains than in the city.'

'Christophe, what am I going to do?' I cried, desperate for some advice. 'I don't want to leave the school in the camp, but I have to follow where he is.'

'If I were you, I'd go back to the camp. If Yussuf really is in Algiers, it will be almost impossible to track him down, especially if he's in the Casbah.'

I remembered vividly my journey through the Casbah as I had tried to follow the whereabouts of the printing press.

'How much longer are you committed to the school?' asked Christophe practically.

'As long as the army are still there.'

'They'll be gone within a month. Go back there for three weeks and in the last week get yourself to Algiers. It will be chaos there as the pied noirs get on the last boats, but in the chaos, you'll have cover and you can find out where he might be.'

'But what if it's too late?'

Christophe put his arm round my shoulder.

'Listen, Marie, if he's really gone there with the FLN, it's probably too late anyway. We don't know what pressure they're putting him under. There's probably some sort of deal that his family in the village will be protected, if he works under cover for them in the Casbah, while the French are leaving.'

'But how could he do that if he used to be part of the French army? Surely they'll recognise him?'

'That might be the point. They'll trust him and he'll be able to report back to the FLN.'

'But what will happen when the pied noir leave?'

'Marie, I don't know the answer any more than you do. If he's proved his worth to them, they might keep him. After all he's got lots of skills to offer his new country.'

I was tearful with the frustration of the whole situation.

'But it seems so unfair. He'd started a new life in France. He's given his life over and over again for his country already. Why bother to kidnap him? Is he really worth so much to them?'

I didn't want to leave that house. Bill and Alice and Christophe seemed so sane compared with anyone else. I knew that I couldn't go alone to Algiers and I had to let Christophe take me back to the camp.

There was only one thing to do – throw myself into the care of the children for my last three weeks there. The end was coming for me and for them, and they knew it.

One night after all the children had gone back to their tents for the evening meal, I found Haiza waiting for me.

'What's up Haiza?'

'I'm not going back for a bit, Marie. My sister can help my mother tonight. I just want to stay in the class-room by myself and think about all we have had here.'

'I'm afraid you haven't had very much.'

'You can't imagine, Marie, what it was like to have something when before we had nothing.'

I was silent. I couldn't imagine what she had salvaged from this small inadequate experience of education.

749

'What will happen to you when the French leave?'

'We don't know.' She stated it simply and without bitterness. So many people were content with 'I don't know' in this country, I thought. I was put to shame. Was it my Western European upbringing which meant that I always had to know about the future and do something about it?

'Can you get back to the village you came from?' I asked her.

'No. I don't think so. Even if we could travel, which is not possible with my grandparents and the babies, it's probably been razed.'

'By the French?'

'Yes, part of their razed ground tactics.'

'If you stay here, how will you get food?'

'The French are bringing in three months' extra supply before they leave.'

Thank God, I thought. At least they've got that much humanity.

'But food isn't the same as education,' Haiza remarked.

I looked at her carefully. She wasn't a conventionally pretty girl, but she had bright, inquisitive eyes.

'No,' I agreed. 'You can manage without education but not without food.'

'It's the only chance I've ever had,' she said wistfully.

'You might get it again?' I suggested hopefully.

Haiza shook her head.

'No. If we ever get out of this camp, I'll have to be married.'

'But you're only fourteen, Haiza.'

She shrugged her shoulders. 'Too bad. My older sister was married at that age.'

'But surely the new national government will make it illegal.'

'It already is. But no one really cares. Families just do what they can to survive.'

Yes, families need to survive, I thought. But some of us are lucky enough to have parents who want us to do more than survive. I suddenly realised how lucky I was to have had parents who at least let me go to Paris, rather than trying to protect their honour or their own financial future.

The last three weeks were worth it, after all. I couldn't give these children better prospects for the future, but I could give them the sense that they mattered – their education, themselves as people and for the girls to be considered as human beings rather than mere fodder for marriage. My heart was desperate for my own loved one, but I learnt to laugh with these lovely young people who had all the odds stacked against them.

When, three weeks later, I arrived in Algiers, my priorities had changed. I still wanted to find Yussuf but I couldn't forget the young people of the camps. I found a French book shop which was just starting to pack up its stock and I bought out their stock of books for children and young people. I wouldn't let Christophe go before he had found me another army truck which was returning to Constantine. Inside the boxes I had a list of names of those who had attended our school. I wrote a letter to the Lieutenant explaining my actions, with a special list of the oldest teenagers who were to receive a book and the younger ones who were to receive the 'bandes dessines'.

Christophe was amused. 'You've really taken them to heart, haven't you? You realise, Marie, that the adults will probably force them to sell the books on the black market to get more food?'

'I don't care,' I insisted stubbornly 'I can't help what happens in the end. But I've never admired anyone more in my life than those teenagers and especially the girls. I want them to know that they haven't been forgotten. And when they're carrying babies, with no hope of education for themselves, they'll be able to read their book in secret.'

He looked in a kindly at me, trying not to disillusion me. 'You never know, Marie. Perhaps they'll be able to read it to their children and tell them what happened.'

Could there be a future for this country, I wondered. Could something good come out of all this waste? I really hoped so.

The city of Algiers was in chaos. Everywhere there were people's belongings piled up on the streets, waiting for the mass exodus which had already started to happen. Some of the pied noirs were trying to sell their houses and furniture, but most knew that it was hopeless. Looting had already started and, once the big passenger boats had begun to depart, it would happen in earnest. Everyone I passed in the street had the look of people who were determined. They were a contrast to the people who were not going anywhere but set on making as much money as possible

751

while there was still time. French troops were still to be stationed there during the hand over to independence, but the government had made them promise not to fight on behalf of the French. Time was running out for the pied noirs.

Strangely, the Casbah itself was a calm place compared to the days when it had been the centre of revolutionary plans for rebellion. The people of the Casbah were not waiting for their victory to be finalised.

I asked to be directed to the house where the printing press had been hidden. It was only the vaguest link with the ALN, but I had to start somewhere. I asked at the goldsmiths for the names of the people and they gave me directions. I knew that I would quickly be lost so I paid for a teenage boy to take me. He didn't speak any French, but I followed him faithfully through the alleyways, remembering my last journey there and the excitement of looking forward to finding out about El Moudjahidine. I supposed that the paper now only had two weeks to remain underground. It would soon become Algiers' key serious daily paper. I admired Algerian tenacity in keeping going through the final years of the French rule.

It seemed like a re-run of my journey three years earlier, only this time there were no French troops in pursuit.

Somehow, I was not surprised when my guide threw open the door of the upstairs rooms and I was face to face with Abdelkrim.

'So, Mademoiselle the left-wing journalist, still sending despatches to your colonial masters?'

His face looked older and he was no longer a physical threat to me, but his attitude had not changed. I would have known that derisive tone anywhere. I knew that it was not chance that he was here to greet me, but I was wary of saying anything which might endanger Yussuf.

I put my dislike and fear of this man in the back of my throat and concentrated on being tough – the only stance which he would respect.

'I have never betrayed you, Abdelkrim, either with the French or with my reports. I've always been a friend to Algeria.'

'So, I understand. But unfortunately, that is not true of your lover.'

'Neither has he betrayed his country.'

'Oh? So, fighting for the enemy doesn't count?'

'Fighting for a fair future for your own country does count.'

'Not when you join with the enemy.'

'In that case, what's the point of having him here if you think he's so useless?'

'Justice.'

'Justice for who?'

'For my country. We can't let traitors get away with it.'

This sort of argument was not going to achieve anything.

'So, where is he?'

'If you want to see him, you'll have to go to Cherchell.'

'Where's that and what's he doing there?'

'It was a French holiday destination, reserved for their elite.'

'What's the point of him being there?'

'He's doing something useful for us for a change.'

'Like what?'

'Helping to unload supplies in advance of independence.'

'I'm sure he's good at doing anything which will help his country. Can I see him?'

He looked cynical.

'Are you sure you want to see him? Now is your best chance of getting out of Algiers alive.'

'I don't care what you say. I want to see him.'

'French women are so romantic.' He said without a trace of humour.

'No. We stick by our men.'

'So, you're prepared to stay with him here after independence?'

I hesitated. I had no idea what would happen to me if Yussuf chose to remain here.

'Wise to be unsure, Marie. I'll get you out to Cherchell this evening and you can make your decision.'

I'd learnt nothing about how he'd been abducted or blackmailed but at least I was going to see Yussuf and he was still alive. I didn't want to spend more time with Abdulkrim in Algiers. I'd no doubt that he was the source of power for the fledgling independence movement in the capital, but I didn't trust him or his talk.

In the event, I didn't have to undertake any undercover work. I took a perfectly ordinary ride in an Algerian taxi to Cherchell. If it had been the centre of the French tourist scene, it was now deserted. The hotels and well-kept grounds along the coast looked incongruous as if they had nothing to do while waiting for the next influx of holidaymakers.

I was taken down to the small port, where there were still a few yachts moored, but most of the activity was centred round an old fishing boat, which was docked there. I watched from just above the pier where large crates were being unloaded. I recognized one of the figures as Yussuf. At least he was in good health, I thought.

I was made to stay in the taxi and watch, but I dared to ask the driver one question.

'What are they bringing in?'

'Guns.'

There didn't seem any point in commenting. That means guns against their own people and any remaining pied noirs, I thought.

Suddenly all the work seemed to stop. The driver took me out of the car and down to the jetty.

'Don't say anything,' he warned. 'You will be told what to do.'

Yussuf was lined up with four other men against the counter where the crates had been piled.

The captain of the ship – I assumed that was his role from his air of authority rather than from his dirty overalls – stayed on the boat. He spoke in Arabic to all five of the men.

Then he turned to me.

'As a foreign journalist, you will get on the boat first. Then these others will follow.'

I didn't dare ask anything. I tried to look at Yussuf as meaningfully as I could, but I didn't know how much any of them knew about our relationship and there didn't seem any point in giving away unnecessary information. As long as he was getting on the boat with me, I didn't care.

The taxi driver walked over to the gangway with me.

'Thank-you,' I said unnecessarily, as if he was an employee helping a passenger.

Once on the boat, I turned around and saw the men walk up to the gangway. One of the sailors indicated where I should sit and sat next to me.

As the third man walked onto the gang plank, the other two, including Yussuf, were stopped.

He was looking at me and suddenly mouthed, 'I love you,' in English.

In an impossible five seconds, the gang plank was removed, and the two remaining men forced back into the office against the counter and the taxi driver and another office worker turned the guns on them.

# Chapter Fifty-Three

It needed two men to hold me down and to stop me jumping off the boat to get back to the landing stage.

I can't explain how that journey from Cherchell to Cassis passed. I screamed, I cried, I hit the boat, I hit the captain and anyone else who came into my striking range. The sailors had nothing to say. Why were three of the workers allowed back on the boat and two of them killed? Why had they allowed me to see Yussuf alive for an hour, gave me hope of his release and then had him killed in front of me? Had I caused him to be killed by coming to Algeria and searching for him? Was it all part of Abdulkrim's malice because he hated and despised me? And, most of all, how can someone who is so beautiful and honourable be wiped out in ten seconds? How can a human being, who takes so long to develop into the person he becomes, his brains, personality and emotions, be wiped out just like that? And how can such terrible injustice take place in a world where we believe in goodness?

Questions I had seen asked the world over by those who suffer the untimely death of loved ones. It doesn't matter how many times you've seen it in the experience of other people. It makes no difference to the enormity of your own terror and disgust. For a few minutes on that boat, I slipped off to sleep and for a moment on awakening I had forgotten what had happened, so the terrible realisation started all over again. The men on board were not unkind. They made sure I was safe and brought me hot drinks. But there was nothing they could say. They probably had no way of knowing what was going to happen before they embarked, and they almost certainly didn't know Yussuf.

When I clambered onto the tiny landing stage at Cassis, I just walked through the Calanques. The unforgiving landscape of the huge boulders, cliffs and crags, unrelieved by greenery, suited my mood. I didn't want to walk amongst human beings who were happy with their own lives. I didn't want to live. Life had no meaning for me. But I knew I wouldn't die either. I'd never been quite brave enough to consider taking my own life and, though I stared down at the impossible heights of the Calanques, it merely served to intensify my terror of life.

I wondered whether to go and stay with the Tribiers. They would have been so welcoming, but they didn't know Yussuf. They knew tragedy of course – which Jew after the war in Europe didn't know it? But I couldn't cope with their kindness and the beauty and purposefulness of their home.

Eventually I managed to find a bus to Marseille and then went up to Paris by train. One morning, after a night in dishevelled clothes, I arrived at Mathilde's door. She saw immediately the terror of what had happened etched onto my filthy, fatigued face. Wisely she didn't ask any questions but drew me in to help me get showered and changed. I was so exhausted that I couldn't speak. She gave me hot chocolate, dressed me in her pyjamas and put me to bed.

I don't know whether she ever went to work that day, but later she told me that she had called in at the office for short spells but kept coming home to check whether I was still asleep. Forty-eight hours later I started to explain a little bit of what had happened, but she let me go at my own pace over the next few days. My life had stopped. I had no idea of where I was going to live or how I was going to earn my living. I didn't even want answers about what exactly had happened to Yussuf.

I lived with Mathilde for six months. I reported back to my editor, André, about what had happened with the education project in the camps and wrote a few articles about it, especially to satisfy those who had supported it financially. The future was just a grey mist in the morning settling on the flat landscape of Les Landes and refusing to dissipate in the sun.

Most of the pied noirs were back from Algeria, the majority settling in the South of France but also a minority came to Paris. It seemed incredible that we had at one time supported the heady claims of Algérie Française . France had forgotten Algeria quite quickly. The students of the Sorbonne in the 60s were too young to remember it. They were concerned with their own freedoms and rights. I felt restless and uncertain what to do. I couldn't go on relying on Mathilde for ever, even though in the intervening months, I had given up my flat and moved in with her.

One evening I had just set the table for our evening meal and Mathilde had returned from work. It seemed strange that I was now in the position of housekeeper and chef, but it seemed like the least I could do, when Mathilde was the only one of us who was earning. She had picked up her post which had arrived earlier that day, while I prepared the asparagus for our entrée. Suddenly I heard a gasp. Two minutes later I walked in with the wine uncorked to find out what had happened.

'Are you alright, Mathilde?'

'I suppose so. I'm not sure.'

'What do you mean?'

'I've just been told that Jules has died.'

'I'm sorry.' I wasn't quite sure how to react considering her lack of enthusiasm for him as a husband.

'Well, I'm sorry too as it happens. Not for myself. We were finished long ago. But for him. I'm not sure he deserved this.'

'What?'

'He stayed in Algeria after independence and was murdered.'

'Oh! my God! By the FLN?'

'No. By Yamina's family.'

'Why?'

'Apparently a killing of honour. He dishonoured her by his affair with her.'

'But she wanted it.'

'OK, so it's some arcane notion of morality. Probably also to distance themselves from our family and our money under the new regime.'

'That seems a bit unfair when you consider how well the whole family must have done out of it.'

'No doubt, but actually that wasn't what made me gasp.'

'You mean that there's something worse than the murder of a husband?'

'No. Something better.'

'Sorry?'

'Jules, it seems, got a lot of the money over to France before independence. He's left it all to me.'

'Wow, Mathilde! So, he did have some respect for you after all!'

'Perhaps. Or maybe in the end he didn't want it to go to an Algerian family he didn't trust, even though he loved Yamina.'

'I can see that. Perhaps they were so disappointed that they killed him.'

'And perhaps Yamina had an affair with him because she was hoping her family would do well out of it.'

'All sorts of possibilities, I agree. But the point is, Marie, what am I going to do with all this money?'

'I've no idea, Mathilde. It's completely up to you. And you don't have to think about me, you know. It's about time I got out of the way anyway. You've been supporting me for too long.'

'I'm really happy to have you around and, since you've had such an awful time after Yussuf's death, it's right for you not to work.'

'Sure. But that can't go on for ever.'

'That's true but only for your own sake, not for mine.'

Mathilde's news pushed me to think about my own circumstances more seriously. I couldn't face going back to international journalism. I knew that I had an excellent reputation and could have travelled anywhere in the world for my profession, but my experience of war zones and deep personal loss had taken away all the glamour and excitement associated with my job. The 1960s had changed France for me. I no longer had a connection with the post-war world where I had become an adult. My political position was even shakier than it had been before. I no longer wanted to work for avowedly left-wing papers. But I didn't believe in the politics of the right either. I wasn't sure that I could cope with the pettiness of local news.

It was strangely the news of another death which finally jolted me into action. My mother had died very suddenly of a stroke in Les Landes and Mathilde and I went to the funeral. My father looked lost and unsure of himself without a complaining, nagging partner. Arthritis was having an effect on his ability to go out hunting and he had never been capable of managing the small holding himself without my mother's hard work.

Travelling back to Paris from the funeral, Mathilde made some suggestions.

'How about us both moving back to Les Landes?'

'You're joking? We'd be so cut off. And you've never lived there.'

'We wouldn't be so cut off if we moved to a bigger town like Labouyère.'

'Alright. What would you do?'

'Possibly have a small holding?'

'But my father already has one.'

'OK. So, we could help him with his. Maybe I could do a part-time office job at the same time.'

'But what would I do there?'

'Had any thoughts about your future?'

'I know I have to leave journalism. I know this might sound crazy, but I have occasionally thought about teaching, after my experience in the camps, but I don't know whether that is in any way realistic.'

'Of course, it's realistic, Marie. If we lived at Labouyère, at least while you do your training, and travel to Bordeaux, and then we can decide what to do after you've finished. If you wanted to teach locally, we could take over your parents' house and your dad could live with us. He doesn't strike me as being able to manage the place by himself.'

'But, Mathilde,' I objected, 'the place is a mess. It's had nothing done to it for years.'

'True, but it's a perfectly solid structure. I could put some of my money into it, so we could modernise it, provide a flat in it for your dad, and that would be sorted.'

Moving back to Les Landes! I'd been so keen to leave it, but I knew that deep down I missed the lakes and the pines and the seashore.

One weekend we explained the idea to my father, while we were visiting, and he had had time to think about the future after the funeral. He didn't say much – it wasn't his way to be outwardly enthusiastic – but we could tell he was quietly content with the decision. The same weekend he broached the subject of my relationship with my mother.

'Don't think badly of your mother, Marie. She didn't have much help in her life from me and I was a disappointment to her.'

'She didn't exactly go about asking for help in the right way, did she?'

760

'No. The only thing which kept her going was you.'

'Me? I thought she was disgusted with me?'

'She was very proud of you, Marie. She kept all your articles from the newspapers.'

'And I never knew!'

'She wasn't very good at expressing pleasure.'

'Maybe no one had ever expressed pleasure in her,' commented Mathilde wryly. 'I lived like that for years myself. Until you rescued me.'

'That was just a chance encounter.'

'Chance encounters can change your life. Your mother wasn't as lucky as I was.'

# Epilogue

And so, our lives change their rhythm according to our age and circumstances. While I completed my teacher training in Bordeaux, Mathilde and I rented a small house in Labouyère. Mathlde took a part time office job in a local garage and spent long weekends at my parents' small holding, learning the ways of the farm and transforming its output.

Three years later I got a job in the local school at Mimizan.

Local schooling was so much more up to date than it had been in my day, though I missed the opportunities to warm my feet at the wood-burning stove at lunchtimes.

That September, as I welcomed my new pupils for the year, I looked at the home details of their registration, and realised that one of them lived near Eulalie, in the farmhouse where Alain had been brought up.

'That means his family were probably the ones who originally betrayed Alain's family and took over the house as a reward,' I confided to Mathilde in the evening. 'It makes me feel angry and also worried about meeting the parents.'

'Think about all the revenge attacks after the war in Paris,' she suggested. 'Think about all the killings and counter killings in Algeria. Who have they benefitted? No one. Leave the family alone and concentrate on a new generation.'

And that is what I decided to do – to look to a new generation of children who always offer hope for the mistakes that the older generation have made.

Once we lived at my parents' small-holding, Mathilde took on the task of changing and updating the house. She even turned the barn into extra living accommodation 'so that we could have people to stay', which turned out to be a real forward-looking move as Les Landes became a holiday destination for the rest of France, and not just for the rich, as it had once been.

Two years after we had moved, there was a knock on the door one Saturday morning.'

'Marie'

'Yes?'

'You don't remember me?'

I looked hard at him. Underneath the beard there was something familiar, but I still couldn't place him.

'Daniel,' he announced triumphantly, 'and my sister, Devorah. Do you remember?'

I yelped in wonder and amazement.

'Come in! Come in!'

'I can't believe it, first of all that you're alive, secondly that you managed to get out of the USSR.'

He grinned. 'It's quite a story, believe me.'

'I don't have any difficulty believing you. Where's Devorah?'

'She's in Bordeaux arranging her transfer papers. Luckily for us we found our French birth certificates. Devorah's marrying a French man we met in the kibbutz in Israel and I'm going back there after the wedding.'

'Daniel, this is the most marvellous news I've had in a long time.'

I introduced him to Mathilde, who knew the background to his story already.

'Don't tell me you got out through Vladivostock!' I said unbelievingly, remembering the Japanese fishing boat and my arrest by the GRU.

'Afraid not, Marie. It took a lot longer than that. Fortunately, Kruschev's thaw provided us a way out.'

'How long ago?'

'About six years now. We went straight to Israel.'

'And you stayed all that time in that camp and survived?'

'Not only survived but acquired some good scientific skills – all down to you, Marie. You made sure we got to the right place.'

'And Nikolai?'

He looked sombre.

'I'm pretty sure he didn't make it. There were too many people after him.'

'And I wasn't able to save him.'

That was three men I'd seen go to their deaths.

'You can't save everyone,' said Daniel in a soft tone.

'I wish.' But then my tone changed.

'Knowing that you and Devorah are alive is the best news I've had in a long time.'

'Devorah said that if I found you, I was to invite you to the wedding next week. It's on a Saturday and of course your friend here can come too.'

Mathilde tried to protest. 'I'm sure you've got far too many people to invite as it is.'

'Well actually, we don't. François's family have lots of guests, but on Devorah's side there aren't many at all. We'd be delighted if you would come too. Especially as she's going to be living in Bordeaux, so you can get to know her. She'd love that.'

'

# Further Reading

If you wish to follow up on the historical background against which this fictional story is set, you may enjoy reading the following: -

### FRENCH HISTORY

Cruel Crossing by Edward Stourton : Black Swan 2014

The Resistance by Matthew Cobb: Simon and Schuster 2009

Visit the Jean Moulin National Centre, 48, rue Vital Carles 33000 Bordeaux

### RUSSIAN HISTORY

Where the Jews Aren't by Masha Gessen: Random House 2016

Gulag : A history by Anne Applebaum: Penguin 2004

The Whisperers: Private Life in Stalin's Russia by Orlando Figes: Penguin 2008

### ALGERIAN HISTORY

A Savage War of Peace: Algeria 1954 – 1962 by Alistair Horne: Penguin 1977